ALEXANDER'S GENERALS

by
Stuart Slade

LION BY LION
PUBLISHING

Dedication

This book is respectfully dedicated to the memory of Diodorus Siculus the founding father of written history.

Acknowledgements

Alexander's Generals draws very heavily on The Library of History written by Diodorus Siculus who quoted an older and now lost history of the Diodochi Wars by Hieronymus of Cardia. Other key sources were "Ghost on the Throne" by James Romm, "The Seleucid Army" by Bezalel Bar-Kochva, the "House of Seleucus" by Edwin Robert Bevan, "The Rise of Parthia in the East" by Cam Rea and "Dividing the Spoils" by Robin Waterfield.

I must also express a particular debt of gratitude to my wife Josefa for without her kind forbearance, patient support and unstintingly generous assistance, this novel would have remained nothing more than a vague idea floating in the back of my mind.

Caveat

Alexander's Generals is a work of historical fiction set in the period immediately following the assassination of Alexander the Great in 323 BC. This period is known as the Diodochi or Successor Wars. The events described within this story actually took place and most of the characters appearing in this book really did exist. As far as possible, the characterizations of these long-deal politicians and generals are as accurate as history permits with the provisio that the histories were written by the winners. Other characters exist only as fiction and any resemblance to any person, living or dead is purely coincidental. An appendix is provided to distinguish between the two groups.

Copyright Notice

Contents

Books In This Series
Available From

LION BY LION
PUBLISHING

A Mighty Endeavor	(1940)
Winter Warriors	(1945)
The Big One	(1947)
Anvil of Necessity	(1948)
The Great Game	(1959)
Crusade	(1965)
Ride of the Valkyries	(1972)
Lion Resurgent	(1982)
High Frontier	(1986)

Coming Shortly

Kazan Thunderbolts	(1943)

iv

PROLOGUE
THE RECRUIT

Prologue

CHAPTER ONE

IGRAT

Market Square, Close to the Esagila, Babylon, 322 BC

"That doesn't sound good." The echoes of the woman's scream had been drowned out by a dull roar of cheering. As it faded away, the woman screamed again. "Can you see what's going on Gusoyn?"

The man driving the team stood up in his seat and looked ahead. "There is something going on at the Esagila, Parmenio. I cannot see what." Gusoyn was still trying to cope with the enormity of discovering his heritage and swung between amazement at what the future held for him and confusion at how normal life was in the immediate present. One good thing, he did have a partner, somebody to share his life with. For a man who had thought himself doomed to loneliness, that was a gift worth almost any price.

"Take us closer." Parmenio gave the order reflexively, more as a reflection of his desire to know what was happening around him than curiosity over the event. Gusoyn urged his team forward and the cart moved forward until it was at the edge of the crowd, in the shadow of a tall wall. In the meantime, the unidentified woman had shrieked twice more, her cries agonized and desperate.

"What's happening?" Parmenio spoke to a man standing nearby, his eyes riveted on the scene.

"Woman was caught stealing from a man in the Esagila. That blasphemy could bring the wrath of Marduk down on us. Marduk's our protector, if he turns his face from us, the whole city will be doomed. So, the priests are having her scourged."

Parmenio looked at the stage by the Esagila gate. A naked woman was hanging between two pillars, her feet barely touching the ground. As he watched, one of the priests took another swing and her body convulsed again.

"Who is she?"

3

Prologue

"I don't know." The man was irritated at the distraction from watching the spectacle. "I've seen her around, a cheap whore and a thief, that's all."

"Seems a bit harsh." Parmenio wasn't very interested. The woman was a thief, she'd known the risks she was taking, now she was paying the price.

"This is only the start. You see those oxen there? When the scourging is over, they'll use those to pull her legs apart until her hips crack open like the wishbone in a chicken. Then they'll leave her to die." The man licked his lips in anticipation.

Unnoticed behind them, Lillith got out of the cart and vomited in the angle between a wall and its supporting buttress. A woman behind a nearby market stand gave her a cup of water and a rag to clean her face. "Parmenio, get her out of there."

"She's a thief."

"Killing her is one thing, torturing her like that is different. Kill her if you've got to, but stop that." Lillith had her own, deeply personal reasons for hating what was happening. "Besides I've got a feeling. . . . ."

Her words were drowned out by another scream, one that ended in a sob. Parmenio nodded. He had no particular objection to executing a thief, but this was excessive. He made his way through the crowd, Gusoyn and Apollo behind him in the position normally occupied by servants and bodyguards. They *were* bodyguards, they were *not* servants, but it suited the situation for them to play the latter part as well. The whole situation had Parmenio worried. He liked to prepare for his actions and on this occasion there had been no time to plan ahead. Fortunately, he looked the part of being wealthy and powerful and that helped him through the crowd.

He took another look at the woman when he reached the platform. She was young, slender, her head down, her black hair covering her face. Her back and hips were covered in blood, so much so that Parmenio could only imagine the mangled flesh underneath. Even as he watched, she was cut down from the two pillars and collapsed in a heap on the wooden floor. Some of the priests were moving the oxen into place, others were bringing up two lengths of rope, loops ready to fit around her ankles. She crawled across the platform, begging the priests not to kill her, ending up kissing the feet of the senior priest, her hands on the back of her head, fingers in her hair. Some of the priests laughed, others got ready to fit the ropes to her feet and get the oxen moving. Before anything else could happen, Parmenio addressed the Senior Priest directly.

"Your Most Holy Reverence, this city has seen so much bloodshed." *That was true*, Parmenio thought, *after Alexander was killed a few months ago, there has been all too much blood flowing in the streets.* "Surely a better way to appease the wrath of Marduk would be to honor his temple with gold and precious stones, to make his most holy of statues finer and more noble than they have ever been before. Allow me to buy this worthless whore for 10,000 in coin and Marduk will be well pleased."

"And why would you want this blasphemous wretch." The woman was still tearing her hair, trying to kiss his feet and he kicked her away.

"I have a great estate not far from here." That was true, although the estate was newly-purchased. Parmenio had allied himself with one of Alexander's generals, Seleucus and the money flowing in from that alliance was more than enough to buy his family a proper home. "I have slave workers in the fields, they will appreciate a woman to enjoy. For as long as she lasts."

The priest frowned. "You could buy a slave girl for one fiftieth of that money."

"I could, but my slaves have been without a woman for years. When they get one, they will tear her apart. An innocent slave girl does not deserve such a fate, but this one. . . ."

The priest nodded slowly, thoughtfully. "A fitting fate indeed for a whore who blasphemed against Marduk. And your offer, 12,000 coin I believe you said, will be a fitting tribute to assuage Marduk's wrath."

Money was always the best route to a priest's heart, Parmenio thought. The crowd had realized that the execution was over and started to disperse, grumbling with disappointment. Apollo had gone to get the gold, Gusoyn climbed up on to the platform and picked the girl up, swinging her over his shoulder. Parmenio handed the gold over and they were on their way back to their cart.

"You managed it?" Naamah was astonished. "I thought they were having far too much fun to let you get away with it."

"Told you he would." Lillith was conceited. "You owe me ten coin."

"And you owe us twelve thousand." Lillith's eyebrows rose as Parmenio gestured and Gusoyn unloaded the girl into the back of the cart. She was slumped on the floor, apparently unconscious. "Right, let's get on our way home. Our new home that is." He and Gusoyn went around to the front of the cart leaving Apollo with Lillith, Naamah and Shammuramat to look after the new arrival.

That was when the girl came to life. She'd landed in the cart with her right arm doubled up underneath her head, her legs apparently tangled but when she started to move, she moved very fast. She pushed with her legs, lunging forward while her right hand emerged from her hair holding a small knife. In one smooth flowing motion, she slammed the knife into Apollo's shoulder, twisted it, and jerked it out. Then, she was heading out over the tailgate of the cart.

Hitting somebody isn't just a matter of strength, it's also a matter of technique. Due to a lifetime's training in the Macedonian martial art of Pankration, Parmenio had both, and his hand caught the girl across the face as she started to jump out. The force of the blow was enough to send her back into the cart, sprawled across the decking, the little knife left uselessly on the ground outside. Parmenio picked it up. It was indeed tiny, the blade narrow and barely more than two inches long. For a second, the back of the cart was a frozen tableau, the girl on the deck, her eyes blazing hatred at Parmenio, Lillith cradling Apollo in her arms moaning 'my baby, my baby' as she patted ineffectually at the blood streaming down the left side of his tunic. Parmenio stared at the girl in disbelief. "She's one of us," were his only words.

"Later." Naamah pushed Lillith out of the way and tore open Apollo's tunic.

"Is it bad?" Gusoyn's voice was anguished.

"Very. That girl knows how to use a knife." Naamah had a water soaked rag and was cleaning the blood away. "Even in that condition, she was barely a knife-blade's thickness off. Gods, I can see the artery in the wound. If she's nicked that...." There was a long, aching pause, "no, we're safe. The blood isn't from there." She started padding fabric into the wound and tying it into place.

Parmenio pointed at the girl, his finger barely an inch from her eye. "If you hurt one of my people again, I will kill you. Understand?" The girl nodded, slowly, the hatred still in her eyes. "Where was that knife?"

"In her hair. She had it hidden in her hair." Shammuramat was disbelieving.

Parmenio was confused. "If you had a knife, why didn't you try and escape? Or try to kill yourself to avoid what they had planned for you?"

"Because I wanted to kill the priest. I'd have done it too if you hadn't shown up. I'd wormed my way so close to him, I would have put that knife through his eye before anybody could have stopped me." Her voice was attractive, soft and husky despite the tightness caused by pain and exhaustion. "Let me go or I'll get my nails into the face of one of your women. You'll kill me but I'll shred her."

"We've got a real wildcat here." Shammuramat was still stricken with disbelief.

"I know. You go up top with Gusoyn, get us out of here. I'll stay here. As for you, wildcat, just one word. Don't. You won't succeed, you're too badly hurt to make an escape possible and a naked woman in your condition won't get very far. So, don't. Odd as it may seem right now, this is the best place for you."

Estate of Parmenio, Seleucia-on-the Tigris

"What's your name?"

"You bought me, you can call me what you like."

Parmenio sighed. The young woman was lying on a couch in a small room, face down. Even so, she still managed to transmit a wave of hate. "I asked you what your name was."

"Why should you care? So you can tell your slaves what to call me when you throw me to them?"

"You are not going to be thrown to the people who work here. I told the priests that so they would sell you to me. Now, what is your name?"

The girl paused for a moment. "Igrat." The voice was sulky but calmer.

"Very well Igrat. As soon as Naamah, she's the one with red hair, has finished patching up Apollo she'll be here to look after you." There was a rustle behind him. "Speaking of whom, how is he Nammie?"

"Resting, he's asleep but Gusoyn is with him. He'll call if there are any problems. Apollo should be all right but he's lost the use of his arm for a couple of weeks while that wound heals and he'll have an impressive scar. Wildcat here really knows how to stab somebody."

"Her name's Igrat. Do you need help."

"Around her, I need a bodyguard." Naamah looked down at Igrat and astonished herself by having a brief masochistic fantasy. "So stay please. Do we have hot water?"

Parmenio called out and a servant brought in a bowl, still steaming from the fire. Naamah soaked a cloth and started to wash the matted blood from Igrat's back. The girl yelped and tried to get away.

"Shhh, shhh, stay still. I've got to get these wounds cleaned or they'll become corrupted and ooze poison. And me getting to them soon is the best way of avoiding scarring. You don't want more scars than you can avoid do you?"

Igrat shook her head and lay still, biting her lips and whimpering. Four bowls of water and a pile of rags later, Naamah sat back, slightly puzzled. "Well, there we have it Parmenio. I thought it was going to be much, much worse. I thought the hooks on the scourge would have torn her flesh off, I was expecting to see her spine and ribs. I don't think they used a scourge though, just a normal multi-tail whip. She's got welts, a lot of them and quite a few have broken the skin, mostly where they cross."

She patted Igrat on the back of the head. "You'll recover Igrat and the scars will fade. I just don't know why they didn't use a scourge on you."

"They wanted me to live longer."

"That sounds like it. I'm going to inspect you now, for other injuries." *And for sickness*, Naamah thought, *given the way you've been living, the Gods only know what you're infected with*. Her hands ran quickly over Igrat's body.

"Enjoying yourself?" To Parmenio's surprise, Igrat's voice was almost droll. "Lots of well-bred ladies like to paw their maids."

"Perhaps I am. But you're not a maid. Did they kick you? Hit you in the ribs? Have you any trouble breathing? Pains in the chest?"

"No."

Naamah nodded. Her ribs weren't broken.

"How is she Nammie?"

"She's a very sick woman, mostly from today's adventures. You did a number when you hit her boss, she's going to have that bruise for weeks. I don't think she'll scar but it's hard to tell with us."

Namaah sat back a little. "Are you listening Igrat? Good. You have to keep the sun off your back while you heal. Don't go outside without being covered up, try and keep in the shadows as much as you can. I'll give you some ointment to rub into the skin. Now, next thing, I want you to wash three times a day, all over, your whole body. I'll make you shampoo for your hair, you must wash it every day without fail. Understand? She's got headlice Parmenio, we're all going to have to be careful until they're gone. Now Igrat, I'm going to give you some wine, it's got something mixed in with it to make you sleep."

Igrat looked highly suspicious. Naamah was slightly annoyed. "Oh don't be foolish. If I wanted to kill you, I'd cut you here." She touched Igrat's thigh very high up on the inside, again she astonished herself when her finger lingered for a split second longer than necessary.

"You'll bleed to death in a few seconds. Or I'll get Gusoyn to come in and kill you. After what you did to Apollo, he'd be grateful for the chance. You need sleep, I'm making sure you get some. Gods Parmenio, this one is suspicious of everything."

Estate of Parmenio, Seleucia-on-the Tigris. Six hours later

In the early hours of the morning Igrat eased herself off the couch, moving slowly since her muscles had stiffened with the long rest. She'd pretended to drink the drugged wine but hadn't and then she'd waited until the house was quiet. The people who owned her had left clothing for her and she dressed quickly. Then she looked around. There was nothing of value in the room. To her surprise the door was unlocked and she let herself out and started to search the house. She quickly found a knife; it was blunt but a few hours work with a stone would solve that. There were no gold pieces she could find but there were some ornaments that could have value. She'd only just pocketed them when somebody lit the lamps. Even in the dim glow, she could see that everybody was present.

"That balances out the 10 coin you won yesterday. Naamah sounded satisfied.

"Sit down Igrat. We've got something to tell you and now is as good a time as any." Parmenio was speaking calmly and quietly. "What do you think about secrets?"

Igrat cursed to herself, that was a killing question. Secrets got people killed. A girl who had learned something she shouldn't would get beaten, at best. More than one girl she knew had been killed for learning the wrong piece of information at the wrong time. "I think they are very dangerous. People who learn secrets are killed by them. I prefer not to know them, Sire." She held her breath, *was my answer mature enough to imply experience and wisdom, cautious enough to imply prudence and foresight. Was that a good answer? And have I kept the sulkiness and hatred out of my voice?*

"That's a very tactful answer. Igrat, this is a house of secrets. Everybody here has them and we prefer to keep them to ourselves. We've found we can do that better if we work together. This is also a house of refuge. One where people who have secrets can shelter amongst others who face the same problem. In this house, learning secrets, having secrets, does not endanger your life. It makes you one of us." *And if we told you now what the biggest secret of all is, you would think we are all mad.*

Igrat cursed again to herself. *Am I slipping, to allow somebody to see what I am thinking.*

"Don't worry about the fact that you don't believe us, your face isn't showing it. It's just a hard thing to believe, that the secrets that endanger your life can also be the key to safety. Just count yourself fortunate that Lillith recognized you as one of us. That's why I saved your life." The last wasn't quite true, he'd saved it because gratuitous cruelty wasn't in his nature and seeing it had appalled Lillith. But, those were details.

"Is this true?" Igrat was looking around, seeing the others in the dimly lit room nod. She looked around and her eyes narrowed as she saw how closely Gusoyn and Apollo sat together and noted their body language towards each other. *Yes, this is a house of secrets and I've just learned at least one of them.*

"Igrat, you've got three choices. You can leave us now, you needn't steal anything, we'll give you clothes, money to help you restart your life somewhere else. But, I warn you, you are really in no condition to do this, I believe if you try, you'll be dead within a week. But, if you want to, it's your life. You can leave if you wish." Parmenio pauased for breath.

"Secondly, you can stay here until you've recovered, then you can leave. Again, no need to steal, we'll give you what you need. That gives you a much better chance but be warned. If you carry on living the way you have been you'll get caught again and the mob will kill you. And that leads to your third choice. Stay here with us, become part of our family. Because we are a family we can all cover for each other, help each other. And we can keep us all from loneliness. It's just better being part of a family, being with people you can trust."

"You'd trust me?" Igrat couldn't believe it. Then a thought struck her. "In the cart, you said you'd kill me if I hurt one of your people again. But if I join you, I'd be one of the people you'd kill to protect wouldn't I?"

"She's getting the message." Shammuramat chuckled.

"That's right Igrat. When you join us, you've got all of us between you and anybody who might want to hurt you. And the same applies in reverse of course."

"Suppose one of you wants to hurt me?" Igrat was staring at Apollo, his left arm tightly bound to his chest to stop it moving. She'd done her best to kill him, and, by the sound of it, only failed by the tiniest of margins. She guessed if he moved his arm before the wound was healed, there was a danger the great blood vessel that fed his arm could rupture.

"Anything that happened before you joined us, to you or by you, is forgotten. The ledger starts fresh. It's like any family, if somebody here does something against you, you're entitled to retaliate in a suitably ingenious and humorous way. The more humorous, the more respect you'll earn. We're a family Igrat, an extended family and one that's growing slowly as we find more people like us. But still a family."

Igrat stared around the group and slowly thought the problem out. There was only one logical answer and she gave it. "Please, may I join your family?" The people in the shadows nodded. "You know I've got no money or anything." She didn't know how to say the next bit, she didn't want to live on charity but she couldn't see any other way. She just looked around helplessly.

"Can you read and write Igrat?" Lillith asked, "and how old are you?"

She shook her head. "I can't. And I don't really know. I was brought up by the women working in a brothel. They told me I was found outside the door, a baby bleeding to death. I can't do any of those things."

"Don't worry, I'll teach you. And don't worry about money either, you'll find your place in the world, we all did."

Everybody relaxed and sat more comfortably. Igrat felt something she'd never experienced before, acceptance. She understood now what a family meant, something also she'd never known before. And, as her understanding of acceptance grew, the sullen anger and resentment at the world that had filled her ebbed away. She'd never understood how much the grimy shroud of bitterness and rage that she'd wrapped around herself had warped everything she'd done, right up to the time she'd stabbed Apollo. Suddenly, she realized that there had been no need to stab him, let alone try to kill. It had been her own hatred for the world that had driven her to do so, not the need to escape. She suddenly caught his eye. "I am sorry Apollo, I am so, so sorry."

He waved his right hand dismissively. "Don't worry about it. Just teach me how to use a knife like that when we're both better."

"Anything else we need to discuss before we go to bed? Oh, Igrat, take your wine this time. Nammy tells me you really do need to sleep. And it'll help you forget the Esagila."

"Uh, since we're dealing with Macedonians, I'm going to use the Greek form of my name from now on." Shammuramat looked around. "Semiramis."

"Now, there is a problem coming up. There's a war starting and I'm going to be planning Seleucus Nikator's campaigns for him." Parmenio glanced at Igrat. "I don't grow wine, I fight wars. And win them. This time around, I'm going to make sure Seleucus wins. It'll take time. Years probably and I'll be away for long periods. Out of touch. That's going to be a problem."

"I suppose we could hire messengers." Lillith didn't sound convinced.

Prologue

"You don't need to." Igrat was feeling drowsy from the wine but her mind still galloped ahead, still trying to absorb the wonderful sense of belonging. "I can be the messenger. Look, Apollo and Gusoyn must stay here to protect our home right? And you three are great ladies, you can't go following armies, you'll be robbed and killed. But I can. I'm a whore and a thief. I can go anywhere and nobody looks twice at the camp followers. Why should anybody think I'm anything other than what I am. I'll just be one of the baggage train, and I can get your messages through."

"She's right you know." Lillith sounded impressed. "See, Igrat, I said you'd find your place. We'll start your lessons tomorrow, right?"

"Right. Now I must sleep. Naamah, thank you for looking after me." She went over to Naamah and whispered something in her ear that made her flush. Then she went back to her room.

"Can we trust her?" Shammuramat spoke very, very quietly.

"Of course," Parmenio replied. "She's family now."

CHAPTER TWO

FAMILY

Estate of Parmenio, Seleucia-on-the Tigris

Igrat was laying on the stone floor of the temple, pinned down by the weight of men sitting on her. They were crushing her, holding her down by their sheer weight, squeezing her chest and slowly suffocating her. She'd fought hard, in the process hurting some of them badly, and now they were taking their revenge. Some of them were holding her legs apart while the rest took turns forcing themselves on her. She had one card left to play, a tiny knife hidden in her hair, but she knew she was going to die and she had one last blow to strike at the world around her. That knife was the tool she would use to do it. When the time was right, she would drive it right through the Chief Priest's eye. She managed to twist her head and she saw the figures around her change. They weren't priests, they were demons, their eyes glowing brilliant red as they used her. Any hope she had left collapsed. She wasn't going to die. She already had. She was in Hell and this was her fate for all eternity. Then, the scene shifted again and suddenly, she was one of the demons, her eyes glowing red, assisting in the abuse of the helpless, sobbing woman beneath them.

Then, Igrat woke up, she was conscious of the room around her and the bed she was sleeping on but the dream wouldn't stop. It was weird, she could see everything around her, the shadows on the wall that told her it was late morning, the crumpled bedding damp with the sweat from her nightmare but still the dream went on in her head, mixing with reality and distorting it. She knew it was a dream but still she couldn't make it stop.

She sat up, shaking her head and an appalling reality dawned on her. It was late morning and she had no money for food or for her lodgings. She had to get some fast, steal some coppers, perhaps pick up a careless man in the market who she could rob while he enjoyed her. Then, another realization dawned on her, or rather memories of the weird meeting the night before, and she knew that was something she wouldn't have to worry about again. She'd been invited to join this family and she'd accepted. She belonged here and that realization stopped the dream and drove it away. By the time she stood up it had gone almost completely and she could barely remember it.

The room was small and bare, just a couch, a chair and some clothes laid out on it. Heavy linen, they would be hot to wear but Igrat remembered the instructions she'd been given. *Don't let the sun shine on your back or you'll be scarred.* She remembered more instructions, *bathe yourself all over, three times a day, and wash your hair with the shampoo I give you, every day.* The best thing now was to do as she was told, to show that she accepted this place and was grateful for her acceptance into it by causing as little trouble as possible. Then, she looked around the room, where to wash and how?

Behind her, a maid cleared her throat. Obviously she had heard Igrat wake up and had brought hot water for her to wash with. Igrat smiled at her, but the smile died on her lips for the maid was looking at her with obvious and open contempt. That made her anger start to boil again but she battered it down. The girl was a maid in the house of a rich and powerful family, Igrat knew she was a copper-coin whore and a sneak thief who'd been stupid enough to get caught. Of course the maid looked down on her, she had every right to.

"Is there a mirror here?" Igrat asked the question, tentatively, uncertain of what privileges she was allowed. Polished mirrors were expensive and perhaps this family did not trust her near one. But the maid had a silver mirror and held it up for Igrat to use. She turned around and looked over her shoulder, gasping at the sight. Her back, from just below the neck to half way down her thighs, was a mass of purple bruising and livid crimson welts. Worse, it was streaked with blood and Igrat saw that some of that had been smeared on her bedding. She turned and looked at her face. One side was recognizable but the other was disfigured by a massive purple bruise with the white of her eye reddened. She remembered the man called Parmenio had hit her and she'd been shocked by the power in his fist. Obviously she'd under-rated him even so.

"I must wash."

The maid nodded and pulled her through to a small room, bare except for some stone benches around the walls. She put the jug of hot water down and took some cloths from one of the benches, soaked them and started to wash Igrat down. The water ran pink on to the floor and her back burned so badly it made her cry. After the maid had washed her back for her, Igrat took the cloth and finished the job. As she did so, she shook her head. The words *she's a very sick woman*, ran through her head. She hadn't realized just how badly battered she was. Parmenio had been right, if she had tried to leave in this condition, she would have died.

The maid cleared her throat again. It was time for Igrat to wash her hair. The maid poured hot water over her head, then added a liquid from a small flask. "The Lady Naamah made this for you herself."

It was the first time the maid had spoken to her and Igrat was caught by surprise. The liquid smelled of rosemary and sage along with the tallow-soap. There was something else in there as well, something that made it thick and runny. Igrat and the maid worked the stuff through her hair, feeling it sting as it met her scalp.

"Close your eyes, you don't want this to get in them." The maid spoke quickly, before pouring another liquid over Igrat's head. It smelt of chrysanthemums with a sharp, acrid tinge and Igrat felt it burn her scalp. The maid rubbed it well in. "The Lady Naamah made this as well, it kills lice. She makes us all use it."

More hot water was poured over Igrat's head, washing the soap and liquids out. Finally the maid produced a metal comb and started running it through Igrat's hair. She yelped as the comb caught in the knots and tangles but the maid continued combing her mane out. When she had finished, Igrat opened her eyes and looked into the bowl. It was full of hair that had fallen out with the combing and the mass literally seethed with vermin. "The Lady Naamah wants you to take that to show her."

It was probably the first time in her life that Igrat had been really clean. The maid handed her a loincloth and Igrat started to tie it on, fastening the tapes on one side in a clumsy knot. The maid clucked in dismay, slapped her hands away and retied the tapes in an elegant bow. The she handed Igrat a white linen tunic, a long one that reached the floor. Igrat gathered it around herself, then tied it in place with a girdle around her waist. If she'd been going outside, she would have worn a shawl as well, one that was placed over her head and wrapped around her like a cloak. But, for inside, the tunic was entirely enough. With a pair of sandals on her feet, Igrat was ready to face the world, or, at least, this small part of it.

The room was airy and well-lit, the sun streaming between the pillars that lined the outside wall. Igrat obeyed the orders she'd been given and kept out of the direct sun. She'd have done that anyway. Over the last couple of years, she'd noticed that the noon-day sun hurt her eyes. Now, more and more, she was keeping to the evening when the light was soft and there were shadows to hide in. There was a woman on a couch in the room, reading a scroll. She had a helmet-like layer of short-cropped red hair and it was the color that gave her away, Igrat recognized it immediately. The woman was Naamah. She looked very different from the night before when she had been wearing an ornate hairstyle. Igrat cursed herself, *of course she looked different, she is a Great Lady. Important people never wore their own hair, only ever used wigs. It was the very poor women who had to use their own. Poor women like me.* Igrat went over to her and dropped to her knees, bending her face down low.

"There's no need for that." Naamah was amused more than anything although the truth was she didn't like excessive genuflection. "We are the ones who own this house, it's ours and the servants work for us. Don't act like one of them or they'll run rings around you. Now come and sit beside me."

Igrat did as she was told, for the time being anyway. "A maid told me to bring this to you."

She passed Naamah the bowl containing her hair combings and the vermin in them. Naamah had a wooden stick and pushed the mess around, looking at it. Igrat watched Naamah's lips tighten slightly in disgust. Eventually, Naamah gave the bowl to a maid with instructions that the contents should be burned immediately.

"Just lice, nothing worse. No worms or ticks. You're lucky but I want to look at your scalp in a day or two. I'd prefer to shave your head first but you'll need your hair. Would you like something to eat?"

Igrat blinked at the way Naamah had skipped around topics. "Please, if it wouldn't cause problems."

Naamah rang a bell. "Drop the submissive act, it doesn't suit you and it makes us wonder what you're up to. You're part of this family now, remember. Look on me as your mother."

"That would mean I'd have to try and cut your throat."

Naamah laughed delightedly. "That's better. Now you're our wildcat again. You remind me of my grandchildren, they wanted to torture me to death. Tried to as well but Lillith and I outsmarted them. Take a word of advice Igrat, never deny your nature. You'll have to pretend you are something you are not all the time, so your true nature is all you can hang on to."

Naamah looked up at the servant girl who had anwered her call. "Girl, get fruit, olive oil and fresh bread. Fresh mind you, not the old stuff."

The maid left quickly and Naamah grinned again. "Servants are always trying to put one over on their masters. Given a chance we'd have got yesterday's bread and they'd have kept the fresh stuff in their quarters."

"What happens if you catch them, they get beaten?" Igrat tried to keep the bitterness out of her voice but couldn't. Where she had come from, anybody who tried to get an edge over the wealthy and powerful got a bad beating at best. Her back was a proof of that.

Naamah shook her head. "My husband never allowed servants in our household to be beaten. He said that any plot to destroy a household always started with information gained from resentful servants. He also said loyalty had to be sent down before anybody could expect it to come back up. Good advice and very true. So servants don't get beaten here."

"Parmenio is your husband?" Igrat spoke carefully. She needed to know just what the relationships were around here.

"No, although we do sleep together. My husband was a man called Sammael and he died a long, long time ago."

Igrat thought about that for a long time. Were the stories she had heard in the marketplace about some people having lives lasting far beyond the normal span true? If it was, what had she done to deserve such a gift? A maid brought bread, oil and fruit out. Igrat and Naamah ate quietly together. Eventually, Igrat managed to get out the question she'd been turning over in her mind. "We're his harem aren't we?"

"Sammael's? Gods no. He's been dead for years." Naamah knew exactly what Igrat meant but decided to play dumb.

"No, Parmenio's. I don't mind, its little enough payment for the shelter here."

"Number one, you're family now, there's no need for payment and when you start your courier runs, if anything we'll be in your debt. Those runs will be risky. Number two, no, we're not Parmenio's harem. The truth is that it's hard to say what we are. We're unique and we make our own rules. We all have our roles to play. Lillith is our book and records keeper. She also organizes all our finances and invests our money. Semiramis is our court princess, she keeps us advised on what's going on politically. For a number of reasons, I have to stay out of sight for a few years so I'm running the household."

"There's still us four women though. And Parmenio's the only real man...."

"I'd be careful saying that." Naamah's voice was sharp. "You've obviously guessed about Gusoyn and Apollo but don't you dare think any the less of either of them because of it. Their relationship is one of the little secrets this household keeps but it's their private business. In fact, all of the couples in this house are the private business of the two people in question."

Prologue

Igrat's mouth set. She was trying to conceal her thoughts but not succeeding very well. *Two men of their age, it was scandalous.*

Naamah knew exactly what Igrat was thinking. "Anyway Igrat, you invited me into your bed last night remember?"

"That's different, we're women. And you want me, I can tell. There's no need to be embarrassed about it, a lot of great ladies like to have a bit of trash in their beds now and them."

Naamah sighed, Igrat's sense of her own worth was atrophied to the point of non-existence and she wondered if it would be possible to rebuild it. "Igrat, you're only trash because that's the way you look at yourself. You'll find people mostly take you at your own valuation of yourself. Think of yourself as being a person of value, a great lady, that's how you'll get treated. I don't mean putting on airs or acting parts, just respect yourself. Recognize and appreciate your virtues, acknowledge your faults and try to do something about them. Self-respect is something you don't have any of at the moment, so try to develop it."

Naamah hesitated, she was dealing with emotions entirely strange to her. "And yes, I am attracted to you. You do realize you are as seductive as the Succubi don't you?"

"Me?" Igrat was disbelieving, her hand instinctively touching the massive bruise on her cheek.

"Yes, you. Look, let's be honest about this. None of the women here up to now have been great beauties. Men dance attendance on me until I look at them then they run screaming out of the room." Naamah looked up and Igrat saw her eyes for the first time. Utterly dead, their muddy green the color of corruption and decay. She caught her breath and her hand moved to cover her mouth. "Not pretty are they? Lillith and Semiramis have looks that men describe as showing character rather than being beautiful. That's fair and it's no insult but classical beauties they are not. You, Igrat, are a classical beauty, the sort of woman men fight to the death over. We'll teach you how to paint yourself and dress so that your beauty can flower but we couldn't turn you into the toast of Seleucia unless you had the looks to start with. And you do, never forget that."

"Never forget what?"

Lillith and Apollo had entered the room and Lillith had picked up on just the last remark. Igrat rose as they entered. "Lady Naamah was telling me of the arrangements here and what everybody did. Lillith, if there is anything I can do.."

"You've done quite enough." Lillith's voice was tart.

"That's enough of that." Naamah's voice was even sharper and it made Lillith blink and draw back.

"You can't blame Igrat, Lillith." Apollo smiled at Igrat and gave her a little salute with his good hand. "She thought she was being taken away to a rather nasty death so of course she tried to run for it. I just got in the way, that's all."

"Apollo, can I do something for you?"

Apollo ran his eyes over Igrat and smiled gently. "Don't take this personally..."

"She knows, Apollo."

"In which case, Igrat, you can peel me some grapes. Can't do it with one hand."

Igrat laughed delightedly, took the bowl of grapes and settled down next to Apollo. Her fingers moved deftly as she stripped the grape of its skin, then she popped it in Apollo's mouth. By the time he chewed and swallowed it, she had the next one waiting. Then she dunked a piece of bread in the olive oil for him to chew on.

Across the room, Lillith watched the display with a complex array of mixed feelings. She'd long ago accepted Apollo's sexual orientation, but in many ways he was a replacement for her own long-lost children and she also had a mother's wish to see him settled down with a nice girl. This was the closest he'd ever got, but the problem was that Igrat wasn't anywhere close to anybody's definition of a nice girl.

"Igrat, we should start your lessons as soon as possible." Lillith seized on that excuse to get her away from Apollo. "It's easy for children to learn to read and write but adults find it much harder. You'll have to get fluent in Greek as well."

"I speak some Greek already." Igrat smiled at Lillith who realized her ploy had been rumbled. As if to drive the point home, she peeled Apollo another grape and fed it to him. "I learned it from the soldiers."

"Well, that's a start, but you'll have to learn a lot more. Also high-class Attic Greek not the Koine street version. And you must learn to read and write, without those skills you're helpless. Even with that knife of yours, you can't defend yourself properly unless you are literate."

Igrat nodded. She didn't quite understand what was so important about reading and writing, she'd done all right without them for years. Then she stopped herself. *Had I done so well? I lived covered in dirt in a small room, selling my body for coppers and stealing whatever and whenever I could. All*

19

the time, these people, people who could read the scratches on papyrus and make them in reply, they'd lived in palaces like this. I wasn't living, I was surviving.

"We can steal a lot more with a pen than by cutting purses you know." Apollo was droll, he was thoroughly enjoying both the attention and the opportunity to twist Lillith's tail a little.

"I once got five silver pieces when I stole a man's purse." Igrat spoke with just a little pride. "And he couldn't do much about it without his wife finding out where he had lost it."

"We once removed half a King's treasury just by writing a puzzle." Apollo reminisced, causing both Naamah and Lillith to get nostalgic looks on their faces. Then, one of the doors banged and Gusoyn came in, dusty and travel-stained. Apollo got up quickly, almost pushing Igrat to one side and hugged his partner. "You made good time."

"Easy on a horse." Gusoyn handed his cloak to a maid and tried to settle down with the food.

"You, bath." Naamah and Lillith spoke almost in unison. Gusoyn was definitely 'horsy'.

"First things first. Igrat, I went back to your lodgings, tried to get your things. I'm sorry, the man who owns the place had already sold them, he claimed you owed him rent."

"That's not true! I paid him up to tomorrow." Igrat was indignant, but also very upset. Her tiny handful of possessions were all she had to show for her life. Now they were gone and she truly had nothing.

"I guessed that and he admitted as much when I pushed the matter. Anyway, he'd sold your clothes and so on to a market stall. I got him to give me the money since you didn't owe him anything." Apollo looked down and saw that Gusoyn's knuckles were skinned. Obviously the discussion had been a bit more intense than he was letting on.

"Anyway, I went to the stall, your clothes had gone." *Torn up and sold for rags* thought Gusoyn *but no need to say that.* "But I did get most of your jewelry. The stall-keeper was quite upset that she'd been sold stolen goods so she gave me the money she'd taken for the things she'd sold. She pointed out a few people who'd bought some pieces and I used some of the money to buy them back for you. Anyway, here's what I could recover and here's the money I got. It's not much but it's a start."

"You went all the way back, just to get my things? After I knifed your friend?" Igrat was genuinely amazed, not least because she understood that the task of recovering her property could not possibly have been as easy as

20

Gusoyn had made out. She also had spotted the bruised knuckles. The knowledge also left her bewildered because she didn't know how to thank him. Nobody had ever done anything for her that required her thanks. She opened the two cloth bags Gusoyn gave her. One contained a silver coin and some coppers, the other her jewelry.

Looking around the house she'd found herself in, she realized how cheap and tawdry they were. Even the most expensive ones, the ones she'd stolen rather than bought, were rubbish compared with the things that were around her. Even so, she treasured them. "Thank you Gusoyn. I don't know how to say it properly, but thank you. Let me peel you some grapes."

"I'll take you up on that. After I've had a wash." Lillith and Naamah both nodded emphatically.

Igrat looked at the coins and made a decision. Whatever else she had to do, she would try to be honest here. Even that led her into uncertain ground since she wasn't entirely certain what honesty was. Nobody had ever explained it to her. "Lillith, take these. First part of the money I owe you for buying me away from the priests."

Lillith looked at the coins, a pitifully small amount by the standards this family was used to, but she also understood why Igrat was offering them. "Igrat, that money came from family funds rather than my personal holdings. Those coins are old and worn, you'll need them when you start carrying messages. It would look odd if you had new gold coins. So, you keep them as your travel funds, I'll record the amount against our family account and note it was given back to you to cover your expenses as our messenger. All right?"

"I think so."

"Igrat, you'll have money of your own soon enough. If you wish, I can manage it for you, at least until you've learned enough to do it for yourself. Managing money is a skilled art, one few people learn to do well."

"I'd take her up on that offer Igrat. Lillith manages all of my money and she does it better than I could." Apollo smiled at her and pointed to the grapes. Igrat returned the smile and started peeling grapes again.

"Mine too." Naamah nodded. "But it's your decision Igrat."

In truth, Igrat was thoroughly confused. Her ingrained caution warred with her desire to be part of the family. And then there was Gusoyn who had bruised his hands recovering her things. *Having done that for me, how can I not take his advice? Won't he be offended if I don't? I don't want to offend anybody, least of all him.* "That's good advice, Gusoyn, thank you. Lillith, when I get some money of my own, would you manage it for me please? "

Prologue

Lillith nodded. "I'll be happy to. And I'll teach you how it's done."

Estate of Parmenio, Seleucia-on-the Tigris. Two Weeks Later

"What are you looking for?" Igrat was sitting down, leaning back against Naamah who was searching methodically though her hair.

"Small patches of red skin in your scalp, shaped like rings. If I find them, we've got problems, curing them is very hard. But, you seem to be clear. The lice have gone from your hair, we haven't seen any for days now."

"Are you going to check my hair down there." Igrat moved her hips suggestively. "You seemed to enjoy doing that last time."

"Not this time, you're clean down there as well, given the way you lived, that's little short of miraculous. I think it's time for you to move out of here now."

"Why?" Igrat sounded disappointed. "I was getting to like this little room."

"It was only temporary, it's the one we use for visitors whose hygiene we're not sure of. Now, you can move to your proper room. Lean forward so I can see your back."

Igrat did as she was told. The purple bruises on her back were beginning to yellow at the edges and the red welts were losing the worst of their scarlet anger. Naamah touched one with her nail and Igrat mewed slightly, pulling forward. "Any numbness in your fingers and toes? A tingling feel perhaps?"

"No, never. I've been beaten before, you know." The bitterness was back in Igrat's voice and she fought to keep it suppressed.

"I don't doubt it. I suppose you deserved it."

"Not always. Sometimes the client liked to end up by beating the woman bloody. Trouble is, we don't always spot them in time."

Naamah sighed to herself. She found herself wondering if this sort of thing had been happening in Shyt'tim under Sammael. She'd seen some of the low underlife of the city but never anything like the degraded brutality Igrat so casually took for granted. Sammael had been so proud of the city's reputation of being somewhere women could live safely. For all that, had there been women like Igrat there who were exploited the same way?

Naamah took Igrat by the chin and looked at the bruise where Parmenio had hit her. That, too, was healing. A quick look at the eye showed that was blackened but undamaged.

"He really knows how to hit somebody, doesn't he?" Igrat sounded impressed.

"It's a thing called Pankration. Most of the Macedonian nobles are taught it from childhood. You'd do well to remember that. Now, no headaches or anything, no blurring of sight?"

"None. In fact I see better now than I did when I was younger. It's just my eyes hurt in bright light."

"So do mine. It goes with our condition. Look, come with me, I'll take you to your room now. While we're doing that, I'll give you a guided tour of our home." She led the way into the main living area of the house. "This bit you know, it's the public area and the living space. Imagine this house as a big, hollow square. This is the top of that square and the largest part. Gardens are in the middle, all our private rooms look out on to them.

Naamah went over to a heavy door set in one corner of the wall. "This leads to the women's quarters. If Parmenio was an old-fashioned sort, he would turn the key on it when he is out of the house, so we'd be locked in. But he's a modern fellow and Macedonian rather than Babylonian so the door is never locked." Naamah giggled. "Not that we'd let him get away with locking us in anyway. Men's quarters are the other side of the garden. This place is quite empty, there's a lot more space than we need right now. We're guessing it will fill up as we find more of us. This is my room, when Parmenio's here, he shares it with me."

There was a hint of a claim and a warning in Naamah's voice and Igrat took due notice of it. Not that she intended to challenge Naamah or anybody else. Especially not Naamah since she had a suspicion that challenge would be ended by a dose of something in her food or wine that wasn't intended to heal her hurts. But there was another reason as well. When she'd first arrived here, she'd hated Parmenio for hitting her face. Now, she understood why he'd been so angry and she looked on him differently. She'd never had a father but she guessed that if she'd had one, she'd have felt the same way towards him as she was beginning to feel towards the Macedonian general who'd sheltered her. For the first time in her life, as far as she knew, Igrat had met a man she didn't feel driven to seduce.

Naamah was looking at her with amusement on her face. "You think I'm warning you off, don't you? Well, I am but not for the reason you think. You're learning the family secrets one by one so here's another. Parmenio's son, Philotas, was killed, murdered. How, why, doesn't matter but it happened. It tore Parmenio apart and he still hasn't really recovered. But, he respects you, likes you."

"He respects me?" Igrat was incredulous.

"Sure. From the moment he found out you had a way to escape either the prison or a really foul death and traded them both for a chance to kill your enemy, that was a mindset he understood and respected. Igrat, Parmenio is beginning to look on you as a daughter, a replacement for his lost son. So don't do anything to hurt him, understand? Because if you do, I'll get mad at you. This is your room here."

Naamah opened the door and stepped in. Igrat followed her and gasped. Compared with the bare room she'd been living in so far, this was a palace. Of course, even the bare room she'd been in had made her sordid lodgings back in Babylon seem good. But this room was opulent. She could feel her jaw dropping as she looked round, taking in the furniture and the decorations. And the bed, one larger than she'd ever seen before.

"Here's the key Igrat. There's no need to lock the door at night but you probably feel more at ease if you do. One thing, if you go on a courier run, you'll need to use the other room until we're sure you're clean. No offense but it's better that way."

"What's all this with being clean?" Igrat wrinkled her nose slightly. "I mean it feels nice and my hair doesn't itch all the time but all this washing?"

"I've been around a long time Igrat, and I've noticed something. When plague starts, it always does so in the poorest, dirtiest parts of town and spreads out from there. It spreads like water, you know? In a pool, not odd patches here and there. Just as if it was passing by contact. I've also noticed the cleaner places are, the fewer times plague can get to them. Once Lillith, Apollo and I rode out a plague that killed thousands. We slammed our doors at the first sign of it and didn't let anybody near us until it had burned itself out. I believe that keeping clean is the secret of avoiding plague so I insist on it. And, be honest, it feels better, doesn't it?"

Igrat nodded, causing her hair to ripple. She touched it, spreading it out between her fingers. "My hair, it's never felt so good. I tried to wash it once and it was awful, a tangled mess that took days to get right. What's in that soap you gave me?"

"The hair shampoo? Oh, I infuse some olive oil with rosemary and sage. That means I put a pot of the oil and herbs in some boiling water so it doesn't overheat and leave it for a while. Then I mix the scented oil with tallow soap and blend in an egg. Then I mix it all with some beer. You had the right idea but your hair has oil in it that it needs. Soap on its own takes it out so my shampoo puts it back in, that's all.

Igrat was wandering around her room, picking up things and looking at them, acting for all the world as if she was a young child with her first toys. The sight saddened Naamah, she was becoming aware of the fact that Igrat had never really had a childhood. She'd been fighting for survival ever since she'd been a baby. Her suspicion of everything, her defensiveness, all were products of that battle. She watched Igrat open a cupboard and heard her gasp at the clothes inside. "Are all these for me?"

"They are. Some are mine, some Lillith's, they're ones we got tired of. They'll be a bit big for you but they'll do until you can buy some of your own."

"Do I have to pay for these?" The suspicion was back in Igrat's voice. She was very well aware that trapping a woman into debt was a very good way of turning her into a slave, She'd seen it done all too often and had people try it on her. Efforts she had always dodged.

"Of course not. Look on them as a welcome home gift. The things in this room belong to the family so they're yours as much as anybody else's. You can get your own things later. Your jewelry is in the box by the way."

Igrat looked at the jewelry box on a small table. Quietly she knew that the box was worth more than her small collection of jewels. "How can I buy things? I don't have any money."

"Parmenio will talk to you about that. He's had an idea. There are a lot of people who need to have things carried from one place to another. Valuable things, documents, whatever. A reliable person who can carry them safely can earn a lot of money. His idea is that he'll front the operation so people don't need to know it's you carrying the package. We'll charge high for the service of course." Naamah smiled, it was remarkable how almost anything could be turned into a profitable business once Lillith had put a little thought into it.

While she had been speaking, Igrat had moved and was standing by her bed, feeling it. "This is beautiful, I've never had anything like this."

"Not even when you were working?" Naamah smiled again to take the sting out of her words.

"No. Usually I did it standing against a wall in a back alley somewhere." Igrat's face showed her distaste and a flicker of shame. Then she smiled in return, a playfully wicked smile. "Why don't we try my new bed out together? Nobody around to disturb us."

Naamah felt herself flushing bright red. "Umm, nothing personal but I'd rather not. Not now."

She watched Igrat half-turn, looking back over one shoulder, one eyebrow raised, her face in a knowing smile. "What's the matter, afraid you might like it?"

"Actually I am, yes." Naamah's flush deepened and she felt herself fluttering, not least because she pictured herself taking Igrat up on the invitation. She needed to move away from the subject quickly before she changed her mind. "Why don't I show you the rest of our home? Where the servants' quarters are and where the storage rooms and so on are situated."

"That will be nice." Igrat's voice was grave but the laughter bubbling beneath it was threatening to burst through and her eyes were shining with enjoyment. Suddenly, both women realized just how long it had been since Igrat had ever had any real cause to be happy. Naamah didn't know how to answer but she didn't get a chance to reply.

The mood was broken by another bang on the door and Parmenio strode in. He grinned at Naamah but made straight for Igrat who flinched, fearing she'd done something wrong.

"Igrat. We're going to need your courier services sooner than we thought. Naamah, how soon before she can start travelling?"

"Two weeks, perhaps three. Why?"

"Antipater, Craterus and Antigonus are forming an alliance against Perdiccas. The whole Diadochi are going to break wide open. War's coming people, we'd better get ready to ride it out." He thought for a second. "This is going to be fun."

PART ONE
THE FIRST DIODOCHI WAR
(322 – 320 BC)

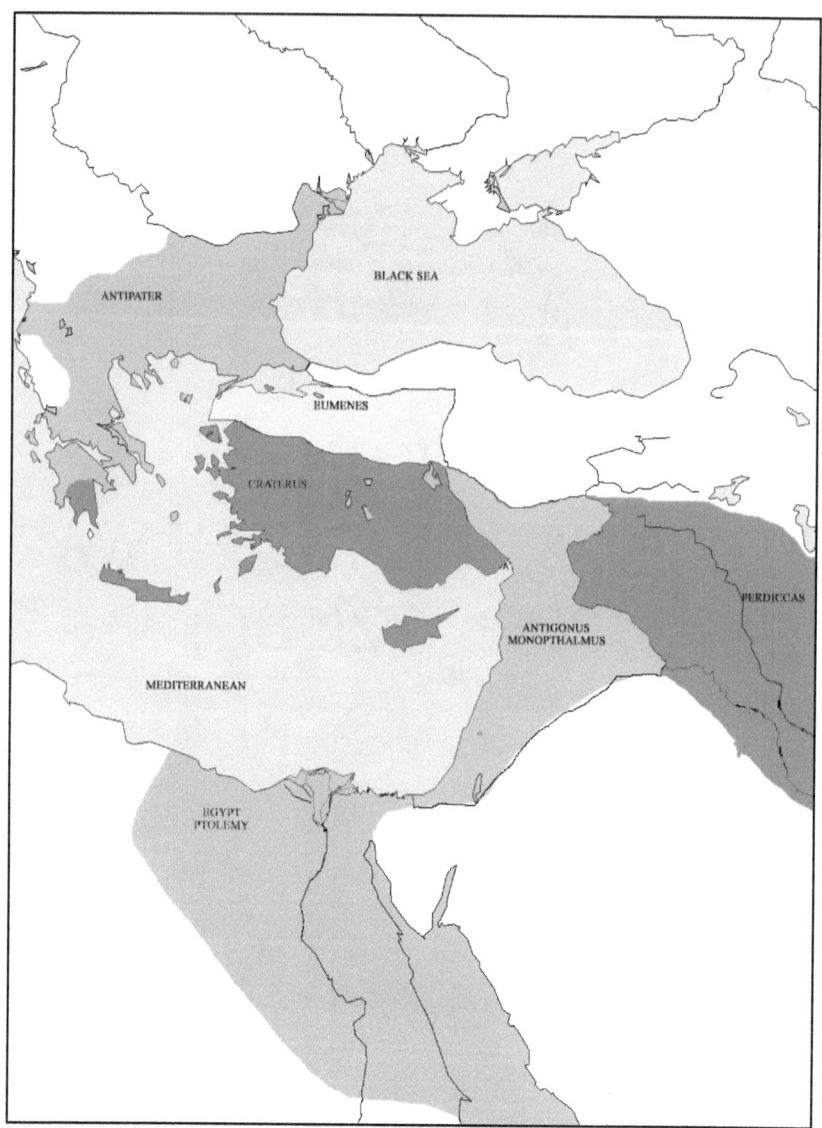

The Alexandrine Empire at the start of the First Diodochi War.

CHAPTER ONE

MANEUVERING

Palace of Seleucus Nikator, Seleucia-on-the Tigris

"I should get word to Antipater, declare my allegiance to him. As commander of the Companions, my position will be crucial." As a statement of intent, it was fairly weak but Seleucus Nikator still glanced around him. The room was empty save for Parmenio but his words had been treason to Perdiccas and that could buy them both a gruesome death.

"Are you sure that's wise?" Parmenio spoke mildly. As far as Seleucus knew, he was Parmenio the Elder's son. A favored son, whose existence had been kept secret because, as Parmenio's preferred heir and designated successor, his very life would be in danger from the jealousy and spite of Alexander. The same jealousy and spite that had led to Parmenio's 'murder' by Alexander's assassins. What Seleucus didn't know was the murder attempt had failed and there was no secret son. Just Parmenio and the finest strategic brain in the vast, sprawling Macedonian empire.

Seleucus stopped dead in his tracks. He was already beginning to learn that this strange man, this unknown son of Parmenio whose identity would be highly suspect had be not borne such a remarkable resemblance to his father, had an uncanny sense of what would happen if any given combination of events came to pass. "But I am Court Chiliarch, the senior officer in the Royal Army after the Regent and commander-in-chief to Perdiccas. If I turn away from him, his doom is sealed."

"Indeed it will. That's the problem really, Sire. The alliance is between Antipater, Craterus and Antigonus. They're all Satraps. Antipater has Macedon, Illyria, Epirus and Greece. Craterus shares those with him and is Guardian of the Monarch as well. Antigonus has Asia Minor. You're the Court Chiliarch and commander of the Companions, certainly. That makes you a vital part of victory but once victory has been won, a deadly threat.

You'll be the weakest of the four in the alliance and the one without a geographical power base. You'll have a powerful army but no home base and without anywhere to run to. And, your presence reduces each of their spoils from a third of the Empire to a quarter. So, put yourself in any of the three's shoes, what would you do?"

Seleucus mulled the matter over. Parmenio the Younger's words made common sense, all too much common sense. "I'd have me assassinated as soon as Perdiccas was out the way."

"I agree, very sensible thing to do. So we'll have to try and avoid that, won't we? What we have to do is make sure that, when you change sides, you do it when you have things to bargain with. Declare for Antipater now and you'll have nothing in your hands when the time to negotiate comes. You'll be hanging out to dry."

"So I have to stay with Perdiccas? He wants power for himself, he'll tear down everything we've built. Antipater wants to keep the Empire whole."

"Sire, the Empire is dying anyway. It's too big for one man to control, even Alexander couldn't do it. His control never really extended beyond the footsteps of his Army. The question is really what sort of successor system do we want? A weakly-linked federal empire? A series of smaller but centrally-controlled empires with a balance of power between them? Those are questions for the future. What we have to work out now is how you're going to dominate whatever does come next. You do want to dominate what comes next don't you?"

Seleucus nodded. Parmenio reflected that all the Macedonian generals were far too ambitious for their own good. Not that he, Parmenio, was any less so but he had time on his side. He could afford patience. After all, he had created this situation quite deliberately. Not even his family understood the care and exquisite timing behind the assassination of Alexander. That timing had been critical and Parmenio had been waiting patiently for the stars to fall into place.

The delicate timing had created a situation where Alexander had died leaving no clear heir. His half brother Arrhidaeus was a half-wit and fit only to be a figurehead, not capable of ruling independently. Alexander's wife, Roxana was pregnant, but even if the child was a son, which was by no means certain, it would take at least fifteen years for him to reach a suitable age to take power. So the death of Alexander had caused paralysis at the center of the system with the only certainty being that, whichever heir was selected, a long regency would follow. That was what suited Parmenio perfectly. The choice of regent had the potential to decide if Alexander's empire would survive intact. Or not as the case may be.

The prospect of the regency had split the Diodochi, the hard core of Alexander's Generals and his closest companions, wide open. Perdiccas had been Alexander's senior commander at the time of his death, and he wanted to wait for the birth of Roxana's child, and if he was a son declare him to be King Alexander IV. Perdiccas would then be regent to the new monarch. Eventually a compromise was agreed. Arrhidaeus would be declared to be King Philip III. He would be joint monarch with the infant Alexander IV, who had now appeared on the scene. Perdiccas would be epimeletes – either guardian or regent for the new kings, neither of whom was capable of ruling. He would have overall command in Alexander's Asian empire.

Parmenio wanted him dead, wanted that very badly. But Parmenio was a patient man.

"So what do we do?"

"We side with Perdiccas as you say. Don't declare for him, just side with him as if it was the natural thing to do, which it is of course."

"And go to war with Antipater, Craterus and Antigonus?"

"I don't think so, that group are still posturing. Ptolemy in Egypt is the one who really wants to set up as an independent empire now. He's the one Perdiccas will hurl his armies at because he's the one really serious threat. Take him out and things start to drop into Perdiccas's lap. Also there's bad blood, a lot of bad blood, between Ptolomy and Perdiccas and that will affect both their decisions. Perdiccas will attack Ptolemy and that's where the war will start. That will give you your chance, Perdiccas isn't the general he thinks he is, he'll botch the initial assault."

"But the other three?"

"Oh them? No problem. Craterus wants his own fiefdom as well. Now, Eumenes is a loyal Perdiccas ally right? Especially since Perdiccas helped him conquer Cappadocia and Paphlagonia. Craterus will hit Eumenes hard to take him out, depriving Perdiccas of his northern ally. But if we can hold up there, it should be possible to take out Craterus. With the north in chaos and the south bogged down in the Nile, that's when we're really valuable. We'll sell out both Perdiccas and Eumenes to Antipater at a time when their heads are worth anything we chose to ask for them. And what you'll ask for is Babylon and the East."

"Why Babylon?" Seleucus was genuinely confused.

"Because it's the center of power in this part of the world. Why do you think one empire after another has grown up here? Antipater and Antigonus don't understand that, they're fixated on Macedonia and Greece. But, it's here the real power lies. By the time they realize that, it'll be too late. And,

31

by the way, by selling out Perdiccas then, Ptolomy will owe you. That's an alliance worth having."

"You think we should trust Ptolemy?" Seleucus was incredulous.

"Trust him? Gods no. But, he's sharp, shrewd and knows what he wants. His own empire. As long as you're valuable to him, he'll be a good ally. Remember this Sire, trust is great but commonality of interests is better. Mutual value is best of all. Never trust a man who does things because he thinks they're the 'right thing to do', but a man who looks to his own interests, those you know when to trust."

Rear Area, Army of Eumenes, Cappadocia, 322 BC

"It looks like we're on the losing side." Igrat looked around at the scene surrounding the wagon she was riding in. To her, it seemed like chaos and disaster, there were wounded men to be seen, some hobbling on crutches, others trying to rest in the shade of the few trees that surrounded the camp. Other men skulked in the shadows, *deserters* she thought, *the ones who had found that going to war wasn't the romance it was supposed to be.* There were other carts as well, some selling wine, others bread and meat. A few were trading in armor and weapons, presumably either war loot or taken from dead soldiers, not that there was much difference between the two. Then there were the women in the camp. They had already seen her and their expressions were not welcoming. They were country women, hard, tired and prematurely aged, Igrat knew she looked young and fresh and she was from the cities. That made her a serious threat to their business. She knew she would have to be very careful or she would get a knife slashed across her face and she guessed repairing that kind of damage would be beyond even Naamah's skills.

"We're not on anybody's side Iggie." Callicrates the sutler was also looking around at the scene. "This doesn't look too bad, the backwash of every army looks like this, winning or losing. There's a bad feel to the air though, I don't like it. You'd better watch your step."

The warning was both sincere and an offer, Igrat knew what he meant and it was worth considering. She'd met him two weeks earlier as he was setting out from Seleucia with a cartload of sale goods and struck a deal with him. For five gold coins she would stay with him for the time it would take to ride up here and he could enjoy her without further payment for that time. She'd thought of asking for a silver coin but she remembered what Naamah had said about valuing herself and demanded five gold expecting to be negotiated down. It had stunned her when he had agreed on the spot and seemed well pleased with his bargain. Of course he had made most of his money back by renting her out on the way up but she'd expected that. He'd been fair, he'd divided the money he'd got evenly with her and he'd stayed close by when she was working. Once, a client had got too rough with her and the sutler's fists had seen him off very quickly. Igrat was happy with the arrangement she'd made. It could have been a lot worse and she'd got to this camp far faster than anybody could have expected.

"Hey, Attalus! How goes things?" Callicrates waved vigorously, attracting attention from a number of bystanders. Only one responded, another sutler who returned the wave and hurried over.

"Callicrates! I should have expected you to turn up. You've left it a bit late though, most of the traders are pulling out soon. Don't want to be here when the camp gets overrun."

The sutler nodded. He'd meant what he had said when he claimed that he and his fellow traders weren't on anybody's side but it still wasn't smart to be in camp when the army they were following lost. The winners would treat anything and anybody they found as their rightful loot and woe betide those who resisted them. A careful trader would be somewhere else when that happened and return a few days later when the furor had died down. The camp women would be well-advised to do the same, the victorious soldiers would help themselves to their stock-in-trade as well.

"What's happened? Last time we heard, everything was quiet up here."

"Where have you been?" Attalus looked at Callicrates' companion and whistled. "Now I see what you've been doing, no wonder you were too busy to keep up with the news. Surprised you can stay awake. Still, you always did like to go first-class."

Igrat raised an eyebrow and smiled. "You'll have to speak with my partner here if you want to ride the same way."

"Partner is it? Callicrates, you old dog. Where did you find her? Anyway, you did miss the important news. Neoptolemus of Armenia, has changed sides. He declared for Craterus and deserted Eumenes just as Craterus's army was preparing to cross the Hellespont. Eumenes was supposed to prevent Craterus crossing but fat chance of that with Neoptolemus changing sides like he did. Craterus is across and his army, combined with that of Neoptolemus are charging across Phrygia. At least Eumenes had the sense to pull back rather than get trapped out there but his back is to the wall now. He can't retreat any further. He has to fight, in a day or so, the battle's on."

"Can't Eumenes win?" Igrat didn't like what she was hearing. Her question got her a long-suffering glance from the two men.

"Of course not." Attalus spoke to her with weary patience, the same tone an adult used when explaining things to a young child, a tone that made Igrat decide that he would shortly mislay some of his more valuable property. "Eumenes isn't a general. He was Alexander's principal secretary and keeper of the Royal Journal, I guess he was one of Alexander's closest associates but never a general. Anyway, the troops hate him, he's Greek, not Macedonian. It's questionable even if they'll go through the motions of fighting for him. Craterus will walk all over him."

"Well, it's too late to do anything now. We'll sleep here and decide what to do in the morning. We're in the camp now Iggie, I guess our deal is over. Unless you want it to continue?"

Igrat thought carefully. "If everything is this bad, there's no point in me staying on. Will you be going back South?"

"Probably, try and sell my stock on the way. Better to sell at a small loss than getting a total write-off when it's looted. Same deal?"

"If I decide to go south, yes." She noted the expression of delight on Callicrates face. "But for one night, I'm going to look around, I've never seen anything like this before. Can I use the back of the wagon? I've got a few girl-things to do."

"Of course, but you be very careful out here. This is a rough place. Attalus and I are going to have a drink. At his wagon if you need help."

The two men went off to seek solace in a jug of wine while Igrat slipped into the covered back of the wagon. Mixed up in the stock of trade goods was her bag, a blanket folded into a sack that she could slip over her shoulder if she had to walk anywhere. First thing out was a box containing make-up Naamah had made for her. She quickly lined her eyes with kohl, then wiped a slight hint of fine olive oil over her cheeks. Then she dusted her face with the powders Naamah had matched to her normal skin colors, highlighting her cheekbones and complementing the black of the kohl. Finally, she painted her lips with her red-dyed wax and honey mix. Semiramis had taught her how to use the cosmetics and, by the time Igrat had finished, she could barely recognize herself. Then, she took a tunic that Lillith had given her and slipped it on. Lillith's clothes suited her better than Naamah's which wasn't surprising considering the Igrat was much closer to Lillith's coloring. Finally, she took a shimmering silk shawl, draped the front edge over her head so that it hung down around her, leaving her face bare. She drew it close, then fastened a silk girdle around her waist to hold it in place. A pair of sandals finished off her dress and she was ready to complete her journey. All she needed to do was pick up the scrolls she had been entrusted with and she was off. Night had fallen and it was a good time to make her delivery.

There was a clearly defined path that led from the camp-follower's area to the regimented lines of tents that marked the quarters of Eumenes' Army. Igrat had only just started to follow it when a group of three camp women came out of the darkness. They were talking amongst themselves and Igrat could hear the ugliness in their tone.

"She'll be around here somewhere. Run her out before she takes all the good trade."

"Hey you." Another woman snapped at Igrat, "Have you seen the new . . . ."

One of her companions jabbed her in the ribs and the woman stopped short, looking at Igrat more closely. When she spoke again, it was in a much more subdued and deferential voice. "I am sorry, Lady, I did not mean to disturb you."

Igrat did a double take, then realized the women had mistaken her for the wife or concubine of one of the Macedonian officers. That meant they believed disturbing her was a serious, potentially fatal, mistake. One word to her supposed husband and the women would be literally skinned alive for their rudeness to her. The Macedonians didn't care about what happened to the local women, but lay a hand on one of theirs and their vengeance would be swift and savage. When she'd been on the other side of that divide, Igrat had railed against the injustice of it, now she was protected by the same rule, she saw it as being entirely reasonable. She looked down her nose at the camp women, a very good approximation of the arrogant manner adopted by the Macedonians who had torn the Persian Empire apart.

"Watch your mouth." Igrat snapped the phrase out in Attic Greek, using up about a third of her vocabulary in the process. Then she switched to Koine, her stumbling and mispronunciations would be mistaken for an Attic speaker trying to use the street language. "Mind your business and let others mind their's. If there is any trouble here, I'll see you answer for it to the Guard."

The women paled at the threat and backed off into the darkness, mumbling profuse apologies as they did so. *People take you at your own valuation* Naamah's words rung in Igrat's mind as she approached the military camp.

"You stop!" The guard snapped the words out. "Business here?"

"Business indeed." Igrat slipped the shawl off her head, posed and winked at the Guard. "My client had me brought up all the way from Babylon for his pleasure and he's waited long enough for a woman to be uncomfortable sitting on his horse."

First Diodochi War

The Guard laughed at the picture of a Macedonian officer sitting painfully on a horse, scanning the horizon for his long-awaited relief to arrive. "Whoever your client is, he's got taste, I'll give him that. Now, if you want some real men, we're off duty in two hours."

"Five gold coins?" Igrat swung her hips and lifted an eyebrow.

The Guard gulped. "Gods, you must be good. Beyond our means that."

"Perhaps after the battle? I give discounts to winners."

"That'll be us then." The Guard smiled broadly. In his eyes, it wasn't often he got to exchange words with a high-class woman like this. "Don't know what's got into Eumenes, but he hasn't put a foot wrong since we got here. We all thought we were doomed when he took over, him being a Greek librarian and all, but he's dodged every trap, got us out of every tight hole and bloodied Craterus's point troops a couple of times into the bargain. Now we're giving battle, he must have something in mind. Look, here's a pass Lady, if you need to get out again, just show it to the Guard."

Igrat took the wooden disc and smiled her thanks to the guard before setting off into the camp. She was looking for a tent with a specific mark, a circle with two dots and a curved line inside. It was the agreed mark for Parmenio's tent, Igrat still couldn't read properly so the sign was as good an identification as it came. It took a few minutes but she found it, a larger and more ornate tent than most with two guards outside the entrance.

"Stop Lady. You can't go in here."

"I am expected. Please tell the General that Igrat is here, in accordance with his orders, concerning the matter of Antipolis. Make sure you mention my name." The man hesitated. "I do not think the General will be pleased if I am delayed."

The guard went inside and Igrat heard a mumble of voices followed by a sharp command from Parmenio in a voice that reminded her of the time in the cart when he'd hit her. The guard returned and ushered her through the tent flap.

"Parmenio my Lord, I am here at your command. How may I serve you?" As she spoke, she rolled her eyes at the guard's departing back.

"Well, I trust." The Guard safely out of the way, Parmenio took Igrat into the rear portion of his tent where they could speak privately. As he did so, she looked around, seeing the maps spread on the table and the armor hanging on its hooks from the wall.

"How did the trip go Igrat?"

"Very well, I made it up in two weeks. I've got your scrolls here." She reached into her bag and pulled them out. Unobtrusively, Parmenio checked the seals. Igrat caught the movement and laughed. "Parmenio, I couldn't read them even if I'd opened them. There are advantages to having an illiterate messenger you know."

"Not you Igrat, but they may have been stolen, read and returned on the way up. Never take things on faith, always check everything out. Two weeks is good time, you beat the official messengers by a wide margin. No sign of them yet. How did you do it."

"Whored my way up. Made a deal with a sutler and he gave me a ride in exchange for me giving him some. We're both happy and he might give me a ride back down on the same terms."

Parmenio laughed and shook his head. "Sit down and help yourself to some wine while I read these."

There was silence in the tent for a few minutes while Parmenio read the dispatches and Igrat sampled his wine. It was very good, much better than the jugs Callicrates had brought up. Eventually, Parmenio dropped the scrolls with a satisfied sigh.

"It's going well?" Igrat was still concerned at the sentiments in the sutler's camp.

"Very well. The Egyptian campaign could hardly be going any worse. Perdiccas's army has reached the eastern branches of the Nile, but he's stuck in front of the river and the earthwork defenses Ptolemy has thrown up. He's losing men in fruitless attacks and his Army is losing its spirit. Seleucus should be able to move soon. Any verbal messages?"

"Of course." Igrat closed her eyes and concentrated, then started to repeat the first message from Naamah. Listening, Parmenio could hardly believe it was Igrat speaking, her husky tones were quite different from Naamah's gravel-like delivery but Igrat had the pauses, cadences and phrasing perfectly. He was in no doubt what he was hearing was exactly, word-for-word, what Naamah had said and how she'd said it. Igrat finished with an admonition to Parmenio, instructing him to take care and not get himself killed. Then she opened her eyes.

"That's goes for all of us you know. We'd all be really angry with you if you get killed."

"I'll try not to. Any more messages?"

"Of course." Igrat closed her eyes again and repeated the message from Lillith, reeling of some figures to reassure Parmenio that the family was doing well despite the outbreak of war. Once again, she had the distinctive pitch and intonation of Lillith's speaking style perfectly and again, Parmenio was left in no doubt he was getting the message word-for-word perfect. It was the same with the messages from the rest of the group, even though the contents were similar, Igrat had the delivery of each down perfectly. Parmenio was fascinated by the ability.

"Just how do you do that?"

"Remember messages? I always have been able to. Since I could never read and write, I had to be told everything and the only way I could use what I'd been told was to remember it exactly. If you have messages for us back home, I can do the same for you. But, Parmenio, business. Everybody in the sutler's camp thinks you are going to lose, yet your soldiers think you'll win. What's happening?"

"Battle's going to start, day after tomorrow. Igrat, it's pretty unusual for soldiers to believe they are going to do anything but win but this time they're right. The sutlers are wrong."

"They say Eumenes' Army is outnumbered three to one and since he's a Greek, they hate him. They're planning to pull out soon."

"It's not three to one, Craterus and Neoptolemus have 40,000 men between them. I've got 25,000 and I'm fighting on ground I chose a long time ago. A lot of the men know I'm Macedonian, although there are several different stories of just who I am, and they know Eumenes is a figurehead along for the ride. The rest think that Eumenes has been inspired by the Gods so they're putting their prejudices aside for the while. All in all, they're happier than they let on. Soldiers always grumble Igrat, it's a good sign. Even better if they complain about the food. The time to watch out is when they get sullen and stop moaning. I must admit, the bit about the sutlers planning to leave is worrying. If the men are worried about their baggage and wives, that's a real problem."

Igrat thought about that and an idea formed in her mind. "Parmenio, can you loan me two hundred gold?"

Parmenio started at the amount. "What for?"

"The sutler I came up with has a friend who warned him to leave. If I can persuade them to stay and buy up the trade good of those who plan to leave, it'll make people think twice about leaving. Callicrates said he wouldn't even cover his costs if he sold his trade goods on the way back south so the other traders will be happy to part with theirs at cost or less. They'd rather stay and take a chance on a profit than a certain loss. It's the dead loss of losing they fear and if Callicrates is staying and has the confidence to buy them out, they will stay as well."

Parmenio thought it out and decided it was worth trying. He went over to a chest, got out the coins and put them in a leather pouch before giving them to Igrat. She hung it around her neck, slipping the pouch under her tunic.

"Parmenio, how did you know the battle would be here?"

"Igrat, imagine you're being chased by a savage dog."

"Don't have to imagine, been there. There are those who think unleashing a savage dog on a woman is funny."

Once again, Parmenio reflected on the different worlds he and this woman had come from. "Well, you're being chased by a savage dog, there are two paths ahead of you. Which do you take."

"The one that offers the best chance of escape of course."

"And which one does the dog take?"

"The one I did of course." Igrat paused for a second. "Ahhhh."

"Exactly, Craterus has been chasing us across Phrygia and all the time we've been leading him here. Because here, I can win if I had ten thousand men against his forty thousand. He's got his neck stretched out across a block and I am going to drop an axe on it."

"Look, this is how it's going to happen. The weakness of every Army is its right flank. You see, the individual soldiers in the Phalanx carry their shields on their left arm. They use it to protect the soldier to their left, not themselves. This means that the men at the extreme right of the phalanx were only half-protected. In battle, opposing phalanxes exploit this weakness by attempting to overlap the enemy's right flank. To stop that happening, commanders put their elite heavy infantry, the hyspasists on the right of the Phalanx to guard its flank. Conversely, they put their heavy and light cavalry on their left so that it can attack the vulnerable enemy right."

Igrat was staring at the wooden blocks on the map, trying very hard to understand, not least because it was obvious that Parmenio was happy and telling her about this was giving him a lot of pleasure. "But you haven't got much on your right at all."

Parmenio grinned triumphantly. "No, I haven't. Just some auxiliaries, mostly archers and slingers and light cavalry. Eumenes is commanding that force. But my right is guarded by something much better than troops. See how the whole battlefield slopes off to my right? Well, the river drains into that ground to my right and it's a swamp. Oh, it looks firm enough and a man can walk across it although if he stands too long in one spot, the water will start to ooze out. But if he runs, he'll break through the surface and into the mud underneath. Horses will bog down even more quickly. And Craterus doesn't have much in the way of heavy cavalry, instead he's got the chariots Neoptolemus of Armenia brought with him. Now, chariots with scythed wheels are deadly if they can get up to speed and hit in mass but in that swamp? They'll be up to their axles in mud before they can get into a trot.

"In the center, Craterus's phalanx will have to advance up the slope towards mine. That's a rocky broken slope and his men will find it impossible to hold formation and keep their sarissas under control."

Parmenio thought for a second. "This is one situation where he would have been better off with the old doru but never mind. My phalanx, formed up and on smooth ground can hold him even though it's only half the size of his. And everything else, my heavy infantry, heavy and light cavalry, all of it, is on the left, behind the high ground. When they charge, its smooth going and all downhill slamming straight into Craterus's right."

"And then you will win." Igrat spoke firmly and with total conviction.

"And we will win. Craterus's troops will fold because they're mercenaries and there's no money to be made in fighting a losing battle. Neoptolemus will fold because his troops will realize they are doing all of the dying and they'll end up the filling in a meat-grinder unless they back off."

"And now my part is to persuade the sutlers to stay so your men know their rear is safe." Igrat went over to Parmenio, took his hands and lifted them so they touched her cheeks. "You just be sure you don't get killed all right?"

Parmenio started slightly, the gesture Igrat had made was that of a daughter speaking to a loved father. He hadn't quite worked out what his relationship with Igrat was, but now she had taken that initiative and made a decision, it was one he very much approved of. She bowed to him, then left quickly.

Estate of Parmenio, Seleucia-on-the Tigris

"You can't leave it there!" Apollo sounded indignant that Igrat had broken off her story to drink some wine and eat some of the skewers of meat that had been brought in. "I want to hear about the battle."

"And I want to hear how you left here with a couple of silver coins and came back with a purse full of gold and a wagonload of loot."

"Are you sure you want to know how Igrat managed that?" Gusoyn spoke dryly.

"I think we'd all like to know how she managed that. But I want to know how Parmenio is doing up there. Nobody around here thought Eumenes had a chance until news of the battle came in, now they're in a state of shock." Semiramis looked around at the group. Igrat was a natural story-teller, she'd got them caught up in her account of her journey up to Parmenio's camp and the events in there. Everybody was waiting for the next installment.

"Well, all right then." Igrat looked at the wine on the table, and saw that the jug was empty. "But we'll need some more wine."

Rear Area, Army of Eumenes, Cappadocia, 322 BC

Igrat walked back along the path towards the area where Callicrates and Attalus had drawn their wagons up side-by-side . Around her, other sutlers were already starting to load up their wagons and preparing to leave. Nobody had said anything, nobody had made a decision but there was an unspoken agreement that it was time to get out before troops from Craterus and Neoptolemus overran the campsite. Her mouth twisted slightly. *People were a problem, they always had been.*

To her relief, the two sutlers she had marked out as the start of her scheme hadn't started packing up yet. She knew it was much easier to stop somebody from doing something than that to change their minds once they'd started and what she had in mind was going to be a hard act to sell.

"Hey Igrat! Hurry up if you want to come along, we're going to leave."

Callicrates called out to the familiar figure on the path but when she stepped into the lantern-light he sucked his teeth in shock. He'd known Igrat was beautiful but seeing her made up and dressed in fine clothes, he realized now she was much more than that. "Gods, you look incredible. If you'd dressed like that on the way up we'd have made a fortune."

"We wouldn't have made anything at all, the clients would have been scared off by the cost. Dress to match the market, Callicrates. And why are we leaving?"

Attalus sighed wearily. Callicrates's companion might have been a sight for sore eyes but she was a woman and didn't understand things. She'd had this all explained to her and still she didn't understand. "Because Eumenes is going to lose and we don't want to be overrun here. We'd lose everything. So we get out fast and save what we can."

"Eumenes's Army isn't going to lose. I've spent the last couple of hours, ever since dusk, up in his camp with the officers. They all are sure that their Army is going to win."

"What do they know?" Attalus was openly scornful in a way that made Callicrates look at his friend sharply, he might have been an old friend but he looked on Igrat as his woman and didn't take the note of contempt well.

"More than we do. Firstly, Eumenes isn't commanding, there's a Macedonian general up there, a real one, one who has never lost a battle. All the men up there speak well of him. And this battlefield is carefully chosen. It's narrow, the enemy army is being funneled into a restricted area so their extra numbers won't mean much."

Although she didn't realize it, Igrat was repeating Parmenio's lecture world-for-word and her voice even sounded like his. "And the odds aren't that bad anyway. Craterus has been losing men all the time in the advance across Phrygia, stragglers, garrisons, losses from ambushes. Eumenes has been picking up men as he retreated. Now, the odds are much better."

"Who is this general who makes such a difference?" Attalus was almost at the point of jeering and silently Igrat blessed him. She could wrap Callicrates around her fingers and the hostility to her from Attalus would push him into agreeing with her.

"Parmenio."

"That's ridiculous. He's been dead for ten years or more." The sneer was obvious and Callicrates shifted irritatedly.

"Not the father, the son. Parmenio's son, one whose existence he kept a dark secret to protect him from Alexander." Igrat repeated the agreed-on cover story with real conviction. Sincerity was always crucial and nobody was better at faking it than Igrat. "I've seen him, he looks just like Parmenio the Elder's picture. The troops and officers are saying his arrival is a sign from the Gods. So, we're staying."

"That's all right for you to say, but we could lose everything."

"Have you any idea what happens when a group of drunken soldiers get hold of a woman? If she's lucky, she dies quickly. If she's not, she gets torn apart and left still living. I'm risking a lot more than just everything. But there's more to this than just staying. We can make our fortunes here."

"How can we do that Iggie?" Callicrates was thoughtful, and the idea of making a fortune appealed to him.

"Everybody else is pulling out, right? Just as you were planning to do. They'd sell their goods for what they can get, say one part in ten below cost, is that right?"

"If we were very lucky. Two parts in ten below cost is more likely, three parts in ten if the Gods turn their faces from us."

"Oh, they will, Callicrates, one thing one can always count on with Gods, they will turn their face from you when you need them."

The sutler blinked slightly at the blasphemy and the venom behind it. "Three part in ten then."

"So, we go around all the sutlers now. We have some gold and we use it to buy their goods, two parts in ten below cost. You said it yourself, it's better to accept a small loss than a large one. When the Army of Eumenes wins, we'll have a monopoly of what all the soldiers want. We can charge what we like and then use the money we gain by buying up the loot from when Eumenes' men raid the enemy camp. They'll sell it at rock bottom prices for more money to buy drink and women. We'll have a near-monopoly of that as well. We buy low, sell high, use the money to buy low - again and sell high – again. We could make 50 coins for every ten we start with. Or a hundred. "

It wouldn't be quite that profitable and everybody knew it. When word that Callicrates and Attalus were staying and buying out their rivals started to spread, quite a few of the sutlers would realize they knew something that the others did not and they'd stay to share the loot. Some might even start buying up the stock of the faint-hearted as well. For all that, the prospects of making an immense profit were tantalizing. All that was necessary was the means to turn prospect into reality.

"All well for you to say, but where do we get the gold?" Attalus had changed from jeering to grumpy. Amongst other things, he'd noted that Callicrates had subtly shifted his position so he was sitting beside Igrat. That small move spoke volumes. He wasn't being asked for his opinion on what to do, rather he was being asked whether he wanted to be a part of a policy already decided.

"You have some coin put away I'd guess. And I can make a contribution as well." Igrat reached under her clothes and fished out the pouch of gold, spilling the contents into her lap. The two men gazed at the golden flood and then looked at her.

"Where did you get that from Iggie?"

"I told you, I've been up with the Macedonian officers."

"You couldn't have earned that much in a couple of hours, not even with looking the way you do."

"Who said that? And who counts the contents of their purse before a battle?"

"You stole it?" Attalus breathed the words almost with respect. "Gods, girl, you've got nerve. The Macedonians would burn you alive if they'd caught you."

"I never said I stole it." Igrat looked around. "Well, do we start buying or let this opportunity slip by?"

Attalus and Callicrates exchanged glances. "We'd better get to work before the others actually leave."

CHAPTER TWO

BATTLE OF THE HYLLUS RIVER

Right Flank of Eumenes Army, Hyllus River, Border of Cappadocia

A lesser man would have been insulted. Eumenes had been relegated to commanding the right wing of his own Army, and a pretty puny right wing it was. About 500 auxiliaries, a mix of Parthian bowmen and Rhodian slingers, and the same number of Prodromoi light cavalry. Less than a thousand men all told and undoubtedly the weakest forces in his Army. His command wasn't just tiny, it was weak to the point of being feeble.

That made no sense at all. Everybody knew that the right flank was the weakest part of a phalanx-based army. That was why it was always guarded by the best troops available, the hypaspists and the Companion cavalry. Not this rag-tag bunch of auxiliaries and skirmishers. To an observer, the conclusion was obvious. The librarian and archivist Eumenes who only knew of war from the reports of others had believed the myth that the phalanx was the decisive part of his army and loaded all his strength into that, leaving his flanks bare and exposed. A man who had never commanded any serious military force in his life couldn't be expected to understand that the phalanx was there simply to fix the main body of the enemy in place and allow other forces to do the killing.

Eumenes knew that nobody could have expected him to have understood that, and that was a fair expectation because he hadn't. The man really commanding this Army, the man sent by Seleucus Nikator to aid him, had understood this and much more besides. Eumenes had taken his lessons to heart. The right flank of the Army was defensive, intended to protect the phalanx. The center of the Army, the phalanx was the pinning force, the fulcrum upon which the army rotated. The left flank was the offensive arm, that would crush the enemy right. Over the on other side, Craterus and

Neoptolemus were seeing just what Parmenio wanted them to see, an Army that apparently had all its strength concentrated in the center. They saw the puny right and even more inconsequential left and thought that was all. What they didn't see, and couldn't, because Eumenes' center was at the top of a long slope and they were looking up at it, was that the right and center were stripped down to the bare minimum. Of Eumenes' 25,000 men, fully 16,000 including all of his Companion and Thessalian cavalry, his hypaspist elite infantry and a second phalanx, were loaded into that left flank, concealed behind the ridge formed by the rising ground. When the time was right, they would pile into Craterus's right flank, a flank guarded by only 2,000 hypaspists.

A lesser man would indeed have been insulted by his command of a thousand men from the army that was nominally his but Eumenes was not such a man. He knew his limitations and understood why he had such a limited role. He also knew that what he had to do was critical, he had to stop the chariots and heavy cavalry blow that was about to descend on his handful of men. He also knew exactly how he had to perform that task. He was a man who knew his limitations and this one was well within them.

"Here they come boys." Eumenes heard the shouting from the officers as they saw the whole left wing of Craterus's Army surge forward. The Army of Neoptolemus had more than 300 scythed chariots backed up by heavy cavalry. If they could sweep aside the auxiliaries and light cavalry in front of them, and nobody on that side doubted that they should be able to do so, Neoptolemus would be able to send his own infantry in to roll up the phalanx and that would be that. It should have been a quick, relatively painless victory scored by two professional commanders over a hapless, bungling amateur.

The spray shimmered in the sun as the chariots and cavalry crossed the River Hyllus. That was another mistake that Eumenes was supposed to have made. Craterus assumed he would have read the reports of the Granicus and not realized that the Hyllus was a very different river from the notorious Granicus. The Hyllus had gentle, sloping banks and a shallow, firm bottom. To horses and chariots it formed no obstacle at all while to infantry it was, at best, an inconvenience. The obstacle that Craterus imagined Eumenes was depending on hardly existed.

And yet, the evidence was there. It was here, in this valley, that the Hyllus left the bed of impermeable clay over which it had run so far and ran instead over permeable chalk. Even as the chariots and cavalry crashed through the river, water was draining out through sink holes in the river bed into a bowl-like, clay-lined depression on the southern side of the river. There, unable to flow out, it stagnated, turning the soil in the bowl into a glutinous stew. The sun had baked the first few inches into a hard crust, leaving the wet ground underneath continually saturated by the river water running past. Even then there was one last clue to warn the unwary, the grass was a thick, lush green, quite at odds with the parched brown of the surrounding hills.

None of the warnings registered as the chariots plowed into the swamp, the narrow wheels breaking straight through the crust and into the mud below. To the horses pulling them, it felt as if the drivers had suddenly thrust a spear through the wheels so great was the jerk as the chariots slowed down and started to sink. They reared up, their hooves breaking through the crust as well, causing them to panic as they too started to struggle in the sludge. Ironically it was the chariots at the front that got furthest before they ground to a complete halt, their progress served to churn the ground, destroying the crust and bringing the marsh beneath to the surface.

To Eumenes, the first sign of the impending disaster was the change in the motion of the horses. Their smooth gallop changed into a series of lurching leaps as they struggled to get clear of the mud. He watched intently as the chariot charge degenerated into chaos, the chariots piling up as more and more entered the swamp. They had crossed too fast, the change from firm footing to nighmarish treachery too sudden for the charioteers to respond. The cavalry following them tried to avoid the log-jam of wrecked and stranded chariots and struggling horses but the swamp extended all along that portion of the river bank and there was no way around it. Only by going upstream could they avoid the trap and that would take them straight into the waiting sarissas of the phalanx drawn up along the ridgeline. They knew better than to charge uphill into the hedgehog of spearpoints presented by an undisrupted phalanx. Even if they hadn't their horses did. No horse was foolish enough to charge straight at such an obstacle.

Eumenes watched with satisfaction as the massive blow aimed at his right degenerated into chaos and futility. He heard his commanders giving the orders for the slingers to use staff-slings and he watched the Rhodians prepare their weapons. A small lead shot inserted into pouch, two slow rotations to seat it properly, then a single savage swing that hurled it out towards the stranded chariots. The Rhodians weren't quite the best slingers around, the Balaeric slingers had that honor, but they were easily good enough. With a staff sling, a Rhodian could throw his lead shot some 600 yards and the range was much shorter than that. They fired, slowly and deliberately, conserving their precious lead shots and aiming carefully at the most dangerous targets, the archers and the charioteers themselves. The Armenians started going down, slowly at first, then more quickly as the slingers got the range. Trapped and under the galling long-range fire, the charioteers abandoned their vehicles and started to pick their way back across the swamp, leaving a steady trail of their dead behind them.

Eumenes waved his arm and his auxiliaries started to move forward, slowly, carefully, being sure to keep Craterus's left at a distance as he did so. He kept his light cavalry in hand. Their role was to guard against an unexpected breakthrough, not achieve anything spectacular. An unspoken duty was to ensure that the auxiliaries didn't turn tail and run. If they tried to the cavalry would cut them down. But, this day, there was no need for that. The retreat of Craterus's left was rapidly turning into a rout when Eumenes's troops got close enough for the slingers to switch to normal slings and the archers to begin their work. It was more than enough, the enemy cavalry and the survivors of the chariots couldn't take any more. They started to exchange arrow shots with Eumenes's men who were edging forward through the churned-up mud of the swamp. As they did, they were crowding the enemy cavalry back against the river, pinning them down.

Estate of Parmenio, Seleucia-on-the Tigris

"Right, so the Armenians got stuck in the mud. That's all very well but what was Parmenio up to?" Apollo was leaning forward, trying to catch every word that Igrat said.

"Patience, Apollo, Igrat will get there. At least we know where that cartload of goodies came from. Why did you bring it here, I'd have thought it would have been simpler to have sold it up there?" Semiramis was curious, the description of the battle was bringing back memories with a vividness she had long forgotten.

Igrat shook her head. "We got in first, bought up everything we could get our hands on, especially the wine, and then sold it for top-plus prices when the soldiers came back after the battle. We cleaned them out selling wine at three or four times the usual price and then gave them back the gold buying the loot from Craterus's camp off them at one coin in ten of the real price. By the time the other sutlers came back, we had the cream of the loot, worth fifty, sixty times as much in gold as we had started with. Then, the other sutlers flooded the market and knocked the bottom out of prices so we got out of there. We split the loot up three ways and I brought mine back here, I thought that Lillith was the financial genius, she could do a better job of turning it into cash that I could. Where is my cart by the way?"

"In the courtyard, Gusoyn is watching the servants while they unload it into our strongroom. There's ten thousand coin in that cart at a guess." Lillith was smiling broadly, at the thought of that much gold in the family accounts made her forgive Igrat for the stab wound that had almost killed Apollo. "That's five for you Igrat, five for the family."

"Take it all, I owe you so much money."

"No, not a good idea. People who are short of money do foolish things to get some so it's in our interest for all the family to be rich. The rule is, every time somebody earns money, half goes into the family funds, half is theirs. And you will need money, you can't wear cast-off clothes all the time."

"These cast-offs as you call them are better now than anything I ever had before. Strike a deal? You take four thousand off my share and that's a third of my debt paid. I'll keep the other thousand." Lillith thought for a second and nodded.

"Do we have to pay the cart driver?" Apollo was looking at three long cloth-wrapped packages in the corner. Igrat had brought them in but not explained what they were.

"No, I've done that." Igrat smiled. "Ride for a ride, he had me every night on the way down. He's happy."

"Exhausted but happy." Apollo returned her smile.

"I hope so, or I'm losing my touch. Now, want to hear more about the battle?"

Center of Eumenes Army, Hyllus River, Border of Cappadocia

Leonnatus gave profound thanks for the fact that he had a real general to serve. He'd almost been in despair when he heard that Eumenes was commanding the army and he'd started to make some very discrete approaches to Craterus about changing sides. Of course, Neoptolemus deserting to Craterus had ruined the situation for everybody else. It was the old story, the first people to recognize the winner and change sides got the good deal. Everybody else would be lucky to get the leavings.

Only, looking over to the right, Leonnatus saw that Neoptolemus had made a bad mistake. His assault on the flank of the Army had been a disastrous failure. The chariots were sinking in the mud, their horses fighting to get free of the morass that threatened to drown them. Around them, the light auxiliaries and Prodromoi light cavalry were filtering past, moving over the swamp in a way that the chariots and heavy cavalry could only dream of. One by one, the stranded chariots were being isolated and their crews killed. Some of them anyway. Other charioteers had surrendered and joined the slingers and bowmen in cutting the horses loose and getting them out of the mud. Eumenes was commanding out there and doing well which only went to prove that even a Greek could fight when told what to do by a Macedonian.

That's what had changed Leonnatus's mind about switching his allegiance. The arrival of a real Macedonian general, not just any one but a son of the great Parmenio, who bore a startling resemblance to his murdered father. It was Parmenio who had led them here, Parmenio who had chosen this battlefield where the ground was doing more to destroy Craterus's Army than the troops had done, so far at any rate. It was Parmenio who had stationed his phalanx along this ridgeline and ordered his troops to spend two days clearing their ground of the loose rocks that were everywhere. Those rocks had been rolled down the slope so that Craterus's phalanx would have to scramble over them on the way up. Looking down, Leonnatus could see the effect of that, the men laboring up the slope were in sad disarray that got worse as some of the larger rocks at the top of the slope were rolled down in their general direction. Most didn't make it to the attackers, getting lodged on the way down but even the threat was enough to split the ranks up still further.

For a combat formation that depended on men advancing together, shoulder-to-shoulder, the rock-covered slope was a disaster. By the time Craterus's phalanx reached that of Eumenes, they were exhausted and the ragged ranks were irretrievably disrupted. Instead of striking Eumenes' center as a solid blow, they were arriving piecemeal and were helpless before the array of sarissas pointing down the slope at them. Even worse, they knew they were helpless before that array and their spirit was more than half broken before the first sarissa thrust out.

That wasn't the case with the men under Leonnatus's command. Their spirits were sky-high and not just because of their advantage. Something had happened the night before, something that gave new heart even to the most pessimistic. A beautiful woman had suddenly materialized in the middle of the camp and gone to the General's tent. Well, that wasn't so unusual, Generals liked to get laid before a battle just as much as the commonest sarissaphoros. After all, who knew if they would get the chance to do it again? But, they hadn't. The General and the beauty had spent an hour discussing the plans for the battle! A dedicated General might give up the chance of a beautiful woman to ensure victory but a woman give up a tryst with a powerful General? Impossible. There was only one plausible explanation. The woman wasn't human. She had to be Athena Alcidemus, the Goddess of Victory herself, come down to give her blessing on Parmenio's plans. Leonnatus knew that, every man under his command knew that. Today their victory was divinely inspired, the very Gods themselves were looking down and aiding them. As his phalanx stepped forward to engage center of Craterus's Army, every single sarissaphoros in Eumenes's center knew for an absolute certainty that the day was already won.

For all the weakness on one side and the strengths on the other, the casualties were few and more by clumsiness than intent. Craterus's men knew they couldn't break through the phalanx facing them so why waste lives trying? Just go through the motions and buy time. Leonnatus's men knew that even with divine help, their own phalanx was too thin and spread out to develop the mass needed to punch through the enemy center. Most of all, both phalanxes were mercenaries, men whose living was war. They'd die if they had to, that was their profession, but there was no need to die unprofitably. They had no interest in the issues behind this battle, other than the commercial benefit of being able to say they'd been on the winning side at the Hyllus. In any case, one day the positions might be reversed and they'd be on the winning or losing side and they would hope to receive the same consideration. Above all they remembered the Granicus and Alexander murdering 18,000 Greek mercenaries in cold blood. Oh, he'd said it was because they were Greeks fighting for the Persians but everybody knew it was because they'd soundly thrashed the "Great" Alexander and he'd only been rescued from ignominious defeat by the skills of Parmenio. Nobody ever wanted that act of barbarous brutality repeated.

The sarissas weaved and interlocked, pushing back and forth but neither side had the desire to force the issue. Some of the sarissaphoros even grinned broadly at their opposite numbers, so sure were they that mass killing wouldn't be necessary. Craterus's blow on the right flank of Eumenes' Army had been checked, now his center was fixed and deadlocked. All that was left was the blow about to fall on Craterus's right flank and that Parmenio the Younger was commanding himself. Suddenly, Leonnatus wondered if he knew what had happened to his brother Philotas and he felt very sorry for Craterus.

Right Flank of Eumenes Army, Hyllus River, Border of Cappadocia

Parmenio checked his right flank and center. The force under Eumenes was pushing Neoptolemus back through the swamp while the center was holding perfectly. Craterus's hypaspist infantry guarding the right flank of his Phalanx had advanced over the river, past the field of rocks and were now moving up the slope towards Parmenio's position. There were 2,000 of them, about the same number of prodromoi light cavalry and a handful of auxiliaries guarding the camp. Five thousand at best and only 2,000 of them were really good troops. Parmenio's right flank had 16,000 men, a phalanx of 6,000 sarissaphoross, 2,000 hypaspist infantry, a thousand heavy cavalry and the rest were light cavalry. They were in line now, but as Parmenio gave the starting wave, only the Phalanx started to move. It was the right of his force and would take the lead as his assault started. His men would be moving in oblique order, the blows multiplying in force as each segment of the line struck home.

Craterus's hypaspist infantry saw the phalanx appear over the ridgeline and moved to counter it. This was their function after all, to defend the vulnerable right flank of the Phalanx now fighting in the rocks. The two forces collided and came to a halt in a welter of screams and blows, sarissaphoros and hypaspist fighting with all the fury that the men in the center so singularly lacked. Parmenio took a quick glance, once again, the phalanx was doing its work and the enemy hypaspists were pinned down, locked in place by the need to fight the great sarissas that threatened to tear through them. It was time, and he gave his second order, sending his own hypaspists over the ridgeline and down towards the now-exposed enemy right flank. With Craterus's flank guard firmly locked in place and fighting for its life, all that was in front of Eumenes's elite veterans was a gaping void.

Craterus's men weren't fools, their commanders saw what was developing, recognized the oblique order attack and guessed what was coming next. They were already flanked and Craterus's hypaspists would soon be enveloped and destroyed unless they got out of there. That was the point of the hypaspists, a phalanx by its very nature was locked on a single course and would move in a single direction. Turning one could be done but it was hard and the unit would be helpless while it tried. The hypaspists could turn and change direction but now, with their flank already under threat, the only way out for them was straight back. They started falling back, urged on by the points of the merciless sarissas but there was a problem. The same field of rocks that had crippled Craterus's center now acted as a barrier against retreat. With Eumenes's hypaspists already on their right flank and quickly moving behind them, Craterus's right started to disintegrate.

Time to move. Parmenio waved again and this time it was his heavy cavalry that started to move forward, in a wedge-shaped formation with himself and his personal guard located securely inside the point. He had to go with them, this was *the* decisive charge after all and inside the point of the wedge was just about the safest place available. Parmenio had strong opinions about generals getting killed, most of which rotated around the word 'don't'. Too many battles had been lost because one of the commanding generals had gone down with delusions of being a line soldier and been picked off. Still, as the heavy horse picked up speed going down the slope, he had to admit that cavalry charges were fun.

He even took the time to glance quickly over to his left. Craterus had his light cavalry over there, screening against an attack on his right flank although he'd never expected an oblique-order assault of this power. The enemy prodromoi were forming up to catch his heavy cavalry in the flank, Parmenio recognized that their commander was no fool and had seen the only way out of this mess. Then his own prodromoi came over the ridgeline and made straight for them. Parmenio recognized that he had been right, the enemy prodromoi commander wasn't a fool, outnumbered two, almost three, to one and already isolated from the main body of the army, it was time to leave. Craterus's prodromoi, the last organized unit on his right flank, broke and fled. Behind them, two squadrons of Eumenes's prodromoi pursued them, the other three swung round and made a wide arc. They would be heading behind the enemy main camp and cutting it off. Parmenio and his heavy cavalry were simply going to crash straight through that camp.

Ahead of him, Parmenio could see, framed neatly by his horse's ears, the camp guards. Lightly armed auxiliaries, with sword and short doru spear and little armor. A few arrows and slingshot rounds came out but few and wild. In response his heavy cavalry, cataphracts was the name that was being used more frequently since the idea of Alexander's companions was falling into disrepute, lowered their xyphon lances and headed straight for the ragged rows ahead. They never reached them, the line broke before the cataphracts could slam into them. They ran, and in doing so far more died than would have done if they had stood their ground. The xyphons caught them in the back and hurled their broken bodies to one side. A few of the lances shattered with the blows and their users dropped the remnants to draw their swords. As they did so, they were racing through the enemy camp, screaming women frantically trying to get out of the way, the sutlers desperate to try and save what they could of their stocks. Parmenio noted with amusement that his cataphracts were trying not to ride down the women. After all, they were worth good money when the battle was over.

Over it was, Parmenio never doubted it. Behind him, Craterus's right flank was in chaos. Craterus's hypaspists were already throwing down their arms while Parmenio's were starting to roll up the phalanx stalled on the rock-covered slope. They were mercenaries all and they'd negotiate a deal up there, Parmenio knew it and his own men would rejoice in the reputation of a company that had held off a force four times its number. Behind him, heading north out of the camp was a small group of men, almost certainly Craterus and his personal bodyguard trying to escape. They had no chance, Eumenes's prodromoi were already out there and even as Parmenio watched, the party was surrounded and brought to a halt. He held his breath for a second in case Craterus decided to go down fighting but he didn't have the stomach for that. Knives in the dark and whispered accusations were much more in his line. The prodromoi had his group surrounded and were bringing them back.

That just left the left flank under Neoptolemus and that was something to worry about. There were 10,000 men over there, mostly heavy cavalry and chariots. They'd been bloodied, badly so, and their cream was stranded in the swamp but if they got their act together they could still turn this battle around. Parmenio's own force was scattered, the horses winded, the infantry tied down in dealing with what was left of Craterus's army. A well-timed heavy cavalry charge could work wonders. Parmenio wondered if Neoptolemus had it in him.

Right Flank of Eumenes Army, Hyllus River, Border of Cappadocia

The situation was almost comical. The cream of Neoptolemus's Army was stuck in the mud and its men were working with those of Eumenes to try and get the horses out of the swamp before they exhausted themselves and drowned. Eumenes was under no illusions about the motivation. Those carefully trained war-horses were worth a lot of money and every one that his men rescued could be sold for a good amount of gold. From the other point of view, every one that Neoptolemus's men rescued was one less they would have to buy back at ruinous price. Commercial interests had largely overridden the demands of war and rescuing the horses was the prime interest of both sides.

Not all of them though, a large portion of Neoptolemus's cavalry was still stuck the other side of the swamp and the Armenian king was trying to get some organization into them. Eumenes guessed what he had in mind, there was a narrow strip between the swamp and the rocks that was good, solid ground. Neoptolemus intended to use that to get his cavalry around the edge of the swamp and then assault Eumenes. It might work, but the strip was narrow and Eumenes knew his Rhodian slingers and Parthian bowmen could turn it into a killing ground. And the battle was almost over.

Any fool could see that. Eumenes might be a Greek librarian but he was no fool. Parmenio's cavalry was in Craterus's camp, the right flank behind them was in ruins and had already thrown down their arms, the great phalanx that had formed his center was already collapsing as the mercenaries who made it negotiated a deal. Even from here, Eumenes could see there were strangely few bodies on the ground. There were few indeed where the two phalanxes had been pushing against each other and even over on the other flank, after the cavalry charges, the carnage was nothing like the scene here in the swamp. It had been the Neoptolemus's Armenians who had done the dying.

Despite that, Neoptolemus was trying to get his heavy cavalry organized for a charge along that narrow bridge of dry, smooth land. Eumenes could see him riding backwards and forwards along their ranks, see him shouting and waving his xiphon. Eventually, he gestured violently at the area where Eumenes's prodromoi were gathered and jabbed his xiphon in their direction, wheeled his horse around and set off.

Eumenes could not help but reflect that if this had been a tale told by a storyteller in a marketplace or recorded on one of the scrolls in his library, the cavalrymen would have been so impressed by the oration that they would have followed their leader through that narrow defile and staged the charge that snatched victory from the jaws of defeat. But this was reality and Eumenes was already learning how far reality was from the official accounts he had spent most of his life responsible for filing and preserving. As Neoptolemus rode off, a few of the cavalrymen made mocking salutes while others shifted uncomfortably on their horses but not one followed their leader into the charge.

Neoptolemus, his eyes fixed firmly ahead, plowed on and he must have covered at least a hundred yards before the anvil dropped. He looked over his shoulder to realize that he was alone, that his men had deserted him. Eumenes couldn't blame them, they'd done more than their fair share of dying and the battle was already lost. Pointless deaths were, well, pointless. Neoptolemus was still in shock from the realization that he was charging more than 500 light cavalry on his own when the first slingers started their throws. They beat the Parthian bowmen by only a few second.

The horse screamed as the lead shot thudded against its body and arrows smacked into it. It reared, and in doing so threw Neoptolemus, probably buying him a few minutes more life. He staggered to his feet, then fell again as a javelin thrown by one of the prodromoi struck him. Eumenes waved and the fire ceased. Then, he rode his own horse over to the scene and looked down. Neoptolemus's mount was on the ground, writhing from the penetrating arrows and the broken bones caused by the lead slingshots. The king himself was clambering to his feet, trying to draw his sword. Eumenes slipped from the saddle and drew his own.

"There's no need for this. It's over. Leave it." Eumenes's voice was almost desperate. He had hated Neoptolemus for the betrayal that had allowed Craterus to cross the Hellespont unmolested but to cut a man who was already beaten and badly wounded down didn't sit right with him. Then, in a flash of inspiration, he knew why he would never be a true warlord or successor to Alexander. It didn't matter anyway. Neoptolemus had his sword out and rushed Eumenes who parried the blow expertly. This wasn't war, it was dueling with swords and here Eumenes year's in the palace served him well. He was no sarissaphoros, no warrior, no strategos but he had practiced with a sword all those years and a duel between two men was something he knew all too well.

Neoptolemus started giving ground almost immediately as Eumenes parried his thrusts and countered with blows of his own. He fell back, yard by yard until he was back on the swamp where his great assault had foundered and there his feet broke through the dry crust and he staggered from the lost footing. Eumenes's sword sliced out, cutting the great artery in Neoptolemus's leg, sending a spray of blood skywards. That was the only dramatic part, then Neoptolemus just collapsed in the mud and died. *There had to be*, Eumenes thought, *more to the death of a King than that but there wasn't. Just bleeding to death in the mud.*

Eumenes walked along the strip of dry, smooth ground that had lured Neoptolemus to his death. The Army of Neoptolemus was before him, waiting to see what would happen next. Eumenes summoned his strength and gave the firmest, loudest shout he could.

"Send me your leader so we may discuss the terms I offer you."

Estate of Parmenio, Seleucia-on-the Tigris

"Oh my." Apollo was impressed, as much by Igrat's story as by the battle itself. "I mean I knew Parmenio was a General and all that but I never even guessed he could do things like that."

"Parmenio isn't just a General." Igrat spoke with some vehemence and the other women smiled to themselves. Parmenio's self-confidence and good humor gave him a magnetic attraction and even the street-hardened Igrat appeared to be succumbing to it. "He's a Strategos, a strategist, that's a step up from being just a General. Anyway, Lillith, you keep the family records. Parmenio asked me to give you this."

She took a scroll out of her tunic and passed it over to Lillith who took it with a measurable amount of apprehension. She opened and read it and, as she did so, her mouth twisted slightly. "Did you know this is your death sentence?"

Igrat went white. "No. he told me...."

"Don't worry, I'm just teasing. You do know what it really is?"

"I can't read it yet, but he told me what it was."

"Lillith, stop it." Naamah almost snapped the words out. "What's Parmenio done? Don't tell me he's married Igrat?"

Lillith laughed and watched Naamah and Semiramis waiting impatiently for her to tell them what the scroll contained. She glanced at Apollo and he winked back at her, he at least had already guessed it. "This scroll, signed by both Parmenio and Igrat, is formal notification that he has adopted Igrat as his daughter. There's a note in the adoption scroll that this is a private measure between them, defining their relationship, and doesn't affect her position with regard to the family as a whole.

There was a moment's silence as the news was absorbed and then Igrat found herself being grabbed and hugged, passed around the room from one person to the next.

"What's happening?" Gusoyn spoke from the door, he'd stepped through it as Igrat started making her second trip around the room.

"Parmenio's adopted Iggie as his daughter." Lillith spoke with a degree of satisfaction. Privately she'd been worried about the group's stability with four unattached women. With Igrat defined as Parmenio's daughter, that eased the relationship problem a bit. It had been easy at Delphi, with one woman serving as the Pythia the other paired with Parmenio. Or, that had been the theory.

"That is very good." Gusoyn grabbed Igrat and gave her a squeeze. "Parmenio needs somebody to keep him down to earth, without it he could lose touch with the rest of the world."

Igrat stared at him for a second. *Had he known what had almost happened after the battle? Surely not, the official messenger was still on his way down and he didn't know that part of the story.* "Thank you Gusoyn, that's a lovely thing to say. Look, I'm glad you're here now. I've got something for you and Apollo."

Igrat reached into the bag that was by her couch and took out two small pouches. "One of the Armenian chariots was crewed by a pair of identical twins. They got trapped in the marsh and tried to fight their way out rather than surrender. Didn't have the money to pay ransom I guess, and didn't want to be sold as slaves. Anyway, the Parthian bowmen killed them both. I was doing some business with the Parthians and I got these."

She opened the bags and took out two gold rings. "These are exactly identical. I've spent a couple of days trying to spot differences between them and I can't find any. So, I thought you could have one each. I know you have to be careful in public because your relationship would cause a scandal, but with these, you can wear them and everybody else will think they are just soldier's rings. But you'll know that they mean more than that."

Silently, Gusoyn took the rings, put one on his own finger and then took Apollo's hand and slipped the other on to his finger. Then he held his hand so the two rings were side-by-side. "Igrat, I don't know what to say. That's the nicest thing you could have done for us."

Igrat was crying slightly. "They're all right? Really? I never got presents for anybody before and I was so afraid I'd be doing something wrong."

"What Gusoyn said Iggie." Apollo spoke as quietly as Gusoyn had done. "To have thought of us in the middle of the chaos up there, to have found a gift so thoughtful. I honestly don't know how to thank you."

Naamah sniffed. "Typical of Igrat, gets all the men presents but forgets about us women." A chuckle ran around the room, breaking the mood perfectly. "And what's all this about doing business with the Parthians?"

"I didn't forget about you." Igrat was slightly indignant. "And I wasn't doing what you think with the Parthians, not then anyway, that came later. Some of their women had lost their men and the only way they could get some money to live on was to sell their equipment. The sutlers were going to cheat them, buy for a silver coin stuff that was worth ten or twenty gold coins. I made Callicrates and Attalus pay a fair price, made them realize that treating the women right would mean we could overcharge the men more later and they'd still thank us. Worked too. Anyway, I got these for you three."

Igrat got up and fetched the packages from where they rested against the wall. She handed them out and the women opened them hastily.

"Bows Iggie?" Lillith's voice was curious. Semiramis was handling hers with the familiar muscle-memory of long practice.

"Bows. We might have to defend this place and with Parmenio off at the wars, we've only got Apollo and Gusoyn to do so. Now, we can't fight with swords and spears but I saw how well the Parthian bowmen did in the battle with these bows and we can fight with them. We can back our men up with these once we know how to use them."

"I can't even pull it." Naamah was struggling with the bowstring.

"There's a trick to it, one I'll teach you." Semiramis pulled her bow back to the chin, feeling the wood flex in her hands as she did so. "These are superb bows, but all the Parthian ones are. Keep the wood oiled and waxed, it'll last forever. And Igrat is right, with these we can scare off robbers and brigands."

Semiramis didn't mean brigands and everybody knew it. Word would get around of a house with four women in it and only a couple of men to defend them. Men would come in the night and Lillith shuddered at the thought. "Well, Igrat has this household down pat doesn't she. Brings jewelry for the men and weapons for the women. Tell us how you got all this stuff Iggie."

Camp of Craterus, Now In Eumenes' Hands, Hyllus River, Border of Cappadocia

The scene was utter chaos as the aftermath of battle slowly sorted itself out. The Army of Armenia, or what was left of it, was already starting the long trek back to their home territory. Their commander had ransomed them with the gold that was supposed to have been their pay and the best of their horses. In exchange, they had got their freedom and their women and that was all. They would walk back home with their tails between their legs, a beaten army with a dead king. For them, the Hyllus had been a disaster unmitigated by any hint of relief.

The rest of Craterus's Army was milling around under the watchful eyes of Eumenes's men. Some of the mercenary regiments had already changed sides, more would do so while others would lose men individually as they sought a better deal with the regiments under Eumenes. The auxiliaries and levies were already quietly leaving, some trying to slip away without paying ransom, the others succumbing to the inevitable and parting with their pay in exchange for a safe conduct home. By the end of the day, Eumenes's war chest would be bulging with gold.

So would the cash boxes of the sutlers who had stayed with the winning army and none more so those of Callicrates and Attalus, and that of Igrat now she had established her own. They'd already done well, cleaning out most of the stock of wine they had bought the night before and turning it into gold. Now, the two men were buying up all the wine from Craterus's sutlers who were desperate to sell almost at any price before their wagons were looted and the wine was taken for nothing. Better one coin in ten than none. But, that would come later, when the aftermath of battle was cleared.

Igrat had taken the two hundred gold she had borrowed from Parmenio and was on her way to where he was standing. She was acutely conscious that she had only a limited time to move freely before drink and armed soldiers made it too dangerous for her to do so. By the time she had edged closer to Parmenio, Craterus had been dragged in front of him. Igrat looked around and there were two pairs of oxen waiting and, with a thrill of horror, she knew what he planned to do.

"Craterus, I see that the day did not go well for you." Parmenio spoke loudly so his voice carried around the troops. The noise and movement ceased and people drifted over to see what was happening. "As badly as the day went for Philotas when you manufactured your charges against him. It wasn't enough for you, just to have my brother killed was it? Alexander would have just executed him but you wouldn't allow that. You had to persuade him to torture my s. . . my brother to death and have my father killed. Well, now the day is mine."

His voice dropped slightly and took on an almost friendly tone. "Not long ago, some people were going to kill a friend of mine, somebody I care for, by using oxen to pull her legs apart until her hips cracked open. In honor of their gods they said. Well, I stopped them from doing that but the Gods demand their honor and my murdered family demand your blood. So we'll try that trick out here."

"No!" Igrat gasped the word out as the oxen were brought forward. Parmenio spun to look at her, his eyes ice cold but the skin around them red and stretched. Igrat was in no doubt he was furiously angry with her and she suddenly had a vivid mental picture of her stretched out over a rock while men cut out her tongue. Nevertheless, she was committed and she kept going. "Parmenio, you can't do this. You're not that kind of person and it'll destroy you. He could do it. You could kill him in battle or to get information or many other ways, but not like this. The memory of it will eat you alive. Let me do this, I'll turn his death into a joke so that if he's remembered at all, it is with contempt."

Parmenio looked at her, thought and then nodded but his eyes were still ice cold and rimmed with anger. Igrat walked over to where Craterus was kneeling, held down by two of Eumenes's men. She patted her hair as she did so, removing the tiny knife that was hidden there. Parmenio saw it flash slightly in the sun but few others did. Even then, the blade was so small that it was hard to see.

"See the great Craterus!" Igrat's husky voice didn't carry as well as Parmenio's had but it did so well enough. "Kneeling before a camp woman like a slave." Her fist lashed out and struck him on the side of the neck. The knife blade was barely a quarter of an inch wide and two inches long but it severed his carotid artery perfectly. Her voice rose slightly in scorn as she held the blade up. "The great Craterus, killed by a camp woman for his ring." Then she grabbed his hand and pulled a ring off. "A cheap fake ring at that."

The audience laughed, more to please her than with genuine humor. Craterus lay on the ground, blood spreading from the wound in his neck. "The great Craterus, killed by such a tiny tool. I wonder if his tool is any bigger?" She made a great play of looking under the dying man's tunic and shook her head sadly. "No, he couldn't deflower a mosquito with that." This time the roar of laughter was genuine and the last thing ever Craterus heard was his defeated army laughing at him.

Igrat cleaned her knife and returned it to the sheath hidden in her hair. Parmenio looked at her steadily then made a gesture, summoning her to approach him. "Two down. Igrat, come with me."

In Parmenio's tent, he sat at his table, pointedly not offering Igrat a seat. She braced herself for a blast but instead, his voice was mild and gentle. "Igrat, you've indicated that you'd like to be considered my daughter. Did you mean that?"

She thought for a second and nodded. "Please Parmenio, I've never had a father, I think I need one."

"I wouldn't disagree with that. Can you read this scroll?" He held it up and Igrat shook her head. "It's a formal declaration of adoption. If we both sign this, you will be my daughter in everything but blood. We'll keep the news in the family though, otherwise your usefulness as a messenger will be over. Can you sign your name?"

"Lillith taught me, in Attic Greek."

"Excellent, do so." Parmenio watched as Igrat slowly and clumsily signed her name. Parmenio signed his own and then gave her the scroll. "Give that to Lillith. Now, one of the jobs a father has is to chastise errant daughters. Igrat, you will never, ever contradict me in front of my men again. Never. What do you think would have happened to you if you'd tried that on Eumenes or Leonnatus?"

The vivid scene she had imagined came back to Igrat's mind, making her shudder. "They'd have cut my tongue out?"

"Perhaps. More likely spread-eagle you face-down on the ground with a rock forced into your mouth and then have his men stamp on the back of your head. This is an army, we do things quickly and simply here. Igrat, a commander must be seen by his men as omniscient and infallible or they won't obey him when it matters. Understand?"

Igrat sighed and nodded, then slipped her shawl of her shoulders and stood by the tent-pole, reaching up to grip it firmly over her head. Parmenio laughed quietly. "Igrat, first lesson in being a daughter, a father who loves his daughter may often threaten to beat her but rarely actually does. This once, we'll take the threat for the deed. Just don't ever do it again."

Igrat nodded and picked up her shawl. "I brought the gold I borrowed back father. We've made a fortune out there."

"Lillith will like that. She has a tax-collector's heart. Now, get along and make preparations for your trip back, I've got messages that need to go home."

Igrat left the tent and made her way back through the camp. She could sense the mood was changing, slowly but surely as the shock of the fighting faded and drinking started to have its effect. She found Callicrates outside a roped-off enclosure containing the women from Craterus's camp. Men were already starting to go inside.

Callicrates explained what was happening to her. The regiments that had decided to change sides and join Eumenes's Army didn't have to pay ransom and they were allowed to collect their women from the enclosure. So were the men who had decided to join Eumenes's Army on an individual basis. They'd collect their women and their pay and be assigned to units to replace casualties. As Igrat watched, one Regiment that had served with Craterus and now owed allegiance to Eumenes collected its women. Igrat saw the women crowding towards the edge of the enclosure as their men approached and ran to meet them. A few women were left standing. Their men hadn't made it out of the battle alive.

"What happens to them?" Igrat was curious. "Sold as slaves?" Callicrates shook his head and pointed. A youngish soldier went to one of the women and spoke to her. She was crying but she went with him out of the enclosure. "That was kind of him, there were more beautiful women there."

"He's a smart lad, especially for one so young. That woman knows camp life, knows where to get food, where to wash clothing, how to look after her new husband's equipment and tend to his wounds. She'll look after him well, and his comrades will respect him for protecting one of their women. He's done well for himself. The young camp women might be better-looking but they won't be able to serve him as she will."

"We have an interest in this?" Igrat was curious.

"I struck a deal with Eumenes's treasurer, we bought the agency on these women, we keep any ransoms paid and auction off the unclaimed women. We'll make enough money on this alone to keep us rich for months."

Other men had take the widowed women away. Igrat noted that Callicrates had been right, the experienced women who were familiar with camp life had no shortage of suitors. The women in the enclosure thinned out quickly. Once the soldiers who had changed sides had collected their women, the men who were simply going home took their place. They would have to pay ransom, both for themselves and their women and Igrat wondered quietly how many women would find that they were worth less to their husbands than a few day's wages.

Eventually, as dusk was falling, those women who had men of their own had been claimed and only the camp prostitutes and other unattached females were left. Their bodies would be rented out to the unattached men. Igrat looked at them emotionlessly, she knew that had the battle gone the other way, she would be standing out there but the thought didn't really disturb her. Her services had been sold before, by her and by others. It was the way the world worked.

A few other women were walking around, some carrying weapons and armor. "Widows of our men who died. They're looking to sell their husband's equipment so they can live until they find another man." Callicrates went over to one group of three women and offered them a silver coin each for their men's bows and armor.

Igrat looked at them and remembered when Parmenio had spent his family's money to rescue her. The memory made her realize that she owed more debts than she knew, debts that couldn't be measured in gold. She went over to Callicrates and pulled his arm. "How much is that equipment worth, really?"

He thought for a second. "Ten gold coins, perhaps twenty. If it's in good condition. Those bows look perfect."

"Give them fifteen each. They've lost their men today, they don't need to be cheated as well. I'll take the bows."

Callicrates started to argue but Igrat changed her stance slightly, one leg crossed over the other. The message was simple, *pay them or you don't get any*. He shrugged, the amount was tiny compared with the amount they had made this day. Then he went off to set up the auction of the remaining camp women. The three women bowed to Igrat, then made their way into the throngs of people gathering.

As Igrat turned to go she bumped into a man behind her. They'd come apparently from nowhere, out of the gathering dusk and her heart missed a beat. Then one of them smiled at her.

"We heard you speak up for our women. We are Parthians, we do not forget our debts or those who speak for us. A small gift for you Lady. Know that we are grateful."

As they slipped away, Igrat opened the pouch. It contained two perfectly-matched gold rings.

Estate of Parmenio, Seleucia-on-the Tigris

"And that was it. We set out next day, back down here. Parmenio is following me down, he'll be here soon. Not for long, he has to go south for the fighting there. I'll be staying until the next group of messages have to be carried."

"How do you do it?" Semiramis was professionally curious. "The couriers are picked men with picked horses yet you beat them back by a day or so."

Igrat shrugged. "I think it's because I never stop. I eat and sleep on the carts and when one stops I switch to another. The couriers say they don't stop but they do. When they change horses, they have things to do and it takes an hour or more. There are formalities and paperwork they must do. They have to prove who they are and where they are going. Then there are people asking them for the news. It all takes time. Meanwhile, my cart is moving steadily. Might be slower but it moves every hour of every day."

"You must be exhausted." Apollo was curled up in Gusoyn's arm, the two of them still looking at their rings.

"And we never got Iggie a coming home present." Gusoyn sounded seriously regretful.

"Oh I think we have the perfect present for her." In the background, Semiramis caught Lillith's eye and the two women grinned at each other before looking down at Naamah sitting in front of them.

CHAPTER THREE

REMOVING THE OPPOSITION

Estate of Parmenio, Seleucia-on-the Tigris

"Three down." Parmenio's voice was laced with satisfaction. Once he had thought that only killing the people responsible for Philotas's death himself would satisfy his need for revenge but it had turned out that wasn't true. Killing by remote control was just as satisfying, as long as the guilty died, it was enough.

"Three?" Naamah spoke up from where she was sitting with Igrat. Relationships had changed around a little since his adventures in Cappadocia. Now, Naamah spent most nights in Igrat's room while Parmenio himself was sleeping with Semiramis. It was a bit odd, Parmenio had been in no doubt that one of the women would have ended up partnering Igrat but he had expected it to be Lillith. She'd had too many unhappy experiences with men. Naamah had been much more fortunate.

"Perdiccas is dead. Seleucus Nikator came through as expected. The official reports giving confirmation have just arrived."

"Weren't the ones I brought confirmation enough?" Igrat sounded slightly indignant although the sleepiness in her voice disguised it.

"They were indeed, that allowed me to get us properly positioned for the next phase of the game. We're now associated officially with the party of Seleucus which will allow me to make sure he is awarded Babylon when the mess caused by this war gets sorted out. But, having the official documents in hand means I can now officially admit to knowing what happened out there. That 24 hours difference was critical Igrat."

Igrat settled back on her couch, a satisfied expression on her face. Parmenio reflected that her offer to be a courier had proved to have been sent from the Gods. Not only did it allow the family to keep in touch through the chaos of a civil war, Igrat had turned out to be incredibly good at the job, slipping through the backwash of the armies in ways that made ghosts seem clumsy and incompetent. He still couldn't work out how she, effectively cadging rides on carts, could beat official couriers who were supposed to have fast horses and priority on the roads. He was just deeply grateful that she managed it.

"So, where do we go from here?" Semiramis was professionally interested, at one time, long, long ago, this kind of civil war had put her in power and into the history scrolls. The machinations of political power still fascinated her.

"Once we have Seleucus set up as satrap here? Making sure he stays in power of course. Old Antigonus One-Eye is going to want him out as soon as possible and we want One-Eye deceased with equal dispatch. Once we've taken him out, any hope of getting Alexander's empire back together will be gone. Not that there's much chance of that with Perdiccas dead and buried."

"Does the official report say whether they managed to find all the pieces to bury?" Igrat sounded interested. "Come to think of it, what does the official report say? And how does it fit in with the reports I brought back?"

"Well, settle back one and all, and let me read the whole dire story."

Memphis, Nile River, Egypt, 321 BC

"Do we know where Antipater is?" Seleucus Nikator couldn't quite believe he was having this conversation. His guards had told him that a Lady wished to see him and added that she wished to speak to him over 'the matter of Antipolis'. That had been the agreed code word but he had been expecting the messenger to be a man, not a woman. Especially not a beautiful one. Yet she was here and very obviously the messenger in question. After a few minutes discussion, he was convinced she was conveying the spoken messages as accurately as the documents she had brought conveyed the written word. Yet, he still could not imagine what Parmenio thought he was doing, entrusting work this important to a woman.

"He's in Cicilia at the moment, trying to reorganize what is left of the Army of Craterus. Which isn't much by the way but what there is, he's assembling so he can bring them down to the aid of Ptolemy. That's a measure of how short of men the alliance of Antigonus and Antipater is after the Hyllus. They haven't told Ptolemy yet, they're letting him think there is a strong army on its way down to help him against Perdiccas. He doesn't know the Army he was counting on either lies dead on the banks of the Hyllus or is now part of the Army of Eumenes."

It was eerie, if Seleucus ignored the husky female voice speaking, the words, the way they were used, even the pauses and body language adopted while speaking were all those of Parmenio. With a flash of insight, he realized that this was the best of all security precautions. If Igrat was being forced to send a false message, all she had to do was not mimic the supposed sender and the recipient would automatically be alerted. "You need to know what is happening here?" It was not, of course, a question.

"Parmenio needs to know how well Perdiccas is doing. He says the time to move is very close, when Ptolemy Soter finds out he's been tricked, he won't be at all happy. He'll also guess than when the Army of Eumenes joins that of Perdiccas, Ptolemy won't be satrap of Egypt much longer either. He'll be desperate to get Perdiccas removed from the field before Eumenes and his men arrive. So, your offer to join him in an alliance will be heaven-sent. But, Ptolemy is smart, he'll know that the move will be impossible once news of Eumenes's victory reaches them. Any idea of when that will be?"

"A week at least, perhaps two at most. The messengers got sick." *That was one word for it*, thought Igrat.

"How do you know all this?" Seleucus was fascinated.

"I'm just repeating what I was told. I don't understand much of what's happening and I try not to. If I understood it, you might get my opinions, not Parmenio's. And mine aren't worth anything."

Seleucus nodded. *That sounded fair.* "Very good, now listen. Perdiccas is camped outside the city of Pelusium on the approaches to the Nile. His attempts to cross the river have been a disaster. His first shot was to clear out an old canal and lower the river so his men could cross easily but there were some bad rainstorms around then and the river flooded, destroying all his work. The men, the officers especially, thought that was a sign the gods were against us and there was a lot of talk then about going over to Ptolemy. For once, Perdiccas actually listened to people, he called the commanders together, plied us with gifts and promises, made a few inspiring speeches and won us all over. At least, he told us he had another plan to cross the Nile although he didn't elaborate on it. Anyway, he warned us to be ready to break camp, then set out that evening with his army. Didn't tell anybody where he intended to go which was probably a good idea. If we'd known what he had in mind, he'd never have got out of that meeting alive.

Fortress of Camels, Nile River, Egypt, 321BC

"He can't be serious." Seleucus Nikator looked at the fortress the other side of the river and shuddered. The river was deep and fast-flowing and

First Diodochi War

Ptolemy Soter, ever the fortress-builder, had thrown up impressive sand embankments topped with parapets. Even before the assault had properly started, they could hear the trumpets blasting and the shouting of the officers inside the fortifications summoning the defenders to the walls.

"He is, I suppose he was thinking the overnight march would catch the fortress by surprise. Well, so much for that. What's your part in this?"

"I've got the cavalry, I'm to intercept the forces of Ptolemy when they march up to relieve the fortress and cut them up while they're still in march order."

"You're well out of it then." Dromichaetes looked grim with good reason. "I've got to take the phalanx over the river and storm the walls. Just cross the river, climb those walls and stroll in. A walk in the park."

"The phalanx?" Seleucus was incredulous. The phalanx had many virtues but forcing a fixed, heavily defended position was not one of them. "Against a fortress like that, Perdiccas must be mad."

"You know him, he commanded the phalanx under Alexander so the phalanx is the be-all and end-all of warfare. Only, he's thought about the walls. We've got four elephants right? Well, they're going in first and they're going to take the fortifications apart you see. And, the back rank of the phalanx will carry ladders instead of sarissas and they'll throw them against the walls and we'll just climb up. Carrying sarissas of course." Dromichaetes looked grim. "Seleucus, there's some personal things in my tent, can you make sure my family get them?"

The day was dawning and there was just enough light for Seleucus to see that the tough old Sarissaphoros had tears trickling down his face. He'd been in many battles seen many men die but he'd never led them to certain death before and knowing he was doing so now was hitting him hard. Seleucus leaned over from his horse and grabbed the old man's arm. He squeezed it and nodded, there was nothing else to say and nothing else to do.

The sun continued to rise and Seleucus sat on his horse, watching the spectacle unfold. It was impressive all right, there was no doubt about that. The phalanx was advancing towards the river bank, the elephants in the van. The, as they entered the river, the currents and soft, shifting riverbed started to take their toll and the solid ranks started to sway and bend. That was not good, not good at all. When they were halfway over, Ptolemy himself and his troops did appear, coming at a run out of the fort, forming their own phalanx in defence of the Fortress of Camels. The two formations clashed, their sarissa's locking as each tried to force the other back by sheer weight. The locked phalanxes wavered and bent but the troops of Perdiccas were slowly gaining the advantage. They pushed Ptolemy's men back towards the fortress, slowly gaining ground between the fort and the river. Then, to cover the retreat of his phalanx, Ptolemy ordered his slingers and bowmen to open fire on the advancing men of Perdiccas. The shot and arrows rained down but Perdiccas's sarissaphoros were not frightened, but boldly assaulted the fortifications. They set up the scaling ladders and began to climb them, while the elephants started tearing at the palisades.

Seleucus watched as Ptolemy threw himself into the front of the battle with a detachment of picked men around him. He went from danger point to danger point to encourage the other commanders and their men to face the danger of battle. One moment he was taking a sarissa and posting himself on the top of the outwork, trying to put out the eyes of the leading elephant. The next, with utter contempt for danger, he striking and disabling those who were coming up the ladders and sending them rolling down, in their armor, into the river.

Seleucus found himself quietly cheering the man on. He was a true Macedonian, fighting in a way that made every man proud to be with him. The reckless disregard for death was contagious and his companions fought just as boldly, taking the three remaining elephants head-on and killing their riders. Without humans to direct them, the three great beasts gave the battle up as a bad job and wandered away.

Yet bravery was not just the reserve of Ptolemy and his men. They drove Perdiccas's sarissaphoros back, into the river where crocodiles were already waiting to gorge on the dead and the wounded. The phalanx reformed, weakened and bloodied but still the dreaded Macedonian phalanx and advanced again on the Fortress of Camels. One again, the desperate fight around the walls took place, the soldiers of Ptolemy having the advantage of the fortifications higher ground and those of Perdiccas being superior in number.

Once again they were driven back and forced to reform in the river while the ever-growing number of crocodiles feasted on the harvest of dead and dying. Yet again the phalanx went in only to fail again before the personal prowess of Ptolemy whose examples and exhortations to his men to show Perdiccas just what bravery truly meant. One wave followed another but each was weaker than the last and the fight each time was just an instant shorter. Finally, as the sun was starting to set, Perdiccas gave up the siege and went back to his own camp.

That night, Seleucus rode to the camp and found the tent of Dromichaetes. The old Sarissaphoros had died in the river, just as he had known he would. His body had been taken by a crocodile so he wouldn't even get the warrior's funeral rites he had deserved. Seleucus collected the man's possessions and put them into a pack.

First Diodochi War

Memphis, Nile River, Egypt, 321 BC

Seleucus Nikator took the bundle out from his own pack and put it on the table in front of Igrat. "You are a courier, a trusted one. Please take these back and see they get to the family of Dromichaetes."

"I will. So, that was when Perdiccas was killed?"

"Not quite, no. You have to understand the man Igrat. Perdiccas was a man of blood, one who usurped the authority of the other commanders and, in general, wished to rule all by force. He brooked no argument, sought no other opinion, respected no advice. He was a dark man whose cruelty and suspicion engendered only fear, not love. Even Roxane feared him and it was Perdiccas who forced her to have Barsine Stateira murdered. So there was no chance then of organizing a plot against him. But, he played into our hands. Breaking camp at night, he marched secretly northwards to a place where it happens that the Nile is divided and makes an island large enough to hold with safety and form the base for a very large army. To make the march faster, he left the baggage train behind, including all the food and, of course, the soldier's possessions and their women.

"When he got there, he ordered his men to cross the river, driving them on with curses and accusations of cowardice After the fighting around the Fortress of Camels when more than two thousand of them had died, those accusations destroyed what little loyalty they had left for him. Soon, the soldiers were only crossing with difficulty because of the depth of the river. In the middle, where the current was fastest, the water came up to the chins of those who were crossing while the current buffeted their bodies and hammered them with their own equipment. I had my cavalry downstream, trying to catch the men who were being carried away by the river and bringing them safe to the other side but that was little enough and the number of men carried away soon overwhelmed us.

"That was the odd thing you see, at first only a few men got swept away by the current but as the crossing went on, more and more lost their footing. The explanation was simple enough, Perdiccas hadn't bothered to do any scouting and nobody had inspected the ford before his men started to use it. So, nobody knew that ford wasn't rock but just compacted sand and clay. Perdiccas sent the elephants and light cavalry over first and the sarissaphoros afterwards and between them they broke up the compacted soil and the current carried the mud away downstream. So the ford was hollowed out and after a third of his army was over, it became unusable. Of course, he wouldn't accept that and he kept ordering the men on the bank to attempt the crossing. For a while, those who knew how to swim well and were the strongest succeeded in swimming to the island but only by throwing away a good deal of their equipment and they were exhausted by the effort. The weaker or less-skilled swimmers were swallowed by the river, others were carried by the current to the shore held by Ptolemy, but most of them, the crocodiles got them.

"This was a real disaster. It wasn't just that another two thousand men were lost, among them some of the prominent commanders, the part of his army that had crossed was not strong enough to fight the enemy and those left on the nearer bank were equally unable to resist an attack. The real damage though was in the mind of the Army. Perdiccas had lost all authority and the troops began to look to Ptolemy. Word spread that Ptolemy was generous and fair and granted to all the commanders the right to speak frankly. What is more, he had secured all the most important points in Egypt with garrisons of considerable size, which had been well equipped with every kind of missile as well as with everything else. This explains why he had, as a rule, the advantage in his undertakings, since he had many persons who were well disposed to him and ready to undergo danger gladly for his sake. He did not rule by fear as Perdiccas did.

"In the midst of this word came from the Ptolemy himself. He had found the bodies of the men who had been washed up on his bank of the river and had them burned with all the honors due to soldiers who had laid down their lives. Then, having bestowed on them a proper funeral, he wished to send the bones to the relatives and friends of the dead. The time was right at last."

Meeting Place, Banks of the Nile Near Memphis, Egypt, 321BC

"It is an honorable thing you have done Ptolemy Soter. An act of mercy that the Gods will see and cannot fail to reward, for such a deed shows true nobility of soul."

"The Gods will do what they will Seleucus Nikator, and we will do what we must. Honor demanded that the dead be treated with respect even if they were not respected in life."

So he's heard. Just how many spies does he have in our camp? Ptolemy was known for the efficiency of his intelligence. "And allies should be respected as well. We are fortunate to have Eumenes, who even now closes on us with reinforcements." *And thank the gods for the strange beauty who brought that news so fast. And to Parmenio for finding her and winning the battle that gave her news to bring.*

"What?" Ptolemy sat back in his saddle from shock. "Eumenes is in Cappadocia, pursued by Craterus."

"Not anymore." *He doesn't know. Gods be praised, he still doesn't know.* "There was a great battle at the River Hyllus. Craterus is dead as is his ally Neoptolemus. Eumenes is victorious, much of Craterus's Army has joined him and he is on his way down here with almost 40,000 men. He took the best of his own army and Craterus and sent home those of lesser quality. Once he is here, the men will regain their hearts." Seleucus eased back on his saddle and feigned puzzlement. "You did not know of the defeat of Craterus? Antipater did not tell you?"

"I know nothing of this. I still do not. I have heard what you say. Do you have proof of this?" Ptolemy was stunned by the news but it explained much. The messages from Antipater in response to Ptolemy's appeals for help had been vague and indecisive. Now he knew why and when he read the scroll Seleucus handed to him he could see that the news was accurate. The scroll might be forged but its content rang true.

"If the troops learn of this, they will be heartened even after the losses of today. The opportunity to oppose Perdiccas will be gone and you will face the might of both armies. Almost 80,000 men. You will not be able to stop them Ptolemy Soter."

"So what do you propose Seleucus Nikator?"

"The men are demoralized, their hearts are filled with lamentations and mourning, that so many men having been senselessly lost without a blow from an enemy. Now is the time, I and my companions can exploit this mood and overthrow Perdiccas. His army can join with yours, not with that of Eumenes and together we can fight him."

"And your price for this?" Ptolemy was genuinely curious, this was a development he had not expected.

Seleucus took a deep breath and made his play. "A deal in two parts. With Perdiccas dead, the war is over. Eumenes can be hunted down and beaten, that is Antipater's affair." And without Parmenio there to hold his hand, that won't take long. "So, I shall be recognized as Perdiccas's successor in command and also awarded the Satrapy of Babylon."

Ptolemy frowned, not in disagreement with the demand which was reasonable given the situation but with the choice. Syria he could have understood, or one of the Asia Minor satrapies but Babylon? An impressive city perhaps but far removed from the center of power in Macedonia. It was a backwater. "And the second part?"

"Is between us alone. An alliance a firm and solid one. Ptolemy, Alexander's empire is dead, collapsed. The very fact we speak here today shows that. Chaos is falling and in such extremities, a single man may easily be torn down and never see his assassin. But two men, trusted friends, each with his back braced firmly against the other, they can survive. Egypt and Babylon could be such friends. We know Antigonus Monophthalmus and Antipater will be coming after us sooner or later. Each wants to rebuild the empire under their own image and will eliminate us before they turn on each other. But, you and I understand one thing, that the Empire was too big to be ruled by one man. We are content with what we have and do not seek to expand. Yet, together, we have the space and depth to resist them. If they come for Egypt first, Babylon gives you depths and a refuge. If they come for me, Egypt does the same for us. That is my price for the head of Perdiccas, Ptolemy Soter. Babylon for me and an alliance for us."

Seleucus saw Ptolemy Soter staring at him, calculating the odds. If Parmenio was right, one thing would count uppermost in Ptolemy's mind, the fact that Antipater had hung him out to dry, left him alone to fight the Army under Perdiccas. Would that be enough? Seleucus had barely the time to ask the question when he saw Ptolemy's hand stretched out to him. "Agreed."

Riding back to Perdiccas's camp with the bones of the dead on packhorses behind him, Seleucus made his plans. His first step was to collect about a hundred of the commanders led by the illustrious Pithon, a man second to none of the Companions of Alexander in courage and reputation. They were outspoken in condemnation of Perdiccas and his abuse of the troops so it took but little in the way of persuasion to have them agree with his plans. Accordingly, they assembled outside the tent of Perdiccas with the ruse that they had important news for him. And so they did for as he came to speak with them, Seleucus cut at the back of his knees with his sword and Perdiccas, hamstrung, fell to the ground. As he tried to drag himself away, the men fell upon him with knives and their sarissas, cutting and chopping at his body until only fragments were left.

Then, the commanders assembled the men and spoke to them, advising them that Perdiccas had died and that Pithon commanded the Army with the aid of Arrhidaeus under the leadership of Seleucus Nikator. They were ending this foolish war that had cost so many lives for so little gain and forming an alliance with Ptolemy. This was met with cheers for Ptolemy's estate had only grown with each hour that had passed. Then, Ptolemy himself had come and greeted the hungry troops, providing them, at his own expense, with grain in abundance for the armies and their women given both food with the other needful things. So Perdiccas, after he had ruled for three years, lost both his command and his life in the manner described.

Memphis, Nile River, Egypt, 321 BC

Seleucus Nikator leaned back, his tale finished at last. Igrat looked at him and smiled. "Parmenio will be pleased with all of this. He told me to tell you he will be with you at Triparadisus."

Seleucus returned her smile, this time with relief. "I will be pleased to see him by my side." *Because that way I will know he is not at somebody else's side* he added to himself.

73

First Diodochi War

Estate of Parmenio, Seleucia-on-the Tigris 321 BC

Parmenio laughed delightedly as he related the last bit. "You really think he thought that Igrat?"

"Certainly, it showed on his face very clearly."

"Oh well, he'll learn. Now, people, tell me about all the changes here."

"That's something Lillith and Semiramis can tell you about. I'm exhausted, I need to sleep. With your permission father, I'll take my leave." Igrat looked at Parmenio, seeing him smile and nod, then rose to her feet. Naamah did also.

"Do you need to speak with me?" Her voice was tentative and a little embarrassed. Parmenio shook his head. Igrat took Naamah's arm, turned her towards the door to the women's quarters, then put her hand between her shoulder blades and pushed hard. Naamah staggered slightly then left the room ahead of Igrat, her head hanging slightly. As they left, Igrat turned slightly and winked at the rest of the family. When they'd gone, Parmenio laughed quietly.

"That's something I never thought I'd see. Naamah being submissive."

"Does it really surprise you?" Semiramis spoke with a little heat in her voice. "Look on this from her point of view. She's been in charge ever since she and Lillith left Shyt'tim. She's taken every decision, planned every action and she's done it well."

"We alternated at being the Pythia when we were at Delphi." Lillith objected.

"You alternated at being Pythia, but Naamah called all the shots and made all the decisions. Right?"

Lillith thought for a second and nodded.

"Bear in mind, she was brought up to be a Queen, not a King. To support the King, to help execute his decisions, to give him wise counsel and to run his household, yes. To actually rule, no. Somebody else always had that responsibility but then the whole load was dumped on her. But she was thrown into a position where she had to rule and make decisions and her survival was dependent on making the right ones. And she's being doing that for how long? I had that burden for twenty years and by the end I was sick and tired of it. I was only too pleased when my son tried to assassinate me and I got the excuse to quietly vanish. But nobody was there to take over from her. When Apollo arrived, he was a man in the group but he was too young, too inexperienced and lacked the steadiness of character to take over." She glanced apologetically at Apollo who nodded in agreement with her assessment.

"So when you turned up Parmenio, you were a Godsend to her. And what was the first thing you had her do? Assassinate the ruler of the known world in front of a room full of highly suspicious people without them even beginning to realize what was happening. But she did it, and she pulled it off. Do you even begin to comprehend what an achievement that was? And what it took to walk out of that room without giving any sign that the impossible had been achieved? Now everything's changed, we're at war and you're in your element. You've taken over running this group and are steering us through the storm, doing so very well may I say, even if you are killing all your personal enemies in the process.

"The important thing is that Naamah had been able to put aside the burdens she's carried for so long. She's letting Igrat make all the decisions, tell her what to do and when. She's relaxing in a bath filled with a complete lack of responsibility for anything. She's on holiday and she's going just a little bit wild. For all the years, she had to maintain her dignified, conventional persona, which is, by the way, the real her. Now she can throw that aside, defy conventions and indulge herself. Her affair with Igrat is just a part of that, it's something new, exciting, and more that, slightly scandalous.

"Add in something else. You know Igrat when we found her. Quite apart from everything else, she had no pride, no self-respect and her self-image was about as low as one can get. Something that should tell you how bad that situation was, when she got here, she was covered in dirt, unpainted and utterly ignorant. For all that she was still very attractive yet she sold herself for a copper coin or two when she could easily have been paid in silver. She charged what she thought she was worth and that was virtually nothing. Ever since then, we've been trying to build up her self-image, give her some self-respect. Being our courier and doing so well at it was a big step. Another was you adopting her, that did more for her pride than anything else."

"It was either that or have her tongue cut out, I couldn't let her defy me in public. She either had to have a position that allowed her the privilege or be publicly punished. She was too useful as a courier for the latter so it had to be the former."

"That's terrible." Lillith was appalled.

"No, that's sensible." Semiramis was amused. "If a camp woman spoke to me like that, I would have had her skinned alive and rolled in salt. Anyway, having an affair with Naamah with Igrat calling all the shots had done her a lot of good as well. She's got a Queen doing her bidding in bed and who's there because she wants to be. That's given Igrat a sense of pride and responsibility. She's come a long way from the vicious, self-loathing gutter-cat we picked up. Anyway, once Naamah finds unrestricted hedonism and lack of responsibility tiresome, she'll revert to type. Give it a few months."

"She might have to end her holiday up sooner than that. How did this all get started anyway?"

"Now that," said Lillith, "is a story. It was the night she came back from her first courier trip to Cappadocia, the one where she brought back her adoption scroll. She'd brought us all presents from the trip, something she'd never done for anybody before, I think primarily because she'd never had anybody to give presents to. So, we wanted to give her one and Naamah had been fluttering around her like a moth around a candle."

Estate of Parmenio, Seleucia-on-the Tigris, 322 BC

Igrat closed the door on her room and was about to lock it when she paused. There was no need to lock the door here, for the first time in her life she had somewhere she was safe. She put down her travel bag and rooted around in it for a moment, drawing out a small package. In it was a pair of small golden statues, presumably two of the Greek goddesses. There were names written on the bases but she couldn't read them, not yet. The statues had come from Attalus. She had stolen them as a measure of revenge for the way he had treated her. She put them up on a shelf, one high up in the room. She didn't know which Goddesses they were and she wasn't really sure that gods and goddesses existed but until she was sure, she guessed a little respect would do no harm.

Her thoughts were interrupted by a knock on the door. That itself was unfamiliar, never in her life had people had the consideration to knock before entering. They'd always just pushed in and left it to her to try and throw them out if their presence was unwelcome. Here, as with everything else, it was different. This was her room and people asked before entering. "Come in." Even saying the words was a pleasure.

The door opened, somebody was pushed in, and the door closed again. Now standing inside her room was Naamah, naked except for a coronet of flowers on her head, a loose garland hanging around her neck and another around her waist. Igrat looked, feeling her eyebrows rise in surprise, then looked again. Sure enough the flowers were all she was wearing, even Naamah's feet were bare.

"I'm your welcome home present." Naamah's voice was shaky and she kept clearing her throat. Her face was pink with embarrassment, the flush starting to spread.

It has been a long, long time since Igrat had been embarrassed by this kind of situation and she was having a hard time stopping herself laughing. "Who thought of the flowers Nammie?"

"Lillith. She said it would add a festive air to the evening." The two women looked at each other then both burst out giggling.

"So you're all decked out for the sacrifice then?" Igrat dabbed at her eyes, carefully removing the smear where the kohl on her eyes had run.

"I am." Naamah's face went from light pink to deep red. "I suggested they used the flowers to tie my hands but Semiramis said that would bring back bad memories for you."

"She was right." Igrat remembered times when she had been pushed into a room with bound hands and none of them had seen a pleasant outcome. Then she saw Naamah was still standing by the door. "Come in properly and sit down."

Naamah looked around, there was nowhere to sit but the small couch where Igrat was seated and the bed. Naamah sat on the edge of the bed covers, her back straight, looking around nervously. Watching her, Igrat suddenly realized she was frightened.

"Nammie, there's nothing to be scared of. What's the matter?" Naamah glanced down, the flush in her face returning. That was when the truth dawned on Igrat. "Oh, I see, you've never been with another woman before?"

"Never. I'm sorry" The flush on Naamah's face deepened.

"No need to say sorry. I thought you'd lived in a harem? The storytellers say all sorts of things go on there."

Naamah laughed and her embarrassment faded again. "Don't believe everything you hear from the storytellers. Lillith and I both were part of my husband's harem certainly but I never slept there and I don't think Lillith did very often. She had her own room while Sammael and I had our own apartment. I spent all my time, when I wasn't being the High Priestess or other things, there. The only time I went to the harem at all was when running his household called for it. I don't know if others were the same but Sammael's was a happy place. The women were all well-looked after and protected, Sammael told them they could leave if they wanted to but none ever did. They knew that anywhere else would be much worse for them. I guess a few of them went with each other, must have done I suppose, but they must have been very discrete. Lillith can tell you more but from where I was, all the stories you hear about orgies and lechery and cruelty were quite wrong." Naamah's blushing had faded and her face had the curiously happy-remote look it always wore when she was lost in her memories of her life with Sammael.

Igrat slipped off her tunic and sat down beside her, then reached out and gently eased Naamah back so she was laying down on the bed. "Nammie, you've taught me so much about keeping clean and looking my best. Now, let me drive and I'll teach you a few things."

Estate of Parmenio, Seleucia-on-the Tigris, 321 BC

"And you two were listening outside the door of course." The mock-severity in Parmenio's voice was almost comical.

"No, we weren't. Well, only until we were sure that nobody was upset or offended. Then, when everything was going well, we left them." Semiramis paused for a second. "What did you mean 'She might have to end her holiday up sooner than that'."

"Soon, I'll have to go to a place called Triparadisus in Syria. There's going to be a meeting of the remaining Diadochi there to try and divide out power again now the war is over. Seleucus is the hero of the hour of course after killing Perdiccas but we need to be in his party. I want to take you and Naamah with me. We'll be going to Pelusium first to meet up with Seleucus Nikator and Ptolemy Soter, then going as a party to Triparadisus.

"Are you taking Igrat?" Semiramis was curious.

"I haven't decided. She's our best method of getting messages around, faster and more reliable that official couriers. So, the question is, do I leave her here so you can get a message to me quickly if something goes wrong here or do I take her with me so I can get a warning to you if everything goes wrong in Triparadisus? What do you think?"

Semiramis thought carefully. "If something goes wrong here, by the time the message gets to you, even with Igrat carrying it, and you get back, it'll be too late to do anything except bury us. On the other hand, if everything goes wrong up there, the extra warning we would get by a message Igrat carries could be vital. We'd have at least a day to do something before the official news arrived. So I would counsel you to take Igrat with you."

Parmenio nodded. "Makes sense."

"I also counsel you not to take Naamah. It's too soon after Alexander died and all it would need is one person to recognize her and the connections would fall into place. I know what you have in mind, a few convenient illnesses but it's too soon. Far too soon. Naamah needs to remain out of sight for another few years. Take me as your consort and Igrat as your daughter and all will be well. Lillith and Naamah have a good double-act and this time they have Gusoyn, a mature and steady man to help them. This is my counsel." Across the room, Gusoyn nodded in acceptance of the compliment. Semiramis didn't hand them out very often.

"As you said, wise counsel is the duty of a queen. Consider your advice taken. Should we get the love-birds and tell them?"

"I don't think so." Lillith was hard put to stop herself laughing. "I think Naamah's a bit tied up by now."

Parmenio shook his head. Life was definitely full of surprises.

City Walls, Pelusium, Egypt, 321 BC

"So you're Parmenio the Younger." Ptolemy Soter looked at the man curiously. He was shocked to see that the family resemblance to his father was very close. It was almost as if Parmenio the Elder hadn't aged since his middle years. "You show the family face. I read about the Hyllus. That was a noble victory indeed. Your father would have been proud of you."

"Thank you Ptolemy. He taught me everything I know. If only he'd lived longer we might not be here today."

"True words. What happened to him was a foul crime, the darkest of all blots on Alexander's name." Ptolemy drew a deep breath and looked at Parmenio. "And I have much guilt in this matter. Some of the blame lies with me."

"How so Ptolemy?" The name Ptolemy Soter had a question mark by it in Parmenio's mental ledger.

"I was supposed to be there, my official duties demanded it. But I neglected them in pursuit of my own interests and was away on my own business when the situation fructified. Had I been doing my duty as I should, I would have been there and would have put a stop to the stupid business. But I was not and so blame falls on me. If you wish to claim a blood debt, Parmenio's son, I would not dispute it." Ptolemy grinned. "I would try to stop you collecting it though."

Parmenio stared at him carefully and made his decision. Ptolemy would never know it but his words and the sincerity behind them had saved his life. "There is no quarrel between us Ptolemy Soter. So if one day I slap your army around, it will be business, not personal."

Ptolemy and Seleucus both burst out laughing. "That is fair." Then Seleucus dropped his voice. "I never realized that beauty you use as a courier is also your daughter."

"Let us keep that our secret. Her anonymity is her best protection and she is the best at her job I have ever seen. Her skills are a priceless advantage to us."

Ptolemy and Seleucus both nodded in agreement. Following steps behind them as befitted the womenfolk, Igrat heard the compliments passed on her and her head straightened slightly. Beside her, Semiramis, her bow hidden under her shawl, marked the reaction and she smiled to herself.

Parmenio sighed slightly and looked around. As the three men had walked quietly by the city walls, their steps had brought them near a watch-tower that was under repair. The sun had set and night was falling fast. Parmenio reflected that he could see better in the dark now than he had when he was young, a truly remarkable thing that was matched only be the fact that the women in his family saw even better. Then, a movement caught his eye, up on the wall by the watch-tower. A shadow moving at first, but one that quickly resolved itself into a man with a bow. Parmenio moved fast, diving across the party and bringing Seleucus down behind a pile of rubble.

"Get down, ambush!" Ptolemy reacted just as fast, diving behind a small cart loaded with rubble. He just made it because the whirring noise of arrows was in the air. Two bounced off the rubble sheltering Parmenio and Seleucus, a third slammed into the wood beside Ptolemy's head. Then there was another whirr and Parmenio marked how curious it was that a friendly arrow going out had so much of a different sound than an unfriendly one coming in. Parmenio even believed he could hear the soft thud as it slammed into the target's heart. The bowman pitched off the wall and fell to the ground beneath and this time there was no mistaking the dull thud of the body landing.

Even as he fell, another of the assassins rose to loose off an arrow. He was looking around, trying to find where the counter-fire was coming from but bewilderingly he could see nothing. Unknowingly, he had actually seen Semiramis and her bow but he was looking for a man and he simply didn't bother to pay any attention to the two women. Before he realized his mistake, another outbound arrow found its mark and his shot was aborted. Parmenio watched the arrow fall from his fingers as he collapsed and fell from the wall. The third assassin fired off a shot, not at his targets but at the mysterious archer who had killed his comrades. The effort was fruitless for his arrow missed its mark and the return shot did not. Soon he, too, lay with his two friends, dead at the foot of the wall.

Parmenio checked around and stood. Behind him, Semiramis had her bow at the ready, an arrow nocked and the string drawn, her eyes skimming the parapet for any more movement. He nodded to her, there would be time for thanks later, and then saw Seleucus and Ptolemy standing.

"Don't touch those arrows!" Semiramis's voice was commanding and Ptolemy froze as he reached out. Semiramis picked up one of the arrows and inspected it carefully. The arrowhead was unusual, a four-bladed cross and there was a thick gummy substance smeared between those blades. "They're poisoned."

Ptolemy pulled a face that registered anger and disgust. "We owe your wife much, Parmenio. It is a debt that will not be forgotten."

He paused slightly. "You have a formidable family it seems."

"You have no idea." Parmenio's voice was droll.

"We can't leave them around. Somebody might pick them up and be fall victim to the poison meant for us." Igrat was looking around very carefully before she left the cover of a pile of building materials. "And Naamah may want to look at the poison."

"A considerate thought and a worthwhile suggestion. Naamah is a healer?"

"She is, and knowing what this poison was may help her tend to a victim if it is used again." Igrat looked at the poisoned arrows and shuddered, imagining one of them biting into her body.

Parmenio was much more interested in practical things. "Any idea of who these assassins were, my wife?"

Semiramis looked at the bodies and again at the arrows. "I think the poison is oleander sap. And the assassins were Lycaonians."

Seleucus looked at Ptolemy. "Antipater."

"Of course. I think a message in return is in order?"

Seleucus nodded and drew his sword. Half a dozen blows later, the bodies of the three assassins were headless and their heads rolled in a cloak for delivery back to the man who had sent them.

Parmenio went over to the watchtower. The floor within was made of flagstones, freshly laid. It was a moment's work to lift them and barely more than that to dig a pit to hold the headless corpses. By the time the three men had finished, there was no trace that the three assassins had been buried under the flagstones. They grinned at each other, there was nothing like an escape from death followed by a surreptitious burial of the would-be killers to cement a friendship.

Parmenio looked at the others and decided a little advice was in order. "Take a word of advice, if you can find women skilled with weapons, use them as your bodyguards. Nobody takes women seriously and that killed those men. By the time they realized we were not where the threat lay, they were already dead." Parmenio looked around. "Antipater took his shot, he'll know we'll be watching out now. And, with his ploy failed, we're in position to get all we need. I think the Partition of Triparadisus will run in our favor don't you?"

CHAPTER FOUR

ISOLATION

The Riverview Inn, Triparadisus, Syria 321 BC

"Well, I can't see the river." Parmenio grumbled.

"You can if you sort of climb on the cabinet and push yourself right over to the left." Semiramis started to demonstrate. "Then if you stick your head out of the window, and look along the wall, you can just see the river. A little bit of it anyway."

"That's hardly a river view is it? That's more like a contortionists nightmare."

Semiramis snuffled with her laugh. "Well, what do you expect? We're not part of the official delegations and we've got to keep a low profile. Seleucus Nikator really doesn't want you talking to any of the other Diodochi in case they lure you away from him. You're his ace, his trump card, the General who wins all his battles for him. I bet he has nightmares at the thought of losing you."

"He does." Igrat spoke up from the corner of the room. "He has bad nightmares, the maids at his official residence here speak of them with fear. They think he might be possessed."

"Oh come on, he's not a bad sort as over-ambitious would-be emperors go." Semiramis snuffled again, she'd caught a cold somehow and it was at its most unpleasant. The strange gift that the three people in the room shared seemed to help them when they were ill but it didn't protect them completely. A cold was still a real discomfort, it just didn't last as long as it did for others. "And he pays well."

"I should hope so. He's managed to get his hands on most of Alexander's treasure, even though Ptolemy got the body. More gold than he can comfortably spend, even in a war. We've got Lillith hard at work multiplying our income from Seleucus, she's doing quite well. Thanks to Igrat, she gets a jump on the news from the conference here. Her latest scroll said she's been playing grain futures. She used the advance news of Antipater's election to buy up stocks just before the price rose and sold at a handsome profit. Then, when he appointed Seleucus Satrap of Babylon, she sold short just before the price slumped and made another satisfying pile of gold."

"I didn't understand that bit at all." Igrat was reading one of the scrolls Lillith had sent her, slowly and painfully, her finger moving along the line of text, her mouth forming the words as she read them. She was fluent in Koine street-Greek now and nearly as proficient in Attic Greek but her reading was lagging behind her speech and her ability to write fell behind that.

"Lillith knew that the price of grain would fall once Seleucus was made Satrap of Babylon and the prospect of war faded. So, she sold grain she didn't actually own at the then-current price but for delivery a week later. Then, when it came time to deliver the grain, she bought it at the new, lower price and delivered it. The difference between the price she was paid and the money she had to pay out was her profit on the deal." Semiramis paused to wipe her nose. "It was your message that made it possible, most of the city was expecting Antipater or Antigonus would start a war over Babylon, causing the price of grain to rise. If that had happened, Lillith would have had to buy the grain for more than she had been paid and would have lost on the deal."

"So, Lillith sold something she didn't own." Igrat was frowning in confusion. "I tried to do that once, sell something I didn't have but the mark found out. He had me raped and beaten. How come Lillith gets away with it?"

Parmenio sighed inaudibly. "When a great lady sells something she doesn't own, it's called speculation and it's legal. When a street woman sells something she doesn't own, it's called fraud and she gets punished."

Igrat's face brightened. "Ah, that I understand. Why didn't you say so before? Now, will somebody tell me why this is the Riverview Inn but we can't see the river without giving ourselves injuries?"

"It might have had a view of the river once. This is an old building after all and we know the Orontes has changed course several times." Semiramis smiled before a sneeze caught her by surprise. "Or perhaps the original owner got the idea looking at a river. Perhaps he just liked the sound of the name. I once owned an inn called the Red Wall but it wasn't red and it wasn't near a wall."

So why did you call it that?" Igrat was curious.

"Because I bought the property on the anniversary of the day my Army took Rossim. They stormed the walls of the city and slaughtered the defenders upon them so that the wall ran red with their blood. And so my inn was called the Red Wall."

"Charming." Parmenio muttered. To him, war was a tool he used to achieve a specific end, he didn't relish it and its carnage the way Semiramis did. All that concerned him was whether the butcher's bill was justified by the end he was pursuing. More loudly, he asked, "So, what is the court word on Antipater's decisions?"

Semiramis spent most of her time with the ladies attached to the Diodochi attending the conference. They were remarkably well-informed and she had proved able to assemble a reasonably accurate picture of what was going on in the meeting hall, one that Parmenio was using to validate the progress reports he had been given by Seleucus and Ptolemy. The confirmation of those two in their holdings, the latter by way of the fact that nobody had the military power to shift him and the former because Antipater didn't wish word of his botched assassination attempt to leak out. Nobody would object to an attempted assassination, that was a standard part of Macedonian politics after all, but news of such a comprehensive failure would badly damage his reputation.

So, Antipater had swallowed his pride and enthusiastically endorsed Ptolemy's proposal that Seleucus be made Satrap of Babylon. He had, however, made Antigonus general of the royal army in place of Perdiccas, making sure that his son Cassander was Chiliarch to Antigonus. That was, in Parmenio's opinion, a wise precaution since it would prevent Antigonus from going off the deep end in pursuit of his own ambitions. Antigonus had also been assigned the task of finishing the war against Eumenes and Alcetas. *That*, thought Parmenio, *offers me the chance of taking down the next name on my list.*

"He's carved up Eumenes's possessions. He's given Cappadocia itself to Nicanor, while Great Phrygia and Lycia have been confirmed as the possessions of Antigonus. Of the minor provinces, Antipater has declared that Caria should be in the charge of Asander, Lydia should be ruled by Cleitus, and Hellespontine Phrygia has been given to Philip Arrhidaeus."

"So Arrhidaeus controls the Hellespont does he. That puts him between Antigonus and Macedonia and old One-Eye won't like that at all. I sense a rift in the alliance of those two developing. One we should get to work widening as quickly as possible."

"You won't be the only one." Semiramis's face suddenly screwed up and she gave an explosive sneeze.

"How so?"

"Eurydice isn't well-disposed to Antipater either. She used her marriage to Philip Arrhidaeus to force her way into the meeting hall and delivered, in person no less, a harangue against Antipater, which her secretary Asclepiodorus had written for her."

"I heard about that from Seleucus. We were pretty much agreed that it didn't mean anything. Eurydice doesn't have any real power or influence, she may hate Antipater like poison but she can't do much to him. Unless she gets an ally that has real power, she's going nowhere."

"What you might not know is that she's well on her way to getting that ally. It's whispered that there is one in Antipater's camp who is inclined to support her."

"Who?" Parmenio thought for a second. "Polyperchon? Surely not. He's been with Antipater for years, they fought the Lamian War together and Antipater made him regent of Macedonia when he set out for the war against Perdiccas. He can't have turned against Antipater."

"He hasn't and that's the problem. Antipater has made Polyperchon his heir, overlooking Cassander. And Cassander is furious about it. Not that Antipater cares much."

"Gods, that'll do it. Cassander is a great one for dynastic succession, which is probably the only way he'll get his hands on power. This'll split Antipater's position wide open."

"Then why did Antipater do it father?" Igrat was curious. Having grown up on the streets, she found the dynastic conspiracies of the aristocracy bewildering. She was rapidly coming to the conclusion that there was very little difference in actions between the great ones and the petty criminals she had grown up with. She'd schemed and plotted to get a better street corner to sell herself from while the Diodochi and their women did the same with whole countries. Then she had the startling thought that she was one of the Diodochi women now and she'd slipped into the role with little effort. Obviously there was as little difference as she'd assumed.

Parmenio thought carefully. "Antipater is a great believer in the Alexandrine inheritance. He wants the empire on his terms and under his control. Oh, he recognizes that it's too big for one man to rule directly but he sees himself as the first amongst the Diodochi, treating them as local administration rather than independent rules. Old one-eye sees himself the same way but they both want to establish the system first and decide who runs it later. Antipater is probably all right with that, he's as old as I am and hasn't got our gift. But Cassander, that's another matter. He hates Alexander and his memory, I remember him saying that it made him feel ill just to pass a statue of the man. I know how he feels by the way. Cassander wants to tear the whole edifice down and build anew simply because Alexander built the original. So, since Polyperchon is Antipater's man, he got the big prize to maintain the Alexandrine inheritance. I'd even guess that Antipater is quite happy to see Antigonus take over in the long run with Polyperchon just being an interim stage."

Parmenio got up and walked to the window, looking out at the street below. Out of curiosity, he peered left, along the wall, but he couldn't see any hint of the Orontes. "That has to be it. Antipater is hoping that Polyperchon in Macedonia will hold everything together long enough for Antigonus to get the east settled down. Then, he'll die and Antigonus will take over the west as well. There we have it, the Empire reformed. But Cassander will want to rule as his own monarch, subject to nobody. Putting him in power means that the civil wars will continue."

"So, where do we go from here?" Semiramis was dabbing her eyes.

"Igrat, do you miss Naamah?"

"Not really, not the way you mean. Oh, it's been fun I agree and she was a nice present but we're more or less over. We both prefer men anyway. Let me guess, you want me to go back to our home." It was a flat statement, not a question.

"Indeed I do. We need to tell the others what is happening and give Naamah a warning that we will need to use her services again. I'll check with Ptolemy and Seleucus in case there are any other messages that need to go back to Babylon. But, the word to Naamah is the key. With Cassander and Antipater on the outs, things are opening up again.

Palace of Seleucus Nikator, Seleucia-on-the-Tigris, 320 BC

"It's a disgrace. An unforgivable insult." Seleucus Nikator spoke comfortingly and sympathetically. At the same time he was reflecting that this was a problem he would have to consider himself. He was well on his way to founding his own empire, the Seleucid Empire had a nice ring to it. It was an option that he'd never thought of until Parmenio had sat down with him and laid out the route by which it could be made to happen. But, there were problems he'd never thought of as well and one of them was the succession. The very fact he was having this conversation proved the thorniness of the problem an imperial succession posed. Alexander hadn't solved it, or so everybody said. In point of fact, Seleucus wasn't to sure about that. He'd been there when Alexander was dying and had been asked to whom he left the empire. Seleucus had been sure that he'd said "to Craterus" but Antigonus had insisted the words had been "to the strongest". The problem was the two sounded so alike in Attic Greek, but Alexander and Craterus were both dead now. Dead and in their graves, just as he, Seleucus Nikator, would be one day. He was determined he would not leave the same question of an heir to tear his new Empire apart.

"My father always hated me." Cassander spoke with bile and venom dripping through every breath he took. "Nothing I ever did was ever good enough for him. All he ever did was speak about Alexander and the marvels that man could achieve. Whatever I did, Alexander had done it better. Whatever I said, Alexander had said something wiser or wittier. Every time I drew breath, I got told that Alexander had drawn it deeper and better. Well, Alexander's dead, good riddance to him. Would that my father would follow him."

Seleucus pretended to be shocked by the outburst. "A father's wishes must be sacrosanct, you know that Cassander. Antipater has appointed Polyperchon as his heir and as a dutiful son you must follow his wishes. A father's word is law, he is the master of his family. If, in his wisdom, he has appointed Polyperchon to be his successor and given him your rightful inheritance, then as long as he lives those wishes are the last word on the subject."

"As long as he lives." Cassander spoke thoughtfully. "There's the rub. He is a sick old man."

"None of the Companions of Alexander are feeble, Cassander. They are tried by time and tempered by hardship. Your father's health may not be excellent but he has many years left in him yet. And with every year that passes now that he has appointed his heir, the position of that heir will strengthen and your own will weaken. I am sorry, despite the wrong that has been done to you, I see no way of saving your position. You will be what you are now, the messenger of Antigonus, for the rest of your life."

"NO!" Cassander exploded, crashing his fist on the table. Across the room, Seleucus's bodyguards started to draw their swords and, although Cassander had no way of knowing it, in the shadows a Parthian bow was drawn and nocked, the arrow pointing directly at his heart. Cassander looked around, realized his position and forced himself to calm down. "No, Seleucus Nikator, I will not accept that."

"As long as Antipater lives, you have no choice."

Then Antipater will not live thought Cassander. *His day is done anyway and his ways are those of the past. Good riddance.*

"Then, Seleucus Nikator, we must pray for a solution should we not? Perhaps I should pray to the gods in the hope they will see the justice of my cause and give me relief."

"That would be wise Cassander. The gods can often provide solutions to problems that we mere mortals could never think of. Here in Seleucia-on-the-Tigris we have temples that are rich in gold and please the gods greatly. Pray in one of them, and I am sure your words will be heard." Seleucus nodded and a servant sounded a gong. From the shadows, a lady-in-waiting emerged, having been careful to leave her bow behind. "This lady will take you to the temple of Daron, the God of Medicine. There perhaps you will find the solution to all your problems."

Cassander got to his feet and bowed respectfully to his host. Then he rose to his feet and followed Semiramis out of the room.

Temple of Darus, Seleucia-on-the-Tigris

Cassander knelt before the altar to Darus, his sacrifice placed perfectly on the grating over the fire, the scent of roasting meat and herbs filling the temple. There was something about the smell of cooking meat that soothed the soul and brought about reflection in the minds of those who prayed here. It was late evening, the skies were already darkening with the onset of dusk and the inside of the temple was shadowed and dim.

"May I have the honor of praying beside you?"

It was a woman's voice, probably one of the priestesses Cassander thought. "The honor would be mine. A priestess of Darus?"

"In a manner of speaking." The woman's voice was pitched very low although the words were clear. The delivery was slightly odd, the voice rougher than normal for a woman, as if the speaker had gravel in her mouth. "You have told Darus of your problem and the answer is easy to find. A sacrifice will solve most problems if the timing is right."

Cassander looked down. At his feet was a small bag, one that had not been there a few minutes before. "As you said my Lady, a solution is easy to find."

"You suffer from the circular sores in your hair? So many do. The powder in yonder bag is a sovereign cure for them. Take one tenth of the contents of that bag, make it into a paste with water and spread it on the sores. Do this every day for ten days and the sores in your hair will be gone. But I counsel you this. Be careful never to swallow any of that powder or apply it over an open wound for this can be most injurious. Above all, I counsel you, never mix the whole contents of that bag with a glass of wine and drink it for then, a slow death will be certain with no way of saving you."

Cassander picked up the bag and stowed it carefully in his belt. "Thank you La......" He was speaking as he turned to face the woman who had spoken but she had already gone.

Headquarters of Eumenes, Cappadocia, 320 BC

"When you find the bastard, thrust a sarissa up his ass." The angry roar echoed around the campsite.

"He is joking isn't he?" Phoenix of Tenedos sounded distinctly concerned.

"No." Pharnabazus had served with Eumenes a lot longer than Phoenix and knew that the Greek librarian turned general could be very unforgiving to those who crossed him. "This mess is the last thing he needed right now, with Antigonus Monophthalmus coming out of winter quarters at last."

"Phoenix, get in here, right now." The sound coming from Eumenes's tent sounded remarkably like a female elephant giving birth.

"Well, it was nice knowing you Phoenix. Wave goodbye from your stake, won't you." Pharnabazus grinned at his friend and ducked to dodge the dope-slap Phoenix aimed at the back of his head.

Inside Eumenes's command tent, the General was staring at the map showing the latest reports of Antigonus's movements. He was consolidating his forces after the winter, bringing his men in and assembling his army. When he'd finished, he would outnumber Eumenes by at least two to one. Eumenes was also assembling his army and he was hoping he could move fast enough to hit Antigonus while his forces were still dispersed. Then, Perdicatus had gone and staged this stupid mutiny. He knew why of course, he was Greek and still people remembered that he had been Alexander's archivist, not one of his generals. Even the victory on the Hyllus hadn't changed that. Too many people knew that he hadn't masterminded the stunning defeat of Craterus, the strategist sent by Seleucus to aid him had done that. Now, Parmenio's son was gone, called back by Seleucus, and Eumenes was on his own. A lot of his army had very little faith in his ability to win again.

"You know what's happened?" Eumenes barked out the question as Phoenix entered.

"I heard there were problems assembling our Army, yes."

"Problems? That's a good word for it. Perdicatus and his entire command have mutinied. 3,000 men and 500 horse. They've set up camp three days march away. May they all roast in hell, I need every day to move against Antigonus and then that swine has to go and pull this. I want you to take four thousand men and a thousand horse. Get there as fast as you can and get rid of Perdicatus. On second thought, bring him and his fellow officers back here alive if you can. We'll make an example of them."

"What about his men?"

Eumenes stopped, breathed deeply and calmed himself down. "They're just following their leaders, they probably don't even know they've mutinied yet. Bring them back, we'll disperse them amongst the other units. With a little kindness, we can win them back."

Phoenix nodded in agreement. "Very wise, we will need those men when we come to take on Antigonus. The longer we get delayed, the greater our need becomes."

"I know. We must hit Antigonus before his forces are assembled. If we can move against him within a week, we should have the edge in numbers. So waste no time Phoenix, make a forced march all the way."

Headquarters of Antigonus Monophthalmus, Cappadocia, 320 BC

Antigonus threw down the message scroll with frustration. "That young Phoenix shapes well. Covered three days march in a night and crushed that mutiny by noon the next day. That speaks of a man whose men will follow him. And to crush the rebellion without bloodshed, this also speaks well of his common sense."

"Not quite without bloodshed sire. Perdicatus and the officers who were his fellow-mutineers got impaled on Sarissas in front of the assembled Army. And may I remind you that Phoenix does serve the enemy."

"The opposition, Alcetus, the opposition. Not the enemy, for a commander in the opposition one day may serve us the next. To win and hold loyalty in times such as these is as valued a gift as any other. Eumenes did well in solving his little problem although I wish he had taken longer to do it. We need time, Alcetus, time more than anything else, more than men, more than cavalry, more even than elephants. My Army is scattered all over Asia Minor and I need to buy time. I thought I had it with Perdicatus but he failed me."

"That's not why Eumenes impaled him though."

"No, not for failing me, I never expected him to achieve very much and that mutiny was a long shot at best. Although the men would have come in useful, it would have reduced the odds against us quite markedly. No, Eumenes impaled him to discipline his Army, to show them that he was in charge. That tells us he has a problem with ensuring the loyalty of his men."

"After winning at the Hyllus and killing Craterus and Neoptolemus? A victory like that should have won the hearts of his men."

"Yes, it should and it hasn't. There's something we are missing here Alcetas, something important. I can't see how a man who spent his life recording Alexander's self-glorifying tracts could suddenly turn into the general who took Craterus's army apart. There's whispers that the gods themselves helped him out on that one, some even claim that Athena Alcidemus herself commanded his army for him. That makes as much sense as anything else I suppose. Still, Perdicatus's mutiny does suggest one thing, where there is one disaffected subordinate there may very well be more. Make some inquiries, find out of there are any other candidates who might wish to change sides."

Ruined House, Foothills of the Cappadocian Plain, 320 BC

"It will be mostly a cavalry battle."

"So much is obvious."

"And Eumenes has command of five thousand cavalry while you have but two thousand."

"I also have thirty elephants."

"A mighty force indeed, and one that would be devastating against an unsupported phalanx. But this will be a cavalry battle and your elephants will be cut off and hamstrung by our superiority in cavalry." Apollonides leaned back, eying Antigonus Monophthalmus speculatively.

"If Eumenes retains the use of his cavalry, that is so."

"And why should he not? His phalanx outnumbers yours by two to one. And the Argyraspides have no equal in your army."

That made Antigonus think. Eumenes had consolidated his own hypaspist infantry with those who had rallied to his side and in doing so had re-created Alexander's elite corps of hypaspist infantry, the Argyraspides so-called from their polished silver shields. To make matters worse, the new corps had a core of veterans from Alexander's unit. It might be that most of them were over 60 years of age but they were still the most experienced and dangerous foot soldiers on the field. Eumenes had been lavishing them and their families with riches and honors. Most of the gold he had taken from Craterus's treasury had found its way into their hands. That made them loyal as well as lethal, they were too rich to change sides.

"Even the Argyraspides cannot stand on a cavalry battlefield. They can fight their way out, perhaps, or die gloriously but on the plain before us it is cavalry that will win the day. And that man who commands the cavalry on the winning side might do exceedingly well for himself."

Apollonides sat bolt upright. After the exchange of commonplace statements of the obvious, Antigonus was finally getting to the point. "Such a man might indeed. But not one who commands two thousand horse against five thousand."

"But the man who commands seven thousand? There would be much scope for a man to enrich himself with gold."

"And land, such a man might earn himself a satrapy all of his own."

"Indeed he might, if his intervention was well-timed and decisive. Honors beyond land and gold may also find their way to him."

"It would be all a question of timing then." Apollonides wasn't asking a question, he was simply stating a fact.

"It would. All generalship comes down to timing and a man who wishes to be appointed to such a rank would have to show that he had a fine sense of timing. Too early and Eumenes would leave the field, his army largely intact. Too late and his superiority in numbers would have gained too much of an advantage to be easily offset. Yes, Apollonides, to demonstrate good timing would be the key to a long and successful career. If such a man might be found."

"I do not think you will have much trouble in recognizing such a man, Antigonus Monophthalmus.

Right Flank, Army of Eumenes, Cappadocian Plain, 320 BC

The Argyraspides were his trump card. Eumenes had spent lavishly building up the unit, separating it from the rest of his army. Even its camp and baggage train had been isolated from the rest, not least because he guessed the resentment it would cause if his other troops saw the extent to which the Argyraspides had been favored over them. Still, today was the day in which it would all pay off. The Argyraspides had 4,000 men, all on his right flank, with support from almost a thousand slingers and bowmen. In his center was his phalanx, 15,000 sarissaphoros strong and perfectly drawn up. There was no rocky slope to disrupt the advance of a phalanx here, his 15,000 men would meet the 7,000 of Antigonus and overwhelm them. Over on the left, his 5,000 cavalry were poised ready for the charge that would destroy the Army of Antigonus.

Eumenes was satisfied by the result of his efforts. In a week he had concentrated an army of 25,000 men and managed to catch Antigonus with barely half that number. Another week, ten days at the most and Antigonus would have doubled the number at his command and that would have made things difficult.

Eumenes was under no illusions about his skills as a general. He needed a numerical superiority to win. At the Hyllus River he'd seen what a real general could do and he knew that Antigonus was as good as they came. As good as Parmenio the Younger? Eumenes knew that he lacked the knowledge to make the comparison. In military affairs, he had reached only the first level of wisdom, he knew enough to know how little he knew. But he did know that Parmenio the Younger spoke of Antigonus Monophthalmus with professional respect.

Earlier, Eumenes had seen just what Antigonus could do when he put his mind to it. He'd launched a dawn attack on Eumenes's picket line along the hills that bordered the Cappadocian plain. He'd pushed those pickets in with little difficulty and now, sitting on those hills, he had a bird's eye view of the upcoming battle. Still, that wouldn't help him now.

The center of Eumenes's line advanced and the phalanx collided with the one forming the center of Antigonus's line. Antigonus's phalanx was Macedonian, brave men hardened by battle, but they were sorely outnumbered and they started to be pushed back. Men were falling, a few here, a few there, nowhere in numbers enough to cause concern. Looking at the fight, Eumenes saw the difference between this battle and the one along the Hyllus. There, the two phalanxes had been going through the motions, little more than pretending to fight while the issue was decided elsewhere. There, the battle had been fought by mercenaries whose only interest was surviving the day and collecting their pay. Here, Antigonus's men were professionals, enlisted and retained by him. They were fighting hard for their lord and in doing so forced the mercenaries who served Eumenes to do so also. He guessed that already more men had died in the two phalanxes than had fallen in their equivalents at the Hyllus and the day was yet young.

Yet, Antigonus's men were indeed being forced back. The hypaspist infantry guarding the right of the Antigonid phalanx was already hotly engaged for the Eumenid phalanx overlapped that of Antigonus and would destroy it had the hypaspists not held it back. Eumenes cursed to himself, on this level plain he lacked the ability to oversee the battlefield and then he understood why Antigonus had gone to such lengths to claim those low foothills.

One thing he could see, Antigonus was committing his elephants into the battle on his right flank, using the 30 animals to support his phalanx and crush the effort to envelop his right. That meant, of all Antigonus's forces, only the two thousand cavalry in front of Eumenes remained uncommitted. That meant the time was right, and he gave the order. His slingers started hurling their lead shot at the Antigonid cavalry while the bowmen moved forward to bring them under fire. Eumenes had a simple plan, the cavalry would be stung into charging the auxiliaries, then his Argyraspides would counter-charge and destroy them while they were tied down fighting the auxiliaries. It was a bit hard on the auxiliaries though, but the prospects of enveloping and destroying the Antigonid army was too good to allow a few auxiliary troops to stand in the way.

As his right became engaged, pinning down the Antigonid left, Eumenes knew what would be happening. Seeing his troops become engaged, Apollonides would bring his cavalry down in a mass charge, sweeping away what was left of the Antigonid right and completing the destruction of the army. He raised himself in his saddle, peering through the dust and haze to see his cavalry start to move. It was odd, the combination of the heat, the sun and the dust seemed to distort things, it was hard to work out quite what was happening but the charge looked wrong somehow.

Then, helplessly, Eumenes watched while his cavalry smashed into the rear of his phalanx, turning his whole left flank into a chaotic whirlpool of men, horse and elephants.

Rallying point of the Army of Eumenes, evening.

"How many, Phoenix, how many do we have?"

"Six thousand Sire. The Argyraspides formed square and escaped almost intact. We fell back with them on their baggage train. We have picked up two thousand more, mostly auxiliaries and some sarissaphoros from the phalanx. The light cavalry are with us also. But six thousand men and horse are it. The rest are dead or with Antigonus."

"Damn Apollonides. Damn him to the hells and back again." Eumenes stomped backwards and forwards, his body jerking with rage as he imagined what he would do to his cavalry commander when he got his hands on him. "We had him, we had Antigonus right where we needed him."

"Antigonus wouldn't have accepted battle if he had not known of Apollonides treachery."

Pharnabazus spoke carefully, an experienced general would have guessed that the crafty old One-Eye would never have accepted battle with the odds against him unless there was a trump card hidden in his sleeve. Just as Parmenio the Younger had refused battle until there was a trump card hidden in his sleeve. Eumenes might not appreciate the insinuation that he was too inexperienced for this kind of war.

Pharnabazus had, though, misjudged his man. Eumenes knew all too well that the disaster had been his and his alone. He should have guessed, but he knew he had been too blinded by his numerical superiority and the chance of scoring a victory against the fabled Antigonus to be suspicious enough. He was also honest enough to admit that he had wanted a chance to prove that he could wina battle against the top rank of the Diodochi commanders without Parmenio the Younger's assistance. Still, his investment in the Argyraspides had proved its worth.

"What now Sire?" Phoenix sensed the danger to his friend and moved in to divert Eumenes attention.

"We got to the fortress of Nora. It's small enough for the army we have left to defend with ease but its strong. Gods is it strong, the buildings are on the top of a lofty crag, and the Armenians have reinforced it over the years. Even better, they stocked it up with grain, firewood, meat and salt, ample keep us supplied for many years. We can sit out a siege there. We've seen reversals before, we'll see them again."

"We will allow ourselves to be besieged, sire?"

"We cannot continue to fight in the open field. We have little in the way of other choices that offer us hope. Remember this, As long as we stay in the field, we stay in play and that's all that matters. We just have to wait our chance, that's all."

Headquarters of Antigonus Monophthalmus, Caccadocian Plain.

"The final total?"

"There are eight thousand dead Sire. We took the entire supply train, so that Eumenes' soldiers are both dismayed by the defeat and despondent at the loss of their supplies. In addition to the five thousand of Apollonides cavalry, more than 6,000 of Eumenes's men have joined us. Allowing for our losses, we now have about fifteen thousand men and seven thousand horse. And our thirty elephants as well. We seized a great sum of money besides."

Antigonus nodded. Once his army was fully assembled, there would not be a commander in all Asia who had the forces necessary to compete with him. It was time to build his own empire on the ruins of the Alexandrine imperium. Just finish a few loose ends off and then it would be time to deal with those who were left. *Of whom Ptolemy and Seleucus topped the list.* Antigonus decided that he would no longer take orders either from the satraps or from Antipater. *I am my own man and they will rue the day they had thought otherwise. My forces increase, my war-chest builds and those who defy me will learn the error of their ways.*

"Eumenes, where is he?"

"Heading for the fortress of Nora sire."

Antigonus cursed. The fortress was as secure as any could be made on this earth. He would have to maintain the pretence of being well disposed toward Antipater a little longer.

"So the rat heads for his hole. Very well. Pursue him there, then surround the fortress with double walls, ditches, and palisades. We'll bottle him up there where he can do no harm. Then we'll...."

He was interrupted by a messenger on a horse, galloping in at an indecent rate. Around him, the guards made a wall, partly to prevent him doing harm had he so wished, but also to render aid for the man was clearly exhausted. After the confusion straightened out, he was brought over to Antigonus.

"Sire, I bear terrible news. Antipater is dead."

Well, that means I won't have to pretend to be well-disposed to him any more. Antigonus's face showed no sign of his triumphant thought. "This is terrible news. How did this happen?"

"He had a meeting with Cassander and Polyperchon to discuss the succession and to make arrangements for the future. They had a great feast to celebrate their reconciliation and much wine was drunk in toasts to their future. During the night that followed, he was taken ill. Nobody thought much of it at the time. It seemed like just a little stomach upset, perhaps too much wine having soured his stomach. So minor he did not pay it any heed and he set out on the next stage of his journey. But it did not clear up and the ride caused him increasing distress.

"After five days, he took a great turn for the worse. He became confused and was no longer sure of where he was or what he had to do. He could not eat or drink without immediately vomiting up whatever he had consumed. Amidst all this, he had terrible stomach cramps and his bowels ran like water. His suffering was dreadful and he could not rise from his bed. Yet, his head was so inflamed that he could not lie still and his mouth drooled beyond control. After a week of great anguish, he slipped into a coma and died."

The messenger paused to take breath. "Cassander and Polyperchon have each accused the other of poisoning the great Antipater. Great is the anger and rage that now divides them. Cassander has claimed his inheritance and he and Polyperchon are at war. All Greece and Macedonia look set to be their battle ground."

"Thank you, you have done well. Guards take this man away and treat him well, he has done his duty nobly." *And given me the chance of a lifetime.* Antigonus added to himself.

First Diodochi War

Estate of Parmenio, Seleucia-on-the Tigris, 320 BC

Parmenio unrolled the scroll Igrat had brought from Seleucus and read the contents, a grim smile of satisfaction spreading over his face. *Naamah has done well. With Cassander and Polyperchon at war, nobody will care what we are up to stuck out here. There are so many advantages in being removed from the scene of a conflict.* That was when he opened his mental ledger of debts to be repaid. In the fading light of evening, his words were clear and unmistakeable. "Four down."

PART TWO
THE SECOND DIODOCHI
WAR (318 – 316 BC)

Second Diodochi War

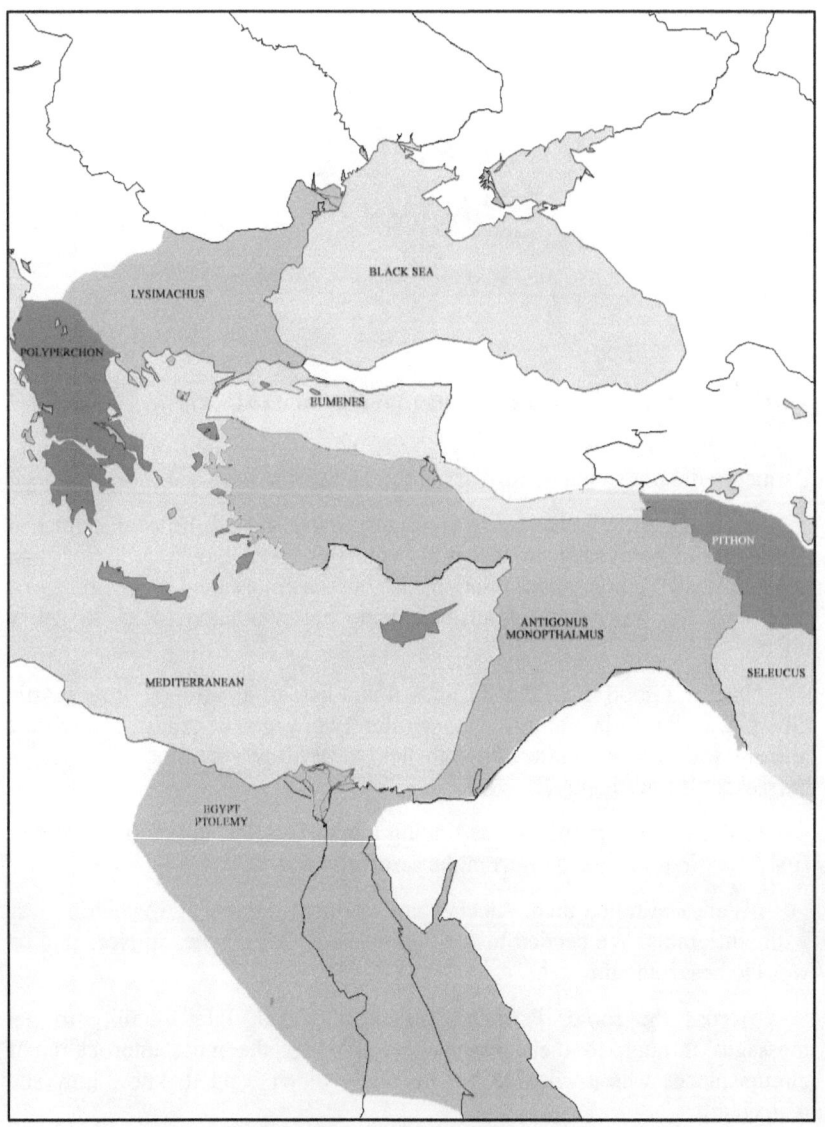

The Diodochi Satrapies at the start of the Second Diodochi War.

CHAPTER ONE

ALLIANCES

Estate of Parmenio, Seleucia-on-the-Tigris, 318BC

"Gods, does this mean I'm going to have to kill him or something?" Parmenio did not sound unduly perturbed by the prospect.

"Of course not." Naamah was slightly indignant. "Lillith told him that she had your permission to accept his courtship. And she made it clear that she didn't want a permanent relationship, but was more than happy to have a temporary liaison. Alcetas is a good man, there's nothing for us to worry about."

"Isn't it a good thing that Lillith's found herself a partner?" Igrat's Attic Greek was becoming almost fluent after two years of study. Her Koine already sounded authentic although her vocabulary was more suited to a barracks. "If she's happy?"

"Lillith's main problem was finding a man in Seleucia you hadn't got to first." Semiramis looked up from the scroll she was reading.

"Well, she failed then, Alcetas had me three months ago, when he was with Antigonus. We needed to get that package to Eumenes in Nora and he was the best route through."

Across the room, Parmenio shook his head. Igrat's ability to get messages through to their recipient even under the most improbable of circumstances was invaluable but he really didn't want to know how she managed it.

Igrat noticed the gesture and raised one eyebrow. "Naamah's right, he is a good man if unimaginative. I was with him for a week and I was in the Lioness position every night. But isn't it better Lillith should have a partner?"

"Iggie, unless you get killed by a jealous wife or have an unfortunate accident, you're going to outlive every partner you have. You're going to lose people you care about. Eventually, outside this small group, you're going to

102

lose everybody you care about. That's just one problem with our gift. Iggie, you will lose everybody you love outside this group. That will hurt and you have to decide whether it's worth the pain to have a companion for a few years. Not forgetting that having a companion from outside our circle raises the possibility that we'll all get discovered. You stay with him long enough, he'll notice you're not ageing."

"Nammie, I've never been faithful to a man in my life. I've never been with one long enough for him to look at me that closely."

"That's true. Our Iggie leaves her men just before they notice their purse is missing." Semiramis was laughing and her amusement took the sting out of her words." Iggie responded by sticking her tongue out at her. The exchange had all three women chuckling. In his corner, Parmenio shuddered slightly. He'd never had a daughter before. His late wife had only given him sons. Normally that would be a blessing and something to make a husband proud but it had left him at a disadvantage when dealing with Igrat. He had an uneasy suspicion that, as her father, he was supposed to do something about her blatant lack of morals but he had no idea quite what. And her skills were far too useful to be lightly discarded.

"Poor Parmenio. A lifetime of commanding armies and he ends up besieged by a houseful of women." Naamah spoke with mock sympathy, but while doing so, she stretched her hands behind her head and lifted one leg so her robe fell clear to expose her. Igrat had been giving some basic lessons in seduction and Naamah was putting them into practice. So, all three women suspected, was Lillith. Right at this moment, in Alcetas's home.

"Are you sure I don't have to kill him?" Parmenio decided a little goading of his own was in order. "This is my household after all and that makes you all my property so it could be argued . . . . ." He ducked quickly to dodge the fresh olives thrown at him by Naamah and Igrat.

Semiramis just grinned at the exchange. "Careful girls, or he'll lock you in the women's quarters before he goes off to war again."

Naamah shook her head. "Over his dead body."

"No need to be so extreme Nammie." Igrat looked smug. "the first thing I did when I started to live here was to find out how to slip that lock. If he tried, I'd have us out in five minutes."

"Now that makes Igrat what I would call a really useful member of our family." Semiramis was approving. "But, now that we mentioned the war, what's going on Parmenio? Everything seems to have been pretty quiet since Antipater got his."

Second Diodochi War

Parmenio quietly sighed with relief and thought the situation over. "As far as we're concerned, everything is pretty quiet. The reason is that Cassander and Polyperchon are competing for the throne of Macedonia, which is why Antipater had to die when he did of course. The conflict caused by his, err, tragic, demise has focussed the eyes of everybody on Macedonia itself and we've been more or less forgotten. We've bought two years already and we'll get at least two more out of the present situation. Antigonus is stuck in Cappadocia, besieging Eumenes in Nora. He's trapped there, Eumenes can't get out but old one-eye can't get in. He can't strip his troops away to move on Macedonia because Eumenes has just enough men in Nora to stage a break-out if Antigonus leaves. So from our point of view, everything is going well. We're getting ready to resist the moment the situation breaks loose."

"You think Antigonus will invade then? The part of Semiramis that had been an Assyrian warrior-queen ran over the prospect with glee. "And we will fight him?"

Parmenio saw her expression. She was a warrior certainly, but to her, the fighting was an end in itself not a means to a more valuable conclusion. She needed a sharp dose of reality. "He will, yes. Either us of Ptolomey, and I think it is likely to be us first. But fight him, no. I said resist, not fight. When he comes, we run. We head south, link up with Ptolomey's forces and resist from down there. When the invasion comes, it's a rock-hard certainty Antigonus will take Babylon and kick Seleucus out, kill him if he gets the chance. So we don't give him that chance. We evade, hit his supply lines and outposts and generally make his life miserable. But no battles. When Antigonus hits us he's going to have at least 90,000 foot and 20,000 horse. Plus elephants, at least thirty and possibly as many as fifty. There's no way, no way at all we can fight an army that big. So we nibble him to death."

Semiramis was disappointed. Parmenio looked at her and decided to finish off the plan. "Give it a couple of years and we can make this area too much trouble for Antigonus to hold. He'll have to pull out. Then we all return. Antigonus and I will fight it out sooner or later."

"A fair fight." Semiramis's eyes lit up at the prospect.

"Gods, I hope not!" Parmenio was appalled at the prospect. "Never, ever fight fair. Only fools do that. I'll be spending every hour between now and then making sure the fight is as unfair as possible. Always, always load the dice people. Igrat knows that don't you?"

Igrat chuckled. "Always. A knife in the back beats a fair fight any day. Or across his throat while he sleeps." She thought for a second. "When I was in Nora, Eumenes seemed quite confident he would get out. The package I took to him and Hieronymus seemed to cheer him."

"So it should, it was the keys out of that place. Antigonus has to break away so he can take his army to Macedonia. So, he'll talk to Eumenes, try and renew their former friendship, and tried to persuade him to cast his lot with him. Now, given the information we sent Eumenes showed him just how desperate Anigonus is, we can assume that Eumenes will insist upon greater concessions than his existing circumstances justify. In fact, it wouldn't shock me if he thinks he ought to be given back the satrapies that had been originally assigned to him and be cleared of all the charges Antigonus and Antipater engineered against him. That's more or less what the information Igrat brought back from her trip to Nora told us. How was Eumenes taking his siege there by the way?"

Igrat thought carefully for a second. "He seemed quite cheerful. He told me that he had experienced many and various changes in the circumstances of his life and knew well that Fortune makes sudden changes in both directions. He's convinced that the remaining Diodochi would have need of him because of his judgement and his experience in warfare, and even more because of his unusual steadfastness to any pledge."

To the amusement of her companions, her voice had taken on the pitch and intonations used by Eumenes and it seemed as if the Greek librarian himself was in the room with them.

"That's rich. He's fought two battles, lost one and I won the other one for him. He has as much experience in warfare as a chamber pot. As for his steadfastness. . . ." Parmenio snorted disdainfully.

"Does that make him any the worse that any of the others? There isn't a real king amongst them." Naamah knew exactly how a real King behaved, she'd been married to one. She also knew how a real queen behaved because she had been one and in her opinion only Olympias even came close to qualifying from the present crop.

"Not in any real sense." Parmenio thought carefully again. "The whole concept of royalty in the kings of the Macedonians is an empty pretence. There hasn't been a real king since Phillip II. The people coming to the front now are not royalty but men of ambition. Antigonus is the most ambitious of them all. Ever since he was appointed supreme commander of Asia by Antipater, and put in charge of the Army of Asia, he's been filled with pride and arrogance. No way is he going to take any more orders from the kings, nor from their guardians. Good for him, he's got the largest and most powerful of the armies, he can use it to gain possession of the treasures of all Asia. If he can break loose from his siege at Nora, there's nobody who can stand against him."

"And that's a good thing?" Semiramis was lost. Her definition of warfare was a straightforward lunge at an enemy, slaughtering anything and everything that got in her way. It had worked in her day, it didn't work any more but she found it difficult to adjust to the constant maneuvering and bewildering shifts in alliances.

"A very good thing. He collects all the loot in one place and I can take it off him. Along with his head, of course. But, the loot comes first."

Fortress of Nora, Cappadocia

"Well, what is the message?" Eumenes stared at Hieronymus. "What does Antigonus have to offer?"

Hieronymus stared at his friend and ally. "As Seleucus Nikator told you he would, you are offered gifts many times the value of those you have received to date, a greater satrapy, and in general to be the first of Antigonus' friends and his partner in the restoration of peace to the Empire. His message contains an account of the meeting he has held with his existing allies. He doesn't say so specifically but he was advising them of his design for gaining imperial power. He made it clear that he considers only two options for those around him, to support his plan for Macedonia or to oppose him. He invites you to share in his undertakings, and says that, after receiving an oath-bound pledge, you will be freed from this siege. He says he is minded to go through Asia, remove the existing satraps, and reorganize the positions of command in favor of his friends.

"Seleucus Nikator won't be pleased to hear that."

"Seleucus Nikator is weak and a fool. After the death of Perdiccas, he could have had anything he wanted. Instead, he settled for a back-country satrapy that is far removed from the center of power. In doing so, he showed he lacks the heart and stomach to be a real ruler of consequence. He hoped that being based in Babylon, he would be away from the fighting and would be left in peace. For such spinelessness, he deserves to lose everything."

"Seleucus Nikator has stood beside us so far. Without him we would never have survived the first battle let alone maintained our lives and our presence here."

"A single fortress, besieged and isolated. Such assistance he provides us."

"He keeps us advised of what is happening. Without him all we would know of the events in the rest of the Empire would be what One-Eye wants us to know. We would be in a position of weakness and helpless before him. Now, knowing what we do, we have room to maneuver again."

"And what do we maneuver with? We have five hundred men with us and we can gather perhaps two thousand more from the remains of your army that has gone to ground and remained hidden. Those men are loyal to you and can be trusted. But 2,500 men? Not enough there to change the outcome of a skirmish, let alone a war."

"We maneuver with knowledge, Hieronymus. Antigonus is not the only player in the game. Seleucus sent us also a letter from Polyperchon. He promises us five hundred talents of gold to compensate us for the losses we have suffered to date and instructions to the generals and treasurers in Cilicia directing them to give us five hundred talents and whatever additional money we request for raising mercenaries. Polyperchon also says that if we rally to his cause, he will write to the commanders of the Argyraspides, ordering them to place themselves at our disposal and to cooperate wholeheartedly us. The regents for the kings offer us supreme command of all Asia whereas Antigonus offers only his friendship if we bow down to him."

"So, the regents or the generals, that is the question. Do we remain loyal to the Alexandrine inheritance or throw our lot in with those who would engrave their own names in stone to replace his?"

"That is what Olympias herself asks."

"We have had a letter from Olympias?" Hieronymus was astounded.

"By the efforts of that beauty Seleucus uses as a courier, yes. Before you condemn Seleucus Nikator, remember he has come from nothing to being a Satrap and he knows how to recognize talent. His courier got in and out of Nora by herself when twenty thousand of Antigonus's men have failed to do so. He knows how to use people and we must assume he knows how to use us."

"If we wish to be used."

"Of course, that goes without saying. But there is much bad blood between Antigonus and Seleucus, why I do not know. That must bear in our calculations also. But Olympias asks us if she should remain in Epirus and place no trust in those who are supposed to be guardians of the kings, but are really trying to transfer the kingdom to themselves. Or, should she return to Macedonia and fight for the rights of the Kings alone? You see how this ends Hieronymus. If we accept the offer of Antigonus, we may as well place him on the throne right now. But if we side with the Kings, we will never get out of this fortress."

"And if we side with Antigonus, we may as well throw ourselves on our swords before he does it for us. We will not live long enough to see the dawn rise on his new Empire. But if we do not, then we will die here in Nora and never see that Empire."

"There is one other thing to remember Hieronymus. I am a Greek, not a Macedonian and have no claim to the royal power. The Macedonians, whose command Antigonus has offered me and who will be subject to me, are those who have only months ago decreed my death. All those who occupy military commands are filled with arrogance and are aiming at winning noble office and great power. Powers and offices that I cannot, and never will be, able to grant. To them, I will be an object to be despised and at the same time envied. I will be an obstruction on their road to power and this will place my life in danger. Not one of them will willingly carry out my orders or do anything other than conspire against me. Antigonus knows that he will not have to raise his hand against me, there are all too many others who will do that for him."

Headquarters of Antigonus Monopthalmus, Asia Minor

"What is that damned fool doing?"

"Eumenes Sir? He has accepted our offer and left the fortress of Nora, pledging allegiance to you. Sir, I must tell you that our allies are disturbed at this. All wonder at the incredible changes of fortune that has seen Eumenes condemned to death by the kings and generals of the Macedonians, but now, forgetting their own decision, they have allowed him to escape punishment. They see you entrust him with great power in Asia. They ask whether, having experienced such a reversal in his fate, will he not adopt a bearing too high for mortal weakness? In short, Sir, they ask whether he can be trusted not to change his allegiance again."

"How many men has he accumulated?"

"Two thousand, five hundred Sir." Apollonides had anticipated the question and had the figures to hand. "All foot, he has yet to acquire cavalry to back up his infantry."

"After the last battle, does that surprise you? Next time Eumenes marches into battle, the rear half of his phalanx will be stepping backwards to guard his rear." Antigonus laughed grimly. "We can expect Eumenes to place little faith or trust in his cavalry from now on." *As little as I place in you, for a man who will sell out one commander will sell out another just as easily.* "But he is on our side for the moment and if he changes, he is still out of Nora and that makes him easier to deal with. I have other things to do."

"Sir?"

"Arrhidaeus, of Hellespontine Phrygia, has laid siege to the city of the Cyziceni. It is a strategically most important and very large city, one that is an ally and not guilty of any offence. Also, by doing so, he clearly intends rebellion and is converting his satrapy into a private domain. These are grave offenses, made all the more so by the fact that I want that city myself. As an ally if possible, by occupation if not. So, I will take a relieving force to Cyzicus and end this outrage. The rest of my army, under Menander, will remain here and watch for signs of treachery on the part of Eumenes."

Palace of Seleucus Nikator, Babylon

"Antigonus Monopthalmus is our primary enemy. Should we not join the alliance forming against him?" Seleucus Nikator voiced the idea tentatively.

"From one point of view, that may very well be the best way to jump. Old One-Eye is going to come at us sooner or later and the more we can chew his army up before he gets here, the better. Eumenes is going to pull in a lot of support when he declares for the regents. Mostly, because he's a foreigner and will not be able to advance his own interests beyond that of being a General. That means he can't harm the cause of the regents or go down with a bad case of the god-like delusions. A disease, by the way, of which Old One-Eye has a particularly bad case. That makes him a powerful friend who will protect the satrapies of those who rally to his side but be unable to do more than that. Antigonus had made it clear that he plans to redistribute all the existing satrapies this side of the Hellespont so even if the undecided groups rally to him, there is no guarantee that he will either protect their satrapies for them let alone give them others also."

"But Antigonus has a huge army and a great following." Seleucus was thoughtful, weighing the politics of Asia as he tried to work out what would happen next. "That is a weight that will take much overcoming. I think it is critical which way the first few uncommitted satraps jump. If they declare for Eumenes, then they will create an avalanche in his favor. If they opt for Antigonus, then the avalanche will benefit One-Eye."

"I agree" Parmenio was impressed; *Seleucus Nikator is learning fast.* "So, we had better try to get the avalanche falling in Eumenes's direction as quickly as possible. We can start to use that war chest we have sitting around. Now is the time when gold will be more lethal than a sarissa. But, as far as our own actions are concerned, we should delay as long as possible but when prevarication is no longer an option, we should declare for Antigonus."

There was a clatter as Seleucus dropped his wine goblet. "Parmenio, are you mad? You already admit he will be coming at us sooner or later. To forestall him seems a better plan."

"He will come at us sooner or later, personally, I would prefer later. As he sees the alliance building against him, he will be desperate for reinforcements. So, he will cast his eyes here, hoping to defeat us and absorb our Army into his own. That will also serve to clear his flank and remove the risk of us stabbing into his heart from below. But, if we are already his allies, fighting by his side, then he will gain nothing from such an assault. Indeed it will cost him dear for he believes we will not go down quietly. His losses might be such that the even the troops he will absorb from us will leave him weaker than before.

"So, we bribe the uncommitted to join Eumenes, thus increasing the threat to Antigonus while also making our alliance with him all the more valuable. By the way, we need to get word to Ptolemy, warn him of what is going on. In the longer term, when Antigonus turns on us, his allies, he will sorely damage his reputation and raise doubts from those who might otherwise sympathize with him. That is a consideration for the medium future. In the short term, we must keep Antigonus at bay and, ironically, that means getting closer to him."

"Keep your friends close, but your enemies closer." Seleucus nodded. "This makes sense. But suppose Eumenes gains so many allies he wins this war? We'd be on the losing side and pitched against the Regents."

"Won't happen. Look at the situation. In reality we're going to have two wars here with only a tenuous connection between them. We'll have Cassander and Polyperchon fighting it out in Greece and Macedonia while Eumenes and Antigonus slug it out in Asia. The connection really is tenuous, the two wars will be about as independent as they get. The only connection between them of any value is going to be by sea and Ptolemy has a fleet that can sever the connection any time he wants. All he needs to do is give the word. Now look at the situation with different eyes. All the support that the Regents will be getting via Eumenes will be in Greece and Macedonia. We don't care who wins there, Polyperchon or Cassander, it means nothing to us. Neither is a threat. We care about Antigonus and Eumenes, the former being an actual, very serious threat, the latter being a potential threat. So, all the allies we buy for Eumenes will actually be fighting for Polyperchon and will not benefit Eumenes at all. Antigonus will see them as his enemies certainly, but in reality, they're almost irrelevant. All they do is make us more valuable to him."

Palace of Olympias, Epirus, 318 BC

"Your Royal Highness, there is word from Eumenes."

"Speak." Olympias stared down at the messenger who was prostrate on the floor in front of her.

"Eumenes wishes to make it known he has always observed the most unwavering loyalty toward the kings and to the Alexandrine inheritance. The treachery of Antigonus and his many acts of rebellion against the kingship show that he has no honor and that the gods themselves have turned their faces from him. Eumenes says that he swore allegiance to Antigonus in the belief that Antigonus still served the kings. Now that he is in a state of rebellion against them, Eumenes will stand by the intent of his oath of loyalty. The son of Alexander is in dire need of help because of his orphaned state and the greediness of the commanders, and Eumenes believes that it is his duty to run every risk for the safety of the kings."

"Gods, that Greek Librarian talks too much." Olympias waved her hand irritably, as if brushing away a particularly annoying fly. "So, he has rallied to our cause."

"That is so Your Majesty. He further advises you to remain here in Epirus for the present until the war should come to some decision."

"In other words, he demands that I stay out of his way." The messenger could think of no way to answer that would not immediately cost him his head. He was saved from destruction by Olympias continuing without waiting for a reply. "And how much gold will Eumenes's loyalty cost me."

"None, Your Majesty. Indeed, he was promised no less than five hundred talents in gold for refitting and organizing his Army but he refuses to accept them. He says that he has no need of such a gift and that the monies would be better spent in raising troops to support Polyperchon."

"The Greek refusing gifts of gold? Then what does he want in their place? High office? Marriage into the Royal family?"

"Your Majesty, Eumenes wishes it made clear that he has no desire to hold high office. Even the position of command he now holds is not of his own will, but was forced on him by the treachery of Antigonus and the wishes of the kings that he undertake the great task of bringing Antigonus to meet his just fate. Serving the kings and furthering the interests of the Alexandrine line is all that he has ever wished."

Olympias leaned back in her throne , trying to see what Eumenes had to gain by declaring for the regents in such an open and blatantly provocative manner. It was very hard for her to accept that one of the commanders had loyalties that could not be bought. In the previous war, she had assumed that their loyalty went to the highest bidder and nothing she had heard or seen since then had altered that opinion.

"Where is Eumenes now?" Perhaps his movements might tell her something that his words did not.

"Your Majesty, ten days ago, Eumenes ordered his men to break camp and prepare for forced marches. He departed from Cappadocia with about five hundred horse and more than two thousand five hundred foot soldiers. Such was his urgency that he did not wait for reinforcements who had promised to join him."

Second Diodochi War

"And the reason for this great resolve is?" Olympias was growing more suspicious. To move with such speed suggested a great aim indeed and there was only one she could think of that would merit abandoning reinforcements when so clearly they were needed.

"Your Majesty, when General Menander heard word of Eumenes declaring for the regents, he acted on his orders from Antigonus and marched on Cappadocia with 15,000 men. When I was sent to carry these dispatches, he was three days behind Eumenes and hotly pursuing him. Eumenes has declared his intention of crossing the Taurus and entering Cilicia. There he will join with the Argyraspides and turn to fight Menander. He will still be outnumbered but with the Argyraspides on his side, he believes victory will be probable. He also believes that rather than fight the Argyraspides, Menander will retreat to Cappadocia and await reinforcements from Antigonus.

Headquarters of Eumenes, Cilicia, 318 BC

"Sir, Antigenes and Teutamus, the leaders of the Argyraspides request entry to your company."

"They are most welcome. Ask them to enter." Eumenes looked up from his map table. This was going to take some fine maneuvering.

"General Eumenes, in obedience to the letters of the kings, we bid you welcome to Cilicia and congratulate you on escaping the vile treachery of Antigonus Monopthalmus. We bring three thousand Argyraspides with us and willingly submit them, and ourselves, to your orders."

"Not to my orders, valiant comrades, but those of the regents of whom I am merely the agent. No magistracy is mine for I am Greek and thus excluded from the power that belongs of right to the regents and the Macedonian kings they represent. This was made most obvious to me by a strange vision I had while waiting in the Fortress of Nora. I believe that it is necessary to disclose this vision to you all in the name of harmony and the general good.

"While I slept at Nora, the great Alexander himself came to me, alive and clad in his kingly garb, presiding over the council, giving orders to the commanders, and actively administering all the affairs of the monarchy. Then he turned to me and said 'Eumenes, you have been brought to this dire pass because you remained faithful to me and my line. Do not despair because you will rise again and your integrity will be well rewarded. But, I warn you this, do not follow the examples of my other Companions who now consider themselves greater than me or mine. Remember always that you serve me and my line and victory always will be yours.' Then, the Great

Alexander left and from that night on I slept untroubled, knowing that He Himself approved of my actions.

"And so, I think that we must make ready a golden throne from the royal treasure, and that after the diadem, the scepter, the crown, and the rest of the insignia must be placed on it. Every day, we should offer incense to Alexander before his throne and hold our meetings in its presence. In this way, we will show that our army receives its orders in the name of the king just as if He were alive and still at the head of his own kingdom. Then, when the Kings come of age and take power in their own right, the throne of Alexander and the army of Alexander will be there, waiting for them."

Eumenes finished his speech and looked at those he had addressed. To his disbelief, he saw tears in the eyes of Antigenes and Teutamus. The grizzled old Argyraspides had been moved by his words. Had he been alone or out of sight, Eumenes would have shaken his head at the sight but to do so now would be to dilute the impact of his proposal. Quietly, he wondered if they realized the full impact of what he had proposed. Now, to engage his army would be to make war on Alexander himself. That might not concern Antigonus or Menander too much but to the simple, superstitious sarissaphoros in the ranks, it would create an ill state of mind. That, as Eumenes had learned at the Hyllus, was a major factor in who would ultimately win the battle.

"Is there gold for such a proposal?" Antigenes asked the question but the hope that there was shone clearly through his words.

"There is indeed." Eumenes had thought this out very carefully. "And Antigonus himself gave it to us. Another sign I believe that Alexander himself sits with us. At the Hyllus, my troops captured the treasury of Craterus and Neoptolemus, thus returning the gold of Alexander to those who were loyal to his inheritance. Although some was lost to Antigonus, the great majority was saved and taken to Nora. It was carefully preserved throughout the siege of Nora and now it can be used for its rightful purposes. Using it we can procure a magnificent tent with the throne, diadem, scepter, and Alexander's favorite armor. In that tent, we can all make sacrifice from a golden casket of frankincense and other kinds of incense. Once we have paid due respect to Alexander we can deliberate upon those matters that require our attention."

"What should our next step be?" Antigenes was looking on Eumenes with growing respect. He had come to this meeting out of reverence for Alexander but also filled with envy for the man who had so rapidly recovered from almost total defeat to secure a place of high command. Now, that envy was already being worn down and replaced by loyalty.

Second Diodochi War

"The Argyraspides total some 3,000 men. To those we may add the 2,500 men and 500 horse I brought with me. Menander has 15,000 men although the word from my scouts is that news of your arrival has caused him to slow his pursuit. I would suggest that we send out the most able of our friends with ample funds to engage mercenaries. We do not fight for our own profit but for the glory of Alexander's line so all that we have should be devoted to that end. Then, once the levies have arrived, we can engage Menander and teach him the folly of facing those upon whom the Great Alexander smiles. Does this seem a worthy plan?"

Teutamus nodded. In his eyes, Eumenes had done more to cement his position by regarding himself as an equal with the other commanders and seeking their favorable opinions on his plans than any display of force would have done. In consequence, he looked on the Greek Librarian with a level of goodwill that had previously been absent.

"I think this is an excellent plan. A small Army of great quality may beat a much larger force for a limited time but numbers exact a price all of their own. To have a future we must expand our forces. I counsel that we send our agents into Pisidia, Lycia, and the adjacent regions, where the love of Alexander remains strong and a zealous enrollment will bring many troops to our hand."

"This is true." Antigenes also was impressed by the attitude Eumenes was adopting. "I suggest also that we send agents through Cilicia, Syria and Phoenicia for the reasons that my old comrade has suggested. It would also be worth recruiting in Cyprus. I would caution though, that we should offer pay that compares with the best that is available and better than that Antigonus will spends. But, of the men attracted by that gold, we should take only those who are strong and experienced in war. Plus the recruits who are both able and willing to learn from their betters."

Marvellous, just what I intended. Eumenes thought. *One day, this won't be so easy.* "Wise counsel indeed comrades. We shall do as you suggest. Now, will you do me the kindness of introducing me to your men so that we may all become comrades in the service of the Great Alexander?"

Palace of Ptolemy Soter, Memphis, Egypt

"And so, the recruiting campaign by Eumenes was wildly successful, many recruits travelled of their own free will, even from the cities of Greece, to serve under his standard and be enrolled for the campaign against Menander. Eumenes has now more than 15,500 foot soldiers and 2,500 horse gathered together. Menander, disturbed by the cult of Alexander growing in Eumenes's Army and concerned at his growing disparity of numbers, has fallen back into Cappadocia and is appealing to Antigonus for help. Antigonus himself is tied down at Cyzicus and can send none. We will not be seeing Menander around much longer and with him, a quarter of Antigonus's army will be gone."

Igrat opened her eyes and looked at Ptolemy. "Enjoying the view?" The voice was her own, not the tones and inflections of Parmenio she had used to deliver the spoken message that had been entrusted to her. It had a droll tone to it that made Ptolemy smile. He had indeed been enjoying the view down the front of Igrat's tunic although that hadn't prevented him from absorbing every word and nuance of the messages. It would, in his opinion, be a very sad day for the world when a leader got criticized for eyeing a beautiful woman.

"You're a beauty Igrat. If you weren't the daughter of my friend and ally, I would steal you away."

And you wouldn't say that if you had seen me as the dirty, unkempt copper-coin whore who arrived here. Igrat's thought was concealed by a smile that was dual-purpose, an acknowledgment of the gallantry and recognition of the value of her deception. She had gone to great lengths to make sure that she was only ever seen as a beautiful lady of quality by those to whom she delivered her messages. Those who saw her in her copper-coin whore persona never knew that she had messages to carry. In that division lay her safety and she was very well aware of it. *Except there are two men outside my family who have seen me as both. Attalus and Callicrates. They saw me in both guises before I understood how critical it was that they should not. Now, they are a danger to me, one I should eliminate.* That thought shocked Igrat. *Gods, I'm starting to think like a Macedonian. I'll have to stop that.* "Well, you might not have to steal."

Ptolemy returned her smile. "I would take no liberties with your family, I already owe your father a great debt for grave transgressions generously forgiven. Your grandfather was my oldest friend yet I failed him. We were somatophylakes together. You know what they were?"

"The seven personal bodyguards of Alexander. My father has spoken of this." *Whoever my real father was and I doubt if my mother, may she rot in hell, even knew that. I may be a whore like her but no baby of mine will be left to bleed to death in the garbage.*

Ptolemy noticed the quick frown that had creased her forehead. "Is something troubling you?"

"No, just making sure that all the messages I have to pass were relayed properly."

Some of Ptolemy's women came in bearing food and wine for the Satrap and his guest. "I sort of inherited the royal harem." Ptolemy explained.

"Local custom and following it keeps the people quiet. Egypt is my powerbase, securing it and keeping it tranquil is my first priority."

Igrat was looking at the group of women. There was a strange feeling in the back of her head, the same one she got when she returned home after one of her journeys. *Ptolemy wasn't one who had the gift* she thought *so one of his women must be. I wonder which one.* Before she could follow up on the thought, the women withdrew.

"Igrat, most of the messages you carry are in your head. Those that are written could be stolen I suppose but not the ones in your mind. Forgive me for asking this, but what would you do if you were taken and tortured for the information you carry as spoken words?"

Igrat gave him a beaming smile. "I suppose I would scream. A lot."

Estate of Parmenio, Seleucia-on-the Tigris, Babylonia

"Tell me Parmenio, is this war going to be fought out entirely by writing letters to people?" Naamah dipped her bread in the olive oil bowl and munched on it. "Good bread this. New baker?"

"Lillith's invested some of our money in setting him up. She thinks that when times get hard, people will always want bread. You're right, he does bake good bread. Nice and crusty without being hard. As to the war, yes, you're right there as well. This part of it is all about writing letters."

"Then why am I still here? Shouldn't I be carrying some of them?" Igrat pulled off a cluster of grapes and started peeling them.

"Not your thing, the truth is we don't care whether these letters really get to their destination or not. We use you when a message has to get through and get through fast. The less we use you the better, for your sake as well as ours."

"Ptolemy seemed worried about me getting caught. He only knows me as your elegant and so-refined daughter. He's never seen the real me." Igrat's voice had changed slightly with the last sentence, the elegant Attic Greek being corrupted and vulgarized by a Koine accent. Naamah caught Parmenio's eye and her mouth twisted slightly. Even after four years, Igrat still had a self-image problem.

"You still don't get it do you?" Parmenio was mildly reproving. "My beautiful elegant daughter is the real you. The street woman is a shell you had to adopt to survive. Now, she only appears when you need her."

"He's right Iggie, nobody can make a marble statue out of pig dung. There had to be a beauty hidden there before we could turn you into one. We just dragged the real you out into the light."

"Don't like the light. Hurts my eyes." The words came out mixed with grape.

"Same for all of us. Tell me, Parmenio when the fighting starts, will the phalanx's bear down on each other wielding letters?" Naamah dunked another piece of bread and started nibbling the crust.

Parmenio laughed at the picture of his sarissaphoros wielding scrolls like spears. "If there was a way of doing that, Eumenes would have thought of it by now. Everybody is still jockeying for position, so far it's us, Ptolemy and Antigonus against Eumenes and the regents. That's one reason why you're getting a rest Iggie, Eumenes knows you by sight and there's nothing urgent enough that makes asking you to take the risk worthwhile. Standard couriers are quite adequate and we need to have you around in case we have to beat one to its destination."

Parmenio wondered at that. It was a mystery that still confused him. *How could Igrat slip through the backwash of a war so quickly that she could beat an official courier to his destination. When she cadged rides on carts and he had specially-selected horses and a clear road?*

"Anyway, Ptolemy is still writing his letters to Antigenes and Teutamus, exhorting them not to pay any attention to Eumenes and to swear allegiance to Antigonus. He's also written to the commanders of the garrisons in Cyinda, protesting at their payment of subsidies to Eumenes. He's urging them to declare for old One-Eye and has promised to guarantee their safety. He's even moved his fleet to Zephyrium in Cilicia to add weight to his words. That, by the way, puts him in a nice position to cut the link between Eumenes and the Regents.

"All in all, it's a good effort on his part, all he's done is waste some letters and get some sea-time on his fleet but it looks good to Antigonus. We've thrown a few letters around ourselves for the same purpose. It's a fine balancing act, making like good allies without actually doing anything."

"Are you getting anywhere with all these letters? Any of Eumenes's allies changed side yet?" Naamah finished her bread. "The cooks have made stew of meatballs in a rich savory sauce. They smelled good. I hope Ptolemy is having his food tasted?"

"Yes, he is. We ate together before I came back. Food, wine everything was tasted."

"Good for him. Although nothing can stop a skilled poisoner." Naamah had very good reasons for knowing that, reasons that Igrat was only just beginning to realize. "Parmenio, Eumenes losing any of his allies?"

"Gods, I hope not. I want them all where I can see them."

Second Diodochi War

Parmenio waited while the servants brought in a steaming bowl of small meatballs in a rich sauce. Naamah reached out and took a spoonful for herself. After a couple of minutes she nodded and dismissed the maids. "It is good. Dig in."

Igrat reached out and ladled out a portion of the dish for Parmenio who took it with a smile of thanks. Naamah smiled to herself at the scene. Although she didn't realize it, Igrat was becoming a real part of a family at last.

"Naamah, aren't you taking a risk by tasting the food yourself. Igrat sounded worried. Although their brief affair had ended years before, the women had remained good friends. In a strange way, each was the other's mentor in areas of human experience that the other had been ignorant. In Naamah's case, the experience had been eye-opening and made her understand how sheltered her life had been. There had been a whole world in the streets whose existence she had never suspected.

Naamah shook her head and dropped her voice. "Not really, I've been a herbalist for so many years, I've built up a sort of immunity to most of the things we're likely to run into. We're not quite as vulnerable to poison as those around us. Not quite, with us a poisoner would have to work a little harder. There are a few things, some of the poisonous mushrooms for example, that will infallibly kill us. But, mostly, if poison will kill a normal person, it'll make us really, really sick but I'll be a little less sick than you. Anyway, I know what to taste for. For example, this has got hemlock in it . . . ."

She watched while Parmenio spluttered. "Just joking."

Parmenio took another lump of bread and started to wipe up the sauce in his bowl with it. "Anyway, our letters won't do any good. The kings and Polyperchon, in his role as their guardian have sent their own endorsing Eumenes as their commander-in-chief and damning Antigonus as a traitor and defiler of the Alexandrine legacy. Olympias has done the same, telling the commanders that they should serve Eumenes in every way, since he was the commander-in-chief of the kingdom. She has also damned Antigonus to the hells and back again. With some very colorful embellishments by the way."

"What about us?"

"We're pointedly left off the 'may your bones crack and your penis rot' list. So's Ptolemy. That tells us how much Olympias is behind what's going on. You can bet she knows exactly what we are up to and why. So, she's leaving the way open for reconciliation. Oh, we got some 'rally to the cause of the Kings' letters as well but the damnation and cursing was missing. I got the feel she was just going through the motions.

Parmenio thought for a moment, weighing the strategic situation. "So, yes, in a way the picture is quite right. The sarissaphoros are fighting with letters right now. Of course it won't stay that way. Eumenes is moving in on Menander even while we speak."

CHAPTER TWO
BATTLEFIELD DECISIONS

Center of the Army of Eumenes, Tarsus, Cilicia, 318BC

"It's quite a jump from Nora." Hieronymus looked at the headquarters with satisfaction. It was lavishly furnished, the food was excellent and the wine better. "Antigonus must be ruing the day he lifted the siege of that fortress. A pity Seleucus has changed sides though."

"He's weak and foolish. He's just trying to buy Antigonus off. Everybody knows Antigonus will be coming after him soon so he's trying to buy some time. That's all. He doesn't matter to us one way or the other. At the moment, we're old One-Eye's primary target, making me the Regent's appointed Commander in Chief has displeased him greatly. And he fears the magnitude of the power that was being concentrated in me. He sees me as Polyperchon's choice as the strongest enemy of all who would become a rebel against the monarchy. Anyway, even Antigonus is out of play at the moment. All he can do is write letters and send agitators. The only army in the field against us is the force under Menander and that's today's order of business."

"The balance favors us. Menander has sixteen thousand foot and nine hundred horse. We equal him in foot and have a three-fold superiority in horse." Hieronymus looked uncomfortable with the latter, after the disaster before Nora, neither man had much faith in the reliability of cavalry.

"We do better than equal him in foot. Phalanx for Phalanx we match but we have the Argyraspides as well. I have them on our left flank with the cavalry far out on the left. Even if they betray us, they will be too far removed for the betrayal to matter. Menander has concentrated all his men in his phalanx, both his flanks are weak. Our right is weak also, but the power of our left is overwhelming.

120

Left Wing of the Army of Eumenes, Tarsus, Cilicia, 318BC

"The center is deadlocked – as usual. Time to move." Antigenes looked over to where the two phalanxes were 'locked in combat'. *Waving their sarissas at each other would be more like it,* he thought. *It was interesting how more and more of the successor generals were concentrating on the Phalanx and ignoring the rest of their army. It was as if all the lessons of Alexander were being forgotten.* Ahead of him, the Argyraspides were formed up, their formation perfect. They might be the oldest men on the battlefield, some well into their sixties, but they were feared and deadly fighters.

Teutamus was inspired by the sight and by the feeble force of five hundred hypaspist infantry in front of them. Inside himself, he was relieved that Antigenes had talked some sense into him. A few days before, he had been contacted by an old friend, Philotarsas, and given a letter from Antigonus that offered him great gifts and greater satrapies if he would change sides and secure the support of his acquaintances and fellow citizens among the Argyraspides for a plot against Eumenes by corrupting them with bribes. Antigonus had added that there were at least thirty other agents, suborning additional commanders and if Teutamus wouldn't go along with the offer, he would die when the inevitable defeat of Eumenes took place.

Teutamus had found his tentative approaches to various other commanders were unlikely to find solid ground so he had abandoned that effort and instead concentrated on persuading, and bribing, Antigenes, to betray Eumenes. It hadn't gone the way he had expected though. As they had drunk wine and broken bread together, Antigenes had displayed his great shrewdness and trustworthiness and shown him that it was to his advantage that Eumenes rather than Antigonus should remain alive. He'd shown Teutamus that if Antigonus became more powerful, he would inevitably would take away their satrapies and set up some of his friends in their places; So Teutamus had abandoned his scheme and once again given his loyalty to Eumenes.

Now, Antigenes dropped his hand and the Argyraspides moved forward, their ranks in perfect order. Ahead of them, Menander's hypaspists were already beginning to shift nervously and Teutamus suddenly realized that this was going to be one of those occasions when the defense in front of them would break before the assault actually charged home. And, as the Argyraspides picked up momentum, that is exactly what happened.

Rather than face the invincible veterans of Alexander's Army, Menander's hypaspists broke and ran. It didn't save them, for as they fled, the cavalry out on the far left charged, hitting the mass of fleeing troops in their disarray, trampling them down under their hooves. A feeble counter-charge by Menander's own light cavalry was swept away in the maelstrom and Menander's flank dissolved in utter chaos. His center followed suit, with the Phalanx outflanked and the Argyraspides closing rapidly on their exposed sides and rear, the troops decided they had much better things to do than get killed. Somewhere in the chaos and confusion of the disintegrating army, Menander died. In one sense, he did so alone despite the wreckage of his army around him, for in crushing the flank of his army and rolling up its center, the Argyraspides had not lost a single man.

Center of the Army of Eumenes, Tarsus, Cilicia, 318BC

"We've picked up most of Menander's army. Even allowing for our losses, we've nearly twenty five thousand foot and five thousand horse. If they stay loyal."

"You doubt that?"

"I have every reason to. That gibbering idiot Philotarsas is back. He's brought a letter from Antigonus to the Argyraspides and the other Macedonians, reminding them of the death sentence against you and urging that they seize you quickly and put you to death. Otherwise, he will come with his whole army to wage war upon them and will inflict grave punishment upon those who refused to obey him."

"Are they listening to him?"

"They have heard the letter read to them. If we hadn't won such a victory today and if Menander's head wasn't on a stake in front of your tent, then I would suggest you find a fast horse and a well-concealed hiding place." Hieronymus grinned. "Now, with about a quarter of Antigonus's Army either dead, running or in your Army, they're a bit perplexed. They've got a straight choice, side with the kings and receive punishment from Antigonus, or to obey Antigonus and be chastised by Polyperchon and the kings. They're still talking about it."

"Well, we'd better discuss it with them hadn't we." Eumenes sighed and stood up. Running armies was a complex thing and making sure they stayed his army was more complex than most. He had never recovered from the shock of seeing his cavalry plowing into the rear of his foot soldiers and turning what should have been a great victory into catastrophic defeat.

Inside the commander's tent, the assembly of officers was in disarray. Nobody seemed to be in charge, there was no form to the discussion and, while the troops were in this confused state, nothing was likely to get done. Eumenes saw that Hieronymus had been right, had not the day been marked by such a devastating victory, this meeting would have been threatening. Now, it was rudderless, lacking direction and purpose.

There was a sudden silence when Eumenes entered and he made a great show of reading the letter. Then he looked up and appeared to be in deep thought. "Antigonus writes well doesn't he?"

The first words fell into the silence and drew attention to him. "He has a good hand, clear and easy to read. This is fortunate because it makes it all the more obvious how little he has to say. He says I am condemned to death. Well, that's true, of course, he has condemned me to death. But the Kings, the son and the brother of the great Alexander, and their guardians led by Polyperchon have made me commander-in-chief of their armies. In spirit, Alexander himself sits with us and his hand has guided us today in a great victory, a victory we won in his name. So who has greater weight?"

Eumenes lifted up his left hand. "Antigonus who writes so well and whose excellent hand makes clear the treachery of one who has become a rebel." Then he lifted his right hand. "Or the Kings who carry on the tradition of our greatest leader, those who have dedicated their lives to guarding those kings and we who are guided by the spirit of Alexander to win great victories."

Eumenes made a show of weighing the two and then crashed his right hand down to the table. "Not much of a choice is it?"

"It is well that Antigonus writes so clearly for he reminds us that he deals in lies and treachery. How many have allied with him, only to see their satrapies taken from them and themselves cast out or killed? How many have allied with him on the promise of great rewards yet been paid only with their deaths? Who now trusts him? Look at those who are his allies. Seleucus the weakling who starts at shadows and who lives in fear of losing his backwater province. Ptolemy, corrupted by the vices of the Egyptians and who spends his days idling in his Egyptian harem. And who else is there? Why, nobody. Only those degenerates and none other. Are we equal to such apologies for rulers that we should bend our knee to a rebel in the hope he might condescend not to steal everything we have. Are we not better people than that?"

The roar of cheering swept the room and Eumenes quietly sighed with relief. "Now, with Menander dead and his army destroyed, where do we go from here? I tell you, we go for the head of Antigonus. We've chopped off one of his arms today, let us cut off his legs tomorrow and his other arm the day after, Let us see how well he writes then, hey boys?"

Another roar of laughter swept the room. "After all, what does one call a man who has no arms and no legs?" Eumenes waited while people anticipated the answer. "Why, anything we like because there's not a damned thing he can do about it!"

Another roar of approval, mixed with laughter, greeted the punchline. Eumenes let it continue for a moment, then lifted a hand to quieten it before it had time to subside. "So, what do we do and where do we go? First of all we shall break camp from here and invade Phoenicia. We have more than twenty five thousand foot and five thousand horse. Why Phoenicia you might ask. Because there we can gather ships from all the cities and assemble a considerable fleet. This will allow Polyperchon to win control of the seas and bring reinforcements of the Macedonian armies safely for us to use against Antigonus whenever we wish. Also Phoenicia has riches they may contribute to our war-chest so that those who are loyal to us can be paid in gold, not with promises conditional on a victory whose attainment lies in the far future. And why else do we go to Phoenicia first? Because where else are the most beautiful and affectionate of women who will reward us all for the victory we have won today?"

Listening to the cheers, Eumenes knew he had won. *Promise the men victory, gold and women and they'll follow their leader anywhere.* "And what, you may ask, will Antigonus do about this. He'll come for us, that is certain. But, his army is spread all over Asia and he cannot concentrate it in time. We will move first, we will move fastest and we will take his army on piecemeal. Every victory we will swings the odds still further on our favor. Yes, one day the soldiers in his army may well want to enjoy the favors of Phoenician women – but they'll have to beg you for your permission first!"

The cheers were thunderous and spread from the assembly tent across the camp. Eumenes looked around at his army. He had come a long way from Nora.

Palace of Seleucus Nikator, Babylon, 317 BC

"We have a problem in Macedonia."

Listening to the complaint, Parmenio wasn't quite sure whether Seleucus was asking a question or stating a fact. Either way, it really didn't make much difference.

"I don't think so. The situation there is actually quite favorable to us. We appear to be backing Eurydice and Cassander as part of our alliance with Antigonus and with Eurydice assuming the administration of the regency, that means we are in a position of influence with the ruling power. But, we are also backing Olympias and Polyperchon and keeping them well-supplied with gold and information so when Polyperchon moves against Cassander, we'll be well-placed there. Now, our real ally, Ptolemy, has got his fleet between Polyperchon and Antigonus. That looks as if he's cut Eumenes off from support but actually it works the other way. Those ships are preventing Antigonus from coming to the support of Cassander. Only that hasn't dawned on Antigonus yet."

How do you keep track of all this?" Seleucus was genuinely fascinated. "We seem to be backing everybody against everybody else."

"It's just a talent I think. Anyway, we are; we and Ptolemy. We're guarding each other's backs while the rest of the Successors tear each other apart. It's not so hard to keep track of really. No harder than running a major battle. The fact is that the battle between Eumenes and Antigonus is a nice, self-contained little war that has very little effect on anything else. Eumenes has been wintering his army in Phoenicia, Antigones around Susa. Neither are of much concern to us at the moment. As long as they keep battering at each other, they're not battering us. The only thing that slightly concerns me out there is that Eumenes is doing much better than I'd expected. For somebody with virtually no military command experience, he's done remarkably well."

"You don't think he'll defeat Antigonus surely?" Seleucus sounded disbelieving. A Greek librarian beating a hardened Macedonian general wasn't a comfortable thought.

"It's hard to say at this point. If Eumenes had moved at the end of last year and gone straight for Antigonus, he would have been in with a good chance. His Army was large, hardened by campaigning and flushed with victory after Menander got his. But, he chose to go to Phoenicia instead. Now, he wintered well there, that's for certain, but his Army has lost its edge. They got soft and used to living in luxury over the winter and they've got used to having their wives around. Antigonus made the better choice for winter quarters, soft enough to keep his army alive, hard enough to make sure they kept their edge. Eumenes won't have the easy time of it he had last year. On the other hand, he's had a string of victories behind him and that'll hearten his men.

"But, from our point of view, the critical things is that they should keep fighting. That's all that matters to us. The moment they stop, whoever won will come after us and we have to have our plans in place for that. And they are. As soon as the army approaches, we'll be out of here. I'll be taking the Army south and dancing around while you head for Ptolemy. That's when the others are going to start learning why we chose to be based out here."

"And what about Cassander?"

"The lad has done well. We're supporting him as well by the way."

"I might have guessed." Seleucus was amused at the situation as the full extent of the web that was being woven on his behalf became more apparent. "I suppose the fact that he took Athens a few weeks ago is working for us into the bargain?"

"Of course, he's established an oligarchy in Athens and placed Demetrius of Phalerum in charge there. That cleared his rear and he's moved south into the Peloponnese to campaign against Polyperchon. Now that was a smart move, there's no doubt that Polyperchon is the most dangerous of his enemies and moving south put a lot of pressure on him. That, of course, meant that our aid to him became that much more important."

"Aid to Polyperchon or Cassander?"

"Polyperchon. We've sent him gold to hire more mercenaries and we have ships offshore to pull him out if Cassander breaks through. But that won't happen, you see, we sent word to Eurydice, telling her that a great army under Olympias is about to descend upon her. That threw her into a panic and Eurydice has sent a courier into the Peloponnesus, begging Cassander to come to her aid as soon as possible. She's getting desperate; her antics at Triparadisus have caused her to be isolated from the majority of the Diodochi and her arrogance has alienated the rest. She thinks that by plying the most active of the Macedonians with gifts and great promises, she will make him personally loyal to herself. Now, Cassander wants her, both on a political level and on a personal one so she has good reason to think that. Foolish mistake to mix business with pleasure. So, he's going to break off, release the pressure on Polyperchon and head north. Worst strategic mistake he could possibly make."

Sutler's Caravan, Approaching Euia, Macedonia.

"You interested in a little trade?" The guards at the checkpoint were crowded around Callicrates cart. They had stopped the caravan with the official excuse that they had to check for spies and hostile messengers. The real reason was to shake the Sutler down for a portion of his stock-in-trade. Then, they'd spotted Igrat and had become inordinately interested in her stock-in-trade

"All of you?" Igrat did a quick count. Six. "Fifty copper each for the first three, thirty each for the second pair, twenty for the last one. I won't be at my best by then."

The soldiers laughed uproariously, encouraged by the flip of Igrat's eyebrows. Then she frowned slightly. "That one there, the youngster. He looks like a newbie to me."

"Nikomedes? Just joined us last week." The sergeant in charge had recruited the boy himself. "Fresh off a farm, can't even handle a Sarissa yet."

"The question is, can he handle his Sarissa?" Igrat's sally caused another outburst of laughter and she relaxed. Once she had them laughing with her, they weren't a threat. "Well, Nikomedes, can you handle your Sarissa. Ever done it with a girl?"

"Of course I have." Nikomedes was defensive, afraid of being teased by the veterans over his lack of experience. Behind him the veterans caught Igrat's eyes and shook their heads.

"Well, that's a pity. Because us working girls have a tradition. If it's a recruit's first time, he gets it free and he goes first. Now, tell me the truth. You used your Sarissa yet?" Nikomedes flushed and shook his head. "Well, hop up into the back then. Rest of you, decide who goes when."

There was a round of cheers as the boy scrambled into the back of the cart. Igrat sorted out a few things and put some rolled-up blankets down on the wooden floor. "Support for my back" she explained. "Now, be nice to a girl and spit on it before you stick it in."

Ten minutes later, the recruit jumped down from the wagon, grinning broadly at the other men. The Sergeant climbed up next. Igrat stretched out her hand and counted the coppers that he gave her. *A hundred of them?*

"For the boy as well. We did a collection while you were breaking him in. That was a nice thing to do for him, we thought you shouldn't end up short."

"Thank you." Igrat gave him a smile. "Look, leave the Sutler alone will you? You take some of his stuff, he'll take it out on me."

The Sergeant nodded. "There's plenty coming through, we'll make it up from the next one. And I'll have a word with him before you two move out. Now, brace yourself girl, veteran coming aboard."

An hour later, the Sergeant waved Callicrates through the checkpoint. "Just remember, Greek, that's a nice girl you got back there. You rough her up and we get to hear of it, it'll go badly for you."

Callicrates gulped and nodded, only too pleased to be through the checkpoint with his goods untouched. As the checkpoint faded into the distance, Igrat scrambled out of the back of the cart and on to the seat beside him. "You all right Igrat?"

"A bit sore. I had a soft winter and need to get back into the business. Those were Polyperchon's men?"

"That they were. Doesn't matter too much for us of course."

And there you are much more wrong than you could ever believe possible. Igrat thought. She had critical messages for Polyperchon and Olympias. She doubted that the soldiers would have found them though, she'd spent the last hour laying on top of them. Beside her, Callicrates started whistling cheerfully. If this trip went as well as their previous ones, he would be rich enough to retire, buy a farm and give up chasing around after armies.

Second Diodochi War

Headquarters of Polyperchon. Euia, Macedonia

"There is a lady to see you Sir." The Royal Guard, one of Olympias's trusted veterans spoke from the door of the room.

Polyperchon frowned. He had many more important things to do that worry about women, no matter how highly-bred. Olympias and her wretched arrogance caused him more trouble than he could easily cope with. "What does she want?"

"She claims to have messages. From our allies."

Polyperchon frowned at that. His only official ally was Aeacides of Epirus and he was here, in this room. Of course, it was also whispered that they had other allies, secret ones whose names should not be spoken. "Send her in."

The woman who entered from the darkness into the yellow light of the candles was obviously wealthy and of good family. Her hair, carefully dressed, her clothes rich and costly, her jewelry more so. Obviously a woman of good family and Polyperchon wondered what she was doing here and why she undertook the dangerous role of messenger. When she spoke, it was in fluent Attic Greek. "You are General Polyperchon?"

"I am, and this is my ally, Aeacides of Epirus."

"I am commanded to place these messages in your hands and yours alone. I also have words for you." The woman closed her eyes and continued speaking but her voice was subtly different. The husky tones were still an obviously female but the way she spoke, the way she used words and the spacing between them was achingly familiar to the General. He'd heard somebody speak like that before but he couldn't place where or when.

"The Army of Eurydice and Cassander is rotten. The men have no faith in their leaders nor do they owe loyalty to them. They respect the position of Olympias as mother of the Great Alexander and remember well the benefits they received at the hand of Alexander. Their allegiance hangs finely in the balance and it needs only a slight gesture of greatness to swing them over to your side. That will be all it needs to restore Olympias and the son of Alexander to the throne."

"I planned to end this campaign with a single decisive battle." Polyperchon stared at the beauty who had brought the messages. "I had not thought that this was possible. Who sent these messages?"

"One who has your interests at heart." *And that is a lie of such proportions you could not believe its full extent* thought Igrat. "I will stay here with you until the battle is joined or the Army of Eurydice collapses. My presence is your surety."

Polyperchon nodded. "And you had better hope that the words that you have brought are true."

Polyperchon's Center, Battlefield of Euia

The two phalanxes were arrayed on open ground, their ranks opposed, the sarissaphoros staring at those ranged against them. Both flanks were weak, both commanders had placed the greatest portion of their strength in their phalanx. The commanders on Polyperchon's side heard the trumpets blaring out their commands and saw the enemy phalanx start to move towards them. They also heard the eerie swish as the sarissas swung down from their vertical carry position to the horizontal attack. But, mindful of their orders, they gave no command and their men stood at rest.

The phalanx of Eurydice closed on them and then stopped. Their sarissas swung again, this time from horizontal to a downward slope that rested their points on the ground. The Army of Eurydice had surrendered without a blow being struck.

Court of Olympias, Amphipolis, Greece

"And so you thought that Philip III Arrhidaeus and Eurydice could escape my Kingdom?" Olympias looked at the two prisoners who had been brought in chains before her. Both had been roughly handled but of the two, the woman was by far the worst off.

"This is not your kingdom." Eurydice spat the words out, the hatred within them obvious to all. "My husband is the rightful king of Macedonia and successor to the Great Alexander. This is our Kingdom, our Empire. You are nothing here."

Sitting quietly in one corner of the throne room, Igrat winced at the words. She was in no doubt of the psychotic cruelty that lay inside Olympias. It was her attempt to poison Philip III Arrhidaeus that had left him in the pitiful physical and mental state that had debarred him from being appointed King. Olympias frightened her and all she wanted was to get out of this court as quickly as she could. Once she was outside, it would take but a few minutes for her to revert to her street whore persona and disappear into the mass of camp followers where she would be safe.

"You think you should have a kingdom do you?" Olympias's voice cooed seductively and every syllable dripped venom. "Well, I have prepared one for you."

She gestured with one hand towards a small room, barely large enough for two people to lay down within. Philip and Eurydice were dragged over to it and thrown in. Then, masons walled up the entrance, leaving only a tiny slit.

Second Diodochi War

Estate of Parmenio, Seleucia on the Tigris

"What happened next?" Lillith asked the question gently, it was obvious that the scene in Olympias's court had shaken Igrat deeply. That their street-hardened alley-cat had been so frightened was more disturbing than her description of the events themselves.

"She kept them in there for days, many days. Just gave them enough food and water to keep them alive. She would stand outside the chamber they were walled up in for hours, taunting them, asking them how much they liked their new Kingdom."

Igrat took a deep draught of wine and steadied her voice. "And she told them that one of them would be released if they killed the other. She had a single knife thrown in there with them. But they refused to betray each other. Then she had thrown in a rope and said that if one of them hanged themselves, the other would be released. This caused the dispute she had hoped for because each one wanted to die so that the other might live. In the end, Philip took the knife that was in their prison and stabbed himself.

"Eurydice laid out the body of her husband, cleansing its wounds as well as the circumstances permitted. Then, in the presence of all the priests prayed that the way she and her husband had been treated might also one day fall to the lot of Olympias herself. Then, Olympias went mad with rage and had a poisonous viper brought. She took the snake and passed it into the cell where Eurydice was confined. Then she had the masons seal up that slit so there was no way out for woman or snake. And so Eurydice died, alone in the darkness with only a deadly viper to accompany her."

Igrat was crying quietly as she finished the story and Naamah went to her, cushioning her head on her shoulder and patting her gently. The thought of Eurydice, alone in the total darkness of a walled-off room waiting for the bite that would kill her was chilling.

"Father, if it is possible, please don't send me back there. Olympias is insane. After she killed them, she had Nicanor, Cassander's brother killed along with hundred of the most prominent Macedonians from among the friends of Cassander. Nobody is safe anywhere near her."

"You won't be going back there Igrat. Olympias has made a terrible mistake with those killings. They will cause everybody to hate her ruthlessness. All Macedonians will remember the words of Antipater, who advised them never to permit a woman to hold first place in the kingdom. She's signed her death warrant, it's just a matter of time now. We've no more interest in her or her grandson."

Igrat nodded and left with Naamah. Parmenio stared at the wall for a few minutes before making his final comment on the tale. "Five down."

Headquarters of Eumenes, Carianas, Phoenicia, 317BC

"Seleucus and Pithon are above themselves. Since Eurydice and Cassander were defeated, they come snivelling to the Kings, attempting to desert Antigonus before it is too late. As for Ptolemy, he spends all his time plotting the recovery of Phoenicia. He cares nothing for anything but his own interests."

Don't we all. Hieronymus allowed the vaguely mutinous thought to pass through his mind unchecked. Eumenes had changed over the last year, the almost magical reversal of his fortunes and a few strategic military victories had given him the idea that he was a great commander. *Better than his enemies had thought, yes. But great? That remains to be proved.* "The defeat of Eurydice and Philip III Arrhidaeus was a great blow to Antigonus that is certain. But what Olympias has done since then? Eumenes, it does not sit well with the men. There is discontent in their talk around the camp fires and they ask if the Gods would smile on those who continue to support a desecrater of tombs and defiler of the dead."

"That will change with another victory. The men have gold, they have women. Once we have won another victory, all their doubts will be pushed to one side. And, with Antigonus gone, we can turn to Greece and deal with our problems there."

"Antigonus is not so easily brushed away."

"He will be. He brought his men down from Colchis through Armenia to Arbela. They broke winter camp early and have marched cold and hungry while our men have wintered easily in the lush lands of Phoenicia. We will march on Antigonus and then we will indeed brush him away."

"Seleucus of Babylonia lies beween us. What is his word?"

"Same as that from Pithon of Media. Seleucus says that he is willing to be of service to the kings, but he will never consent to carrying out my orders, because the Macedonians in assembly have condemned me to death. Our army will be his response. We will march through Syria with the design of making contact with the upper satrapies. Once they see a Royal Army on their borders, they will remember the debts they owe to the Great Alexander and rally to the cause of his grandson. Then we will turn south, follow the Tigris and thus split Seleucus and Pithon away from Antigonus. Then we may defeat them all in detail.

Parmenio's Center, Thapsacus-on-the-Euphrates

"The army is not as large as I had feared." Seleucus stared at the campfires stretched out along the banks of the Euphrates. "He has fifteen thousand infantry and thirty-three hundred cavalry still?"

"He has." Parmenio was watching the campfires as well. "But he's got command problems even so. Look how his men have spread out along the banks of the river. We're about to teach him why that is a very bad idea."

"With only Prodromoi light cavalry and light infantry? The Sarissaphoros are far behind us." Seleucus was curious, what was unfolding before him was something he had never seen before. He had an idea he was seeing the birth of a new form of warfare.

"I've been reading accounts of the latest battles, both the one's fought between Pithon and Peucestes here and between Cassander and Polyperchon in Macedonia. They're all saying the same thing, the Diodochi are placing more and more emphasis on their phalanx and their supporting forces are withering from neglect. They are forgetting the lessons of combined arms and instead just relying on their heavy infantry. The result is that their mobility is falling. Back in the old days, Eumenes would have moved much faster than this.

"I suppose though it's largely inevitable. Most of the forces below are mercenaries and they want to get paid, not die. When two phalanxes stand there and wave their sarissas at each other, the casualties are slight. We're about to change that. Wars are won by destroying the enemy's ability and willingness to fight. We're about to show them that fighting Seleucia means a blood-letting. We're also about to show them that it isn't profitable. This is our first real blow Nikator, we're starting the process of educating our opponents in what picking a fight with us will mean."

Prodromoi Light Cavalry, Thapsacus-on-the-Euphrates

"Are the men ready?" Alcetas had his cavalry drawn up behind a low ridge just short of the Euphrates.

"They are Sir. They wait for the signal and their hearts are stout."

As well they should be. A quick raid, in and out to grab the gold and the women. A perfect operation to please the troops. Not an honorable battle though, more like bandits raiding in the night. In fact, exactly like bandits raiding in the night. Alcetas didn't quite know what to make of this plan or of the man who had conceived it. He was supposed to be a great general, a strategos who had learned his trade from his father, the great Parmenio himself yet there had been no great battle, no overwhelming victory. Instead, he had fallen back in front of Eumenes's force, drawing them deeper and deeper into hostile territory. This was the first offensive action he had taken and, whatever it was, it certainly wasn't a set-piece battle.

His household was equally strange. Alcetas had been carrying on a liaison with one of the ladies of Parmenio the Younger's house. He had been prepared to make an honorable offer of marriage but Lillith had refused him and Parmenio seemed quite happy with that. *Would not the master of a household be outraged at the seduction of one of the women there?* None of this made sense.

Up on the ridge, there was a gentle rustle as the slingers got ready. Alcetas spurred his horse and his light cavalry surged forward, their spears lowered for the attack. As they crested the ridge, he saw the campfires strung out along the river. His cavalry charge would be striking one extreme end of the line. He would overrun that, swing parallel with the river and roll up Eumenes's camp sights. As they did so, the slingers and archers spread out along the ridgeline would hit the men ahead of him as they tried to organize the defense. Once the camps were being overrun, the orders were simple, loot them of their treasure and seize as many of the women as possible. Kill the other camp followers and destroy anything that cannot be carried away. That part of his orders did not sit well with Alcetas.

Ahead if him, there was a blare of trumpets as the lookouts saw the light cavalry pouring down the slope towards the camp. Men from the tents started stumbling out, trying to buckle on their armor and seize the weapons that were by their sleeping quarters, but the slingers on the ridge let fly with their first salvo and men began to fall as the heavy shots thudded into their unprotected bodies. Then, the Prodromoi were into the camp itself and any hope of an organized resistance was over. Those men who tried to stand were speared by the cavalry and left to lie in the dirt, the rest started to run, no doubt reasoning that they needed space and time to organize a resistance. The problem was that the cavalry was moving faster than they were and the running men were mercilessly cut down.

An army loses more men when it breaks than it does when it stands. Parmenio the Younger's strangely flat voice echoed through Alcetas's mind as his cavalry swung around to follow the retreating men and hunt them down. Behind him, the light infantry and auxiliaries were already following him down the slope, seizing the abandoned camp. Already, women were being dragged from their tents and herded backwards, the Sutlers hauled from their wagons and killed, their goods seized and carried off. Fires were spreading as the infantry seized brands from the campfires and used them to torch the tents and wagons. Alcetas heard the screams as those who had tried to hide there were forced to choose between being burned alive or carried off.

He had more important things to worry about though. Ahead of him, the defenses were beginning to solidify as Eumenes's men recovered from the shock of the raid. They were becoming organized, their ranks forming even as the shot and arrows from the ridge felled a fair share of their number. The wild charge of the Prodromoi was slowing and Alcetas guessed it was time. As if to confirm his judgement, he saw a hedge of spearpoints ahead of him.

That was the sign he had been ordered to look for, when the first phalanx started to form he took his trumpet and blasted out the signal to retire. His sub-commanders took up the call and, rather than throw his cavalry on to the waiting sarissas, he and his men fell back. Behind him, the light infantry heard the signal also and started to retire to their ridge with their loot and captives.

Parmenio's Center, Thapsacus-on-the-Euphrates

"I can't understand why they didn't follow us?" Seleucus Nikator asked the question and waited to file away the answer. He'd already learned his first lesson, always ask, never assume or, even worse, be too proud to ask. "His men must be furious."

"Furious, humiliated and quite a few other things. But, he has only heavy cavalry and heavy infantry. Even with captives and loot, we can move faster than he can. He is smart enough to realize that trying to catch us will just be setting himself up for another ambush. I taught him that when we were retreating across Cappadocia. Anyway, we did what we intended to do. He'll spend more time every night now fortifying his camps and that'll slow him down. He'll keep a higher percentage of his men awake on guard and the rest will sleep in their armor and that will tire them out. Both those things favor us. Now it's your part in all this."

The disengagement from the Army of Eumenes was completed and the force was resting after their night attack. Parmenio wasn't worried about a pursuit, he had other cavalry out, watching the enemy for any signs of movement. Meanwhile, the army had other things to do. The loot from the sutler's wagons was piled up in the camp and the captured women were penned in a corner of the area. Seleucus was already riding down to speak with them. Parmenio felt a move beside him and was on his guard but it was Igrat, in her noble lady guise, and sitting astride a horse.

"I didn't know you could ride Igrat."

"Gusoyn taught me, during the months I wasn't travelling much. Father, I don't like this." She gestured down at the captive women waiting to be sold. "You took those women from their families. If I'd been in that camp, I'd be down there with them."

"War isn't nice Iggie, sometimes we have to do things that are pretty bad. This is one of them. I want the men in Eumenes's Army to be worried about their families. Now, raids like this weren't rare once. They have a purpose and they serve that purpose. Only, that purpose has been forgotten and raids like this have fallen into disuse. Last night, we taught Eumenes why he had to defend against them. If it eases things for you, those women won't be any worse off than they were before. Most will be taken by the unattached men in our Army, the rest will be sold off and probably bought by us officers."

Igrat looked down and saw Seleucus Nikator speaking to the men gathering around him. He pointed to one of the Prodromoi and his voice carried clearly. "You, I saw you in the charge last night. You took down that Sarissaphoros in fine style. Alcetas, that man deserves promotion. And that slinger, you there. To hit a running man at that range was an example to us all, an extra piece of gold for you." The cheering men surrounded him and she saw the chosen men being eyed enviously by their comrades. To be noticed so favorably by the king, even if he didn't claim that title yet, was a major step forward for them.

Seleucus lifted his hand and the tumult quietened. "In recognition of your achievements last night, I forgo the commander's share of our loot. It will all be apportioned between you, equal shares for every man regardless of rank. Those of you who wish to take a woman from the captives may do so, her value to be deducted from your share of the gold." Another burst of cheering. "As for the wine." There was a quietening around him. "Equal shares for all – and I will drink your health with mine!" The tumult resumed and Seleucus dropped off his horse and made his way amongst his men, slapping backs and exchanging jokes. Parmenio nodded contentedly, Seleucus was doing his job and Parmenio would continue to do his.

Prodromoi Light Cavalry, Thapsacus-on-the-Euphrates

Alcetas looked up at Parmenio sitting on the ridgeline and looking down. There was a young woman beside him Igrat his daughter. Alcetas noted that she was riding her horse astride his back, like a man, not side-saddle the way a lady of quality would normally ride. Another strange thing about that household. Did Parmenio the Younger not control his womenfolk properly? Or did he use them the way he used his armies, as pieces on a board to be maneuvered? And that their strange behavior was to meet with ends of his own, that possibly only he knew?

There was a knot of men gathered around the enclosure where the captive women were corralled. Some were already speaking to the women inside, doubtless making their agreements with them. A few couples were already making their way to Seleucus's treasurer, advising him that they had taken a woman in lieu of part of their share of the loot. There weren't quite as many as he'd thought, the Prodromoi were mostly young men who had no need of a camp-wife yet while the slingers and archers had theirs already.

By the time the men and women had made their bargains, there were still a small number of women left. Alcetas saw Seleucus buy most of them. Presumably for his palace staff. Parmenio bought two including one who was very young and had been pulled away from an older woman who was being taken by one of the Prodromoi. *Just a little bit too old to be left with her mother, too young to accept what was happening. Perhaps Parmenio wanted a maid for his daughter?*

Sharing out the gold was an operation that took most of the rest of the day. The men got their shares and most of them parted with a coin or two to add to the shares of their officers. The King might have said equal shares for all but a wise soldier bought favor with his officer. And so it was that the Seleucid Army won the battle of Thapsacus.

Camp of Eumenes, Thapsacus-on-the-Euphrates

Hieronymus felt his eyes watering from the stench of the burned tents and wagons. And from the smell of the burned flesh within them. The raid had been devastating for the camp that had been hit. The bodies of the dead seemed to be everywhere although, intellectually, Hieronymus knew that if he had seen them on a battlefield he would have counted it as but a light loss. It was the circumstances that made the difference, the surroundings of a ruin camped, the number of the dead who were women. The older ones, he noted, the younger ones had been carried off. All too many of the dead had men grieving beside them and all too many of the men were veterans. The older men had the older wives and they had had longer to become a firmly-fixed pair. Now that pairing had died on the point of a Prodromoi spear.

"I sent to Seleucus in order to ransom the women who were taken." Eumenes spoke dully, still shocked by the ferocity of the raid and the fact it had taken place at all. "I offered to pay for them in gold, from our treasury but the offer was refused. The women were taken and they will remain taken. Our men will not see them again."

He looked around at the burned section of the camp. "Why? Why did they do this? They killed the sutlers, what did they have to gain from that? Many times they killed them and just burned their goods. They had no need to kill and why burn what they could not use? They killed the women they did not want. Why?"

Faced with questions he could not answer, Hieronymus just looked around at the ruins. "Perhaps Seleucus was sending you a message. That if you wish to make war upon him, then the price will be steep and bloody. You should know that Seleucus has sent an ambassador to Antigenes and the Argyraspides, asking them to remove you from your command. They refused to listen of course."

"Their loyalty deserves praise and rich reward. See to it. We must prevent this kind of night-time raid from happening again. In future we will cease marching an hour earlier than usual and we will fortify the perimeter of the camp. The men will remain close together with the camp guard quadrupled. Each man will sleep with his weapons and armor to hand."

"That will slow our march down greatly. With every day that passes, Antigonus grows stronger. His men recover from their forced winter march and eat well in Susiana."

"That cannot be helped. We will march to the Tigris and make our base three hundred stades north of Babylon. Once there, we shall summon the armies from the upper satrapies and to make use of the royal treasure to pay them and our men. And, so reinforced, we will advance on Susiana."

"There is a problem Eumenes. Our scouts are reporting in, the land on our route between the Euphrates and the Tigris has been plundered, whereas that on the other side of the Tigris is untouched and able to furnish abundant food for an army. Seleucus and his troops remain well-fed while we must scavenge for every mouthful of grain."

"Then we will have to divide the army into three columns and take different routes to the Tigris. Also, distribute to the soldiers rice, sesame, and dates, since the land produces these in plenty. And spread word amongst the men that Pithon of Media has been defeated by Peucestes and that the Army of Peucestes will be joining us at the Tigris."

"Is that so?" Hieronymus hadn't heard the news.

"I hope so."

Headquarters, Seleucid Army, Tigris River, Babylonia

"Well, Pithon is out of the game." Seleucus Nikator took an almost delighted relish in the news.

"I know." Igrat had got back with the news from Pithon the previous day. In her inimitable style, she had beaten the official courier by more than twenty four hours. One again, that margin of time had proved to be priceless. Parmenio couldn't help reflecting that, as a courier, she was probably doing more to change history than he was commanding armies. That had led him to speculate on the value of information as a strategic tool. She was on her way back home now, escorted by a Prodromoi cavalry detachment under the command of a young Parthian officer named Derya Shafrid. Parmenio had noted that the two of them had been together a lot recently. *Interesting, still, back to business.*

"Pithon made a bad mistake when he had Philotares, the former general of Parthia, put to death and installed his brother Eudamines as the new Parthian general. That made all the other satraps in the area nervous and they joined forces against him. Quite reasonably as a matter of fact, Pithon did have plans for them that weren't entirely in their interests."

"What were they?" Seleucus had an idea what the answer would be.

"He planned to kill them, just as he plans to kill you." Parmenio had been perturbed by that. He had long-term plans for Seleucus Nikator. "Anyway, they campaigned against him in Parthia and drove him out. There were a couple of minor engagements but, in them, he lost a lot of his key people. Anyway, he's on his way down here where he's going to ask you for aid in recovering Parthia and securing his hold on Medea."

"I think not. In fact, I'm sure not."

"A very wise decision. What he means by you aiding him is you getting assassinated and him replacing you here. But the problem is, the damage is already done. Pithon was, nominally at least, the ally of ourselves and Antigonus. And Ptolemy of course but our Egyptian friend doesn't feature in this. So, by alienating all the regional satraps and making them combine their forces under Peucestes, he's presented Eumenes with a ready-made allied army. And that is a problem.

"Peucestes has his own army with him, giving him ten thousand archers and slingers three thousand Sarissaphoros and a thousand horse. He's been joined by Tlepolemus of Carmania, who has one thousand five hundred sarissaphoros and seven hundred cavalry. Sibyrtius of Arachosia, brought a thousand sarissaphoros and six hundred horse. Androbazus of Paropanisadae has with him twelve hundred sarissaphoros and four hundred cavalry. Stasander of Danginê has fifteen hundred sarissaphoros and a thousand horse. Finally, they have Eudamus with five hundred horse, three hundred sarissaphoros and forty elephants. That gives them a phalanx of 5,500 sarissaphoros, 10,000 light infantry and 3,700 cavalry. And the forty elephants of course."

"Forty elephants. They are the decisive weapon of course. Antigonus has thirty and they decide the battles for him. We need elephants of our own."

"We do indeed. I'm working on that. The real problem is going to come when Peucestes links up with Eumenes. Eumenes is reassembling his army on the banks of the Tigris and he's got 15,000 Sarissaphoros and 3,500 cavalry. The united army will therefore have a phalanx of more than 20,000, the 10,000 slingers and archers and more than 7,000 cavalry – and the elephants. With that force and with his elephants checkmating those of Antigonus, he can fight old One-eye and win."

"And so our position is decisive after all." Seleuscus seized on the concept with glee. "We are the balance of power, neither Eumenes nor Antigonus can move against us until after they have dealt with each other. But neither can deal with the other until we support them and upset the balance. But, the moment we do that, the very person we have supported will come after us. So we stay out of things."

"Exactly, we make overt friendly noises to Antigonus who is the greater threat. Covert friendly noises to Eumenes who is the lesser threat. But we undertake as little positive action as possible. However, there is one thing we do need to do and that's get Eumenes out of our country. Still, I've got a plan for that."

Seleucus laughed. He had been expecting Parmenio to come out with a plan to deal with the invasion by Eumenes. Seleucus had only ever been a relatively low-ranking cavalry commander, unfamiliar with the higher arts of command. Now, he was learning them from an obvious master and he greedily absorbed every lesson. He was well aware that, had it not been for Parmenio, he would probably be laying dead on one of the battlefields that marked the internal conflicts of the Diodochi.

"What have you in mind Parmenio?"

"Well, it seemed to me that Eumenes's men are dirty and exhausted after their long march from the Euphrates. I thought I would give them a bath."

Old Canal, Banks of the Tigris

"Dig harder! The spade is brother to the sword." Parmenio yelled the encouragement out to the teams of men clearing the mouth of the old canal. He had a substantial number of his infantry down in the canal bed, heavily reinforced by teams of workers conscripted from the nearby villages. He had more infantry and cavalry strung out south of the worksite, guarding against the possibility that Eumenes would realize what was happening upriver from his position and move to stop it.

Parmenio moved away from the digging and inspected the stakes that were being driven into the canal mouth. Digging away the earth that blocked the old canal was one thing but when the water burst through, it would drown everybody who had done the digging. The stakes would prevent that. Once the earth barrier crumbled, the stakes would hold just long enough to allow everybody in the canal bed to escape. They'd been given their orders. "When the trumpets sound, run. Don't hang around because if you do, you'll drown." He couldn't help wondering why the entrance to the old canal had silted up, from what he could see, once the dam caused by the silt and sand was breached, the water flow would be strong and fast. Already the pressure from the Tigris was starting to push through the weakened barrier.

As if to confirm his thoughts, the trumpets suddenly blared out their warning. More and water was finding its way through the plug at the entrance to the old canal and it was carrying away the dirt faster than the diggers could move it. The workers ran for the banks and started to scramble up, trying to get clear of the steadily increasing flow that eddied beneath them. Those already out or stationed at the top of the bank were reaching down, trying to grab the hands of those underneath so they could be hauled to safety. Parmenio slid down from his horse and joined them, reaching down and pulling the workers underneath him up to the security of the bank.

That meant he never saw the barrier that separated the old canal from the Tigris collapse. The earth went first, the flow of water through the weakened barrier had finally reached critical mass and what had been a solid mass of sand and silt suddenly turned into a viscous slurry and flowed away. That left just the line of stakes and, deprived of support, they stood for only a few seconds before they too were swept away by the flood. A tide of water, mud and debris was flowing down the channel towards the camp of Eumenes.

"Did everybody get out safely?" Parmenio shouted the question. The answer wasn't actually important to him but the fact that he had asked the question was. Around him, the officers quickly counted up the men in their digging teams and shouted back the totals. They'd been lucky, everybody in the canal bed had got out safely although the last to climb the banks were decidedly wet. The stakes had held the tide just long enough. "Well done. There's fifty copper coins as a bonus for every man here, soldier and civilian alike. A gift from Seleucus Nikator."

A roar of cheering went up from the workers standing on the bank. The civilians had assumed that, having been dragged from their homes and put to work, they would be discarded without any ceremony once the job was done. Fifty coppers was hardly a princely reward but it was a very good wage for a night's hard digging. The civilians went back to their homes, coin jingling in their belts and favorable thoughts about Seleucus Nikator occupying their minds.

Camp of the Army of Eumenes, Banks of the Tigris

"They've tried again." Hieronymus made the report with a certain element of scorn. Deep inside himself though, he was worried by the way this campaign was shaping up. Eumenes was advancing ever-deeper into the hostile lands of Mesopotamia without coming to a decisive battle against either Antigonus or any of his allies. Instead, his army was being slowly hobbled by the succession of raids on his baggage train. Hironymus couldn't quite understand what was going on there, certainly the raids had created havoc amongst the long column of families, camp followers and sutlers that trailed behind the Army but its fighting strength remained unharmed.

"Tried what?" Eumenes was irritable. He had assumed that this advance to threaten the northern flank of the Seleucid Army would force Seleucus into battle. That just hadn't happened.

"Seleucus and Pithon have again tried to persuade Antigenes and the Argyraspides to remove you from your command. They asked why the Argyraspides were preferring, against their own interests a man who was a foreigner and who has been responsible for the deaths of many Macedonians. Once again, Antigenes and his men were in no way persuaded. He and his men have remained loyal to you."

"And so they should, with the amount of gold we have given them and the arrogance we have tolerated from their ranks." Eumenes stared at the map spread on the table before him. He had chosen this position carefully, he had the Tigris to his back and that would provide him with a source of fresh water as well as securing his rear. His army was encamped in a bend of the river with a depression in front of it. A strong position indeed Eumenes thought. Two thirds of its perimeter guarded by the river, the remainder with a steep uphill march for the attacker before a battle could be joined. To a casual viewer it seemed as if Eumenes had camped his army on a hill so great was the difference in elevation but the river said that was not true. Everybody knew that water flowed downhill only, never uphill. It wasn't that the area Eumenes had chosen for his army was much elevated, it was that the area surrounding it was so low.

His thoughts were interrupted by a faint sound of thunder. "It's not the season for storms is it?"

"Not for several weeks Sir. But, that's not thunder. It's a continuous roll not . . . . ."

The water hit Eumenes's camp with all the force of a battering ram. The old canal had led directly from the river to the depression in front of the camp and that path was as steeply down as the climb from the depression to his camp was sharply up. As a result, the torrent had gained force as it descended. *Why was that?* Eumenes thought, the scholarly part of his mind taking over while the disaster beneath unfolded. *Why does water always flow downhill?*

The scene was made worse by the fact that, while Eumenes and his army were camped on the high ground by the Tigris, the baggage train had congregated into the depression that lay on front of it. Weeks of being raided by light cavalry with the victims being killed or carried off and their property burned had ended the easy-going ways of Eumenes's Army. Now, the wagons and tents had been packed together, within an easily defensible perimeter and guarded by off-duty soldiers. That had always been the way things were done in the past, when night cavalry raids were a common threat, but the virtual cessation of those raids had led to complacency and neglect. Now the raids had returned and complacency had exacted its usual price.

Still, the tight perimeter and the guards had almost ended the threat of the raids. The massed incursions with killing and burning had ended and been replaced by slingshot stones and arrow shots out of the darkness. Now, one threat had been replaced by another that was more dire in the extreme. The water from the canal rolled through the baggage train, throwing down the tents and trapping those inside. Some managed to fight their way out of the entangling tents only to find themselves in the fast-flowing avalanche of water. Those who could swim, did. Those who could not joined the ones who had not escaped from the tents in drowning.

The waters rolled on, swamping the campsite and sweeping away the people who had been settling down for the night. The sutler's wagons were lifted off the ground, turned over and rolled along, the jugs of wine shattering as they hit the ground. Soaked bags of wheat burst open, the other goods scattered in the flood as the wagons gave up the struggle to stay intact and broke up. Some of the sutlers fled, abandoning goods and wagons. After the night raids and the killings, this was just too much. There were easier ways of earning a living than this and those had the advantage of being less dangerous. Others stayed and tried to salvage their goods from the torrents that still poured into the camp area. The task was hopeless and the unlucky drowned in their efforts. The rest made their way to the depression rim where their fellows were already gathering. Misery shared wasn't misery reduced but some company was better than none.

Dawn, Camp of the Army of Eumenes, Banks of the Tigris

"Sir, the sutlers are leaving."

"What?" Eumenes seemed stunned by the catastrophe. He looked down at the wreckage of his baggage train and heard the wailing of the survivors. The area was still flooded and it represented a serious obstacle to moving an organized army. With the river behind him and the flooded depression in front, Eumenes's safe base had turned into a deadly trap. One he honestly did not know how to get out of.

"The sutlers Sir. They've had enough. They're leaving." Hieronymus spoke the words with what amounted to fear. The army depended on the sutlers for supplies and all the various commodities it needed to remain a viable community. An army without sutlers would soon cease to be an effective force.

"Then stop them."

"How?" Hieronymus almost snarled out the question. "They've already lost everything but their lives and a lot of them have lost that as well. What can we threaten them with? And to what end? They have lost everything they brought with them. Wine, food, cloth, metal, everything. If they leave, some may come back with more goods although the prices they will charge will be higher than anything we have ever seen before. What do we gain by keeping them here now their goods are gone?"

Eumenes nodded dully and went back to staring at the ruined camp. *Why is it I keep getting hit by things I never thought of?* The question tormented him. First treason, then night raids, now using the water itself as a weapon against him. Every time he seemed to gain the upper hand, something completely unexpected would dash the cup from his lips.

"Antigenes of the Argyraspides wished to see you."

"Antigenes, how are your men? Has this latest blow struck them hard?"

Antigenes laughed at the idea. "No, sir. We have our own camp and it has guards and it is in a secure area. We were untouched by the flood and our guards kept out the stragglers from those who were less careful. The Argyraspides are professionals and the heirs to the Alexandrine tradition. It is not for us to be careless or ill-disciplined. We guard what is ours and protect those that are ours also."

The arrogance of the Argyraspides is insufferable Eumenes thought. *And the reason why they keep a separate camp, under heavy guard is because it is stuffed with gold, the product of thirty years campaigning. They have whole families there, wives, children, grand-children, married and intermarried so that the entire unit is more like a family than a fighting force. And yet they are a fighting force, one without equal. Against them, even twenty elephants must retreat.* "That is good news Antigenes."

"What do we do now?"

That is a good question. Eumenes cudgelled his brain, up to now he had remained inactive, not knowing how to deal with the situation but being so was a luxury he could no longer afford. "We have small boats, many dozens of them. Each can take a boatman and perhaps four soldiers. We will use them to ferry men to the other bank of the Tigris. Seleucus has only cavalry over there, his light cavalry. If we land enough troops, they can establish a secure base and we can probe out from there. We can find out what we are up against, locate the main body of Seleucus and see how many days we have before a battle will be forced upon us.

"We will pull back by nightfall. A small detachment like that will be overwhelmed if we leave it unsupported. Also, find some local inhabitants of the region, that old canal fed into this depression, there must be a way that it will drain it also. Once we find that drain and dig it clear, we can make the way passable again. We will assemble with the satraps in Susianê and join with their armies there."

Second Diodochi War

"Do I look right?" Igrat stared into the silver mirror her maid was holding up.

"A better question would be whether you know what you are doing." Lillith was watching Igrat get ready for the visit of a suitor. "You do understand that this man is serious, don't you? He isn't trying to seduce you, he is courting you, and doing so correctly and properly. That alone shows you his intentions are both serious and honorable. It would be . . . cruel . . . to lead him on for your own amusement. Who is he anyway?"

"Hipparchus Derya Shafrid. Commands five hundred Prodromoi. His men have been escorting me back from Parmenio's headquarters. He said that it would be dangerous for me to make the journey alone. Stragglers from the armies are all over the area. So he got permission to detach some men to protect me."

"Protect you?" Lillith was incredulous. "Who are you and what have you done with the real Igrat?"

Igrat snorted with laughter. "Lillith, I'm travelling as Parmenio's daughter, remember. A lady. Not a camp whore. Nobody who knows me as one should see me as the other. And I don't want Derya ever to see me the way I am when I'm working."

Lillith's jaw dropped. "Gods have mercy on us. You do love him don't you?"

"He's kind, and nice and he respects me. When we came back, he took the chance to ride close to me but never tried to push himself. Just spoke pleasantly to me. Lillith, he treated me as a lady."

"That's because you are one now, dear. You're the only one who doesn't understand that. Now, check your make-up one last time. You've chewed some mint like Naamah told you to make sure your breath doesn't smell bad? Good, let's get going."

A few minutes later, Igrat was sitting on a bench in the garden between Semiramis and Lillith when Gusoyn and Apollo brought Derya Shafrid in. Shafrid made respectful bows to each of the three women, starting with Semiramis who gave him the expected glower of disapproval. Lillith received his greeting with an almost complete lack of interest while Igrat looked down shyly. All exactly as custom demanded. Then, Shafrid sat between Gusoyn and Apollo, both of whom had daggers openly displayed, a warning that they would be quick to defend Igrat's honor.

The conversation that followed was mostly between Shafrid and Semiramis. In it, each asked about the other's families and customs. After an appropriate period, Igrat asked if Shafrid would like to see the gardens and the party rose to make a tour. At some point in the walk, Igrat and Derya Shafrid ended up walking beside each other, carefully separated by slightly more than an arm's length.

Headquarters, Seleucid Army, Tigris River, Babylonia

"I have sent word to Antigonus, warning him that the satraps and their armies have joined with Eumenes and that his plan to follow Eumenes close on his heels before his strength should be increased is now outdated. I have counselled him to check his speed and begin to reinforce his armies by enrolling additional soldiers. This has turned into a war that calls for large armies and for no ordinary preparation. I have advised him to be ready to receive soldiers from us also and that we have made a pontoon bridge over the Tigris River so that he might bring his army across, and set out against the enemy." Seleucus Nikator relaxed in his seat. In some ways he had the hard part of this, he was used to to simple, direct action and the duplicity needed to keep Eumenes and Antigonus at each other's throats was foreign to his nature."

"Excellent. And the Satraps?"

"I made sure they got the message from Polyperchon and Olympias, instructing them to join Eumenes and war upon Antigonus. I checked the wording first, it says nothing about who should have the supreme command."

"Even better. A divided command is no way to fight a war."

CHAPTER THREE

BATTLE OF PARAITACENE

Estate of Parmenio, Seleucia-on-the-Tigris, 316 BC

"But I don't want to leave our family." Igrat was weeping, distraught at the possibility she might have to leave the home she felt safe in. Lillith hugged her and stroked her hair.

"It's inevitable, Iggie. If you accept the proposal from Derya Shafrid, he'll expect you to leave here and go and live with his family." Naamah was sympathetic as well and was all too aware of the problems this situation could cause. The dashing prodromoi officer might be prepared to turn a blind eye to his beloved's background and life but his family would not. Living in their home, Igrat would be in considerable danger from relatives who considered her unworthy of their son's affections. A poisoned cup of wine might well be the kindest fate she could expect from them. "I don't recommend that."

"Nor do I." Parmenio was concerned by the situation. From a practical viewpoint, he didn't want to lose Igrat's services as a courier but he had a father's concern for her safety as well. And for her happiness, the problem being that matching up all three would be a strategic trick that matched anything he'd pulled off to date.

"But, he loves me." Igrat blurted the words out between further outbursts of crying. Lillith and Naamah exchanged glances, the anguished plea had been much more revealing than she had intended.

"Do you love him though?" It took Semiramis to ask the question that had occurred to everybody else. Tact had never been an Assyrian strong point. The question stopped Igrat in her tracks and she looked confused. "Well, do you?"

"I don't know." Igrat was hesitant and bewildered by the question. "I don't know what it feels like to love somebody. I've never had anybody love me before."

"Can we deal with practicalities please? Philosophy can wait." Parmenio wanted the discussion kept within areas he was able to deal with. "Iggie, as head of this household, I have to approve any proposals for marriage and negotiate the terms and conditions of the alliance. Those terms have to benefit both families and the members thereof. Because I am who I am, that also means the strategic interests of Seleucus Nikator have to figure in the negotiations. Finally, because we are who we are, we have to watch who we associate with very carefully. At the moment, Derya Shafrid is in his early twenties and looks it. You are in your middle thirties and look as if you are early twenties. What is going to happen in fifty years time when he is in his seventies and looks it while you are in your eighties and still look as if you are in your twenties?"

"You won't survive in a Macedonian aristocratic household." Naamah's voice was pitiless. "Nobody is better than you at surviving on the street, but in that kind of household, you're out of your depth. I've lived in deadly decadent courts all my life and I still have to keep my wits about me just to survive. You won't. Oh, they'd die just as quickly if they had to live on the street where they're in your world. But in theirs, I'd give it a week before you get poisoned or wake up with a silk cord around your throat."

"Why don't you just sleep with him? You do with everybody else." Semiramis was at her tactless best again.

"But he loves me. Not just having sex with me. I never knew there was a difference until we met."

Parmenio sighed. *Really maneuvering armies is much easier than this.* "He's outside, waiting I presume?"

"Cooling his heels like a good boy." Lillith was droll. "In accordance with tradition, Gusoyn is keeping him amused with tales of the ghastly fates that befall people who disrespect the women of this household."

"Better bring him in then, before Gusoyn scares him into ignominious retreat. Rest of you, make yourselves suitable for strange company." Parmenio watched while the women pulled on shawls and arranged themselves properly. His household had a reputation for liberal and relaxed attitudes but he didn't want that to go too far.

When Gusoyn ushered Derya Shafrid in, Parmenio inspected the young officer closely. He was fit, handsome and didn't have any obvious signs of degenerate behavior or poor character. He had an excellent military record and his superiors spoke well of him. Shafrid came from a noble family but seemed free of the vices that afflicted so many from such backgrounds. Indeed, one of his superiors had commented on his loyalty and his reluctance to criticize others without giving them a chance to speak in their own defense. He was, in fact, the sort of man every father wished his daughter would marry.

"Strategos, I think you for welcoming me to your home and for agreeing to consider my proposal for your daughter's hand." The formal greeting was smooth and sincere.

"You are Hipparchus Derya Shafrid? Why do you wish to take my daughter to wife?" Parmenio's voice was blunt and hostile.

Shafrid didn't blink. "Because her smile lights up my day and she fills my world with joy. When I am with her, I wish no more from life. When I am away from her, the desire to return to her is my only thought."

"And that, Iggie, is the definition of love." Naamah whispered the words very quietly into Igrat's ear. Lillith nodded almost imperceptibly. Both women had heard many protestations of adoration before and knew the real thing when they heard it. What surprised both of them was Igrat's attitude. She had the feral look in her eyes that told them she'd retreated to what they called her alley cat mode. Naamah understood why, Igrat was in unfamiliar terrain and felt threatened by her inability to cope with the situation. So, she'd returned to her roots where she was on her own ground.

"You realize Igrat is my adopted daughter only. She was born of the lowest class. Marrying her will gain you no special preferment. Nor will it bring you any great fortune. She will bring with her only that which is rightfully hers." *And that is a lot more than you might think, lad. Since paying off her self-assumed debt to us, her work has seen her prosper.*

"I do not ask preferment other than that I win with javelin and sword. Igrat has told me of her background and it does not matter to me. I am of sufficient independent means to provide us with a household that meets with your approval." Shafrid stood before Parmenio with his back straight.

"Household, now that is another point." Parmenio liked the young officer but no way was he going to show that yet. "You know of Igrat's background; how will your family accept her?"

"They will not, Strategos. That is why I will provide our own household where she will be free from victimization by spiteful tongues."

"So you are prepared to give up wealth, position and influence for her?"

"No, Strategos. I will gain my own wealth, position and influence by my achievements. And those in my family who do not approve can choke on them."

That time Parmenio couldn't stop himself grinning. *This young man is a lad after my own heart.* "Very well, if Igrat decides to accept your proposal, then I will permit the marriage. However, there will be conditions. Igrat is a vital part of my command staff. How and why is no concern of yours. The first condition is that you will never ask her about the duties she undertakes for me, what they are or how she performs them. They will be a mystery in her life you will not seek to illuminate. Secondly, I have need of a light cavalry unit attached to my headquarters, for security and other special duties that might be needed. It will be of one thousand prodromoi. I will require you to accept the rank of Chiliarch and command that unit. On occasion, the duties of that unit may be to assist Igrat in hers. As such you, and it, will obey her orders as if they were mine. Thirdly, this isn't just a family estate, it is a military command post. You will not establish a household of your own. Instead, you and Igrat will become part of this household, living in a detached building in this complex as members of this family with all the privileges and duties that entails. Do you accept these conditions?"

Shafrid didn't hesitate. "I do."

"Then take Igrat outside and make your proposal to her."

Once the couple had left, Naamah raised her eyebrows. "A thousand light cavalry Parmenio? An excessive headquarters guard?"

Parmenio shook his head. "The game of march and countermarch between Eumenes and Antigonus is reaching its climax. Eumenes is a better commander than any of us thought but he isn't as clever as he thinks he is. Antigonus has herded him towards the Kuh Rud Mountains of Persia where the land is is cut by many narrow valleys and has many lookout posts that are high and close together. Antigonus has put lookouts with the loudest voices on those posts. Since these posts are separated from each other by the distance at which a man's voice can be heard, those who wish to raise the alert can pass it to the next and then on in the same way until the message reaches old One-Eye at the border of the satrapy. Eumenes screwed Antigonus over at the Coprates River and cost him about 4,000 men there but he's running out of ideas. In a month, two or three at the outside, those two will meet in battle and end the game. Then, Antigones will be coming after us. That prodromoi force is the bodyguard for the rest of you getting the hell out of here and setting up in Egypt."

Naamah looked suspiciously at him. "Did you send our alley cat out to hook a promising prodromoi officer for that reason?"

"No, just for once, things worked out right. They do sometimes. We're going to have to play this carefully. I want Shafrid and his cavalry here in case you have to make a rapid exit but equally I don't want them too close.

There's too many secrets in this house for that. We've got another problem as well. Eumenes is heading for Persepolis. That's where the campaign will end. As far as Eumenes is concerned, he's in end-game right now. He just doesn't know it yet. Anyway, Igrat can get married when she gets back from her next trip. I need her to get an urgent message through to Antigenes and she's the only person who can do it."

"You're going to get her killed one day." Naamah sounded deeply saddened. "I hope she has some chance of a normal life first."

"She lost the chance of having a normal life the day her mother left her to die in the trash. Naamah, we're all what the world has made of us, her as much as anybody else. Purely by chance, she's found something that she's superbly good at and it's become the center of her life. Take it away from her and there's little left other than the wildcat we found at the Esagila. If she gets killed, she dies knowing she had a place in the world. If her work as a courier dies, I honestly believe she'll wither away."

Camp of the Army of Eumenes, Pasitigris

"We're too far south. We have to head north to link up with Olympias and her Army in Cappadocia." Eumenes looked at the maps spread out in front of him.

"Antigonus is in Media." Hieronymus knew the positions without looking at the map. "If we head north, he will fall upon our flank. Olympias is in Cappadocia?"

Eumenes nodded. "I received a letter from from Orontes, the satrap of Armenia. He informs us that Olympias, associating Alexander's son with herself, had recovered firm control of the kingdom of Macedonia after slaying Cassander, and that Polyperchon had crossed into Asia against Antigonus with the strongest part of the royal army and the elephants and was already advancing in the neighbourhood of Cappadocia. I have ordered it to be carried around and shown to the commanders and also to most of the other soldiers. Once we can join with Polyperchon, Antigonus and his allies will be unable to stand against us."

"I disagree." Antigenes was emphatic. "We should fall back on the coast. The march inland was a mistake and we should recify it. We should always have our backs to the sea. The way Seleucus and his prodromoi cavalry are harassing our rear proves that."

"Harrassing our rear is just about all that Seleucus Nikator has done." Hieronymus was slightly amused by that. "He moves his troops around, seeming to support Antigonus, but always arriving just a little after the event. Actually he does nothing of any note. Except those cavalry raids of course. I doubt if more than a small handful of his men have lost their lives in the service of Antigonus. But, that is of no concern to us. What does matter is that those who have come down from the satrapies are anxious about their own private affairs. They believe that it is essential to maintain control of the upper country."

Eumenes stared at the map again. There was something he knew that Antigenes and Hieronymus did not. The letter allegedly from Orontes was a forgery. Eumenes had had it prepared to restore the morale of his army that had been harmed by the march inland. Cassander was still alive and fighting. Olympias and her army were still in Macedonia and showed no sign of moving. Therefore, any hope of actually linking up with them was futile. Therew as another factor to be considered in all this. The first stage of the journey north would be through an enclosed valley, torrid and lacking in provisions, but the rest was over high land, blessed with a very healthful climate, heavily overgrown and containing food and supplies of every kind. Even better, those who inhabited the countryside were the most warlike of the Persians. Almost every man was either a bowman and a slinger, and the density of population, made it a recruiting ground that far surpassed the other satrapies. The retreat favored by Antigenes and the Argyraspides might serve their ends but it would bring him nothing.

"Antigenes, your counsel is always valued and I prize it above all others. But this time, I fear that other demands must weigh against its acceptance. If we advance inland, we will pass through areas rich with supplies and men who will leap to our colors. We must take that route so that we will be in the best of conditions when the armies meet. We march for Paraitacene."

Camp of the Argyraspides, Pasitigris

"Despite your failure to rally to his cause, Antigonus is still prepared to forget your intransigence and welcome you to his cause." Igrat was reciting the words she had been given. If Antigenes closed his eyes he could see Antigonous speaking so accurate was her mimicry. "He makes you this offer now. He urges you not to obey Eumenes but to put trust in himself. He will allow you to keep all that you have gained in forty years of warfare and in addition he will provide every man of the Argyraspides a large gift of land where they may settle and live out their lives. Those who wish to return to their homes may do so, laden with honors and gifts. Those who have not seen enough of war, and wish to continue bearing arms will be assigned appropriate posts in his army."

Igrat handed over a scroll with the offer detailed within it. She watched him read it. "I am instructed to add that this offer only holds good until the time battle between Eumenes and Antigonus is joined. Once that has happened, then you must take what fortune decides for you."

Second Diodochi War

Antigenes looked at her with contempt that came very close to loathing. *Just how the hells did this woman manage to get into his camp? His guards hadn't reported a woman of noble birth gaining entry.* "Your words urge treason and treachery. Perhaps I should return you to Antigonus with your lips and tongue cut out?"

"I have been threatened with worse. Some have even tried to carry out those threats. They do not change the words I carry or my duty to repeat them to you." Igrat stared at Antigenes, her heavy-lidded eyes piercing through his bluster to the man beneath. In some ways, he resembled the man she had adopted as her father but there was a critical difference. Parmenio thought several moves ahead and guarded against outcomes he did not wish. That was Igrat's talisman, one she hung on to when the world about her grew threatening. She always believed Parmenio had forseen the danger and provided her with a way out.

"Do you have other messages before your power to speak is taken away?"

"I do, a message from Seleucus Nikator. He makes no offers and attempts no bribes. But he does remind you of a story from his youth. It seems that once a lion, having fallen in love with a maiden, spoke to the girl's father about marriage. The father said that he was ready to give her to him, but that he was afraid of the lion's claws and teeth, fearing that after he had married her he might lose his temper about something and turn on the maiden in the manner of a beast. In order to win his love, the lion decided to remove the obstacles in the way. When, however, the lion had pulled out his claws and his teeth, the father, perceiving that the lion had thrown away everything which had made him formidable, killed him easily with a club.

"Antigenes, Seleucus Nikator reminds you that your present position relies entirely on the supremacy of the Argyraspides. They are your claws and teeth and only their fighting skills makes you formidable. Once they have surrendered, you will be utterly helpless. When Antigonus has mastered the Argyraspides in battle, that very moment he will execute its leaders. Thus warns my master, Seleucus Nikator. Tonight's offer has, at its core, life. To refuse it means your death."

"Then, you may keep your power to speak. Use it to go to Seleucus Nikator and tell him that his warning fell on deaf ears. The Argyraspides will listen to neither threats nor promises."

Igrat rose and left the palladium. Antigenes watched her leave and turned to one of the Argyraspides officers. Seleucus Nikator's message had caused him to modify his plans slightly. It was not desirable for him to be directly involved in the murder of Seleucus's messenger, not when the message brought had held a shadow of conciliation. Instead, there would be an unfortunate accident. "Pass word to the guards on this camp. I do not know how she got in, but she will not leave alive. Tell the guards to kill every woman of quality attempting to leave the camp."

Parmenio's Field Headquarters, Paraitacene, 316 BC

"So, how did you get out of there?"

"Same way I got in here." Igrat seemed inordinately pleased with herself. "I keep telling you, nobody looks at the camp followers. Father, you and Derya rode within two arm's length of me when you two arrived and neither of you saw me. Derya has an excuse, he's only ever seen me as a member of your household, never as a street whore. You have, you're one of two people who has seen me as both yet even you never recognized me. The Argyraspides guards killed three or four women who were unlucky enough to be in the wrong place and look the wrong way at the wrong time yet they let me go without a second thought. Well, not quite true, they did have second thoughts but they were naughty, not deadly. They were on duty and couldn't have me so I promised to see them right when I got back."

"Did we really ride that close to you?" Parmenio couldn't believe it. *Surely she's exaggerating to make a point?*

"You did. Really. You and Derya were talking about arranging the pig dance for our wedding. And about getting a cavalry detachment up to the Paraetaceni ahead of Eumenes before he could get established into a solid defensive position."

Parmenio shook his head. He remembered the conversation he and Shafrid had been having as they arrived in the camp and he replayed the sights around them in his mind. There had been the usual crowd of camp followers around them but even with Igrat in front of him, he couldn't recall seeing her. "You'd better not tell Shafrid about that."

"Father, Derya must never know what I do on these missions." For the first time in her life Igrat was ashamed of her conduct and didn't want the man she loved to know what she had done. For reasons she couldn't understand, she found it very important that he should think well of her.

"I've made that very clear to him. On the grounds that your anonymity is your greatest protection and that one question from him, heard by the wrong ears, could condemn you to a lingering death. Which is quite true by the way. Believe me, nothing guarantees his lack of curiosity more than that. Anyway, you were right. Eumenes broke camp early and headed for the Gabiene. He's actually done very well, he's split Antigonus away from Pithon and ourselves and put himself in a position where he can defeat us in detail. That's why Shafrid is taking the cavalry to block his passage. Old one-eye will owe us after this, although he'll never admit it. Basically Eumenes made an idiot of him. Again."

"When I left, the soldiers were bolting down their food and wine and throwing their kit together. That's how I knew they were moving out in a hurry. Usually they take their time over their meals and pack their belongings with care. Not this time."

"He did more than get his army moving fast. He bribed some mercenaries in his army to desert to Antigonus and reveal that Eumenes had decided to attack the camp during that night. So, Antigonus drew up his forces in the hope of ambushing Eumenes as he made his approach. That, of course, meant that Antigonus had to postpone his own plans for a move and distracted him. He was so concerned with dealing with the situation that he failed to notice that Eumenes had got the start of him and was marching at top speed for the Gabiene. Strategically, it was a beautiful move. The Gabiene area is unplundered and filled with grain, fodder all the other provisions needed for a great army. Even better, the terrain itself is seriously defensible with rivers and ravines that were hard to cross."

"Anyway, Antigonus finally realized he had been played for a fool, again, and set off in pursuit. It's not the first time Eumenes has outgeneralled him and I hope for Eumenes's sake that he doesn't let Antigonus catch him alive. That doesn't look immediately likely though, he's got a start of two watches. Old one-eye isn't going to catch up easily. So its up to Pithon and I to save the situation. You know, if I was to charge one-eye for all the good ideas I've given him, he'd be broke by now. Anyway, I'm taking the cavalry ahead, Pithon following as soon as he can get the rest of the army together."

Forward Detachments, Army of Eumenes, Paraitacene, 316 BC

"How did Antigonus manage that?" Eumenes was stunned by the sight of the enemy cavalry pickets stretched along the ridgeline. "He's still behind us and not moving very fast."

"That's not Antigonus. That cavalry belongs to Seleucus Nikator." Antigenes peered at the cavalry lined up on the hills. "That's his prodromoi. Light cavalry only. They've played hell with our baggage train for the last couple of years but they're no match for a regular army."

"Seleucus Nikator. And that means Parmenio the Younger is up there. You weren't at the Hyllus River, Antigenes. He never gives battle unless he has already loaded the dice in his favor but you'd never know it because he hides everything except the things he wants you to see. We see a weak force of light cavalry because that's what he wants. I wager he is hoping we'll attack uphill hoping to disperse them and then he'll hit us with his real army.

At the Hyllus, he used the ridges to hide his heavy cavalry and hypaspists. He's doing the same here. He forgets that I'm wise to his tricks."

"If he's the man his father was, then he hasn't forgotten anything. But, you are right. We cannot afford to assume that what we can see is all there is. We can sweep prodromoi aside but if there are cataphracts with infantry support up there and we attack off the line of march, we're the ones that will be swept aside. Well, you will be. The Argyraspides have nothing to fear of course."

Eumenes swallowed a bitter rejoinder to Antigenes's insolence. It made matters worse that he knew the Argyraspides general was right; even in the middle of a catastrophe, the old veterans would just form square and march off the battlefield. He knew he had little choice, he had to halt his march and draw up his army on the assumption that there would be an engagement immediately.

Prodromoi Cavalry, Army of Seleucus Nikator, Paraitacene, 316 BC

"An impressive sight." The valley below was filling up as the Army of Eumenes came off the line of march and started to deploy in front of the sparse line of light cavalry. Derya Shafrid would have been a lot happier if there had been an equivalent army behind the prodromoi pickets but there wasn't. The thousand cavalry strung out along the ridgeline was it. It was the largest, most powerful unit that could move fast enough to occupy the area before Eumenes could do the same. The problem was that it was little more than an insignificant dot before the 35,000 strong army Eumenes was deploying.

"Not as much as you might think." Parmenio was reflective as he carefully analysed what the sights below really conveyed. "He's putting most of his light cavalry out on the left wing. There's a lot of them, six thousand I would guess, but they're a mixture of small groups. There's not much cohesion there. Hit them hard enough and they'll split up. Thracians won't bleed to support Arachosians and Stasander won't go out of his way to win glory for Cephalon. The real worry is those elephants. I count 45 of them on his left and another forty in the center. I don't think I've ever seen that many on a battlefield before."

"The Phalanx is forming up." Shafrid watched the army dropping into ranks.

"It's too large. Eumenes is falling into bad habits. The purpose of the phalanx is to fix the center so that the wings can pivot smoothly. Anything more than that is a waste of men. I count 20,000 men at least in that Phalanx down there. He could do the job with half that number. That Phalanx is too large, too unwieldy and there are too many different groups forming it. It's not just too big, it's much more vulnerable than he thinks it is."

"Look, there are the Argyraspides." Shafrid sounded excited and even Parmenio felt a surge of awe at the sight of the veterans. The noonday sunlight shone off the polished silver shields, of the three thousand men, undefeated troops, the fame of whose exploits caused much fear among those they faced. *That was probably their greatest weapon*, Parmenio thought, *they are invincible because everybody thinks they are.*

"Heavy cavalry on his right wing. I count two thousand of them, and another forty elephants. A hundred and twenty five in total. I never knew that were so many elephants in the world." Shafrid sounded awed by the sight and Parmenio could sympathize with him. *Eumenes must have scoured the region and brought every elephant he could find.*

"I can count reserves of three hundred heavy cavalry. That's it. Eumenes has blundered badly there. He's loaded his army up front; gives him a lot of power at the start but if things start to go badly, he won't be able to recover. Always keep a good reserve Derya, at worst it'll give you a chance of swinging a battle your way, at best it'll save your life and win the war."

Shafrid nodded and mentally noted the lesson. He was beginning to realize just how much expertise lay in the head of the man he was with. As the realization sank in, respect for him and his duty to a prospective father in law were being supplemented by genuine admiration and devotion. He had been drawn into this strange family by his love for Igrat; now he realized that he was bound to it by far more than that. "Strategos, over on the ridge to the south. The lead elements of the Army of Antigonus have arrived."

"About time too. Time for us to leave, we've taken enough chances up here. We'll head back to camp, get you married and still be in time for the battle. By the time Antigonus has got himself in order and Eumenes changed facing to meet him, it'll be late afternoon. That's when the fun will start."

Headquarters, Army of Antigonus, Paraitacene, 316 BC

"Come home carrying your shield, or carried on it." Igrat's traditional words to a husband heading out to battle had meant more than they might suggest. She had stood beneath his horse, holding its head as he had mounted up and there was a lock of her hair safely placed in Shafrid's belt. These were the duties and privileges of a wife, something that Igrat had never thought she could be or would want to be. The marriage ceremony had been hasty, the pig dance abbreviated and Parmenio had only managed to delay the messages from Antigonus long enough to get the couple a few minutes privacy. Even so, Seleucus Nikator had taken time out from preparing for the impending battle to spend a few minutes honoring the wedding with his presence. This had not gone unnoticed by those who monitored the constantly shifting patterns of relationships in the Satrap courts.

"It is fortunate that my decision to send the cavalry on ahead stayed the retreat of Eumenes long enough for us to catch up with him." Antigonus Monopthalmus spoke with almost sanctimonious self-satisfaction. Shafrid caught Parmenio's eye and the two exchanged knowing glances. The overwhelming ego of Antigonus would bring him down one day. Both men were sure of that, Parmenio because he had carefully planned just that, Shafrid because he was learning to have absolute faith in Parmenio's judgement.

"My valued ally Seleucus Nikator will take charge of the left wing of my Army, facing the heavy cavalry and elephants that form the right wing of the Army of Eumenes. Seleucus, old friend, you will take the mounted archers and lancers from Media and Parthia, a thousand in number, men well trained in the execution of the wheeling movement; and twenty-two hundred Tarentines, men selected for their skill in ambushing. You will also command a thousand cavalry from Phrygia and Lydia, the fifteen hundred with Pithon, the four hundred lancers with Lysanias, and in addition to all these, the prodromoi cavalry who defied Eumenes this morning.

"The center will be the Phalanx, 28,000 men strong, more than nine thousand mercenaries, three thousand Lycians and Pamphylians, then more than eight thousand mixed troops in Macedonian equipment, and finally the nearly eight thousand Macedonians. These men will be under my personal command." Again, Parmenio and Shafrid exchanged glances. *If Eumenes had too many men in his Phalanx with 20,000, what does that say of Antigonus with 8,000 more? Too much in the center, flanks too weak.*

"The right wing will be commanded by my son Demetrius who today fights in company with his father for the first time. He will command five hundred heavy cavalry made up of mercenaries of mixed origin, then a thousand Thracian heavy horse, five hundred more heavy cavalry from our allies, and the thousand Companion cavalry.

"Of our 65 elephants, the strongest thirty will support the right wing with the rest placed before the phalanx. We will advance in oblique order with the battle decided on the right wing. In the name of Alexander, I command you all to do your duty."

Headquarters, Left Wing, Army of Antigonus, Paraitacene, 316 BC

"Who wants a pet elephant?" A roar of laughter went up from the ranks of cavalry as Seleucus Nikator rode through them. Even from a distance of a few hundred yards, the forty elephants that reinforced Eumenes's right wing were imposing beasts. "When we capture them all, the first forty men to ask, regardless of rank, get one as a pet."

That got Seleucus a rousing cheer from the assembled cavalry. Nobody took him seriously of course, every man knew that simply keeping an elephant fed was a massive burden for a single family. Even so, the elephants were becoming a vital part of the armies fighting out these succession wars. To Parmenio, sitting on his horse in the midst of the Seleucid cavalry, it was another sign of how the succession wars were changing the armies. What had once been finely-balanced combined-arms tools were degenerating into massive phalanxes backed up by elephants. All the lessons that had been so painfully learned during the construction of the Macedonian Empire under Phillip the Great and Alexander were being forgotten. At times, it seemed to Parmenio that he was the only one who remembered them. Then it occurred to him that, had he not had the strange gift of extended life, he would be dead by now and those lessons truly would be lost in the past.

"Demetrius is in trouble." The messenger rode up to Parmenio, his horse lathered from the ride across the battlefield. "His heavy cavalry is bogged down fighting the superior numbers of Eumenes."

Parmenio acknowledged the information with a nod. "Well, it isn't taking long for that plan to break down did it? The next thing will be that the two Phalanxes will meet head on and they'll deadlock. With his right and center fully engaged, Antigonus will be wide open to an attack from the Argyraspides. They'll hack a hole in his line and then everything will start to fold up. Eumenes will have out-generalled Antigonus again and he'll win another victory. Like all the others, it won't mean anything because the way he's learned to fight pretty much guarantees an indecisive result, one way or the other."

Parmenio thought for a second. "Right, the original plan Antigonus came up with is a dead loss. That frees us up to do something useful. Lysanias, take your lancers and mounted archers from Lydia, ride out around Eumenes's right wing and making an attack on the flanks. It's not safe to take those elephants head on but your mounted archers can wound them with repeated flights of arrows. Use their mobility to keep out of trouble, we're trying to make a nuisance of ourselves here. We're not trying to win the battle single-handed yet although it might might very well come to that. Probably will in fact. And much thanks we'll get for it."

Lysanias drew himself up in his saddle. "Will you remind the men of their duty before we advance?"

Parmenio sighed and shook his head. This was another bad habit Antigonus was falling into. Men had to be led by encouragement and example, not driven by threats and browbeating. Parmenio raised his voice so that those nearest him would hear and carry his words to the rest. "I most certainly will not. Every man here knows his duty and I already know that every man here will do all of that and much more besides. What need is there to demand that which is freely given? I will only say that, when this day is over, I will be honored to share wine with these men. Now, outflank those elephants and do as much damage as you can to them. If you're attacked, fall back fast enough to avoid getting involved in a slugging match. With a little luck they'll break ranks to pursue you but don't worry. Their weight makes them formidable in place but it also means they can neither pursue nor retire when the occasion demands."

The lancers and mounted cavalry started to move far off to the left, looping around the right wing of Eumenes's army and closing in on the elephant-reinforced heavy cavalry. Parmenio watched them, his eyes measuring distance and time. "Well, this will throw a little confusion into the pot. Nobody's taken on elephants with light cavalry before."

"Can we do it?" Shafrid sounded doubtful.

"Of course not. Only elephants can drive elephants from the field. But, Eumenes doesn't know that. All he will see is his right being flanked and assaulted. He'll think, quite correctly, that it has to be reinforced. Now, he's got virtually no reserves and he's not going to throw 300 heavy cavalry against ten times that number of lancers and mounted bowmen. So, he'll have to pull in troops from his left wing and move them across the battlefield. That'll weaken the force opposing Demetrius and give the young lad a better chance of achieving something."

"Suppose Eumenes doesn't fall for the bait?" Shafrid was fascinated by the way the possibilities for the battle branched out. He was beginning to realize there was much more to this general thing than he'd realized.

"Then we'll have to make nuisances of ourselves until he does." Parmenio grinned broadly at his son in law. "We've got a lot of options for that. And with both Eumenes and Antigonus fixated on their Phalanxes in the center, neither of them really cares what we are doing over here. We'll have this battle won before either of them can stop us."

Battle Headquarters, Center, Army of Eumenes, Paraitacene, 316 BC

"General, Seleucus Nikator is attacking the elephants on our right wing. With horse-archers. They're starting to push back our right. The messenger's voice was shaky with a combination of panic and exhaustion. Threading his way through the battlefield had not been easy

Eumenes grimaced. "Damn Seleucus and his prodromoi. They've been tasking us for a year or more. What is Parmenio up to this time."

Eudamus and Ceteus exchanged glances. Whenever Seleucus Nikator appeared on the scene, Eumenes would speak of the strategos who worked for him and planned all his battles. He couldn't seem to accept that one of Alexander's generals could produce the schemes that were being woven around him. *It had to be some strange strategos nobody has ever heard of. No matter what he does, Eumenes will never forget that he rose to the position of general from that of court librarian. He will never accept that generals know what they are doing and that some unidentifiable outsider does not.* Eudamus looked up from his thoughts as Eumenes summoned him.

"We need to reinforce our right wing. Take the lightest and most mobile of the uncommitted cavalry on our left and cross behind our center to engage Seleucus's cavalry. You drive them back and the elephants will regroup and follow you. Push them all the way back to the foothills."

"Demetrius is driving hard at our left." Ceteus spoke diffidently. This battle made him nervous, there was something about it that did not seem right. He devoutly wished he was somewhere else, a feeling reinforced by news from the elder of his two wives. She was pregnant again. Given her age, that was something of a miracle and he wanted to be with her.

Eumenes shrugged dismissively. During the times the armies had been wintering, he had studied all the old records and come to the conclusion that keeping a reserve force was pointless. What mattered was throwing the largest possible army into the early stages of the battle and so gaining the initiative. Once that was done, it was much easier to hold the initiative and exploit it. Any contingencies that arose could be accommodated by moving troops in the line around. It was so obvious a matter that he couldn't believe that he, a mere librarian had spotted it while the professional generals had overlooked its importance. "Demetrius is an inexperienced youth. He will not achieve much of note. We can weaken our forces there without risk. Eudamus, why are you still here? You have your orders."

Prodromoi Cavalry, Army of Seleucus Nikator, Paraitacene, 316 BC

"I hear that congratulations are in order." Alcetas hoped that he had kept the bitterness and anger out of his voice. *Who was this Prodromoi officer to have his proposal to a woman from the house of Parmenio the Younger accepted and his wedding honored by the presence of Seleucus Nikator himself when my own desire for an alliance had been rejected by a woman of that household? What kind of household was it where women were allowed to decide on the acceptability of such an alliance?*

"A hasty marriage on the very cusp of a battle." Derya Shafrid had a happy smile on his face. The ceremony had been slotted in between the Generals getting their orders from Antigonus and transmitting those orders to their troops. "The gods have smiled on me today. Now, I must earn the fortune they have bestowed."

Not if I can help it, you bastard. You're a Parthian nobody and you get to marry a noblewoman under the eyes of our Satrap. I'm the descendent of the kings of Macedonia and my proposal to a woman of the same household who cannot even walk properly is refused. But battles are unpredictable things and a prodromoi commander might well get a spearpoint in his back when he least expects it.

Alcetas watched Shafrid wheel his horse and rejoin the special unit of a thousand prodromoi he had been appointed to command. Every one of them was a picked man, chosen because of a reputation for skill and daring. That was another thing that rankled with Alcetas. *I led the charge at Thapsacus, that unit should be mine. I even recognize one of the men in it, a prodromoi who had been publicly praised and promoted by Seleucus himself after the Thapsacus. Even the rankers get preferment that is denied to me.*

"Alcetas, word from Seleucus Nikator. A force of cavalry under Eudamus has detached from the left wing of Eumenes's Army and rides to attack Lysanias. The attack on the elephants has drawn away the light cavalry and elephants on Eumenes's Right and opened up a gap between them and the Phalanx. You will take your Phrygian cavalry and advance into that gap, taking Eudamus in his flank." The messenger wheeled his horse and rode off to where Shafrid was waiting with his thousand prodromoi.

I know who that order came from and it wasn't Seleucus Nikator. I'll be damned if I run around at his bidding while he gives his daughter to a nobody and denies me a cripple. I'll obey orders but in my own good time.

Alcetas ostentatiously stretched before moving to join his thousand Phrygian and Lybian heavy cavalry. By the time he had finished a leisurly review of the battle and relayed the orders he had been given, the moment had passed and Eudamus's horse were closing in on the detachment of Lysanias. The gap he had been expected to exploit had been filled as the Argyraspides advanced and fell upon the left flank of Antigonus's Phalanx.

Extreme Left Wing, Army of Antigonus Monopthalmus, Paraitacene, 316 BC

"The enemy is closing fast."

Lysanias saw the truth of that cry right away. The enemy heavy cavalry and elephants should have been unable to close in on his horse-archers and lancers but they'd been reinforced by a thousand or more light cavalry and they were at least as mobile as his own men. More so, it appeared that Eudamus had picked the lightest-equipped and most mobile of his cavalry to mount the attack. The enemy heavy cavalry was milling around, trying to form up, and the elephants were close to panic from the volleys of arrows that were being fired into them. Their riders were struggling to bring them under control but the great beasts were recalcitrant.

"Fall back! Archers, give us some covering fire." Lysanias called ut the orderrs and watched the archers changing targets from the elephants to the light cavalry. Hitting a light horseman with arrows fired from the back of another horse was more difficult than it sounded. Few of the newly-arrived light cavalry went down but the arrows at least caused some to swerve and bought a little time. That was what Lysanias needed, time to get his force reorganized and in proper formation. He led his troops backwards, hoping to get them in hand before he ran out of open ground and the foothills to the north closed in.

Headquarters, Army of Antigonus Monopthalmus, Paraitacene, 316 BC

"General, the Phalanx is collapsing. All is lost."

Antigonus staggered slightly with the impact of the news. The collapse of a Macedonian Phalanx was unprecedented. Phalanxes had been stalled or driven back but for one to collapse completely had never been contemplated. "What has happened?"

"Our left, Eumenes ordered an attack on our left and has scattered it. The troops are retreating towards the hills. The Argyraspides have moved into the gap and rolled up the left of the Phalanx and are destroying it from there. Already we have lost many men and there is no end to it.

The Argyraspides, always the Argyraspides. They may be fathers and grandfathers but their hardihood and skill means that none can withstand their might. Even though there are only three thousand of them, they have become the spearhead of Eumenes whole army. One way or another, they have got to go. In the meantime, Eumenes has pulled off yet another victory.

"Pass the orders to the remainder of the Phalanx and the right wing. Tell them to break off contact and retire to the mountains. We will establish a rallying point for those who escape from the rout. The organized parts of the Army will remain under my personal command as a rearguard.

Extreme Left Wing, Army of Antigonus Monopthalmus, Paraitacene, 316 BC

"Here we go." Shafrid heard the glee in Parmenio's voice. *The sun is setting so we might be able to disengage in darkness but we've lost the battle surely. So what is the Strategos so happy about?* "Take your Prodromoi and hit Eumenes's cavalry in the rear. Fast, don't throw the chance away as Alcetas did. I'll take his heavies and hit the Argyraspides in the rear.

Shafrid suddenly realized what was happening. The pursuit of Lysanias had drawn the troops of Eumenes's right wing far away to the left while the advance of the Argyraspides as they rolled up the main Phalanx had taken them far to the right. Between them was a gaping void, similar to the one Alcetas had failed to exploit earlier, but much wider. Shafrid spurred his horse and shouted out to him men "You want to get drunk tonight? Well, the wine's over there."

His horses were fresh, rested and well fed. The thousand tore over the ground and fell upon the flank and rear of Eudamus's cavalry with a ferocity unmatched by any of the fighting seen thus far on the left flank. Most of Eudamus's cavalry was so intent on closing with the survivors of the archers and lancers assigned to Lysanias that they didn't see the blow coming out of the gathering dusk until it was on top of them. The prodromoi were lightly armed and equipped but mass, speed and surprise made for an irresistible blow. Eudamus and his cavalry broke before the charge and were driven into chaos. Beside them, Lysanias had rallied his own weary troops and managed to join in the charge. Their horses exhausted, they couldn't keep up with the prodromoi but they didn't have to. The archers fired volleys into the heavy cavalry while the lancers peeled away to attack the elephants.

In the face of the onslaught, the whole right wing of the Army of Eumenes crumpled while the prodromoi rode through the wreckage, hacking down anybody who attempted resistance. In the thick of the fighting, Shafrid heard a scream of warning from a group of heavy cavalry. "Flee, for they fight like daimones."

Parmenio had an intuitive sense of what was happening on the battlefield. He had seized control of the thousand heavy cavalry nominally commanded by Alcetas and was already getting them moving. There was little difficulty in doing that for the men had been shamed by their commander's failure to advance when ordered and did not wish to be known as cowards who hung back while better men fought for them. The charge wasn't well-organized or in proper formation but it was the right move at the right time.

The heavies plowed into the mass of troops engulfing the left wing of the Antigonid Phalanx, putting the majority of the troops there to flight and killing a great number of them. That was when Parmenio saw why the Argyraspides were so feared. With an attack in their rear materializing, they calmly disengaged from the task of hacking up the Phalanx in front of them and formed square. Then, equally calmly they started a march to the rear, protected by the prickling hedge of their sarissas. Momentarily, Parmenio saluted the men who pulled off such a remarkable feat, then got back to work.

By this time, the prodromoi under Shafrid had hacked their way through the disorganized mass of light and heavy cavalry that had once been the right wing of the Army of Eumenes and were crossing the battlefield to fall on the right flank of the Eumenid Phalanx. Parmenio spurred his horse and led his heavy cavalry to support him. In the rapidly-gathering darkness, the men in that Phalanx only saw themselves outflanked by thousands of enemy cavalry. None of the disparate groups in that Phalanx were ready to die for the others and they all broke. The Phalanx dissolved into a mass of men running for the rear with the two masses of cavalry closing in on them for the kill. All that saved them was the night; the cavalry had to slow their headlong charge since going over broken ground at full gallop in the darkness was suicidal for horse if not for man also.

Battle Headquarters, Center, Army of Eumenes, Paraitacene, 316 BC

"What happened?" Eumenes was shocked into near-catatonia. A few minutes before, he had decisively won the battle, now he faced an equally complete disaster. On the plain below, a remarkable situation was taking place. Both phalanxes had been broken, one by the Argyraspides, the other by the cavalry of Seleucus Nikator. As a historian, Eumenes wished it was daylight so he could record the sight for posterity.

"It was the elite cavalry regiment of Seleucus Nikator. The Daimones Prodromoi. They took us in the rear and they fought possessed by the dark forces. They slaughtered all before them and the gods turned away all our weapons from them." Eudamus was frantically making up whatever excuses sounded reasonable.

"Oh don't be so stupid and superstitious." Eumenes was furious and his voice took on a whining child-like quality as he mercilessly mocked the cavalryman. "They were possessed by dark forces. They were protected by magic. Don't talk like a whimpering girl. They outfought you, Just admit it.. Sound the trumpets, order the men to fall back on the hills. Although it is already lamp-lighting time, the moon will rise in an hour or two and it is a full moon tonight. It will give us enough light to fight by. This battle is not over yet. We will rally our troops and put their entire forces into the battle once more. Our men are still filled with zeal and we can form our line four thousand paces to the rear. See to it."

"Sire," Ceteus knew the sound of a man fooling himself with false optimism when he heard it. "the men are indeed filled with zeal still but they are also exhausted by marching, by their suffering in the battle, and by lack of food. However much they may wish to fight, they cannot. We must give up the battle and go into camp."

"We cannot do that. We must retain possession of the battlefield and control the disposal of the bodies to put my claim to victory beyond dispute."

"Sire, the men cannot do it. And, with respect sire, we cannot force them into the line by punishment for there are many who dispute your right to command, and the time is not suitable for chastising those who disobey. Sire, never give orders you cannot enforce."

Headquarters, Army of Seleucus Nikator, Paraitacene, 316 BC

"Is it always like this?" Igrat's voice was hushed. She and Naamah were sitting quietly in their tent, waiting along with the rest of the women for the Army to return. Only then would they learn if their men had survived.

"Always." Naamah spoke equally quietly. She had spent all too much of her time with Sammael waiting for his return from a battlefield. She had the experience to know not to allow her mind to dwell on what might have happened but Igrat did not. She had never cared about anybody enough to worry about their return before and her mind was filled with fears of what might be.

"All we know is that we won. Antigonus is making his infantry camp on the battlefield by the bodies. To possess the fallen is to be victorious in battle. So, we won. Parmenio and the others will be counting heads right now, finding out who has lived and who died. That'll take time. Nobody's fought a battle this late before."

"They're coming in!" The shouts that were going up all over the camp were jubilant.

Igrat leapt to her feet to run outside but Naamah grabbed her arm to stop her. "No. We're the family of the commanders. We have to be calm and show absolute confidence in our men. We know everything went well for the Army. So, wait for a moment, compose yourself and then walk outside with grace and dignity. Igrat, if Derya didn't make it, save your tears for later. Alive or dead, you must honor him."

The women gathered their robes and left their tent. The cavalry regiments were already well into camp, the horsemen surrounded by women checking to see if their husbands had survived the battle. A group of horses were being led in, each with a shrouded figure over its back. Igrat watched as the figures were reverently taken down and the faces exposed. The wails from the women who had lost their men started to pierce the air. Then, she saw Derya Shafrid leading his prodromoi cavalry in. Their lances were stained with blood and their shields battered but there was no doubt. Her husband of less than a few hours had lived and won honor on the battlefield. She ran over to him and seized his horse's head so that he could dismount. The beaming smile that greeted her made the wait worthwhile.

A few yards away, Parmenio had dismounted and was speaking with Seleucus Nikator. "We pulled it off, Sire. It was touch and go for a few minutes but it all went more or less as we thought."

"As you thought Parmenio, I have no doubt as to where the credit for this victory should lay. I've got the losses from Antigonus. In this battle three thousand seven hundred of his infantry were killed. Eumenes lost five hundred and forty, none of them Argyraspides."

"We've got fifty four dead." Parmenio was pleased by the small butcher's bill. Unlike Semiramis he took little pride in more blood flowing than was strictly necessary. "We won't know how many cavalrymen Eumenes lost until morning. The battlefield is strewn with them. At least nine hundred would be my guess."

Seleucus nodded and started to circulate amongst the men, slapping backs and praising individual men for some deed of valor, real or imagined. As he did so, he made his way to the women surrounding their dead. He spoke softly to them, speaking quiet words of comfort mixed with promises that they would be properly cared for and their needs met from the royal purse.

Eventually he came to Derya Shafrid who was holding Igrat by the waist. "Shafrid, it is hard to single out any one of your men for all are so loaded with honor that other men can only envy them. And none have covered themselves with honor more than their commander who has led them to a great victory against a force forty times their number. On his wedding day as well no less! Oh, fortunate and lucky bride to have such a man as husband!"

Igrat flushed bright red as the roar of cheering went up from the prodromoi, mixed in with some ribald jests about her prospects for a truly memorable wedding night.

Parmenio had joined the group and he winked at Igrat. "Your majesty, there is something we have learned from prisoners of Eumenes's cavalry. Such was the ferocity of this regiment and so bravely did its men fight that they call it the Daimones Regiment. Since we cannot honor each man individually as they deserve, let us honor them all collectively by adopting that name, a name won fairly on the battlefield. After today, even the Argyraspides will fear the name of the Daimones Regiment!"

The thunder of cheering was renewed. Parmenio waited for a second and then continued. "And all praise must also go to Alcetas without whom this battle would have been less convincingly won. He received orders to advance yet knew the moment was not right and held his hand until the perfect time was reached. It takes much courage to fight well in battle but much more for a commander to disobey an order he knows is mistaken for if he is wrong, then the penalty will be dire. All hail Alcetas for his brave and noble spirit."

Alcetas heard the words and his heart filled with hatred for the man who has spoken them. *Others had been rewarded with honors and coin. The prodromoi under Shafrid had been singled out by becoming a named regiment, an honor held by very few. All I received was a few words and even those contained a double edge.* Then he forced a smile to his face and went to where Seleucus was waiting.

Headquarters, Army of Antigonus Monopthalmus, Paraitacene, 316 BC

"We have to fall back and reorganize. We can rest for a day to bury the dead and the troops can forage for food. We'll send the wounded and the heavy baggage back to Susa. The rest of the Army will fall back on Gamarga. The land there is unplundered and can supply our army with everything needed for its support. That herald from Eumenes? The one who wanted to plead for the return of the dead? Detain him and let him go in the evening with word that we will bury the Eumenid dead the next day. Only, we'll break camp overnight and institute a series of forced marches to gain seperation from Eumenes."

At the back of the crowd, more or less hidden by banners, Parmenio shook his head. "And that, Sire, is how to toss away the fruits of a victory. A day's rest I can swallow because Eumenes isn't in a position to move far anyway. We should be on the move all right, but straight at the Army of Eumenes. We've got a chance of finishing him off right now. Old one-eye is throwing away everything his men died for today. I don't know about you, but I don't think we should let him do that." Parmenio was speaking quietly but Seleucus Nikator heard the words and knew they rang true.

"What can we do?"

"Get our cavalry moving again. We'll follow Eumenes ourselves and pursue him the way he should be pursued. He'll be heading for Gabiene which suits us nicely. We'll get him tangled up in a battle. That'll give Antigonus the choice, he can sit back and watch us take on Eumenes alone or he can do a winter forced march to join in. He'll remember what happened today where we salvaged a situation he had comprehensively lost. He won't want word to spread that we, despite being heavily outnumbered, finished off Eumenes in a few weeks after he'd failed for four years. So he won't leave us to win on our own. He'll do the forced march and the last battle will be fought on the Gabiene. Good place for a final battle as well, the ground should see both armies chewed up nicely. That'll buy us another year before one-eye comes after us."

"Suppose he joins up with Eumenes to wipe us out?"

"Very unlikely on both counts. He hates Eumenes for out-generalling him over and over again. Eumenes hates him for betraying the King and fears him. If they both overcome that background, they still won't wipe us out. We'll go back to outmaneuvering them. We're still the only people who make war on the baggage trains. Nobody else has seen why we do that yet. If they stick together to invade us, it won't help them when they run out of food and water and the sutlers won't risk coming near them."

"Your Majesty, strategos, there has been an important development." The messenger had the wits to keep his voice down but the attention of the room was fixed on Antigonus and ignored him completely.

"Speak." Privately Parmenio thought that anything would be preferable to listening to Antigonus explaining for the tenth time how he had lured Eumenes into a trap.

"The Army of Eumenes is retreating even as we speak. They are withdrawing towards the Gabiene, some nine days march distant. But, the elephants are not yet able to move. They need fresh food and water after the efforts and injuries of today. They are but a few hours away and cut off from all assistance."

"Get Shafrid without delay. Tell him to urge his regiment to be ready for a movement carried out with all speed and while they do so to report to me for orders."

"We're going to move on them?" Seleucus Nikator was nodding as he put the bits of the puzzle together.

"Oh yes. We can do a lot of damage very quickly here if we move fast enough." Parmenio paused as Shafrid joined them. "Derya, you got here fast?"

"I used your messenger to send orders to my regiment and came at once. We going to win another battle for old one-eye?"

Parmenio grinned. "In a manner of speaking. We're going elephant-hunting."

Daimones Regiment of Prodromoi, Gadamala

"They didn't last long." In Parmenio's eyes, the rout of the Eumenid light cavalry had been almost comical. The light cavalry that accompanied the elephants had consisted of a force of not more than four hundred men.

The night before, Shafrid's men had painted a daimonic symbol on their shields and the mere sight of the thousand men in the Daimones Regiment had been enough to send their opponents tumbling backwards in chaos. Left alone and isolated, the commander of the elephants had arranged them in a square with the baggage train in the centre and a handful of heavy cavalry guarding their the rear. He was now trying to fight his way clear but having a very hard time of it.

"Mmmm, baggage." Shafrid watched his men decimating the heavy cavalry rearguard with a professional eye. The heavies couldn't compete with the lightly-equipped prodromoi in this kind of running battle. Already their horses were tiring and their close formation breaking up under the unrelenting pressure.

There was another advantage of the kind of war Parmenio was introducing. The constant attacks on the enemy baggage trains was steadily transferring wealth into the hands of the Prodromoi without draining Seleucus's war chest. Already it was becoming known that the Selucid Army was a place where much money could be made by a skilled fighter yet where lives were spent with the most grudging and miserly of hands. Parmenio had asked Lillith to look at the numbers and she had come to the conclusion that, so far, this war was running at a profit. For Seleucus Nikator at least, for Antigonus, not so much. In fact, the war was slowly draining resources away from Antigonus and into Seleucus's treasury.

Below them, the heavy cavalry gave it up, throwing their xyston lances down in despair. The prodromoi had been harrassing them with arrow fire but always dancing just out of reach. The surrendered cavalry were surrounded by a group of prodromoi and led away from the scene surrounding the elephants. Parmenio guessed they would soon be made an offer they couldn't refuse and would be joining the Seleucid Army. There the combination of good pay, appreciation of virtue and the knowledge that their lives would not be thrown away as part of a meaningless gesture would turn necessity into loyalty.

Meanwhile, the elephants were in desperate trouble despite their square. They were receiving wounds from all directions and were not able to injure their enemies in any way. As with the heavy cavalry before them, they were becoming exhausted from the running fight. *That's the problem with elephants,* Parmenio thought, *virtually impregnable in defense as long as they can stand still but they're slow to maneuver and their endurance isn't that good. Odd for such huge beasts. There must be a better way to use them than this.*

The surrender of the heavy cavalry had opened up the rear of the square and the Daimones Regiment was already exploiting the gap. The elephants were holding firm but their formation was inevitably breaking up. Their crews could see that the Seleucid cavalry was forcing their way into the elephanteer's baggage train and they knew what that meant. The prodromoi would take the goods, wealth and women they wanted and burn or kill the rest. That meant death for their wives and slavery for their daughters. The elephanteers were not cowardly men and they would have died for their leader and their pay. That wasn't the option facing them though. With their support gone and their baggage train exposed, they faced capture and ruin. The only choise they had was whether that happened before or after the Prodromoi had finished with that baggage train. They were reasonable men but they would not stand and watch themselves become paupers while their families were destroyed. Before the prodromoi could begin their grim work, the standards of the elephant formations dipped.

A few minutes later, Parmenio and Shafrid rode through the elephant lines, counting the number of beasts that had surrendered. There were more than forty of them with three more killed. Overall, Eumenes had lost a third of his elephants in this one raid. He'd lost something else as well. Amongst the dead was Ceteus. He'd been killed by arrows while trying to rally the heavy cavalry and his body in the gilded armor of a general had been recovered and was now surrounded by his men. Parmenio found it an interesting question whether they were doing so out of respect or awaiting an opportunity to strip it of everything valuable.

That was when he realized he was wrong. Two women were having a violent argument that, to Parmenio's experienced eye was about to turn into a serious catfight. The men around the body had seen the prospect as well and were waiting for the fight to start. Soldiers being soldiers, they were already placing bets on who would be the winner. Parmenio decided that intervention would be a good idea. *Quite apart from anything else, we may need to get out of here fast,* "What's going on here?"

"They are the wives of Ceteus, Sire." Cambyses, commander of the elephant regiment formerly part of the Army of Eumenes, explained. "The younger is Indian. She claims the right to be burned on her husband's funeral pyre. The elder disputes that, saying that although she is Greek, she is senior wife and deserves that honor. The younger has responded by saying the elder is pregnant and thus disqualified. They are on the verge of fighting."

Parmenio shook his head. The ways of the Indian lands were incomprehensible to him. "So I can see. The whole idea is barbaric. Is the elder wife pregnant?"

"She is, sire."

"Then tell her she should be ashamed of herself. Her duty now is to the child of Ceteus, ensuring he grows up a credit to his father. As for the other woman, tell her that she is now a prize of war and that her fate is in my hands not hers. Burning herself alive on her husband's pyre is not an option for her."

"It is a deterrent against wives poisoning their husbands, Sire."

"I don't care. Tell her that if she ends her life without my permission, her body will be desecrated and thus she will never see her husband in the afterlife. Make that very clear, understand?"

Cambyses went over to the two women and very roughly pushed them apart. Then he spoke to them, obviously angry and with his arms waving furiously, The older woman burst into tears and was taken away by a pair of servants. The Indian woman was shouting back, her arms also waving. That was when she was grabbed by two of Cambyses' men and dragged off. Parmenio guessed she would be in chains fairly shortly. Derya Shafrid had ridden up while he was watching the incident and made his report.

"Parmenio, our scouts report that an enemy rescue party is approaching. Fifteen hundred of the strongest cavalry in the Eumenid Army and three thousand light infantry."

"Right, Derya, get your regiment formed up and ready to act as a rearguard. Time we got out of here."

Headquarters, Army of Seleucus Nikator, Gadamala

The cavalry herded the elephants into the camp with style and finesse. To anybody watching, it would seem that they had been herding elephants all their lives rather than just a few hours. All over the encampment, children were running out to see the great beasts. A few, the quicker thinking, had brought fruit or handfuls of fodder which they gave to the animals as they were paraded in. The elephants took the gifts carefully, their trunks reaching out for the food with a gentle care that was remarkable for such big animals. Parmenio could swear that the elephants receiving the gifts were grinning broadly despite the arrow wounds in their flanks.

"We're not going to be very popular with old one-eye, Parmenio." Seleucus Nikator sounded very unimpressed with the idea of Antigonus being angry with him. "They were going to start maneuvering against each other again but this raid has put a stop to all that. Eumenes has ended his retreat and is getting into position along the Gabiene. Antigonus is ordering his army and his allies to march across the desert rather than follow Eumenes directly. That way, he's hoping to catch Eumenes before he is properly formed up and thus he'll have the advantage."

"Nobody ever said old one-eye was stupid." Parmenio thought carefully, weighing time and distance. "We'll do as he asks, only a little slower than he intends. We'll let his army do most of the fighting for us. We need to get an enclosure set up for the elephants. I've talked to the men in the unit and the elephants don't really understand that they shouldn't take what they want. If they're left to wander around, they'll eat everything in sight. The whole unit has joined up with us by the way. I promised them they could keep their baggage train and all it contained."

"Are our cavalry happy with that?" Seleucus was anxious about his men. Half the strategy slowly unfolding was to create a perception that the Seleucid Army should be a good place to soldier and a place where good soldiers would want to serve. He had taken achieving that end to heart and by doing so had turned perception into reality. It was apparent when the men in his army were alongside those of Antigonus and Eumenes. Soldiers of the Seleucid Army had a swagger about them that could only come from pride in themselves and genuine respect for the man they served. What was even more impressive was that the men who joined them from forces they had defeated soon picked up the same confident swagger.

"They ran off the light cavalry and captured the heavies. So, they got the baggage from both. By the time the heavies bought back their women, there was more than enough gold to keep our cavalrymen happy. We're waiting to hear from the light cavalry but they don't usually yield much in the way of loot. By the way, word is spreading that you gave money, protection and words of comfort to the women of men who lost their lives in your service. They know Antigonus would never have even thought of doing that. People are beginning to look to you as a fair and just ruler and that's going to be worth a lot when the showdown comes."

Seleucus nodded. He'd made a discovery that he hadn't expected. It felt good when the members of his Army and its baggage train recognized him and their eyes showed affection and respect. "I suppose I'd better go and tell Antigonus that we've ruined all his plans again. He'll be shouting for hours. If we start to move tomorrow?"

"That should do nicely."

Parmeno saluted and headed off to his own tent. He reflected that it seemed emptier without Igrat's irreverent presence and he realized he actually missed her. It hadn't been like this before, even when she'd been away for weeks on a courier run her presence had still been tangible. He started to unlace his armor but was interrupted by a cough from behind him.

"You smell of elephant. Bath. Now." Naamah was standing behind him, grinning broadly. She waved her hand in an exaggerated motion of trying to brush the animal odor away. She dropped to her knees and started to unlace his greaves. That was actually the duty of Semiramis as his acknowledged partner but she was away. He finished removing his cuirass and carefully put it on one side. Naamah looked at it, frowning slightly. "Should not your armor be gilded as befits a great general?"

"If I want to get killed, yes. That's not in my job description. My role in life is to win battles, not get killed in them. Today, the gilded armor worn by Ceteus almost certainly got him killed. I'll stick with the same armor everybody else wears."

Parmenio stopped suddenly, an eerie realization dawning on him. *In our own separate ways, Igrat and I do the same thing. I wear the armor of a common soldier, she fades in the mass of camp followers. Both of us survive by making ourselves as inconspicuous as possible. That's probably as good a recipe for survival as people with our gift can find.*

"Your Majesty." In the background, one of the maids had been preparing the hot water for Parmenio's bath and getting ready some scented soap that Naamah had made. The maid had seen Seleucus Nikator step in and stopped those preparations immediately.

"Parmenio, it's official. We're in disgrace. Antigonus went berserk when he head about our raid. It didn't help matters that even his son was laughing when he heard that we'd captured a third of the Eumenid elephants without losing a single man. He wants them by the way. Demanded them in fact."

"Tell him to go capture his own. Anyway, those elephants are exhausted and wounded, they're not fit for battle. I'm going to send them back to Babylon so they can rest. Anyway, now we've got some elephants, I want to think about them. We're using elephants wrong, I don't know how we should be using them but this habit of spreading them along the line to stiffen the infantry isn't the way."

"I told Antigonus that the elephants we had captured were ours and if he wanted more elephants he should go out and find them himself. That's when he started bouncing off the walls. When he stopped shrieking, he appointed Pithon commander of the left wing for the battle that's coming up. We'll be under his command."

Parmenio and Naamah exchanged glances. The prospects of Pithon remaining in good health had just suddenly deteriorated. They didn't even need to discuss the matter.

Meanwhile, Seleucus was looking around the tent. One thing that always impressed him was just how clean it was. He knew that Parmenio's staff were fanatics about keeping everything spotless but the fact they managed to do so even in the middle of a campaign was impressive. He also noted the bath full of steaming, scented water. "You don't believe in hardships, do you?"

"Any damned fool can be uncomfortable." Parmenio sounded content. "By the way, two women we brought in were the wives of Ceteus. They had strange ideas abouting burning themselves on his funeral pyre. We need to find something to do with them."

"I've had a talk with Eunike. She is with child and understands her duty now the shock of widowhood has worn off. She will bear Ceteus's child and raise him as befits his father. I have promised her that she can live at my court, under my protection, as a tribute to her late husband's valor. And I will make sure his posthumous child is well provided for. The Indian woman's name is Kavita and she is a very different matter. She's determined to join her husband in death."

"Let her go. She has no place in this Army and her future is grim. If she wishes to end her life, let her."

Seleucus started at Igrat's voice. He wasn't accustomed to women who openly commented on the affairs of men. Looking around he saw her behind him, a saddened look on her face. He shook his head. "I cannot, in conscience, do that. Her reaction now is the product of grief and shock at the loss of her husband. As that fades, she will discover new interests in life. She'd better, she'll stay in chains until she does."

Seleucus looked carefully at Igrat. She had entered the tent on the arm of her husband and was looking around suspiciously. Then she openly sniffed. "Father, elephant smell, bath."

"She made me bathe as well." Derya Shafrid looked affectionately at his wife.

"Keeping clean is the best way to avoid disease. And it stops wounds becoming infected."

Parmenio looked at Igrat for a moment, first seeing the ragged, filthy, bruised and blood-stained creature he had rescued from the Esagila, then the elegant, confident woman she had become. The strange thing was that earlier he had missed her presence in his household but now she was here, the brassy irreverence that surrounded her was still absent. She looked at him and he knew she had shared the same revelation.

"Derya, with your permission, I will help my father bathe?" Derya Shafrid nodded, feeling in his heart that this household, strange though it was in so many ways, was more of a family to him than his own had ever been.

Parmenio settled down in his tub, feeling Igrat starting to wash the dust and sweat off his back. As she did so, her voice was very quiet. "Father, don't shut me out of our home. I know I'll only have Derya for a limited time and I never want to be lonely again."

"You're never shut out Iggie, and you never will be. It's just at the moment, you're in his household, not ours. Or, rather, you have your own household which is a part of our larger establishment. Be warned though, the prodromoi are brave and dashing but their officers tend not to live very long. You'll be back here sooner than you might wish."

Second Diodochi War

CHAPTER FIVE

BATTLE OF THE GABIENE

Headquarters, Army of Antigonus Monopthalmus, Gabiene, 316 BC

"Damn Seleucus. That raid of his has trapped us into this battle before our army can regroup." Antigonus Monopthalmus stamped backwards and forwards before the map on his command table, trying to deny the obvious that was in front of him. The Army of Eumenes was drawn up in defensive positions along the Gabiene and, for once, Eumenes heavily outnumbered his opponent. For a commander who had made a habit of winning battles against the odds, that was an unusual situation.

"Form the Phalanx in the center. We'll put all our 22,000 infantry into it. Demetrius, take eight thousand horse and form our right wing. I will join you there myself. Pithon will take the left with a thousand light cavalry. Where is Pithon?"

"He is severely ill, your Majesty. He runs a great fever and his bowels are seriously disturbed."

Antigonus shook his head. With Pithon ill and Seleucus disgraced, there was nothing much he could do with his left. "We will spread the elephants, all 65 of them, across the whole front, filling the spaces between them with lightly-armed auxiliaries. Eumenes has 30,000 infantry in his Phalanx and has massed six thousand cavalry on his left. He has only a scattering of light horse on his right. Demetrius, the cavalry engagement on our right will decide the battle. He has spread his eighty remaining elephants to reinforce his front. Once we have routed his left, we will be able to roll up his army."

"Where are the Argyraspides?" Demetrius was adding up the odds and he didn't like what he was seeing. *Could it be that Seleucus Nikator knew what he was doing when he got himself excluded from this battle? My father dismisses him as a treacherous lightweight with an army of cavalry unfit to stand alone on a battlefield yet he won the Battle of Paraitacene however much my father claims otherwise. And what was my father thinking of anyway? Seleucus's cavalry and his infantry would have evened this battle up. As it is, we don't have a left wing to the Army. And turning the right of a phalanx can be decisive.*

Demetrius got his answer sooner than he thought. Antigenes had spurred his horse opposite the place where the phalanx of Antigonus' Macedonians was stationed, and shouted at them, "Wicked men, why are you sinning against your fathers, who conquered the whole world under Philip and Alexander? In a while you will see what the Argyraspides can achieve."

The response from the Antigonid Phalanx was immediate. A barrage of angry cries rose from their ranks, not directed at Antigenes but at Antigonus. The men in the Phalanx claimed that they were being forced to fight against their kinsfolk and their elders. That alone was enough to drive Antigonus to fury but his temper was made worse by the roars of approval from the ranks of Eumenes. The men in the Army of Eumenes were cheering and demanding that he lead them against the enemy as soon as possible. When Eumenes saw their enthusiasm, he directed his trumpeters to sound the signal for combat and the whole army to raise the battle cry. Then his phalanx started to roll forward against the smaller, already-disorganized Antigonid Phalanx.

The battle had already started between the elephants. The two lines had split up into a number of pairs where the riders of the elephants were thrusting at each other with long spears. For all the noise and dust that the elephants made, as far as Demetrius could see the elephanteers didn't actually do anything very decisive. About the only significant thing that he saw happening was that one of Eumenes' leading elephants fell after having been engaged with the strongest of those arrayed against it.

It was time. Demetrius sounded the 'advance' signal and led his men straight into the mass of Eumenid cavalry opposite him. As soon as the two masses of cavalry closed, Demetrius, at the lead of his forces, lost all control of them. His world contracted to the men he was fighting, a radius of a few feet around him. Despite that limited knowledge, he realized the cavalry battle was fierce with Eumenes' men being superior in spirit but those of Antigonus having the advantage in number. In the thick of the fighting, Demetrius realized that the scene along the elephant line was being repeated. Many men were falling on both sides but the battle was deadlocked without either force having a clear advantage. To make matters much worse, the dry, dusty soil was being thrown up in choking clouds and his ability to control the battle slipped still further away. Soon, the cavalry battle was nothing more than men randomly hacking at each other in the smothering clouds of dust and hoping they were fighting foe not friend.

Second Diodochi War

Hill Overlooking The Left flank of Antigonus's Army, Gabiene

"It's sheer butchery down there." Derya Shafrid looked at the cloud of dust that was enveloping the two armies. Neither had a serious upper hand but both were hacking away at each other despite the indecisive nature of the fight. "What's happening with them?"

"It's the inevitable result of concentrating the Army into the Phalanx and ignoring everything else. In every battle since Alexander died, the Phalanx has grown and the other forces withered. Except us of course which is why nobody can predict what we'll do next. We're breaking the rules they set up for themselves. But, Derya, when one's two worst enemies are making a complete mess of the battle, it's rude to interrupt them. The question is how we can exploit this situation to our advantage."

"The baggage train?"

"That will do nicely. We've got almost a completely free hand. The fact that we're in disgrace means that Antigonus won't even talk to us while the dust and chaos down there means nobody can see what we're doing. We can pull a flank attack on Eumenes and grab his baggage train. In fact, we can do something that has never been done before. We can seize the baggage train belonging to the Argyraspides. Take your regiment, Derya, and the rest of the Median and Tarentine light cavalry, and seize that baggage train. Do it with as little bloodshed as possible. This time, don't massacre anybody. I want that baggage train as close to untouched and undamaged as we can manage. Keep it all as intact as possible. When this battle is over, possession of that baggage train will decide who will really win this fight."

A few yards away, Naamah saw the two men sitting on their horses and then Derya Shafrid riding away to his command. She didn't worry overmuch about what was happening. She had a patient to care for. Pithon was in his tent, prostrated by the agonized flux that had gripped him shortly after the evening meal the night before. Naamah entered his tent, wrinkling her nose at the ghastly smell. Pithon saw her, gasped, then screamed as another violent spasm sprayed blood and other fluids from his rear end. Naamah inspected the product and noted that the violence of the emissions was fading slowly. Her patient was recovering although he had a long way to go before he would be capable of resuming command here. That didn't surprise her, the instructions she had been given were to disable him, not kill him.

"So, how are we doing?" Her voice was bright and professional, as befitted a healer ministering to a patient. Pithon's moan was enough of a response. *Time for a little good advice even if it wouldn't have helped you last night.* "We told you not to eat that meat. Anybody could tell it had gone rancid. You know more people die of sickness on campaign than in battle.

Rotten food is as lethal as a sarissa. Next time, don't eat anything that smells foul."

Peithon moaned again and Naamah made a tutting noice. "Bad Pithon. Bad, *bad* Pithon. No battle for you."

Argyraspides Baggage Train, Gabiene

"Cavalry! Enemy Cavalry!"

The desperate warning cry went up from the relative handful of men guarding the Argyraspides baggage train as the horsemen swept out of the dust to assault the camp. The maneuver had gone completely undetected, not least because the camp was some five miles to the rear of the Eumenid Army. That meant that it was isolated from any help even had the men of the Argyraspides realized the disaster that was about to engulf their baggage and families. The camp area was crowded with women, children and other persons who were useless for fighting but had few defenders. With all the fighting men gone, those defenders were mostly young boys who had barely started their training.

Against the battle-hardened Daimones Prodromoi, the Median horse-archers and the Tarentine lancers, they stood little chance. A few stood their ground and were killed, the rest broke before the cavalry charge and were quickly captured. For almost 30 years the baggage train of the Argyraspides had been inviolate, protected by the fearsome reputation of the 3,000 veteran soldiers who made up its core. Now, four thousand cavalry under the command of Derya Shafrid slammed into the rear area guard of 1,500 men under Peucestes, satrap of Persia, and scattered them in panic. The rout was contagious and in the dust and confusion, the entire right wing of the Army of Eumenes fell apart. That was of little concern to the cavalry of Seleucus Nikator that had just seized the richest prize ever to appear on a Diodochi battlefield. In their eyes, Antigonus had relegated them to the rear. He just hadn't said whose. That oversight had made them all rich.

The main problem was restoring order to the baggage train that had just been overrun. Shafrid was trying to keep his troops in hand and prevent the raid turning into an orgy of rape and looting. That was why he had the Medians and the Tarentian cavalry providing perimeter security while his own Daimones Regiment actually occupied the camp. Even so, the women and children were running in panic. They knew what a successful raid by Seleucus's cavalry meant. The cavalrymen would take the women and treasure they wanted and kill the rest. Most of the wives of the Argyraspides matched the ages of their husbands and knew that few, if any, of them would be taken as captives. A middle-aged woman experienced in camp life might find somebody who would take her but one in her fifties or sixties was denied even that faint hope. They knew this raid meant death for them and their wailing filled the dust-laden air over the baggage train.

Headquarters, Army of Eumenes, Gabiene

"Our right has collapsed. The center and left are holding."

Eumenes stared at the map in front of him. The dust was turning what should have been an orderly battle into chaos. "Assemble the remaining cavalry troops on our left wing and consolidate it with the survivors of the cavalry from our right. We'll support the Argyraspides as they assault the right of the enemy Phalanx and start to roll it up. As they do that, we'll pass behind them and show the trust placed in us by the kings is not misplaced by forcing our way towards Antigonus himself. Order Peucestes and his reserve to join us as well."

"Sire, Peucestes has already fallen back to the river and cannot reassemble his forces. The enemy prodromoi under Seleucus have utterly disorganized him." Hieronymus of Cardia already believed this battle was lost. Why, he wasn't quite sure but the crushing victory everybody was expecting hadn't taken place. Somehow, the momentum of the battle had changed and he wasn't certain why. With a flash of insight he suddenly understood that his inability to comprehend why the flow of the battle was changing direction was why he could never be a general. From that insight came another, Eumenes didn't know why either.

Eumenes cursed. *It was as if the Gods are punishing me for daring to take the field with a superior force instead of relying on their favor to balance inferior numbers.* "What of the Argyraspides?"

"There, the news is better. The Argyraspides in close order fell heavily upon their adversaries, killing some of them in hand to hand fighting and forcing others to flee. They were not to be checked in their charge and engaged the entire opposing phalanx, showing themselves so superior in skill and strength that of their own men they lost not one, but of those who opposed them they slew over five thousand and routed the entire force of foot soldiers, whose numbers were many times their own."

A messenger came in and handed a scroll to Eumenes. When he spoke, it was with a voice already crushed. "Seleucus Nikator has entered the battle on our right. His cavalry has taken our baggage trains. All of them."

Eumenes stared at the wall of his tent, remembering the scenes from the Thapsacus onwards. Baggage trains burned and devastated, the sutlers either burned in their wagons or speared as they tried to flee. Worst of all the women. The younger ones that could be sold for coin and those desired by the raiders had been carried off, the rest killed. That was why Eumenes had been forced to leave a substantial portion of his forces with the baggage trains. Now, the same thing had happened in the middle of a battle. *What sort of mind would think about raiding baggage trains in the middle of a major battle?* "Do as I said, assemble the cavalry. We ride to the aid of the baggage trains."

That was when he realized why the baggage trains had been raided in the middle of a battle and who had thought of the idea.

"Sire, what about the Argyraspides? Without cavalry support, they will be taken in the rear and surrounded."

That made Eumenes stop dead. The truth was that the Argyraspides had won his battles for him. With a sudden clarity of vision he realized that his battles had all been about keeping the enemy forces from stopping the Argyraspides doing their work. Now, if he went to the aid of the baggage trains, he would be deserting them. "Get word to them. Order them to abandon their attack and form themselves into a square. They must withdraw safely to the river, where they can form a proper defensive position."

"There is another problem. Dusk draws near. We cannot get to the baggage trains before nightfall. We must seek a meeting with Antigonus and arrange a truce. We must buy back our women and the baggage."

Eumenes looked around him in despair. *How could this situation have fallen apart so quickly? My Army won't fight until the baggage trains are rescued or ransomed.* "Very well, make the arrangements."

Headquarters of the Argyraspides, Gabiene.

"We will slaughter you all for this. Your women and children will weep bitter tears over your bodies when they are sold into slavery." Antigenes was furious with the Seleucid cavalry that surrounded his unit. More specifically, he was consumed with hatred for their leader who seemed vaguely amused by his threats.

"Antigenes, you may very well do that. But you will be a lonely, impoverished man who has buried his entire family by the time you do." Parmenio looked down from his horse at the enemy commander. "We hold your camp, we hold your baggage train, we hold everything that you have won in thirty years of warfare. But, we are reasonable people. We will release your women and children alive and unharmed. We will even return your baggage and loot, save for twenty parts in a hundred which we will keep to cover our expenses."

"You cannot fight war like a man of honor. Instead, you attack those who cannot defend themselves."

"We'll make that twenty five parts in a hundred. You might want to accept that before I remember that you were going to maim and mutilate my messenger and make it thirty. As to your baggage trains, you made that possible. There was a reason why baggage trains and camps were always heavily guarded. There was a reason why commanders held a reserve to deal with situations like this. You and yours have ignored those reasons and done neither. Now, you pay the price. Oh, and there is one more item to be added to the cost of that lesson. You will take Eumenes prisoner and deliver him to Antigonus. With the compliments of Seleucus Nikator."

Antigenes seethed with anger but he was in an impossible position and knew it. He'd been trapped with only one way out and it was humiliating. Nevertheless, if he did not take it, his own men would remove him from command of the Argyraspides. "Your terms are accepted."

Headquarters, Army of Eumenes, Gabiene

"What the devil is going on?" Eumenes knew that the day had not gone well for his army but he still held a strong position along the Gabiene and with the night to reorganize the army, he would be able to resume the fight at dawn. On the other hand, he also knew that the Phalanx of Antigonus had been shattered by the Argyraspides again, this time with almost half its number dead, wounded or fled the battlefield. Antigonus had also lost the cream of his heavy cavalry. That left him with only his elephants and his prodromoi light cavalry. At dawn, the Army of Eumenes would be ready to fight, the Army of Antigonus would not. *So what is all the tumult about?*

Antigenes and half a dozen of the Argyraspides forced their way into Eumenes's presence, swords drawn. Eumenes didn't need telling that his guards outside were already dead. "So, Antigenes, you have betrayed me at last?"

"I have no choice Sire. Not with our families and baggage held hostage by Seleucus Nikator. We have negotiated with Antigonus and Seleucus for the safety of our families and the recovery of our baggage, and after receiving pledges we have enrolled in Antigonus' army.

"It's all over Eumenes, we folded first and got the good deal. Already the other satraps and most of your other commanders and soldiers are deserting you. They also must think of their own safety and that of their family. None want to see their wives and children sold into slavery or dying on the end of a prodromoi lance.

"Our agreement is to deliver you to Antigonus with the compliments of Seleucus Nikator. I suggest you spend the time until then working out what deal you too can strike."

"You have betrayed me."

Antigenes sighed. "It's nothing personal. Just business."

Headquarters, Army of Antigonus Monopthalmus, Gabiene, 316 BC

"You need to remember this, Igrat. Record everything you have seen and will see here. Then, when asked, tell the story in your own words. Not mine or Seleucus's but yours. That way, people will believe you and know what happens to those who make agreements with Antigonus Monopthalmus."

It had happened at dawn. The Argyraspides had spent most of the night reorganizing their baggage train and seeing to the needs of their families. Then, as the sun rose, they had found themselves surrounded by the infantry of Antigonus and disarmed. More than ninety of their senior officers had been led away, including Antigenes himself, Eudamus, Celbanus and Teutamus. During the night, Antigonus had ordered his men to dig deep pits near his camp and the Argyraspides officers had been thrown into them. There, they waited. Meanwhile, the rest of the Argyraspides had been dispersed in twos and threes. Some had gone back to their farms with their families to live out their lives in retirement. Others had been sent to units far away, units whose commanders had been given orders to get the old veterans killed as quickly as possible. The legendary Argyraspides were no more. Never again would their silver shields turn the course of a battle.

Dozens of carts pulled up beside the pits and started to unload their cargoes of oil-soaked straw into them. The men in them had been shouting abuse at Antigonus and his army, accusing the general of treachery and dishonor while goading the army with the number of times they had been defeated by the Argyraspides. When the implications of the oil-soaked straw sank home, those insults changed to panic-stricken cries as they tried to scale the walls of the pits. But, there were spearmen at the top who pushed them back in to the ever-increasing depth of straw. Soon, the men inside were almost buried. Some remained silent, others wept or prayed. Then, Antigonus himself threw a lighed torch into each pit.

The oil-soaked straw didn't flare up into a ball of flame as wood might have done. Instead it burned slowly and steadily, eating across the width of the pits. Without the roar of the open flames, there was nothing to hide the agonized screams from inside the pits as the men in them were slowly roasted. They echoed around the whole camp, seemingly carried skywards by the pyre of foul-smelling black smoke. Most of the men looked away as the nightmare went on and on. Most of the women in the area either fled or put their hands over their ears as they tried to shut out the sounds of the men dying in the pits. Only Igrat seemed unaffected, standing erect and motionless as she tried to put every single detail of the awful scene into her memory.

Second Diodochi War

"Does she have to see this?" Derya Shafrid was whitened with horror at the mass burning.

"If she doesn't, Antigonus will suppress all word of this atrocity. His allies need to know just what his word is worth and she's an unimpeachable witness. Over the last few years, everybody has learned to trust her words. What are you doing here anyway?"

"Seleucus found out about this an hour or so ago and sent us to guard you. He was afraid Antigonus might try and put you in there as well. You've got a thousand loyal Daimones Prodromoi watching your back." Shafrid paused, noting with heart-felt relief that the screaming was finally fading away as the victims in the pit finally died. "We've done some pretty bad things but never anything like this. Seleucus would never allow this to be done in his name. Not once he had given his word."

"That's why we fight for him, Derya, not for Antigonus." Parmenio sighed, *that much is true but there is more besides.*

"And what of Eumenes?"

Parmenio looked again at the pits, blessedly silent now. "He'll have no faith in Eumenes' promises because of the latter's loyalty to Olympias and the kings. He tried once before, at Nora in Phrygia, but Eumenes still supported the kings most whole-heartedly. And Eumenes out-generalled him over and over again. I fear that Eumenes will envy the men in those pits by the time Antigonus has finished with him. Or would, if he gets the chance."

Parmenio looked around and saw the members of the Daimones Regiment scattered around. Their positions looked random but actually they could quickly converge to get him a safe route out. Derya Shafrid knew his trade well and Parmenio mentally saluted him for that. Around them, the foul, stinking black smoke still welling up from the pits seemed to form a shroud.

A few hundred yards away, Eumenes was sitting in an iron cage, awaiting his fate. When he heard somebody enter the room, he assumed it was his executioner. Instead, it was a woman, one with chestnut red hair. She was modestly dressed in shawl and tunic and her eyes were downcast. Eumenes looked at her and wondered if or where he had seen her before. "Come to look at the prisoner?"

Naamah ignored the gibe and sat down just out of reach of the cage. "I have come to help the prisoner. Antigonus betrayed Antigenes just as Antigenes betrayed you. All the officers of the Argyraspides have just been burned alive. Slowly, so their agony would be prolonged. Antigonus hates you for your victories over him and plans a worse fate for you. You are to be starved to near-death and then roasted over a slow fire."

"You will help me escape? What do you wish for your reward?" Eumenes realized she was telling the truth. Antigonus was slowly going mad with power and lust for slaughter.

"I ask no reward. And the escape I offer you is a final one. You will cheat Antigonus of victory one more time." Naamah produced a small bottle from under her shawl. "Drink this. It is a painless way of escape made with the finest wine I could find. In a few minutes you will feel a tingling in your fingers and toes. It will spread up your arms and legs with coldness following it. When the coldness reaches your chest, you will die. It is the way out I have chosen for myself and my friends should we ever find ourselves where you are now."

She put the bottle down where Eumenes could reach it and stepped back. He took it and inspected the contents. Then he looked at her again and saw the dead green slime color of her eyes and it jogged his memory. "I know you, you were the healer in Babylon who tried to save Alexander."

"Actually, I was the one who poisoned him. Well, one of the ones who poisoned him, I've never quite worked out how many times he was assassinated that night. I think there were at least three separate poisoning attempts at that banquet. But, mine worked. Take the potion, Eumenes."

Eumenes looked at her, uncorked the tiny bottle and quaffed the contents. "A fine wine indeed, I think, with an unexpected kick in the tail. Thank you, lady. Before it takes effect, a question. What of the historian Hieronymus of Cardia? I always held him in honor."

"Now he enjoys the favor and confidence of Antigonus and tells of his great victories over you."

Eumenes nodded and then felt the tingling sensation in his hands and feet. It spread quickly and behind it, his limbs felt cold and numb. Before the numbness reached his chest and the world went dark he blessed the poisoner who had enabled him to beat Antigonus one last time.

Naamah slipped out of the room and made her way through the camp, her shawl drawn modestly over her face. She saw Parmenio riding out with his Prodromoi escort and caught his eye. She nodded and read his lips as he said something quietly to himself. "Six down."

Estate of Parmenio, Seleucia-on-the-Tigris, 316BC

'Well, that's it. We did well during the war and our investments have multiplied our wealth several times over. We're now officially rich beyond our wildest dreams." Lillith closed the family books and sat with a smug smile upon her face. "Best of all, I've made sure that we're mobile. If we need to, we can get out of here with everything we possess at a few days notice. We will get a few days notice won't we?"

"We will, hopefully a bit more than that." Parmenio paused, then continued "Nearly everybody gets notice of a disaster but the problem is they only realize it in retrospect. Campaigning season is over for this year so we have time to catch our breath. Antigonus has seen his army badly cut up. In the last two battles he lost almost half his men and word of his betrayal of the Argyraspides has spread so he is trouble finding new recruits to replace his losses. All that means we have a year or more but when things do go down, we'll need to recognize the warning signs. All of you, keep your eyes and ears open. Anything that seems wrong, make sure we all know."

"Reports and despatches." Derya and Igrat Shafrid had arrived from Babylon with the latest intelligence reports from Seleucus Nikator. Standing slightly behind her husband, Igrat winked at the others. Just for once, she wasn't carrying the documents in question. Parmenio wondered how much sooner they would have arrived if she had been their bearer. Igrat quietly got her husband a glass of wine and a plate of food from the side table while he sat down with the men. Then, she joined the other women present. Naamah and Lillith exchanged glances, Igrat was playing the role of a dutiful wife just as well and completely as she played every other role in her life.

Parmenio was reading the scrolls quickly, skimming the contents. As he reached the end he looked up. "Igrat, you need not worry about going back to the court of Olympias again. She's dead."

Igrat visibly relaxed. Derya looked at her curiously. "You've been to that court and met Olympias?" Then, he realized he was setting foot into areas he was better off not knowing about. "Sorry I asked. Parmenio, what happened? Last I heard, she was ascendent in Macedonia?"

"The torture and murder of Eurydicê and King Philip did for her. Just as the treatment of the Argyraspides is hobbling Antigonus. After Eurydice's Army collapsed, Cassander headed north, recruited a new army and besieged Tegea in the Peloponnesus. Well, he got hung up there while he started to build siege towers and ladders to storm the walls. That was when he got word of what Olympias had done to Eurydice. Then, Oympias made matters worse by descrating the tomb of his brother Iollas. Right up to that point, everything had been business, not personal but from that point, everything changed. He wanted Olympias dead and he was perfectly happy to pay for that with his own life and the lives of his entire Army. The killing of King Philip changed everything for his army as well. They might not have much love for Cassander but the wanton murder of King Philip was more than they could stomach.

"Anyway, Cassander negotiated a deal with the people of Tegea and set out for Macedonia with his army with massacre on his mind. Of course, this threw the whole balance of power in the area into complete confusion. The army of Callas was waiting to attack the cities of the Peloponnesus once Cassander had cleared the way in. Now, with Cassander heading north as fast as his army could march, all they could do was twiddle their tumbs waiting. So, Cassander ordered them to break off the planned attack and head east to engage and defeat Polyperchon. Meanwhile, to get at Olympias, Cassander had to march through the pass at Thermopylae."

"That place again?" Semiramis sounded curious.

"That place again. It's just about the most strategic pass in the whole of Greece. Any campaign fought out in Greece is going to end up in a confrontation there sooner or later. This time it was the Aetolians, who wished to please Olympias and Polyperchon, that had occupied and barred Cassander from the passage. Cassander, who managed to find wisdom in the middle of a roaring rampage of revenge –which is quite an achievement by the way – bypassed the pass and used boats and barges to transport his army north. That put him ahead of the Aetolians who were trying to find other passes to block only to discover Cassander kept getting to them in front of him.

"Cassander might have been mad with rage but his strategic moves were brilliant. Polyperchon and Olympias had been split apart and could be defeated in detail. Polyperchon and his army were in Perrhaebia with a superior army under Callas closing in on him. With that threat in place, there was no way he could move to support Olympias who had Cassander closing in on her with a massively superior army. So, she did the only thing plausible under the circumstances. She headed for the fortress of Pydna so she could try and sit out the crisis there. I assume she wanted to try and buy time for Polyperchon to break free and come to her aid. Or at least somebody. Only, her murder of Eurydice and Philip meant that nobody wanted to lift a finger on her behalf. Just to make matters worse, even though she knew she was going into a siege, she made no effort to provision Pydna. Not only was the city short of food before the siege even started but she filled it up with useless mouths. She didn't even have much of an army in there with her. Basically just her court pretend-soldiers and some Ambracian cavalry. Oh yes, and a group of elephants that promptly started to eat what little reserves of food she had.

"So, once Cassander had surrounded the city and laid siege to it by land and sea, Olympias and her followers started getting very hungry very quickly. Her pleas for help got quite a bit more desperate. We got one by the way and so did Ptolemy. That was about the time we cracked the Army of Eumenes open at the Paraitacene. We didn't move on it and nor did anybody else. The few that tried saw their armies mutiny. One of her allies even deposed their king and switched sides to join Cassander. That started a ripple effect that was felt all the way down to Perrhaebia. When Callas closed in on Polyperchon, he bribed the entire army to change sides. That they did and poor Polyperchon was left standing on the battlefield with his own personal bodyguard and nobody else. They're still running. Olympias was left sitting in Pydna without a single ally to break the siege.

"After that, it really didn't take long. The few supplies in the city were rapidly exhausted. The garrison sawed up wood and fed the sawdust to the elephants for want of proper forage. Their own rations were the slaughtered pack animals and horses. They ran out as well of course. The elephants died of starvation, the cavalry ate their mounts and then starved themselves. That was for the people who were armed, the unarmed citizens in the town were reduced to cannibalism. Within a week or two, the city was filled with corpses and their stench was unbearable, not merely to ladies who were of the queen's court and addicted to luxury, but also to those of the soldiers who were habituated to hardship. The result was pretty much inevitable, what was left of the garrison deserted to Cassander. Antigonus could learn a thing or two from that boy. He welcomed all of them, treated them in most friendly fashion, and gave them food and gold. Then he sent them to their homes to tell of the weakness of Olympias and the generosity and honor of Cassander. If anybody was thinking of helping Olympias, that finished their ideas on that score.

"Olympias tried to make a break for it on a quinquereme but Cassander had expected that and he intercepted the ship in full view of the city. That was when news of the defeat and death of Eumenes came in and it finally made Olympias admit defeat. She asked for terms and was told only her unconditional surrender would be accepted. She persuaded Cassander to grant the single exception that he guarantee her personal safety. And so it was that Olympias surrendered to Cassander. That was when Olympias suffered for the way she had treated people when she held power. Good lesson here people, be careful who you step on when you are on the way up for you will meet them again on your way down. The relatives of those whom Olympias had slain accused her in the general assembly of the Macedonians on charges murder, treachery and torture."

"Coming from Macedonians, that's rich." Naamah's voice was droll. There was a ripple of laughter around the room. Parmenio tried to look offended but failed dismally.

"Well, Olympias wasn't present and nobody, but nobody was willing to speak in her defence, so it wasn't surprising the Macedonians condemned her to death. Cassander fulfilled his pledge to her by warning her of the death sentence and advised her to escape. He even offered her a ship to carry her to

Athens. Of course, by accepting that offer she would be condemning herself to exile and would end any pretensions of power she might retain. Olympias, however, refused to flee and declared herself ready to be judged before all the Macedonians. It was too late, she had already alienated far too many people and a mob assaulted the palace, overwhelming the two hundred guards Cassander had placed there. They dragged Olympias out and literally tore her apart. The survivors of the guards say that she met her death with great dignity and uttered no ignoble or womanish pleas.

"I resent that." Semiramis was mightily offended. "Last time I killed somebody, he wept like a little girl. Womanish pleas indeed.

"Last time you killed somebody, he fell off a wall with your arrow in him and uttered no pleas on the way down, ignoble or otherwise." Parmenio was amused.

"There were three more while you were away." Gusoyn joined in for the first time. "Bandits who thought they could rob an estate while the owner was away at the wars. Lillith and Semiramis got one each with their bows and we handed the third over to the local magistrate. He took a dim view of bandits trying to rob the homes of men who were away fighting for their king and had him executed. That was when we got the ignoble pleas Semiramis mentioned. Much good that they did him."

"Word has spread around the marketplace of how Seleucus aided the women left widowed by soldiers who died in his service. That he spent time to speak with them and give words of solace has made a better impression on people than the coin he gave them for their support. 'Any king can give coin but a only a good king will take the time needed to speak with the lowest of his subjects.' That's what people are saying." Igrat added the comments thoughtfully. It wasn't often that the streets and markets spoke well of those who ruled them.

Parmenio nodded, equally thoughtful. The time would come when that growing loyalty would be seriously tested. "That's good to know. We've got the winter ahead of us, it's time to think of a few ways to keep Antigonus amused."

The room emptied as people retired for the night. Parmenio was left in a dim room, lit only by the single remaining lighted lamp. He thought about the death of Olympias before rising himself and putting out that last lamp. As he did so, he spoke two words in the darkness. "Seven down."

189

PART THREE
THE THIRD DIODOCHI
WAR (315 – 312 BC)

Third Diodochi War

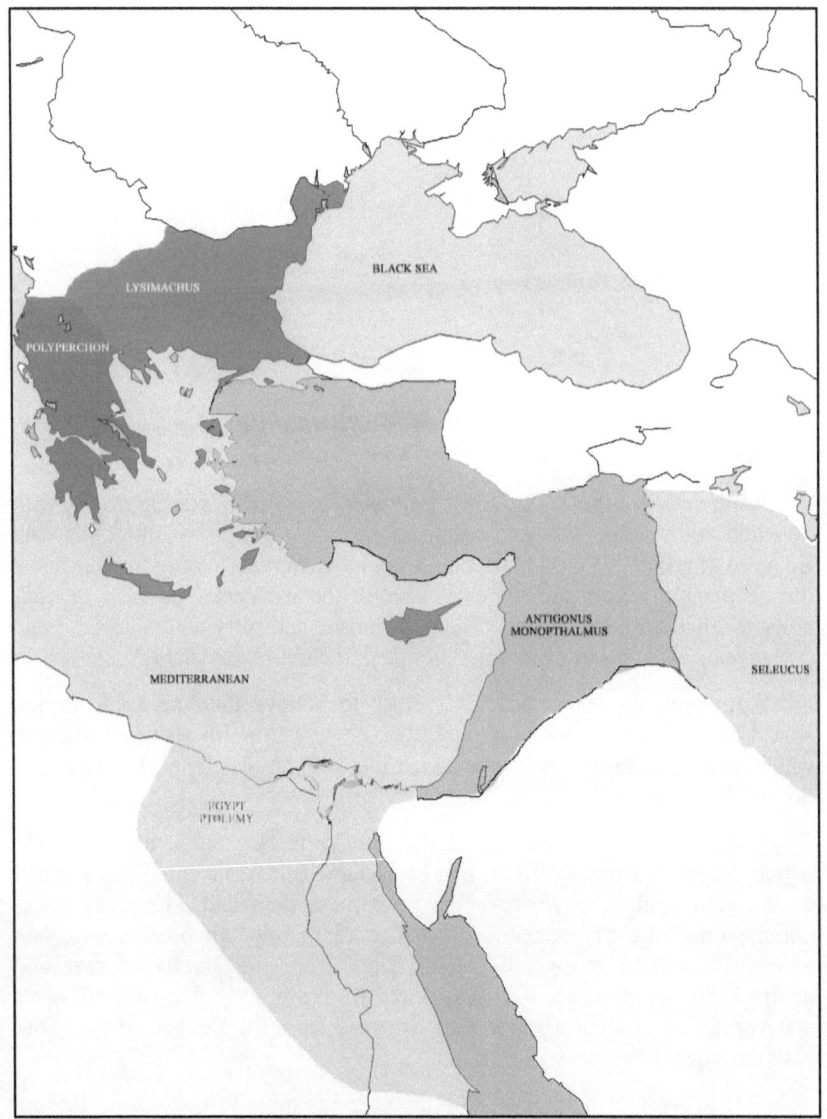

The Diodochi Satrapies at the start of the Third Diodochi War.

CHAPTER ONE

A WAR OF GOLD

Headquarters, Army of Antigonus Monopthalmus, Media, Winterset 315 BC

"And so it is that Pithon buys the loyalty of your wintering troops with Seleucid gold." Hippostratus passed the message through to Antigonus with a degree of relish. "Would that I could say he buys their loyalty in your name but he plans a revolt and hopes to exploit the weakened position of your army to his own ends. He distributes promises and gifts with a lavish hand that reveals his support from your enemies. Such base treachery."

Antigonus shook his head. "I refuse to believe that the noble Pithon would conceive of actions so base. Did he not rise from his sick-bed when he was near death and command the attack that brought Eumenes down? Is this not so Hieronymus?"

Hieronymus of Cardia caught the faint, lingering smell of the pits in which the Argyraspides officers had been burned. It was a smell that seemed to surround Antigonus wherever he went these days and Hieronymus was not the only one to notice it. With it were mixed two other odors, less pungent but even more subversive. They were the smells of fear and mistrust. "It is indeed so, Pithon suffered from a bloody flux of the bowels that would have killed a lesser man yet rose from his sickbed to carry out your commands."

"There we are then. Hippostratus, your attempts to undermine Pithon, the hero of the Gabiene, are transparent and futile. How dare you impugn the honor of a man who had gained preferment for merit while serving under Alexander and who is at this very time the trusted satrap of Media. I can only wonder at the pettiness of a man who would try and disrupt my friendship for our greatest general. Be gone from my sight and let me not see you again until your conduct on the battlefield has restored my faith in you. Hieronymus, write a letter for me to Pithon. I will display my faith in him with more than mere words. I appoint him as overlord of all the upper satrapies with command of an army sufficient for their safety. Soon I will be moving on our next campaign and I need a trusted man who can rule in my name. Pithon is such a man and I would have all here know it."

Palace of Seleucus Nikator, Seleucia-on-the Tigris, 315 BC

"Well, that worked better than we expected." Seleucus Nikator couldn't believe that the simple scheme had actually succeeded in taking out a rival. He laughed again, shook his head and drank from a goblet of wine.

"It did, although Antigonus is becoming swept up by suspicion of all around him. He sees plots and schemes in every shadow and is always on his guard against treachery. A man false to his word will always believe that others are false to him. In this case, his betrayal of the Argyraspides has meant that everybody is suspicious of everything he says. Not one of them believes Antigonus and he knows it. So his mind defaults to betrayal and treason. So, he is determined to strike first and that gives the whole cycle a further deadly twist. Of course, it all added to the picture that Pithon really was planning a revolt. He'd already corrupted a large number of minor leaders in the most distant parts of Media, who had promised to join him." Parmenio helped himself to more wine.

"And so Antigonus lured him to his court and killed him." Seleucus considered the implications of that and found them terrifying. "A short term gain for him, for it is no easy matter to arrest a man by force when he has curried favour with the entire army. But, in the longer term, people will now treat every invitation from Antigonus as a trap, even when couched in the friendliest of terms. No guarantees will be held sufficient. Even the friends of Pithon wrote to him, telling him of his great prospects under Antigonus. So, when the letter from Antigonus asking him to come as soon as possible, that he might discuss the necessary matters for his next campaign with him, Pithon believed it. It must have been quite a shock for him when he was accused before the members of the council, convicted and executed."

"He quite lost his head." Parmenio spoke solemnly and Seleucus couldn't help but laugh at the pun. "Anyway, Orontobates has been appointed satrap of Media and Hippostratus has been made general with an infantry force of thirty-five hundred mercenaries. Antigonus himself is moving to Ecbatana with his army. His war chest is twenty thousand talents of uncoined silver. We have a hundred times that amount in silver and gold and more besides. He's getting ready to move but he won't start quite yet. Anyway, we haven't quite finished playing campaigns with his head yet."

Seleucus looked confused. "But we are already preparing to retreat from Babylon when Antigonus attacks. Funds are being distributed to our most loyal supporters so that they may use them in the harassment of Antigonus. Yet, the delay is still worth achieving?"

"Any delay is, for it means that Antigonus is dancing to our tune. And it means that we get more time to ensure that he gets the proper reception when he runs into our towns. Anyway, some of our gold has gone to Meleager and Menoetas, good friends of Pithon who were disgusted by the treachery of his death. I believe you met them when Perdiccas met his end. Anyway, they've linked up with the survivors of Eumenes' Army and in all have some eight hundred light cavalry. Their first target has been the Medes who have remained loyal to Orontobates. When they started their attacks and showed that Orontobates could not or would not defend against them, the most important of the Medes, one Ocranes, changed sides and joined them. Now, they harrass the army of Hippostratus. That won't make a great deal of difference to us directly but it will add to the difficulties Antigonus will experience in keeping his Army supplied."

"He will loot the countryside instead." Seleucus sounded saddened by the thought.

"He will indeed, and much good it will do him. He has to hold the cities and that means he'll have to send out foraging parties to bring the supplies in. Not many of them will survive the attempt. Antigonus is going to find that he might control Babylon and the larger cities but we'll control the surrounding countryside. Meanwhile, the cities will be restive and his garrisons will start to lose men from disease, desertion and the odd murder. He'll find that people, when given a choice between a man with a reputation for brutal treachery and a ruler who rewards loyalty with coin and kindly words, they'll chose the latter.

Seleucus drank deep of his wine and contemplated those words. The idea of being a good and kindly ruler had agreed with his personality and it had pleased him when it coincided with the needs of his kingdom. "Pithon was a good man, a great soldier and a noble servant of the great Alexander. I was close to him when we removed Perdiccas from power. He was a man second to none of the Companions of Alexander in courage and reputation."

"That he was." Parmenio sounded saddened as he, too, drank of his wine. *Eight down.*

Headquarters, Army of Antigonus Monopthalmus, Aspisas, Spring 315 BC

"They have awarded me the title of King of the Persians." Antigonus looked around suspiciously, keen to detect the whiff of treachery from anybody who might disappove of his receipt of a kingly crown. For, by accepting it, Antigonus had put an end to the fantasy that he was merely a Diodochi, ruling as regent for the heir of the great Alexander. Now, there was no doubt that he saw himself as Alexander's successor. "This means that the satrapies here now owe allegience to me as their king. I will permit

Tlepolemus to retain Carmania, and likewise Stasanor to retain Bactrianê for they are both loyal and honorable men in whom I place my trust."

And when they hear that, their sleep will be much disturbed. Today when men hear they have the trust of Antigonus, they make their final arrangements in expectation of death at his hands. Hieronymus was well aware of the difference between Antigonus and Eumenes and knew his transfer of loyalty from one to the other had not been an improvement. *But, the only choice was to join the others in the burning pits. And keeping Tlepolemus and Stasanor in place is a wise more for it was not easy to remove them by sending a message since they had conducted themselves well toward the inhabitants and had many supporters.*

"I also appoint Evagoras in the place of our lamented friend Evitus as Satrap of Aria, and permit Oxyartes, the father of Roxanê, to keep the satrapy in Paropanisadae as before. But, Peucestes is disloyal and jealous of my kingly title. There is no need for a satrap in Persia any more so I take his rank away from him.

And so Peucestes will be filled with hope for other things and will deceive himself with vain expectations before he is removed from the country and probably from life. Hieronymus wondered whether Peucestes would find his way out of this trap. *His bungling idiocy at the Gabiene suggests that he probably doesn't deserve to.*

"Your majesty, Xenophilus, the supervisor of the treasury at Susa, desires to see you." The court herald announced the arrival with pomp and ceremony.

"I am always pleased to welcome Xenophilus, whom I honor among my closest friends. Xenophilus, how fares my noble ally, Seleucus Satrap of Babylonia?"

"Babylonia prospers, your Majesty and in display of its loyalty, Seleucus Nikator sends you the golden climbing vine of Susa and a great number of other objects of art, weighing all told fifteen thousand talents of gold. In addition, he offers you in friendship five thousand talents in coin, and another five thousand from the spoils of Eumenes. In all, these supplement your treasury by twenty five thousand talents."

I wonder if Seleucus intends to provoke Antigonus into doing something foolish. Hieronymus had an idea that was exactly what Seleucus Nikator had in mind. *Twenty five thousand talents is a flea-bite compared with the wealth Seleucus has acquired. While Perdiccas, Antipater and Eumenes fought over territory, Seleucus acquired as much of the Alexandrine treasury as he could and that was all of it. How much has he got? Two hundred or three hundred thousand talents or ten times more? Easily that and he sends a mere twenty five thousand to Antigonus?*

"It seems to me that Babylonia could make a greater contribution to the funds of our alliance than this." Antigonus's voice thundered across the room. "Go to Seleucus and tell him that in twenty-two days I will arrive in Babylon. Once there, I will demand an accounting for the revenues, Seleucus has received from his Satrapy. Then we will see if twenty five thousand talents is the best he can offer."

"Your Majesty, Seleucus is not bound to undergo a public investigation of his administration of his country which was given to him in recognition of his services rendered while Alexander was alive. And as ruler of Babylonia, it is for him to decide what funds he should commit to your mutual interests. But, I will carry your message to Seleucus Nikator in the sure knowledge that he will honor you with gifts suitable for a king of your standing."

Gods, Seleucus is provoking him. Hieronymus watched Xenophilus turn and leave the room with his head held high. What Hieronymous did not see was a young woman in the shadows slipping away as well. *Delivering a message like that took courage. I wonder what gifts Seleucus has in mind? A basket of elephant dung perhaps? Whatever it is, the Third Diodochi War has started this day.*

Estate of Parmenio, Seleucia-on-the-Tigris, 315BC

"Fourteen days left. How long to pack up and head for Egypt?" Parmenio took the message from Igrat and once again gave thanks for her inexplicable ability to travel far and fast. She had beaten Xenophilus back by three days. The supervisor of the treasury at Susa was still hurrying down to Babylon, not knowing that the key items of his news were already known to everybody who mattered.

"Five days." Lillith ran through the inventory in her head. "What transport will we have?"

"The elephants and Derya's cavalry as escort. Seleucus will be getting ready to leave with you as well. I'm counting on seven days lead. Somebody will tell Antigonus where you're going."

"What about this place? Burn it?" Lillith winced at the financial dead loss that would represent.

"No, I like this house. We'll get it back when Antigonus leaves with his tail between his legs. But, leave it a bare shell. Take everything, all of you. Don't leave old one-eye as much as a fouled loincloth."

"Wait a minute, father, you said 'Seleucus will be leaving with you as well'. Meaning that you won't be coming with us?"

"That's right. I'll be staying on here with the Army while we pull back south and east. This campaign is going to be a tricky one and it'll need my personal attention."

"Then I'll stay on with you."

"No, you won't Igrat. I need you with the rest of the family in Ptolemy Soter's palace."

"You do need me. Suppose you need to get a message back to Egypt?"

"I won't. Or, if I do, a standard courier will do. Your services will be needed in Egypt. While I keep Antigonus chasing his tail in our eastern provinces, Ptolemy will be assembling a coalition in the west and lining us up with Cassander and the surviving regents. You might well be the key to getting that done. Your ability to be a skilled and reliable messenger is changing history. That's a responsibility that will be heavy on you sometimes."

"Cassander and the surviving regents? That'll be a trick knowing how he feels about Alexander and the family." Semiramis was curious.

"That's a problem that will solve itself very shortly. In fact, the process of solving it has already started. He's married Thessalonicê, who is Philip's daughter and Alexander's half-sister, and thus established a connection with the royal house. That makes him the prime candidate to gain the Macedonian throne and puts Roxanê and her son squarely in his way. A pity, for Roxanê is a beautiful and pleasant woman. I hope Cassander doesn't kill her and her son slowly or that she doesn't die as messily as Olympias did. She deserves better. But I don't give her more than a few weeks now. She's no longer useful to anybody and a nuisance to some. The only thing that's keeping her alive is that he knows the effect that Olympias's murder of Eurydice had on the common people and he doesn't want to be in the same position. Also, Cassander is beginning to realize the effect the treatment of the Argyraspides by Antigonus is having and he doesn't want to be seen in the same mold. So, he's placed Roxanê and the child in custody and transferring them to the citadel of Amphipolis. He's ordered that their servants and pages be taken away and that they should no longer have royal treatment but only such as was proper for any ordinary person of private station. Once she's forgotten, she and her son are dead."

"That's sad." Igrat seemed genuinely upset, something that startled those around her.

"That's Macedonian politics." Parmenio sounded grim. "That's why I want you all out of here. All of you, with no arguments. Naamah, you'll be in charge until we get back together again."

Semiramis bristled at that. In her eyes, Naamah had been a Queen but she had been an Empress and, anyway, Assyrians had never taken well to being under somebody else's leadership. Also, she was Parmenio's partner. Parmenio noted the reaction. "I mean it, Semiramis. If we were going to be fighting, you'd make the better leader but that isn't the way its going to be. The job of this family over the next few years is to avoid the fighting and avoid getting mixed up in the internal battles going on. For that role, Naamah is the better leader and I want you to understand that. If you don't, just remember that I'm Macedonian as well." Parmenio grinned to take the sting out of the threat but it was there and everybody knew it.

Semiramis settled back, prepared to accept the inevitable. Just barely.

Baggage Train, Army of Antigonus Monopthalmus, 315 BC

The baggage train had made slow progress since Antigonus had left Aspisas. An unordered mass of wagons and camels, it stretched for miles with two thousand light cavalry desperately trying to keep it in some form of order and closed up into an area that could be reasonably defended. They were having a hard job of it and not just because the occupants of the train were slovenly civilians. Emotions were running high in the train and none of them did the people riding on the carts credit. Greed was a major part of those emotions. Everybody knew that Antigonus was moving his treasury of sixty thousand talents in the huge convoy. It was even easy to see where, for the treasury wagons were guarded by hyspasists at least five hundred in number and all skilled veterans. There was the hope in every man's mind that somehow he would get access to the hoard and live to tell the tale.

Mixed in with greed was fear. Everybody knew that the Seleucid Army was small compared with the immense host gathered by Antigonus. It was rumored that the Army of Antigonus marched on Babylon with more than 90,000 infantry and ten thousand cavalry plus seventy elephants. Against them, Seleucus had barely 15,000 infantry if that and thirty thousand cavalry. Plus the forty elephants they had taken from Eumenes. The problem was that the Army of Antigonus wasn't here and nobody knew where the Army of Seleucus was. It had vanished along with almost every trace of Seleucus' administration. Any hope of loot from the Seleucid lands was fading fast. The country seemed to have been stripped clean. Add in the known proclivity of the Seleucid cavalry for massacring baggage trains and there was much cause for fear.

"Sire, bandits have attacked again!" The cavalry officer rode up in a cloud of dust that rose from the parched road surface in a billowing, choking, fog. Anatolios Metrophanes wheeled his own horse around to hear the rest of the message. "At the end of the baggage train. The bandits waited until there were no cavalry around and are burning the carts."

Third Diodochi War

There were fifty men on horseback around Metrophanes and they formed around him for the ride back. This was the problem, if he rode to the scene of every attack, his horsemen would be worn out and, in any case, the raiders would be gone by the time they got there. If he didn't, the raiders would continue their ghastly work and the demoralized baggage train would fall apart.

It didn't take long before the pyre of black smoke showed him where the raid had taken place. A group of five wagons had become separated from the rest. Not by much, perhaps only a minute's ride, but enough for a group that had only carts and camels. The raiders had swept in, killed the occupants and burned the carts before fleeing. There had been other sutlers and camp followers not far away but they hadn't even tried to aid the victims. Metrophanes knew why; men riding to the aid of those attacked would be ambushed and killed. Their responsibility was to their own families, not strangers. And yet, when their turn came to be attacked, they would also die unaided.

There was a body nearby, a woman her clothes blackened from fire. Undoubtedly she had been hiding in one of the carts when the raiders had set in afire. She had taken the chance of running rather than the certainty of burning only to be speared in the back and her broken body cast contemptuously aside. Not far away was the body of the only casualty suffered by the raiders. Metrophanes climbed down from his horse and looked at the corpse. An older man, his face scarred and one eye lost. Not a soldier, a real bandit. Metrophanes took his knife and sword and checked his belt. There was a gold coin in it, not something that a bandit would normally have and it betrayed what this raid really was.

He held it up so that it gleamed in the sunlight. "See, Seleucus will not fight us man to man. Instead he slaughters the defenseless with gold coin."

His call was met with silence and that disturbed him more than the raid had done. As he was remounting, another officer galloped up. "Sire, bandits have attacked again! At the front of the baggage train."

Escape Party of Seleucus Nikator, Heading for Egypt, 315 BC

"Does he have a name?" Naamah spoke to the Indian Mahout who was controlling the elephant she was riding.

"Certainly, Highness. He is Dilipa Ganesh. The elephant to our right is Vasu Pankaja and the one to our left is Krishna Ravi. Then we have Kumara Drupada in front and Gopala Mahesha behind."

"Dilipa Ganesh appears a cut above the others. Is he their leader?"

The mahout beamed at the compliment paid to his elephant but shook his head. "No, Highness. The leader is always the oldest male. That is Jaya Sushila, over there. The great king Seleucus Nikator rides him as is right and proper."

Naamah looked at the elephant pack. There were five rows, each of eight elephants making a compact box that was at once easy to protect and easy to defend. Seleucus was, of course in the middle with his court carried on four elephants. Dilipa Ganesh was behind and to the left of him. Outside the elephant box, the men of the Daimones Prodromoi patrolled the flanks. Naamah had already noticed that Derya Shafrid was leading his troops with a little more dash and energy than the role actually required. *It is amazing*, she thought, *what a man will do when he knows his beloved is watching.*

"This is much more comfortable than I had thought. Quite different from riding a horse."

"Highness, once used to travel on an elephant, a horse is a poor and tiring ride. See how easy the motion of Dilipa Ganesh is? His steps over the ground are so smooth that we might think we were sitting in our own homes. As long as we do not make him run, we can go further on a sack of food than any other animal."

"That's strange, I thought elephants were greedy."

The mahout laughed. "They are like children, Highness. They will eat everything they can find at once and overfill themselves then complain when they are hungry again. They will even cry when told they have eaten enough and must wait for their next meal for more. It is necessary to be stern with them for their own good and give them only the food they need."

"Get stern with such a great animal? Suppose you upset him?"

"I say again, they are like children, Highness. In their hearts they know we look after them and do what is needed for their own good. So they may be upset with us but it fades quickly and is forgiven. But I caution you, Highness, with all respect. Never make an enemy of an elephant for he will not forgive or forget. Once he is your enemy he will be so for life. You may not meet again for ten years but when you do he will remember and perhaps he will crush you in your tent that night."

"Who would want to make an enemy of such a great and noble animal?" Naamah looked at the elephant and swore it smiled and winked at her.

"None who desire to live, Highness. But do not be afraid for Dilipa Ganesh already is very fond of you and the other lady. I can tell this."

Naamah glanced behind her to where Igrat was sitting with the other members of the elephant crew. There were four soldiers on board, two armed with sarissas and two bowmen. Igrat was talking to them but her conversation was very different from the bawdy and suggestive tone she usually used when speaking with the rank and file of an Army. Instead her behavior was quiet, refined and modest. Intriguingly, she was being treated with elaborate courtesy and respect. Both attitudes were entirely suited to the fact that she was the wife of a senior officer speaking to men reporting to her husband.

Naamah was struck by the way the new personality had emerged when it was needed. She was well aware that there was a massive difference between Igrat's character and conduct when she was traveling with messages and when she was delivering those missives. She had also become aware that her almost-sisterly behavior as a member of the household was a separate character but Naamah had assumed that represented the real 'her'. The vicious wildcat she had been when they had first met was another character again. Now she had to ask herself, *which of any of these characters was the 'real Igrat'? Were any of them? Does Igrat even have a character of her own or is she always a reflection of what the situation around her demands if she is to survive?*

Naamah blinked for a second then returned her attention to the Mahout of her elephant. "I am sorry, I never asked your name."

"I am called Gopala, Highness."

"Well, Gopala, when we next rest, may I give Dilipa Ganesh an extra piece of fruit as a reward for his loyal service to his Majesty?"

"He would be most grateful for that, Highness." Naamah saw the smile of satisfaction on the mahout's face and realized that before she had met Igrat, she would never have thought to ask the man's name or whether she should give his elephant a piece of fruit. It wasn't just Igrat who had been changed by her arrival into their household.

Palace of Seleucus Nikator, Babylon, 315 BC

"He's gone. Everybody and everything has gone." If Hieronymus of Cardia had had the courage he would have been laughing at the frustrated expression on the face of Antigonus Monopthalmus. Both of the palaces belonging to Seleucus Nikator were empty, deserted stripped shells. The summer palace at Selucia-on-the-Tigris and the great formal palace here in Babylon had that in common. Whatever they had been once, they weren't it any more.

"Perhaps this is for the best. It spares me the duty of laying violent hands upon a man who has been my friend and trusted ally. By condemning himself to exile, Seleucus has surrendered his satrapy without struggle or danger. Let him live with Ptolemy in exile and be a burden on the resources of Egypt."

Well, that's new. Hieronymus wondered if Antigonus had finally begun to understand the damage to his reputation caused by his betrayal and execution of so many men who had trusted him. *Has the fact that he sits here in this empty shell of a palace alone finally sunk in on him?*

"Sire, the treasury is empty. Every gold coin has gone, every item of value vanished. All that is left is the gift that Seleucus promised you as being suitable for a king of your standing." The supervisor of the treasury of Antigonus was terrified at what he had to say next and Hieronymus wondered if his idea of a basket of elephant dung had been correct. "He leaves you a single mud brick of the worst and lowest quality with the invitation that you make it the foundation of your empire."

Oh that's good. Better even than the basket of dung. Hieronymus watched Antigonus carefully, waiting for the explosion of rage that he felt certain would come. But, the general just shook his head. Before he could make any reply, there was a major disturbance and a Macedonian officer entered the room with three Chaldean astrologers in tow.

"Noble Antigonus, I am Alcetas an officer whose heart had always been yours to command. These astrologers have words for you that I believe you should hear. I have heard their words and am troubled by them for these men are reputed to possess a great deal of experience and to make most exact observations of the stars."

Hieronymus watched Antigonus shake his head. It was well known that Antigonus despised prophecies of this kind and, on other occasions, had simply killed the astrologers who suggested that a course upon which he had decided was unwise. This time, though, he seemed to be genuinely interested in what they had to say. A wave of his hand gave the astrologers permission to start.

"Your Majesty, if you allow Seleucus escape from your hands, the consequence will be that all Asia would become subject to him and you yourself will lose his life in a battle against him. This is written clearly in the stars as is the alternative. Bring down Seleucus and send him to death now and you will reunify the empire and your name will exceed even that of the great Alexander in glory."

"Alcetas, what do you hope to gain by bringing this to my notice?"

"Only to serve you, Noble Majesty, in whatever capacity I can."

And if, One-Eye, you believe that, then your wits are addled and you should take up a more fitting profession. Such as linen-weaving. Hieronymus didn't know what was motivating Alcetas but he guessed it was little to do with any loyalties he felt. There was something very strange about the man. At first he seemed a typical Macedonian nobleman yet underneath it was an undercurrent that had the same repulsiveness as a poisonous snake moving through tall grass. It was very well hidden and perhaps only a skilled observer of human nature might have seen it but as a historian, Hieronymus was aware of it.

"Then we will put you to the test. You will take two regiments of cavalry and pursue Seleucus. Once you have caught up with him, you will slay all who are with him but bring him back here alive that he may answer the charges that should be brought against him."

Alcetas saluted and turned away, his face beaming with fulfillment. *Just what the devils is he up to? And has Antigonus realized that with 2,000 of his cavalry escorting the baggage train and now another 2,000 chasing Seleucus, almost half of the mobile part of his Army is out of his control.* Hieronymus had spent enough time with Eumenes to recognize a game being played and he was suddenly aware that neither Antigonus nor Alcetas were writing the rules.

Baggage Train, Army of Antigonus Monopthalmus, 315 BC

"Sire, another ten men deserted over night, taking their horses and weapons with them." Anatolios Metrophanes heard the report with something approaching despair. The number of cavalry at his disposal was shrinking steadily, mostly from desertion but also from arrows fired out of the darkness or cunning ambushes that would wipe out a small patrol of three or five horsemen before they could realize they were in danger. It was a fair bet that most of the deserters had already found their way into the ranks of the Seleucid cavalry. Antigonus might have occupied Babylon but Seleucid gold was out there somewhere and gold coin was dispensed with a liberal hand to the deserving. For every piece of gold in the treasury of Antigonus, Seleucus had ten or more.

"What of the civilians?"

"They continue to desert as well and the number of those doing so grows quickly. Word has already reached the others that those who abandon this baggage train and go home will pass unmolested. The sutlers may risk their own lives for profit but those of their wives and children?"

"Well, the more that desert, the fewer we will have to protect." Metrophanes understood what was happening all too well. The constant desertions and attrition were wearing down his numbers while the constant raiding meant they were wearing out their horses riding to each point of attack. Worse, the growing numbers of ambushes meant that he was having to keep his men together in ever-increasing groups. Fewer men in larger groups meant more and more of the baggage train was unguarded and it took longer to respond to each attack. The path that this would follow was all too obvious; it would not be long before the cavalry was spending all of its time defending itself and the baggage train would be open to looting.

He sighed and urged his horse over to where the hyspasists were gathered around the treasury wagons. That was when an important point struck him. Antigonus did not have one talent of gold for every ten owned by Seleucus; he had none. All his gold was here. Suddenly, Metrophanes realized that this baggage train wasn't a backwater command of no importance. It was the key to the whole invasion of the Babylonian Satrapy. If Antigonus lost this gold, he would have no money to pay his mercenaries and his great army would start to fall apart.

"Basilius Sophocles, how went your night?" Metrophanes called out to the commander of the hyspasists. The officer waved cheerily but when he arrived to speak to the cavalryman, his face was grim.

"More deserters slipped away overnight. We have to slow down, my men are exhausted from marching in the heat with their armor."

"We can't. There are raiders all around us. If we stop for a day we will never get moving again. the only thing that is preventing the raiders from assembling around us is our continued motion. And Antigonus waits for us in Babylon."

"Which is still many days march away." The treasury of Antigonus had made much of the journey to here by boat but that option was no longer available.

"Chiliarch, raiders! At the rear of the baggage train!"

That cursed cry. "More bandits?"

"No, Sire, Prodromoi. They are not striking and running but have seized the end of the baggage train and are putting it to fire and sword."

Metrophanes wheeled his horse again and set off with more than eighty cavalrymen around him. This was different, he could sense that the appearance of regular cavalry meant the battle against the baggage train had reached a new phase. Bandits, a more polite name might be auxiliaries but the truth was they were bandits, were one thing. Regular cavalry were another. Ahead of him, the rear of the baggage train had dissolved into chaos. Dozens of wagons were burning and the bodies of the camp followers were strewn all over the ground. He had hoped that his arrival would catch the looters by surprise but he had already been spotted and the enemy cavalry were forming up. Metrophanes saw his own cavalry had been dispersed by the ride down and were in no fit condition to make a charge – or withstand one.

The light cavalry ahead of him were supported by mounted bowmen and the arrow salvo reduced what little order there was in his formation to utter chaos. Outnumbered, dispersed and disorganized with men and horses already going down from arrows, there was no chance whatsoever of beating off the raid and precious little of surviving the attempt. Metrophanes had resigned himself to death while trying when he realized the arrow shower had stopped and the enemy cavalry had disengaged. They were pulling out, using the fire from the mounted bowmen as cover while they retreated with their loot. The raid was over.

It had, however, done enough damage to make Metrophanes wonder if this baggage train was every going to reach Babylon. A dozen or more horses were down, some with their riders pinned under them. The rest were winded and incapable of another charge. Above all, the fact that he had faced prodromoi supported by mounted bowmen sounded a note of doom. Bandits and raiders were one thing, they could create problems but they were soluble ones. If Seleucid regulars had joined the battle of the baggage train, they must believe they were getting near the endgame.

Alcetas's Column, In Pursuit of Seleucus Nikator

"They have at least a week's lead over us. That means they must be half way to Egypt by now."

"They have elephants. That means they can move thirty miles a day, no more than that. And they must stick to routes that have plenty of fodder for the horses as well. They are two hundred miles in front of us, three hundred at most. If we ride hard we can catch them in four or five days."

Alcetas was grimly determined to catch up with the escape party he knew had to be heading for Egypt. He had even obtained a good idea of the route they would be taking and knew that he could cut across some inhospitable areas that were denied to the elephants. Four days to catch them was ambitious but it was just possible. Five days was the most likely. Six at the outside."

"We'll kill the horses if we drive them like that."

"You think Antigonus will care about that if we bring Seleucus back? We can always get fresh horses but the opportunity to catch Seleucus and his treasure will not repeat itself. Now, we ride and if you can't drive the men to catch up, then I will find somebody who will.

Escape Party of Seleucus Nikator, Heading for Egypt, 315 BC

Naamah was holding a fresh apple and sensed Dilipa Ganesh watching her. His eyes were fixed on the apple and she could sense the message he was trying to convey. 'I am but a poor elephant, ill-fed by a cruel master. Please give me your apple so I may finish my day's work before I starve.' To Naamah's amazement, a tear trickled out from the corner of his eye. She reached out and offered the apple to him, feeling the incredible dexterity which he took it from her fingers with his trunk. Igrat was holding another apple and the elephant repeated the same trick with her.

They really are just like children. Naamah smiled as the elephant, finally convinced there was no more food to be cadged, ambled off to drink some water. *He hasn't realized that those two apples came from his mid-day feed.* She waved to Gopala and then continued to walk the cramps out of her legs. "If he was a beggar in the marketplace, that elephant would be too fat to move."

Igrat chuckled at the image. It had been a long time since she had begged for food in a marketplace but she could envisage the scene easily. "He'd have people lining up to buy fruit so they could give it to him. Don't tell Lillith that or she'd organize a business where people were paying to feed her elephant for her. Then she'd expand it to every marketplace in the kingdom."

"And find a way to evade paying the taxes on the income." The two women exchanged looks and laughed. Lillith's ability to squeeze money out of any situation was notorious.

Their rest was interrupted by a patrol of four horsemen riding in fast. They dismounted so hurriedly that one of them actually fell over when he got to the ground and rolled in the dirt before leaping to his feet. Then, they ran over to Derya Shafrid. Neither of the women could hear what they were saying but the response was instantaneous. The cavalry commander was suddenly the center of rings of activity as sub-commanders ran to their men and started the process of mounting up.

"This doesn't look good." Naamah's comment was dry but she didn't get a chance to elaborate further. One prodromoi ran up to them, already breathless. "Noble ladies, mount your elephants immediately. We must move on without delay."

"What's happening?" Naamah started to ask but the man was already running around the file of elephants to which he had been assigned.

"Don't argue, Nammie. Just do it." Igrat was unconsciously repeating Parmenio and was using his speech patterns in doing so. That made Naamah start for a moment but Gopala was already bringing Dilipa Ganesh over. The two were hauled up into the howdah by the animal's crew. By the time they had settled in, Dilipa Ganesh was already moving out of the shaded clump of trees where they had been resting and the box was forming up around them.

"What's happening?" Naamah repeated her question.

"The cavalry scouts reported a large body of cavalry to the east of us, riding hard this way, highnesses. Our Chiliarch believes that they are sent by Antigonus to detain us. Or worse. But, we have an advantage in that our horses are fresh and rested. To have caught up with us so quickly means they must have been pushing their mounts hard. Both horses and men will be tired beyond belief." The sarissaphoros returned to scanning the horizon, looking for threats. "See, highnesses, the cloud of dust on the horizon? That will be them. They are well behind us still but the harder we make it for them to catch us the better."

Naamah looked at the dust cloud, far off on the eastern horizon. "To catch us up, they must have known exactly where we were going. I wonder how they knew that?"

Baggage Train, Army of Antigonus Monopthalmus

"We can't go on like this." Basilius Sophocles looked at the scene of the ambush with something close to despair. More than thirty of his men were dead, at least two dozen more wounded. To make matters worse, they hadn't even seen the bowmen and slingers who had wrought havoc on the formation of hyspasists. The shower of heavy lead shots had come without warning, bringing down his men with crushed skulls and shattered limbs. Arrows had killed still more. By the time his men had organized themselves into some sort of formation, the worst of the ambush had been over and the attackers had already faded away.

Anatolios Metrophanes agreed. The fight at the head of the baggage train convoy had brought the entire column to a halt and it would be the devils own work to get it moving again. After a week of almost continuous ambushes and raids, his cavalry was down to less than half its original strength. The actual losses to combat and desertion were less than that and the deserters far outnumbered the killed and wounded. The problem was the horses. Too many of them had collapsed from exhaustion due to the constant riding backwards and forwards along the column of wagons. He could see that the battle here had pushed the hyspasists to the end of their endurance as well.

He looked around, measuring the terrain. The treasury wagons and the hyspasists were on a small rise, hardly deserving of being called a hill, but one that offered some command of the surrounding ground. The problem was that the broken rock fields that surrounded them offered all too much cover for an enemy. It was afternoon, though, and it looked most unlikely that he would find a more secure position by dusk. That left the task of getting what was left of the baggage train into cover. In truth, that was not as hard as it would have been a few days earlier. The number of sutlers and camp followers who had deserted far exceeded the cavalry and hyspasist losses. Also, there was water here. That was the deciding factor and Metrophanes made his decision.

"I agree. We must rest and gather our strength. We will bring the wagons in and surround this hill with them to form a perimeter. You must gather the treasury wagons in the middle to form a final redoubt. We will then garrison the walls we have made and make our stand."

"What about the civilians?" Sophocles knew what he wanted as an answer to that. *The civilians are just useless mouths who get in our way. Whatever this cavalryman might want to believe, this is our last stand.*

"If they wish to go, they can, but they leave the wagons." Even as he said the words, Metrophanes knew that he had made a terrible mistake. Word of his decision would ripple down the column and those at the rear would be leaving with their wagons before they could be stopped. He had just signed the death-warrant for the baggage train.

Headquarters, Army of Antigonus Monopthalmus, Babylon

"Now he's founded a city of his own, Cassandreia in Pallenê." Antigonus was bristling at the actions he saw as presumptious.

"He hasn't really founded a new city. He's just united several existing towns that were clustered closely in the peninsula with an existing city, Potidaea. He's populated the new areas with the Olynthians who survived the destruction of their city. Those were not few in number and now they are fanatical in their support for Cassander. Viewed objectively, it is a skilled move on his part. Since a great deal of land, and good land too, is included within the boundaries of Cassandreia, and since Cassander is very ambitious for the city's increase, it has the prospect of great future importance. The people there see themselves as much strengthened and enriched and have vowed to make great progress and become the strongest of the cities of Macedonia." Hieronymus looked up at Antigonus. "Cassander becomes more powerful daily."

"And the strength of Polyperchon and his son Alexander wanes in the same proportion." Antigonus wasn't very happy about that either. Despite their enmity a few years earlier, he had thrown his power and influence behind Polyperchon when it had seemed that the veteran general would crush Cassander. He realized that decision to recreate the alliance with Polyperchon had been strongly influenced by the years they had campaigned together under Alexander. What Antigonus didn't understand was why

Third Diodochi War

Cassander had committed himself so solidly to Seleucus and Ptolemy. That just didn't make sense at all. Now that Polyperchon was watching his position in Greece and Macedonia collapse, it appeared that the alliance between Seleucus, Ptolemy and Cassander was growing in power in the west just as quickly as Antigonus was watching his power growing in the east.

"We must take action to change this state of affairs." Antigonus was all tooa ware of how pompous that sounded. "Polyperchon is a lost cause?"

"Indeed so, your majesty." Hippostratus sounded positively oily. "He was under in Azorius but the death of Olympias caused him to despair of success in Macedonia. He fled from the city with a few followers. He joined up with Aeacides in Thessaly but the number of troops he gained by doing so was of no great account. The latest word is that he has withdrawn into Aetolia where he retains some level of popular support. He seems to believe that he can wait there in safety and observe the changes in the situation that might bring about a change in his fortunes."

"I doubt if Cassander will go along with that plan." Antigonus spoke drily. "There is only one army left in the whole of Greece and Macedonia that can oppose his will. That is under the command of Alexander, son of Polyperchon, and is currently holding the Peloponnesus. The area he controls is not great but it is strategically important and by being so must represent the last card in Polyperchon's hand. It is not hard to see what Cassander will do next. Destroying Alexander will leave Polyperchon neutralized and harmless. Our course is obvious, we must support Alexander with troops and coin. By keeping the son in play we repair the position of the father."

"Therein lies a problem." Orontobates had remained silent up to this point. "Our baggage train from Media has been under cosntant attack for a week or more now. We ave received a message from its commander but a few hours ago. They have been forced to halt not far from Cyaxares and move into a defensive position. They plead for assistance in escaping the trap that is closing in on them"

"Then mount a relief column from Cyaxares." Antigonus was enraged that he even had to say something so obvious. "Why should we worry about a baggage train anyway?"

"Your majesty, Cyaxares remains loyal to Seleucus. We would have to take the city before we could mount a relief column from it. And we must protect that baggage train for your treasury is within it. All sixty thousand talents of gold is there."

Antigonus took a moment to absorb what he had just been told, then he went slowly white as the implications of the situation sank in. *Without that gold I have no money to pay the mercenaries that are the backbone of my army. Yet Seleucus has all the gold he needs and more. Without that baggage train my army will desert and become his army. Only with the death of Seleucus will my position be secure. This is the meaning of the prophecy I was given. All depends on Alcetus killing Seleucus and us relieving the baggage train under siege at Cyaxares. There is nothing I can do now about the former but the latter is within my power.*

"Assemble the troops. Hippostratus, you will march on Cyaxares with thirty thousand men and relieve that baggage train."

The Open Tap Bar, Babylon

The bar looked like one of the better kind. Pharnabazus thought for a few seconds, weighing its virtues but the sight of the women lounging provocatively against the bar decided him. Babylon had been a great disappointment to him. He had expected it to be packed with entertainments for all tastes and stations in life but all he had seen were seedy dives suitable only for the rankers. This was the first bar he had found that looked fit for an officer's attention. *It really is most annoying. I've fought for five years to get here, first with Eumenes and now with Antigonus. I've survived the battles in Cappadocia, the siege of Nora, the Thapsacus, Paraitacene and Gabiene plus more than I can remember. And now, I can't even get a decent drink and an indecent woman. Perhaps Phoenix was right, I should have stayed in the barracks and got drunk there.*

He swept the curtain aside and entered. There was a sudden silence as he did so, then the noise of a busy evening in a bar returned but there was a subtly different tone to it. Before it had the normal sounds of boisterous entertainment, now it was the sounds of people trying to sound like they were part of a normal evening's boisterous entertainment. Pharnabazus slammed his coin on the bar. "Wine. The best you have."

He knew this night out was a mistake. If the flask of wine that had arrived was they had, then this was a really poor house. The stuff was barely better than vinegar. He forced a few gulps down, more to feel that he hadn't wasted his coin than a desire to drink the thin, sour brew. He paused and looked around with a conspicuous lack of interest. Everybody was studiously ignoring him.

"Buy a girl, a drink?" The woman's voice was as unattractive as the wine, equally thin, equally sour. She smelled bad even to somebody who had spent five years soldiering and had smelled the decay of a battlefield. She was heavy-set, her features coarse and lacking the refinement to be of expected of anybody but the lowest class of peasant.

"Here take it." He passed her the flask and watched her take a swig out of it without any obvious sign of disgust. Perhaps her ability to taste things has decayed along with the rest of her. *Still, that wine must have something to it. She's beginning to look a little less horrible.*

"If that was your best wine, what in the name of all the Gods must your worst be like?" Pharnabazus shuddered at the thought.

"The same. We only have the one." The man serving the wine was surly and his attitude oozed dislike for the Antigonid officer. That didn't worry Pharnabazus very much; he was feeling a little light-headed but he really didn't care whether they liked him or not. As long as they feared him.

"You want better wine? I know where there is some." The woman sounded bored as she started her customary pitch. "You can buy a flask or two there and we can share it."

Pharnabazus felt that his light-headedness had turned to dizziness but it really mattered very little to him. He followed the woman out of the bar and saw her turn down an alley that led off between two taller buildings. He stepped into it, the buildings cutting off the light from the full moon and the stars. That was when she tripped him.

He staggered and fell against the wall, suddenly realizing that he had fallen for the oldest trick in the book. Three men had emerged from the shadows and they were closing in on him fast. He tried to draw the long knife hidden under his cloak but the woman grabbed his arm and stopped him long enough for them to close in with their own knives. Pharnabazus felt a heavy blow to his stomach and the grinding cold of a stab wound there. He slid down against the wall, already aware of the smear of blood he had left behind him. The men were stabbing him over and over again, needlessly for he was already dying. The last thing he remembered was the attackers running away down the alley and the woman from the bar spitting on him.

Meeting Place, Babylon

"You left the money in his purse?"

"Of course. Those were the orders. Thirty copper coin."

The three men and one woman had gone to the meeting place after the attack. Word had spread around the Babylonian underworld that attacks on Antigonus's soldiers would be well-rewarded. It was nothing as definate as hiring people to carry them out. Just that those who did so would get coin in generous amounts. And they did. People knew Seleucus Nikator was a man who kept his word. The instructions were strange though, coin in the victim's purse was to be left untouched, its value to be added to the reward for the attack.

"He was an officer as well." The woman added the comment.

"That's very good. There'll be a bonus for that. Ten copper coin each for you, and eight each to replace the coin you left behind. Oh, we'll call it twenty coppers each."

"Thank you, sire." All four were more than grateful for the reward that amounted to much more than a usual night's work. They slunk off into the darkness, more than aware there were guards they couldn't see who were there to protect Seleucus's man.

Behind them, Callicrates made a note in his ledger. It had no names, no identities, just a list of coin paid out. Before Antigonus had arrived, Callicrates had been approached by agents of the king who had told him he was a known and trustworthy man. Gold coin had been lodged with him, enough to pay for the rewards made to those who stabbed Antigonid soldiers in the darkness. He'd been cautioned never to make promises he couldn't keep and ensure that every man and woman got at least the rewards they had been promised and more besides. If he had to use his own funds as a result, he should do so and they would be refunded. The campaign was already working. It was becoming rare to see a soldier out on his own. Now, they usually moved in pairs or more. Even so, they walked carefully, avoiding shadows and other dark places. The whole city was their enemy and they knew it. *The officer who had died this night was foolish indeed.*

Then Callicrates paused. *I wonder what happened to Igrat? Is she out there with a knife, bringing down unwary Antigonid soldiers? It's been a year or two since I saw her last. I hope she's safe.* He sighed again and folded up his ledger before leaving for the next rendezvous. Around him, the men in the dark watched and made sure he was protected from harm.

Escape Party of Seleucus Nikator, Heading for Egypt, 315 BC

The elephants had formed into a defensive square, packed closely together so that nobody could slip between them. The auxiliaries surrounded them to guard the great beasts from attacks by light infantry who might stab them in the belly or hamstring them. Outside the square, the Daimones Prodromoi Regiment was ready to attack the Antigonid heavy cavalry when it made its move. To the mahouts on the elephants, this was a familiar situation, one that previously had ended in them ceasing to serve the Eumenid Army and transferring to that of Seleucus. They assumed that if this day didn't go well, they would be changing armies again and fighting for Antigonus. After all, wars were wars and elephants were elephants.

Arrows were rattling off the chain mail that protected the howdahs on the elephant's backs. They were striking with remarkably little force. Many simply slid off the elephant's skin without even scratching it and the rest hardly did any greater damage. Semiramis watched them and sniffed in contempt. "The arrow shower. Their bowmen are firing as many arrows as they can without drawing their bows fully or even aiming properly. They think it will demoralize us and cause the elephants to panic. It'll work against inexperienced troops but against us? They're just wasting their arrows." Her voice only carried to the elephants on either side of hers but the message was relayed along the line. It steadied the elephant crews.

In front of the box, the armored, mounted bowmen of the Antigonid force were advancing slowly as they fired, their horses in little more than a slow walk. Even from the distance between them and the elephant line, it was easy to see that their horses were exhausted and had been ridden hard for days. In contrast, the Seleucid cavalry were well-rested and their horses were fresh. They'd moved into a carefully-chosen position before they broke into their charge. Although the Daimones Prodromoi had horse-archer detachments, Derya Shafrid had chosen not to use them. Instead, his men hurled javelins at the enemy horse, and then charged home with the sword. The Antigonid horse-archer line broke up in chaotic confusion and fled. Shafrid had his men well in hand and they let the surviving horse archers go. It was more important to conserve their horses' strength than to go chasing after a defeated enemy.

The arrow shower attack had been intended to break up the elephant formation and it was followed almost immediately by a heavy cavalry charge. The mass of armored men swarming over the ridge was awe-inspiring, a never-ending torrent that seemed to turn the whole hillside black. Semiramis wasn't impressed. She had noted the way the horses were moving and the raggedness of the formation. These men and horses were just as tired as the archers had been. The sarissaphoros and archers aboard the elephants were getting ready to withstand the charge. The sarissas were already lowered, forming a hedge of points ahead of the elephant line. The bowmen, aided by the height above the battlefield conferred by the elephants and the steadiness of their mounts gave them an advantage the Antigonid horse archers had lacked. There was no shower of low-powered arrows here; the archers drew their bows with the full weight of their bodies and their shots were carefully aimed. The arrows punched through the cataphract's armor and the horsemen started to go down.

"Shoot at the horses!" Semiramis was as good as her word. One of her arrows took a cavalry horse full in the chest and it tumbled down in a somersault, bring down the horse behind it. The cavalryman was trapped underneath the dying animal and was crushed as it threshed around. The elephant-archers saw the effect and took followed Semiramis's example and the horses started to go down, taking their riders with them and breaking up what little remained of their formation.

The combination of the deadly arrow fire, the hedge of spear points and the horse's fear of elephants meant the cavalry charge never struck home.

Despite the best efforts of the heavy cavalrymen, the horses veered away from the elephant square and went to one side or the other. Soon, the cataphracts were riding around the elephant square not through it. All the time, the arrows from the elephant archers were exacting their toll. The archers didn't have the deadly precision that Semiramis took for granted but they were good enough and the ground started to be littered with the bodies of horses and men. The charge had failed and the only question was when the Antigonid heavy cavalry would retreat.

They never got the chance. The Daimones Prodromoi had regrouped and their counter-charge took the Antigonid cataphracts in the rear. The heavy cavalry shattered with the blow. The unlucky ones were trapped between the Prodromoi and the elephant line, the lucky ones had a clear line of retreat and fled.

Headquarters, Antigonus's Intercept Force, Heading for Egypt, 315 BC

Alcetus watched the cavalry charge disintegrate with despair. The plan had been simple and workmanlike, the archers to disrupt the elephant square, the cataphracts to break it and slaughter everybody inside. He'd succeeded in catching up with Seleucus Nikator's party but breaking the group of 40 elephants and a thousand light cavalry was proving much harder than he had expected. His casualties were mounting steadily and he had nothing to show for it.

It was time to roll the dice again. He drove his horse forward and led his commanders down to intercept the retreating cataphracts. It took a major effort to halt their flight and turn them around but he managed it and in a few minutes he had a mixed group of cataphracts, horse-archers and lancers assembled. By this time, the surviving cataphracts down by the elephant square were in desperate straits and on the verge of surrender. Alcetus led his cavalry down to relieve them. With the Seleucid prodromoi fully involved in finishing up the fighting by the elephant square, he had a fleeting opportunity to trap them the way his heavy cavalry had been trapped. He intended to make full use of that chance.

On Dilipa Ganesh, Seleucus's Escape Party

Igrat had never felt so helpless in her life. Her skills with a knife were useless here. In fact, everything she depended on for her survival was useless in this battle. All she could do was watch while Naamah and Semiramis used their bows to pick off Antigonid cavalrymen while the two sarissaphoros used their spears to protect the elephant line. The sudden counter-charge by the Antigonid cavalry had changed the battle again. Now, it was the Seleucid prodromoi who were trapped between the two Antigonid forces. In this situation, their light armor and weapons put them at a grave disadvantage compared with the cataphracts that formed the bulk of their enemies. It was only the support from the elephant line that was allowing them to survive.

Igrat watched Derya Shafrid lead a counter-charge against a group of cataphracts who were about to cut down some of the prodromoi. The attack struck home but the details of the fight were lost in the swirling clouds of dust thrown up by the horses. She relaxed slightly as the Antigonid cataphracts broke and fled, then a little more as she saw her husband and his men ride clear of the fight. That was when her heart felt as if it had stopped completely. Derya Shafrid's head was down and another group of cataphracts was closing in on him and his companions. She watched in appalled disbelief as he slumped forward over his horse's neck and rolled to the ground.

"Gopala, we have to help him." Igrat's desperate scream cut through the noise of the battle that seemed to dominate everything else.

The Indian mahout said nothing but kicked Dilipa Ganesh behind the ears. The elephant started to move forward, breaking out of his usual leisurely walk into a strange gait that was still a walk but a very fast one which covered the ground remarkably quickly. Beside him, Vasu Pankaja, Krishna Ravi, Kumara Drupada, and Gopala Mahesha also broke away and joined their team mate in the charge. Igrat looked behind her. The elephant square was breaking up with the rows of elephants that formed its sides swinging around to join the charge into the mass of fighting cavalry.

By the time the elephant charge struck home, the forty beasts had formed into an echeloned arrowhead that plowed straight into the enemy cavalry. Dilipa Ganesh thrust his tusks into the side of one cataphract horse, the ivory slicing straight through the protective chain mail and sending the horse staggering sideways. Another elephant used its trunk to pluck an Antigonid rider from his horse and hurl him through the air. The elephants had changed, their gentle child-like disposition gone. They were screaming with rage, their trumpeting drowning out every other sound as they tore at their enemy. On their backs, the howdah crews were stabbing with their spears while the archers pumped out arrows at the targets surrounding them.

The horses couldn't stand it. Never very fond of elephants at the best of times and already exhausted from days of hard travel, they panicked and fled, taking their riders with them. They could outrun the elephants, that they knew and all they wanted was to get away from the huge, smelly, noisy creatures that had so suddenly turned savage. Within seconds of the elephants starting their charge, the battle was over. The Antigonid cavalry had been utterly routed and was fleeing. Behind them, the ground was scattered with the dead and wounded of both sides.

Dilipa Ganesh slowed down to a halt as the Seleucid forces gathered themselves back together. Several of the men were off their horses and gathered around their commander to protect him from any Antigonid stragglers. Naamah was already sliding of her elephant's back and running over to where he was laying. Igrat was only a few steps behind her.

"You, you and you, get the men together, collect our wounded. Gusoyn, Apollo, divide them out, those with minor wounds who can survive without immediate attention, those who have severe wounds that need to be treated now if they are to survive and those who cannot be saved." Naamah was rapping out orders without any question in her mind that they would be obeyed. Another figure was sliding off an elephant behind her. "You, get cloth for bandages."

"I hear and obey." Seleucus Nikator might have sounded droll but he was already at work as commanded.

Naamah recognized his voice. "My apologies, your Majesty, but every minute we work now will save lives."

"We must move soon." The deputy commander of the Daimones Prodromoi was worried the enemy might regroup and return while the Seleucid party was utterly disorganized. The unexpected elephant charge had won the battle for now but it could resume at any time. To his dismay, everybody completely ignored him.

"How is he?" Igrat's voice was agonized but she knew enough to keep out of Naamah's way when she was working on a patient.

"Bad. Very bad indeed. Arrow wound in the shoulder, lance wound in the small of the back." Her hands moved swiftly as she felt the bones. "His back isn't broken. It all depends on how much damage there is inside. There's things in there, if they start to bleed he's done. Cushion his head for me."

Igrat dropped to her knees and moved her husband's head so it was in her lap. One of the cavalrymen ran up. "Highness, we have the wounded divided as you commanded. Many have light wounds and are being bandaged by your friends and some will die regardless as you warned but three need your help now."

Naamah thought quickly. "Iggie, take over here. Keep pressure on this shoulder wound. It's in the same place you stabbed Apollo once but the gods only know how much damage is in there. The wound in the back isn't bleeding too badly. Lillith, help Iggie with that back wound. Just keep pressure on it. You've got to stop that bleeding before I can do anything else to help him."

Naamah ran off to where the critically wounded had been gathered. Igrat was weeping as she tried to keep her husband from bleeding out. "Why isn't she helping Derya?"

"Because if he is bleeding inside, he will die anyway. If we can stop the wounds bleeding outside, he may live. We can do that as well as she can and there are others who need her help more." Lillith had worked with Naamah in the aftermath of a battle before and knew what she was doing. That, she knew, didn't make it any easier for people who had to watch while their loved ones waited for care.

The men around them were looking confused at the way their wounded were being treated. Normally, the wounded got rough care from their comrades, not this kind of organized treatment. The deputy commander of the prodromoi decided it was time to try again. "Your Majesty, we must move on."

Seleucus Nikator, his arms full of cloth for bandages shook his head. "If we can save the lives of men who risked theirs for me, then we stay here until our healer says otherwise."

It seemed like hours before Naamah returned although in reality it was only a few minutes. "Lost one, the other two will make it. For a while anyway. Now, let's look at this."

She pulled the wadded cloth Igrat was holding over the shoulder wound away. "Bleeding here is stopping. Hold tight, we can uncork the wound now. Iggie, I couldn't do this before, he'd have bled out in seconds."

She broke the arrow shaft close to the skin, then gripped the arrowhead and pulled it through the shoulder. Once it was out, she looked at the points. "Normal barbs, clean and not poisoned. So far, so good." Her hands moved swiftly as she replaced the wadded cloth with bandages. "This wound must be kept clean and dry. That's your job from now on Iggie. Turn him over please."

Derya Shafrid had passed out when the arrow had been pulled from his shoulder. Naamah was grateful for that. Her hands moved again, probing the wound in his back and cleaning out the dirt that was caking it. Eventually she relaxed, wiping the blood off her hands on one of the rags Seleucus had brought. "The lance point didn't go deep. It went in a little then was deflected sideways, away from his backbone. That caused a big wound with much exposed muscle damage. That lance point was filthy and that is very bad. If the wounds don't get infected and if there is no internal damage I missed, then he'll live. Iggie, there's two big ifs there. You've got to look after him and keep these wounds clean while they heal. Look at the wounds often to see if there is any black or green showing. Smell them and tell me immediately if you even think there is decay. The wound will smell of rot before you can see any sign of it. Don't try and convince yourself you didn't smell anything bad. If we catch infection early, I can do something to stop it but if the wounds mortify and the rotting sickness starts, we must let him go.

There would be no kindness in doing otherwise. Do you understand all that?"

Igrat nodded, tears still streaming down her face. Quietly Naamah wondered if this was the first time if she had grieved for anybody other than herself. "He's bandaged, now I have to attend to anybody else who needs it. Anybody with untreated wounds, line up here to be washed and bandaged. Apollo, Gusoyn, there are a couple with leg wounds. Bring them over will you."

There was a good-natured jostling as each cavalryman tried to impress his friends with his courage and fortitude by pushing others forward to be treated by Naamah first. While she, Lillith and Semiramis washed and bandaged, one group of cavalrymen were standing to one side talking amongst themselves. By the time the wounded cavalrymen had been treated, their group had grown. Eventually, one of them walked over to where Naamah was sitting with her family.

"Highnesses, no noble ladies have ever worked for our wounded like this before. We wanted to thank you for all you have done for us. Also, for the way you led the elephant charge that saved our Epihipparch and the rest of us. We'd be honored if you permitted us to consider you as being part of our regiment."

"The honor is ours." Naamah was too tired to reply but Lillith did it for her.

"Thank you Highness." The cavalryman beamed with delight as he turned to the survivors of the regiment. "Hey, horse-lovers. We have some new Daimones joining us."

Baggage Train, Army of Antigonus Monopthalmus

The attacks were incessant, a continuous rain of arrows and lead shot from slingers. The civilians in the baggage carts suffered worst since they had little to protect them and lacked the skills to avoid at least a portion of the missiles. But, the soldiers were going down as well. One by one, a man here, another there. Every one of them reduced the ability of the remaining escort to guard the train. As Anatolios Metrophanes had feared, once the baggage train had stopped moving, it had proved impossible to get it started again. After a few hours, the casualties inflicted on the horses, mules and camels had meant there were not enough to move the carts. Even the cavalry were very short of mounts.

"We've got to give it up. We're running out of water. Another day and we'll be dying of thirst out here." Basilius Sophocles had tried to send parties out to gather water but they had not returned. *Had they deserted or been killed?* He didn't know the answer to the question he posed himself but was realist enough to admit that either was a possibility.

"Hippostratus marches to our relief with 30,000 men. That is more than Seleucus has in his entire army. They will be with us in the next day or two. All we have to do is hold out." Metrophanes sounded desperate and he knew it. Sophocles looked doubtful. He had heard the same thing for days now and the arrival of the relief force was always going to be in the next day or two. He was about to say something when there was a shout of warning from one of the look-outs.

"Riders approaching. Under a flag of truce."

Metrophanes looked out from between the wagons that had been upturned to form a defensible perimeter. A group of four prodromoi were approaching, leading a horse with a fifth man sitting on its back. The riders came close enough to be heard, then the leader shouted out a message that had a jeering note of confidence to it. "We found this man, we think he belongs to you. Listen to what he has to say for it may save your lives. When you have heard his words, if you wish to discuss terms, send out a flag of truce. You may place your trust in it for Seleucus Nikator keeps his word."

Dismounting was a polite word for what the prisoner did when told. 'Fell off his horse' would have been closer. He picked himself off, then ran for the baggage train stockade. Metrophanes could understand his distress, after all, it would not be unknown for a prisoner returned in such a manner to get an arrow in the back. But the four Prodromoi gave a cheerful wave to the besieged baggage train and returned to their own positions. *In a way, that's more demoralizing that killing him would have been.*

"Who are you?" Metrophanes had an unpleasant premonition of what the answer was likely to be.

"My name is Ampelius of Thebes. I was a sarissaphoros in the army of Antigonus Monopthalmus. I marched with Hippostratus to the relief of this convoy. Let me tell you the sad story of his march to Cyaxares."

Army of Hippostratus, Road to Cyaxares, five days earlier.

Ampelius regarded his career as a mercenary sarissaphoros as being an unwelcome diversion from his chosen life as a poet. It had always been his ambition to take up the pen laid down by his honored ancestor Pindar and fulfill his forefather's passionate faith in what men, by the grace of the gods, could achieve. But, Thebes had risen in revolt against Alexander and been destroyed for its temerity. All its people save only priests, the leaders of the pro-Macedonian party and descendants of Pindar were either killed or sold into slavery. And so it was that Ampelius, by the grace of his ancestor, would wield a sarissa rather than a pen and do so for pay rather than the inspiration of others.

"Form the Phalanx!"

The order echoed down the column, sending the sarissaphoros into their positions. The Hekatontarchès and Chiliarchs were ordering the ranks and extending the phalanx to the formation ordered by Hippostratus. Ampelius found himself being positioned five ranks back from the front and about a third of the way from the extreme right into the formation. The phalanx stretched along a ridgeline, a massed, powerful striking force that had few equals. The Seleucid Army had fewer men than this force and only a portion of them were infantry. Also, much of the Seleucid Army was besieging the baggage train five days march away. *Surely this mighty phalanx could sweep all before it?*

When the attack came, it was sudden and unexpected. A force of heavy cavalry swept out from between the hills and descended upon the right of the phalanx. There were at least two thousand of them, armored men on armored horses that disregarded the scattered flights of arrows from the few auxiliaries that were stationed on the right wing. There was a half-thousand of hypaspist infantry to protect the vulnerable flank of the Phalanx and that was it. Suddenly, Ampelius wished that the silver shields of the Argyraspides were there to fight off the cavalry but the Argyraspides were gone, their leaders foully murdered, the hypaspists either retired to their farms or sent to far-off places to be killed.

Lost in the mass of 25,000 sarissaphoros that were formed up into the phalanx, Ampelius saw little of what was going on at the flanks of the huge formation. What he could see was the Seleucid phalanx that was forming up in front of them. It had a front equal to the huge Antigonid phalanx but was much thinner. Two ranks for every five was his guess. He heard the swishing noise as their sarissas dropped to the horizontal position and for a brief second he wondered if they were going to surrender the way the Army of Eurydice had done. A quick look between the shoulders of the men in front of him eliminated that hope for the Seleucid phalanx was already advancing with sarissas levelled. *Ten thousand men attacking twenty five thousand? This is something new.*

There was a much louder swishing noise as the Antigonid phalanx dropped its sarissas to the horizontal. Or, the front ranks did. Ampelius was in the last rank to do so. Such was the depth of the formation that his sarissa only reached a bare arm's length in front of the foremost rank. The crash as the two phalanxes collided was awesome to hear and the clatter of the sarissa points engaging threatened to drown out all else. Behind him, the sarissas of the rear ranks angled upwards for there was little they could do at this point other than provide some protection against missiles for the men in front. Other than that, they were there merely to give weight to the formation and deter the forward ranks from breaking. Not that the sarissaphoros that were now engaged in the fighting had any real ability to do that. This was not a polite jousting with spear points between mercenaries intended simply to keep the generals happy. The Seleucid troops had come in meaning business and they were in a killing mood. The front rank of the Antigonid ranks had been badly mauled before they had realized that they were really fighting for their lives. Now that the point had been made, both sides were fighting hard but, as was the way of things, the fight between the two phalanxes was indecisive.

The lighter Seleucid phalanx was forced back, step by step, but it was a slow process and little seemed to be achieved by it. The Antigonid sarissaphoros made an unpleasant discover at this point. Even though they were advancing slowly, they were doing so over the bodies of the slain and that was enough to disturb their footing and degrade the solidity of their phalanx. Ampelius was so swept up in handling the unwieldy length of his sarissa while not tripping over the dead that it was a few minutes before he realized many of the ranks behind him had vanished.

Baggage Train, Army of Antigonus Monopthalmus

"While we were fighting the Seleucid Phalanx, their cataphracts and hypaspists had destroyed the right wing of our formation. While they were so doing, the prodromoi and auxiliaries had driven back the scattered forces on our left. Although we did not know it then, we were advancing into a deadly trap with the enemy moving to surround us. General Hippostratus saw what threatened and he took the rear ranks of his phalanx and managed to form another that defended our right. More troops from the phalanx were moved to protect our left. This took time of course and while it was being done we suffered grievously. Yet once it was done, and our forces formed a great U-shape, we lacked the strength and ability to advance further. We were in a strong position and were confident of repelling any attack upon us but in the enemy ranks, the trumpets sounded and they retired, leaving the field to us.

"So it was that we won the battle but at great cost. Few survived of the hypaspists on our right and the front ranks of our phalanx had suffered severely. Our auxiliaries were gone completely. Some were killed but others deserted to the Seleucids or simply ran from the battlefield. In total our losses were almost two thousand men of whom a thousand were troops of the most valuable kind. The Seleucid Army had lost barely two hundred. That night, their light cavalry raided our baggage train, killing and burning wherever they could. Many of the women, wives and camp followers, were taken and many more killed to the grief of those men who had survived the battle.

"When Hippostratus started the march the next day, his force was sorely changed. Now, he had barely enough men to form his phalanx since the hypaspists were dead and the auxiliaries deserted. The discontent of the soldiers and their fears for their families were such that he had been forced to detach a large force to protect the baggage train. So, when the Seleucid Army appeared again soon after dawn, he had little choice but to form the same U-shaped defensive position as he had ended the previous day in. So deployed, his ability to move was slight although the fighting was so light as to be barely worthy of the name. For all that, he advanced barely one mile instead of the twenty he had planned. And so it has been every day since. Hippostratus has advanced barely five miles since the first day the armies met and his supplies run low. I was one of ten men sent from my thousand to gather water. We were ambushed by prodromoi and I alone survived to tell you this tale of woe. Think not of relief from the Army of Hippostratus for it is hard put to do more than protect itself."

Metrophanes and Sophocles exchanged glances. If the story they had heard was true, then the baggage train was finished. Already short on food and water and under continuous attack, it was doomed unless relief could come from outside. The question was, though, whether the account they had heard was true. It could be a ruse to bring about the premature surrender of the baggage train and the loss of Antigonus's treasury. Sophocles put the doubts into words. "How do we confirm this?"

"I can take a few men and the remaining fit horses along the road. A few hours hard ride should see if the relief column is within reach or whether it has been forced to a stop."

Basilius Sophocles never lived to see the return of the scouting party. He was walking across the area held by his hypaspists when a lead shot hurled from a staff-sling hit the side of his head. His helmet gave his skull some protection but not enough and some veins inside his brain ruptured with the shock. A few minutes later, he felt dizzy and unable to remain on his feet. By the time he realized how seriously injured he had been, he was already dying.

With their officer gone, the discipline amongst the hypaspists collapsed. The sight of the elite infantry deserting in dozens and with both senior officers out of contact, what was left of morale in the baggage train vanished. The trickle of deserters became a solid stream with the civilians so panicked they even forgot about the gold of Antigonus now virtually unprotected in the middle of the camp. The Army of Seleucus Nikator ceased to be a deadly threat that hung over them and now became the one refuge left open.

By the time Metrophanes and his patrol returned, what was left of the baggage train was in chaos. If the sight of Hippostratus's forces on the horizon, hours ride and several days march away had not convinced him of the futility of the situation, the sight of the encircled baggage train dissolving before him did. His stay in the encampment was brief. He took the standard from the wagons that had once been guarded by the hypaspists, took it outside the improvised walls and threw it down.

Headquarters, Army of Seleucus Nikator, Bakhtiari

"We get our gold back?" Parmenio sounded as good-humored as he felt. The destruction of the baggage train had struck a critical blow against the Antigonid Army. Much more importantly, the 125 great wagons with 60,000 talents of gold on board had been captured intact. That was, of course, why Parmenio had instructed the gold be given to Antigonus. It had made his treasury far too valuable to be left behind while also weighing it down. Now, it had been taken and would be dispersed across the Seleucid Empire along with the rest of the Seleucid treasury, Without his war-chest, Antigonus Monopthalmus was incapable of maintaining his forces. Already he was learning that his writ did not run beyond the footsteps of that army and soon it would be gone when its pay fell into arrears.

"We're taking possession now." One of the cavalry officers was supervising the transfer of the sacks of gold from the existing wagons to Seleucid transport. There, it would go to fund the resistance that was engulfing the Seleucid countryside.

"Make sure you keep enough aside to pay our auxiliaries." The caution was more for effect than anything else.

Arkadios heard the exchange from the lines of men waiting payment for their services. He had been promised twenty coin in gold for his services as an auxiliary in the attack on the baggage train. He knew what would happen next. He would be offered a lesser amount, perhaps five gold or ten if he was lucky. It would be explained that there was less loot than expected, the expenses were greater and the excuses would go on for ever. He would shout and pound his fists on the table and make blood-curdling threats. In the end, he would strike a deal, getting less than he had been promised but more than he had been offered. It was the way things were done.

"Arkadios? There you are. You were offered twenty gold coin for your services?" The treasurer looked at the scroll with Arkadios's mark upon it.

"I am he and that was our agreement." Arkadios got ready for the bargaining.

"Here you are. Twenty coin in gold. And the thanks of Seleucus Nikator for your gallantry. Did you lose any of your men?'

Arkadios shook his head. "The gods smiled upon us. Will you be needing us again?" *To be paid in full without argument is a marvel without compare.*

"Brave men such as yourselves? Of course. Our agents will contact you soon. Same rates of course, more if it is to be a major battle. Timoteus? Over here please. You were promised twenty coin in gold." Again a pouch was handed over. "Did you lose any men?"

"One man killed."

"He had a wife and family I presume. Seleucus Nikator adds seven silver coin to give to them so that they will not starve." The treasurer looked at the bandit and his expression said the rest clearly *And make sure she gets it, we will check.* "Next."

Ampelius wandered around the camp, looking at the scene as the auxiliaries were paid off and the loot distributed. He presumed he was to be sold off as a slave but he was literate, a Greek and that meant he would probably get a good position as the administrator of one of the officer's family. A position where enough coin in transit would stick to his fingers for him to buy his freedom after a year or two. There were many worse things that could happen to a prisoner and he seemed to smell the stench of the Gabiene burning-pits. He and every other soldier he knew were convinced that the Gods had turned their faces from Antigonus Monopthalmus after that atrocity and that he was already doomed.

"Hey, you." The shout came from one of the factors who were organizing the sale of the prisoners. "Ampelius, here, now."

"I am Ampelius." *Here it comes, either I've already been bought by an officer or I'm up for auction.*

"You are from Thebes are you not?"

"I was, a descendent of Pindar the poet. But Thebes is no more. Burned by the great Alexander after it rose against him."

"Thebes lives again Ampelius. Our ally, the great general Cassander was told by the gods in a vision that it was his duty to rebuild the city and gather the survivors that it may regain its former greatness. Cassander marched against Alexander, son of Polyperchon and engaged him at the pass of Thermopylae. There he defeated him easily and drove Alexander's army of Aetolians back from Boeotia. It was then, after that victory, that Athena Alcidemus, the Goddess of Victory came to him in a dream and told him how grieved the gods were that Thebes no longer delighted them with its many songs and poems. She told Cassander that if he rebuilt the city, success would attend him and the kingdom of Macedonia would be his.

"This vision delighted the great Cassander for it foretold of his success and added to his renown. Summoning from all sides those of the Thebans who survived, he at once gained the permission of the Boeotians and then undertook to re-establish Thebes. The task pleasures him for he assumes that this is a most excellent opportunity to set up once more a city that had been widely known both for its achievements and for the myths that had been handed down about it. He also supposes that by this benevolent act he will acquire undying fame.

"And so it is that Cassander has started to rebuild the city for those of the Thebans who survived. In doing so he has drawn many of the Greek cities to share in the resettlement both because of their pity for the unfortunate and because of the glory of the city. The Athenians, for example, are rebuilding the greater part of the wall, and of the other Greeks, not alone from Greece itself but from Sicily and Italy as well, many have erected buildings to the extent of their ability, and others sent money for the pressing needs. In this way the Thebans have recovered their city. The great Cassander has asked of his allies only that if they find Thebans in their armies, or take them prisoner during the fighting with the foul murderer Antigonus, that they offer them the opportunity to return home with such aid and comfort as might be needful."

Ampelius could not believe that his fortunes had changed so much in so short a time. "How may I give thanks for this great kindness? And might I know your name so that I may thank you?"

"I am Attalus, once a sutler but now a factor for the Army of Seleucus Nikator. Come with me that I may give you silver for your journey back to Thebes and introduce you to some companions who are bound for the same destination."

CHAPTER TWO

A WAR OF ALLIANCES

Headquarters, Army of Antigonus Monopthalmus, Babylon, Summerset, 315BC

"All of it?" Antigonus was stunned by the disaster. "The whole train?"

"The Army of Seleucus Nikator fought us every step of the way to Cyaxares. By the time we reached the area, the train had been destroyed. Everything had either been taken or destroyed." Hippostratus took a deep breath for what he had to tell Antigonus would not fall well upon his ears. "Now we know why Seleucus has structured his army the way he has. In Greece, Macedonia and Asia Minor, the areas for campaigning are limited and infantry can march from one to the next with little delay. Out here, in the east, the distances are much greater and to get from one place to the next takes longer. Seleucus's Army is cavalry based and it is more mobile than ours. Not much so, for in truth cavalry do not advance that much faster than men on foot over a period of time. But there is a small difference and in short periods of time, a much greater one. That means Seleucus's forces can engage and disengage at will. We are like a bear fighting a pack of wolves."

Antigonus Monopthalmus felt an upswelling of rage at the comments but the sheer shock of losing his entire treasury had dispelled the hubris that had enveloped him after the Gabiene. With its evaporation, depression had flooded in and made him doubt himself and everything he perceived. One thing he did not doubt was the catastrophic situation he now faced. With his gold gone, he could not pay his army and it would evaporate. If he did not do something about that fast, he would be left sitting on his own in this deserted, stripped shell of a palace.

"There is something else we should consider." Leonnatus, commander of the Babylonian garrison and the Phalanx of the Army of Antigonus spoke gravely. "This city is slowly killing us. Every night we lose four or five men, stabbed in back-alleys, strangled in brothels or poisoned in bars. Our men dare not go out alone for to do so invites death."

"Thieves have always targeted soldiers for the coin in their pouches." Antigonus was still incapable of thinking beyond the stunning loss of his treasury.

"These are not thieves, your majesty. Oh some are and they steal what they can. But the majority leave the coin in the soldier's purses and befoul their bodies. They are killed because they are our soldiers, not because they carry coin and our men know it. Once they went in pairs, now groups of five or six are needed. Many refuse to leave their barracks. Instead they stay there, bored and mutinous. Our sickness rates rise quickly. Chancre and pox spread through our forces in an uncontrollable flood. Your Majesty, we have to get the army out of this city."

"If they don't get paid, they'll be gone soon enough." Antigonus realized that everything now depended on him securing enough gold to keep his army paid. "Very well, we achieve both ends at once. The Army will leave Babylon and march for Cilicia. There we can secure ten thousand talents of gold from the wealth they have in store. That will tide us over until the revenues from the provinces we now control are at our disposal. They will total eleven thousand talents and buy us yet more time."

"Your majesty, our cavalry is sorely depleted. We must hire more." Alcetas was nervous about drawing attention to himself after the fiasco of his attempt to stop Seleucus escaping.

"If we could afford it, we would. What we have now is what we must fight with. No more, no less."

"Cilicia ia part of Ptolemy's sphere of influence. When we march on them, he will treat it as a declaration of war." Hippostratus knew that the Seleucid Army was only a fraction of the size of the forces Ptolemy could put in the field.

"I know. We will send envoys to Ptolemy, Lysimachus, and Cassander, urging them to maintain their existing friendships with us and explain our actions on grounds of great strategic necessity. That also will buy us time."

A courtier entered the room with much deference and genuflection. "Your Majesty. Envoys have arrived from Ptolemy, Lysimachus, and Cassander."

"So much for buying time. Bid them enter."

The three men who entered the throne room were dusty from hard travelling. They made the customary courtesies but briefly, declining the refreshment that was offered to them. That alone, with its implication that food and drink from Antigonus was not to be trusted set the meeting off on a sour note. And so it was no surprise when the envoy from Ptolemy made the desires of the group very clear.

"Antigonus, since the murder of Eumenes, the massacre of the Argyraspides and now the displacement of Seleucus Nikator who was your faithful ally, your power in Syria and Asia Minor has grown to excessive proportions and breaches the Partition of Triparadisus. To restore that agreement, we must insist that Cappadocia and Lycia be given to Cassander, that Hellespontine Phrygia be awarded to Lysimachus, all Syria should be subject to Ptolemy, and Babylonia restored to Seleucus. Furthermore, the treasure seized after the battle of the Gabiene should be divided between those who took part in the battle. If you do none of these things, then the Partition of Triparadisus will no longer be of any significance and we will all join in waging war upon you.

Antigonus felt the hubris rising once more within him and his scream of anger echoed around the room. "Then make ready for war."

Headquarters, Army of Ptolemy, Damascus, Summerset 315 BC

Trumpets echoed backwards and forwards across the avenues leading up to the old palace of Damascus, blending with the cheers of the crowd and causing the clouds of rose petals to swirl in the air. The column of elephants made their way through the celebration, their eyes firmly fixed on the crowd in a sharp lookout for any food that they might persuade the people to give them. On their backs, the court of Seleucus Nikator basked in the attention. The cavalry was formed up behind the elephants, their armor freshly polished, their spearpoints gleaming and the black daimones-head painted on their shields striking awe into the spectators. Word had already spread of the exploits of the Daimones Regiment of prodromoi who had charged and defeated a force forty times their number at the Paraceitene and then defeated the legendary Argyraspides at the Gabiene. Word had also spread of their honor and chivalry when they had returned the women and children of the Argyraspides out of respect for the veteran warrior's courage and many victories. Now, they had escorted the court of Seleucus Nikator over 500 miles across hostile territory, defeating another force many times their number on the way. All so that Ptolemy Soter could be warned of the foul plot Antigonus Monopthalmus was planning against him.

On the backs of the elephants, Lillith, Naamah and Semiramis were returning the waves and salutes of the crowd. Igrat was not to be seen. Her husband was seriously ill, the wound on his back was infected and it was taking every last drop of Naamah's skill and Igrat's care to keep him alive. She had him shaded in the elephant's howdah, protected from the sun and the dust. So had it been every day since the battle on the way to Damascus.

Third Diodochi War

"Was it like this when you were last in Damascus?" Naamah returned a particularly enthusiastic burst of cheering. She knew Semiramis had made a triumphant entry to the city once before. The fact that the entry in question had been five hundred years earlier wasn't public knowledge.

"Of course. The entire population turned out to welcome my army. If they hadn't, we'd have killed them all."

Naamah shuddered slightly. She and Lillith had lived through the Assyrian occupation of the Canaanite lands and they both remembered well how the Assyrian Army had behaved. They'd been lucky, the Assyrian rulers were deeply superstitious and a few well-placed prophecies had worked wonders.

The elephants finished their parade through the street and started to form a long line in front of the reviewing stand. There, Ptolemy, Lysimachus, and Cassander were waiting. Ptolemy's ships controlled the seas and they were a highway that united the new alliance. Antigonus and his allies barely had a ship to their name and those they had were no match for the solidly-built and heavily-armed Egyptian warships. It was a sign of the growing wealth of Egypt under Ptolemy's rule that they were able to afford ships that had no purpose other than making war.

Seleucus Nikator dismounted from his elephant and addressed the reviewing stand. Ptolemy himself left the stand to embrace Seleucus and invite him to join the great alliance that was assembling to confront Antigonus. Seleucus mounted the stand and was embraced also by Lysimachus, and Cassander. Then he addressed the assembled people, bitterly accusing Antigonus of treachery, treason and lack of respect for the emmory of the great Alexander. He pointed out that that Antigonus had removed from their satrapies all who were men of rank and in particular those who had served under Alexander; as examples of this he mentioned the treacherous murder of Pithon, the removal of Peucestes from Persia and his own experiences. All of these men and many more besides, he said, had been guiltless of wrongdoing and had even performed great services out of friendship for Antigonus yet had been denied any reward for their displays of virtue and respecy for tradition. He reviewed also the magnitude of Antigonus' armed forces, his vast wealth, and his recent successes, and went on to intimate that in consequence he had become arrogant and had encompassed in his ambitious plans the entire kingdom of the Macedonians. Finally he ended by reminding all present of the terrible fate of the Argyraspides who had surrendered to him on agreed terms and in good faith yet had been condemned to a vile, lingering death.

The cheering of the Army and citizens of Damascus redoubled at the oration and the scenes of amity between Seleucus, Ptolemy, Lysimachus, and Cassander. The four had already gathered their forces and prepared stocks of arms, missiles, and the other needful things. If anybody had been in any doubt that the Third Diodochi War was starting, they weren't anymore.

Headquarters, Army of Ptolemy, Damascus, Harvesthome 315 BC

"We have news from Cassander." Seleucus Nikator had just received the news by conventional courier. He was beginning to realize the priceless advantages that had been brought by Igrat's ability to slip through the backwash of a war with inexplicable speed. Quite without any malice and with considerable personal regret he had already decided that if he was ever to be at war with forces commanded by Parmenio, finding and killing her would be his first priority. If that eventuality ever arose though, it lay far in the future. As it was, he sorely missed the extra time her abilities brought them. But, she was looking after her sorely-wounded husband and that duty took absolute priority for any wife.

"How fares our friend in Greece?" Ptolemy was the recognized leader of the alliance but the battle-plan to which they fought had been conceived by Parmenio. He had half the Army of Antigonus locked up in Seleucid cities, unable to go outside the walls for fear of the irregular forces that picked off any party smaller than a full thousand. The other half were heading for the Mediterranean coast, straight into the Army of Ptolemy. That Army was dug in at a series of fortresses. While Antigonus was being split asunder in Asia Minor, Cassander was finishing off the Antigonid allies in Greece. In truth, they were few in number for Cassander's rebuilding of Thebes funded by Seleucid gold had won him the hearts of the Greek people and they had flocked to him. Gold was winning this war, not troops although the armies would play their part soon enough.

"Cassander has taken the town of Megara and bypassed the Isthmus of Peloponnesus by transporting his army on barges. From there, he advanced upon Epidaurus and Argos, taking both cities with ease. The occupants of Epidaurus rallied to him, greeting him as a hero and cursing the name of Antigonus and Polyperchon. The Argives maintained their alliance with Alexander and Cassander dealt with them sternly until they were convinced to join him. The last two cities giving their loyalty to Polyperchon were Ithomê and Hermionis and Cassander gained those through negotiation. Despite these advances and the extent to which the people rallied to the cause of Cassander, Alexander refused to venture forth and engage him. So, Cassander has left a force of two thousand soldiers to keep him bottled up and has returned to Macedonia so that his conquests there may be completed."

"You know, we're well out of there." Seleucus rolled up the report scroll and helped himself to some wine. "Greece and Macedonia are impossible; a mass of conflicting interests only held together by a desire to inflict the same poisonous stew on everybody else. Cassander is going to come to grief in the long term. Parmenio believes that it'll take a few years but he'll fall foul of the place just like everybody else."

"In the meantime, Antigonus is going to have to move to support Polyperchon and Alexander or his value as an ally will be gone completely. That means he'll swing away from us and move towards Lysimachus up at the Hellespont. He'll come to grief there, that's bad territory for campaigning. Winter is closing in as well."

"Parmenio believes that Antigonus will winter at Malus in Cyinda before attempting to seize Syria and Phoenicia next year. He's going to split his army again, he has to. He's facing Parmenio himself in Babylonia, you here, Lysimachus in Cappadocia and me at sea. That 100,000 man army he was so proud of is evaporating while we watch."

Ptolemy took another glass of wine. "Antigonus is beginning to remind me of Prometheus, chained spreadeagled on a rock while birds come to eat his liver. I just wish we knew what was happening in Babylonia."

Parmenio's Household, Damascus, Syria, Harvesthome 315BC.

"Just stop whining and consider yourself lucky your spine wasn't broken." Naamah was sharp, decisive and pitiless. "The muscles in your back are permanently damaged, get used to the idea. Compared with what that lance point could have done, you got off lightly. Instead of giving thanks to the gods for your good fortune you wail like a woman. Be careful I do not get robes from Igrat's closet for you to wear. Now, start walking."

Derya Shafrid glared hatred at Naamah but she just raised an eyebrow in response. So, he groaned and started to haul himself along the bars Naamah had the carpenters build for him. His left leg was badly weakened by the damage to the great muscles of his back and he had lost much of the use of his arm. Exhausted by the effort needed to recover from the wounds and frustrated by his inability to resume command of his regiment, he'd been unwise enough to grumble that he'd have been better off dead. That had earned him an epic tounge-lashing from Naamah. One, he had to admit he'd deserved but her words and scorn seared him. He tried to get his mind off the pain in his wounded arm and leg by imagining what his father would have done if his mother had spoken to him like that. He'd probably have been struck dumb with shock. The image actually made him chuckle.

"That's better." Naamah was much quieter and more encouraging. "There's always something in life to laugh about if you look for it. I bet you never knew you'd enjoy your wife so much with her sitting on top did you?" She smiled as Shafrid's brilliant red flush confirmed her statement.

"She is neglecting her duties to our household and our king. She does not say so but I know it. Her father needs her and our war against Antigonus suffers as a result." Shafrid sounded more sulking than disappoving.

"Oh , so you are trying to get rid of me are you?" Igrat had entered the room while everybody else was distracted. "Let me guess, Nammie, he's being lazy again. You know why I had to get on top? When he tried, he fell off. Anyway, Derya, I've brought you a scroll from Seleucus. Of course, if you don't want to read it . . . "

Shafrid stepped forward to take it from her but he nearly lost his balance in the process. Igrat started to move forward to support him but Naamah grabbed her arm to stop her. She'd noticed that the lure of the scroll had resulted in Shafrid taking his first unsupported steps since the lance point had gouged into his back. It had taken Igrat a split second longer to catch on.

"Well, I am no longer prodromoi. I must hand command of the Daimones Regiment over to Aeschylus. In its place I am to command the elephants and to develop new tactics for their use. Apparently, Parmenio has heard of our elephant charge and it has convinced him more strongly than ever that the way we have been using our elephants is wrong. He says he sees the elephant as an offensive weapon, not just a mobile fortress and I am tasked with finding out how to do it. For this role, Seleucus has appointed me phrourarchs."

"Doesn't that mean a garrison commander?" Semiramis had arrived as soon as she'd heard a message had been received.

"Not really, no." Shafrid was reading the rest of the scroll. "It means the commander of a mobile or expeditionary force, independent of higher command. A garrison commander is a harmost and holds position for only one year. A phrourarchs may be a harmost but a harmost never a phrourarchs."

"What else, what else?" Semiramis was desperate to know details of the fighting she knew was going on in Babylonia.

"There is no news. We do not know what is happening back home. We must assume that our father is winning because he never does anything else but the details remain unknown."

The three women exchanged glances, noting how Shafrid had referred to Parmenio as 'our father'. That didn't make the lack of news any less frustrating. Igrat broke the silence. "I'll have to go to him and get word."

"No, you won't." Naamah was firm. "You were told to stay here and use your skills to aid Ptolemy and Seleucus. And now, to aid your husband. What sort of wife are you anyway, to speak of leaving for a long journey when your husband has just received a promotion and you haven't even celebrated it with him yet.

Igrat smiled ruefully, then put her weight on her left leg, her hands spread out from her waist and her head dipped. It was a surprisingly erotic pose and Shafrid took a step forward to embrace her. As he did, she stepped back, once then twice more. By the time he had managed to catch her, he had taken five complete, unsupported steps.

"There," said Naamah. ""You can do it. Properly encouraged."

Headquarters, Army of Seleucus Nikator, Babylonia, Winterset 314BC

"Europos has fallen." The messenger's triumphant words rang around the command post. With the fall of the fortress on the Euphrates, any hope of communications between the forces under Leonnatus in Babylon and Antigonus wintering in Malus had been cut. With it, so had Antigonus's prospects of getting support from any of the Babylonian regions. His invasion of Babylonia a year earlier had started the Third Diodoch War but now his gains from it seemed ephemeral at best.

"Sire, Seleucus Nikator is far away in Damascus. You are here and have won victory after victory over the Army of Antigonus. It would hearten the men greatly and serve us all well if you were to assume the throne in Babylonia. Leonnatus is under orders not to surrender the city to Seleucus on pain of death for him and all his line. But, Antigonus said nothing about him surrendering the city to you." Meleager had an odd smile on his face while he uttered the treasonous words.

Parmenio looked at him with a certain degree of disdain. "Our lord is Seleucus Nikator and you would do well to remember that. I serve him and my ambitions go no higher than to win battles in his service. As to surrendering Babylon, it serves us well to have the city in hostile hands at the moment. It drains what resources Leonnatus has available and keeps him pinned in place." *And if you had any intelligence at all, you might note that all those who have aspired to be anything more than a general have one thing in common. They are all dead. Simply winning battles for somebody else is good enough for me.* "I will assume your words were uttered in a momentary lapse resulting from our great victory today. They will not be forgiven again. Now leave me and consider how your prospects may be improved by a display of loyalty to our Satrap."

The map unscrolled on Parmenio's table showed the situation in Babylonia perfectly. Leonnatus had been appointed Satrap by Antigonus and left with 30,000 men to hold the area. Of those men, 10,000 had been held in Babylon itself and the rest distributed around key cities in the region. Now, all those cities were under siege. They were not a formal sieges; there were no great towers or giant rams battering at the walls. It was simply that any Antigonid soldiers who left the city never lived to return. *I made an error there.* Parmenio thought. *I assumed that we would have to pay all the irregulars we are using but it isn't working out like that. People are fighting our battle for us without pay, for the love of Seleucus. The pre-war investments in coin, time and kindly words have paid off better than we ever hoped.*

"Sire, Arkadios the bandit leader is here to speak with you."

"You mean, Arkadios, a leader of our irregulars and thus a valued ally?" Parmenio was genuinely angered by the messenger's reference. *In truth, Arkadios is a bandit leader but he serves our cause nobly and has fought well. Respect for those deserving of it costs nothing but pays dividends above counting.*

"Apologies, Sire. That is indeed what I meant."

"Then send him in. Without delay."

Arkadios entered the tent and looked around. That caused Parmenio to make a mental note to double the guards for the next few days. *Respect was one thing, failure to take reasonable precautions was quite another. Which brings me back to the problem of Meleager.* "Noble Sire, I bring words from people within Babylon. They say that the troops of Leonnatus are mutinous from want of food and their contempt at the hands of the people of the city. They also say that Leonnatus is preparing an expedition for those troops in an effort to forage for the supplies most needed."

"If the troops are in such sad condition, the fate of the ordinary people must be much worse?" That was a genuine concern to Parmenio though not for any sentimental reason. It was simply that the attrition caused by their actions was an important part of wearing down the garrison. If people were starving, they wouldn't be stabbing soldiers in back alleys.

"They run short and are in want yes. But not so much as the garrison. There are insufficient numbers of men to secure the walls of the city and of those that do, many are hungry enough to turn a blind eye to their duty in exchange for food. So brave men who love and honor our real Satrap smuggle supplies for the people into the city. And, fortunately there is much gold in the city to see that such men are well-rewarded for the dangers they face."

The message there was obvious. Those who gained Seleucid gold by killing Antigonid soldiers or by spreading chancre and pox amongst their ranks used that gold to buy smuggled food and thus survived in greater comfort. Others were aware of that and sought to earn some of that gold for themselves. And so, the resistance to the Antigonids spread. *And to think the gold we took from Antigonus is being used to fund the whole process. Well, make a contribution to funding it anyway.*

Arkadios seemed almost to read Parmenio's mind. "There are those who do not take gold for their loyalty. The women to whom Seleucus spoke comfort in time of their grief and gave coin to ease the loss of their men, now repay him by encouraging others to take up arms on his behalf and denying friendship to those who do not. And there are also those, who having been treated fairly and honestly, repay that trust. The upper citadel of Babylon has openly declared for Seleucus. They fly his banners and the men of Leonnatus do not dare contest it. Yet they ask nothing for their defiance other than to be recognized as true Seleucids."

Parmenio was honestly surprised by the words and the sincerity with which they had been delivered. *Gods, I think I've started something here that we might all live to regret.* "These words of loyalty and honor will be relayed to Seleucus himself. Have you been given aid for the families of your men who have lost their lives in the service of our lord?"

"I have, strategos, and I have added to it from my own pay." Arkadios had seen how the simple act of looking after the families of casualties had brought returns of loyalty and new recruits. So, he had indeed added to the Seleucid silver he had been given for them and seen the rewards bestowed upon him increased in proportion.

"Then, I thank you for the words and news you have brought. Your efforts to support our people in Babylon are most welcome and we will see you benefit from them."

Parmenio watched Arkadios leave and make his way out of the tent. *You may be a bandit leader, but I trust you a hell of a sight more than I do Meleager. That man needs to be very carefully watched.*

Headquarters, Army of Leonnatus, Babylon

"What do we do?" Leonnatus was in despair. Every option he considered led only to an impending disaster. Stay in Babylon without supplies and with every hand in the city turned against him and his army would be gone from deaths and desertion in a few months. Leave Babylon and its walls and his force would be engaged in battle. First by the irregulars who would wear him down, then by the Seleucid regulars who would finish him. If he pulled in all of his troops and concentrated them against the Seleucid Army, then all of the cities they occupied would rebel and he would control nothing outside the footprints of his own Army. If he dispersed his remaining troops out amongst those cities to reinforce their garrisons, they would be defeated in detail.

The worst thing was that every one of those options was already happening to him. He didn't really have a choice which would destroy him, he could only determine which would end his army first. There was something else that he was beginning to finally understand. This wasn't a war between his army and that of Seleucus. It wasn't like the battle between Antigonus and Eumenes where the two armies had fought without the civilians that surrounded them being involved. Here, his thirty thousand men were fighting an entire country. Every person, every single Seleucid was a potential ally, feeding supplies and information to their ruler. Somehow, Seleucus had found a way to mobilize his entire country for war. *The Seleucid Army fights amidst a sea of support that feeds and informs it. That same sea is drowning my troops.*

"There is a strategy that may buy us time." Phoenix of Tenedos had been studying the maps and he believed he had an option. At this point, anything that sounded like an option was more than welcome. "We abandon Babylon and fall back on Ecbatana. We do so by forced marches, leaving behind those who are too weak to maintain the pace. We can spread rumors that Seleucus and his men slaughter all those who fall out of the march to discourage stragglers. As we go, we roll up the garrisons in the other cities and consolidate them with our forces. Ecbatana is a small enough area for us to garrison properly, has a population too small to cause us the problems we face here and is rich enough to support us in comfort."

"You believe that we can march fast enough to make a successful retreat?" Leonnatus was doubtful but he remembered how Phoenix of Tenedos had established a reputation for forced marches.

"I do not know, General. It depends upon the terrain and the state of the men. All I do know is that our destruction is certain if we do not."

Headquarters, Army of Ptolemy, Damascus, Winter 313 BC

"The gastraphetes." Derya Shafrid was more than thoughtful.

"Useless." The reply was swift and uncompromising. The gastraphetes crossbow was a very powerful weapon, far more so than the usual bows, but it was awkward to use and slow-firing. Its power gave it great range but that was hardly significant in most battles where lines of sight were limited to ranges where the power of existing bows was adequate. So, the gastraphetes was a curiosity, an interesting machine but no more.

"But, suppose we mount it on the back of the elephants. The increased height will mean we can fire it over the heads of those below and we can actually use all that power. A bolt from a gastraphetes will transfix a man wearing even the heaviest armor at six hundred paces or more. The elephants can lift far more weight than we are giving them. Why not add a couple of gastraphetes to their equipment for killing heavy cavalry at long range? We could even use them to pick off officers or shoot holes in the phalanx."

Ptolemy Soter nodded and envisioned the results. Despite his initial words, he actually quite liked the gastraphetes and used it in the fortifications that his men threw up every time they stayed in one location for more than a day or so. Fortifications that were causing Antigonus unending grief. "If you're going to mount a crossbow on the back of an elephant, why not make it a bigger one? One that two men operate. That way you'll get some real range, and power that even another elephant may be wary of."

Shafrid thought about that and the possibilities inherent in a very powerful, two-man crossbow. "I will explore that, Majesty."

"Do so. Now, your wife has looked after you long enough and her services are needed again. Please send her in, I must speak with her in private."

Shafrid had long understood that Igrat had duties that put her in regular contact with the highest figures in the disintegrating hulk of the Alexandrine Empire. So it was with a certain level of pride that he ushered her in to Ptolemy's presence before taking his own leave.

"Igrat, the time has come for you to take messages to Parmenio in Babylonia. I have words for you to take with the official despatches. Parmenio needs to know that Antigonus has sent Agesilaüs to the kings in Cyprus, offering them support in an assault upon us. This is of no great concern to us for Antigonus has no naval power yet so his support is words only. Agesilaüs knows that and remains loyal to our cause. But, this will change. Antigonus has collected eight thousand wood cutters, sawyers, and shipwrights from all sides, and one thousand pairs of draught animals carry wood to three shipyards he has established at Tripolis, Byblus, and Sidon in Phoenicia and a fourth in Cilicia. He will have five hundred ships by the middle of the year. At that point, he will attempt to organize an alliance of the Aegean islands against us. As part of that effort, Antigonus has also sent Idomeneus and Moschion to Rhodes where they found that Nicocreon and the most powerful of the other kings there are already our allies and will not listen to his words.

"His own army has split with one part moving to Cappadocia in an effort to confront Lysimachus and Cassander. Finally he has sent Aristodemus of Miletus to the Peloponnesus with a thousand talents, instructing him to establish friendship with Alexander and Polyperchon and, after raising an adequate force of mercenaries, to carry on the war against Cassander."

Ptolemy looked at Igrat whose eyes were blank as she memorized the message. *Now lets see how she reacts to this.* "Finally, we have received a private message from Meleager accusing Parmenio the Younger of treason and treachery. He says that Parmenio has approached him privately with the idea of taking power in Babylon for himself. Seleucus Nikator is at sea with the fleet so this matter has fallen to me to act upon. You are to tell Parmenio of this plot against him, assure him that our faith in his loyalty is unwavering and that we will support whatever action he chooses to take against Meleager. Add that Meleager's life brings no benefit to anybody while his death carries no penalty. The same message, without the last comment, is going by standard courier but by sending it so, Meleager will know his plot has failed and he may take other action. You will get there first so Parmenio can strike before Meleager is warned."

Ptolemy watched life return to Igrat's eyes as she rose. Her voice was its normal, casual self. "Majesty, I must leave immediately. Parmenio is in the vicinity of Babylon?"

"We believe so. We don't know for communications with him are slow and unreliable. I believe he knows as little of what is happening here as we do of how his war progresses. This must change."

Front Line, Army of Antigonus, Siege of Tyre, Winter, 313AD

"We're ordered to try again." There was a distinct lack of enthusiasm in the tetrarchès voice as he passed the order. Technically, his command was of 32 men but now it had twenty. The rest lay dead in front of the walls of Tyre.

"What's the point?" Hyakinthos knew he had been lucky to survive this far and he didn't want to push his luck. Another charge at the walls of Tyre would be the perfect definition of pushing his luck. "There is no breach in the walls to admit us.

"Demetrius Poliorcetes has brought up a great battering ram that needs a thousand men to swing it and the siege tower Helepolis. This time we will break through the walls and overcome the city." Tetrarchès Draco was trying hard to put some enthusiasm into his voice but he was finding it very hard. Demetrius Poliorcetes might be the son of Antigonus and he might have captured some cities along the Cilician coast but everybody knew the gods had turned their faces from Antigonus and even if they hadn't, Seleucus Nikator had soon recovered the captured cities when he turned up with his fleet.

"And the ghosts of the Argyraspides man the walls of the city alongside the living defenders." Hyakinthos was deadly serious. "They have sworn that they will not find peace in death until Antigonus, all his line and all those who serve him have been burned alive just as they were. If we charge again, that fate awaits us."

There was an uneasy silence behind the palisades that protected the besiegers. All too many men remembered the dreadful screaming that had come from the pits where the Argyraspides leaders had been burned and the choking cloud of black smoke that seemed to hang around them for days afterwards. Since then, nothing seemed to have gone right. Every maneuver seemed to have failed, every enterprise had met with ill-fortune. Even the attempt to winter at Malus in Cyinda had been a failure. Constant raids from Ptolemy's fortified cities had disrupted the army's rest and forced them to campaign throughout the year. Even their pay was short and in arrears. The murmur of discontent was running through the army and every day it grew that little bit louder.

The murmuring discontent was silenced by the blast of trumpets as the order to begin the assault was wounded. Tetrarchès Draco left the protection of the palisades and, after a split-second of hesitation, his men followed him out. They were on the left of the assault, heading towards a section where the height of the city walls had been reduced. Further to the right, the great siege tower Helepolis was being hauled forward, men, elephants and horses pulling together in the struggle to get it up to the walls. To Hyakinthos, the siege tower was one of the wonders of the world. 120 feet tall and sixty wide, it had gained Demetrius the nickname Poliorcetes "The Beseiger". Now, it was being deployed against the walls of Tyre.

Ahead of Hyakinthos, one of the men in his file suddenly slumped to the ground. A crossbow bolt was sticking out of his chest where it had penetrated his armor and brought him down. Hyakinthos knew that the fire from the crossbows was only the start of the attrition the men on the walls would exact from those who dared to oppose them. The number of men falling to the crossbow bolts was small but it was still an ominous omen of what was to come. He also had a strong feeling that the generals who had ordered the charge had no real hope it would achieve anything. All that they would do is prevent the defenders concentrating on the sections of wall threatened by the Helepolis siege tower and the great battering ram that was already being edged up to the gates.

Running ahead of him were the small groups of men carrying siege ladders. Their job was to reach the walls and get the ladders up, allowing the men behind to climb to the crest and force their way into the defenses. It was those men who were drawing the bulk of the crossbow fire and their casualties were already grievous. The survivors reached the foot of the walls only to receive the next weapon the defenders on top had waiting. Cauldrons of liquid poured down in smoking streams, olive oil heated to boiling point. Those unlucky enough to be under the cascade screamed in untold agony as the boiling oil drenched them, seeping under their armor and saturating their clothes. *See, the ghosts of the Argyraspides are already starting to exact their revenge. Death from boiling oil is a terrible way to die.*

Other men were dying as rocks dropped from the battlements crushed them. For all the crossbow fire, rocks and even through the horror of the boiling oil, some of the men managed to swing their ladders up so that the top slammed against the battlements. The infantry following started to swarm up the ladders, only to be hurled back to the ground when the defenders pushed the ladders away or smashed them with more great rocks. Even so, a few men managed to gain the battlements and start exchanging blows with the defenders waiting for them. This was the critical part; if enough men could get up on top of the wall and hold a section long enough, others could follow them in the safe zone so created and their growing numbers would overwhelm the defense.

Hyakinthos was getting closer to the ladders now. Soon it would be his turn to try and climb up them and fight the defenders at the top. That was when he heard the appalled shouts along the line. "Helepolis burns! The great tower is burning!"

It shouldn't have been happening. The tower was coated with raw cowhide soaked with water to prevent the defenders from burning it. Yet, the cries were true. Hyakinthos chanced a look sideways and saw that the tower was well-alight, flames and smoke already pouring out of the firing ports cut in the sides. Around the base, the owners of the elephants and draft-horses were already trying to get their animals clear of the tower. If their beasts were trapped under the tower when it fell, their livelihoods would be lost and, quite likely, their lives. *How had the defenders set Helepolis on fire? Was it the ghosts of the Argyraspides striking yet another blow?*

Encouraged by the sight of the siege-tower burning and the carnage inflicted on the men below, the defenders of Tyre had redoubled their efforts. More oil was already well on the way to reaching boiling point and would soon be ready for pouring on the victims. The great ram had already started falling back, its men dispirited by the sight of doomed Helepolis and fearing the barrage of crossbow bolts and rocks that enveloped them. They also knew that the oil was waiting for them in greater quantities than had been seen to date. As they fell back, they drew the remainder of the attacking infantry with them. The cheers and taunts from the men on the walls surrounded them as the attackers scrambled backwards, seeking as much cover as they could from the crossbow bolts that once more were thudding out from the walls.

A few minutes later, they were back where they had started except that the twenty survivors of Draco's files had now dropped to fifteen. The men were sheltering behind the palisades, glorying in the protection they gave from the crossbows and the distance they had gained from the horror of the boiling oil. A Hekatontarchès came up and spoke with Draco, no doubt asking how many casualties had been taken during the failed attack. That was when one of the men called out, asking what had happened to the seige tower.

"The men on the walls threw pots filled with burning naphtha at the tower. Most hit the outside and did not damage but enough went inside to start fires. Helepolis was crowded with men waiting for the drawbridge to drop and the way to open for them to storm the walls. The press was so great the fires could not be fought properly and they took hold. By the time fighting them started, they were already established. Then panic took hold and men started to scream that the ghosts of the Argyraspides had entered the tower and were taking their revenge. There was a stampede to get out and more men died then than were consumed by the fires." The Hekatontarchès shook his head and carried on with his rounds.

"The men inside told the truth." Somebody spoke from the crowd, anonymity giving his voice courage. "It was the ghosts of the Argyraspides. They passed through the wood as if it were air and everywhere they went, the timber burst into flames."

"You see, we are all doomed." Hyakinthos spoke with a funereal timbre to his voice and the men around him nodded in agreement.

Headquarters of Demetrius Poliorcetes, Army of Antigonus Monopthalmus, Gaza, Spring 312 BC.

It had taken long enough but Gaza had finally fallen to the siege engines of Demetrius Poliorcetes. Once again, he had justified his nickname "The Besieger". The problem was that, as Demetrius was well aware, taking a city was one thing, holding it was quite another. With the fall of the city, Ptolemy had taken the field against the army of Demetrius. He was closing in with eighteen thousand foot and four thousand horse. Demetrius had received reports on that army but he wasn't quite sure what to make of them, According to his spies, some of Ptolemy's army were Macedonians and others were mercenaries from various places. However, the majority of Ptolemy's troops were Egyptians and nobody knew how well they would fight. All he did know was that they were well-armed and serviceable for battle. The spies had said something else, something that was highly significant. A thousand of Ptolemy's cavalry were Seleucus Nikator's Daimones Prodromoi regiment. That force had already established a fearsome reputation and many mentioned it in the same breath as the now-extinct Argyraspides.

Damn my father, the casual thought of the murdered Argyraspides had brought doubt to the mind of Demetrius. *Ever since he broke his word to them and slaughtered their leaders, nothing has gone right for us. Every soldier in our army is convinced their ghosts haunt us and will bring about their death by burning.*

Demetrius steadied himself and forced himself to think out the situation logically. Ptolemy had marched from Pelusium and camped outside Gaza. Demetrius had reinforced the garrison of the captured city with troops he had brought up from their winter quarters. Even so, he was still outnumbered. And he was facing both Ptolemy and Seleucus while his father was far away, trying to remedy the devastation wrought by the seaborne raids of Seleucus.

That was another thought that suddenly seized his mind. *My father is far away and presumably any curse that haunts him is equally far away. Although my friends urge me not to take the field against generals so great in renown commanding a superior force, the absence of my father gives me an opportunity. All the ill will that he has generated over the years as a general of long standing has caused every minor irritation to be combined in a single mass grievance. Every decision he has ever made is counted by the multitude against him. I am not my father, we have an opportunity here to start fresh. This may be the opportunity we need to turn this war around.*

The tent where his commanders were waiting was in front of him. Demetrius squared his shoulders and thrust his way inside, taking his position on the raised platform at one end. To his surprise, his arrival was the cause of an enthusiastic welcome with even veteran commanders shouting out praise and encouragement before the heralds called for silence. The tumult quickly ebbed away, leaving Demetrius to look at the officers gathered before him. That was when another thought wormed its way into his mind. *Since my father is already an old man, the hopes of the kingdom, center upon my succession to his throne. Are the Gods bringing me this command and the goodwill of the multitude so that I can repair the shame and dishonor he brought upon us?* He was also aware that many of those who gathered to hear him were not his senior commanders but others who wished to demonstrate their loyalty and respect for him.

And so, Demetrius Poliorcetes raised his hand and started to address those who waited on his words. "The critical struggle that we now face will be decisive. We will not just be fighting a more numerous force, but one commanded by generals who are counted amongst the greatest. Ptolemy and Seleucus took part with Alexander in all his wars and had often led armies independently on his behalf. As far as I know, they have never been defeated in the field. But, they represent the past, not the future and it is time that their ways were ended. Today, we will show them how their successors can fight. Be sure that all those whose actions are deserving will receive generous gifts and I will divide my share of the booty between all those who fight with me today.

"I appoint Athenaeus to command the Phalanx that will have 11,000 Sarissaphoros. Of these, two thousand are Macedonians,, one thousand are Lycians and Pamphylians, and eight thousand are mercenaries. They will be supported by thirteen elephants and a thousand auxiliaries. Our right will have 1,500 cavalry under the command of Andronicus. Andronicus, your task is vital. You will hold your line back at an angle and avoid fighting. I have read of the battles fought by Seleucus and in each case the outcome was decided by an unexpected cavalry charge. You will await that charge and then throw your forces at its flank. I will command our left where we will deploy one thousand cataphracts and two thousand prodromoi supported by thirty elephants. The elephants will advance with the cataphracts and We will crush the right flank of Ptolomy's army, roll up his phalanx and throw him into ignominious retreat."

That brought out another prolonged burst of cheering and Demetrius saw his army was much heartened by his words. So, it was in confident spirit that he left to command the left wing of his army. Yet, one worry still nagged him as his army deployed. *I hope I know what I am doing. I don't want my father to burn me alive.*

Center, Army of Ptolemy Soter, Gaza, Spring 312 BC

"The scouts were right Nik, he is loading his left wing. Really loading it, his right has barely fifteen hundred men. And all his infantry is concentrated in his phalanx. If he's got any reserves, I can't see them." Ptolemy Soter carefully stood on the back of the elephant Jaya Sushila to get the best view of the opposing army as he could. Beside him, Seleucus Nikator was doing the same on the back of Dilipa Ganesh. There were good reasons why neither commander was committing any of their elephants to this battle. One was that their sheer size gave commanders a major advantage when it came to managing a battle. That had already resulted in one hasty change to the battle plan; originally Ptolemy and Seleucus had intended to push hard with their left to crush the enemy right flank but their view of the battle and the reports of the scouts had resulted in a quick change of plan. Now, they were moving the balance of their army to the right to match the formation adopted by Demetrius. That had implications that were not lost on Ptolemy. If Demetrius moved fast, he could catch the Egyptian Army while it was still redeploying.

"I hope Parmenio the Younger was right about the Phalanx." Not that we can do much about it now even if he wasn't. The advice given by Parmenio to thin down the Phalanx to the bare minimum needed to deadlock the opposing Phalanx had run against the grain for Ptolemy. "But I don't have any choice. I'm strictly limited in the number of Greek and Macedonian sarissaphoros available to me and my Egyptians are not trained or equipped to form part of the Phalanx. That means I have but eight thousand men in my Phalanx, outnumbered two to one by Demetrius. On the other hand, those same Egyptians give me a lot of light and heavy infantry to act as skirmishers."

"With respect, your Majesties, I saw for myself at the Paraitacene and Gabiene how the oversized Phalanxes achieved little. Most of the men in them never fought at all. When the Phalanx collapsed due to being outflanked, there was little they could do but join the rout." Derya Shafrid remembered those battles well. It was what had happened after the Gabiene that he desperately wanted to forget. "As long as your eight thousand can hold the center, your Phalanx will have done its work.

Ptolemy nodded in acceptance. Off to his right, three thousand heavy cavalry and three thousand of his Egyptian infantry had formed up at last. Over on his left, the thousand men of the Daimones Prodromoi were drawn up, supported by three thousand more Egyptians. The balance of his Egyptians were spread out, supporting the Phalanx. Even so, to Ptolemy's eyes, his center looked desperately weak. He guessed that Demetrius had seen that as well for his center and left were already starting to move forward. "Good luck, Nik. May the Gods look after you."

With that salutation ringing in their ears, Seleucus Nikator and Derya Shafrid wheeled away and moved to take over the battle developing on the right flank.

Right Flank, Army of Ptolemy Soter, Gaza, Spring 312 BC

The sight of the 30 elephants advancing upon them was a terrifying one. Derya Shafrid understood now how the troops of Alcetas had been demoralized when the elephants had made their unanticipated charge against them. But, this charge had been anticipated. For almost eighteen months, Shafrid had been working with elephants and had developed a sophisticated understanding of their strengths and weaknesses. Some of his ideas were proving more difficult to realize than he'd expected. The two-man gastraphetes was a case in point. What had seemed a simple development had bogged down with the problems of finding materials strong enough to withstand the forces in the enlarged crossbow. But other ideas had proved much more practical.

In front of the right wing, Ptolomy's Egyptian infantry were laying out one of those ideas. Lengths of chain with sharp steel spikes at short intervals, the sets of four spikes being designed so that no matter how they fell, one of the spikes would point upwards. Once the chains had been laid, the infantry had dropped back and were preparing to meet the anticipated charge with bows and javelins.

Shafrid knew that would come later. The first move by Demetrius had been to send the heavy cavalry on his left in a sweeping maneuver aimed at enveloping Ptolemy's right. Seleucus had seen that move develop and had led two thousand of his own cataphracts in a counter-charge. The heavy cavalry of Demetrius had scattered the light auxiliaries and scouts that had been spread out in a picket line but the charge upon them by heavy cavalry drawn up in depth stopped their advance. He watched in frustration as the two masses of cavalry met head-on, at first fighting with spears and, when those shattered carrying on the fight with sword and shield. He forced himself to remain motionless, knowing that the arrow wound in his shoulder had left his shield arm too weak for proper use while the damage to his back prevented him riding well enough to save his life in the bitter fighting that was spreading across Ptolemy's right wing. Even though he understood why he could not join that battle, he held himself to be less of a man for his failure and he thanked the Gods that Igrat was not here to see him hold back from the fighting.

The butcher's bill was growing rapidly with many of the antagonists wounded and, as the fighting became locked in close combat, many were slain on each side. Demetrius and Seleucus were in the thick of the fighting, encouraging those under their command to fight stoutly and not hang back. In truth, their words were not necessary for the horsemen on both sides vied with each other in acts of bravery since their generals were sharing the struggle with them and could witness deeds of valor. Initially at least, the advantage was with the forces of Demetrius but the greater number of cataphracts in Ptolemy's force began to tell. Their heavy armor gave them a level of protection that the Prodromoi in Demetrius's force could not match and the balance swung against Demetrius. Then, with a great shout, the cavalry of Ptolemy Soter broke through and started to drive back their opponents.

With his plan to turn the right of Ptolemy's line foiled, Demetrius ordered his elephants to charge the remaining force in front of him, assuming that the sight of the great beasts advancing on the Egyptian infantry would cause them to break. Shafrid saw the elephants moving forward, urged on into the combat by their Indian mahouts, just as if no one were going to withstand them. Yet the Egyptians did not break. They may not have been sarissaphoros and may not have been entrusted with standing in the Phalanx, but they had been brought up with bow and javelin since childhood and with those weapons they were most skilled. As the elephants came within range, the javelin-men and archers opened fire on the elephants and at those who were mounted upon them.

That was when the spiked chains came into their own for on smooth and yielding ground the elephants possessed an irresistible might but Shafrid had found that the tenderness of their feet made them hard to use where the terrain was rough and difficult. Where their feet were vulnerable to injury, their strength became completely useless.

So it was that, when they came up to the barrier of spikes, the elephants found their feet were severely wounded and they refused to advance further. The mahouts tried to force them forward using their goads but, tormented by the wounds to their feet, the elephants became disorderly. Already, the Egyptian javelin-throwers and archers were sending their missiles in a continuous hail that started to bring down the mahouts themselves and the sarissaphoros who rode with them. Without their riders to control them, the elephants lost interest in the battle and started to wander off. With the surviving cataphracts from Ptolemy's left enveloping them and their mahouts shot down, the elephants decided that enough was enough and they quietly submitted to being captured. With that taking place, the left wing of Demetrius's Army, in which he had placed so much faith, was shattered.

Right Wing, Army of Demetrius Poliorcetes, Gaza.

By the time Demetrius has succeeded in extracting himself from the collapsing ruin of his left wing, he was aware that the battle was turning into a catastrophe. The only thing that was preventing his left from dissolving completely was the exhaustion of the heavy cavalry that had turned back his flanking move and the rest of Ptolemy's forces concentration on capturing the elephants. That, and that alone was buying him a little time to try and shore up his position. Once clear of the ruined left, he started to assess what remained of his Army.

The good news is my center is still holding. Ptolemy's Phalanx lacks the weight and strength to push mine back. I can take some of the troops from the rear ranks and use them to form a new left wing, angled back to protect the rear of my center force. My right is weak, but Ptolemy's is weaker. If I can start to advance there, I can turn this situation around. His Phalanx does not have the strength to face a threat from its flank.

Leaving orders for the rear ranks of his main Phalanx to detach and form a new Phalanx guarding the left, Demetrius rode to the right wing. While hoping that he could lead the cavalry there in a charge on a weak Ptolemaic left, he found that the situation was most unpropitious. Ptolemy's Egyptian light infantry was advancing forward into the gap left by Demetrius's right. The idea of holding those 1,500 cavalrymen back was no longer an option. Already, the Egyptians were moving to positions where their arrows and javelins were harassing the exposed flank of his main Phalanx. Demetrius realized that he had to drive that infantry back. The cavalry charge he had envisaged was now essential to stave off complete defeat, not win a victory.

At first it seemed to go well. The fifteen hundred prodromoi surged forward, catching the Egyptian infantry as they tried to close on the exposed flank of the Phalanx and sent them tumbling backwards with great loss. The charge quickly restored the front line and protected the flank of the Phalanx. Only, in doing so, they had become disorganized and would take a few minutes to reform.

Demetrius didn't have those minutes. Across the gap between the armies, he saw a regiment of over a thousand prodromoi already formed up in perfect order and starting to move forward. As they did, their shields were brought round to the fighting position and he could see they were bright yellow with the black Daimones head painted on them. The cry went up from his own men, "It's the Daimones Prodromoi."

Every man knew what that meant. They were facing an elite cavalry regiment, one that had won every battle it had ever fought and which had defeated even the legendary Argyraspides. They also had a demonstrated propensity for capturing baggage trains and destroying them utterly. With the prospect of their families being slaughtered and their possessions captured or destroyed, most of Demetrius' horsemen were panic-stricken and rushed into a frantic effort to get back and protect their baggage train.

Seeing both their left and right flanks disintegrate, the great Phalanx that formed the center of the Army of Demetrius started to break up as well. It was the men being redeployed from the rear that ran first. Being out of the tight-packed files and being able to see the unfolding disaster on their flanks, they threw down their sarissas and started to melt away. As those near them saw this, they did the same. Demetrius's Phalanx dissolved as completely and as quickly as a piece of salt dropped into fresh water. Demetrius himself was left with a few companions and then, since no one heeded him when he begged them each to stand and not desert him, was forced to leave the field with the rest.

Right Flank, Army of Ptolemy Soter, Gaza, Spring 312 BC

There were benefits to being an elite, named regiment. For a cavalry outfit, those benefits included the best horses that the Army quartermasters could find. As groups of remounts were brought in, the Daimones Prodromoi got to inspect them and pick the best for their own use. The horses themselves understood that they were a picked elite and it showed in their bearing and demeanor.

Aeschylus, successor to Derya Shafrid as commander of the Daimones Prodromoi, felt his own mount surging forward under him as the regiment closed on the enemy in front of them. Yet, even picked men on picked horses, convinced that they were about to add yet further luster to their reputation by inflicting another crushing defeat could not close on the enemy quickly enough. The cavalry of Demetrius had broken and started to run long before the charge of the Daimones Prodromoi could strike home. What should have been a mighty blow as the charge plowed into the enemy turned into a frantic pursuit as the Daimones Parodromoi tried to bring down the fleeing cavalry.

At first, Aeschylus could see that the cavalry of Demetrius was at least remaining in formation, not so much in obedience to their orders but from the sure and certain knowledge that any man who broke formation would be pursued and brought down by a lance-point in the back. Also, the battlefield was open and yielding, and favorable to men who wished to withdraw in formation. Aeschylus knew it would be different where the phalanx was collapsing. There, men would be dying in chaos as the infantry and cavalry tore into them. The only hope defeated men there had was to throw down their arms and surrender. That, at least would be respected for all knew that Ptolemy and Seleucus were honorable men who would keep every promise they made.

The city of Gaza was in front of them and that was when Aeschylus saw a sight that amazed him. The Army of Demetrius had left its baggage trains under the protection of the walls of the city. As the retreating army reached those trains, their formation was dissolving with some of the cavalrymen trying to find their own pack mules and women. Others were trying to enter the city, presumably to do the same for their families inside. As a result, the scene outside the open City gates was complete chaos with a large number of pack animals were gathered together and each man trying to lead out his own beasts first. Incredibly, Aeschylus could see fights starting over disputed ownership of the pack animals. It came to him in a flash that there was so such confusion around the gates that nobody could possibly close them in time. All now counted on dash and gallantry.

The Daimones Prodromoi swept up to the chaotic scene at the gates. At their head, Aeschylus saw a single cart blocking the way through. His horse was tiring from the prolonged gallop and had already given more than any horse could be asked yet he urged it forward and the noble beast responded gallantly. He felt the massive thrust of its hind legs as it jumped the cart and landed the other side, barely interrupting its stride as it did so. He was through the gates and inside the city with his regiment pouring through after him.

Outside the gates, the Army of Demetrius was frantically throwing down its weapons and surrendering. Aeschylus slowed his horse to a canter and reined in beside the city bouleuterion. He had a surrender to arrange.

Third Diodochi War

Center, Army of Ptolemy Soter, Gaza, Spring 312 BC

Ptolemy looked around at the scene. Wounded men were being brought in by their friends and comrades and being treated for their injuries. There was a quick division going on. Men with slight wounds were being given to the camp women who would wash their injuries and bandage them. Some others were being taken to one side, in the shade of the tents and given wine to drink and comfortable bedding to rest on. They were the ones whose wounds were so severe that they could not live. The remainder, the ones who needed treatment now if they were to live, were being taken to an area where skilled healer could do their best for them. Ptolemy saw a flash of red hair as one of the women working there started to tend the wounds of a sorely-injured cataphract.

"Yes, even the most noble of our ladies work for our wounded after a battle. Sometimes I think that when a man sees the wife of a general kneeling in the dirt to treat his wounds, it does him as much good as the treatment itself." Seleucus was looking at the scene with pride. *Quite apart from anything else, the men fight much harder when they know that every effort will be made by everybody, high-born or low, to treat their wounds. Ptolemy has followed our example and brought skilled doctors from Egypt to help with the wounded. And so word spreads and we get the pick of the best recruits.*

Seleucus's musing was interrupted by a prodromoi riding in on an exhausted and near-foundering horse. His eyes took in the bright yellow shield and black daimones head as the rider slid off the horse and bowed before Ptolemy and Seleucus. "Majesties, I bring you news from Aeschylus, commander of the Daimones Prodromoi. We have taken the city of Gaza and secured the surrender of all within it including eight thousand of the soldiers of Demetrius. Aeschylus has given his word that the city shall remain unsacked and that the baggage train of Demetrius will be ransomed for twenty coins in a hundred of its value. By offering these terms, the surrender was won without fighting or the loss of a man."

"That is acceptable." Ptolemy thought for a second. "You mean a regiment of light cavalry took a walled city without losing a man?"

"That is so, your Majesty."

Ptolemy nodded, very respectfully. "That's rare."

CHAPTER THREE

A WAR OF TREACHERY

Army of Leonnatus, Babylon, Springset, 312BC

It was commonplace to hear the population cheering when an army entered a city. The people would pretend to welcome their arrival in an effort to protect themselves from being plundered and looted. Sometimes it worked, mostly it didn't. When an army entered a city, decent women hid from their view in an effort to protect themselves from rape. Sometimes it worked, mostly it didn't. The sounds that surrounded the Army of Leonnatus as their ranks marched through the streets of Babylon were quite different. They were genuine cheers of delight and victory and the strange whooping noise of exhilaration that women made at times of triumph. Only, the Army was leaving the city, not entering it. And the sounds were those of a crowd that had driven a hated invader out.

Hatred. Riding a horse and wearing his gilded armor, Leonnatus found it hard to understand why it was that he and his army were so openly despised. *We behaved as well as any other army when we were in the city. We did not pillage and burn and the amount of rape and looting were no more than any other large group of armed young men in a city of civilians would commit. Yet the whole city turned against us.*

All around him, the banners of Seleucus were flying openly and the cheers of triumph from the crowd redoubled every time a new one broke out. Even those few businesses and households who had shown favor to the invaders were flying the banner of Seleucus now. In fact, they were the most enthusiastic of all in doing so. Leonnatus knew why. The crowds were cheering his departure now, but when he was gone they would turn upon those they regarded as traitors. There would be pillaging, burning, rape and murder tonight and the victims would be those who had been a little too indiscrete with their support of Antigonus. He guessed that the agents of Seleucus Nikator who had masterminded the resistance of the city would protect some of those they regarded as traitors, simply to prevent the attacks on them turn into city-wide looting. But, they would protect the less-guilty by throwing those whose pro-Antigonus opinions had been most obvious to the crowd.

That was when a clod of dung hit Leonnatus full in the face. For a second, in pure blinded fury, he nearly turned his horse on those responsible but he managed to control himself just in time. If he had done so, the men behind would have followed him and the fighting would have become general. With his men strung out in fours through the narrow street and their sarissas split in two for travelling, his army would have been massacred. *That is quite possibly what the organizers of the crowd had hoped would happen. Well, we can disappoint them there, anyway.* "Pass the word, the tetrarchès are to keep control of their ranks. Do not break formation no matter what the provocation."

The dung clear of his eyes, Leonnatus looked around and picked out the person who had thrown it at him. It was a woman, her clothes and demeanor that of a noble lady of the highest class. A woman who would not even have been on the street normally, let alone screaming obscene taunts at the soldiers. He watched her scoop up another handful of dung and throw it at the soldiers. Other women had joined her in doing so and the city street-children saw an exciting new game starting and began to throw mud and dung as well. Leonnatus knew it would not be long before the soft mud and foul-smelling but harmless dung would be joined by stones and rocks. His army would be well-advised to have left the city before the stones and rocks were joined by arrows and javelins.

The shadow of the great gate fell across him and then the city of Babylon was behind. It was only the sun returning after the arch of the gate was left behind but Leonnatus felt and overwhelming sense of relief as if a shadow had been lifted from his soul. He turned to Phoenix of Tenedos, noting the bruise on the man's face where a rock had struck home. "We are well out of that city."

Phoenix nodded, then paused for thought. "Just what, in the name of all the gods, happened to us in there?"

Headquarters, Army of Seleucus Nikator, Babylonia, Springset 312BC

"Strategos, with respect, I must warn you that there is a plot brewing amongst disloyal officers of the Army. A group of those whose ambition exceeds that appropriate for their rank foment discord in the Army and lay plans to assume power here in Babylon. They scheme against you and seek to have you removed from command."

Parmenio looked at the young officer doubtfully. "Do you have any idea who is the ringleader of this plan."

"I believe it is Meleager, Strategos."

Well, it seems that Meleager has approached at least a dozen officers with his mad scheme of whom ten have reported his subversion while two threw him out so hard he bounced. Of course, we don't know how many he has approached who have not thrown him out or reported his approaches. The prospect of a satrapy of one's own is a heady vision.

"This may very well be so." Parmenio appeared to be thinking deeply. "You have acted wisely. The prospects of an officer whose loyalty to our lord Seleucus Nikator has been so clearly demonstrated are great indeed. If indeed Meleager is indeed conspiring against Seleucus then the peril that attends him is equally great. Have you made your refusal to join Meleager public?"

"No, Strategos."

"Then, keep your feelings to yourself and go along with his plans. Identify any other conspirators you may find and report them to me."

The young officer saluted and left. Parmenio leaned back in his seat and allowed himself a grin. *That means Meleager now has ten informants at least surrounding him. He should have realized that a man who changes sides seven times in eight years will have great difficulty in inspiring loyalty from others.*

With that satisfying thought, Parmenio looked at the maps in front of him. Leonnatus and Phoenix were falling back on Ecbatana by way of forced marches. The Seleucid light cavalry was keeping in contact with him but there was little point in exhausting the main body of the army chasing a foe determined to march itself to death while trying to escape. The truth was that Antigonus had made the classic mistake of trying to accomplish everything and had so spread out his efforts that he could concentrate overwhelming strength at no point of any significance. *A large army has limitations all of its own, one of them being that it tempts its commanders into overstretching that force. That's what Antigonus has done and now he is paying for it.*

He continued staring at the map until a rustle by the tent flap broke his attention. What really did distract him though were the contralto words that followed. "Hello, father."

Igrat was standing by the tent entry, smiling broadly. It had been almost a year since Parmenio had seen her and, for a moment, he thought he was seeing things. "Iggie, how did you manage to get here?"

"Usual way although I'm a bit out of practice. Finding you was harder than getting here. I left Damascus three months ago, although it helped when word that Babylon had been liberated spread. Father, I have important words for you." Igrat closed her eyes and started to repeat Ptolemy's message concerning Meleager's treason. Listening to her, Parmenio could hear

Ptolemy speaking with her voice. When she had finished, Parmenio was nodding slowly.

"We're pretty well up on what Meleager has been planning although we didn't pick up on the message to Ptolemy and Seleucus. I'll have to find out what went wrong there. In some ways, it's a pity this little game is ending so early. Meleager was acting as a magnet drawing out any disloyal elements in the army. But, we'll make an example of him and that'll put a stop to any mutinous thoughts people might have. Not that there are many, we've won every major battle we've fought and we're taking city after city. The soldiers like being popular and welcomed as heroes by people and they've noted how loyal the civilians are to Seleucus. That's had an effect on their behavior when they enter the towns that fall. They treat the civilians there as their allies, not a crop to be harvested. We've had some disciplinary problems but far, far less than normal. Now, important things, how is the family."

Igrat relaxed slightly. The content of the verbal message she'd been carrying had distressed her and she'd spent the weeks in transit worrying over whether she'd get it to Parmenio in time. Now she knew he already had the matter under control, things seemed better. "The family is well and prospers. The escape went as planned except that Derya was badly wounded. He has spent many months recovering and is no longer able to command light cavalry. Instead, the Daimones Regiment is commanded by Aeschylus who is as loyal to us as Derya. My husband is now playing with the elephants, trying to find better ways to use them."

"Tell me about that elephant charge."

Igrat told how the elephants had formed up and charged. "It was really strange. You know how gentle and passive elephants are? Well, when they charged, they turned savage. There was one enemy cavalryman laying on the ground and an elephant stamped on him so hard the blood sprayed from his body for yards around. They drove their tusks into the horses and threw the riders through the air. It was as much as we could do to stop them attacking our own people as well. The enemy horses saw what was happening and fled rather than stand against the elephants. Derya believes that if we mount crossbows on the elephants there will be few that can stand against them. He is working on a two-man version of the gastraphetes that will be able to shoot up a phalanx from a distance.

"Otherwise, Lillith is still at work making money for us all. There were big sieges going on at three cities, Joppa, Gaza and Tyre. As a result there is a heavy demand for olive oil to be boiled and poured on the attackers. Lillith's doing well trading in olive oil. Gaza has fallen, Ptolemy thinks that Tyre will fall but Joppa will hold out."

"He's right there. And how is our Lord Seleucus?"

"Playing boats." Igrat grinned at her father and her voice slipped back into the tones and cadences of Ptolemy. "Antigonus built a shipyard at Tripolis in Phoenicia. As soon as it was completed and the first ships laid down, Seleucus arrived with a hundred Egyptian warships that were royally equipped and sailed excellently. He sailed contemptuously right into the shipyard, unloading our troops into their camps. Then, his force burned the shipyard to the ground and killed men from cities who were co-operating with Antigonus. Once the shipyard and the new ships were destroyed, he plundered the lands of those who declared friendship for Antigonus. When all was ruin, the men boarded the ships again and sailed away. Now, those in the remaining shipyards wait in fear for the same thing to happen to them."

"That's a real problem for old One-Eye. The Egyptian ships can concentrate and strike anywhere without warning. So, if Antigonus spreads his troops out to defend everywhere that might be attacked, he'll be overwhelmed where we concentrate. If he concentrates on defending a few points, we can strike where he isn't and make it look as if he is defenseless against us. And if the island alliance we have planned works as well as we hope, we'll have the eastern Mediterranean in our pockets."

"Antigonus claims he will take the sea with five hundred vessels by this time next year."

"I doubt it. I don't think he really understands what's involved. He may build five hundred hulls but getting them to sea will be another matter. If the Aegean campaign goes well, he just won't have enough sailors to provide them with crews."

"And it does go well. He sent Agesilaüs to Cyprus to conclude an alliance with Nicocreon only to find that all the most powerful of the island kings had declared for us. The kings of Cition, Lapithus, Marion, and Ceryneia did concluded a treaty of friendship with Antigonus and promptly got attacked by our allies supported by Seleucus and his fleet. They're going down one by one. The Aegean is our private lake. Apart from that, the real fighting is in Greece and Cappadocia. Cassander is doing well in Greece. Antigonus sent to help Polyperchon and managed to recruit around eight thousand soldiers to fight Cassander. He met up with Alexander and Polyperchon, and, as per instructions from Antigonus, appointed Polyperchon general of the Peloponnesus. Alexander is on his way to meet with Antigonus to settle the terms of a formal alliance." Igrat's voice dropped the sound of Ptolomy and reverted to her own husky contralto. "Father, nobody knows what's going on out here. They need word."

"I'll have to ask you to go straight back with the reports. Basically, we've cleared the Antigonid forces out of the satrapy. What few troops they have left here are either holed up in the cities and unable to move or streaming back in retreat to Ecbatana. Babylon awaits the return of Seleucus with great impatience for the citizens made great efforts on his behalf and ask nothing other than the return of a ruler they admire and respect."

Headquarters, Army of Seleucus Nikator, Babylonia

Parmenio awoke with a hand covering his mouth and two fingers holding his nose closed. Kneeling beside him was a camp woman in a ragged shawl and dirty tunic. As soon as she saw he was awake, her fingers released their grip. Her voice was a quiet, husky contralto and it penetrated what was left of his sleep. "Quiet, father. Assassins come in the darkness. Take hold of a weapon quickly."

Parmenio reached out in the tent and took hold of his xiphos before the full impact of the words sank in. When they did, his own voice was a whisper. "Iggie? What are you doing here? I thought you were on your way back to Damascus."

"Saving your life. When you told me of the plot, I returned to join the camp women and hung around Meleager's positions. I told you, nobody looks at the camp women unless they want some tail. I heard the men talking and of their scheme for tonight. They'd learned that most of the men they thought were on their side had not wavered in their loyalty to you so they wished to strike before you were ready for them. Now, be quiet. They are coming." Igrat was standing with her back to one wall of the tent. She was so completely masked by the shadows that, for a moment Parmenio thought he had been dreaming and that her presence had just been part of that dream. Then he heard the faint rustle of cloth in the darkness and he knew that this was no dream.

That was when he smelled the acrid, choking smoke that told him the tent had been set on fire. His initial reaction was to head for the map and command section that formed the front half of the structure but Igrat grabbed his arm and pushed him towards the back of the tent. There, she had cut a long slit in the rearmost wall and he found himself falling through it into the night beyond. *Just how sharp is that knife she carries?* he found himself wondering. She'd followed him through the slit and was looking at him, waiting for a lead. He pointed off to his left. Men carried their shields on their left arm and their right was more or less unprotected. Going to his left would give him a slight advantage.

There were more than a dozen men waiting just beyond the entrance to the command tent. Parmenio knew that if he had followed his first instincts, he would have come out the front of the structure and been cut down before he had even realized they were there. Thanks to Igrat's warning and the sharpness of her knife, he had escaped that trap. Now he faced another and the odds were not good. Even with Igrat and her undoubted skills with a knife, the odds against him were too great. On the other hand, all he had to do was survive for a couple of minutes and the rest of his army would be running here. Even while he had been weighing the odds, he had moved towards the second from the left of the group waiting for him. They were watching the tent entrance so carefully that they had failed to notice what was happening round them. Parmenio had noticed that before about men used to fighting in the Phalanx; they were fixated on their front and disregarded everything that wasn't in that narrow arc.

The man never stood a chance. At the last second, he heard something that alerted him but it was too late. Parmenio's xiphos took him just under the rib cage, the great leaf-shaped blade slicing across his diaphragm and spilling his intestines out from his ripped stomach. Parmenio swung again, the blade slicing smoothly through the man's throat until the blade jarred against his spine. He was down and he was going to stay down. It was in the follow-through to that blow that Parmenio saw something he could scarcely credit. As the mutineer on the far left had turned to fight Parmenio, Igrat had come running out of the darkness and jumped at him. Her left arm had wrapped around his neck and the combination of her weight, the speed of the run and the downward force of her jump had pulled him off his feet. They crashed to the ground together and her closed right fist punched him in the small of the back, twice. Then, she rolled clear, leaving him writhing on the ground, but with his screams alerting the surviving mutineers. *What in the name of all the gods did she do to him?*

The night darkness that enveloped the camp was broken only by the smoldering camp fires and the flames that were working slowly along the walls of his tent. The thick, heavy fabric burned only slowly and the fire had yet to spread very far beyond its starting point. Parmenio took that all in as he started to move off to his left, trying to gain the advantage of position that might offset the numbers that were arrayed against him. That thought made him frown; there were nine assassins now moving towards him. There had been twelve to start with and that left one unaccounted for. That was dangerous since the man could easily rejoin the battle by sinking a spear into Parmenio's unprotected back.

The line of men were moving towards him and spreading out so that they could encircle him. Despite all the old myths of one man holding off dozens, that could only happen where the ground was so restricted that the many could approach the few in equal numbers. That wasn't the case here. The assassins had planned to kill him quickly as he came out of the tent but that plan had failed. They hadn't given up. The killing would take longer this way and would put each of them at greater risk but the ultimate end was still certain. Already the points of at least four sarissas jabbed towards him and he knew he was being herded backwards into a killing zone.

That was when another sarissa stabbed past him from behind. For one moment of blinding panic, Parmenio thought there were more asssassins behind him but the sarissa parried the thrust from one of the men in front. "Strategos, drop back. We will handle this."

It was the remainder of his guard. They were in a killing mood, there was no doubt about that. Shame and guilt at their charge having been left in danger of his life had combined with their rage at finding eight of their fellows treacherously slaughtered to produce a murderous frame of mind. There were other rumors as well, spreading through the camp so fast that only those familiar with campfire rumor could credit. It was being said that Athena Alcidemus, the Goddess of Victory herself, had seen the foul plot against their Strategos and come down to thwart it. She had warned him of the attack and taken him by the hand to lead him through the solid rear wall of his tent. Then she had fought beside him and killed two of the attackers with a wave of her hand.

"Strategos, armor for you." One of his guards, a grizzled sarissaphoros in his sixties had a breastplate and helmet. They weren't Parmenio's own but he habitually wore the armor of a common soldier anyway. He slipped them on with the ease of long practice. By this time, the assassins were either dead or surrendered. *The intelligent ones are dead.* Parmenio thought grimly. *It is a better death to die on the point of a sarissa or the edge of a sword than the fate that will befall those who did not.* "Strategos, a favor we beg you. Intercede with Athena Alcidemus for us and beg her forgiveness on our behalf. We came running as soon as we knew of this foulness. If there was negligence here, it was the mistake of humans. We meant no blasphemy against her."

"I will do so and I will speak well of the man who thought to bring me armor. As to negligence, a plot by a handful of greedy and impious men is always hard to predict. We will investigate what happened tonight when the dawn comes and there will be no blame assigned where none is deserved." Parmenio saw the relief on the sarissaphoros's face. He would accept the judgment of an investigation and the opinions of his fellows with courage but the fear of being considered blasphemous by the goddess he worshipped was enough to unman him.

"Strategos, we have another of them. And his fate is strange indeed." The surviving assassins, three in number, were already being herded away. Another one of Parmenio's guards was close to where Igrat's first victim was sprawled on the ground. "He bled to death yet there is not a mark on him."

"Athena Alcidemus. She killed him with a gesture." Parmenio heard the word spreading, rippling through the ranks of sarissaphoros in a way that reminded him of a breeze ruffling a field of grain. "The Goddess forgive us the blasphemy of an attack on one of her favorites."

"There is a mark on him." A healer spoke very quietly for Parmenio's ears alone. "Two tiny stab wounds in his back, less than a little finger's width in thickness but deep. One in each kidney. He died quickly but in excruciating pain. Even had he not bled to death, he was doomed. With his kidneys destroyed, he would have died in a week."

"Another one, over here." It was the ninth man, the one Parmenio had lost track of during the fight. He was sprawled on his back, his face twisted in horror and agony. There was no visible mark on him and no blood around his body. Again the swirl of whispers started to spread and the fear in the ranks was tangible.

The healer inspected the body and again his voice was very quiet. "One stab wound in the back of the neck. The same knife and the same tiny wound. This one cut the man's spine and left him unable to breathe. He lay there for several minutes, slowly suffocating, his mind desperately commanding his lungs to suck in air but unable to make them obey. A horrible way to die."

Over in the ranks, the sarissaphoros who had given his armor to Parmenio was speaking quietly. "You see, it was Athena Alcidemus. I've seen her before. She came to visit our Strategos the night before the Battle of the Hyllus. That was almost ten years ago but tonight she looked exactly the same as I remember her. I was on guard duty that night I saw her discussing battle plans with him. I gave her the pass to enter the camp and she spoke kindly to me. And in ten years of fighting since then, I have never suffered a wound or a day's illness. If Meleager and his plots have lost me the favor of the Goddess, I . . . ." The sarissaphoros's voice trailed away

"Has anybody touched these bodies?" A priest of Athena Alcidemus had arrived on the scene. He had been arranging for the purification and funeral rites of Parmenio's guards who had been killed by the assassins. Now, he had to deal with the dead assassins. And the living ones although that would come later.

"I have." The healer sounded abashed.

"Then see us in the Temple of Athena immediately. You must be purified and cleansed after touching such impious foulness. Anyone else who has touched the dead assassins do the same or risk the wrath of Athena Alcidemus." Another ripple of fear went through the ranks and the hatred that was directed at Meleager and his fellow-conspirators redoubled as the men realized his plot had put their immortal souls at risk. "Have the bodies dragged out of the camp by dogs and thrown into the midden. Then kill the dogs and throw their bodies in as well. And all the weapons that were used to kill them. Nothing that has contacted the blasphemers must be left in this camp."

The priest turned to Parmenio and looked at the blood-stained Xiphos. "I am sorry, Strategos, but your sword also must be thrown into the midden. I trust it was not a family heirloom."

"Just a normal xiphos. What is good enough for my soldiers is good enough for me." Parmenio managed to get that out without sounding sanctimonious and a ripple of approval swept across the assembled troops.

Behind him, more troops had finished putting out the fire in his tent. The living section was burned out but the fire hadn't reached the all-important command section where he kept his maps.

Parmenio was studying those maps when he felt a tiny movement in the tent. He looked up to see Igrat sliding into one of the seats. He was about to give her a joking warning about the seats being dirty from the fire but he saw the look in her eyes and bit it back. It was an expression he had never seen before, a combination of misery, despair and guilt. "What's wrong Iggie."

"Me. The reply was decisive and abrupt. It was also so loaded with misery that it made Parmenio's stomach churn in a way he hadn't experiences since Alexander had murdered his son and tried to kill him. Igrat was barely able to keep herself from weeping and her usually contralto tones were blurred with grief. "I haven't changed."

That left Parmenio slightly bewildered and our of his depth. It had been an active night but nothing that a Macedonian general wasn't used to handling. This conversation, on the other hand, was new to him. "Take a deep breath, gather your wits and tell me about this."

"I thought I had changed. When you took me into your family, I realized that the only thing that the way I'd lived had done was to make me and everybody around me miserable. I tried to change, father, I tried so hard. I tried to be nice to people. I wanted to be different so much. Then, tonight, I killed those two men just the way I'd stabbed men before. I haven't changed at all."

So that's it. "Iggie, tonight you saved my life. What you did was to save part of your family. That's a big difference right there. Here's another. I spoke with the healer tonight. He was very impressed with the way you stabbed those two men. The wounds were so precisely placed that a hair's difference either side or up and down would have left them alive to kill you. Yet, I saw one of those stabbings, you were fighting with the man, rolling in the dust with somebody twice your weight and a trained soldier as well. I didn't see the other one, but the healer told me the only way you could have stabbed him like that was if he'd had his arms around you and was bending down towards you."

"He thought I wanted to kiss him. That's supposed to make me feel better? That I'm a skilled murderess instead of an incompetent one?"

"No. You don't understand. Remember when you stabbed Apollo? You missed the artery that would have killed him on the spot. Not by much but you missed. Tonight you showed that you don't miss with a knife. The blade goes exactly where you want it to go. Iggie, you were never as evil or vicious as you made yourself believe. If you were, Apollo would be dead and buried these ten years past. You missed the kill point because deep in your heart that's what you wanted to do. You saw yourself as a spiteful, vindictive killer because that fitted your loathing for yourself and the way you had to live. Now, you have nothing to loath. You're a loving and attentive wife who makes her husband very happy." *We'll forget about the faithful bit.* Parmenio thought. "Tonight you proved you are a brave and dutiful daughter. For ten years, you've been a thoughtful and considerate friend to the rest of our family. You're a loyal servant of your king and that is the most important thing of all. Seleucus Nikator has proved a noble King, worthy of our allegiance, and your service to him has shown faithfulness beyond measure.

"Igrat, you've always had the potential to be a better person than you gave yourself credit for. The very fact that you're questioning what you did shows that you've become that better person. Yes, you killed two men. In the service of your father, your family and your King. Not as part of a sordid crime in the Babylon underworld. There's all the difference in the world, right there. Iggie, we're alike in more ways than you realize. When I fought my first battle, the day I saw what a phalanx does to the people who try to stand against it, then I knew that I had to cut myself off from worrying about what the battles I planned meant to the people in question. If I let myself think about what commanding an army actually meant in human terms, it would drive me mad. You did the same; you had to survive so you did what you had to do in order to survive and cut yourself off from the cost of it. Now, you don't cut yourself off any more. I wish I could do the same."

Parmenio was out of breath and had to stop. Igrat was staring at him with her eyes opened wide. "You really mean all that?"

"Of course. I will say that your knife work was admirable. If you weren't a first-class whore, you'd be an excellent assassin."

He stared at her with open-eyed innocence and Igrat returned the look with confusion. Then the outrageousness of the comment sank in and she suddenly exploded into laughter. "Father, you say the nicest things to me. Anyway, it was all your fault. When we got out of the back of the tent, we could have slipped away. Instead, you attacked a dozen men. I had to do something."

"I'm a Macedonian general, Igrat. I'm supposed to be able to handle situations like that. The guards were coming and all I had to do was buy time. If I'd run away my authority would have evaporated. By the way, only the priests, the healer and I know about those knife wounds. Everybody else thinks those men died without a wound on them. You see, they think you are Athena Alcidemus and you killed them with a wave of your hand. That's very convenient from my point of view."

Igrat paused, thinking over what Parmenio had said to her. "Father, what will happen to the assassins who were taken alive?"

"They'll be questioned. Then they'll be impaled in the middle of the camp. When they are dead, their bodies will be dumped in the camp midden. We tried to find Meleager by the way, but he's made a run for it. We may get him, we may not." Parmenio thought for a second. "There is something else you could do though."

Perimeter, Army of Seleucus Nikator, Babylonia, Spring, 313BC

"You stop!" The guard snapped the words out. "Business here?"

"No, my business is done. For a while, anyway." Igrat looked at the guard. He seemed vaguely familiar to her but she couldn't remember where she had seen him or when.

He, on the other hand, recognized her instantly or so he thought. "My Lady, I beg forgiveness."

"For what?" Igrat smiled at him. Parmenio had asked her to convince this particular man that she smiled upon him still and thus spread word throughout the Army that Athena Alcidemus, the Goddess of Victory, still favored them.

"Our failure to guard the Strategos against the attack of assassins." The old Sarissaphoros was in an agony of fear, believing that he was speaking with a goddess. It had been the center of his beliefs that his apparently miraculous escape from wounds and sickness was the result of their previous meeting and not just the blind chance of the battlefield.

"He who sent for me still lives. What more can a girl ask than that? Anyway, are you not the man who gave the Strategos your armor? Without your act, I might not have received the fee I had been promised." Igrat put a slightly lecherous note into her voice, adopting the coarsened banter that suited the rank and file of the Army. "I might well mark my gratitude with a discount to those who served my client so well. And I would certainly think that those who protected my interests should consider themselves my friends."

Igrat slipped way into the darkness, heading for the sutler's camp. There would be more guards there, Parmenio did not make the mistake so many others had made of assuming that the baggage train would not be attacked. But, by the time Igrat reached them, the lady of quality would have gone and the copper-coin camp whore would have taken her place. Behind her, the old Sarissaphoros felt a surge of relief pass through him. Athena Alcidemus had spoken kindly and she would still look after him.

Headquarters, Army of Seleucus Nikator, Re-entering Babylon, Winterset, 311BC.

Seleucus Nikator knew that sound of the population cheering when an army entered a city meant very little. *That isn't strictly true,* he thought to himself as his chariot moved slowly through the sea of people jamming the streets. *Usually it is a desperate attempt by them to prevent the orgy of rape, pillage and looting that takes place when a city falls. Sometimes it even works. But these are different, they are genuine cheers of delight and victory and mixed in with them all are the strange whooping noise of exhilaration that women made at times of triumph. And mixed up with it all is pride, the pride of a people who know that they share in the glory of victory. This is a sound that I don't think any army has ever heard before.* That was when the realization dawned on him. *They don't see this as my army, to them, this is their army, sharing in their victory.*

That was an insight that made him feel distinctly uncomfortable. But, within the realization was something else, a new way of looking at things. The words he had heard once from Igrat echoed in his mind. 'Any king can give coin but only a good king will take the time needed to speak with the lowest of his subjects.' In a move that horrified the armored cavalry of his escort, he stopped his chariot in the middle of the street and jumped off it. Before anybody could stop him, he had walked over to the crowd and vanished within it. Surrounded by the citizens of Babylon, alone and without weapons or escort, he started seizing people by the arm and congratulating *them* on the great victory that *they* had won, here in *their* city. For a brief second, there was a stunned silence as the crowd absorbed the unthinkable thing that was happening in their midst. Then, they exploded into a great wave of cheering for *their* King. The roar echoed off the walls and roofs, spreading across the city to the Upper Citadel where the banner of Seleucus Nikator flew from the walls as it had every day for the three years the troops of Antigonus Monopthalmus had occupied the city. The cheers from the Upper Citadel echoed back, adding to the tumult.

Third Diodochi War

Seleucus glanced backwards, towards the thoroughly confused troops of his escort and the equally bewildered generals that had been following his chariot on horseback. *Well, all but one of those Generals is confused*, he thought, *I bet that Strategos Parmenio knows exactly what I am doing and why.* That was when he caught Parmenio's eye and saw his Strategos grin at him and make a slight but unmistakable gesture of respect. *Thought so.*

Even while he had been assessing the situation, Seleucus had continued his movement through the crowd, leaving a wake of Babylonian citizens who still couldn't believe that the great Seleucus Nikator had saluted them. Without realizing it, he had been moving towards a great empty table, perhaps one of those used by the city merchants to sell their wares. Regardless, it was what he needed. Tall enough to lift him above the crowd around him, not so tall as to destroy the image that he was part of that crowd. He swung himself up on to the table and looked at the people around him.

"People of Babylon, saviors of the city, victors over the armies of the foul murderer Antigonus Monopthalmus. May our God Mardok shower his blessings upon you and bless you all with long lives and prosperity."

The crowd had quieted when he had started to speak but the invocation of the deity who guarded their city started them off again. Seleucus waited patiently until the noise receded again. "I left this city three years ago as a Satrap, betrayed by those with whom I had served for many years. Antigonus Monopthalmus and his allies had turned on me and the demands of war meant I could not return until their armies were defeated. But, you, the people of this city and the other cities that owed allegiance to me stood firm and fought against the enemy. Now I return to this city, not as a Satrap for that would mean I had been appointed so by others but as your King. Your King, people of Babylon, for you have chosen me to be your leader."

Seleucus stopped and his voice shook with only semi-faked humility. "I will try to be a leader worthy of the trust you have placed in me."

That started the crowd off again. By the time they had stopped cheering, Seleucus had come up with the perfect ending. "People, you won this battle. I cannot take all of you with me in the celebration of our victory so I will ask representatives of you to do so."

Seleucus cast his eyes over the crowd gathered around him, all of them now visibly holding their breaths while he made his choice. His eye fastened on a young couple. They were young, showing signs of the hardship from the long occupation but with the freshness and vigor of youth still about them. The man was obviously wearing his best clothes for the occasion but they were worn and patched. The woman was, at best, commonly pretty but that was so much the better for his motives in selecting her would not be misunderstood. They were no more than average people and that made them the best of all choices for they were those that everybody in the crowd could identify with. And, to complete a perfect picture, the young woman was carrying a young baby. "Would you represent the people of our city on our day of celebration by joining me in our parade?"

The couple nodded dumbly, overcome by the enormity of what was happening round them. Seleucus and his guards helped them mount the chariot and the procession set off again. As it did so, Seleucus realized that with his assumption of the title of King and his speech owing that rank to the acclamation of the people, he had just totally destroyed the last remnants of the Alexandrine inheritance. Behind him, Parmenio had realized the same thing and was grinning broadly.

Estate of Parmenio, Seleucia-on-the Tigris

"Oh no." Igrat was heartbroken. "Why would they do this?"

Her grief was profound and genuine. Parmenio's estate was the only real home she had ever known and the sight of its destruction tore at her. What had once been a beautifully-scaled and proportioned villa was now little more than a devastated ruin. In addition to the damage caused by axe and sledgehammer, the vandals had topped off their work by setting it on fire. The white outer walls were stained black by the smoke, the trails upwards clearly showing how fire had blossomed out of the windows. The exquisite gardens that had surrounded the building had been uprooted and burned. She started to move towards the ruins but Apollo seized her arm. "Stay away from the ruins, Iggie. Leonnatus pulled out of this area months ago and we don't know what happened between then and now. There could be some nasty tricks hidden in those ruins and even if there aren't, vermin and snakes will have moved in. You don't want to get bitten."

"How are we going to fix it all?" Igrat was still distraught. If anything, her distress was deepening as her mind slowly took in the full extent of the ruin.

Lillith shook her head. "We won't. It will cost more to repair the place than it would to start again. We'll get some work teams to tear what's left down and we'll rebuild."

"Why did they do it?" Igrat's voice was weak and wavered as she spoke.

"Because they knew it was Parmenio's home and that he had masterminded their defeat. They couldn't take it out on him so they destroyed his home. If we'd stayed here, our tortured bodies would be in those ruins still." Naamah looked at the ruins carefully, her face expressionless. "And that reminds me. Gusoyn, would you check out the well please. And be careful. If my guess is right, the water down there will be deadly. Even the air could be poisonous. I've seen men go down into wells or caves and never come out. When we found them, there wasn't a mark on them."

Gusoyn nodded and walked over to where the well had been dug, Igrat watched him go. "What do you think is down there?"

Naamah looked at her steadily. "At the very least, a couple of dead goats or sheep. They'll have been rotting down there for weeks. One mouthful of that water will kill even us."

"You said at least?"

"If I was poisoning that well, I'd have thrown some black hellbore down there. Nobody would spot it until it was too late. But, I was thinking that the soldiers who occupied this place probably took some local women to amuse them. When they pulled out, it's good odds, those women went down the well also."

Igrat was nodding slowly. "And I could have been one of them. Or, they were women like me."

Anything else she might have said was cut off by Gusoyn returning, looking immeasurably sad. "You were right, Naamah. The rotting-stench from that well is foul. Worse than any battlefield we've smelled. I tossed a torch down and it went out halfway down. Well's useless, all we can do is fill it in. We can't stay here, can we?"

Namah shook her head. "At the least we'll have to build a new home a few miles upstream. Not downstream. It will be a few years before we can drink the water safely. We can use this land as pasture though."

"Can't we get the bodies of the women out? They deserve a decent funeral at least." Igrat was staring at the well.

"Women?" Gusoyn was confused.

"Naamie thinks that the soldiers who used our home killed the women they kept here and threw their bodies down there." Igrat explained, all too aware that the women might not have been dead when they were thrown down. She had no illusions about the cruelty with which abducted women could be treated.

"There's nothing we can do for them." Naamah was quite firm on that point. "That well is a death-trap. I will not throw life after death without good cause."

Apollo had returned with an odd expression on his face. "I've just been talking to some of our old servants. They came back when they heard that we had. They'd hidden the stuff we'd left behind and now returned it to us, safe and undamaged."

Lillith and Naamah exchanged glances. The only things they had left behind was property they considered worthless yet their servants had risked their lives to hide it for them. Igrat didn't seem surprised though. "You gave them coin for their trouble?"

Apollo gave an exaggerated gesture of shock. "Iggie, you taught me better than that. No. I thanked them warmly for their loyalty and told them we would be building a new home a little upstream. That we would need loyal staff and that there were positions waiting for them should they choose to stay with us. That pleased them greatly and they all wished to return to us. So I gave them an advance on their wages so they could buy new clothes fitting for our improved status. Oh, and they told me who occupied this house and who was responsible for its destruction."

"Who was that." Lillith was trying to hide her curiosity.

"Alcetas."

Lillith nodded. "You were wrong Nammie. This place wasn't destroyed to punish Parmenio. It was destroyed to punish me."

Headquarters, Army of Antigonus Monopthalmus, Celaenae, Phrygia, Winterset, 311 BC

Babylonia and the valleys of the Tigris and Euphrates had gone. All the lands to the east were gone. He had been driven out of Coelê Syria and his hold on the eastern end of the Mediterranean was broken. His allies had lost most of Greece and Macedonia. And the worst thing of all was that Antigonus Monopthalmus had no idea how it had happened. Three years before, he had started the war on Seleucus and Ptolemy with more men under his personal command than they and all their allies had together. He had powerful allies in Greece and Macedonia who dominated the country and held the political leadership in their hands. If ever a war had been won before it started, that one had. And yet, he had lost. His armies were gone, some killed, others deserted to his enemies. Antigonus knew the figures as well as anybody. He had less than five thousand men, supported by about eight hundred light cavalry. Once again the litany of loss ran through his mind. His heavy cavalry had gone, the elephants had gone, the hypaspists were gone, his phalanx was but a weak and feeble shadow of the force it had once been. Worst of all, the gold had gone, stolen by Seleucus. He couldn't hire mercenaries to replace his losses because Seleucus had taken his gold and everybody knew it.

Antigonus stared into the fire that warmed his room and knew that there was more to it than that. Even before the disaster at Cyaxares, the supply of mercenaries had dried up. His recruiters had come back empty-handed yet soldiers had flocked to the standard of Seleucus and Ptolemy. His spies had told him that when Seleucus had started his ride back to Babylon, he had with him but a single regiment of prodromoi light cavalry. Perhaps 800 horsemen, a thousand at most. By the time he had reached Babylon, he had forty thousand men, almost half of whom had deserted from his enemies to join him. Antigonus knew that there was a grim joke running in his army. *When our phalanx advances to engage the Seleucid line, only the Gods know whether it is to fight them or join them.*

Once again, Antigonus looked at the scroll that had been delivered to him. He knew what it was, the terms on which his enemies would allow the war to end. Those terms were brutal. The Partition of Triparadisus was null and void. They would allow him to retain only a part of Asia Minor. He was to cede Cappadocia and Lycia to Cassander and recognize him as ruler of Greece. Hellespontine Phrygia was to be awarded to Lysimachus who would be the new ruler of Macedonia. All of Syria between the great desert and the Mediterranean coast was to be given to Ptolemy. Antigonus was to recognize Seleucus as king of Babylonia and the empire that had been restored to him. The islands of the Mediterranean would continue to live under their existing rulers, all of whom were Ptolemy's allies. They made the terms he had been offered at the start of the war seem almost generous. Now, he was not just being relegated to a patch of Asia Minor, but the poorest and least fertile parts of that area. Combined with his losses in the war, Antigonus knew that his power was broken. Fully two thirds of his empire had gone and with it all the revenues and manpower those lost provinces had brought with them.

There has to be a way back from this. Antigonus stared at the map on his table. Even in the dim light of torches and the fire, it glowered back at him. Ptolemy to the south, Seleucus to the east, Cassander and Lysimachus to the north. That left only the west. *Now there is a thought. My son Demetrius is retreating from Gaza after his defeat there but he is bringing his survivors with him. His last dispatch said that he had three thousand men and fifteen hundred horse. That will give me some eight thousand men and twenty five hundred horse.*

Those numbers guaranteed Antigonus would be acutely aware of the depths to which he had fallen. He was encouraged by the acquisition of a few dozen horsemen where once he had numbered his army in tens of thousands. That brought another thought to his mind. He remembered that Leonnatus was retreating from Babylonia with the garrison of Babylon and that he was picking up other isolated garrisons as he did so. There had been thirty thousand men and another ten thousand at least scattered throughout the country. That was the core of a powerful army, one that could face the Seleucid Army in the field. That was when another point occurred to him. *Leonnatus has three times as many men as I do. When we merge our forces, he could easily replace me. He will have to go before that happens.*

Antigonus summoned Hieronymus of Cardia. "Where is the army of Leonnatus and what is its strength?"

"Sire, the Army of Leonnatus was much weakened by desertions and losses and numbered but ten thousand foot and seven thousand force. His retreat was hard and his gains from the garrisons he relieved barely offset his losses from stragglers and desertion. At Arbela-on-the-Tigris he was met by Seleucus at the head of an army of three thousand foot and a thousand cavalry. He fell upon the Army of Leonnatus at night and in the great confusion most of the soldiers of Leonnatus deserted and joined Seleucus. Leonnatus fled with but a few men left. Of his present location, we know nothing other than that he is somewhere in Medea."

Never had been so resurgent a set of hopes been so quickly and brutally crushed. Antigonus staggered back into his seat, feeling an intense pain in his chest and radiating down his left arm. He breathed slowly, deeply and steadily as his healer had taught him and the pain ebbed away. "Is Medea still loyal?"

Hieronymus of Cardia really wished he was doing something other than relating this tale of disaster. "No, Majesty. Seleucus has comported himself in a way gracious to all and treated his enemies with courtesy and consideration. He bears them no malice; on the contrary, he gives them gifts and keeps him in his court, By these means he makes them his friends and, by advancing them in honor, he wins them over to his cause. All, even the lowest of his subjects, see him as exceptionally gentle and forgiving and inclined toward deeds of great kindness. It is this very thing that most increases his power and makes many men desire to share his friendship. So it has been with Medea. His reputation easily won over Susianê, Medea, and some of the adjacent lands. When he reports to Ptolemy and his other friends about his achievements, he already possesses a king's stature and a reputation worthy of royal power."

Ever afterwards, Hieronymus of Cardia attributed his survival to a herald who chose that exact moment to burst into Antigonus's chamber. "Majesty, your son, Demetrius Poliorcetes, has arrived with news of victory."

In fact, Demetrius could have saved Hieronymus the grave danger of reporting the defeat of Leonnatus but he had spent a few minutes in reconnoitering Antigonus's headquarters. In particular, he was checking for pits and piles of oil-soaked straw. Having found none, he presumed it was safe to enter his father's presence. "Your Majesty, I have to report a victory that lightens the darkness of today. After the defeat at Gaza, we retreated to Upper Syria, assembling a new army as we fell back. Ptolemy detached an army of six thousand foot and three thousand horse under the command of

Cilles the Macedonian to pursue us. They did so without proper care or attention and were were able to engage them under the most favorable of circumstances. Cilles died in the battle but the bulk of his army surrendered to us. Your Army, numbering almost ten thousand foot and four thousand horse, is entrenched in a position of great strength at Myus. We feared that Ptolemy would fall upon in great strength but with the threat to Egypt removed and Seleucus restored to Babylonia, he saw no further gain from campaigning and has pulled back to Egypt. We hold all of Upper Syria, a bargaining tool of great value."

Antigonus looked on his son Demetrius with great favor for his victory and the occupation of Syria had expunged the memory of the defeat at Gaza. *The boy, young as he is, seems to have got out of his difficulties by himself and to have shown himself worthy to be a king. Thanks to him, we have saved something from this wreck.*

PART FOUR
FOURTH DIODOCHI WAR
(306 – 301 BC)

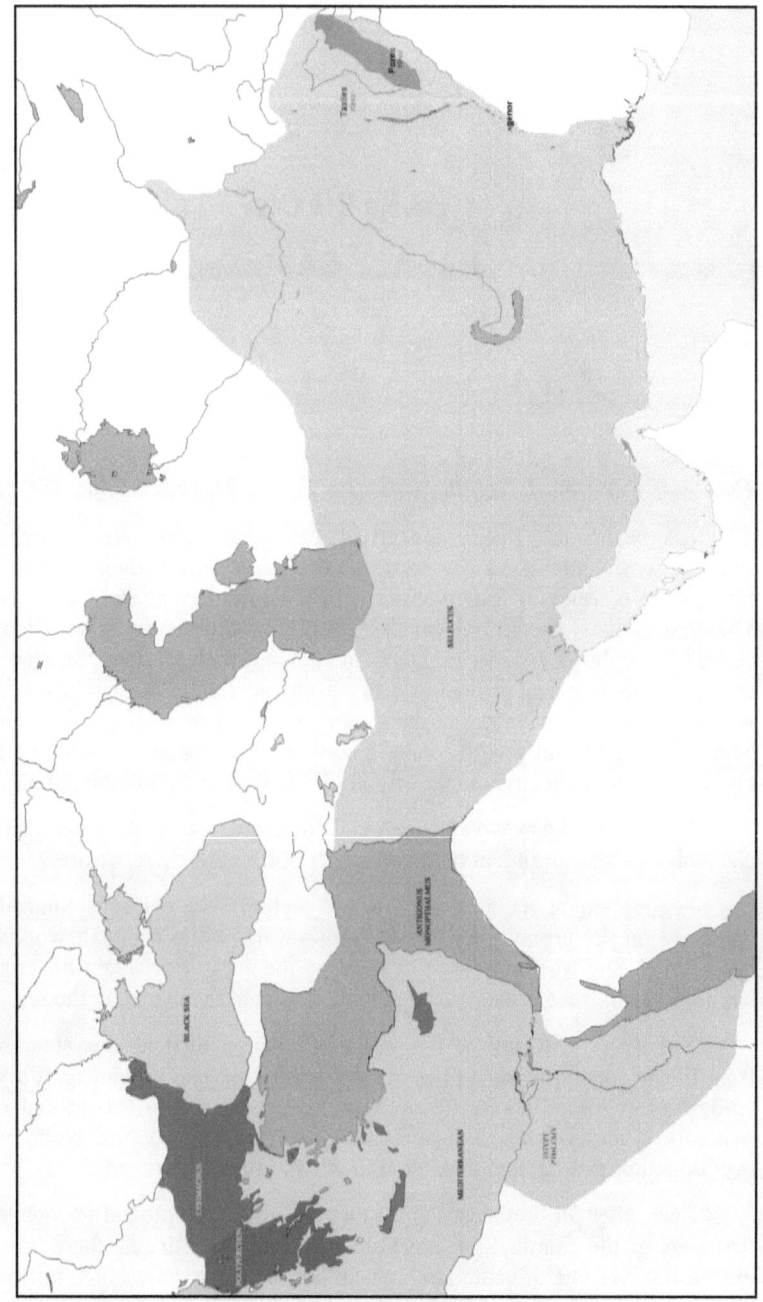

Seleucid Empire 308BC

CHAPTER ONE

PALACE GAMES

Estate of Parmenio, Seleucia-on-the Tigris, Harvesthome, 308 BC

"It's beautiful." Lillith looked at the freshly-completed mural with shining eyes. It depicted the battle at the oasis during their escape from Babylon in a series of four pictures reflecting the key phases of the battle. The first showed the initial cavalry charge of Alcetas being repelled, the second the fighting around the elephant square, the third, the great charge of the elephants that had driven Alcetas from the field. The last showed the wounded Seleucid cavalrymen being gathered and treated. Each scene had been blended carefully with the next so that they looked like a single great mural. The montage covered the whole of one wall and dominated the room.

"The artists did a wonderful job. Worth every coin they charged us." Naamah was also staring at the painting. "Look, Iggie, there we are."

She pointed at an area of the last picture where Derya Shafrid lay wounded on the ground, cradled in Igrat's arms while Naamah worked on his injuries. She was impressed by the way the artist had caught the color of her hair. "I think the artists put too much stress on the aftermath though."

"Not if you ask any of the veterans." Derya Shafrid was standing in front of the section showing the cavalry battle, his arm around Igrat's waist while he reminisced about the fighting. "Every man who was at that battle remembers how you and the other ladies treated our wounds. Nobody had ever done that before, and even now, it is still vivid in our memories."

"Even after all the battles since then?" Lillith had moved to look at the first part of the mural. She had seen the figure of Alcetas there, and her expression was one of acute loathing. In her mind, he represented unfinished business. She also knew that he regarded her the same way and there was no kindliness or mercy for her in the way he wished to close the accounts.

"Even after all of them." Shafrid shifted position uncomfortably, Igrat discretely helping him as he did so. His wounds still troubled him greatly and the strength had never properly returned to his back or sword arm. That helped to remind him that he would have been dead and buried years before had he not been treated on the battlefield and then nursed back to health by the family he now called his own. Instinctively, he drew Igrat a little closer to him, marveling that she was content to be his wife. They had had three years of peace in which her duties had only taken her away for brief periods. About those periods, he never asked. He was aware that to ask such questions could easily bring about her death and that was an event he would not wish to survive.

"You two settling in well?" Gusoyn was admiring the picture of Dilipa Ganesh engaged in crushing an Antigonid cataphract who had been thrown from his horse. Again, the artists had caught the scene perfectly, managing to suggest how the normally friendly and docile elephant had turned into a frenzied killer.

Igrat nodded. Their new home was a development of the same pattern used for their old estate. The original square design mansion had been extended into a figure of eight orientated east-west with the eastern end forming Parmenio's household while the western end was the household of Derya and Igrat. The two homes shared servants whose quarters and the facilities to run the property were housed in the center bar of the eight. The truth was that the area allocated to Derya and Igrat was far too large for them and they only used a portion of it. There was still construction work going on in the rest of their area and would be for a long time to come.

The same applied across Seleucia-on-the-Tigris. What had once been a small provincial town had increased enormously in size as families had moved into the area and settled down. Their influx meant there was far more building work going on than there were masons to do it. As a result, it was taking a long time to get work completed and the best masons were getting more coin for their work than they had ever seen before. One inevitable consequence of that had been predictable. Skilled workers were coming in from towns far away to join in the prosperity. Another was that all the artisans were taking on apprentices and teaching them the basics of their trade. Becoming a mason was a career that offered a bright future and there were more applicants that apprentice positions. So, the best were chosen and the masons earned well for teaching them their craft. As those apprentices gained experience, they were setting out on their own and the spiral of increasing prosperity took another notch upwards.

Seleucus Nikator had added momentum to the process by offering extensive land grants to veterans who elected to settle in the area. It wasn't a new idea, Alexander had done the same, but there was a crucial difference.

Alexander had planted his colonies far away from the heartland of his realm so that the veterans settled there wouldn't be a threat to him. Seleucus was offering the veterans land in the center of his kingdom and close to the important cities. There was a simple reason for that. Alexander had known that the majority of the men in his armies had been mercenaries whose loyalty was bought and could change as soon as a better bid was made. In contrast, the veterans of the Seleucid Army were fiercely loyal to their king. Even those who had joined the army for pay, or as an alternative to paying ransom or being sold as slaves after defeat, had been won over by a King who kept his word, paid his men the wages they had been promised and honored their achievements.

Of course, Seleucus Nikator was a good and just king but he wasn't naive and there was more to his arrangements than simple reliance on men's loyalty. Every town in the kingdom knew how the citizens of Babylon had resisted the army of Antigonus Monopthalmus and made the city untenable for them. They also knew how those citizens had been honored and well-rewarded for their achievements. They also had learned something else; in an occupied city, civilians could resist an army and win. Across the country, the proximity of numbers of loyal, armed veterans near to the cities ensured that the citizens of those cities stayed loyal while the presence of cities full of loyal citizens near to the colonies of veterans ensured those veterans stayed loyal. Each was a check on the other and that made the arrangement a recipe for stability. That stability meant that everybody could prosper. That thought brought a smile to Lillith's face. Her management of the family accounts had seen them gaining a worthy share of that increased wealth.

"His Majesty does well to keep us out of the wars." Kopshape-su-Amunet was looking at the mural as well, and his face was sad at the sight of the men killed in the battle. An Egyptian cavalryman, he had been one of the critically-wounded soldiers from the fighting in Syria. While recovering from his injuries, he had been found and recognized by Naamah. Now, he was part of the household but still trying to adjust to the implications of his unique heritage. He was also suffering badly from culture shock, finding the mostly Hellenistic customs of the household wildly different from the Egyptian mores he had grown up with.

"They're not really wars, not yet." Behind them, Parmenio had entered the room and was shedding his cloak. Quietly, one of the servants took it and left the room. "They're more like skirmishes at this time. Antigonus, Cassander, Lysimachus and Polyperchon simply don't have the strength left for a real war, not yet anyway, and Ptolemy and ourselves have no desire for a slugging match over a few yards of territory. We both want our power bases consolidated before we get into the end game."

"With great respect, Strategos. They may be skirmishes, but men still die, wives are left widows and children orphans."

"Which is another good reason to stay out of them. If I meet any of those men in the afterlife, I want to be able to tell them that I trained them as well as I could, gave them the best equipment we had and used the most effective battle plan I could devise. That we did everything we could to minimize our own losses while maximizing the damage to the enemy. In the end, we had won the day and in doing so made gains that benefitted all of our people greatly yet could not have been achieved any other way. And, all that having been so, I consider that their lives were properly expended. This skirmishing in Syria and Cappadocia fills none of those criteria."

"It is the knowledge that His Majesty begrudges the loss of a single soldier that binds the men to him." Derya spoke carefully and with much thought. "Others may carry out maneuvers that bring only glory to those who command them and death to those who obey, but all the ranks know that is not our way. Even the lowest auxiliary knows that an order that brings death closer to him was issued only because there was no better way."

"You know what the common people say?" Igrat looked around at her family. "Seleucus spends gold freely yet hoards the lives of his soldiers. Antigonus hoards gold yet spends the lives of his soldiers without care."

"Well, most of the gold we are spending belonged to Antigonus once." Parmenio smiled at the memory of the way Antigonus had been hamstrung by the theft of his gold. "What else do the market places say Iggie?"

"Well, the older men are outraged by the new fashions." She stepped away from her husband and twirled around. The tunic she was wearing was armless and much shorter than those worn by the other women, extending only down to mid-thigh. But, underneath it she was wearing a pair of tightly-fitting silk trousers. "What do you think?"

Parmenio studied her carefully. "Interesting, there's not as much of you on display as one might expect. I can't see what the old men are complaining about."

"Mostly, it's the bare arms. The traditionalists think it's indecent."

"They should come to Alexandria." Kopshape was amused at the conservatism of the Persians and at the fact that women's fashions should be the subject of mealtime conversations at what was effectively the command headquarters of the Seleucid Army. "Greek and Egyptian things are merging to produce something new. There, the women have their arms and shoulders bare and the skirts are short, ending above the knee."

"Same thing is happening here; Greek and Persian habits are merging. I'd say most of our soldiers are marrying Persian women. Give it a generation or two and Seleucia will be a very different place from either Ptolemaic Egypt or Macedonia. Igrat, you still wear a shawl over the top when you go out?"

Igrat nodded. "And a veil. There's a lot of Greek and Macedonian women in town now and they find the sun here too strong for them. So they have taken to wearing light veils to protect their faces from sunburn and the local women copy them. Very good for me too."

Parmenio knew what she meant. *Even the light, flimsy veils make it much easier for her to conceal her identity. She's also planted the idea in the minds of Derya and Kopshape that her work for me involves collecting information on how the commoners are feeling and what they think. That's a useful bit of misdirection although it won't really be necessary.* "I'm not sure I like the idea of people walking around with their faces covered. Anybody could be anybody."

"The veil just protects from the sun, Father, and the convention is that married women wear them. They don't conceal much." Then Igrat thought hard. "You're right though. Once a veil is accepted, a darker one than usual would not be noted and it could conceal anything. A man could walk around in a shawl and veil going unrecognized."

Parmenio walked along the newly-finished mural, admiring the workmanship. "The way the artists made each scene flow into the next, it's almost like the pictures can move while they tell the story. They did good work."

"We had a problem with the painters; they didn't want to include portraits of women in it. Said it was immoral to place a picture of the women where it could be seen by strange men. I told them we were Macedonians and our customs were different. They grumbled a bit but a few extra coins soothed their feelings." Lillith snorted slightly at that. She had a feeling their objections had been orientated towards gaining a little extra gold.

Anything else she might have said was interrupted by the servants arriving with the evening meal. It was a plentiful display, honoring the harvest that had just been brought in. The centerpiece of the table was a whole roasted goat surrounded by fresh roasted turnips, fennel and leeks. Other servants brought in flasks of wine and honey-mead. Parmenio took one of the knives off the table and carved himself a section of goat ribs. In doing so, he caught Naamah's eye and she nodded slightly. The food had been tasted before anybody ate it and she hadn't taken her eyes off it since. Parmenio sliced a chop off his ribs and bit into the meat. "Gods, this is good. Olive oil and rosemary?"

"Plus thyme and a little cilantro." Naamah added. As a herbalist, she took great care over the seasoning of the family meals.

"Well, this is better than campaigning." Parmenio tucked into his goat ribs with relish. "Make the most of it while you can."

"We always ate well in the prodromoi. You'd be surprised how many farm animals had to be executed when they developed treasonous tendencies." Derya had carved off a series of slices from the haunch and passed them over to Igrat. She took one slice, folded it over and bit into the tender meat. Watching her, Lillith knew that by the end of her meal, her bowl would be clean and empty. Igrat never wasted food. She'd spent too much of her childhood starving for that.

The way Derya had fetched food for his wife at was one of the many things that Kopshape found hard to accept. He'd grown up in households where the men and women ate separately, the women serving the men and waiting until they had finished before eating themselves. Yet, he had to admit, it was much more pleasant when the whole family gathered together like this. "Wait a minute, I thought you said we were staying out of the skirmishing in Cappadocia?"

"We are, we have another problem though. Anybody ever heard of an Indian prince called Chandragupta Maurya?"

There was a shaking of heads, somewhat diluted by the concentration of people on their food. Lillith was the only one to nod. "There have been some reports from settlers along the Indus have say that he's consolidating the Indian principalities the other side of the river."

"That's what we hear; only our version is that he's finished the consolidation and now rules an Empire that contains almost all of India. Now he's finished doing that, he wants the Indian provinces that Alexander conquered back. He's prepared to go to war over them."

"Why not let him have them? Are they worth so much we should go to war again?" Kopshape sounded suddenly weary.

"Not really." Parmenio was thinking carefully. "The problem is that we can't just give them away. It would be a sign of weakness and we'd have every petty warlord on our borders trying a land-grab. Smacking Antigonus stupid gave us a fearsome reputation in military circles and we need to maintain that. People who think of going to war with us are afraid of what the Seleucid Army will do to them and that's worth more than the lands along the Indus. So, we have to get a decent price for them, one way or another, That's going to be my job. Derya, I want you, Igrat and Naamah to come with me. Gusoyn, Apollo and Kopshape, I want you three to stay here with Lillith and Semiramis."

"And miss the war?" Semiramis was indignant.

"Semiramis, You and Kopshape are the two most skilled fighters we have here, other than Derya of course and he'll be with me. I need you two here in case the house is attacked. Remember what happened to our old home? Well. Alcetas is out there somewhere and we don't know where. In fact, you two will be in a lot more danger here than we will be out on the Indus. There won't be a full-scale war out there if I have anything to do with it but there's a big question mark as to what may happen here."

Semiramis thought that over and nodded. Reluctantly, but acceptingly.

Parmenio gave her a comforting grin. "Don't worry, I'll get you into the middle of a war sooner or later. Gusoyn. You'll be head of the household while I'm away."

"Does that mean I get to claim the ribs off the roast?"

"If you want them. Lillith will be handling the money of course."

"Of course." Gusoyn grinned. "She handles all of mine anyway. Very profitably I might add."

Lillith smiled in receipt of the compliment. In addition to investing the family funds, she'd made it known she would manage the private funds of the family members if they wanted her to. Gusoyn, Apollo and Igrat had taken her up on the offer. Lillith hadn't been surprised by the first two but she'd been amazed and deeply flattered when Igrat had asked her to look after her funds. She'd never believed that Igrat would trust anybody enough for that.

"By the way, it'll be announced soon that Seleucus will be cutting the Land Tax again." Parmenio looked up from his plate of ribs. "On both city and farm land although there will be a bigger cut for the latter. Especially after the cut in farmland tax last year caused us to bring in more revenue from the herd tax and the crop tax than we lost."

"I can see that would make sense." Lillith spoke carefully, "I would wager that when the land tax was reduced, farmers bought enough land to keep the gross tax payment at the pre-cut level. That meant they pushed their harvest of crops up and meant they could graze more animals."

"Why didn't we do that?" Igrat's question came out mixed with goat.

Lillith smiled sweetly. "We did. By the way, we are also making a liturgies, a voluntary payment to fund a project for the public good. In our case, it's for the maintenance of the chorus in the City Ampitheater. There's a drama festival coming up. Hieronymus of Cardia will be reading his latest work, a tragedy describing the betrayal and murder of the Argyraspides by Antigonus."

"Did you hear the market place joke about the theater?" Igrat looked around seeing her family shaking their heads. "Well, a very rich merchant finally achieved his life's ambition and bought a subscription to the best seat in the ampitheater. When he sat there for the first time, listening to the poet reading his new works, he was shocked to see another merchant in the same row but with an empty seat beside him. Since seats in that row were so hard to get, he asked the man why it was empty. He replied that it had been his wife's seat but she had died. 'That's very sad,' the merchant said, 'but couldn't one of your children or another member of your family come?' The other man looked sadder and said "No, they're all at her funeral rites."

Everybody in the room erupted into laughter. Parmenio shook his head, then thought for a second. "I thought Hieronymus of Cardia was sponsored by Antigonus?"

"He was," Igrat had the answer from information gained on her travels. "But he left on a trip to improve his health. He said he wasn't getting enough sleep because he spent every night listening for the sound of pits being dug. Many of Antigonus's captains have done the same. Now, he is left with only his family and those who cannot find patrons elsewhere."

Palace of Lysimachus, Lysimachia, Spring, 307 BC

"Do we really want to ask the aid of Seleucus Nikator? Every time he takes part in a war, his empire gets larger and richer while others do the fighting for him." Lysimachus looked around at his council. "Can anybody explain that?"

There was a general shaking of heads around the room. The way the Seleucid Empire was growing disturbed everybody, not least because nobody could quite work out why it was happening. The Macedonian system had been based on the army; defeat that and the country went down with it. Yet, when the Seleucid Empire went to war, it seemed that their enemies were defeated first and their armies mopped up as part of the aftermath of that defeat. That seemed unnatural, even perverse, somehow.

"We don't need to call for help right now." Leonnatus shared the general feeling of confusion when it came to dealing with Seleucus Nikator. He had never quite recovered from being driven out of Babylon or having his army destroyed as it tried to retreat north. "At the moment, all we face is the people of Callantia, who have driven out our garrison and replaced it with their own." *And I wonder who they learned that from*, he thought. "The city of Istria and a few neighboring towns have joined them but their alliance is weak and will fail under pressure. This is something we can do without invoking our alliance with Ptolemy, Seleucus and Cassander. It is better we do so, for if we ask for aid, we will always be their puppet."

"Leonnatus speaks wisely." Lysimachus was nodding in agreement. "This is a little problem, one that we can handle without assistance. I have heard it said that Callantia is attempting to bring the Thracians and Scythians into their alliance so that the whole will be a union that has weight and can offer battle with strong forces. Even if this is so, we still outnumber them and our army is battle-hardened, tested, and reliable. Their forces will be weak and divided."

"This is so." Leonnatus agreed with that assessment. "The core of their alliance is weak and all they have in common is a desire to gain autonomy. Yet that desire also means that none will yield first place to any other. While the lands of the Thracians and Scythians border upon those of Callantia, they have no interest other than looting the defeated. They will turn on their allies as soon as the gain from doing so makes the act worthwhile."

"And the riches, such as they are, will be in the cities. I wonder if those who have just gained power in Callantia and Istria realize the nature of the bargain they have just struck. I propose that we strike now, and hard. We should advance through Thrace, attempting to draw the Thracians into direct battle. If we succeed and if the Gods favor our arms with victory, then we should cross the Haemus Mountains and advance on Odessus. If the Thracians do not attempt to protect their own lands, we can live off Thracian crops and livestock while we besiege Odessus. Either way, we win. Does this seem a practical plan?"

All those present noted how Lysimachus had consulted with his advisors and treated their opinions with respect. In that, he was a striking contrast with the unyielding autocracy of Antigonus Monopthalmus and Polyperchon. Eventually, Phoenix of Tenedos asked one question. "And where is Antigonus in this matter?"

That caused a pause. Eventually Leonnatus answered with care and precision. "At the moment, Antigonus still looks to his southern and western borders, attempting to increase his power and resources. He is weak in men and coin although his strength in both improves slowly. Now, I believe he has some twenty thousand foot and five thousand horse. He will not come north. Not yet."

Phoenix nodded in agreement; like Leonnatus he had never quite recovered from the shock of the defeat at Babylon. However, unlike his commander, he had returned to Antigonus and sought service with him. That, he had been granted but the constant suspicion and fear that filled the Antigonid court had quickly convinced him that he had made a mistake. Hieronymus of Cardia had summed it up perfectly. "When people smell burning, they do not ask what but who." So, Phoenix of Tenedos had left the service of Antigonus, quietly and at night, and sought opportunities elsewhere. Leonnatus had spoken for him, and so it was that Phoenix was now in the service of Lysimachus.

"His confidence is sorely shaken. Before his defeat by Seleucus, he believed he would win every war that he took part in and that his armies would be invincible. Now, he fears defeat at every turn and explains it all by looking for signs of treachery. Sometimes I think he deliberately incites treason so that he may have the pleasure of executing those who fall into his snares." Phoenix shuddered as the memories of his brief stay in the court of Antigonus Monopthalmus swarmed into his mind. "I think you have the right of this. He will not advance unless he is sure of having massive numbers on his side. And he doesn't have them anymore."

Palace of Antigonus Monopthalmus, Celaenae, Phrygia, Spring 307 BC

"Treason, blackest treason." Antigonus Monopthalmus looked around him with deepest suspicion, trying to see if any of those around him were in league with Asander of Caria. His two chief commanders, Alcetas and Meleager, seemed shocked by the news that had just arrived. For the last two years, they had been fighting a border war with Asander, attempting to nibble away at the territories he held in Asia Minor and Cappadocia. Once, that war would have been an easy victory but Antigonus no longer had the army he had once commanded. Nor, although none would dare tell him so, was he the man he had once been. So, the military operations against Asander had been conducted by Alcetas and Meleager, both of whom had fought with one eye firmly trained on Celaenae.

The strategy had been one of attrition, to cause Asander enough losses and difficulties to make him desirous of peace. It had been fought as a series of small actions, not of any great consequence individually, but together representing an onerous burden. His people had grown restive under the constant burden of a half-war that seemed to cost much yet obtain little. And so, being hard pressed by the war, Asander had come to terms with Antigonus. Under the terms of that agreement he had transferred to Antigonus all his soldiers, he had relinquished the Greek cities he had held and held the satrapy that he had formerly ruled only as a representative of Antigonus Monopthalmus. He had even been made to declare that he remained a steadfast friend of Antigonus. Finally, Antigonus had demanded that Asander give his brother Agathon as a hostage for the fulfillment of those terms.

Once, Antigonus would have been too politically wise to inflict such harsh terms on a man whom he had not utterly defeated. Now, though, after his humiliating defeat by Seleucus and Ptolemy, such cares had been thrown to the winds. All that Antigonus cared about were the 15,000 men and 2,000 horse that Asander of Caria would add to his army and the five thousand talents of silver that would replenish his treasury. With 35,000 foot and 7,000 horse backed by silver coin, Antigonus would be able to start rebuilding his own empire.

And so it was that the greed of Antigonus for both men and coin had blinded him to the unwisdom of his actions. As soon as Asander had taken a few days to reconsider the agreement he had made and had repented of is terms, he had secretly removed his brother from custody and sent emissaries to Ptolemy and Seleucus, begging them to aid him as soon as possible. Yet, that was also the undoing of Asander for the friends of Antigonus who had stirred the population of Caria against him had also found out about those emissaries and relayed their message back to Antigonus. Antigonus, was enraged at this, more than anything else for Asander had not only betrayed his agreement but gone for aid to the two rulers Antigonus despised above all others.

"Demetrius, we will strike at Asander of Caria without delay. His province of Caria is already weak and of dubious loyalty. You will take an expedition there to liberate the cities held by Asander. Under your command, Medius will command the ships and Docimus the Army. You will take five thousand men. Start your campaign with the city of the Milesians, encouraging the citizens to assert their freedom. I will advance overland with the rest of the Army to join you."

"Where will Cassander and Lysimachus stand in this? To move against Caria is against the treaty that we signed with them?"

"Cassander is tied down maintaining his hold on Macedonia and the northern part of Greece. Polyperchon has yet to be defeated and still stands against him. If we can weaken Cassander, Polyperchon will move against him in strength."

Patala, Gandhara, Summer, 307 BC

Once again, the Phalanx was holding its ground, blocking the advance of the Mauryan infantry and thus securing the center of the battlefield. The great strength of the Mauryan infantry units lay in their archers, yet their harassing fire was of little value against the armored sarissaphoros. In contrast, few of the Mauryans wore armor and they fell in great numbers to the constant barrage of arrows and sling shots.

It was the sarissas, though, that were causing the greatest execution. The Mauryan infantry were mostly armed with swords and maces, leaving them helpless against the thick hedge of sarissa points. They didn't lack bravery or skill and they repeatedly hurled themselves against the phalanx, hoping to break or cut their way through but their efforts were futile. Slowly, they were being forced back.

To Parmenio, watching from the back of Dilipa Ganesh, this was a particularly satisfactory outcome. This border skirmish was unimportant in its own right and the ground it was being fought over wasn't worth the bones of a single sarissaphoros. The important factor here was the fact of the fight itself. It was a teaching experience for the Mauryan Army. They were learning that taking on the Seleucid Army meant a bloody fight and a heavy, one-sided butcher's bill. Or, put another way, it was better to negotiate than fight. In the back of Parmenio's mind was one grim statistic. To his certain knowledge, Chandragupta's army contained 600,000 infantrymen. In a full-scale war, he would be swamped. His primary strategic objective was to make sure that didn't happen.

"Strategos, the enemy right flank has crumpled." The words carried up from a cataphract who had ridden in with the news from the cavalry. "Their horsemen engaged us with their javelins to little effect and our charge dispersed them. The prodromoi have engaged the enemy chariots and covered themselves with honor in so doing. The chariots are mostly driven from the field except those destroyed by fire."

Parmenio waved in acknowledgement. The news meant that this particular skirmish was almost over. The nobles who commanded this Mauryan army had been on the defeated chariots. These weren't the light, two-wheeled chariots Parmenio had fought in Cappadocia but much larger four-wheeled vehicles drawn by four or even six horses. Despite their clumsiness, they were regarded as being the rightful mount of the nobility. Also, the occupants of the chariots were the only part of the Mauryan Army that wore proper armor.

In the first battle he had fought against the Mauryans, Parmenio had found them hard nuts to crack until the tactic of setting them on fire by throwing burning torches into them had been discovered. Now, their vulnerability far exceeded their tactical value. It didn't surprise Parmenio that they were quickly vanishing from the battlefield. What it did tell him was that the Mauryan Army was learning more lessons than the ones he intended.

There was something else he had learned from the series of skirmishes along the Indus. The fearsome elephants that had dominated the battles in Cappadocia and Asia Minor were far less formidable than they had seemed from the fighting a few years earlier. The elephants they were meeting now were very different beasts. They were larger and a darker gray than he had seen before. More importantly, they showed a degree of barely-restrained ferocity that the Seleucid elephants couldn't match.

In fact, even the veteran Dilipa Ganesh was obviously terrified of them and it was all his mahout could do to keep him in his position. Given a choice, Dilipa Ganesh would flee rather than stand his ground against one of the Mauryan elephants. Parmenio felt his elephant move underneath him as the nervous beast scanned the battlefield for one of the dreaded rival elephants.

"Flag of truce! Flag of truce!" The cry was being repeated along the line. Parmenio and saw that a party of six Mauryan war elephants had arrived. But, instead of advancing to try and disrupt the Seleucid phalanx, they had stopped and were displaying flags of truce.

If the enemy commander wanted to negotiate instead of fight, that suited Parmenio perfectly. He ordered the mahout Gopala to bring Dilipa Ganesh and the other Seleucid elephants forward. At first Dilipa Ganesh refused, his fear of the Mauryan elephants obvious. Gopala reached down and held a club where the elephant could see it. That did the trick. Followed by the other four Seleucid elephants, Dilipa Ganesh moved forward. Soon, the two groups of elephants were together and the difference in size was starkly obvious. Parmenio didn't like looking up at the people he negotiated with.

"The day is yours." The Indian Commander didn't sound all that upset at the admission. "I request a truce that we may gather our dead and treat our wounded."

Parmenio looked at the man riding the elephant beside him. The Indian commander had a turban with a fine jewel mounted in its center and was dressed in silk robes. They looked sumptuous but Parmenio preferred the protection offered by his battered but serviceable armor.

The Indian appeared to be in his early thirties, clean shaven but with a florid moustache. To Parmenio's surprise, he appeared to be wearing kohl eye shadow. That combined with his heavy eyebrows gave him a slight resemblance to Igrat. Parmenio was very careful not to laugh at that thought. "A truce would be acceptable, especially to care for those who have fought in our service."

The Indian Commander gave a series of orders to his men. Parmenio watched as his officers spread the word along the ranks of Mauryan infantry. The air of relief from those men was palpable. Nobody liked being defeated but facing that hedge of spearpoints was something they did not relish. Parmenio gave his orders and he heard the swishing noise as the sarissas were swung from horizontal to vertical.

Fourth Diodochi War

Behind the Seleucid lines, the camp followers began to set about treating the wounded as they were brought back. What had once been an extemporized process was now a smoothly organized drill. It was one, Parmenio noticed, that the Indian commander watched with rapt attention.

"I had heard how your army fights but I wanted to see it for myself. I had thought that the story of the wall of spears was a fiction, thought up by my commanders to excuse their defeats. But, I see it is not." The Indian spoke Attic Greek, slowly and with much stumbling, but Parmenio had to admit that it was a lot better than his command of the local languages. "That is what you call the Phalanx? How do you get it to change direction?"

"It is. Changing front was a matter that challenged us greatly and it was only after much thought that we discovered how it could be achieved." *By a miracle and the intervention of the Gods.* Parmenio thought. *Once a phalanx sets off, only the Gods themselves can change its course. But I'm not going to admit that.*

"Hmmm." Parmenio caught the suspicion in the Indian's voice. "Another question, why do you bring draft elephants into the battle? They will not stand against war elephants. Especially not mine."

"Your Majesty. I did not know I had the honor of addressing the great Chandragupta Maurya. My apologies for any discourtesy." Parmenio kicked himself for not putting the evidence together faster. In retrospect, he realized that he had been distracted by the kohl Chandragupta Maurya was wearing. *Whatever else you do, do not underestimate this man. He has clawed his way to the top of the Indian aristocracy by sheer, raw talent. In doing so, he is uniting India under a single leadership for the first time in centuries. He is also the key to this situation and I must know what kind of mn he is,*

Maurya laughed in delight. "I was here incognito, as just another one of my commanders. No offense was offered and none taken. You are the great King Seleucus Nikator, successor to Alexander?"

Parmenio shook his head. "I am Parmenio the Younger, Strategos to His Majesty Seleucus Nikator. I represent him in this region."

"A Strategos. I have heard of this rank. A man who is one step above a General, one who decides how a war should be fought. Strategos Parmenio the Younger. I have six hundred thousand infantry, one hundred thousand cavalry, nine thousand war elephants and six thousand chariots. How will you fight us with your forty thousand men and forty draft elephants?"

Parmenio thought about that. "Very, very carefully."

284

Maurya erupted into laughter, a healthy, honest bellow of a laugh. "That is a good start to strategy. Yes. But even with great care, you will be outnumbered twenty to one. This will be a hopeless war for you."

"Perhaps first, we should ask ourselves whether a war is necessary?" Parmenio was taking this very carefully. "There are solutions to wars other than fighting. Especially where the greater interests of both sides might be solved by not fighting."

Maurya stopped laughing and looked at Parmenio hard. "You would be prepared to negotiate over the provinces of Arachosia, Gedrosia, Paropamisadae, and Aria?"

"It is . . . . possible. I have discretion in such matters. We both have greater interests to bear in mind. You have the Deccan provinces issue for example and the question of the South generally, For all your army's size, a few bad defeats would chew it up and leave you vulnerable. The same applies to us. What I have here is barely more than a border guard. We could bring the full regular Seleucid Army here but, fighting such a numerous force as yours would chew us up and leave us vulnerable to our enemies. Much better, I think, that we should negotiate."

"It sounds almost as if you propose an alliance between us?"

"Is not an alliance better than war? Two empires separated only by a border agreeable to both and open to trade between them? Goods and ideas flowing freely backed by trust and friendship. In such a world, each may concentrate on its true enemies and rely on its allies for friendly and profitable discourse."

Maurya nodded carefully. "Such an agreement might well be . . . . . . possible."

Parmenio looked up again at the great dark-gray war elephant. "You keep calling my elephants draft elephants. I can see yours are much greater beasts but the difference you make comes from . . . ?"

Maurya pushed out his lower lip slightly. "Your elephants have been bred in captivity for use as draft animals. To carry loads, to pull and to push, to flatten and build up. But, war elephants cannot be bred in captivity. They must grow up in the wild, then be captured and trained for war. We have great areas set aside in our country where wild elephant herds roam free until we need to capture some for our use.

"Let me give you some advice, Strategos, faced with a male elephant, a female will always run away rather than fight. Faced with a real war elephant, even a male of your draft elephants will run as if it were a female. Do not place reliance upon these draft elephants of yours. They will do well when only faced by men or horses but against real war elephants, they will flee the field."

Parmenio nodded. "Your Majesty, your advice is welcome and shows great sincerity in our mutual desire to avoid war. Perhaps, we could negotiate an alliance in more comfortable surroundings?" *And our casual conversation has just told me where those negotiations should go.*

CHAPTER TWO

STRATEGIC GAMES

Galley **Leontophoros,** *Harbor of Caunus, Caria, Summerset, 307 BC*

Tetrarchès Hyakinthos was quickly coming to the belief that his commander, the famous Demetrius Poliorcetes, had learned a lot from his sieges. Hyakinthos was a veteran of the siege of Tyre and had seen how Demetrius had created new and wondrous machines to help bring down city walls. He also remembered that, for all the ingenuity of those machines, Tyre had never fallen. Gaza had indeed been taken by the Antigonid Army, but it had been recaptured by Ptolemy's forces within days. There was something else as well; he remembered how the great siege tower Helepolis had burned at Tyre. The ghosts of the murdered Argyraspides has passed through the wood, bronze and soaked rawhide covers to burn the tower from the inside out. As a veteran Sarissaphoros, Hyakinthos feared no man, but of vengeful ghosts he was mortally afraid.

In a strange way, that was a comfort to him. Being on a great ship, the largest in the Antigonid Navy, he felt that the ghosts of the Argyraspides would not pursue him to sea. In any case, the *Leontophoros* was like no ship anybody had ever seen before. She had two hulls, separated by a narrow gap, and with a wide, flat deck joining them. On that deck were mounted a battery of catapults. To Hyakinthos's knowledge, nobody had ever built a ship specifically to act as a platform for catapults before. Naval actions were decided by ramming and boarding, not catapults. He did not even know whether it was possible to hit another ship with catapult fire. He did know that Demetrius Poliorcetes has searched through his army to find the most skilled catapult operators he had and concentrated them on this ship. That made serving on the *Leontophoros* and her sister ship, the *Olympias* running just a few sarissa-lengths away, an honor.

They were making their approach to the harbor of Caunus from the west, with the setting sun at their back. The hope was that the glare of the sun beginning to settle on the horizon would blind the defenders and add to the shock of what was happening. Hyakinthos heard the rhythmic thud of the drums pick up tempo. They were accelerating to their battle speed. That was a lot slower than the half-dozen triremes that were escorting them. The *Leontophoros* had three banks of oars, 25 oars per bank and ten men per oar. 1,500 men and for all their efforts, the ship could barely make five knots. The triremes could make at least seven. On the other hand, the triremes needed the speed margin if they were to keep the triremes of Lysimachus away from the *Leontophoros* while she did her work.

"Get ready to fire." Hekatontarchès Draco looked over the bows towards where eight triremes of Lysimachus were clustered in port. Draco was in charge of the four catapults on the *Leontophoros*. He had been with Hyakinthos since Tyre and the two men had a good understanding. Neither liked what they were about to do and both feared that they were about to stir up more angry spirits to torment them. "Load the catapults."

The catapult crews brought out earthenware pots. Each was filled with a light oil chosen for its flammability, and had, as a fuse, a cloth strip soaked in the same oil. The stink of the oil almost made Hyakinthos sick; it was far too similar to the oil that had been used to burn the Argyraspides for any man to be around it and remain easy in his mind. Standing beside the catapults was a man with a lighted torch. When Draco gave the order, the fuse on the jars of oil was lit and the catapults released to send the oil jars arcing towards the enemy triremes. Hyakinthos could follow them easily by the thread of black smoke left by the burning fuse.

Two of the four jars from the *Leontophoros* fell short but the impact of the other pair was marked by a ball of orange fire rising from one of the triremes. It ballooned outwards, snaking up the mast and outlining the rigging in orange fire. Before the fire could develop further on its own, the ship alongside was hit by a jar from the *Olympias* and it too erupted into flames. The two fires wrapped around each other and merged into an inferno that engulfed both ships.

On the *Leontophoros* the catapult crews were working furiously, cranking the winches that drew the catapult arm back. As it bent back to its launch position, another crewman with a jar of oil ran put and loaded the bucket. The *Leontophoros* swerved in the water as the portside rowers backed their oars. Another order, another salvo of four oil-filled jars arched out and burst on the decks of the triremes tied up at the dockside. Even without their added fuel, the fires were spreading so fast that there was no hope of containing them. Hyakinthos saw the crewmen jumping over the side into the water. Some were already on fire and he knew that their jumps were as much to end their agony as a last, desperate attempt to save their lives. Draco was standing beside him and watching the end of Lysimachus's fleet. His words bit deep into Hyakinthos's soul. "And now we are become like Antigonus."

Worse was to come and both men knew it. The oarsmen on the *Leontophoros* and the *Olympias* were coordinating their strokes so the two ships were turning on their axis. In one way, that was a mercy since it hid the sight of the burning triremes and their crews but it brought into view their next target. The city itself. Normally, the city was protected by its walls but with the harbor in the hands of the Antigonid fleet, the *Leontophoros* and the *Olympias* were already within the walls and had a clear line of fire to the heart of the city.

"Prepare to fire on Caunus. Aim at the city center." Trierarch Acacius knew that the catapults wouldn't reach that far but having a distinct point of aim in the fading light would give a more devastating pattern of shots.

"Trierarch, we can't. That's where the women and children have taken shelter!" Draco's voice was filled with horror. Pounding a city with jars of burning oil was nothing new but city walls limited the areas that could be hit to the periphery. The women and children would gather in the city center where they would be away from the fighting and thus relatively safe. Only, this time, the same move had put them directly into the line of fire from the catapults mounted on the *Leontophoros* and the *Olympias*.

"Are you going to tell Antigonus Monopthalmus that he can't do something? Or, that you won't follow your orders? Perhaps you have a desire to end your life sitting in a pit filled with oil-soaked straw? . . . I thought not. Now, load those catapults and keep them firing on the city center. Remember how the citizens of Babylon rose against the army of Leonnatus and drove him from the city in ignoble and womanish flight? Shame on us if the citizens of Caunus were to do the same! If this fate is to be avoided, they must fear us. "

Headquarters of Antigonus Monopthalmus, Caunus, Caria, Summerset, 307 BC

"A messenger from Tralles, Your Majesty. On hearing of the fate of Caunus, the citizens opened the gates and bade our troops enter in peace. And so it is with all the other cities in Caria; all have now been made subject to the rule of His Majesty, Antigonus Monopthalmus! Ptolemaeus has taken Issus and is holding it with an adequate force, compelling that city to support the noble Antigonus."

Antigonus grunted in acknowledgement of the courier's words. He had arrived in Caunus a few hours earlier and spent the time since then inspecting the charred ruins of Lysimachus's fleet and the still-smoldering ruins of the city center. The bombardment by the two catapult ships had been ineffective at first since the burning oil had failed to penetrate the buildings. Then, the ships had switched to using boulders first to open the roofs and crush walls. After that had been done, the burning oil had done its work. The bodies still being cleared from the burned buildings showed that.

"And your part in the capture of Caunus, Meleager?"

That was the question Meleager had feared. He would have loved to have told of a heroic fight on the city walls during which he had led his men in unmatched feats of valor. There was a problem with that. He had indeed been making continuous attacks on the side of the citadel where it was most easily assailed but they had been largely fruitless. Then, the great fires had erupted in the city center and the defenders on the walls had abandoned the walls in a desperate attempt to rescue their families. Meleager had used battering rams to force open the gates but he had been able to do so undisturbed by any efforts on the part of the defenders. His final assault had been unopposed and he had not lost a single man.

He was sorely tempted to create a myth of the battle on the walls but he was realistic enough to know that it would fall apart very quickly. And that he had enough enemies who would make sure that it would do so. That thought gave him the answer. If he couldn't gain glory from the fall of Caunus, he would make allies by ensuring others did.

"Alas, your Majesty, my part was so small and insignificant that it barely deserves mention. All the honor and glory from this great victory goes to the Trierarchs Acacius and Paramonos. Their naval attack on the port and heart of the city opened the way for us to enter almost unopposed. There is much we can learn here for attacks on other cities."

"Coastal cities, certainly. We must build more ships like the *Leontophoros* and the *Olympias*. Order the shipyards to work on them immediately. Meleager, your honesty and forthrightness is pleasing to me."

Who are you and what have you done with the real Antigonus Monopthalmus? Meleager thought. *Honesty and forthrightness usually gets the speaker burned alive.*

At that point, another herald arrived. "Your Majesty, the ambassadors from the Aetolians and the Boeotians, have arrived, bearing gifts of goods and coin. They request an audience and hope that you will consider making an alliance with them."

"Bid them enter."

The Aetolian and the Boeotian ambassadors entered the room and dropped to their knees. "Your Majesty, your exploits fill us all with hope that the dark days currently upon us might be lifted. Lysisimachus has moved swiftly and decisively against the city of Odessus. Beginning a siege, he quickly frightened the inhabitants and took the city by storm. Thereafter he moved with equal speed against the Istrians and recovered their city in a similar way. With his flanks thus secured, he set out against the Callantians. The hopes of that city were raised by the arrival of the Scythians and the Thracians who advanced on the Army of Lysimachus with large forces to aid their allies in accordance with their treaty. But, the Army of Lysimachus, commanded by Leonnatus, met and engaged them at once. His first assault fell upon the Thracians who were so terrified by the force of his assault and the battle-tested courage of his men that they changed sides. The Scythians were then defeated in a pitched battle and left to flee in ignominious rout. Leonnatus pursued them without mercy, slaying many of them and driving the survivors beyond the frontiers. While he was so engaged, Lysimachus encamped about the city of the Callantians and laid siege to it. He promises them no mercy since he is very eager to chastise in every way those who were responsible for the revolt."

Antigonus regarded the Ambassadors with curiosity. "And what part do you play in all of this?"

"Directly, none. Our interest is in Greece. Our province is in the hands of Cassander but our preference is for an alliance with Polyperchon. Yet, the fate of Odessus, Istria and Callentia shows us that we cannot hope to rebel against Cassander and be met with success. We need to have strong support from others if we are to join with Polyperchon. Great Antigonus, we beg you to help us throw off the chains of the usurper Cassander and aid us!"

"And how do you suggest that I do that?" Antigonus was suspicious, looking keenly at the ambassadors in an effort to determine the nature of the trap they were preparing for him.

"Your Majesty, if you advance upon Lysimachus and come to the rescue of Callentia before it falls to sack and rapine, then Cassander will have to respond to this by marching to the aid of Lysimachus. At the very least he will be forced to split his army between the campaign in Asia Minor and containing Polyperchon within the Peloponnesus. We will be able to defeat him in detail, you with your Army here, we with Polyperchon in Greece.

It is a sound plan. Antigonus thought to himself. *Cassander's position, with a potential split in his forces between Macedonia and Greece, has always been weaker than it seems and Lysimachus is a weak ally, of little value except as a sacrifice for obtaining some advantage or other. But, an attack on his ally will indeed force Cassander to come to his aid and split his army before me. Yes, this is a sound plan.*

"Very well. Your words bring much wisdom and I take pleasure in your counsel. The Army of Antigonus Monopthalmus will indeed march to the rescue of Callentia under the command of my trusted general Meleager. I will look to my old ally Polyperchon to assist you in breaking free from the oppression of Cassander's usurped rule."

The Ambassadors backed away, delighted with the promises and kind words they had received. Antigonus watched them depart. *Yes, it was indeed a sound plan that you proposed. But I have a much sounder one.*

Pancratius's Date Wine and Molasses Factory, Seleucia on the Tigris, Winterfall, 307BC

Lillith bit into the pastry she had been offered and savored the taste. "This is exquisite. How did you make it?'

"We start with the date wine." Philemon was very proud of the operation he had started and that pride showed in his voice. "We get the best dates we can find, chop them finely and boil the chopped dates and honey in water for one of the marks on the candle. We take the syrup so made and place it in a fermentation jar to cool. We then add the juice of lemons and a strong tea made by steeping basil and thyme in hot water. Then, we stir in the wine yeast. The fermentation jar is then covered and left to ferment for two days, stirring daily. Now, this is the crucial part. We use a linen filter and strain the liquor into a jar. There is a secret here that you must not divulge. We have a special seal for that jar that allows excess fermentation gas to leave the jar but prevents air from coming in. We then take the jar to the fermentation room and allow the wine yeast to do its work. When fermentation has ceased, we transfer the wine into a clean jar and move the new jar to the maturing room. It's cooler there so the fermentation will not restart. We then leave it to mature. When our taster decides the date wine is ready and stable, we put it into jars for sale."

Lillith listened patiently, knowing that Philemon's expertise was what made this factory such a sound investment. Instead of hurrying him up, she finished her pastry and delicately licked her fingers. Philemon smiled, almost triumphantly, and then continued. "Remember I said the crucial part was when we strained the liquor? We take the solids that have been left in the filter and blend them with crushed nuts and honey. This makes thick paste. Then Allon, the baker you recommended to us visits us, sees how much paste we have and makes a fine flake pastry in quantities to match. He then wraps our paste in his pastry and bakes it. And there, we have our pastry. We do not try to increase production or to lower quality to gain more customers. Instead, everybody knows that there will only be a limited number on a given day and when they are sold, there will be no more until the next batch is made. Those who were disappointed one day come early the next and pay a premium to ensure it does not happen again."

"I can see why. The pastries are delicious. But, I am sorry to say I find your date wine is a little too sweet for my taste."

Philemon nodded. "Between ourselves, I agree. But, we have to go by what the market demands. Most people asked us for a sweeter wine so we had to add extra honey to the recipe. A pity, I find the extra sweetness a little cloying."

"Why don't we do a range of wines? Some sweet, some less so. It would mean we would have to keep track of the batches but the added expense should be small and the extended market should easily cover the cost."

Once again, Philemon nodded. "That would make sense. We could just mark the fermentation vessels with different colors. Blue for sweet perhaps and red for sharp. I'll talk to my brewmaster about this. Now, to business. I have your monthly payment ready."

That made Lillith smile. This was the part of these meetings she enjoyed. Reaching into the pouch at her waist, she took out a square piece of wood called a tallystick. All four faces had notches cut in them that revealed how much Philemon had borrowed to set up this winery, how many repayments he had to make and the amount of each. The most important face was painted red. This showed how many payments had been made. Solemnly, Lillith and Philemon compared their tallysticks, carefully checking each face to ensure the two sticks were identical. Once that formality had been completed and both convinced that all was in order, Lillith took the pouch of money from Philemon.

"The agreed amount, milady. Less one copper coin."

That made Lillith lift an eyebrow. "Why less one copper coin?"

"The price of your pastry, milady."

The two looked at each other and then both erupted into laughter . Eventually, Lillith dabbed at her eyes with a small cloth. "Now, that is what I call responsible accounting. I'll put another copper coin in the bag and we'll be square."

She reached into her bag, took out a copper coin and dropped it in with Philemon's monthly repayment. Then she carefully cut two notches, one in her tallystick and one in Philemon's. Holding the two together, the cuts lined up perfectly. Satisfied, she returned her stick to her pouch and watched Philemon do the same with his.

"Milady, please do not take this the wrong way, but may I urge you to take a little care? For the last few weeks, I have had a feeling that this place is being watched on the days you come here. I mentioned my feeling to Allon the Baker and he has had the same impression. Perhaps somebody knows that you leave here carrying gold coin and wishes to relieve you of it?"

Lillith took a steady breath. "I, too have had a feeling of being watched. Perhaps it is just the way our city has grown over the last few years and become more rowdy. But, my driver is a good, strong man and most loyal. Thank you for your warning though. I will indeed take extra care." *And I think I know who is behind this and what he intends. I am bait and the only difference between me and a goat is that I know that I am bait.*

Outside the Citadel of Oreüs, Euboea, Greece. Spring, 306BC

Phoenix of Tenedos knew that the siege wouldn't last much longer. Since arriving from the court of Lysimachus with a detachment of engineers, he had watched his catapults slowly battering the Citadel of Oreüs into submission. It had taken time but that was the secret of a siege. *Do it slowly, do it right.* Putting down the Callantian revolt had made the Army of Lysimachus experts in bringing down city walls.

"We should get the storming parties ready." Pentakosiarch Phoibos had his five hundred men ready and waiting for the assault. He was interrupted by the rumbling crash of another section of city wall collapsing. Phoenix already had his breach in the wall but he was using the concentrated fire of his catapults to widen it. There was a careful balance to be struck and Phoibos knew it. The wider the gap, the more difficult it would be for the Oreütians to stop the assault parties from streaming through. But, the longer it took to create that gap, the more time the Oreütians would have to build new defenses inside the breached wall.

"Get them ready, yes, but we'll batter those walls for a little longer yet. No reason to lose more men than we have to. With a little luck, the Oreütians will see the breach and realize they can't stop us." Phoenix hoped it would be that way. The rules were simple and clearly understood. Once the walls were breached to the extent that an assault was practical, the city had a chance to surrender. If they did, they would be occupied and relieved of a significant portion of their treasury but the occupying troops would be under control and kept disciplined. If, however, the city refused to surrender and the assault troops had to fight their way in, then the city would be sacked. The survivors of the assaulting troops would be let off the leash and allowed to take whatever they wanted. Gold, goods and women would all be fair game. It would not be a good time then to be a citizen of the town. Plundering, looting and rape could go on for days and the only rule would be 'pillage before you burn.' The problem was that an Army given over to looting and rapine wouldn't be fit for combat for days or weeks afterwards. It had even been known for a Strategos to deliberately accept a friendly city being given over to sack in order to weaken an enemy army before a major battle.

Phoibos shook his head. "Our Chiliarch said that the Oreütians have refused to see reason. They hold fast to the belief that Polyperchon will send men and ships to rescue them before the assault takes place. Damned fools. They gamble their lives and the honor of their women on a hope that Polyperchon will consider them of great enough value to raise our siege?"

"It's not Polyperchon that worries me." Phoenix watched yet another length of the city wall crumbling. "He's old and tired. He and Cassander have been fighting for more than a decade and neither of them have gained the upper hand. Cassander had Macedonia and Attica, Polyperchon has the Peloponnesus and that hasn't changed. Thank the gods that they both had the sense to realize that they weren't getting anywhere and have settled for harassing each other. That's all we are doing here you know. When we take Oreüs, Cassander will have established a position on Polyperchon's flanks, one that will threaten his supply and communications lines. Then, there'll be an adjustment in the status quo. That's all. Frankly, I think Cassander is just waiting for the old man to die."

"Then, if we not fear Polyperchon, who do we?"

"Antigonus Monopthalmus of course." Phoenix shuddered slightly at mention of the name and his nose seemed to catch the scent of burning flesh. "Every time he has tried to solidify his position in Asia Minor, he has come unstuck. The thrashing Seleucus Nikator gave him the last time round was the last straw. Now Antigonus has seized Caria, he'll be looking for other options. He's got an army again, in manpower at least, and he has silver if not gold. And he took Caria from the sea. I think he's looking at Greece right now and measuring his steps across the Aegean. Look at it. Rhodes first, then easy steps across the sea until he lands in the Peloponnesus and joins up with Polyperchon. Then, they take on Cassander and at least drive him back to Macedonia. At some point Polyperchon will find himself sitting in a straw-filled pit and then it will just be Antigonus. If we take the coalition of three who fought him before, Cassander is the weakest. Once he is gone, Antigonus will turn on Ptolomy. Divide and conquer. And that will leave Seleucus on his own."

"Where is Seleucus? It seems strange that he has not become involved in this."

"Out on his eastern borders, so I am told, dealing with some native uprising or other. On the whole, everybody thinks that's a good thing. If we appealed to him for aid, we would get it. We would be treated with honor and respect, given gifts of great value and made welcome members of his court under his personal protection. And, somehow, during the process, we would end up as parts of his Empire."

Phoibos pushed out his lower lip. "So, it's a pit of burning straw from Antigonus or wealth, honor and friendship from Seleucus. That's a hard choice to make."

Phoenix of Tenedos burst out laughing at the sarcasm in Phoibos's voice. "A hard choice indeed. Let us hope we do not have to make it . . . what in the name of all the gods is going on?"

The great fireballs rising over the harbor of Oreüs told him that, whatever it was, it wasn't good.

The Harbor of Oreüs, Euboea, Greece. Spring, 306BC

"Get water on those hides now! And get those ships under way!" Telesphorus of Peloponnesus saw the trails of fire in the darkness as oil-jars arched through the air towards his ships. He had twenty of his own triremes with a thousand soldiers on board, men specially trained for the savagery of a boarding action. Those ships were covering thirty ships of Cassander that were blockading the port. Cassander's soldiers, some three thousand in number, were on shore, besieging Oreüs. That had left his ships vulnerable and they were depending on Telesphorus for protection. He felt that trust deeply and he was determined that the thirty should not be disappointed by the valor of the twenty.

What he had not expected was for Medius of Phrygia to arrive from Asia with a hundred ships. Just to make matters worse, sitting in the middle of the flock of triremes was a huge, double-hulled vessel. Telesphorus recognized it immediately as one of the new catapult ships designed and built by Antigonus. He had heard how two similar ships had fallen on the ships of Lysimachus defending the harbor of Caunus and thrown fire into them, burning and destroying them all. He had heard of that and taken note. Now, his ships had their cloth awnings replaced by rawhide that was already being soaked with buckets of seawater to fend off the threat of burning oil. He had trained his oarsmen to get his ships under way with minimum delay and to move as fast as they could stroke their oars. He had heard how the ships of Lysimachus had been burned while they were motionless at their wharves and he had a feeling the great catapult ships would have a harder task dealing with moving targets.

"Stroke your oars and I'll give you gold to stroke your whores!" Telesphorus's voice roared out, bringing a roar of laughter from his men. His ship, the trireme *Pontos* surged forward as they threw all their strength into their work. Then, there was silence as one of the fire-trailing oil jars headed straight for them. Telesphorus could sense them holding their breath while they waited for the impact.

They didn't have to wait long for the jar struck the rawhide overhead and shattered, spreading burning oil over the hides. Yet, the water and wet skins did their work for the oil spread and flowed over the side into the sea. A few splatters hit the wooden decks but the soldiers raced to throw sand over the pools of fire before the timbers could catch. Water would just spread the flames but sand choked them off at birth.

The oarsmen cheered the soldiers who had snuffed out the flames, rivalry between Army and Navy being forgotten in the triumph over the burning oil. Then, there was a rhythmic thudding as the oarsmaster started beating his drum in a steady measure. The strokes of the oarsmen settled into a steady, synchronized ripple that maximized speed.

Looking ahead of the *Pontos*, Telesphorus saw that Medius of Phrygia was in process of making a bad mistake. His catapult ship had opened fire on the blockading triremes of Cassander and set four of them on fire. That shamed Telesphorus, and he could but hope that his negligence would be made good by the destruction he was about to inflict. For, the triremes of Medius had followed the oil bombardment and were closing on Cassander's ships. In doing so, they had left the slow and clumsy catapult ship behind. It, and a small group of Median triremes, were isolated in the rear of the enemy fleet with the Peloponnesian ships closing in on them. Telesphorus couldn't understand why his twenty ships were being ignored. Then it dawned on him, we *have the seal of Peloponnesus on our sails and the enemy must believe we are allies. Poor intelligence brings its own penalties.*

Pontoswas closing on the enemy catapult ship fast. Telesphorus took a deep breath, *And now it starts.* "Ramming Speed!"

The oarsmaster picked up the rhythm, his drumsticks beating out a wild tattoo that drove the oarsmen into a frenzy of action. Moving fast already, the Pontospicked up yet more speed, swinging towards the lumbering catapult ship. Telesphorus could read her name now, the letters clearly visible. *Amphitrite.* This was when timing would be essential. His men knew what was coming, they were waiting for his word. He stared at the *Amphitrite* looming closer, the beginning of panic clearly visible on her quarterdeck as the officers realized that something was terribly wrong. His mind calculated the speed of his ship, the angle of approach and the distance between him and his target. At precisely the right moment, a moment so finely judged that a novice in shiphandling would call it a miracle, Telesphorus called out his order. "Ship Oars!"

His oarsmen knew what was about to happen and they wasted no time on swinging their oars to the vertical. A split second after their oars were clear, the bronze ram of the *Pontos* slammed into the first oar bank of *Amphitrite*, sheering the catapult ship's oars off in a cacophony of splintering wood. From inside the hull came the screams of the oarsmen as the butt end of the shattered oars crushed their chests and broke their backs. The angle of impact was perfect from Telesphoros's point of view. Instead of getting stuck in the side of *Amphitrite*, *Pontos* bounced down her length, ripping off her oars and crippling her. By the time the trireme's momentum was spent, more than two thirds of the *Amphitrite's* oarsmen down the stricken side were either dead or crippled. More crucially, their oars had been destroyed and there were not enough spares to replace them all. Win, lose or draw, *Amphitrite* was a cripple.

"Follow Me!" Telesphoros screamed the order and leaped the gap that separated the two ships. He was followed by his trained boarding party and as many seamen as could be spared. There were no shields in this fight; the tight, confined spaces of a warship were no place to struggle with a shield – or a sarissa come to that. His men had been trained to fight with a sword in one hand and an axe in the other. Behind them, the seamen had axes and clubs or flaming torches. The battle for the *Amphitrite* was on.

The crew of the catapult ship lacked neither bravery nor skill. They were mostly soldiers, brought in to operate the catapults and they knew their trade. They also knew something else; the *Amphitrite* carried a huge crew compared with the triremes and they outnumbered the boarding party by at least ten to one. And so, although driven back by the ferocity of the initial assault, they quickly regained order and began their counter-attack.

The fight was merciless, with quarter being neither asked nor given. Men died, on both sides, clubbed down, run through with the sword or butchered by the swinging axes. Their bodies tumbled over the side or down into the depths of the ships where the oarsmen were frantically trying to undo the damage from the initial ramming. Telesphoros saw his men giving ground as he knew they would have to, given the odds against them. Yet, they had achieved their goal for behind them, the seamen had reached the lines of oil-filled earthenware jars that waited to be loaded on to the catapults. The jars were thin to ensure they shattered when they struck their target and were no match for the axes wielded against them. The sounds of the jars splintering into shards as the axes did their work were drowned out by the screams and clash of the battle being fought but an arms-length away. And so it was that, at first, the crew of the *Amphitrite* did not notice the thin oil running out across the deck.

It was what Telesphoros had been waiting for. His objective was not to capture the *Amphitrite* for the disparity in the ship's crews made that impossible. Instead, he intended to burn her. He saw the oil from the broken jars start to spread and sounded the retreat. The surviving men from his boarding party immediately started to make their way back to the *Pontos*, hotly pursued by crewmen of the *Amphitrite*. It was when the latter felt the oil under their feet that they knew what fate awaited them. By then it was too late. The seamen from the *Pontos* had already hurled their torches into the stack of broken oil jars and the *Amphitrite* was already burning.

Alongside the *Amphitrite*, the Pontosoarsmen were already using their oars to push their ship clear. The boarding party were leaping from the *Amphitrite* on to the *Pontos*, trying to keep ahead of the flames that roared across the catapult ship's decks. The last few had to jump into the sea and were rescued by oarsmen who swung their blades down and gave them something to hold on to until they could be brought on board. Others had helped their wounded friends escape but, watching the developing inferno, Telesphoros knew that some of his wounded must have been left behind. He resolved, there and then, to make offerings to the Sauadai so that the water-spirits would look after their souls and lead them to paradise.

The *Amphitrite* was beyond saving. What shocked Telesphoros were the explosions that racked her. As the unbroken oil jars were enveloped by the fires, they burst open and sprayed their contents in a blazing rain across the stricken ship. The fires enveloping her spread far faster as a result and had quickly penetrated into the very heart of the ship. Her crew had given up the fight to save her and were jumping over the side in a desperate effort to avoid incineration. Once again, the oarsmen on Pontoswere dipping their blades in the water to try and rescue their fellow sailors. Quite apart from the fact that it was proper and honorable thing to do, Telesphoros approved their actions on practical grounds. The men his ship was rescuing would sign on for his crew and replace the men he had lost this night.

With *Amphitrite* already rolling over as the fires consumed her, Telesphoros had a chance to look around. Off to his left, the trireme *Nereus* had boarded and captured one of Medius's ships. Near her, *Okeanos* had done the same. A third of his triremes, he couldn't make out which one in the darkness, was locked in battle with a Median ship. The rest of his fleet was moving in behind the ships commanded by Medius of Phrygia. The battle with the *Amphitrite* and the triremes with her had delayed the advance of his ships but they were still on their way to join Cassander. The only problem was that Medius's ships were between them.

Suddenly, Telesphoros saw Cassander sailing out against the enemy and realized what was happening. Medius and his ships had assumed that the bombardment from the *Amphitrite* would so distract Cassander that he would be unable to respond to the attack on them. As a result, Medius and his Captains were off their guard. Also, the tide had turned and was now driving their ships towards the lee shore. The same tide was carrying both Cassander's and Telesphoros's ships towards the enemy fleet. Although Medius still greatly outnumbered his enemies and had inflicted greater loss than he had so far suffered, in numbers of ships sunk or captured at least, his tactical position was little short of catastrophic. He could not advance against the tide to engage Cassander nor could he do so against Telesphoros. He could fight where he was and be driven ashore by the winds and tide or he could disengage and head out to sea. Either way, he would be counted as having lost the battle despite a great superiority in numbers of ships.

Medius elected to break off the battle. He and his surviving ships started to withdraw, past the burning wreck of the *Amphitrite*. He had destroyed four ships belonging to Cassander but he had lost one ship sunk and three ships seized with their crews by Telesphoros. His mission, to raise the siege of Oreüs, had failed.

Cassander's Flagship **Lesbos**, *Oreüs, Euboea, Greece.*

"All hail, Telesphoros! Victor of the battle." Cassander's cry echoed around the deck of his flagship.

Telesphoros stopped and shook his head. "My Lord, I failed you. You charged me with protecting your ships inshore yet four of them were lost by fire. I do not merit your praise. At least, let me offer you the three ships we captured as partial replacement for your losses."

Cassander pretended to be amazed at the words of Telesphoros. "You attack one hundred ships with twenty, sink their largest and most powerful and capture three more. And then you apologize for your failure!"

He turned to his officers and spread his hands helplessly, "What do I say? If this is what Telesphoros calls failure, what in the name of all the gods does he call success? Driving a hundred ships before him in headlong flight while rowing a coracle and armed only with a stylus? Telesphoros, you are too modest. Certainly the gods smiled on us tonight and the tide turned at the right time to give us our victory. But it is the duty of a leader to know when the gods have favored his enterprise and take full advantage thereof. It is the duty of an Admiral to know when the tides run and the winds blow and make his plans accordingly. Above all it is the duty of an Admiral and a leader to prepare for battle and be ready for the enemy. Brave Telesphoros, all these things you did. You were prepared for battle and knew what to do and when. The gods may favor us but it is for us to take their favor and exploit it to achieve our ends. So, I say again. All Hail Telesphoros, victor of the battle of Oreüs!"

The cheers of the men on Cassander's fleet echoed across the harbor, not just honoring the victory won the Telesphoros but also the speech of

Cassander that had not only given richly deserved praise but had also provided wise lessons to other men who might wish to emulate the success of Telesphoros.

Eventually, the cries of acclamation died down, and Cassander once again spoke. "Telesphoros, your kind offer of the three captured ships is accepted. Not in compensation for those lost, for losses in war are inevitable and it is to those who started this war we must look for compensation. That is a matter we will take up with the foul betrayer and murderer Antigonus Monopthalmus. I accept your gift to honor your bravery and hereby declare that the largest and most powerful of the captured ships shall bear your name. Furthermore, on behalf of our alliance and with the agreement of the allies gathered here, I appoint you Admiral of all our ships. Lysimachus is away, fighting in Caria but my other ally is here with us. Come, share wine with me and my honored ally, the noble Polyperchon."

Elefsina, Greece, Summerset, 306 BC

"Cassander stays to the north of us, not daring to advance from Chalcis." Ptolemaeus had been sent by Antigonus to attack Cassander on his home ground. He had landed in Elefsina Bay and established his operating base there. He had an army of five thousand foot and five hundred horse while the bay itself was occupied by a hundred and fifty ships under the command of Medius. Ten of those ships were Rhodian. The occupants of Rhodes had declared for Antigonus and supplied him with those ten ships and a force of a thousand foot. "That lack of enterprise opens the way to Athens for us. There, we will be joined by the Boetians with two thousand two hundred foot and one thousand three hundred horse and by the Aetolians with two thousand foot and a thousand horse. Once we have secured Athens and freed it from the oppression of Cassander, we can march north and threaten his hold on Chalcis."

Medius looked at the map that was spread out before him. "Ten thousand two hundred foot and two thousand eight hundred horse. And Cassander has?"

"Eighteen thousand foot and two thousand horse. He outnumbers us now, but Polyperchon moves up from the South with twenty thousand infantry and at least one thousand horsemen. Once he has joined with us, we will have the forces we need to sweep Cassander out of Greece. Then, we can place Heracles, son of Alexander and Barsine on the throne once held by the great Alexander himself."

"That is old One-Eye's plan?" Medius was surprised. It was generally accepted that Antigonus only considered one person a fit occupant for that throne and that was Antigonus himself. Anybody with other ideas usually died.

"It is Polyperchon's price for this alliance. He has Barsine and Heracles in protective custody and placing the son of Alexander on the throne was his one demand. He has been loyal to the Regents and has always acted on their behalf. If he had not been so, this Barsine would have gone the way of Barsine Stateira and her son with her. A few years ago, Antigonus would not have accepted such a demand but now he has little choice so severely has his power been reduced by the war with Seleucus. He needs Polyperchon and his twenty thousand men just as he needs life itself."

"You know you will get no naval support? I have been recalled to Asia with the fleet, to support an advance by Antigonus and his armies on the Hellespont. With Meleager advancing on Lysimachus and Antigonus himself intending to cross over into Macedonia, Cassander and his allies are sorely tried."

Ptolemaeus was surprised. "You are still in favor then? I thought after the defeat at Oreüs, you would be in exile at least. Did Antigonus see reason for once?"

"In a manner of speaking. Antigonus hates defeat but he fears casualties. He knows how thin his resources are. He does not mind a heavy toll as long as it brings victory. It is heavy casualties without victory that really set him off. At Oreüs, we got the fleet out before we lost much and we did damage at least equal to our losses. Antigonus accepted that."

Ptolemaeus looked at the map and drummed his fingers. "How many men is he taking to the Hellespont?"

"Ten thousand foot and a thousand horse."

"And he has five thousand foot here, five thousand in Caria and ten thousand under Meleager advancing on Lysimachus. He has his entire army spread out in small packets all over the region. It seems as if he is trying to take on everything at once and using the smallest amount of force he thinks he can get away with in each attack."

"I think that is exactly what he is doing. He's attacking all his enemies at once in an effort to take them down before they can organize against him. Then, by absorbing the resources he has so seized, he can prepare for either his attack on Ptolemy or to defend against the counter-attack from Ptolemy and Seleucus." Medius looked at the map spread before him. "It is a daring plan but his power is so slight now that he has little else."

"Can he pull it off?" Ptolemaeus was trying to envisage the plan that was unfolding before him.

Medius thought very carefully. "I think he will run wild for six months or a year. Beyond that, I have no confidence at all. Much of it will depend on whether Seleucus returns from his war in the east."

Purushapura Palace, Gandhara, Winter, 306 BC

"Could we beat the Army of Chandragupta Maurya?" Seleucus Nikator relaxed in his seat and drank some of the wine he had been offered. It had, of course, been tasted first. Seleucus had learned a lot from Parmenio's household.

Parmenio thought about that question carefully. "We could, yes. We would need to bring the entire Army here and it would need some deft maneuvering. Maurya's Army is too large; it is clumsy and unwieldy in maneuver and it is too demanding in resources to stay too long in one place. It would be easy to split up and defeat in detail. Its size has a lot of other problems as well. An army that big cannot be properly equipped. He has a lot of infantry but they are unarmored and are armed only with sword or mace. Against a phalanx, they are not quite helpless but they are severely disadvantaged. Their cavalry is basically equivalent to our prodromoi; unarmored and lightly armed. Our cataphracts can dominate them easily."

"Our prodromoi have done exceedingly well in the west." Seleucus was curious to see what the answer to that would be.

"They have indeed and they do well here. But, they have achieved so much on the battlefield in the west because of the mistakes our enemies have made. They chronically misuse their cavalry and we take advantage of that. I do not think Chandragupta Maurya will make the same mistakes. We'll win, but it will be a bloody war and leave our Army in almost as bad a mess as his. Then, two or three years later, we'll have to do it again. We'll be tied down out here, being bled white and our western borders, where the real threat lies, will be neglected. That is a recipe for disaster."

"I agree. But, will surrendering this territory not move the problem west?" Seleucus looked at the maps spread out before him. "This is a lot of territory to lose."

"We're not losing it so much as trading it for things of equal value. We have to accept the fact that our hold on these provinces is very weak. Alexander garrisoned these areas with Greek troops who just want to go home. They've mutinied twice and both times, they just left their cities and started to march back to Greece. These provinces may look Hellenistic at the moment but they are still Indian in spirit. To make matters worse, they adjoin directly on to prosperous and well-populated Indian provinces. To get here, we have to cross desert that is both hazardous and time-consuming. This area will always be more closely associated with India than us. Now, if we give up this territory and move the border back, all that changes. Chandragupta Maurya will have to cross that same stretch of desert to get to us and that huge army of his just can't do it. The new border runs through a range of hills that are hard to cross and easy to defend. We can hold them with a handful of men. Strategically, our position will be much better.

"Now, the agreement we have negotiated with Chandragupta Maurya gets us a good price for the provinces we are turning over. For five years, he will give us gold of value equal to the tax revenues of those provinces. For the five years beyond that, gold equivalent to half the tax revenue of those provinces. We will have a treaty of alliance and friendship, one that profits us both greatly and thus is likely to be kept. If he chooses not to keep it, crossing the desert will take so long and be so arduous we will have adequate warning to strengthen our defenses. And he knows that. I believe that as trade grows, our share of the income from the provinces we are handing over will be greater than that we would get if we retained them under the present conditions. Finally, Chandragupta Maurya has agreed to supply us with proper war elephants, well-trained and with the experts needed to keep them that way."

"How many war-elephants? Fifty? A hundred?" Seleucus's eyes shone at the thought of that increment to his strength. Even in the brief interval since his arrival, he had noticed the greater size and power of the Indian war-elephants.

Parmenio leaned back in his seat, grinning broadly. "A thousand."

Seleucus choked and coughed as a swallow of wine went down the wrong way. Igrat leaped forward and started patting him vigorously on the back. Eventually he managed to catch his breath. "Are you serious? A THOUSAND?"

"Very serious, Nik. A thousand war elephants and a treaty commitment from Chandragupta Maurya to maintain our elephant regiments at that level. As long as the treaty remains in force, of course. That's his guarantee that we won't break the treaty. You see, that's the way this treaty is set up. It's self-enforcing in the sense that any possible gains from breaking its terms will be more than offset by the certainty of major losses. The key point is that he doesn't really want a war with us either. He, like us, has much more pressing issues to deal with."

Seleucus thought about that. "Igrat. What's your feel on this? What do the markets say?"

The question surprised Derya Shafrid. He had long realized that Igrat was on close terms with the leading political powers in the Seleucid Empire but the fact that Seleucus Nikator would look to her for advice drove the point home in a way that nothing else had done.

Igrat thought carefully. Her courier trips, taking her through the streets and markets as a member of the lowest classes gave her a vantage point that Kings and Generals missed completely. These days, gathering information was almost as vital a role as the messages she carried. "My father understates how tenuous our position is here. The truth is that Alexander's legacy goes no deeper than the top layer of administration. The people who live here are Indian and look to India for their heritage, not Greece or Macedonia. They look to Chandragupta Maurya for leadership, not us. If they had the opportunity, they would choose him as their King. Your Majesty, if we try to fight a war here, we would face an armed insurrection from the people as well as the Mauryan Army."

"And we all remember what happened to Leonnatus in Babylon. Why do I think we would face the same resistance in every city we have out here." Seleucus thought carefully. "Parmenio, you have done well out here. This treaty and friendship between us and Chandragupta Maurya is the best way out of a bad situation. I have one suggestion. My daughter, Helen, is unmarried and is at the age when she needs a husband. Ever since the time we stole Eumenes's elephants, she has been served by Kavita, widow of Ceteus and lady-in-waiting at my court. Kavita has taught Helen the Indian language and given her a great affection for Indian culture. Why do we not cement this alliance in blood as well as treasure by marrying her to Chandragupta Maurya?"

Parmenio thought that over. "If both parties are amenable to the arrangement, that will be ideal. We'll send a private message to Chandragupta Maurya suggesting the marriage would be agreeable if he wills it."

In the background, Igrat took note of that. She knew very well who would be carrying that message and mentally started to prepare herself for the journey. She was actually looking forward to it; she found her journeys through the Indian countryside interesting.

Seleucus looked very pleased. "I'll discuss it with Helen but I think she will find the idea acceptable. Anyway, she knows her duty. I understand Chandragupta Maurya is a young man?"

"Very young; no more than his mid-thirties and a man of honor. Nik, what is happening back west?"

"On hearing of Ptolemaeus landing at Elefsina, Cassander summoned his ships from Oreüs and gave up the siege there. He has fortified Salganeus and gathered his entire force at that city. Ptolemaeus moved against the

Fourth Diodochi War

Chalcidians, who he hoped would rally to him but they, like the rest of the Euboeans remained loyal to Cassander. Antigonus has the strategy that, if Cassander remains in Euboea, he might himself occupy Macedonia while it was stripped of defenders, or that Cassander, going to the defence of his kingdom, might lose his supremacy in Greece. Cassander perceived this quickly and responded by leaving his general Pleistarchus in command of the garrison in Chalcis and taking Oropus by storm brought the Thebans into his alliance. Having thus greatly strengthened his position in Greece, and leaving Eupolemus as general there, he went into Macedonia, to face Antigonus.

"Antigonus himself sent an embassy to the Byzantines, asking them to enter his alliance against Lysimachus and Cassander. But, aware of the fate that invariably befalls those who ally themselves with Antigonus Monopthalmus and urged by envoys from Lysimachus, they decided to remain neutral and to maintain peace and friendship toward both parties. Antigonus, furious because he had been foiled in these undertakings and also because the winter season is closing in upon him unusually early, has distributed his soldiers among the cities for winter."

Parmenio thought that over. "What in the name of all the gods is Antigonus up to? He's exposing himself to defeat in detail out there. This kind of strategy with a mix of rapid strikes against all enemies works only if it's carried out with speed and determination. Even then, it's really risky. If ever there was a case for undertaking a winter campaign, this is it. Yet he's gone to winter quarters. Very strange."

"Ptolemaeus is staging winter campaign in Greece all right, but Antigonus is not the man he was, Parmenio. For all that, he's achieved much and has strengthened his position in Caria and Coelê Syria. As he advances, he is recruiting more men. This year's campaigning season has seen him emerge as a player again. How strong a player, we have yet to see."

CHAPTER THREE

TREACHEROUS GAMES

Outside Chalcis, Euboea, Winter, 306 BC

The problem wasn't digging the approach trenches or the arrows coming from the city walls of Chalcis. It was the freezing rain that filled the trenches and forced the men to bail them out. Even worse, they had no buckets and were having to use their helmets. The infantrymen had to stand up to their waists in cold water for hours at time while they cleared their trenches of the accumulated water and mud. Then they had to start digging again. Just to add to their misery, that morning, the ground had been covered with a light dusting of snow. It hadn't lasted long, even the weak winter sun had been enough to melt it off. In many senses, it was the last straw though. The constant cold and wet was hard to bear and foot-rot was spreading through the army as if it were an oil-fed fire. It was whispered that more than one man had lost his feet to the black rotting disease already.

One of the infantrymen, a sarissaphoros named Nikomedes, was staring at a helmet full of water. "Hey, I recognize this lot. I threw it out of the trench just after dawn."

His joke brought a just reward, a bellow of laughter from the men around him. That caused Zephyros, the man next to him, to look at the water thoughtfully. "You know, I think old Nico is right. I remember that water. I pissed in it before he scooped it up and threw it out."

Nikomedes shouted out in pretended outrage and grabbed Zephyros's helmet and defiantly stuck it on his head. Zephyros just shook his head in sympathy. "That won't do you any good. I crapped in that one."

There was another roar of laughter. Suddenly it was stilled as the dreaded figure of their dekarchos wielding his cane. "Get back to work you lazy bastards. If you've still got the energy to cheer, you aren't bailing hard enough."

"I'll bet Seleucus doesn't make his men dig in the winter like this." Nikomedes grumbled quietly. "Or, if he does, he makes sure they get proper equipment and extra coin for their efforts."

He thought he had spoken quietly but dekarchos Petar had heard the remark. "Nikomedes, shut up. Right now, before you get us all into trouble. I know it's just good-natured grumbling as is a soldier's privilege but the generals up top don't see it that way. Too many people have been lured away by Seleucid gold for them to see the joke. So, keep your mouth shut or you may find yourself sitting in a pit full of oiled straw."

Nikomedes looked down and hurriedly continued with his bailing. Zephyros looked at him thoughtfully. *What kind of Army is this where a man can't have a good grumble now and then?*

He was saved from further dangerous thoughts by a messenger riding a horse that pulled itself through the half-frozen mud with difficulty. "Word from the Syntagmatarchis! You can stop digging the approach trenches. General Ptolemaeus, striking fear into the garrison that is holding Chalcis, has persuaded them to surrender. They are opening the gates now."

Sure enough, Nikomedes could see the great gates of the city swinging open. "Hey, what do you know! We get to sleep with women tonight! Whether they want us or not."

The messenger looked down with some sympathy. He had over messages for the officers and they all said the same thing, keep the men under control and don't allow the city to be pillaged. "I fear not. Ptolemaeus has made an agreement with the Chalcidians. The city has surrendered voluntarily with no breach in their walls. There will be no sack of their city. Indeed he has agreed to leave left the Chalcidians without a garrison in order to make it evident that Antigonus in very truth proposed to free the Greeks, for the city of Chalcis is well placed for any who wish to have a base from which to carry through a war for supremacy. We march north to the city of Oropus."

Nikomedes watched the messenger pull his horse's head around and flounder off to the next group of men. "North to Oropus. Well, isn't that just great. We were supposed to be meeting up with the armies of Polyperchon and the Boeotians here. I can't see them, can you?"

Zephyros shook his head. "I have heard that every time a union of our forces has been proposed, there have been delays that postponed our meeting too far into winter. Now, the troops of Polyperchon and the Boeotians have gone into winter quarters. I fear we fight this winter campaign on our own."

Estate of Parmenio, Seleucia-on-the Tigris, New Year, 305 BC

"Forgive me, My Lady, might I trouble you for a moment?"

Lillith looked up to see Korinna kneeling in front of her. She had been one of the family's servants ever since Parmenio had bought her after the Battle of the Thapsacus, twelve years earlier. Now, she had just passed her twentieth birthday and had matured into a handsome woman. [i]We had better get her married off before too long[/i] Lillith thought, [i]her beauty is the sort that fades quickly with age. Come to think of it, she is still a slave here, in theory at least owned by Parmenio. We'll have to fix that as well.[/i] Lillith knew she was probably the only person in the household who knew which of the servants were technically slaves and which were free.

"Of course, Korinna, what troubles you?"

The girl bit her lip and looked down. "My lady, last night I was taking out some trash to the burying pit when two men accosted me. I was very frightened because I thought they wanted to use me but instead they offered me gold if I would tell them about this house. They wanted to know if there was any time when you were alone here. I said not, that although people here came and went, there were always people at home who were very skilled with weapons."

"That was a good answer, Korinna, I'm proud of you. Did they ask anything else?"

"Yes, My Lady. They asked me if you would be going into the city alone and when. They said I would get a gold piece if I told them when you left. Korinna looked down again and her voice shook slightly when she continued. "And they said they would not kill me if I told you of this, but they would cut my face until no man would ever want to look at me again."

Lillith took great care to squash down the surge of sheer, raw fury she felt when she heard of that threat. If Korinna knew how she felt, it would terrify her and she had suffered fear enough. "In which case, it was very brave of you to come to me with this warning. Don't be frightened, we'll make sure you are safe. We may have to send you away for a while. Tell me, do you have a young man admiring you?"

Korinna giggled. "I do. He speaks of asking for my hand but it can't happen. He's a freeman you see and I'm a slave."

"That's something we can fix very easily. I'll write out your manumission today. You deserve it for your courage and loyalty in coming to me." Lillith looked at Korinna affectionately. "You can tell your admirer that he may have your hand if he wishes although I suspect he's more interested in other parts of you. Gusoyn? Ahh, there you are. I want you to take Korinna here and find her admirer and then take them both to the house of Igrat's friend Callicrates. Make sure nobody sees you go there or is aware of who you are taking. Take Apollo with you. Ask Callicrates to shelter them, letting none know they are there, until we can bring them back here. Also, I need to speak with Semiramis and Kopshape. This brooding threat to our safety has gone on long enough."

"Yes, Your Majesty." Gusoyn spoke with a half-smile at the way Lillith had rapped out the instructions. Too good-natured a man to take offense at the usurpation of his prerogatives as head of the household pro tempore, he had, in any case found that patience and humor worked best. Living in a household that contained an ex-Empress and two ex-Queens needed patience and good humor.

Lillith returned his smile apologetically. "I'm sorry Gusoyn, I didn't mean to step on your toes. But the men plotting against us have brought their campaign right up to our home and I want to see an end to it."

"As do I, Lillith. I will do as you ask. Come along Korinna, let us get you somewhere safe."

A few minutes later, Semiramis and Kopshape came in. Lillith quickly explained to them what had just happened. "Anyway, I'm not putting up with this any longer. I doubt if Alcetas is involving himself directly in this; it's more likely that he's staying in the background and working through hired thugs. If we can pick them up, they might be able to tell us where he is and what his plans are."

"If they know where he is, they'll tell us. Eventually. Only question is how much they get damaged first." Semiramis sounded positively enthusiastic. "As for what his plans are, I could tell you that now. Only question is how long he intends to keep you before he kills you."

"It won't come to that of course." Kopshape found Semiramis's attitude disturbing. "We'll make very sure of that."

Purushapura Palace, Gandhara, Late Winter, 305 BC

The great elephants that made up the wedding party made their way down the tree-lined approach to the palace with stately dignity. They'd been dressed in rich tapestries that proclaimed the martial valor and great achievements of both Chandragupta Maurya and Seleucus Nikator. Other tapestries announced the virtues of the bride and lauded her beauty. Much was made of the great love that Chandragupta Maurya had for her and these stories were nothing less than the truth. This might be an arranged marriage, made for purely political purposes, but bride and groom had genuinely fallen deeply in love as well. The elephant's tusks had been wrapped in gold and silver chains while their head-cloths were woven with precious stones.

These were but part of the rich dowry that was being presented to Seleucus Nikator. No dowry had been demanded in the wedding treaty but Chandragupta Maurya had insisted on providing one that would properly honor his new wife. Behind the elephants, a line of dancers put on a performance that awed the audience with its skill and mastery. The music for their dance was provided by a band that marched along behind them. All around, incense pots filled the air with their rich fragrance. It was a wedding procession the like of which nobody in the city had ever seen before.

The elephants stopped in front of the grandstand set up in front of the Purushapura Palace. Chandragupta Maurya dismounted and walked up to the stand, standing tall and facing Seleucus Nikator. "Your Majesty, I would take the hand of your daughter in marriage and have her become my wife."

The music and dancing stopped, leaving the air so still that it seemed time itself had been frozen. Seleucus Nikator gave Helen's suitor the traditional angry, glowering stare of instant dislike. "And who are you that you should make such a demand of me? How do I know that you respect my house and daughter?"

"I am Chandragupta Maurya. Let these six elephants and the treasure they carry be the gauge of the extent to which I honor your daughter."

Seleucus looked at the elephants and then at Helen. "What do you think, daughter of mine? Is the match satisfactory to you?"

Helen looked at Chandragupta Maurya and, when she had caught his eye, put a hand on her stomach and nodded slightly. He carefully concealed his delight at the news she had just given him and instead put of an expression of extreme anxiousness. Helen appeared to think deeply then turned to her father. "I think this may be satisfactory father. They are fine-looking elephants and he is quite handsome."

Seleucus nodded, then took her hand and led her down from the grandstand. "Chandragupta Maurya, I give you my daughter Helen to be your wife. May you look after and honor her as she will look after and honor you."

The cheers of the crowd echoed around the square, then the music and dancing resumed as the bride and groom led the way to where a great fire burned. They exchanged garlands of flowers and then Chandragupta Maurya took Helen's hand and they stretched their joined hands over the fire.

"They are attracting the Goddess Agni to witness their union." Naamah whispered into Parmenio's ear. They watched as the couple took their hands away from the fire and, still holding hands, took seven paces. They each then made a statement in Hindi. The fact that Helen spoke the language so well caused a ripple of amazement to pass through the crowds. Parmenio realized that with that one simple gesture she had won the hearts of the crowd.

"That was the oath of food. He promised to provide for her, she promised to make good use of the food he gives her." Naamah was whispering again while the couple took seven steps and, again made a short statement each. "And that was the oath of health. They promised to look after each other and keep each other in good health."

Parmenio watched while the couple took another seven steps and made a third short statement. By the time they had finished it, Naamah was already explaining. "He just promised to work hard and honestly to support their family and she promised to manage the family well on his behalf. After the next seven steps, he'll promise to provide her with a home and she'll promise to look after it for him. I guess for a King, that's not a hard promise to make."

By this time, Parmenio was looking curiously at her. He knew Naamah didn't speak Hindi yet she seemed remarkably familiar with what was going on. Her next words confirmed that. "Seven more steps and now they'll promise to help each other grow their family and wealth and to give a proper share of their wealth to their country so that it also may prosper. That was the fifth oath. The sixth is to raise their children together so that they grow up to be responsible and honorable people. And, now seven steps more, and we have the last oath where they promise to be faithful to each other. Look, Parmenio, they've taken 49 steps now. They take one last step together . . . . and they are married."

Parmenio looked at her in amazement. "How on earth did you know all that? You don't speak a word of the local language."

"Helen started to describe the ceremony to me and I recognized it right away. It's the old Ba'al wedding ceremony. Apart from the fire being dedicated to Agni rather than Ba'al, it's just the same as the weddings we held in Shyt'tin. Now hush; Helen's going to speak."

Helen was facing her husband and she spoke to him, pitching her voice so her words would carry around the crowd of spectators. "Husband, in my birth-country, it is common for women to take a new name when they marry. This symbolizes the end of their old life and the beginning of their new. It also symbolizes that they are no longer part of their father's family and are now part of their husband's. In accordance with this custom, I now give up my name of Helen. I now take the name of Durdhara. I am no longer Seleucid but Mauryan, no longer Macedonian but Indian."

The cheering from the crowds was deafening. The guards at the palace gates opened them up to admit the gathered population of the city to where a great feast was waiting. Seleucus had declared that all were welcome and that all could join in the celebrations of the wedding. He, Chandragupta Maurya and Durdhara circulated amongst the crowd, discretely guarded of course, and welcomed them on this most auspicious of days. Eventually, Durdhara and a woman wearing the distinctive outfit of a soothsayer joined Parmenio, Naamah and Igrat.

"Uncle Parmenio, my friends. May I introduce Arundhati? She is the soothsayer and prophetess."

The three exchanged cynical grins. Naamah's voice was silky smooth when she asked "And were her prophecies favorable?"

Durdhara looked delighted. Unlike the other three, she had a deep and abiding belief in prophets and soothsayers. "Oh yes, very much so. She says that my husband will not meet death before he is ready for it and that he will not die at the hands of his enemies. She also says that my son will rule after him and, Naamah, the lessons you have taught me will save my husband's life. She also says that the friendship being founded today will last for many generations."

"That's good to know." Parmenio was hard put to stop laughing. To him, the prophecies were just feel-good nonsense cooked up by a clever woman with a flair for the dramatic. "Arundhati, do you have any words for us?"

The woman looked at Parmenio, Naamah and Igrat and suddenly her face was filled with confusion that changed to bewilderment and real fear. She spoke haltingly and hesitatingly to Durdhara who translated her words. "Arundhati says that her vision of your futures is cloudy and uncertain to her. She cannot even see how you will die and that she can usually see for everybody. But, Igrat, she says your beauty will always open doors for you and it will never leave you. But that same beauty means there will always be people around you who will take pleasure out of hurting you and you must be on your guard against them. Naamah, Arundhati says that you have access to the secrets of life and death and you must be sure that you use that access wisely. But, you have been gifted with great understanding and insight. Always trust them, follow your head and ignore your heart when your judgment is needed over when to use one set of secrets and when to use the other. Uncle Parmenio, I don't understand what Arundhati said about you. She said that you will be the mortal enemy of a great evil and you will kill it with fire but when you leave this world, it will be to meet with others not like us. Now, I must take Arundhati to meet my father."

Once they'd gone, the three looked at each other and smirked. Igrat summed up their feelings. "Usual nonsense. A few statements of the obvious, some good advice anybody could give and some 'prophecies' intended to make us feel happy. All mixed up with some mysticism and obscure comments intended to make her sound in touch with things we don't understand. She's got a good act though. I liked the bit about confusion and mists. Since she doesn't know us at all, that covered her against anything she said being obviously wrong."

"She got you right though, Nammie." Parmenio was slightly disturbed by the prophecy about him.

"Of course she did. She's being talking with Hel . . . Durdhara. She knew I am a herbalist and that means by definition I know about both poisons and cures. Nothing surprising there."

"Talking about that, what did Durdhara mean when she said 'the lessons you gave me'?

Naamah shrugged. "I just gave her a basic course in securing her home against attack and especially defending herself and her family against poisoners. Nobody can stop a first-class poisoner but thank the gods there are few of us around. Most poisoners are inept amateurs. Yet, poisoning is still the leading cause of death in aristocratic families. Parmenio, you do realize that even inept poisoners probably kill more people than your sarissas have ever done?"

Parmenio thought about that and he had a nasty feeling she was right. Then an idea struck him. "You know, there's a business opportunity there. We could offer training courses to newly-wed couples. How to protect their families from attack. For a fee of course. Talk to Lillith about it when we get back."

Around them the party was growing in fellowship and good humor. On the grandstand, Chandragupta Maurya and Seleucus Nikator were engaged in a deep and obviously friendly debate over something. Parmenio could see that there was obviously genuine bond of friendship developing between the two men. He took another look around the wedding party and sighed. "You know, this beats the hells out of fighting a war. The only thing I regret is that if we'd thought of this wedding earlier, we might not have had to give these provinces up."

Palace of Lysimachus, Lysimachia, Late Winter, 305 BC

"The winter campaign of Ptolemaeus continues although his losses in men from the weather are grievous. He has taken the city of Oropus and made captive the troops of Cassander stationed there. Thereafter, by receiving the people of Eretria and Carystus into his alliance, he secured the

314

province of Euboea. Now he has proceeded to commence his invasion of Attica. He is moving to seize Athens where Demetrius of Phalerum governs the city. Our spies tell us that the Athenians are sending ambassadors and messages secretly to Antigonus, begging him to free the city. I believe that, when Ptolemaeus draw near the city, the sympathy for Antigonus amongst the citizens will force Demetrius to make a truce and to send envoys to Antigonus about an alliance."

Leonnatus paused to drink some wine. "I believe that after Ptolemaeus has finished seizing Attica, he will move into Boeotia, probably concentrating on besieging Cadmea first. After that, he plans to seize Thebes and advance into Phocis where Antigonus already has much support in on over most of the cities and from all of these he expects to expel the garrisons of Cassander. Of course, by then it will be well into spring and he expects to join with the armies of Polyperchon and the Boetian alliance."

Lysimachus laughed at that. The secret of Polyperchon's change of allegiance had been kept much better than he had expected. Nor had the dispatch of ambassadors from Aetolia and the Boeotia been recognized for the ruse it was. As a result, all of the successes gained by Ptolemaeus in Euboea and Attica were illusory at best. In fact, his advances were doing nothing but drawing him further into a deadly trap and, in the process, revealing all of the secret supporters of Antigonus. [i]Those Athenians who sided with Antigonus so openly will weep bitter tears for their errors.[/i]

"This spring, the armies of Polyperchon and the Boetian alliance will come out of winter quarters and join with Cassander. They will be rested, fit and at full strength. Even though the troops of Cassander have been active all winter, he has withheld them from major fighting and kept them in good spirits. Indeed, the advances of Ptolemaeus are mostly the product of Cassander's restraint. I expect the battle in spring will be at Opuntia. It is a city belonging to the party of Cassander. Ptolemaeus will begin a siege and make continuous attacks until our armies arrive." Leonnatus hesitated. "Can we trust Polyperchon?"

Lysimachus nodded. "We can. He is the last general loyal to the house of the Great Alexander. He tested Antigonus by demanding the throne for Heracles and protection for Barsine, his mother. Antigonus agreed immediately and in doing so showed his hand. For all know that Antigonus will settle for nothing less than that throne for himself and agreeing to allow it to be occupied by another means that occupation will be brief indeed. His agreement means the deaths of both Heracles and Barsine. Antigonus being Antigonus, their deaths would be slow and agonized. Polyperchon will not tolerate that.

315

"There is something else. Polyperchon is old, tired and sick of war. He now rues the day Antipater put him in charge of Greece. All he wants is a quiet and safe retirement. That, Cassander has agreed to give him. A place of honor at Cassander's court and a peaceful life in retirement. The Heracles and Barsine will be sent to Seleucia where they will live under the protection of Seleucus Nikator. All know Seleucus to be a kindly and generous ruler who always keeps his word. By placing them under his protection, Polyperchon has fulfilled his duty to Alexander's blood-line and that means more to him now than idle actions or meaningless title."

Outside Pancratius's Date Wine and Molasses Factory, Seleucia on the Tigris, Late Winter, 305BC

Gusoyn leaned up against his chariot and looked at the woman walking down the street towards him. She was wearing the new-fashion short tunic and trousers under her shawl and her face was veiled. Gusoyn smiled to himself and used the excuse of giving his horse an apple to maneuver himself into her path. When she approached him, he checked the color of her shawl and girdle then addressed her, politely yet none the less ingratiatingly. "Lady, a kind word for a charioteer waiting patiently in the hot sun?"

The woman stopped and looked at him disdainfully. "Are you so impertinent that you would address a respectable lady, unintroduced?"

"My apologies, Lady, I am Gusoyn. A free charioteer in the service of Strategos Parmenio the Younger."

The woman looked a little mollified. A charioteer who was a slave or in the employ of somebody unimportant would almost certainly have been beaten severely for daring to address a lady of quality. But, a free charioteer in the service of one of the most important aristocratic families in the Kingdom was something else. Even the most conservative and prudish of wives would consider exchanging a few words since doing so might secure her husband an introduction to that family. A more adventurous wife might even get a thrill from speaking to a representative of such a family. And, of course, a charioteer had a certain dashing image. Gusoyn could see her come to a quick decision and stop to speak with him.

"I am Phoibe, of the Attacus family. Purveyors of fine silks and borders. Perhaps the ladies of your house may be interested in such goods?"

"Indeed they might. If I may say so, they are noble ladies of great beauty and refined tastes. Especially, when they are required to make an appearance at the court of our most noble king."

"Our family warehouse is just around the corner. Perhaps, if I was to show you some of our latest fashions, you might mention them to your ladies?"

Gusoyn nodded solemnly. "That would be a very good idea."

The woman waved for him to follow her. Gusoyn reached up, scratched his head, and started to follow her. He was stopped from doing so by an apparently older woman suddenly coming out of nowhere waving a heavy stick. She was screaming almost incoherently, "you slut, you whore! Your husband away serving our King and you take up with a charioteer. I told my son what a hussy he was marrying but he wouldn't listen to me. Now, I've caught you in the act and I'll smash in both your skulls."

Despite her old-fashioned ankle-length tunic, heavy shawl and veil, she broke into a run and, screaming incoherent abuse, charged at Gusoyn and Phoibe. Phoibe took one look at her and gasped, "she's mad. Run for your life!"

Gusoyn took her advice and the two of them took off, hotly pursued by the furious mother-in-law and accompanied by gales of laughter from spectators. Gusoyn noted that there was a lot of sympathy mixed in with the laughter, he guessed from women who had had problems with their own mothers-in-law. Then they were around the corner and away, still hotly pursued by the mother-in-law.

The laughter went on, even after the trio had vanished into the group of warehouses that backed on to the main street. The bystanders appreciated the sudden relief from the boredom of an average business day and fell to discussing the display. Within a few minutes, of course, the details had been wildly exaggerated. Only two small groups didn't join in the story-telling. One was an apparently middle-aged couple who had a small cart drawn by a donkey. They had obviously just sold a few amphora of olive oil to one of the shops that lined the street. Now, they were resting and counting their profits before returning home. The others were a pair of men lounging in the shadows, watching the door that served as the entrance to the wine factory.

A couple of minutes after Gusoyn and Phoibe had run away from the mad mother-in-law, Lillith came out and looked with puzzlement at the deserted chariot.

What happened next was a smoothly-oiled operation. A covered cart rolled up and blocked Lillith from the view of the passers-by. Masked by the cart, the two men seized Lillith and bundled her into the back of the cart. While one stuffed old rags into her mouth to muffle her screams, the other tied her hands and feet with leather strips. At the same time the cart driver whipped up his horses and the cart moved off at a smart pace. It had all happened so fast that nobody seemed aware that they had just witnessed an abduction. Across the road, the middle-aged couple finished their break and drove their cart off.

Fourth Diodochi War

Deserted Farmhouse On The Outskirts of Seleucia on the Tigris

The farmhouse had been carefully chosen. The farm had been a marginal one, a case where the land wasn't good enough to support really worthwhile crops. The farmer had eventually stopped trying to make a success of the place and, realizing that the land was worth more as a building site for the city than as a farm, he had put it up for sale. The buildings had been left to rot and that made them ideal for the purpose they were about to serve.

Lillith was unceremoniously turned out of the back of the cart and half-carried, half dragged into the largest of the buildings. Once inside she was dumped on the floor. One of her abductors spoke to her. "Our master orders us to stay here until nightfall before we deliver you to him."

The other one took over and Lillith noted he sounded embarrassed. "He ordered us to defile you while we were waiting. Look, Lady, don't fight. It'll hurt less if you don't fight."

"Actually, it won't hurt at all. Because it isn't going to happen." A woman's voice, one pleasantly familiar to Lillith echoed in the near-empty room. Lillith looked around. Gusoyn, Phoibe, the mad mother-in-law and the couple who had been selling oil had all quietly entered the room. The three women were all still wearing their shawls and veils. That encouraged the two abductors.

"Get out of here. You don't want to get involved in this. Clear out or you'll be sorry. And take your women with you."

"Turn our back on you? I don't think so." The guilt on the abductors' faces spoke volumes. If the newcomers had turned to leave, they would have been stabbed in the back almost instantly. Instead, the mad mother-in-law took off her shawl and veil to reveal Semiramis, grinning broadly. There was a knife in her hand and the blade dripped blood. "Your friend outside is a bit shorter than he was when you knew him. A whole head shorter in fact."

Phoibe took off her shawl and veil. Without them, Apollo was clearly recognizable. "Iggy was right you know. In these things, we can go anywhere and do anything. And be anybody.

"You'd better stay out of the fight, Apollo. Those are Igrat's clothes and if you get them messed up, she'll kill you." The olive oil seller stretched slightly and was instantly recognizable as Hesperos, eldest son of Callicrates. He turned to the 'woman' with him "your turn I think."

Kopshape shrugged off his shawl and veil. "This is good. I did not like those things."

318

The two abductors glanced at each other. What had been two professional thugs against two unknown men and three women had suddenly turned into two against four men. True, one of the men didn't seem to be a professional fighter but, on the other hand, the woman looked fearsome. And she had the blood-stained knife. Nevertheless, fight they had to. Professional ethics demanded it.

As a fight, it was a sad disappointment to Semiramis. As the two abductors started to move, Kopshape's hands snaked out, throwing a length of chain with heavy bronze balls at each end. The chain smacked into one of the abductors legs and coiled around them. They sent him sprawling on the floor but before they did, the bronze balls smashed into his thighs, breaking both thighbones. Gusoyn took out the other abductor. He dodged a wild knife-slash and kicked the man on the knee. In the years they had been together, Parmenio had taught his people, men and women alike, the basic elements of pankration with a heavy stress on the absence of any rules. Gusoyn's kick took out the abductor's kneecap and sent him tumbling to the floor. Gusoyn was on him in a second, grabbing his knife-hand by the wrist and pulling the arm back and up. His fist slammed down, breaking the bone above the elbow. And that was that. Fight over.

Semiramis looked at the scene in utter dismay. "You bastards. A good fight and you finish them off before I get a chance to join in. You might show a little consideration."

Across the floor, Apollo had finished releasing Lillith. He helped her to her feet and she looked down at the two men who had abducted her. "Which one of you threatened to carve up my maid's face?"

Neither answered but the way one man looked at the other made the answer clear. Lillith pointed at the would-be mutilator and looked at Semiramis. "Start with him. Make up for missing the fight."

Semiramis nodded and spoke to the abductors. "Let's be quite clear about this. You are both going to die. Now, I can cut your throats and you'll be dead in seconds. Or I can skin you alive. I've got some hot mustard powder here and after I've flayed every inch of skin from your body, I'll coat you with it. It'll take you a couple of days to die and you'll be screaming for every second of that time. Now, you decide which way you'd go. Who are you working for and where can we find him?"

One of the two abductors decided that a clean death was better than the alternative. "A nobleman called Alcetas. He's waiting at a farm some leagues from here. I'll show you where."

Gusoyn nodded. "I don't think so. Aeschylus is waiting for word and the whole regiment with him. Kopshape, ride to their barracks and give him the information we have. You, tell us exactly where to go."

The abductor looked around and saw Semiramis pick up the bag of mustard powder. He gulped and gave exact directions. With that, Kopshape left.

Estate of Parmenio, Seleucia-on-the Tigris

"And what happened then?" Igrat leaned forward in an intent desire to get to the crux of the story. She was tired and badly wanted a bath but the outcome of the Alcetas affair had to come first.

"Not much to tell really." Gusoyn was smiling. The trap had come off perfectly and he felt he had earned his position as head of the household pro-tempore. "Aeschylus took the whole Daimones Prodromoi which I thought was a bit excessive but apparently they all demanded to go and he had no time to argue. So he took the entire regiment. Alcetas was holed up in a farmhouse just as the thug who talked promised. He had a dozen men with him, hired cut-throats. Apparently, he made an inspiring speech urging them to fight to the death and promising to be by their side. Then he escaped through the back door. His hired men took one look at the better part of a prodromoi regiment surrounding them and gave up. Alcetas thought he had got clear but Aeschylus was not born yesterday. He had some men around back and they took Alcetas prisoner. That is when it got nasty."

Gusoyn paused and looked around. "Those hired men, they talked. The plan was to kill the three men who abducted you Lillith. Then Alcetas and his group were going to head north, to Atropatene. He was going to make you walk the whole way Lillith, barefoot."

Lillith couldn't stop herself whimpering in fear and dread. The others had only a slight idea of how much walking hurt her, even wearing stout sandals and well-padded foot-cloths. Walking that far without either would have been excruciating. "I'd never have made it. I'd have died on the way."

Gusoyn nodded sympathetically. "Well, that got the cavalrymen really mad. You see, they all knew that you were one of the noblewomen who established our tradition of high-born ladies leading the treatment of wounded soldiers after a battle. There is even a story that you stood over a wounded cavalrymen and used a knife to fight off enemies who tried to kill him on the ground."

"I never did that." Lillith was still shocked by the picture of what might have happened to her.

"I know, but that is how legends grow and spread. Anyway, the cavalrymen believe it and when they heard what Alcetas had planned, they decided to give him a taste of his own medicine. They took his boots and made him walk back, lashed to the back of a horse. About half way his knees gave out, possibly from being hit with the butt-end of a xyston. They dragged him the rest of the way. He is in the dungeons now, a real mess. Seleucus will decide what to do with him when he returns. Where are they by the way, Iggie?"

"About three days behind me. I came on ahead with the news. Lillith, Naamah has a whole new series of herbs and spices she found in India. They'll be rare and very expensive for a long time, even with proper trading between us and the Indians. She'll tell you what to get and how to use them. She suggested we could sell imported spices and scrolls that tell of how to use them."

"So, what happened with the war?" Semiramis wanted all the gruesome details immediately. She still hadn't really forgiven Parmenio for making her miss out on a good war.

"There wasn't one really. There were a couple of minor skirmishes, Derya will be able to tell you about those, and then everybody sat down and came to an agreement. Seleucus married his daughter off to Chandragupta and everybody's happy." Igrat kept quiet about the thousand elephants. They were a state secret although how long they would stay that way was anybody's guess.

In the background Kopshape smiled in great satisfaction at the news that a war had been avoided. "Igrat, will you be here long?"

She shook her head. "His majesty has already told me I have some trips to make. We dodged this war, but we won't be able to dodge the next one. Parmenio says that the Antigonid expedition to Greece is going to come to a bad end. That means Antigonus will throw all his weight behind the attack on Cassander. That being a land campaign, it'll leave his navy free for other work. Father thinks that Ptolemy will be the chosen target. And, since we have an alliance with him, that brings us in again. Anyway, I'll be off to Egypt as soon as the rest are back with warnings for Ptolemy to be on his guard and some suggested plans of campaign."

"Don't count on wearing a veil." Semiramis was serious. Igrat's work might have been strange to her but she knew how dangerous it could be. "After our little escapade, the city fathers are proposing the wearing of veils – or any masks that cover the face - in public be prohibited. On grounds that it is a menace to public safety and tranquility."

Semiramis was their court princess and that meant she was the family's eyes and ears in court circles. If the proposal had got that far, it was likely to be acted on. Gusoyn knew that and took it into account. "I can see their point. When word got out of what we had done, everybody had a good laugh. Then, they had a good think and stopped laughing. What we can do, others can and not with our good intentions. We stopped a vicious crime, others could use the same trickery to commit one. No, Igrat, Semiramis is right. There will be an order quite soon forbidding the wearing of veils."

"What do Indian women wear Igrat?" Lillith had managed to shake off the horror that had seized her and was trying to reconnect with what was instead of what might have been.

"They've got lovely fabrics out there. Silks that are richly patterned in glowing colors, much better than anything we have here now. Most of the women at court wear a short tunic or jacket and a long skirt that settles low on their hips. Stomach left bare. And, a shawl over the top of course. Everybody has lots of jewelry. Poorer women wear clothes a lot like ours. That's something else to bear in mind. The cloth, spices, scents we can get from India are superb in quality. We should get in early."

"People, let Iggy get some sleep. We can all ask for her stories of the wonders of India tomorrow. Come on Iggy, I'll walk you to your room."

Igrat and Lillith rose and they went to Igrat's east-wing room. She actually had two rooms, one in the west wing she shared with Derya Shafrid and one in the east that was her own private sanctuary. At the door, Lillith asked the question that had been haunting her since the problem with Alcetas had become critical.

"Iggy, why do all the men I have relations with turn bad? My first husband did this to me," she gestured at her crippled feet, "now Alcetas. Is it me? Do I turn them into monsters?"

Igrat looked at her sympathetically. "No, and don't try and blame yourself. Not that way at least. You don't turn your men into monsters. You have a bad habit of picking men who have the potential to turn into monsters. It's like they've got mental leprosy and you're blaming yourself when things eventually start falling off. You didn't make Alcetas's mental fingers fall off. He did that all by himself. Look, remember what I was like when I came here? I thought all men were like Alcetas and used that as an excuse for what I did to them. Then, when I became part of this family, I learned differently. And it changed my life. It changed me."

"That's not saying there aren't bad people out there. There are, and they aren't all men. Olympias was the worst person I've ever met but she had some good competition. Lillith, what do you think the most dangerous part of my work is?"

Lillith thought about that. "Getting into palaces and so on?"

Igrat shook her head. "That's easy. It's actually delivering the message. There's always the chance that the person to whom I'm delivering the message will decide that the secrets I carry in my head would stay secret if I die. When I'm delivering messages, I make sure that nobody is behind me and I don't eat or drink anything unless somebody else has tasted it first. Even when I was living on the streets, delivering messages was deadly dangerous. Even something as simple as an assignation between lovers could get a girl's throat slit."

Lillith looked at her with horror on her face. "Iggy, I'm so sorry. The day you came in with the news that Parmenio had adopted you, I joked that the scroll you carried was your death sentence. I thought it was funny. It wasn't, was it? It was a horribly, unforgivably, cruel thing to say. You must have thought you were really going to die."

"Let's just say the joke was lost in translation." Iggie smiled comfortingly. "Look, you want advice from a whore? Good place to get advice on men. Think about all the partners you've had who turned bad on you. Think what they were like when you met them and spot what they had in common. Because, turning bad was already there, it is just that you didn't see the signs. So, think them over and learn what the signs are. And watch out for them in future. Here's a start. You know Alcetas had me years back? It was business; I needed his help to get my messages through. When we were in bed, everything was about him. He had me the same way every night and every time all he cared about was how good he thought he was making himself look. He turned bad because he didn't get everything he wanted when he wanted it. That's a warning sign for you. And, if you want more advice, Lillith, just ask. That's the most important lesson I learned when I joined this family. Nobody has to be alone."

Citadel of Cyrenê, Cyrenê, Egypt, Spring, 305BC

"My Lord Hippostratus, envoys from the court of Ptolemy Soter have arrived. They seek audience with you immediately."

That was something Hippostratus hadn't wanted to hear. Since he had instigated the revolt of the people of Cyrenê against Ptolemy, his primary objective had been to place the citadel under siege and bring it down. With Cyrenê in his hands as a secure powerbase, he would have been able to continue with his plan to carve out a state of his own. Cyrenê had seemed ideal for the purpose; isolated on the western side of Egypt and well-removed from the developing war between Antigonus and – well, everybody. He had thought he could be in a strong position by the time Ptolemy got around to doing anything. That obviously hadn't worked. *That leaves only one thing to do. Hear them out.*

"Send them in." Hippostratus watched the three ambassadors file in. "Apollonides, it has been too long since we broke bread together. How do you fair?"

Apollonides carefully considered his reply to that. The truth was that his battlefield betrayal of Eumenes so many years before had effectively destroyed any hopes he had of great advancement. Antigonus had believed that, having betrayed Eumenes so comprehensively, he would do the same to anybody else who trusted him. So, he had shuffled Apollonides off into unimportant side posts and ceremonial positions of little importance. When Antigonus had descended into madness and began executing everybody whose loyalty he doubted, Apollonides had decided he was too near the top of that list for comfort and left. He had sought service with Ptolemy Soter but found the loyalty issue had followed him there. The truth was, changing sides between wars was entirely acceptable but betraying them on the battlefield was not. Ptolemy had given him this mission as a way of demonstrating he had learned that lesson.

"I fair well under the leadership of Ptolemy Soter. He has commanded me to convey a message of mutual benefit to you both. He is distressed to hear of the rebellion of the citizens of Cyrenê and wishes to put an end to the unrest without unnecessary bloodshed. He offers you the position of satrap of Cyrenêica ruling it as your own subject only to your recognition of him as your overlord. You will be responsible for restoring order here and putting down this revolt." Apollonides took a scroll from one of his companions and ceremonially handed it to Hippostratus.

The scroll contained the same offer as Apollonides had related, with the exception of a few florid phrases and meaningless declarations of friendship that were cosmetic only and of little import. The problem was the offer itself. To Hippostratus, Ptolemy's proposal was very reasonable and gave him almost everything he wanted without the need to fight for it. The difficulty lay in the word 'almost'. The proposal still left Hippostratus subordinate to Ptolemy and that defeated the whole object of the maneuver he was engaged in. His ultimate aim was to use a power base in Cyrenêica to depose Ptolemy and rule Egypt in his place. This agreement would forestall that.

For all that, it was a very reasonable offer and one that the citizens of Cyrenê would doubtless find acceptable. If they learned of it, they would demand detailed explanations of why he found it unacceptable. Those explanations would tip his hand and reveal his future plans. The answer to the conundrum was obvious. The citizens of Cyrenê could not learn of Ptolemy's offer. It had to die and that meant the ambassadors who had brought it had to die with it. And that meant war with Ptolemy.

Hippostratus followed that line of thought further. He faced a choice, either accept what he had been offered and give up hope of anything greater or do not do so. If he accepted Ptolemy's offer, there was no reason why Ptolemy couldn't have him called to Alexandria and executed. After all, Antigonus had done similar things often enough. But, if he refused the offer, that meant war with Ptolemy and that, in turn, meant his destruction since the forces available to Ptolemy were vastly greater than his own – all the more so if Seleucus arrived to help his ally. The outcome of the logic was inevitable. If he was to survive, Hippostratus had to acquire an ally and the only candidate he could think of was Antigonus.

That was a problem all of its own. Hippostratus had been a vassal of Antigonus once but had left him to take employment with Ptolemy. Asking aid of Antigonus now meant reversing that act and Antigonus was a notoriously difficult person where changes of allegiance were concerned. Hippostratus had to send him a gesture that would convince Antigonus of his sincerity. One that would convince Antigonus that Hippostratus had committed himself to the anti-Ptolemy cause beyond any possibility of turning back. There were few such gestures that would be sufficient to achieve the desired result.

That decided him. "Apollonides, I will prepare a reply to Ptolemy, accepting his offer, now. You must be tired and hungry from your journey. You will be taken to our guest quarters so you may eat and rest."

After the Ambassador had left, Hippostratus turned to the head of his personal guard. "Intercept them on the way to the guest quarters and take them instead to the dungeons."

"What do we do then, General?"

"Boil them."

Estate of Parmenio, Seleucia-on-the Tigris

"Head's up, everybody. We're at war again." Parmenio strode into the house.

"What's happened?" Naamah looked up curiously.

"Cyrenê under the leadership of Hippostratus revolted against Ptolemy. Ptolemy sent ambassadors to negotiate a compromise, Hippostratus killed them. Boiled them alive and then sent the dismembered bodies back to Ptolemy in grain sacks."

Fourth Diodochi War

Lillith looked at Igrat in horror, remembering what she had said about delivering messages being the most dangerous part of her work. It was very clear to her that she could easily have been one of the murdered ambassadors. She caught Igrat's eye and saw her grimace slightly.

"Ptolemy went ballistic. Especially since Hippostratus signed an alliance with Antigonus and continued the attack on the citadel of Cyrenê with greater vigor. He's sent Agis as general with a land army and also sent a fleet to take part in the war, placing Epaenetus in command. I know Agis, he's inexperienced but capable. The problem is, Antigonus is attacking Cyprus. Igrat, I need to talk to you in private."

The two of them left, Parmenio unlocking the door to his command area. Behind them, Naamah looked at Lillith. "That's unusual, I wonder what they're up to?"

Once in Parmenio's command office, Parmenio sat behind his desk with Igrat taking a seat in front of him. "Igrat, I'm taking you off courier runs to . . ."

"No." Igrat's voice was pleasant but firm. Then she looked at Parmenio and her stomach clenched.

"Igrat, I love you dearly but if you interrupt me again, I will have you whipped until you won't be able to lie on your back for a month. Do you understand me?" Igrat looked at him in shock. She knew the threat wasn't literal, that his words were simply intended to convey how angry he was at her actions, but she also realized she had completely underestimated the severity of what was going on. Also, she suddenly realized that there was more to this particular situation than she knew. Something that had happened had disturbed her father on a very deep, personal level. Unwittingly she had plucked an extremely tender nerve.

Parmenio watched her gulp and nod. "I'm not speaking as your father here, I'm speaking as a Strategos facing an exceptionally complicated situation. To translate that, when a Strategos says 'exceptionally complicated' he means 'extremely dangerous'. Starting again. I'm taking you off courier runs to hostile and foreign powers. There are several reasons for this, not least of which is that Hippostratus's actions have disrupted the normal means of diplomacy. Up to now, Ambassadors have been relatively immune to attack and could do their work unhindered. Murdering ambassadors is a major change in the situation and one of the reasons why this situation is so complex.

"There is also the consideration that you are an extremely valuable asset to our command structure – by that I mean the Seleucid Army command structure. Your ability to get messages through is a priceless combat advantage that must not be risked unnecessarily. Also, it is unnecessary from another point of view. Your unique ability is to get through to where you are going faster that anybody can rationally explain. In the past, when we were fighting for survival, that was an advantage. Now, we're the pre-eminent military power in this part of the world and speed isn't so essential. So, from now on, your courier missions will be restricted to carrying messages from the family to me and from me to people in the Seleucid command chain.

"There's another reason for this change. Igrat, you've been delivering messages for almost twenty years. Too many people on the other side know you. You can still hide in the baggage trains but our enemies must be close to working that trick out. We have to assume they are. You are still safe there for a while since they'll be looking for a woman in her late forties, not her early twenties which is what you still look like. But, runs outside our area of control are getting too hazardous and you are too valuable an asset to lose. So, your outside missions stop now."

"Yes, Strategos."

Parmenio looked at her and nodded to himself. "Do you understand why the scope of your missions has been changed and are you good with it?"

"Yes, Strategos. Father, how did the Ambassdors die?"

"They were taken as they left the meeting room and placed in the dungeons. There a great vat of boiling water had been prepared. Each man, in turn, was placed in a net and repeatedly dipped in the water until they died. They were killed one at a time so each could watch what happened to those who died before them. The last to die was Apollonides. Our spies told us that his pleas for mercy annoyed Hippostratus so much that he had Apollonides's tongue cut out before he went into the water." Parmenio stopped and Igrat was shocked to see the distress on his face. "Igrat, that was how they killed Philotas. I had three sons, my only children. Two of them had already died fighting Alexander's battles and that was how he killed my last child. Then you came to breathe life back into my line. I don't want you dying like that."

So that is it. The news about the Ambassadors has brought all the tragedy of loss back into my father's life and torn open the scars we all had hoped were healed. "Nor do I, Father. It won't happen though. Naamah made me a final friend to escape that kind of fate." Igrat now understood why he had been so angry when she had refused to be taken off her courier runs.

"You and me both. We're still reorganizing our army after our deal with India and it'll be next year before we can move against Antigonus in force.

You've got until then to rest up. After that, you will, I promise, be busier than ever before.

Shahat, Cyrenêica, Summer Solstice, 305 BC

"We don't have a phalanx." Agis made the point politely if a trifle wearily. His whole force consisted of four thousand foot-soldiers, who were lightly armed and well fitted by nature for rapid marching, and more than four thousand mounted men. He had ordered them to carry several days' supply of food that would not require cooking, and, had made a forced march towards Cyrenê, under orders to punish the Cyrenês in whatever way he could.

Being very young and knowing his inexperience, his first act on approaching Cyrenê had been to hold a conference with his veteran officers and ask their suggestions. The problem was that they were men who had grown up with the phalanx at the center of the battlefield and their suggestions had all rotated around adapting the tactics of the phalanx to the circumstances of this battle. Agis believed that way would lead to disaster. "Our strength is in our cavalry."

"Does the General have any suggestions we might consider?" One of his captains, a grizzled veteran, put the question as politely as Agis himself had spoken. Nevertheless, the question had the armor piercing quality of a spearthrust.

"Hippostratus was expecting aid from Antigonus. More to the point, he was expecting veteran Sarissaphoros who would provide him with a phalanx. Without them, he has tried to organize his recruits into a phalanx. But, they are not Macedonians and they do not have the steadiness needed to stand in the Phalanx. Their phalanx will be much weaker than it looks. The only thing weaker than it would be us trying to put our men into a phalanx to match."

"But infantry cannot stop a phalanx, let alone defeat it."

"The Argyraspides did. Over and over again. Every battle Eumenes won was the result of the Argyraspides outflanking and breaking the Phalanx."

"The Argyraspides are dead and gone. Would that they were here, but they are not."

"Then is it not time that the Argyraspides live again?" Agis looked around at his commanders. "The Hypaspists have almost vanished from the battlefield. Armies are like the one we face today. A phalanx with its flanks covered by a small and scattered force of cavalry. The skilled soldier, capable of fighting freely to protect the flanks of their phalanx or assault the flanks of the enemy phalanx, is no longer a common asset. Today, let us return the Hypaspists to their former glory. I suggest we spread our infantry out in a skirmish line. Let us assume that Hippostratus has organized his 2,000 men in ranks of ten. Therefore, the frontage of his phalanx is 200 men. Organized in skirmish order, our men will have a frontage five times that. So, we fight as follows. Our cavalry, outnumbering his horsemen by eight to one will drive them off. His phalanx will advance and we all know the phalanx is invincible from the front. So, the 200 of our men who face that front, retreat before it. The phalanx, which cannot change its course, will continue to advance, being drawn deeper and deeper in. Then, the rest of our men close in on its flanks and rear."

Agis stabbed his sword deep into the sand. "Finish."

His commanders stood looking at the lines Agis had sketched in the sand with the point of his sword. Eventually, the grizzled veteran who had asked for his proposals nodded slowly. "It could well work. If our men are not demoralized by the sight of the phalanx without one of their own to steady them."

"Then we provide something to lift their spirits. Remind them how the Argyraspides preyed on phalanxes as wolves prey on sheep. Suggest to them that silver shields await them once their reputation as a destroyer of phalanxes is established. One might remind them of the great privileges that are bestowed upon elite regiments. First pick of the loot, rewards in gold coin from the King's own hand. The friendship and affection of the most beautiful women. Why, it is even rumored that the Goddess Athena Alcidemus herself married the first commander of Seleucus's Daimones Prodromoi, so impressed was she with his – and their - bravery. All these honors could be theirs provided they earn them on the battlefield."

"But the Argyraspides were murdered."

"Yes, by Antigonus who cares only for gold and accuses those around him of treachery at a whim. We do not fight for such a man. We fight for Ptolemy Soter and Seleucus Nikator. These are men of a very different kind. Is not the proudest boast made by our Royal Ladies of the Court that they kneel in the dirt to treat the wounds of even the humblest soldier? Can any man here think of a time when Ptolemy broke his word? Can any man here think of a time when Seleucus failed to praise and reward those who gave valiant service?"

Agis looked around at his commanders. They were standing tall and straight, their faces glowing with enthusiasm. The grizzled veteran who had led the questioning brought the butt of his half-sarissa down on the ground with a mighty thump and the cry "AGIS!"

The other commanders took up the cry and it echoed around the camp as the spears crashed on the ground in perfect cadence. It spread to the infantry already beginning to form up on the battlefield and the chanting battle-cry combined with the pounding spear-butts to make the very sand shake in fear.

"Earning a silver shield takes more than a single day or a single victory. But, the path to a silver shield starts with the first day and the first victory. Let that path start today!" Agis's last cry echoed around the camp as well and it put fire into the hearts of his men. Every one of them could see himself carrying a silver shield into battle while their enemies fled before them. Every one of them could almost count the plunder that they would win and the women who would flock to them. Some even hoped that their renown might become so great that Athena Alcidemus, the Goddess of Victory herself, might come to them in the night for it was whispered that those she favored never thereafter suffered wounds on the battlefield or sickness when on the march or in camp.

So it was that the Army of Agis took the field at the Battle of Shahat with their hearts filled with enthusiasm and a grim determination to do great things in the service of the their General and their King. Already, the more ambitious amongst them had determined that the achievements of this new regiment of Argyraspides would overshadow the legendary deeds of their predecessors. Some believed that they saw the spirits of the murdered Argyraspides looking down on them from the clouds and urging them onwards to victory. They did not – yet – carry their silver shields but in their hearts and their minds, the spirit of the Argyraspides had been reborn. And so, through their belief, it had.

Center, Army of Hippostratus, Battlefield of Shahat, Cyrenêica

The weakness of his Phalanx was obvious to the skilled eye of Hippostratus. It wasn't revealed in the men themselves but by the tracks they left in the sand. A Macedonian Phalanx would leave tracks in the sand that were as clean-cut as if they had been cut with a knife and straight enough to have been laid down by an architect. The tracks in front of him were ragged and they weaved in and out as the men had lost their station, then regained it.

"Sire, look! They have no Phalanx!" The speaker was waving at the Army of Agis drawn up in front of him. Their center extended far beyond the compact block that represented the Phalanx of the Army of Hippostratus yet the bristling hedge of spear-points was entirely absent. Instead of a rival phalanx, the opposing infantry were spread out in open order.

"What in the name of all the Gods is Agis up to?" Hippostratus couldn't believe what he was seeing. Without a phalanx to hold the center of the battlefield and act as an anchor for the two wings of the army to maneuver, there was no solidity to the battlefield. "Whatever it is, he's sent us a princely gift. Victory."

Hippostratus could see the battlefield developing before him. The absence of a phalanx before him would mean that his own thrust would be unopposed. It would shear through the center of the enemy line and split it asunder. Then with the battlefield center firmly in his grasp, his flank forces, 500 cavalry and the same number of auxiliaries on the left and right, would mop up the disorganized and defeated enemy. The weakness and inexperience of his phalanx was of no great consequence when there was nothing to oppose it.

The effects of Agis's decision to abjure the use of a phalanx were obvious to Hippostratus as the battle developed. The line of infantry was bending backwards as the men within it threw javelins at the advancing phalanx. Hippostratus realized then why Agis had taken the action he had. His infantry were Egyptian, not Macedonian and lacked the Sarissas that made the phalanx so formidable. The Egyptian infantry were trained with sword, mace and javelin, not the deadly Sarissa. The javelins had started to bring men in the phalanx down but in small numbers. Macedonian sarissaphoros would have shrugged off the losses as a necessary cost of doing business but the Cyrenêians lacked that stoicism and fortitude. Men in the ranks twisted and moved to avoid the javelins and, in doing so, caused ripples of movement throughout the ranks that further broke up the cohesion of the phalanx.

It was at that point Hippostratus started to realize things were going badly wrong. The open order line of enemy infantry was still falling back in front of his phalanx but they were thinning out still further. On the other hand, the unengaged portions of the line were thickening and strengthening. That was when Agis's cavalry spurred their horses and moved forward in a coordinated charge on both flanks. They were disciplined cavalry, trained to work as a coordinated team. Hippostratus's cavalry were basically civilians who happened to own horses. Hippostratus saw his horse break and run before the onslaught, putting up resistance that barely even qualified as token. The auxiliaries did not better. They launched a few shots from slings and leased off a few arrows but their effect was inconsequential. Then, they too, broke and ran before the charging horsemen.

With the two forces guarding the flanks of the phalanx reduce to ignominious flight, the unengaged ends of Agis's line started to advance. What a few minutes before had been a bow, pushed back by the phalanx, was now turning into a sack that enveloped it. Hippostratus had been in this situation before, at Cyaxares, and he tried to perform the same maneuver again. He issued orders for his Tetrarchès to take the rear ranks of his phalanx and form another that would defend the right wing of the main formation. More troops from the phalanx were moved to protect the left. His intent was to reform his phalanx into the U-formation that had saved the day at Cyaxares.

Now, Hippostratus learned the difference between the veteran sarissaphoros he had commanded then and the troops he had now. Twenty years of warfare had eroded that hard core of veterans and replaced them with novices lacking in both skill and ardor. As the back ranks of his phalanx peeled away, they did not move to form the flank guard but instead dropped their sarissas and ran for the rear. As each rank did so, the one in front of it saw what was happening and followed them. Hippostratus saw his phalanx dissolve as quickly and as thoroughly as an earthen bank dissolving in a flood. *I am their leader, I must follow them.* The grim words echoed in his mind as he turned his horse to follow his fleeing army.

Before The Walls of Cyrenê

"People of Cyrenê. Soon we will attack with all the vigor at our command and take your city by storm. Troops loyal to Ptolemy Soter still hold the citadel so you have nowhere to shelter. Your goods, your homes and your women will be taken by our victorious troops. The best of these will be kept by them. Others we will sell for gold and silver. You will only be left with those things that none desire. We offer you this alternative only. Open your gates. Hand over to us those who were guilty of the sedition that led you astray that they may be bound and sent to Alexandria. Hippostratus himself shall be likewise handed over and taken to justice for the murder of Apollonides and the other ambassadors. His personal guard who performed those foul murders shall be deprived of their arms before being released. Thereafter, Ptolemy Soter has commanded me to arranging the affairs of the city and listen to any grievances you may have. If there are any genuine faults in his rule and treatment of you, they will be remedied."

The herald settled back. Normally he would have been sent into the city to discuss terms with the city fathers but the treatment of the previous ambassadors precluded that. His announcing the terms from outside was a substitute. The truth was, he rather hoped the terms would be ignored. After such a glorious victory, a man deserved the services of a woman, given willingly or not as the case may be. To his secret dismay, the gates of the city creaked open.

The city fathers had done as promised. The city had surrendered, Hippostratus knelt bound in the sand and the leaders of dissension were likewise prisoners to be taken to Alexandria for judgment. In the case of Hippostratus, there was no need to go to that trouble. His fate was already decided. Beside him, a sturdy hypaspist stood ready. Agis gestured and a second later, the head of Hippostratus rolled in the sand.

Agis rode over to where the bodyguards of Hippostratus stood. They had carried out the murder of Apollonides and Ptolemy Soter had commanded him to punish them in whatever way seemed best to himself. Agis looked at them with loathing. This murder of ambassadors had to be discouraged. Firmly discouraged.

"Companions of Hippostratus. Under the terms of the surrender, you are to be deprived of your arms and then released. We will now keep the terms of that agreement." Agis looked at his army. "Fetch the blacksmiths and tell them to bring their sharpest axes."

Symposium, Home of Parmenio, Seleucia-on-the Tigris

It was an illustrious gathering. Indeed, there had rarely been such a gathering since the days of Alexander and his Companions. The wine flowed as freely as it had in those long-gone meetings and the food, prepared in this household under the close inspection of experts, was as excellent as any that could be found in the empires of those gathered. The first part of the evening had been the formal meal with roasted meats being brought in for the enjoyment of the guests. One the main meal had been consumed, there had been a libation to Athena Alcidemus, the Goddess of Victory, then the evening's drinking session had started.

More food had been brought in. Mostly, they were the tragēmata, snacks such as chestnuts, beans, toasted wheat, or honey cakes; all intended to absorb alcohol and extend the drinking spree. Derya Shafrid had been elected "King of the Banquet" and was supervising the servants as to how strongly to mix the wine. Hieronymus of Cardia had attended to read his latest declamation, an account of how Seleucus had taken the possibility of a devastating war and instead, by skilled diplomacy, turned it into a peace that greatly enhanced the prosperity of his people and the wealth of his kingdom. He had been followed by two of the best singers in Seleucia-on-the-Tigris who had sung the both latest popular songs and the classics in a carefully-balanced mixture.

One ingredient that was not present in the food that was being served was the hellbore that had killed the great Alexander. The person who had administered the hellbore had supervised the preparation of these meals. Even though her intent was to prevent poisoning rather than cause it, she still stayed out of sight. It had been almost twenty years since Naamah had poisoned Alexander and the people in this room included some who had unwittingly watched while she had done it. There was still a chance they might recognize her.

There were many differences also. Some were the obvious ones; there were few survivors indeed of Alexander and his Companions. Parmenio had seen to that. Another was that this symposium was being held in a private home rather than an ornate palace – although this home bordered on being a palace. The great difference though was one that had shocked the guests.

By ancient tradition, the banquet held in the Symposium was strictly reserved for men. Great feasts such as the one served this evening could only be afforded by the rich and in accordance with tradition, women were rigidly excluded. Only, reclining on a couch by the low tables held the food and wine was a woman, clad in a fashionable short tunic and trousers. The fine fabric was richly colored in swirling patterns that showed they had been imported from India at great cost.

Igrat was, as far as anybody knew, the only woman ever to have attended a symposium on equal terms with the men. Considering the other guests included Ptolemy Soter, Seleucus Nicator, Cassander and Lysimachus, that was a remarkable distinction. She had started the symposium perfectly groomed but after an evening matching the men around her goblet-for-goblet, her hair was coming loose and she was bleary-eyed and more than slightly disheveled.

The musicians were playing a bouncing Army ballad with a strong beat that served to keep the ranks in order on the march. Parmenio and his guests were crashing their wine goblets on the table in time with the music and Igrat was joining in the display. Her ability to keep up with the cadence showed a remarkable familiarity with military music.

A strand of her hair had fallen down across an eye. Ptolemy managed to notice it and it set off a train of thought. *She has her own hair. Looks after it but it is her own. Most high-born women wear wigs. Gods, that's how she does it. When she's travelling, she hides with the low-class camp women in the baggage train.*

The cause of the celebration was the alliance that had been formed. The successes of Antigonus Monopthalmus in Greece, Caria and Thrace and brought him back from the brink of destruction and now, once again, he was determined to expand his domains. His latest attempt had been to seize Cyprus from Ptolemy, using the troops he had promised to send to the aid of the late and completely unlamented Hippostratus. Antigonus had signed a treaty with Pnytagoras of Salamis and provided him with reinforcements of men and horse. He'd also supported Pnytagoras with his fleet including a detachment of the dreaded catapult ships.

Using these resources, Pnytagoras had attacked his neighbors, storming the city of Cerynia, killing Praxippus its king and also Stasioecus, ruler of Marion. Pnytagoras had destroyed the city of Marion and transported the inhabitants to Paphos. At that point, Ptolemy had appointed Nicocreon to command an army charged with recovering Cyprus. In a swift campaign, Nicreon had killed Pnytagoras, then captured and sacked Poseidium and

Potami Caron. Sailing without delay to Paphos he had rescued the citizens of Marion and aided them in rebuilding their city. Cyprus was, once again, in Ptolemaic hands. Nobody believed that Antigonus would give up. Cyprus was too perfect a base for an assault on Egypt itself.

The great meeting of the last few days had been aimed at developing a strategy for the final defeat of Antigonus. More realistically, it had comprised Parmenio telling the others how to defeat Antigonus. Conceptually, it was a simple plan. While Ptolemy drew Antigonus westward toward Egypt, Cassander would defeat the forces of Ptolemaeus in Greece while Lysimachus would finish off Meleager. Once the threat of Antigonus's invasion was dealt with, Ptolemy would launch an invasion of Coelê Syria and take the field against the army of Demetrius.

With the secondary theaters eliminated, Seleucus would complete bringing his army westward, link up with Lysimachus and Ptolemy and then destroy Antigonus. The operative word was 'destroy'. Antigonus's power had come back from nothing too often to allow him to survive this war.

"Here." Seleucus Nikator called out to the servants who were keeping the supply of wine flowing. The loyalty of Parmenio's servants was well-known and greatly admired. Already, some of the more enlightened members of Seleucid society were emulating the treatment of household staff that produced such devotion.

Seleucus had brought a series of pouches, containing gold pieces and he distributed them around the servants so that the recipients felt that they had been well-rewarded for their efforts. It was a well-timed gesture for the symposium was winding down since most of the guests were delicately balanced between being paralytic and comatose. The servants were carrying them off to their guest rooms where they would be carefully watched to make sure they didn't choke in their sleep. Soon, only Igrat, Derya and Permenio were left.

Igrat reached up, brushed her hair back, and readjusted her clothes. The disheveled appearance and bleary look from her eyes vanished and she showed no signs of the evening's drinking bout.

"You're stone cold sober! How?" Parmenio was having a job standing up without holding on to something. He knew that Igrat weighed about a hundred pounds if that; he was far more than twice her weight. *Resistance to drunkenness is proportional to body weight. So, how is she sober and I'm not?*

Igrat smiled at him, a touch sadly, a touch triumphantly. "Any woman who attends parties has to learn how to do so and stay sober. It's easy to convince people you're drinking when you're not. Just keep sipping but

335

barely wet your lips each time. People with you'll think that you've been refilling, but they just haven't noticed you doing it. Every opportunity you get, pour the contents of your goblet away. I suppose I've drunk a single goblet of wine if that. The rest of it is in there."

Igrat gestured at her couch. Concealed underneath it was a bronze chamber-pot. It was a simple and familiar enough item; every bedroom had two of them. Only, this one was full of wine. "Father, I need a scribe. I've got everything everybody said this evening locked away in my head and I need to get it out quickly."

Parmenio turned to Derya and grinned at him. "And now you see why your wife is an invaluable part of my command headquarters."

Hall of Judgment, Palace of Seleucus Nikator, Selucia-on-the-Tigris.

Seleucus Nikator swore to himself that, in the interests of justice, he would never hold a court session while suffering from a hangover again. It was immaterial that he was convinced his hangover this morning was the worst known to human history. The very fact that he had a hangover at all was prejudicing him against those appearing before him and he recognized that as being shamefully unjust. Nevertheless, he would soon be campaigning and that meant he had to deal with important cases prior to his departure.

Although an attempted abduction was not the most serious of cases, Seleucus wanted to treat it with the highest priority. By doing so, he could show respect for the house of Parmenio the Younger, demonstrate the high place the household had in his esteem, and also make a part payment for the great services he had received at the hands of that house.

Alcetas had been dragged from the dungeons and now faced him. He was in a sorry state, most people were after even a short time in the dungeons, but he had obviously received rough treatment as well. It was quite clear that the jailors and the common soldiers had also decided to show their respect for the House of Parmenio the Younger and, in particular, for the women of that house who had established the practice of treating their wounds. Not being the most literate or eloquent of men, they had chosen other means to express their anger at Alcetas.

Seleucus had heard the story of how Alcetas had been caught in the trap designed by Gusoyn. He had also heard from the survivors of the men Alcetas had hired. They had been conscripted into one of the Seleucid Army's engineer units and were presently employed in cleaning up after the war elephants. It had, however, been pointed out that in their previous careers as street thugs they had little hope of advancement but in the Army, things would be different and advancement was available to those whose diligence merited it. Assiduous work in cleaning up the mess left by the elephants could result in them being given spades for example.

Alcetas had claimed that his intent was to abduct Lillith so he could marry her. His men had flatly contradicted that and revealed how his plan had been to make her walk until she died.

Seleucus looked at the sorry figure before him, with contempt liberally mixed with pity. "Alcetas, I have to ask one question. Why? You were a well-regarded commander with a record of valor and success in battle. You were in great favor with me and were well-regarded by the House of Parmenio the Younger. You were on the friendliest of terms with this woman, a prominent member of that household. Great honors lay before you, rank and privilege ready to be seized and made your own. And yet, you turned your back on all of this and instead started a descent that led you to the sad position in which you now find yourself. Why?"

Alcetas's voice was angry and loaded with hatred and resentment. "Because I asked for her hand in marriage and she refused me. When I asked Parmenio to overrule her and order the marriage, he refused to do so. This was an insult I could not tolerate."

"Parmenio, I do not wish to intrude upon how you run your household, which stands highest in my favor. Purely for my own curiosity, why did you regard this match as unsuitable?"

Parmenio stood and straightened himself, feeling stabs of pain in his head as he did so. "Your Majesty, my house is cursed with an affliction. The women of our line are few and those that are born to us are barren. I am one of four brothers and so it has been for generations. Alcetas wished to unit our family lines and produce a strong healthy family. This he cannot do with the women from my line. Knowing that she could not bear him sons, Lillith refused him so that he would be free to make another alliance. I will not, on grounds of conscience, force any woman of my family to marry a man she has refused."

"And did you explain this to Alcetas?"

"I did, Your Majesty. He obviously didn't listen."

"You let your daughter marry a prodromoi!" Alectus almost screamed the words.

Ahhh, the old rivalry. Seleucus thought. *There has always been the divide in the Macedonian Army between the infantry and the cavalry. Rivalry was really too mild a word for it. After the death of Alexander, there was open fighting between them that nearly a civil war. That's what is at the real base of this.*

Parmenio looked at Alcetas with something close to amusement. "As everybody knows, my daughter is adopted. She comes from low birth and was adopted because she has unique talents to place at the service of our King. She is not of my bloodline although she is as dear to me as if she was. Her husband proposed marriage to her out of love, knowing her background and desiring her for herself, not for any alliance or advancement she might bring with her. She accepted him out of love and on the same basis. All of that is, however, nothing to do with you."

"I agree. Seleucus had come to his conclusion. "Alcetas, it is obvious that you have surrendered all your prospects, your reputation and your honor in pursuing a grievance that exists only in your imagination. In doing so, you have betrayed everything we stand for as Macedonians. After the death of the great Alexander, some of the Army rose against the rest in an attempt to seize power. The insurrection was put down and the ringleaders sentenced to death. They were executed by having an elephant step on them. I condemn you to the same fate.

"Guard, take Alcetas to the elephant lines and have them trample him."

Battlefield at Opuntia, Summer, 305BC

Nikomedes glanced at Zephyros standing in the file next to him. They were in the front rank of the Phalanx, the place of greatest danger but also where the chance of honors and preferment were highest. They were also warm, something that they would never againt fail to appreciate. There had been times during the horrors of the winter campaign, now far behind them, when they had thought they would never be warm again.

For most of the spring, they had been besieging the town of Opuntia while rebuilding their strength after the losses of the winter. Now, at last, they were back to their pre-winter numbers and more besides. Their ranks had been filled out with mercenaries, hired with Athenian gold, that had doubled their force. Nearly all the Macedonians were in the central phalanx, ten thousand strong. A thousand Rhodian hoplites with large shields and short 8-foot doru spears had been deployed to guard their right while five hundred cavalry defended their left. In other words, the world was back to the way it should be.

Nikomedes knew something else, this was only half the army Ptolemaeus had deployed. There was a second force, hidden behind a ridgeline to their right. It consisted of the Aetolian and Boetian contingents totaling four thousand men and two thousand five hundred horse. Like all

Greek troops, they had only the doru spears but that would not limit for them in their planned role.

As Cassander's eighteen thousand men advanced on the army of Ptolemaeus and were fixed by its phalanx, the Aetolians and Boetians would fall upon its flank. Just to finish off the trap, Polyperchon and his twenty thousand men were moving in to block the retreat of Cassander's Army. When this battle was done, the Macedonian Army would be no more and Greece would be free again.

For twenty years, the successors to Alexander had grappled with the task of fighting wars where the men, weapons and tactics used by both sides were the same. Only strategies differed and strategy had decided this battle. From his position in the front rank, Nikomedes could see Cassander's phalanx approaching. It was a formidable sight, almost twice the number of his own, and its sound was more formidable yet. The hiss of its sarissas as they swung down from the vertical marching position to the horizontal fighting stance echoed across the battlefield. Then, it was matched by the weaker yet still formidable sound of Ptolemaeus's Phalanx bringing down its sarissas.

The two phalanxes squared up to each other, ready to start the brutal business of trying to force the other back. But, with Polyperchon's army already descending on the rear of Cassander's, the battle was already decided.

"What in the name of all the Gods is going on!" Nikomedes heard Zephyros call out. Being in the front rank meant they could see what was going on and it was obvious the plan that had been explained to them was going badly wrong.

The Aetolians and Boetians had unmasked their position early, before Cassander's force had been pinned by that of Ptolemaeus. What should have been a surprise blow that would have swept Cassander's army from the battlefield was now simply an extension to that battlefield. Cassander would be discountenanced by this but he outnumbered his enemies and he could extend his line easily.

That was when Nikomedes realized that the enemy wouldn't have to. For, the Aetolians and Boetians were moving off the ridgeline and into the attack but they were not aiming at Cassander's Army. They were aiming at the thousand Rhodians on his right.

"We are betrayed!" The cry came from his lips for he knew that the attack, outnumbering the Rhodians by four to one could not fail to drive them from the battlefield.

"More than you think." Zephyros was desperate and fearful. Over to the left, the Army of Polyperchon was also making its appearance, not swinging in behind that of Cassander, but beside it to join them. What should have been a battle between roughly even forces was now one in which the balance against the Antigonid army was four to one.

Strategy, thought Nikomedes, this battle is not being won by strategy, it is being won by treachery. *Cassander is not being surrounded by a coalition of all his enemies, he is surrounding us with all of his allies.*

Then, he forgot about what was happening in the desperate effort to survive. The blades of the enemy sarissas were already finding their way through the wall of friendly spearpoints while arrows rained down from overhead. Most of them were stopped by the sarissas held by the ranks behind them but a few got through and the Sarissaphoros started to fall. As they did, the phalanx started to weaken and the advancing enemy spears started to bite home.

While Nikomedes frantically tried to deflect them away from himself while also thrusting at the enemy, his attention was focused tightly on his own three or four feet of frontage. He wasn't even aware of how or when Zephyros had died. It could have been an arrow or a sarissa. All he knew was that his friend was one of the growing numbers of men on the blood-soaked ground under the feet of the phalanx.

The Macedonian Phalanx was invincible from the front and this one was no different. Despite the casualties, despite being outnumbered so badly, the phalanx of grim Macedonian veterans held. It was its flanks that collapsed. Polyperchon's huge force dispersed the scattered cavalry that screened the left flank and started the slow, ponderous swing that would re-orientate their phalanx perpendicular to that of Ptolemaeus. Then, it would roll forward and crush the much smaller force before it. Before it could do that, the Aetolians and Boetians had destroyed the Rhodian contingent and were engaging Ptolemaeus's right. Somewhere in the confusion, Ptolemaeus himself went down.

Even with their commander dead, the Macedonians knew how to conduct a fighting retreat and their phalanx held while they did so. But, there was nowhere to retreat to. Polyperchon's cavalry blocked the way. The phalanx stopped, unable to go forward or backwards. That was when Nikomedes saw the horsemen with flags of truce in front of him. "It's over. Your commanders have surrendered. Save your lives and do the same. There is no need for more of us to die today."

There was a rattling noise that grew in volume as more and more of the Sarissaphoros threw down their Sarissas. Sick with shame, Nikomedes did the same. In front of him, one of Cassander's Tetrarchès was looking at him thoughtfully. "You look like a man of courage and experience. How would you like to fight for Cassander? The standard rate, a tenth of a talent per year."

That was when Nikomedes made up his mind. *There really is no great difference between these sides and I have a wife back with the baggage train. If I die here, she gets taken by another or sold into slavery. Time to look after my family.*

"Sounds good to me." He picked up his sarissa and joined the stream of men who were joining the ranks of the Army of Cassander. Cassander's regiments had casualties to replace and this was the easiest way to do it. That was one of the benefits of winning a battle, the opportunity to recruit experienced veterans from the defeated side. That was a reason why, when an army started winning battles, it kept on winning them.

For the men of the defeated army, joining those who had defeated them was a way of salvaging something from the ruin. How complete that ruin could be was illustrated by the sight of Cassander's prodromoi cavalry in the baggage train.

The Tetrarchès who had recruited him had finished his work and now escorted a group of the recruits back to the captured baggage train. The factors for Cassander's Army had penned the captured women in a rope-bordered enclosure where they waited for their fate with conduct varying from quiet dignity to weeping semi-hysteria. The Tetrarchès escorting his new recruits spoke to the factors. Coin changed hands, a small bribe to ensure that the Tetrarchès got his men into the enclosure quickly, and the factors waved the men into the pen.

Nikomedes looked around the enclosure hoping that his wife Dara hadn't been killed when the camp was overrun. Then, he saw her standing with Zephyros's wife, Eunike. The look of gratitude in his wife's eyes when she saw he had survived and come back for her did much to drive away memories of the battle.

Beside her, Eunike guessed what had happened. If her husband had survived , he would have been here with Nikomedes. She collapsed on the ground, moaning to herself. She faced an ugly future; unless another man offered her refuge in the next few hours, she would become common property, her body made available to anybody who wanted a woman.

The sight made Nikomedes feel almost guilty as he hugged his Dara and set off for the wagons. As members of the Army of Cassander, they were even allowed to find and reclaim their goods. The wagon holding their property had two mounted prodromoi next to it but they seemed genial enough. One of them even grinned at Nikomedes when he heard Dara crying out with delight at finding her precious pots and pans were still safe.

Fourth Diodochi War

By evening, they had set up their home in Cassander's camp and baggage train. Dara was cooking his evening meal, celebrating his survival by taking special care that it would be just the way he liked it. Looking around at his new army and comrades, many of whom he had fought alongside before, Nikomedes couldn't help but think that it seemed as if nothing had changed.

CHAPTER FOUR

NAVAL GAMES

Headquarters of Demetrius Poliorcetes, Carpasia, Cyprus.

"Salamis is the key to holding the island. Once we storm the city, the rest will fall into our hands. The mistake my father made last time was trying to use inadequate forces and relying on local allies to bear the main burden of the attacks. As a result, Menelaüs was able to defeat them in detail. This time around, we're using our own men and we've brought enough to do the job properly. Fifteen thousand foot and four hundred horse supported by more than one hundred and ten triremes, fifty-three heavier ships and a dozen catapult ships. We have enough freighters of every kind to support our strength of cavalry and infantry."

Peucestes nodded in agreement. After ten years in disgrace after the Gabiene, he had finally worked his way back to a command in the Army. In a Macedonian culture where military prowess was the single prime determinant to a man's honor and status, his eclipse had been a crippling blow to his entire family. Now, he had a chance to redeem himself but he had insight enough to understand that he owed the revival of his fortunes to the fact that Antigonus was unable to recruit commanders of greater stature. "We have received word from Rhodes. They refuse to supply any more men or ships, saying that they wish to maintain a common peace with all. I believe that the losses they suffered at Opuntia have opened their eyes to what this war has become."

Demetrius nodded. News of the Battle of Opuntia and the destruction of the Army of Ptolemaeus had spread fast. The Rhodians had lost more than three quarters of their number with the rest sold into slavery. Veteran but defeated sarissaphoros could easily find a new home in the victorious army but the Greek hoplites were the residue of an outmoded means of

343

warfare. They were worth more as slaves than recruits. For a small community such as the Rhodians, the loss was devastating. Demetrius sympathized with them and had not taken action against them despite Antigonus's clearly-expressed desire that he do so. The truth was that Demetrius was beginning to believe that his father had lost the keen edge of intellect that had supported him for his decades of political and military maneuvering. What Peucestes didn't know was that Demetrius had received a letter from his father, instructing him to call together counselors from the allied cities who should consider in common what was advantageous for Greece, and to finish the war with the generals of Ptolemy as soon as possible.

Yet it is not on land where Ptolemy's strength lies. Demetrius stared at the maps before him as a new strategy formed in his mind. *His strength and power are at sea. It is his navy that gives him the options of where to strike and when. The Egyptian Navy dominates the Aegean and splits his enemies into two isolated divisions. Without his Navy, at best we can unite and crush him. At worst, we can isolate Ptolemy from the affairs of Empire and leave him to his own devices on the other side of the Nile.*

His train of thought was disturbed by the sound of a rider arriving. The dispatch was from Anatolios Metrophanes, the commander of his cavalry force. Metrophanes was another commander who had been in disgrace for years and only brought back because of the shortage of officers willing to serve Antigonus. Demetrius took the scroll and read it quickly and then relayed the contents to Peucestes. "Menelaüs has gathered his soldiers from the outposts and consolidated his army at Salamis. He has now left the city and advances on our positions with a force of twelve thousand foot and about eight hundred horse."

"And we have fifteen thousand foot and four hundred horse." Peucestes weighed the odds in his mind. "I don't like our weakness in cavalry."

"We are not fighting Seleucus Nikator and the Daimones Prodromoi are far away. Menelaüs will have to split his cavalry to cover both flanks of the phalanx. We have fifteen hundred hoplites from our allies who can cover one flank while our cavalry covers the other. We still have a slight superiority in phalanx numbers."

"That counts for little." Peucestes had spent his years in exile studying the battles that had taken place since the death of Alexander. "The phalanxes will not be decisive in the center. They will hold each other locked while the soldiers wave their sarissas at each other. The hoplites will stall the cavalry on one flank but that's all and on the other, the cavalry will be evenly matched. This battle will achieve nothing."

Demetrius saw why Peucestes had not been gifted with success on the battlefield. He was skilled enough when looking at battles in isolation but he lacked the vision to put them into a wider context. That was why he had failed at the Gabiene.

"There are times, my friend, when an indecisive battle can achieve more than the most decisive of victories. This is one of those cases. We will move to meet Menelaüs and our armies will engage. The conflict will be blood but ultimately indecisive. Menelaüs will then have two choices, he will either stay in the field and try to engage us again with less hope of success than before. In doing so, he will leave Salamis open to our attack. Or, he will return to Salamis and position himself in the city where the city walls will offset his weakened state. If he does that, we will, of course, besiege him."

"Salamis is heavily fortified and will be a hard not to crack open."

"I've cracked harder, but that is not the issue. With Menelaüs bottled up in Salamis, Ptolemy will come to his aid and to do that he must come by sea. Rescuing Menelaüs means the Egyptian Navy will be entering these waters where we can engage it at great advantage. If the gods smile upon us and we win that engagement, Salamis will fall and the way to invade Ptolemy's base of power, Egypt, will be opened. Is not the conquest of Egypt a valuable prize to be won by an indecisive battle?"

"if we win the naval battle here."

Demetrius looked at the harbor where the *Leontophoros* and the *Olympias* were leading four more of the huge catapult ships in. "The gods of battle are always fickle. But this time, I think they will turn their faces from Ptolemy and his ships."

Palace of Ptolemy Soter, Memphis, Egypt

"Thank you, Thaïs, for your time and effort on my behalf." Igrat's gesture of respect was genuine and heartfelt. She had been a regular visitor to Ptolemy's palace for years and, during that time, she had been quietly instructed by the famous Athenian courtesan Thaïs, on how to conduct herself in the high company she met. As Thaïs had carefully imparted her lessons, she had opened up a whole new world for Igrat. What had started as a simple instructor/student relationship had ripened into a firm, lasting friendship with Thaïs becoming Igrat's mentor. In some ways, Thaïs had become the mother Igrat had never had. The fact that Thaïs was Ptolemy's concubine and confidante was another benefit of the relationship.

"It is my pleasure Igrat." Thaïs looked at her and sighed. "I wish I could keep my beauty as you are doing, but having three children dictated otherwise. Still, they are a joy to me even though they are not in the royal line of succession. I have taken great pains to ensure that for those in the line of succession all too often have a short life. Berenice's children are welcome to that. Take my advice, Igrat, and stay out of any line of succession, the risks exceed the benefits. Now, may you enjoy good fortune and come to see me again soon."

Igrat walked through the corridors towards Ptolemy's rooms. She knew this would probably be the last time she would be visiting this palace since it was about to be replaced by a new and more luxurious establishment at the new city of Alexandria. The guards saw her approach and quickly opened the doors to allow her entrance. She made her obeisance to Ptolemy, then sat before his great desk.

"Your Majesty. I bring news from Seleucus Nikator and words from Strategos Parmenio the Younger. The news is held on these scrolls, but the words are these. The operations of Antigonus in Attica have failed disastrously with his entire expeditionary force being defeated in battle. Cassander now hold Macedonia, Attica and Peleponessus. Now, he will march to the aid of Lysimachus as do the armies of Seleucus. Also, Roxane and Alexander IV are dead, poisoned on the orders of Cassander. Barsine and Heracles are in the hands of Cassander and their fate is uncertain. Their safety was promised to Polyperchon but . . . . .

"Parmenio counsels, do not be drawn eastward for that will play into the hands of Antigonus and Demetrius. They plan to assault you here in your power base and drive you from your throne. Crossing the Nile is impossible due to your well-constructed defenses so they will try to land on your coast. Therefore, Parmenio counsels you to build up your coastal defenses and preserve your fleet for that great battle."

As always, Ptolemy was fascinated by the way Igrat's voice had caught the flat, uninflected delivery of Parmenio. He looked at her intently. He had learned something about her, something very important, at Parmenio's symposium but when he had woken up, the memory had gone and, strive mightily as he had, he could not make it return. "Good advice as one would expect from the master, but, overcome by events. I have had word from Menelaüs, now besieged in the city of Salamis. He implores me to send aid as my interests on the island are in danger. He took the field against Demetrius with a force of slightly lesser size and, in a battle of short duration was overwhelmed losing almost a thousand killed and three thousand taken prisoner. At first Demetrius distributed those captives among the units of his own soldiers; but they remained loyal and deserted back to Menelaüs at the first opportunity. The few that were left were sent to Antigonus in Syria. Menelaüs, after having been defeated in the battle, had missiles and engines brought to the walls of Salamis, assigned positions on the battlements to his soldiers, and made preparations for siege.

"According to Menelaüs, Demetrius is preparing siege engines of very great size, catapults for shooting bolts and ballistae of all kinds, and the other equipment that would strike terror into the defenders. He has also built a new siege tower, named Helepolis in honor of the one lost at Tyre. It is 90 feet wide and 180 feet tall, armed with catapults and a large number of ballistae; and has a crew of more than two hundred men. Menelaüs believes that once the siege engines are deployed, the city will fall.

"That being so, I will have to send an expedition to Cyprus in order to break the siege before the city is stormed. Tell Parmenio that I value his advice above all others and would normally follow his counsel unquestioningly but the importance of Cyprus is such that this time I cannot do so. I am sending one hundred and forty warships and two hundred transports carrying twenty thousand foot and five hundred horse. They will be enough to drive back Demetrius and raise the siege of Salamis."

Palace of Cassander, Pella, Macedonia, Late Summer, 305BC

"The Lady Barsine, and her son, Heracles." The page announced the two who had been summoned to the presence of Cassander. The doors to the throne room opened and they were ushered into the presence of Cassander, now bearing the title of King and undoubted ruler of all Greece and Macedonia. The truth was that Barsine and Heracles were a problem. The official story was that Heracles was an illegitimate son of Alexander the Great, fathered when Alexander had taken Barsine, daughter of Satrap Artabazus of Phrygia, as his mistress.

The truth was that the whole story was suspicious. There was no record of Barsine bearing Alexander a son and there were many who thought that the young man was an imposter, chosen because of a superficial resemblance to the great Alexander. Descendent or not, the two were a problem. Roxane and her son, an undoubted child of the great Alexander and officially titled King Alexander IV, had died only a few weeks before. Their food had been dosed with an extract of hemlock but they'd been separated on a pretext in the brief period between them consuming the poisoned food and the symptoms starting to appear. That way, each had died, believing the other had been allowed to live.

Cassander looked at the two kneeling before him. He had both liked and respected Roxane. Her upbringing as a Bactrian princess had not equipped her to deal with the murderous infighting that distinguished the Macedonian court. Nevertheless, she had managed to maintain her dignity during the chaos that surrounded her and her son. That was why he had arranged for the two to die a merciful and painless death. On the other hand, Barsine and Heracles were opportunists who had taken advantage of the long civil war to enrich themselves. The truth was, he doubted that Barsine had ever been

Alexander's mistress as she had claimed. But, Polyperchon had believed her and the safety of Barsine and her son had been the price of him changing sides.

"Barsine, you and your son are an inconvenience. I have arranged for the two of you to be taken to the court of Seleucus Nikator where you will live in retirement. You will have no royal privileges and will have the status of a private citizen. Do you understand that? The world will hear no more of you and the alleged son of the great Alexander."

"Heracles is the illegitimate son of the great Alexander and rightful . . ." Behind Barsine, a man stepped silently forward. He grabbed her hair, jerked her head back and cut her throat, skillfully and with great efficiency. Behind her son, another guard thrust downward with a sword, sliding it into the soft triangle of skin between Heracles's neck and collar bone. Heracles joined his mother, dying on the floor in a spreading pool of blood. With the deaths of Alexander IV and Heracles, the Argead Dynasty that had ruled Macedonia for four hundred years became extinct.

Cassander looked down at the bodies. He had buried Alexander and Roxane with honors but that would not be the case here. "I said that the world will hear no more of them. Destroy the bodies and get rid of what remains so nobody ever finds them."

Outside the Walls of Salamis, Cyprus, 305BC

There was a reason why Demetrius Poliorcetes bore the nickname of "the Beseiger". A capable commander in the field, he came into his element when faced with a walled and defended city. The city of Salamis was no different from any other. Its defenses were formidable and had been heavily reinforced by Menelaüs. Catapults and other heavy weapons had been mounted on the walls and commenced a steady bombardment of the surrounding forces. Demetrius had retaliated by building siege engines of his own, of unprecedented size and power. And so the great duel between besieger and besieged had commenced.

Slowly, Demetrius had gained the upper hand. His troops had dug parallels, trenches that allowed them to approach the walls of the city without exposing themselves to the deadly fire from crossbows and catapults the defenders had relied upon. He had brought his siege engines right up to the city walls and replied to the fire from them with a shower of missiles. Slowly and methodically, he had cleared the battlements and suppressed the fire from them, That had allowed him to bring up battering rams that had started the process of shattering the walls with their blows.

Demetrius was indeed skilled at his craft but that didn't make the siege easy. Since those within resisted boldly and opposed his engines of war with other devices, for some days the battle was doubtful, both sides suffering hardships and severe casualties.

Nevertheless, the progress of the siege was inexorable. The defender's casualties mounted with none available to replace the dead. Weapons and ammunition were expended, food and other supplies were eaten. Worst of all, the battering rams had their effect and soon whole lengths of the wall was falling. By evening, the breaches in the walls were practical and the city was in danger of being taken by storm. Demetrius knew that allowing the defenders time to restore the defenses was neither wise nor prudent but the truth was that the coming of night had prevented the mounting of an immediate attack. So, he elected to wait until dawn before demanding the surrender of the city.

As it happened, he never got the chance. At midnight, Demetrius was inspecting the siege lines when he saw the city's few remaining catapults firing bales of straw and dry wood at the siege engines. They were followed by a barrage of fire-bearing arrows from the walls. The wood of the siege engines was dry and the burnings traw quickly set it ablaze. Demetrius tried to come to the rescue; but the flames had already established themselves. By the time the fires were brought under control, the engines were completely destroyed and many of those who manned them were lost.

Demetrius was surveying the disaster when a messenger rode in on a horse that was near foundering. "General! Word from Kition. Ptolemy has set sail, rounding the south eastern headland of Cyprus and heading north up the coast to Salamis. He will be here tomorrow!"

Demetrius sighed with relief. The siege of Salamis had suddenly become unimportant. The fate of Cyprus would be decided at sea.

Ptolemy's Flagship Andromeda Approaching Salamis Bay

The fleet of warships arrayed across the entrance to Salamis Bay was impressive even to Ptolemy. He had brought the cream of the Egyptian fleet to this engagement, leaving behind only the older and less powerful ships. Spread out beside him were one hundred and forty quinqueremes and quadriremes. He had placed the large quinqueremes on his left, closest to the shore with the smaller quadriremes in his center and right. That was counter-intuitive; a more conventional disposition would be to place the quadriremes with their two rows of oars with two oarsmen per oar inshore where they would be able to maneuver in the shallow water better than the quinqueremes with their extra row of oars. But, Ptolemy's priority was to clear the way for the more than two hundred transports following which carried fifteen thousand foot-soldiers. His plan was to use the powerful left wing he had created to clear the Antigonid fleet out of the way and let the transports through so they could land their troops and break the siege of Salamis. That was why he had taken command of the left wing himself.

The center of his fleet was commanded by Telesphorus of Peloponnesus. He had been sent to Ptolemy by Cassander with high recommendations as a skilled and determined admiral. His task was simple; he had to hold the center while Ptolemy's ships destroyed the enemy right. Then, he would join the surviving ships from the left wing and roll up the center and left of the Antigonid fleet. Finally Ptolemy's right, the smallest and weakest of his ships, were there simply to hold up Demetrius while the rest of his fleet was destroyed. There was one other factor that influenced Ptolemy's decisions and it kept running through his mind. *Parmenio may be the great master of war on land but this is at sea. Here, I will show him that I am his equal.*

Next to him, Trierarch Meladen was waiting for the order. Ptolemy turned to him and gave him the expected words. "Send the signal. Battle speed."

Meladen nodded and raised a highly-polished shield so that the sunlight reflecting off it flashed across the ships. Each ship, seeing the signal, relayed it to the rest so that the order spread down the long lines in mere seconds. The drums picked up the beat, their hammering echoing in unison across the sea as the oarsmasters kept their ships in the neat formations that added the power of numbers to the individual strength of the ships. The flashing signals had another role. They would be seen by watchers on the walls of Salamis and they would send word to Menelaüs that the great stratagem was under way.

The previous day, Ptolemy had sent messangers to Menelaüs with orders to prepare the sixty ships in Salamis for sea. The plan was that they would sortie from harbor, force their way past any ships Demetrius had left to guard the harbor entrance and fall upon the rear of the Antigonid fleet. With their reinforcement, he would easily be superior in the naval engagement since he would have two hundred ships in the battle. *I just hope those damned messengers get through. This is one time I could really use Igrat. She'd have got through to the city, delivered the message and got out again. In fact she'd be here beside me now with her hair and make-up perfect. I wonder how she does it. Still, never try to understand women, that way lies madness.*

Ptolemy looked ahead, to where the Antigonid fleet was approaching. They had obviously gone to battle speed as well for the gap between the two formations was closing quickly. One thing Ptolemy saw immediately was that Demetrius had loaded his left flank just as he had done. The other was that the Antigonid fleet was much more varied than his own. He could see a wide range of ships, heptaremes and hexaremes mixed in with the more normal quinqueremes and quadriremes. However, what seized his attention were the twenty of so very large ships at the rear of the Antigonid left wing. They were decaremes, very wide in proportion to their length. Even though they were using all the power of their ten banks of oarsmen, they were still having trouble keeping up with the rest of the fleet. Ptolemy had never seen such ships before, but he had heard of them Catapult ships.

Galley Leontophoros, *Bay of Salamis*

"Get those catapults ready!" Tetrarchès Hyakinthos looked down the deck of the *Leontophoros*, making sure that the new, enlarged crew was working well together. Demetrius had reinforced the crews of his ships with the best of his army and equipped them with additional oxybeles and ballistae mounted on the prows. He had ordered other preparations made as well. Looking at the decks where the ammunition was stowed, Hyakinthos could see no jars of inflammable oil. It was a deadly enough weapon but the loss of *Amphitrite* had shown it was too dangerous to the ships that carried it. Instead, the *Leontophoros* carried a large supply of stones that had been carefully rounded and smoothed. At first, there had been grumbling at the work involved but tests ashore had shown the catapults had thrown smooth, regularly-shaped boulders further, faster and more accurately than unhewn boulders. And that demonstration had stopped the grumbling instantly.

Another glance, this one down into the lower decks of the ship, showed that the oarsmen were working perfectly. The three men per oar on each of the two lowest row and the four men on the highest row were keeping perfect time as they drove the ship forward. Skilled oarsmen were in critically short supply and the use of multiple men per oar economized on them. The catapult ships got priority in receiving the best oarsmen since coordinating the rowers on each side of the ship was crucial for accuracy. The crew of the *Leontophoros* had learned a lot since the ship's debut at Caunus two years earlier.

One last check, the bolt-firing oxybeles torsion-crossbows forward were loaded and ready. It was whispered that, when the available horsehair had proved too weak for the oxybeles, the women had cut off their hair and offered that instead. Hyakinthos hadn't seen many bald women around the naval bases so he assumed that was just a story. He encouraged the story though. If the men believed their women had given up their hair to help gain victory, failing to honor their sacrifice by winning that victory would be an unbearable shame.

The *Leontophoros* and her fifteen sister-ships were supporting the left wing of the Antigonid fleet, consisting of seven Phoenician heptaremes and thirty Athenian quadriremes plus ten Antigonid hexaremes and ten quinqueremes, The wing was under the command of Medius of Phrygia. Facing them were forty Egyptian quadriremes. In his two years of naval service, Hyakinthos had learned a lot about ships. He had learned that a homogenous group of ships was superior to a squadron made up of varying types. He also knew that the quadriremes with their two rows of oars with two men per oar, were the fastest ships present. The only problem was, with only two men per oar, they put a heavy burden on the availability of trained oarsmen. Nevertheless, their speed made them dangerous opponents. That also made them priority targets.

"Prepare to fire catapults." The cry came from Hekatontarchès Draco who was watching for Admiral Medius's signal. There was a long flash of light from the quarterdeck of the flagship. "Fire!"

Behind him, Hyakinthos knew, the four catapults had fired simultaneously. He knew that the catapult deck was now a scene of frenzied action while the catapult crews and their Army assistants were pulling back the firing arm and placing the next rock in the holding scoop. He saw none of that happen. What he did see were the black dots of the rocks going overhead in a long arc that terminated around the bows of one of the quadriremes. He'd overestimated its speed slightly and the rocks had gone into the water just in front of it. By the look of it, it had been a common mistake and none of the catapult ships had scored a hit with their first salvo.

"Hold this range!" If his guess was right, Hyakinthus thought that the next salvo of four boulders would strike the quadrireme dead amidships.

"Fire!" Again, the thud of the four catapults firing almost simultaneously accompanied Hekatontarchès Draco's command. Hyakinthus could see that this time his aim was true. The rocks landed slightly at of amidships, one going into the water on each side, so close that the spouts from the near misses drenched the decks. The other two crashed into the hull, sending splinters of wood flying upwards.

The effects of the hits were instantaneous. The quadrireme spun around, the oars on its port side in a hopeless tangle that spoke of serious carnage on its rowing decks. At a complete standstill, the galley started to list. *Water is obviously flooding in somewhere* thought Hyakinthos. *I wonder if one of our rocks went through the bottom of the hull? If so, she's finished.*

While the oarsmen on the *Leontophoros* pulled desperately on their oars, determined not to allow others to advance any faster than they, the design of the catapult ships betrayed them. The ships were slow and clumsy and the swift quadriremes and hexaremes started leaving them behind. The pounding of the catapult ships had already made its contribution to victory though; by the time the advance guards of the Egyptian and Antigonid ships collided more than a dozen of the former had been sorely injured by the rocks thrown at them. The odds now favored the Antigonid wing and they made the most of their opportunity.

All the ships, Egyptian and Antigonid rushed to the encounter in a terrifying manner. Those equipped with the oxybeles used them to hurl heavy darts at the opposing ships. As the combatants closed, the soldiers on board hurled their javelins in a shower, bring down the men who dared to expose themselves to the fire when enemies were within range. It was a desperate fight for each set of crewmen to try and force their opponents to take cover for the ships had come close together and the encounter was about to take place with great violence. The Antigonid crews knew that they had superiority of numbers thanks to the bombardment of the catapult ships. On the Egyptian vessels, the soldiers on the decks crouched down and the oarsmen, spurred on by the oarsmasters, bent more desperately to their oars. They knew that battles were won and lost when the ships came to close combat.

Standing on the bows of the *Leontophoros*, Hyakinthos heard the drums of the oarsmasters break out ito the wild staccato hammering and he imagined he could hear the captain's crying out "Ramming speed! Ramming Speed!" He imagined he could see the sterns of the quadriremes digging in as the ships accelerated, driving the opponents together with dreadful force and violence. In the frantic chaos of the collisions, some of the ships swept their opponents oars so that the ships became useless for flight or pursuit, and the men who were on board, though eager for a fight, were prevented from joining in the battle. Such Antogonid ships were left behind but the Egyptians ships so stricken were immediately engaged by the Antigonid heptaremes and quinqueremes.

Outclassed in men and numbers, the Egyptian quadriremes fought valiantly against the larger, more generously crewed heptaremes and quinqueremes but already having suffered severe loss and having no ability to maneuver, they quickly found surrender unavoidable.

Not all the ships that aimed at their opponent's oarsmen struck that mark. Where the ships had met prow to prow with their rams, they were left locked together and unable to either board or ram. The soldiers on board engaged each other with darts, slingshots, arrows and javelins and caused great execution on the others since the mark was close at hand for each party. Meanwhile, their captains tried to disengage and draw back for another charge that would put their ships and crews in a more advantageous position.

But, the issue was most decisive where the captains had delivered a broadside blow and the rams had become firmly fixed in the enemy hull. There, the soldiers leaped aboard the ships of the enemy and engaged in vicious hand-to-hand fighting, receiving and giving severe wounds with the axes and swords that they carried. Not all of them even made it to the deck of the enemy ship for certain of them, after attempting to board their prey missed their footing, fell into the sea, and at once were crushed between the two hulls. Others were killed with spears by those who stood above them and thrust them into the sea. But the rest made good their intent and succeeded in gaining the enemy decks.

There, they slew some of the enemy and forced the others along the narrow deck. Their feet found it hard to gain a secure footing on decks that were slick with blood but that did not prevent the boarding party from finally driving the defenders into the sea.

To Hyakinthos watching the fighting as the *Leontophoros* lumbered slowly towards the scene, the fighting was varied and full of surprises. Many times he saw groups of men trapped in an apparently hopeless position, weaker and in a worse position than their opponents, gain the upper hand because of chance movements of ships and waves or because of the height of their ships.

Now was the time when the heptaremes and quinqueremes with their extra tier of oars had an advantage over the lower-slung quadriremes. So it was that many times, those who were stronger were foiled by the resulting inferiority of position. Hyakinthos quietly dreaded joining the desperate fighting on the ships and felt his stomach relax when the *Leontophoros* began to turn so that her catapults could be brought to bear on the ships at the center of the Egyptian line.

This day he had learned a great lesson. *In contests on land, valor is made clearly evident, since it is able to gain the upper hand when nothing external and fortuitous interferes; but in naval battles there are many causes of various kinds that, contrary to reason, defeat those who would properly gain the victory through prowess. That is why the fact of being a man of the sea always stands over and above which side we fight for and when ships are lost, saving the lives of the sailors becomes our highest concern.*

Over on the shore, Hyakinthos could see that the first survivors of the sinking ships were reaching the shore. Demetrius had positioned cavalry along the shoreline with instructions to aid the shipwrecked sailors reach safety. Indeed, he had promised each of them a silver coin for every sailor they rescued, Antigonid and Egyptian alike.

He is not his father's son. Demetrius Poliorcetes is a man of honor, thought Hyakinthos as he watched a cavalryman gallop his horse into the surf to aid a sailor who had run out of strength just short of safety. Then, he turned his attention away from battle and shoreline alike in order to prepare his catapults for the next phase of the attack on the Egyptian fleet.

Patronis, *Flagship of Menelaüs, Harbor of Salamis*

"I don't think Demetrius likes Antisthenes very much." Menelaüs looked at the harbor entrance where ten quinqueremes had been stationed to deny him exit. "The harbor has a narrow exit but it's not that narrow and our triremes can go into the shallow water where those quinqueremes cannot. Antisthenes has been given an impossible job here."

"Demetrius is a general, not an admiral." The Trierarchs commanding the *Patronis*, Hegesippus of Halicarnassus, sounded thoughtful. "He probably thinks the added size and power of the quinqueremes combined with the narrow exit will offset the inferiority in numbers. So it might, were the numbers closer. They aren't, it won't. Battle Speed?"

"Battle speed." Menelaüs agreed and heard the oarsmaster's drum pick up speed. He was rapidly coming to the opinion that the trireme was the best of all the varying types of ships taking part in the battle. Although both the trieme and the quinquereme had three banks of oars, the quinquereme had two extra men to row them. That gave extra power but it also made the hull wider and the ships draw more water. That made them slower than the triremes. The only real advantage the quinquereme had was that its larger crew made it more effective in boarding actions. *These triremes really are ideal. Faster than the more powerful ships and more powerful than the faster ships. And they're just about the least expensive to build and crew.* "Open fire with the oxybeles!"

With that order, numbers told instantly. With each Antigonid quinquereme having six or more triremes firing upon it, the crews were overwhelmed almost instantly. Menelaüs could see them scattering on the exposed quarterdecks, those reacting too slowly being hurled from their feet by the power of the torsion catapults. The catapult crews were cranking frantically on their weapons, drawing back the strings against the tension of the twisted strips of oxhide. Then, they unleashed another salvo of bolts, this time aimed at the hulls of the quinqueremes and, in particular the oar ports. The chance of getting a bolt through the ports was close to that of threading needle but one or two bolts made it and crashed into the oarsmen. The effects were instant, the carefully timed cadence of the rows of oars collapsed in a steadily-spreading ripple of chaos. The stricken quinqueremes swerved off their course while the oarsmaster frantically tried to restore order on board. To the great disappointment of Menelaüs, none of the quinqueremes actually ran aground but their formation was broken.

The triremes were already level with the disorganized mass of quinqueremes and the oxybeles fire was steadily growing more lethal as the range closed to minimum. None of the quinqueremes were actually badly damaged but the disruption to their oarsmen was rendering them largely ineffective. One of them was staggering helplessly, both banks of oars in a hopeless tangle. Hegesippus couldn't resist it. "Ramming Speed!"

With the oarsmaster beating a wild tattoo on his drum, the *Patronis* surged forward towards the stricken quinquereme. Hegesippus aimed the bow of his ship very carefully at the point where the lead oar on the target passed through its port. The angle of impact was going to be as fine as he could make it. "Ship Oars."

The oarsmen on the *Patronis* swung their oars out of the way just as the bronze beak on their trireme scythed through the quinquereme's port bank of oars to the cacophony of shattering wood and screams from crippled oarsmen. Below the waterline, the same bronze beak crushed in the timbers of the quinquereme's side. Nowhere was the damage great enough to cause immediate danger of sinking, but water seeped in over most of the ship's length. The quinquereme started listing and her captain tried desperately to regain enough control to beach her.

By that time, his ship and the rest of the Antigonid quinqueremes were being left behind by the fleet of triremes that passed them by in the shallower waters on either side of the main channel. Ahead of him, Menelaüs could see the brawl on the right wing of the Antigonid fleet as Ptolemy's main thrust pushed it in.

Demetrius's Flagship Katsonis, *Center of Antigonid Fleet, Salamis Bay*

Demetrius Poliorcetes had stationed the lightest ships in his fleet in the middle of the line under the overall command of Themison of Samos. The right wing was commanded by Pleistias of Cos, who was the chief pilot of the whole fleet. That right wing was now in desperate trouble. Ptolemy had stacked his heaviest ships and most skilled commanders against Pleistias and his ships and easily routed those stationed opposite him, sinking some of the ships and capturing others with their crews. To make matters worse, Menelaüs had broken out of Salamis harbor and his sixty triremes were bearing down on the Antigonid fleet.

The key was going to be how well the Antigonid center held. Essentially, they were fighting delaying action while the Antigonid left shattered Ptolemy's right and Ptolemy's left drove back the Antigonid right. The two fleets were pivoting around their centers and that meant the center that held steadiest would win the battle. Both sides knew it and he crews in the two centers fought accordingly. As each ship, Egyptian or Antigonid, was boarded, its decks became the scene of unparalleled hand-to-hand fighting. Demetrius fought most brilliantly of all, having taken his stand on the stern of his heptareme. The *Katsonis* had been rammed and boarded by two of Ptolemy's quinqueremes and their crews had poured over the side.

It was fortunate that a heptareme carried such a large crew since a smaller ship would have been overwhelmed almost instantly. Even with the extra oarsmen joining in the battle, the fight on te decks was a desperately close thing. A crowd of men rushed upon Demetrius, but by hurling his javelins at some of them and by striking others at close range with his spear, he slew them; and although many missiles of all sorts were aimed at him, he avoided some that he saw in time and received others upon his defensive armor. Of the three men who protected him with shields, one fell struck by a lance and the other two were severely wounded. Finally Demetrius drove back the forces confronting him, and managed to created a rout that drove the boarding party back over the side. Unsatisfied with that result, he led a charge that took his men over the side of the *Katsonis* and carried the fight to one of the Egyptian quinqueremes.

So lost had he been in the desperate fight, it was only when the quinquereme in question surrendered that he happened to glance up at the flags. Their position had changed and told him that the wind now blew from the south. Even more critically, the movement of the ships had changed, revealing that the tide had turned. With both tide and wind running to the north, the tactical situation had changed drastically. Although the battle had started with Ptolemy's ships approaching from the south, the great wheel made while the two fleets pivoted on their centers had reversed that. Now, it was Ptolemy's warships that were to the north with those of Demetrius to the south. And that put the Antigonid fleet between Ptolemy's warships and his transports. Even worse, from Ptolemy's point of view, the wind and tide made it very difficult for his ships to return south to protect the defenseless transports that the same winds and tides were carrying into the arms of Demetrius.

Home of Parmenio, Seleucia-on-the Tigris, Summerset, 305BC

"The losses in warships were about equal." Igrat was relaying the messages she had received. They constituted a desperate plea for help from Ptolemy who had lost the cream of his fleet and army in the catastrophic battle. "Both sides lost about forty ships, sunk or captured, leaving Ptolemy with eighty and Demetrius seventy. But, Demetrius's ships captured almost the entire transport fleet with Ptolemy's army helpless on board. Two hundred transports and twenty thousand men. Not only has Ptolemy lost his ships and men, he has virtually made a present of them to Antigonus. He has had to abandon his plans for another attack on Coelê Syria and concentrate on the defense of Egypt. He stands in grave danger of being invaded by what was once his own army."

"Not as much as he thinks." Parmenio thought the matter over. "Summer is almost gone and the weather is beginning to close in. Demetrius has a nasty choice ahead of him. If he attacks now, he'll catch Ptolemy at his weakest with the core of his army gone and his fleet gravely weakened. But, he'll face the onset of the winter storms and a great danger of having his own ships dispersed. Also, he may have taken the key centers on Cyprus but the island as a whole is still hostile to him. If he is tied down with an attack on Egypt, he might find Cyprus has slipped through his fingers.

"On the other hand, if he spends the winter in Cyprus, he can consolidate his hold there and be ready to launch an attack on Egypt when spring rises. But, by then, Ptolemy will have rebuilt his army and made a good start on reconstructing his fleet. The defenses on the coast will be in better condition too.

"Then there is our position. If Demetrius stages his invasion now, we can't get troops there quickly enough to help our ally. In fact, right now, there is little we can do to help him other than send him our best wishes. But, if Demetrius leaves his attack on Egypt to Spring, we can have a substantial force to aid Ptolemy."

"If you were Demetrius, father, what would you do?"

"I wouldn't be in this position to start with." Parmenio stared across the courtyard where a fine rain had covered the trees with a silvery, glistening coat. "I think Demetrius knows that as well. It's Antigonus who is driving things. He's more than 80 years old and his time is limited. He wants to settle all his scores before his years finally catch up with him."

Parmenio paused again. "You know, that's one advantage we have. We don't have the burden of years pressing in on us, forcing us to make hasty and ill-considered decisions. We've got time on our side. Time is our ally, not our enemy. We need to use that. We have to slow Antigonus down a bit. A death in the family might do nicely."

"There's one other thing, Father. In his report on the battle, Telesphorus of Peloponnesus places great importance on how his oxybeles crossbows did great execution on enemy ships. Derya's been trying to get a very powerful crossbow mounted on our elephants for years but with no success. Scaling up the gastrophetes just isn't working. If it's light enough, it lacks the strength and if it's strong enough then it is too heavy. But, suppose we scaled down an oxybeles, rather than scaling up a gastrophetes?"

Parmenio thought about that too. "That might work. I'll talk it over with him."

"Could you wait a little?" Igrat was concerned. "If I get back from a mission and suddenly this idea is brought up, he'll add everything up and know I brought the reports describing the battle. Then, he'll know for certain what I do. I don't ever want him to know what I do to get these messages through. He'll think less of me if he realizes how I do what I do."

"You've been married twelve years now." Parmenio smiled gently at his adopted daughter. "I think he understands you better than you think. And values you more than you realize."

Palace of Antigonus Monopthalmus, Antigonia, Summerset, 305BC

"Phoenix is a great loss to us all." Demetrius had hastened from Cyprus on news that his brother was critically ill but had arrived too late for the funeral. Antigonus had buried Phoenix with royal honors and delayed any advance on Ptolemy until the required period of mourning was over. In the view of Demetrius, the loss of his brother was indeed a great one but the loss of time was more so. The days were ticking by, bringing the storms of winter that much closer. The previous winter had come early, been harder and had stayed later than anybody had expected. There was no reason to believe the coming one would be any better. "What happened to him? All I heard was that he had been taken ill."

Antigonus Monopthalmus looked up from the reports he was reading. "Seleucus offered his services as a mediator in ending the war with Ptolemy. He's trying to buy time for his ally of course. Some of his ambassadors came here to negotiate. After they left, Phoenix fell ill. He complained of ringing in his ears and was unable to keep his balance. The next day, he complained of great thirst that no amount of wine or water could slake. His tongue and throat started to swell and turn black. Then his heart rate slowed down and he died."

"Poison?" Demetrius asked the obvious question. Poisoning was so common that hemlock was nicknamed 'inheritance juice'.

"Perhaps. If it was you or me, I would say certainly. But why Phoenix? He was no soldier, no strategist. He was removed from the succession for exactly that reason. There was no reason to kill him."

Demetrius had an uneasy feeling he had the answer to that question but he couldn't quite put his finger on the thought. "When do you wish me to stage the invasion of Egypt. We have the ships and men ready in Cyprus."

"We will not be invading from Cyprus. I intend to lead the invasion of Egypt myself, by way of Coelê Syria. I will have our whole Army, totaling more than eighty thousand foot soldiers, about eight thousand horse and eighty-three elephants." Demetrius noted the pride in his father's voice. The rapid expansion of the Antigonid realm and its meteoric growth in military power had been an unparalleled achievement. It was hard to remember that just five years before, Antigonus had been hard-put to raise ten thousand men and hadn't had an elephant to his name. Now, he had the eighty three survivors of the 120 brought back by Eudamus. The forty four survivors of the hundred brought back from India by Alexander were split between Ptolemy and Lysimachus.

"So, if we are not to mount our assault from Cyprus, then why did we take the place?"

"Because I told you to, runt." Antigonus snarled out the words, then got his temper back under control. "When we took Cyprus we drew Ptolemy into a trap and neutralized his Navy. Now, we have a hundred and fifty warships and as many transports. As my army advances along the coast, you will follow us, using your ships to secure my flank and the transports to keep us supplied with food, water and equipment. Most especially, you will keep the elephants supplied with fodder. They will be the critical advantage when we meet the Army of Ptolemy. We will proceed first to Gaza where your ships will rendezvous with us. You will bring one hundred and thirty thousand measures of grain from Cyprus. The men will carry ten days of rations each and we will carry the arrows and catapult stones on the wagons."

"Your Majesty, the setting of the Pleiades, will take place eight days after you plan to advance from Gaza." Pleistias of Cos was deeply concerned. The setting of the Pleiades marked the approximate end of the campaigning season. It might be possible to campaign on the Nile in winter but at sea, storms and adverse winds would make the proposed naval support hazardous in the extreme. A naval expedition of this scale after the setting of the Pleiades was fraught with peril. "A naval campaign this late in the year is tempting fate."

"Fate will do as I tell it to do." Antigonus almost screamed the words out. "The Fates had determined that I would die in obscurity, remembered by nobody yet it was my will that confounded them. The fates had determined that I would never again command an army of any importance yet now I have, once again, almost a hundred thousand men to do my bidding. You are men afraid of danger and that makes you barely men at all. It is the will to win that decides battles and wars and if you lack the will to win, I have no use for you."

Antigonus stormed out of the room, leaving a stunned silence behind him. It was eventually broken by Demetrius who looked around the others, trying to gauge their attitude. "It looks as if we are going to force a crossing of the Nile. Does anybody know what defenses Ptolemy has built along the West Bank?"

Pleistias nodded. "There are fortresses at all the primary crossing points. They have stone walls, twice the height of a man, topped with the most powerful oxybeles crossbows known. They can drive a bolt right through a man and still have enough power to kill his friend standing behind him. In front of the fortresses are deep ditches, dug when Ptolemy's engineers prepared great sand ramparts. Those ditches adjoin the Nile and can be flooded at a moment's notice. Even when not flooded, water seeping in from the river has created a marsh at the bottom of those ditches. That marsh is infested with crocodiles, snakes and other vermin.

"To storm the west bank, we would first have to cross the river under fire from the oxybeles. Then we would have to descend into the ditches and cross them while those above us throw great stones and javelins down upon us. Then we would have to climb the ramparts, the sand of which has been left uncompacted so that it flows like water when climbers attempt to find footholds. Having done all that, we would still have to face the fortresses and storm their walls. As a finishing touch, there are paved roads behind the fortresses and ramparts so that men may move rapidly from unattacked areas to reinforce those that are being assaulted."

"No defense line is impregnable. They all have weaknesses. Where is the weakness here?"

"A simple one, my Lord Demetrius Poliorcetes. The defense line ends at the coast. It does not extend out to sea. The weakness of this defense is that we can sail around its northern end and land on the coast behind it. Then we can take the ramparts and the fortresses from the rear without having to cross the Nile. But, by the time we get there, the setting of the Pleiades will have taken place and the season of storms will have fallen on us. We may get the troops ashore but keeping them there?"

"Sixteen years ago, Perdiccas tried to force a crossing of the Nile and he failed every time losing thousands of his men in the attempt." Philotarsas looked up at the rest. "Sixteen years ago. We can be very sure than in every one of those years, Ptolemy has improved the strength of his fortifications and increased their strength. Can we break through now where Perdiccas failed?"

There was a dead silence. Philotarsas looked around at the others and suddenly realized what he had said. Perdiccas had indeed tried to force a crossing of the Nile and lost thousands of his men in the effort. And then, he had been betrayed and murdered by his own commanders. To a mind as filled with obsessive suspicion as Antigonus, references to Perdiccas might well be taken as incitement to do the same again.

Demetrius's Flagship Katsonis, *Center of Antigonid Fleet, South-west of Gaza*

"Our luck isn't going to hold much longer." Pleistias of Cos looked to the horizon where the lowest member of the Pleiades had just sunk from sight. It was obvious that the other six were on the verge of doing so. "The records show that the first storm after the setting of the Pleiades is a bad one. The earlier it comes, the worse it will be. If the wind blows from the north as well, then we will truly know that the Gods have turned their faces from us. Last year, there was snow in Gaza during the first storm of winter. And that was from a north-easterly wind."

Demetrius looked at the stars and the clear night air. He couldn't quite put his finger on why, but there was something threatening about the weather and a distinct air of tension on the ship. Even since he had set sail from Gaza several days ago, the weather had been calm, so much so that he had his transports towed by the swifter warships. Something had changed this night and Pleistias had ordered the tows dropped. Now, each ship was free to maneuver as it could. That was going to make it harder for his ships to keep station on the great Antigonid army moving along the coast.

His thoughts were interrupted by a bang and rattling from the single sail mounted amidships on his heptareme. "Wind is picking up, Navarch Pleistias."

Pleistias glanced up at the sail, as much to hide his smile at the acknowledgement of his leadership of the fleet as to check on the wind. "It is picking up, yes. But it is also beginning to shift. We have had an east wind so far and that has aided us greatly. If it shifts southerly or a point to the north, then we have nothing to worry about. But a stronger northerly shift this late in the year, that would be another matter."

"I sense something is wrong." Demetrius had almost been afraid to say that, in case voicing the words would make his fears real.

"You are developing a seaman's eye. Yes, there is something wrong. The stars shine too brightly and steadily and that suggests the temperature will fall. The sea is moving slowly and the waves look as if they are reluctant to break into spray. These are not good signs. Excuse me, My Lord." Pleistias went over to where a seaman was watching the sails and the weather vane. When he came back, his face was deeply troubled. "It is as I feared, My Lord. The wind is indeed changing. It has shifted so that it is now east of northeast and continues to back. I fear it may be a northeasterly by dawn."

Demetrius nodded in acknowledgment. "If we face a north-easterly, how bad will that be?"

Pleistias thought carefully, weighing the wind, the weather, the sea and the stars. "If the wind remains mild, we will have cold and rain but no more. That will not be so bad, it may even give us a chance to refill our water casks. But, a stronger north-westerly wind will drive us south and that way is the coast. The nearest coast town in that direction is Raphia, a city which affords no anchorage and is surrounded by shoals. It will offer some shelter from the weather but at great risk."

"Order the men to be ready to open the water casks and collect as much rainwater as they can." Demetrius was going to end there but decided to explain himself. *After all,* he reasoned, *I might be wrong.* "If there is a bad storm coming and there are no ports within reach,. We may be stuck offshore for days. Topping up our drinking water supply might be the difference between life and death."

"It might indeed." Pleistias was impressed, not by the forethought but by the fact Demetrius had taken the trouble to explain his action. "I will pass the order to the other ships while we have the chance."

As the night wore on, Demetrius found himself pacing the quarterdeck of the *Katsonis,* drawing his cloak closer around him as he did so. Yet, it was with surprise that he realized he was uncomfortably cold. The starshine had, if anything, become brighter and the movement of the sea was oilier. He touched his nose and was shocked to feel it chilled.

"Wind, north east." The voice from the seaman watching the wind vane was neutral yet Demetrius caught the concern that it hid.

"The wind is changing faster than I expected." Navarch Pleistias had finished his round of the ship. "General, I have great concerns about the weather."

He was interrupted from saying anything more by a loud bang from the sails and an alarmed cry. "Navarch! The wind has changed. It now blows from the north!"

"May the Gods have mercy upon us." Pleistias whispered quietly to himself. Then he gathered himself. "General, we must prepare ourselves immediately. A change in the wind that quickly is the worst of all possible omens. We must get ready to ride out the storm. The wind will be strong and from due north. If we do not take the greatest of care, it will drive the entire fleet on to the shore."

"Can we take shelter under the lee of the land to the north?" Demetrius pointed to the low, irregular black line on the northern horizon.

"General, there is no land to the north. What you can see are the oncoming storm clouds."

Demetrius was appalled at how fast the weather deteriorated once the wind had swung to the north. The heptareme started to roll as the waves picked up strength. The black clouds rolled across the sky, shutting out the stars as abruptly and as finally as shield blocked out the light from a candle. That was when he could feel the chill on his face grow raw and painful as the wind became stronger. Soon, the wind in the ropes that held the main mast up started making a tattle-tale sound as the wind shook them. The rain had already started, first a sparse splattering that ran on the decks and turned them into slippery expanses where a careless step could break a man's leg but steadily growing in strength until rivulets of water were running through every dip and cranny.

Even so, it was a shock akin to a physical blow when the storm winds first struck the *Katsonis*, sending her lurching sideways with wild waves breaking over the railings. The winds took the rain and turned it from droplets into a blinding, hissing sheet that drenched everything in its path. No longer was it possible for a man to stand on the quarterdeck. A rain-drenched cloak gave no protection from the howling winds and the bitter chill. All the men on the *Katsonis*, could do was take cover from the gale and pray that the Gods would spare them. At the helm, Pleistias fought to keep the bows pointing at the waves.

Through a brief gap in the storm, Demetrius saw the fate that awaited the *Katsonis* if Pleistias lost his battle. The quinquereme to port, the *Matrozos* allowed her bow to fall away from the waves. The next surge started to roll her over. He wasn't quite certain what happened then. Most likely, the *Matrozos* still had her lowest row of oar ports open and the water had flooded in through them. Whatever it was, the *Matrozos* didn't stop rolling and return to her normal stance. Instead, she kept rolling over until she capsized. The winds and waves tore at her as if they were jackels tearing at a dying prey, ripping at her until she broke up. Then, the *Matrozos* was gone and her crew with her. By the time dawn came, a late dawn held at bay by the black clouds, two more quinqueremes had followed her.

Dawn brought little relief. The northerly winds had strengthened still further, driving the ships apart. There was no fleet then, just a steadily-dispersing group of ships, each desperately fighting for her life against the implacable, remorseless storm. Demetrius had joined Pleistias on the tiller, taking his lead from the wily, experienced Navarch and throwing his strength into the desperate battle to keep the *Katsonis* afloat. The temperature was still dropping and, soon after the time dawn was supposed to have broken, the ship faced a new enemy. Demetrius saw that the rain wasn't just soaking everything. The water was freezing, coating the wood with a thin film of ice that grew steadily thicker.

There was no sign of a change, no sign of a let-up in the howling winds or the bitter, freezing rain. Demetrius lost track of time in the tempest. There was no sense of the passing hours, no sense that the storm was going to end or ever could. The off-duty oarsmen had nothing to do; they huddled in the lowest part of the ship where they thought their weight might help prevent the ship from rolling over but they knew to open the lower oar-ports would be suicide. The wilier of the oarsmen had found the canvasses that were used to shield the crew from the sun and spread them over the soaked, freezing men so that they might have at least some shelter from the deluge of wind-driven freezing rain. The men took it in turns to man the top tier of oars and try and provide some degree of forward movement. While they did so, they looked out for each other. A man who was suffering too badly from the cold would be unobtrusively moved to the center of the groups where he would be warmed by his friends. A fitter man would take his place on the oars until he too suffered too much form the cold and freezing rain. Then he, too would be brought in and his place taken by a man in better condition. For all their efforts, the men on the oars had little help for the sail was long gone, ripped to shreds by the wind.

It seemed like the storm never would end but it did. The wind started to shift back to the east, the rain softened and the bitter, biting cold eased slightly. It was still a storm, the worst any man on the *Katsonis* had ever known but by comparison with what had gone before, it was a blessed relief. Demetrius could take his eyes from the tiller and, for a moment think of things other than the desperate battle to keep his ship afloat. When he spoke, his voice was cracked by strain and exhaustion. "Where do we go from here?"

"That all depends on where here is." Pleistias could hardly speak through his exhaustion. "Before we do anything, we have to find where we are. We haven't seen the sun or stars for two days. Or something like that, I lost track of time in that storm. We could be anywhere. We don't even know for sure where our bows are pointing. All I do know is that we're in deep water, out of sight of land."

"Are we the only ones left?" Demetrius was still trying to absorb the disaster.

"No. Of the transports carrying the supplies and ordnance, some will have been overwhelmed by the storm and destroyed, and others will have turned in time to run back to Gaza. The rest will be scattered and lost just as we are. The warships, the biremes and hexaremes will have faired better, their double banks of oars mean they sit lower in the water and are less likely to be turned over. The triremes and quinqueremes, they have three banks of oars but they'll probably have made it. The heptaremes and larger ships? We survived by a miracle and miracles don't happen very often."

Pleistias opened the chest where the charts were stored. By a miracle they were still dry. "The northerly wind should have blown us south on to the coast but our oarsmen saved us from that. How, I cannot explain other than to say the God themselves must have breathed extra strength and courage into them. We must have gone at an angle and the westerly shift n the wind will have reinforced that. So, we should be here. Somewhere."

Demetrius looked at the circle on the charts, north of the Nile delta. "That's Ptolemy's territory. If we go south, we beach ourselves and deliver our lives into his hands. That might be the best way for the men."

But not for you. Pleistias thought. <u>Ptolemy will look on you as a gift from the Gods. He will demand a great ransom and when your father refuses to pay it, your life will be forfeit.</u> "There is a better way. The wind is from the north east so we row south east, into the wind. Slowly at first, give the men time to recover, but as their strength comes back, we pick up speed. I believe that south east will take us to Casium. This place is not very distant from the Nile, but it has no harbor and now we are in the stormy season will be impossible to make a landing there. We will be in sheltered waters but we will have to cast our anchors and ride the waves at a distance of about two stades from the land. And there we wait until the surf dies enough for us to make a landing."

Bay of Casium, Ten Days Later

"And so it was that we were encompassed by many dangers; for when we arrived here, the surf was breaking heavily, and if we attempted landing, there was the prospect of the ships foundering with their crews. To make matters worse, since the shore was in enemy hands, the ships could neither approach without danger, nor could the men swim ashore, and what was worst of all, the water for drinking had given out and they were reduced to such straits that, if the storm had continued for a single day more, all would have perished of thirst. When the sun rose the next day, all were in despair and already expecting death, but overnight, the wind had fallen, and the banners of the Army of Ptolemy had vanished. That was when we knew that the Army of Antigonus had arrived and driven away the shore guards. Our men were thus able to leave the ships and recuperate on shore while waiting for those vessels that had become separated from us."

"Your Majesty, you should know that our crew owes its survival to the forethought of your son who ordered that our water casks be topped off before the worst of the storm hit. It was that extra water that allowed us to survive the additional days we spent waiting offshore. Those days also forced us to watch while three quinqueremes made it to the safety of the bay yet were lost when shortage of water forced them to risk exposure to the waves and surf and there foundered. At least, the Gods be praised, some of the men from these swam to the shore and there were cared for by Ptolemy's men."

Antigonus looked up from the reports on his desk. "Your heptareme, a handful of triremes and quinqueremes , a greater number of biremes and quadriremes and a small fraction of the transport fleet are all that are left to us. The wreckage of the rest and the bodies of their crewmen are stretched all the way along the coast to Gaza. While we marched here, through wind, rain and snow, I thought much about your plan to land men from the sea to outflank Ptolemy's defenses and saw great merit in them. Now that option has been taken from us."

"I fear it may never have been practical, Your Majesty." Demetrius sighed, admitting to himself that his father had once again been right although, quite possible, for the wrong reasons. "After the storm subsided and the men rested, I took a small group of ships, *Katsonis* and three quadriremes, along the coast, behind Ptolemy's fortress line. We first sailed to Pseudostomon, but when we approached the coast, we were found the town was protected by a strong garrison who met us with a heavy and very accurate barrage of bolts and other missiles of every kind. Driven away from there, we sailed to Phatniticum. This was but a small village and I hoped that we could land a small force of soldiers at night who would storm the place and put the villagers to the sword. That would, at least, spread fear and despondency in the countryside and force Ptolemy to divert his forces further. But, the charts we have of the area were inaccurate and one of the quadriremes ran heavily aground. We took off the crew and soldiers but had to leave the ship behind.

"To make matters worse, the soldiers we had landed reported that the adjacent coast was naturally fortified by swamps and marshes. They could not approach Phatniticum and soon the alarm began to spread. Accordingly, we picked up the landing party and retraced our steps here. One other thing we did observe. Ptolemy has already occupied every landing-place along the river with strong guards and constructed many river boats, all equipped with ordnance of every kind and with men to use it. There is no possibility of landing on the coast, even if our fleet had remained intact. We will have to break through Ptolemy's defenses on the Nile by frontal attack."

Antigonus looked at the maps and absorbed the reports he had been given. "You are right. We will move the Army to a new base camp at a distance of two stades from the river. Then we will survey the defenses Ptolemy has built and select the weakest point for our assault."

Elephant Lines, Ecbatana, Seleucid Empire, Winter, 305 BC

"The oxybeles was the answer, Strategos. We have discarded any idea of using the gastrophetes and instead built a smaller version of the oxybeles used on ships. We have changed the fighting howdah on the back as well. It now has a single oxybeles at the front and two other soldiers with sarissa and bow. They have greater protection than before. Where before the mahout sat exposed on the neck of the elephant, now we have provided him with wood and chain mail protection."

"It looks a bit like the prow of a ship." Parmenio looked at the great war-elephant with its new-model howdah. "You've given the elephant more protection as well."

"Chain mail to protect his eyes, chest, legs and belly. We have been careful to keep the weight to a minimum but the load each elephant carries is still increased. But, our new elephants are much stronger than the ones we had before. And fiercer. Unlike the pack-elephants we were using earlier, these ones relish the opportunity to go to war. Let me show you how these oxybeles work. We've set up some targets."

Derya Shafrid led the way to a stretch of open country. A few hundred paces away, a series of dummies had been set up, straw men with old, unserviceable armor but arranged in the form of a phalanx. "Strategos, imagine this is the final battle against Antigonus. Ahead is his phalanx, holding the center of the line. Now, our elephant regiments approach to make their attack. The phalanx braces itself for the charge, but what is this? Our elephants are slowing, standing off at a range outside the normal bowshot."

Shafrid gave the signal and there was a whistling sound from a line of ten elephants simulating the massive force that the Seleucid Army now deployed. Parmenio could see the black streaks of the bolts before they thudded into the targets. When they did, the effects were catastrophic. The front line of the 'phalanx' was swept away. Many of the straw dummies disintegrating completely with the power of the blows. Most of the bolts went straight through the first dummy they struck and brought down a victim in the second rank. A few even made it to the third rank. Parmenio could easily imagine the devastation the volley would have caused on a tightly-packed pahalanx.

When he looked at the elephants, he could see the men in the howdahs were spinning cranks on their oxybeles, heaving the arms of the crossbows back against the torsion of the tightly-twisted skeins of rawhide. With their oxybeles reloaded, their leader gave a signal and another salvo of bolts shot out, scything into the ranks of targets.

"The tactics we have devised are that the elephants will move forward slowly, firing salvo after salvo of bolts into the phalanx. Light infantry will advance with the elephants, checking for spikes on the ground or other anti-elephant measures. Because the advance moves slowly, they will have time to cleat such obstacles." Shafrid looked grim. "By the time the elephants reach the phalanx, it will have been completely disrupted. They will crush what is left."

Parmenio nodded, imagining the effect of the elephants advancing into the shattered phalanx, the sarissas from their backs cutting down men and driving the rest to flight. "This is what we have been looking for. You have done well Derya. How many of our elephants are so equipped?"

"So far, but a hundred. We are making the new equipment in quantities enough to arm one regiment every two months. By the end of winter, half our force should be armed in the new style. But, I have one more thing to show you." Shafrid produced an oxybeles bolt, one that had a strange cylinder wrapped around its middle. "Our musicians, of all people, came up with this."

Parmenio looked at it closely. There were a series of holes in the front end of the cylinder and more at the back. Shafrid handed one of the bolts up to an elephant crew who loaded it on to their oxybeles. When Shafrid signaled they fired. Instead of the usual whistle, the bolt gave out a loud scream as it streaked towards its target. Horses shied away and their riders were hard put to stop them bolting. Even the great war-elephants seemed disturbed by the noise.

"Imagine hundreds of those bolts going out at once." Shafrid's eyes were shining. "The screamers are slower and penetrate less than the regular bolts. They are also slow and costly to make. But, one salvo of them should break an enemy's will to fight before the battle even starts."

Fortress of Camels, Nile River, Egypt, Winter, 305BC

"I thought you said the walls of the fortress were two or three times the height of a man. That we could cope with, but this?"

Demetrius pointed at the Fortress of Camels guarding the crossing point. Sixteen years earlier, the fortress had started the destruction of the Army of Perdiccas. Then it had been low sand ramparts backed by wooden galleries. Now the walls were much higher and were dressed stone. He had no doubt that Ptolemy had occupied the most of the other strategic points along the Nile with trustworthy garrisons in heavy, well-designed fortifications. Whether he had missed any was the object of the present reconnaissance exercise.

"They've been rebuilt since I was here last." Pleistias shook his head. "Two or three times the height of a man they were then and that stopped Perdiccas. Those walls must be five times the height of man. At least. The river keeps us well back and those ditches will stop us mining the walls. It will be long-range catapult fire to breach those walls."

"No. Can't be done. Those walls are designed to resist catapult fire. See how they are angled? Catapult rocks will deflect off them. Believe me, I know siege warfare. Ptolemy has done the impossible. That fortress can't be cracked open. The only way to take it would be to cross elsewhere, isolate it and starve the garrison out."

"And everywhere we can cross has an equal fortress guarding it. How many have we looked at so far?"

"Too many. While we've been fighting wars, Ptolemy has sat back and built up his defenses. The gods alone know what Seleucus has been up to although I rather suspect we might find out soon. What are they up to?" Demetrius pointed at a fleet of small boats, approaching the landing-place.

Pleistias listened to the shouts echoing across the water. "And so the game starts. Ptolemy is proclaiming that he will pay a premium to any soldiers who desert Antigonus, a tenth of a talent per year to auxiliaries, two tenths to each of the ordinary soldiers, three tenths of a talent to cavalrymen, four if they bring their horse, and one talent per year to each man who has been assigned to a position of command. At a guess I would say that Seleucus was unable to get his army here in time to help his ally so he sent something even deadlier. Seleucid gold. Hello, there goes one."

One of the mercenaries hired by Antigonus had obviously decided that Demetrius was right and an assault on the fortress would be suicidal. He'd flung aside his shield and sarissa, then dived into the water to swim to the nearest small boat. He reached it safely, was hauled aboard and obviously welcomed warmly with a goblet of wine. Cheers echoed out from the walls of the fortress as the deserter poured a little of the wine into the river as a libation and quaffed down the rest. The small boat had already set out for the far bank of the Nile. *Ptolemy up one, Antigonus down one.*

The example set by the first deserter was being followed by others. It was obvious that an urge to change sides had fallen upon the mercenaries of Antigonus, and it transpired that many even of their officers were inclined for one reason or another to desire a change. As each man reached the waiting boats, they received the same warm welcome, cheers and a goblet of wine. "Pleistias, we'd better put a stop to this or we won't have an army by dawn. Station bowmen, slingers, and many of our catapults as we can bring up to the edge of the river. The slingers and archers are to fire on any troops who try to desert, the catapults and ballistas on the small boats. Drive them back. If the deserters pour any more wine into that river, the crocodiles will be as drunk as victorious troops after a battle."

"His Majesty Antigonus orders your presence." The messenger had an air of arrogance about him that made Demetrius want to impale him on a sarissa. However, it was a trait shared by many of Antigonus's messengers, one that stemmed from their master. The messenger led them along the bank of the Nile towards a great fire that had been set up where most of the army could see it. Close to it was an iron cage. As they approached, Philotarsas was dragged out and despite his desperate struggles, was forced into the cage.

"He tried to accept Ptolemy's invitation to desert. But, he was caught by loyal troops and sentenced to be roasted to death in full view of the Army." The messenger seemed to relish giving the account. Demetrius could see what was intended. Metal bars attached to the iron of the cage were thrust into the fire. As heat from the fire spread along them, they would warm the cage and slowly bake the occupant. Fortunately for Philotarsas, that didn't happen. Obviously, the oxybeles crews on the fortress walls had seen what was planned and decided on a mercy killing. A dozen or more bolts streaked across the river. Some missed completely, others bounced off the bars of the cage but a few struck home, killing Philotarsas instantly. Demetrius couldn't help but feel that the incident had underlined the difference between Ptolemy and Antigonus more effectively than any bribes could have done.

Antigonus was staring at the maps in front of him as his commanders assembled in the tent. When he started to speak, there was a sudden lack of confidence in his voice that sounded alien and unfamiliar. "I have assembled you here because we face a critical decision. The Gods have turned their faces from us by destroying the fleet of transports that was to keep us supplied. As a result, food for the men and fodder for the beasts is falling short. Our naval force is of no use to us since the coast has been occupied in advance by the enemy. The fortifications we face are of the most formidable kind any of us have ever seen and the way to them is checked by the width of the river.

"Now, I have received dispatches from home, dispatches that have taken weeks to arrive here." Demetrius thought that was ominous. *Why can't we find couriers who can bring us dispatches as swiftly as those used by Seleucus.* "Cassander has defeated the armies sent against him and now occupies all of Greece. He has sent a message offering me peace. I told him that the only peace terms I would offer were that he would surrender all that is his and subjugate himself to me. Today, I received his reply. It consists of one word. Karýdia."

Demetrius found it extremely hard to stop himself smirking at that. Antigonus had paused to take a breath, but continued almost immediately. "I have also received word that contains Cassander's true reply. He has provided Lysimachus with a large proportion of his Army and the united forces under command of Lysimachus have crossed the Hellespont into Cappadocia. The inhabitants of Lampsacus and Parium came over to him willingly and he has taken Sigeum by force. All of Hellespontine Phrygia has fallen into his hands and his general Leonnatus with six thousand foot-soldiers and a thousand horse has taken the city of Synnada and the great royal treasure it contains."

Gods have mercy on us, it's Cyaxares all over again. I recognize the mind behind this; Seleucus has been playing us right from the start. Unless we move very fast, we'll still be stuck here battering on these fortifications while Seleucus and Lysimachus destroy our base. Demetrius gulped in dismay. "Your Majesty, how many men does Lysimachus have?"

"Including those operating as a detachment under Leonnatus, forty thousand foot, six thousand horse and thirty elephants. To add to that, Meleager, has deserted us and made common cause with Lysimachus. Now, the Army of Lysimachus is going into winter quarters. He will be wintering his army at our expense this year."

"Then we have a chance, your Majesty. If, now, we make the quickest possible withdrawal, break camp and speedily return to Syria, we can position ourselves to defeat Lysimachus when the spring comes. Once that is done and our rear areas are clear, we later make a campaign here with a new fleet and more complete preparation. Then, the Nile will be at its lowest and the great fortifications will be more vulnerable."

Antigonus nodded. "Sound advice, my son. We will do as you say.

CHAPTER FOUR
FINAL GAMES

Home of Parmenio, Seleucia-on-the Tigris, Early Spring, 303BC

"Right, people. It's time. The Army is moving out. Igrat, Naamah, Semiramis, you are with me. Derya is already up with the elephants getting them on the move. We'll be joining him. Aeschylus is riding out with the Daimones Prodromoi in a few hours. We'll be riding with them until we link up with the elephants. Semiramis, you'll be joining the Daimones Prodromoi as one of their troopers. It's up to you to win acceptance from the rest. Try not to get yourself killed."

The look on Semiramis's face was one of pure delight. She had no doubt that, as would be the case with any new recruit, she would be the subject of intense hazing from the veterans of the elite regiment. The fact she was a woman would just add to that. She already had some plans for hazing them right back. Parmenio looked at her and nodded. "Seleucus and the rest of the command staff will be riding with the main body of our army. They're heading out now as well. We're going to be moving forty miles a day. The elephants a little less. In three weeks, we'll be taking on Antigonus in open battle."

"Do you need me to carry messages, Father?" Igrat was rather hoping she would have to go to the elephant lines up at Ecbatana so she could join her husband.

"Not yet. We will soon though. At the moment, everybody knows what they have to do. It's called a concentric advance. All last year, Lysimachus fell back across Cappadocia, leading Antigonus south and east. Remember, Igrat, how we led Craterus to the Battle of the Hyllus River? Well,

373

Fourth Diodochi War

Lysimachus is doing the same thing. While he's been doing that, Ptolemy landed in Coelê Syria and is advancing across Syria proper to take Antigonus from the west. We'll be coming up from the south. Just to make life even easier, Antigonus has assembled all his troops into a single army. He lost the last war we fought because he split his army up and was taken down in detail. Now, he's gone to the opposite extreme. He's risking everything on a single toss of the dice. He's even brought Demetrius over from Greece."

Parmenio thought for a second. "Actually, that was a pretty smart move. Demetrius was sent there to force Cassander to pull his troops back from Asia Minor but it didn't work. He and Cassander just stalled each other, swapping a few unimportant towns here and there. So Antigonus brought him back. It's given him a hell of an Army, eighty thousand men and fifteen thousand horse. And eighty elephants which he thinks gives him an advantage."

A ripple of laughter ran around the room. Everybody in the room knew just how many elephants would be part of the Seleucid Army. Parmenio looked around. "Everybody clear? Gusoyn, you're head of the household pro tempore. Try and do as good a job as you did when we went to India. Apollo, Kopshape, help him. Lillith, make us lots of money. If this goes right, we'll be at peace after this last battle. Naamah, get your herbs and medicines sorted out. There's going to be a lot of wounded and that might include us. So, as much as an elephant can carry. We ride in four hours."

"Where's the battle going to be, Father." Igrat was taken back to the time when she had first watched Parmenio at work before the Hyllus River. She knew that he had planned exactly what was to happen.

"Ipsus."

Headquarters, Army of Lysimachus, Ipsus, 303BC

Lysimachus stared at the map on the table in front of him, trying to work out what to do. The truth was, he was outnumbered two-to-one across the board. His 35,000 men in the phalanx faced 60,000 deployed by Antigonus. So many men had Antigonus that he had deployed three phalanxes side-by-side. Lysimachus had 5,000 light troops on his right flank facing 10,000 of Antigonus. On his left flank, he had 10,000 cavalry facing 15,000 of Antigonus. There was nowhere he could see that gave him an advantage. This battle had all the makings of a first class disaster. The natural course would be to retreat again, just as he had been retreating all the previous year. The problem was that this was the selected battlefield, this was where Seleucus and, if possible Ptolemy, were to join him. If he retreated from here, the junction of the three armies would be disjointed and Antigonus would destroy them in detail.

"What do we do, Sire?" Leonnatus sounded depressed.

"We stand and fight. We trust Seleucus. He promised to be here and he is a man of his word. He gave us his promise and it would take all the Gods working together to make him break it. He must be shown that he can trust us as much as we trust him." Lysimachus was aware how naïve that sounded. Trust was not a virtue often practiced between the Diodochi.

"He could be setting us up for destruction." Leonnatus also thought Lysimachus was being naïve. "Seleucus always ends up enlarging his territories during a war. He could leave us to be destroyed by Antigonus and then fall on the Antigonid Army when it has been weakened by us. Then, he would end up with our territory as well as that of Antigonus."

"He could do that, yes, were he not Seleucus Nikator. Can you think of a time when he has done something so base?"

Leonnatus thought carefully and shook his head.

"Nor can I. So, we trust him. His Army will be here."

For the rest of his life, Lysimachus would believe that a spy for Seleucus had been listening to the conversation and signaled the perfect moment for an entrance. Because, as soon as the last words were out of his mouth, any reply Leonnatus may have made was drowned out by the blast of trumpets sounding. "The Daimones Prodromoi! They are here! The Daimones are here! Seleucus Nikator has arrived!"

Lysimachus stepped outside his command tent and looked at the serried ranks of prodromoi entering his camp. They were hardened veterans, each with the yellow shield painted with a black daimones head that was the sign of the elite regiment. Every man watching knew of the Daimones Prodromoi, the legendary light cavalry who broke phalanxes, captured walled cities and had driven enemies forty times their number from the field. Looking at the grim-faced veterans, Lysimachus's sarissaphoros realized that the stories and legends were true, that this Regiment had achieved great things and would do so again. They banged their sarissas against their shields to salute the cavalrymen and cheered when the Prodromoi raised their xystons to return the honor.

A group of men peeled away from the cavalry and made their way to Lysimachus's command tent. In their middle, a figure dismounted. He was clad in the stained, battered armor of a common soldier and had a Xiphos hanging from his belt. "Your Majesty, I am sorry we are later than planned. I am Parmenio the Younger, Strategos to Seleucus Nikator. May we enter your command tent to discuss plans for the battle?"

You mean so you can give me your orders. Lysimachus thought. *Well, at least you wish to do so out of sight of my men. And you have won every battle you have ever fought, even against great odds. So, you will give your orders and I will listen and obey.*

Inside the tent, Lysimachus quickly showed Parmenio the dispositions he had made. Parmenio said little but took in the details. Eventually, he nodded. "You had a bad situation here, but nobody could have done a better job of using what you had to best effect. Let's just reinforce what you have done already. Leonnatus, you command the right?"

"I do."

"I have brought twenty thousand light troops, mostly hypaspists, slingers and bowmen with me. We will assign them to you along with ten thousand cavalry. With that force, you should dispose of Antigonus's ten thousand light troops with every prospect of success."

"Will the Daimones Prodromoi be amongst them?" Leonnatus suddenly realized he was seeing a great victory form before his eyes.

"Of course."

"Then our victory is assured."

"I hope so. Lysimachus, there is not much we can do to reinforce the center, but then, we don't need to. We'll thin your phalanx out a little but when it meets the phalanxes of Antigonus, neither will be going anywhere. We'll be loading our left wing heavily. Once we've wrecked Antigonus's cavalry and light troops, his phalanxes will be surrounded and we'll crush them from the flanks. Who's commanding his cavalry?"

"Demetrius."

"Good. That works for us. You've got a good phalanx, Lysimachus, mostly Macedonian veterans. Antigonus's phalanx is mostly made up of mercenaries. You're not as outnumbered there as you fear."

"Parmenio, Antigonus has eighty elephants, we have but thirty. And he places them to strengthen his center."

"Don't worry about them. We may have left our heavy infantry behind but we brought up our own elephants. And they are proper war-elephants. They'll be on our left wing."

Lysimachus's eyes lit up. "You've brought more elephants? Thank the gods for that. How many?"

Parmenio grinned wolfishly. "Eight hundred."

Alexander's Generals

Encampment, Army of Lysimachus, Ipsus, Just After Dawn, 303BC

"If we can survive this one, we're finished with the Army. We have enough gold to live the rest of our lives in comfort. So, it ends today. After this one, we go home." Nikomedes meant every word of the promise. It had been a long march from the time he had first picked up a Sarissa. First, across Greece, then this advance into Cappadocia and retreat into Phrygia. He had taken his chances all too often. So, in a different way, had Dara. Every battle fought had meant the chance of a battle lost and for her, that meant terrible danger.

He remembered what had happened to Zephyros's wife, Eunike. He barely remembered Zephyros but the fate of Eunike still haunted him. She had been left unprotected when Zephyros had been killed and hadn't been claimed by another soldier. That night, the factor responsible for disposing of the captured women had rented her out to anybody who wanted her. Later, when the encampment had settled down for the night, she had hanged herself in a wagon. The thought of Eunike suddenly took Nikomedes back fourteen years to when he had been a fresh recruit. They had stopped a sutler's wagon at a roadblock and there had been a girl for hire in the back. She had been his first and so she hadn't charged him. Nikomedes wondered what had happened to her *probably long dead and in her grave.*

Dara adjusted his neck-cloth so that it protected his skin from the harsh edges of his armor. She had cleaned everything she could and made sure that her man looked his best. Who knew, he might catch the attention of an officer and be rewarded with an extra coin or two of silver. She knew that the Army of Seleucus had been arriving all night and Seleucus was a man who rewarded generously those who served him well. She had already decided that she and her husband would settle in Selucia; all that was left was to convince him that doing so was his decision. "Look after yourself, husband, and come back safely to me."

Nikomedes nodded and set off for where the Phalanx was assembling. As he left the infantry encampment he glanced over his shoulder, into the great bowl that lay behind the positions held by the Army of Lysimachus. What he saw there made him stop in his tracks. The bowl was full of elephants, more elephants than he had ever seen in his life. Hundreds of them and they all wore the colors of Seleucus Nikator.

"Hurry up there!" The Lochagos, the commander of a hundred men, shouted at Nikomedes, drawing him away from the awe-inspiring sight of the elephants. "Their Majesties Lysimachus, Seleucus and Antigonus send their compliments and ask that you take your place so they can start the battle!"

The Lochagos looked at Nikomedes closely. "Good turn-out. Nikomedes isn't it? I want you in the back row as deputy commander of the file. We're forming up in tens. If Timotei buys it, you take command of the file. Now move!"

Nikmedes took his assigned place and screwed the two halves of his Sarissa together. The back row was, at once, the safest and most dangerous part of a battlefield. If things went well, he would spend the battle just standing there watching the front ranks do all the work – and take all the casualties. If things went badly and the phalanx was taken in the flanks and rear, it would be the men at the rear who would die first. *Here we go again,* he thought to himself.

Elephant Lines, Army of Seleucus, Ipsus, Just After Dawn, 303BC

The breath of the elephants was steaming in the morning chill. Although the sun was up, there were still traces of darkness left that had yet to be dispelled. Igrat had wrapped herself in a fur cloak against the chill but she still clung on to Derya Shafrid as he made his way down the serried ranks of elephants. Sixteen regiments, each with fifty elephants and all were armed with the oxybeles crossbows in addition to the archer-spearmen in the howdahs. She and her husband has spent the last few minutes together in their tent, with soldiers from Derya's regiment carefully keeping guard to ensure they were not disturbed.

"His name is Jayanta Prabhakar." Derya explained to Igrat. "He is my command elephant and I'll be riding him today."

Igrat looked at the great beast towering over her. In the weak morning sun, he looked almost black and his eyes seemed to glow with ferocity. He was indeed a quite different kind of elephant from her old friend Dilipa Ganesh. She got the feeling that Jayanta Prabhakar had inspected her, decided she wasn't on the list of people to be squashed today and lost interest in her. Accordingly, she was quite surprised when he lowered his head so she could seize his tusk and perform her wifely duty of holding his head while her husband climbed on board. When he was safely in his seat, her voice rang out across the elephant lines. "Husband! Come back carrying your shield, or carried on it!"

The cheers of applause that responded to her cry echoed down the lines as the elephants started to move out. She stood motionless as they walked past her, the ones that came nearest to her taking great care not to crowd or distress her. They weren't in fighting mood yet and were still good-natured, gentle beasts . She knew that would change very, very soon. With the elephants moving out and with her husband now lost to sight, she turned and set off to Parmenio's headquarters tent.

By the time she got there, the sun had risen properly and the day was beginning to warm up. One of the six soldiers with her took her cloak and carried it for her yet his hand remained firmly on his sword. These men were her bodyguards, the most trusted members of the Daimones Prodromoi and their orders were to guard Igrat's life at all costs. If the day started to go badly, her ability to get messages through to their destination might well be the key to saving the situation.

"Strategos, do you have orders for me?"

Parmenio looked up and saw her but he didn't smile. "Not yet, Igrat. Please take a seat and wait. You've organized a good horse?"

"The best the Daimones Prodromoi could offer me."

Parmenio said nothing but went back to staring at the model of the battlefield in front of him. As always, this one had been chosen long in advance and the maneuvering of the last year had been intended to bring the armies to this place at this time. The key to the battlefield was a long, curved ridge, shaped like a bow that bulged out towards the positions held by the Army of Antigonus. The phalanx of the Army of Lysimachus was already forming up along that ridge. In the cup formed by the bow, the left and right flanks were also forming up. When the time came, they would swing out and take their place on either side of the phalanx. Until then, they were masked from sight by the ridgeline and by Lysimachus's cavalry pickets.

A messenger came in and gave Parmenio a tablet and read it. As he did so, he began to relax and, for the first time, smiled at Igrat. "And so it begins. Antigonus's troops are forming up on the secondary ridgeline. We've got the main one so he's using the next best. We've passed the first critical point; Antigonus has committed himself to battle here today. I was afraid he might disengage. But, he knows our main body is still two days march south of here so this was his chance to destroy us in detail."

There were colored wooden blocks on a small table beside the model battlefield. Parmenio took three red wooden blocks marked with a painted sarissa and placed them on the secondary ridgeline. Other blocks quickly followed as the reports came in from the watching scouts. A huge block of cavalry on the Antigonid right, a smaller, weaker block of light troops, supported by bowmen and slingers, on the Antigonid left. As the Antigonid formation became more apparent, Igrat could see that Parmenio was mentally checking it off against his own expectations. She watched satisfaction mixed with more than a little relief spreading across his face.

"It's going the way you want isn't it, Father?"

Parmenio nodded, his eyes still calculating. "There are more than two hundred thousand men on the field. By the far the biggest battle I have ever fought. But, answering your question, oh, yes. It's going the way I want.

Headquarters of Antigonus Monopthalmus, Ipsus, Early Morning, 303BC

Antigonus Monopthalmus watched the build-up of the Army of Lysimachus on the ridge before him. As far as he could seethe opposing army was barely more than half the size of his and was much lighter in the heavy infantry sector. That encouraged him, although he cursed Lysimachus for seizing the great curved ridge that dominated the battlefield,. He had been concerned at the news of Seleucus Nikator's army arriving in the night but it seemed as if only cavalry and light troops had joined the Army of Lysimachus. Antigonus had just received reports from his scouts that the main body of the Army of Seleucus was still on the road, two days away.

Another in a long stream of messengers had arrived, sent to tell Antigonus that more of his units were in position. That made his battle line complete. He was throwing everything he had into the great assault that would open the battle. There were no reserves. He was aware of the dangers that presented but he hoped to avoid them by seizing and holding the initiative. If he was dictating what happened and where, then the lack of reserves would not matter.

"Peucestes, you will lead our left wing and advance upon the Army of Lysimachus. Drive them off that ridgeline so that we can have a full view of the battlefield. With ten thousand men and thirty elephants, you should have little difficulty in driving the five thousand men facing you into dishonorable flight. Demetrius, prepare to take the cavalry on our right wing for a charge. Once we have seized good observation positions on our left, disperse the cavalry if front of you. With both flanks in our hands, the battle will be ours."

Peucestes saluted and took to his horse. As he galloped past the massive Antigonid array of three phalanxes, together more than two and a quarter miles long, he marveled at the sheer concentration of power that it represented. In front of the three massive phalanxes were fifty elephants already beginning their advance upon the phalanx of Lysimachus. That was when Peucestes saw something that worried him. Lysimachus seemed to have a lot more elephants than he was supposed to. The scouts had said he had but thirty but Peucestes could count at least a hundred. They looked different as well, larger and darker than the elephants he was familiar with. Then the scene was left behind as he joined his own troops.

In a way, the fact he was opening the battle was an honor and a sign of his rehabilitation. Ahead of him, the thirty elephants he had been assigned were moving forward to seize the ground between his light troops and those of Lysimachus. That was the value of elephants, they were mobile fortresses that could seize and dominate terrain. In the absence of other elephants, there was little an army could do to remove them. For a moment, Peucestes thought he would have an easy run in but those hopes were quickly dashed. As his thirty elephants moved towards the ridge held by Lysimachus's light infantry, a formation of elephants crested the ridge and started to advance. Peucestes saw that they were smaller and a lighter gray than the great elephants that confronted the Antigonid phalanx. The spies had reported Lysimachus had thirty elephants. Peucestes realized that meant the elephants in the center had to belong to Seleucus.

The two lines of elephants met with great vigor, each group apparently determined to show they could match the courage and ferocity of the newcomers. The elephants of Antigonus and Lysimachus fought as if nature had matched them equally in courage and strength as well as being equal in number. The archers in the howdahs fired on their opposite numbers mounted on the enemy elephants and on the light infantry who were beginning to surge forward around them. That was when Peucestes started to realize that things were going wrong. There were far more light troops facing him than he had been led to expect and a higher proportion of them were bowmen and slingers. Additional regiments were still crossing the ridge held by Lysimachus and the number deployed was now at least equal to his own.

"Seleucus. It has to be Seleucus." The comment escaped from Peucestes without him being aware of it. *Seleucus must have sent his cavalry, light troops and elephants on ahead while he follows up with his main body. Even if we win this battle, we will still have to fight another against them. Just how many light troops has he added to the Army of Lysimachus?*

Peucestes watched his own light forces move up around the battling elephants and come within range of Lysimachus's forces on the ridgeline. The slingers were already beginning to exchange shots, using staff slings to gain the extra range they needed. The exchanges were largely ineffectual, harassing fire at best but they did establish that the assault was in hand. Peucestes started to move up, aware that the increasing number of enemy troops formed on the ridgeline would soon make a formal assault too hazardous to contemplate. He would have to move fast if that was to be avoided.

He wheeled his horse and galloped over to where his two regiments of cataphracts were assembled. His thinking was simple; a cavalry charge using the heavily armored cataphracts could get him on to the ridgetop before the Army of Lysimachus had properly established its grip up there.

He was well aware that he had already missed the most propitious moment for the attack but he had to do something in the face of a battle that was going very wrong. Peucestes gave his orders swiftly and wheeled to lead the charge.

His heavy horsemen started to lose momentum as the ground rose towards the ridge crest. There was, after all, a reason why heavy cavalry did not charge uphill unless there were no other options. Peucestes was grimly aware that he had already run out of other options. He focused on the forces holding the ridge ahead of him. They'd been joined by some cavalry who were forming up almost directly in front of him. A glance to his left showed another regiment forming up there. The latter, he recognized; prodromoi light cavalry. The ones in front were different, unfamiliar to him. It was only when the first shower of arrows descended on his cataphracts he realized he was facing Parthian horse-archers. Protected by their chain mail armor, the cataphracts didn't suffer that greatly from the arrow shower but their semi-protected horses did. Dozens went down as the Parthian arrows pierced their light mail and struck deep into their bodies. As the lead horses went down, the ones behind reared and fell over the bodies of their leaders. The formation and momentum of the charge was broken, irretrievably broken.

Peucestes felt a burning pain in his side. One of the arrows had found a weak point in his mail and struck home. It wasn't the worst thing that happened that moment though. Over on his left, the regiment of prodromoi swung their shields from the carry position on their backs to the fighting stance on their arm. That showed the front of the shield to their victims. A yellow shield front with a black daimones head painted on it. Peucestes heard the cry go up from all over his hard-pressed army. 'The Daimones Prodromoi!' As if responding to the call, the Daimones Prodromoi broke into a charge, heading straight for the stalled cataphracts.

There was never any possibility of the armored horsemen holding their ground. Weakened by the Parthians and stalled on unfavorable ground, their position was already disadvantageous. The Daimones Prodromoi were charging downhill, on fresh horses that were the best mounts army quartermasters from four armies could find. Most importantly, they were the Daimones Prodromoi and everybody knew that those who faced them, died. The survivors of the two cataphract regiments broke and ran long before they received the charge. As they did so, the infantry on either side of them started to do the same.

Peucestes felt the wetness running down his side inside his armor and knew the arrow wound was serious. He still turned his horse to face the oncoming prodromoi. A few of the cataphracts, shamed by their inglorious flight turned to charge with him. In doing so, they had simply swapped a shameful flight for a glorious death. Their small charge was a weak and feeble thing compared with the power of the massed veterans they faced. Peucestes couched his lance, curing the steadily-growing weakness in his left side as he did so. When his charge met that of a prodromoi, each lance struck the shield of the other and both lances shattered with the force of the impact. Peucestes felt the numbing shock of the blow in his left arm and also felt the wetness in his side grow faster as the power of the lance strike opened the wound still further.

The exchange of lance blows had been a disaster for him. His weakened left side had left his shield improperly supported and it had been thrown from his arm. Now, he had only his sword left. He wheeled his horse to face his assailant and drew his sword. His enemy had done the same and the two men galloped straight at each other. The sound of their blows echoed across the battlefield, eclipsing even the trumpeting of the elephants, but Peucestes saw his slashing blow fended off by the yellow-and-black shield. For a split second, he thought the Daimones face was laughing at him, then he felt the counterblow cut into his shoulder. It left him dizzy, sickened and stunned, incapable of remaining on his horse. He tried, but he couldn't stop himself rolling sideways, out of the saddle and on to the ground already being churned into mud by the horses.

Peucestes somehow managed to drag himself to his feet, using his sword to push himself upwards. He staggered towards his opponent, his sword moving in what he imagined were clever cuts but were actually barely more than random waves. That was when he felt a massive blow in his back and saw the blood-dripping point of a xyston lance emerge from his stomach. He realized that while he had been getting up, another cavalryman had simply ridden up behind him and impaled him on his xyston. *That's terribly unfair* he thought as he once again fell to his knees. Then he realized that the Daimones Prodromoi were elite veterans. They got that way by fighting to win, not fighting fairly. As his vision dimmed, he saw the horseman who had dismounted him riding up, his sword held for the stroke that would take his head. And that was all Peucestes ever saw.

With the commander of the left wing dead, the cataphracts in flight, Lysimachus's cavalry flooding into the Antigonid formations, and the rest of the Lysimachan infantry swarming down off the ridge, it was hardly surprising that the whole Antigonid left folded. The regiments of archers, slingers and skirmishers surrendered as Leonnatus and his infantry closed in on them. It was that, or be cut down and have their families sold into slavery.

The elephants knew the drill very well. They had changed sides so many times over the years that they knew exactly what would happen. The humans would surround them and lead them away to their new army where they would make friends with the soldiers and cadge some of their food. They really found it very confusing since they couldn't work out what all the fuss was about. But, the elephants didn't realize this was the last battle they would take part in. They may have fought for Eumenes and Antigonus and who knew who else. Some had even fought for the great Alexander himself, the man who had brought them so far from home. But, they were draft elephants, not war elephants and from now on they would fetch and carry for their new masters. Their time on the battlefield was over.

Headquarters of Antigonus Monopthalmus, Ipsus, Morning, 303BC

"Reverses and misadventures are part of life. We must accept what the fates decide and move on. Armies have suffered tactical set-backs before and will do so again. Now, we must just deal with this one."

Antigonus Monopthalmus looked carefully at the map before him, absorbing the situation that had developed on his left. It had been the arrival of Seleucus during the night that had changed everything. Instead of meeting a mere 5,000 auxiliaries under Leonnatus, the attack by Peucestes and his 10,000 had run into 25,000 hoplites, bowmen and slingers backed up by 10,000 cavalry. *It's hardly surprising his attack failed,* Antigonus thought, *Peucestes did well to buy as much time as he did. While Leonnatus sorts himself out, we have a chance to remedy the problem.*

"The phalanx on our left will withdraw to the ridge. There, it will reform at an angle of 45 degrees to the line formed by our center and right phalanxes. That will protect our left flank. Our auxiliaries there are broken but Leonnatus and his light troops cannot break a phalanx. My son, Demetrius will attack the enemy cavalry in front of him and drive it from the field. The phalanx on our right will follow him into the attack and establish a position on our right, angled at 45 degrees to our center and parallel to the phalanx on our left. Then, with our army in position, all three phalanxes will advance in an oblique order attack."

Cavalry, Left Wing, Army of Lysimachus

This was his first battle and that made the orders he had received all the more galling. He had his own command of two thousand horse added to the ten thousand of Lysimachus and had been put in charge of the combined force. That had pleased him greatly but what had not done so was the task he had been assigned. He had to receive the anticipated charge form the fifteen thousand men under Demetrius and allow them to force him back. If that meant fleeing in apparently womanish and dishonorable panic, so be it. He would get a chance to correct the impression later. Antiochus also minded what his father Seleucus had told him. "If Parmenio tells you to stand naked on the back of your horse and sing lewd drinking songs while servicing a slave-girl, do it. For, somehow, that will bring about victory.

And victory is what is important, not any loss of dignity we might temporarily suffer in its pursuit."

Up ahead of his command, Antiochus could see Demetrius's cavalry breaking into a slow, steady trot. Contrary to the heroic declamations read by orators, heavy cavalry didn't immediately charge at a full gallop. Doing that would exhaust the horses quickly and bring about disaster. Instead the horses would trot into position and then break into a canter when the charge started. They would only go to a full gallop for the last few lengths, just enough to build the momentum they needed.

"Advance to contact!" Antiochus shouted out the order. He had briefed his ten Epihipparches carefully, knowing that in the heat of battle, the desire for glorious victory would overcome knowledge of the lethal trap they were setting up. Each Epihipparch had equally carefully briefed his two Hipparches. One would advance quickly to counter the Anigonid cavalry charge while the other hung back. Then, at a moment judged appropriate by the tardy Hipparch, he would cause his command of 500 horsemen to break and ride for the rear. Because each Hipparch would judge that moment for himself, the unengaged half of the cavalry would run for the rear in a random chaotic pattern that would look just like inexperienced cavalry breaking. The inevitable result would be the troops already engaged would see themselves left unsupported and join the rout. Antiochus knew that Parmenio was betting that Demetrius would be unable to resist pursuing the Seleucid cavalry that had so often defeated his father.

Around him, his cavalry broke into a trot, then a canter. At a precisely-timed moment, the horses lunged into a full gallop and the two formations slammed into each other. Antiochus was nearly lifted from his saddle as his xyston sliced past the shield of an Antigonid cavalryman and struck him solidly on his chain mail tunic. He struggled to stay mounted, knowing that to fall to the ground in this cavalry melee would mark him for almost certain death. *There must be a better way to ride a horse than this. One good swing with a weapon or one good, hard blow and it's out of the saddle and on to the ground.* He clung to his horse's neck for a brief second and watched his opponent slide to the ground beneath him, his mail already soaked with blood from the gaping wound in his chest.

By the time he had heaved himself back so he was properly seated, his horse had already brought him around to his next opponent. Cavalry horses were trained to fight as well, supplementing their human's efforts with their own kicks and bites. Antiochus realized that his mount had already got a couple of good kicks in at enemies who got in his way. Somehow, he couldn't quite remember how or when, he had drawn his kopis cavalry saber and he used it to slash at a cataphract who was closing in on him. He felt the shock in his wrist as his slash was intercepted by the cataphract's shield but before the enemy could counter-strike, the two were separated by the swirling battle. Another Antigonid cavalryman replaced him but before Antiochus could strike at him, the man was brought down by a lance thrust. It was one of Antiochus's bodyguards, making sure that their leader stayed safe in the chaos of the mounted battle. Yet another enemy cavalryman was trying to engage him. Antiochus parried his sabre swing with his kopis and then counter-thrust. He thought his sword had bitten home into the man's arm but again, his opponent was carried away by the wild fight before he could confirm what had happened.

Looking around him, Antiochus suddenly realized that his cavalry were falling back as the regiments behind him started to retreat. Even though he had expected it – counted on it – the sight still shocked and shamed him. For a brief second he felt like making a wild, desperate charge against the enemy cavalry in front of him but common sense and the discrete obstruction of his bodyguards stopped him. He turned his horse's head and broke into a full gallop for the rear. It took a brief interval for the Antigonid cavalry to realize that their enemy had broken and another for them to set out in pursuit. By that time, there was a gap of a hundred paces or more between the two forces. The Antigonid cavalry then started off in pursuit, grimly determined to close the gap and put the seal on their victory.

Seleucus Nikator had spent much good gold on his cavalry horses. They were carefully-bred, well-fed, in peak condition and well-trained. As the Seleucid and Lysimachan cavalry streamed for the rear, those advantages were rewarded. Far from closing the gap, Demetrius and his cavalry were slowly being left behind. Then, Antiochus rounded the edge of the ridge on which Lysimachus had made his position and saw the long line of elephants waiting in its lee. More elephants than he had ever seen in one place before. Ahead of him, the regiments of cavalry that had led the rout had suddenly swung around and formed line. As the rest of the horsemen came level with them, they also swung around and fell into place. There were even carts waiting for them with xystons to replace the ones broken in the initial fight. As the returning cavalrymen pulled into place, the men on the carts threw them xystons and javelins. Within seconds, what had apparently been a broken, routed mass had returned to being a disciplined, compact and re-armed formation. And it was one that thirsted for the opportunity to prove its retreat had been feigned.

Cavalry of Demetrius Poliorcetes, Army of Antigonus

"Oh, crap!" Anatolios Metrophanes realized what had happened as soon as he saw the broken Seleucid cavalry almost magically reform in front of him. He, like every other cavalryman in the pursuit had reveled at the sight of the vaunted Selucid cavalry fleeing before him. Only, no broken, fleeing enemy could reform so fast or so well. *We've just ridden into a trap.*

All around him, the Antigonid cavalrymen were trying to turn their horses and get clear before the trap closed on them but the sheer momentum of their charge defeated the efforts. Over to his left, Metrophanes saw what the ridge had concealed. A vast sea of elephants, some of which were formed into a long line that was already advancing on the mass of cavalry in front of them. Others, the larger portion, were in a great block that was already moving forward to attack the right hand phalanx of the Antigonid line. The infantrymen were too far back to see what awaited them but Metrophanes realized they were in mortal danger. *I never knew there were this many elephants in the whole world.*

It was amazing how quickly the elephant line advanced. As the elephants moved forward in that strange gait that was just a very fast walk rather than a run, yet covered ground at impressive speed, the line began to split into two. The two halves started pivoting so that the line now formed an inverted Vee with the Antogonid cavalrymen trapped between its limbs. The Seleucid and Lysimachan heavy cavalry was also moving into position so that it capped the open top of the Vee. At that point, the elephants raised their trunks and gave a roaring battle-cry. Three hundred elephants trumpeting in unison was a truly terrifying sound and the Antigonid horses, never fond of elephants at the best of time, panicked. They reared, swerved, kicked out at each other. Anything to get away from the huge, smelly beasts that made such frightful sounds. Even before the elephants engaged, the Antigonid cavalry formation was coming apart at the seams.

The sound that followed was even worse. A deafening, high pitch scream that seemed to fill the air around them and tear the very sky apart. Metrophanes saw the heavy cataphracts hurled from their saddles with the force of the impact from the crossbow bolts. Horses hit by the bolts were thrown to the ground. *The oxybeles, nothing else has that kind of power. Seleucus has mounted oxybeles crossbows on his elephants.*

For the 15,000 cavalrymen trapped in the triangle, the casualties from the oxybeles salvo were not that much of a problem. A couple of hundred men at most had died in the crossfire from the two angled rows of elephants. The disaster was the screams of the bolts as they had raced through the air. The already-panicking horses were completely demoralized by the sounds and attempted to get away by any means they could. They bucked and surged, racing this way and that, trying to find a way out of the area they had been penned into. Some threw their riders, either accidentally or deliberately, in the effort to escape. The horses collided, the stronger barging the weaker out of their way, only to be knocked aside themselves when they met a yet-stronger horse. And, all the time, as the great V of elephants advanced, the triangle in which the Antigonid cavalry was trapped, shrank.

Fourth Diodochi War

Desperately trying to regain control of his horse, Metrophanes realized an important truth. Neither the Seleucid nor the Lysimachan cavalry were destroying the Antigonid cavalry formations; the Antigonid cavalry was destroying itself in the panic-stricken chaos of the triangle. He desperately tried to regain control of his horse, anything to find a way out of this killing ground. *But, what to do? My horse will not, absolutely not, charge those elephants. If we try and break out through the cavalry sealing the exit, we'll be hitting formed-up, re-armed cavalry in small packets. They'll cut us down without even needing to draw breath. There is no way out. This trap is complete.*

His thoughts were interrupted when another panic-stricken horse, frantic with fear, crashed into his. The other horseman had no control at all over his mount and was thrown when his horse reared up and tried to kick Metrophanes and his mount out of his way. Then the attacking horse collapsed on to the ground with an oxybeles bolt through its neck. Metrophanes realized that, depending on which row of elephants the bolt had come from, the bolt must have missed him by less than a finger's length or an arm's length. *And yet, that was no closer to death than I am now.*

The wild chaos was beginning to slow down, not because the horses were any less frantic but because the advancing V of elephants had so reduced the area of the triangle that the horses were crowding up against each other and had progressively less room to move in. Yet, the shower of arrows from the archers on the elephants and the periodic salvos of oxybeles bolts never stopped. *Why don't they stop? We're beaten, we've lost. All we can do is surrender.* The words echoed through Metrophanes's mind. Then, the answer struck him with the clarity of deathly insight. *They don't want us to surrender until we've been butchered. They're making a statement, that after today, anybody who fights for Antigonus will die on the battlefield.*

Metrophanes looked down and realized the reason for the clarity. An oxybeles bolt had struck him in the chest. It had penetrated his chain mail at the front, gone right through him and its point had penetrated the mail at his back. He could feel his strength ebbing fast as the blood drained from his body. *Why didn't I feel that?* He never got an answer to the question. As the world around him seemed to fade away he fell sideways from his horse but never felt the cavalryman next to him push his lifeless body away.

Parmenio's Headquarters Tent, Mid-morning, Center of the Army of Seleucus-Lysimachus, Ipsus

"How's my boy doing?" Seleucus's voice broke the silence in the command tent.

Parmenio looked up. He'd just finished updating his map after the last set of reports had come in. "Your Majesty. I pleases me to report your son,

Prince Antiochus, has distinguished himself greatly. He pulled off two difficult maneuvers in quick succession, fought bravely on the battlefield and even ensured the replacement equipment was waiting for his men in the right place and at the right time."

Seleucus Nikator smiled, then dropped his voice to a confidential whisper. "Really? How did he really do?"

"As I said, Your Majesty, he distinguished himself greatly. I wouldn't say he covered himself in glory for the role assigned to him wouldn't allow that. But, he had the fortitude and foresight not to try. Arranging for resupply of xystons and javelins where and when they were needed was a stroke of true genius. I could make a strategos out of him."

"I'd like you to try once this war is over. I am going to appoint him as co-ruler, a junior king if you like, so the succession will be properly defined. I will not have this endless series of wars tearing my empire apart after my time is over. The better trained he is, the better it will be for my Empire. Now, how goes the battle?"

Parmenio led his King over to the great model of the battlefield. "That's the current situation, your Majesty. We've kicked in the flanks of Antigonus's Army. Both are gone. His right and left are both wide open. He pulled his left-hand phalanx back to cover the exposed left and he'll try and do the same with his right. It's too late though. We're already extending past the line of his left phalanx and our elephants are lining up to take his right hand phalanx apart. That'll just leave his center and it will disintegrate. If we let it. Now, Your Majesty, why are you here? Your assignment is to bring up the heavy infantry. If this battle goes sour on us, and it still could, we would fall back on them and try again."

Seleucus blinked slightly at being questioned, but reminded himself of the unspoken deal that existed. He would rule while Parmenio won his wars for him. It was an agreement that had withstood two decades of almost constant warfare. "I wanted to see what was going on up here so I could decide whether to continue to march to the battlefield or get my troops into line. I know you have Igrat here and she could get my orders back to the rest of the army faster than a messenger on a galloping horse. So I came on ahead with a detachment to join you. What are the casualties so far?"

"For us, fairly light. We've had about two thousand dead so far, split evenly between the left and right flanks. We're bringing the wounded in now and the women are hard at work. As for Antigonus, I'd estimate his casualties at around twenty thousand to date. Mostly, they're the cavalry on his right. We haven't got an accurate figure there yet, the bodies are two and three deep in the killing ground. I wouldn't go there if I were you."

"We're destroying his entire army, aren't we?" Seleucus was horrified at what was unfolding on the battlefield.

Parmenio shook his head. "That isn't the aim. The aim is to make this such a massive defeat that, even if Antigonus survives, his credibility as a commander will be gone. We took a big step towards that when we destroyed his cavalry. It's been a long, long time since anybody has inflicted a defeat like that. But, over on the left, we're just doing dummy charges and showering the left-hand phalanx with arrows from the horse-archers. We've also shifted the Daimones Prodromoi into a position where they threaten that phalanx's baggage train. With their reputation for pillaging baggage and growing demoralization at the hands of the horse-archers, Antigonus is going to have to watch his men throw down their sarissas soon.

"Is Demetrius Poliorcetes still alive?" One of Seleucus's companions spoke. Parmenio recognized him as Telesphorus of Peloponnesus, a naval commander highly regarded by Cassander and Ptolemy.

"We don't know. He was with the cavalry when it charged into our trap. Frankly, we've got better things to do right now that go through the bodies looking for him." Parmenio was interrupted by a messenger arriving. He read the dispatch and moved the block representing the largest formation of elephants forward. It now directly faced the right-hand phalanx of Antigonus's line. Behind them, the 300 elephants that had destroyed the Antigonid cavalry were reorganizing and forming up into a second assault block.

"At Salamis, he had his cavalry lined up along the shore, waiting to rescue any sailors who swam ashore. A lot of seamen, ours and theirs, owe their lives to that gesture. If he survived, I would ask that he be treated with kindness. He's not his father's son."

Seleucus nodded in agreement. "I had heard of his concern for the shipwrecked seamen and also that he tries to shield those around him from the tyranny of his father. Parmenio, if he has survived, I would like to see him honored for his actions. Now, I need to get word of the situation here to the main body."

In the corner of the tent, Igrat got to her feet. "Would you wish me to take them, Your Majesty? I have a good horse and bodyguards to get me through."

Seleucus Nikator shook his head. "No need for your skills now, Igrat. If the situation was going bad, then I would accept your offer gladly but time now is no problem. I'll send a normal dispatch rider."

Igrat nodded and sat down again. Parmenio winked at her. He wasn't certain yet that this battle would not go sour on him and he wanted her available if it did. The next few hours would be critical.

Daimones Prodromoi, Right Wing, Army of Lysimachus Mid-morning

"Hey, snake-eater. Going to have a sarissaphoros for dinner?" The prodromoi looked around and laughed at his sally. The other men in their ten-man Lochos joined the merriment.

Semiramis laughed as well. Her nickname in the Regiment had come from an incident just after she had joined them. Some cavalry troopers had slipped a snake into her bedding as a practical joke. Then, they had waited outside to hear her screams when she found it. Only, there had been a complete silence. Eventually, overcome by curiosity, they had looked inside to see what was happening. Semiramis had caught the snake, killed it, skinned it and was threading the meat on to a skewer prior to roasting it over an open fire. Thanks to Naamah's lessons on how to season meat, it had actually tasted pretty good. And so, ever since, she had been "snake-eater".

"Naah, they're tough and stringy. All that marching you see. Now a nice, tender, juicy prodromoi, seasoned with olive oil and garlic of course . . ." Semiramis looked hungrily at the prodromoi who had started the joke and licked her lips. "Now, that would make a dinner worthy of the name."

"Quiet, you lot." Privately, their Lochagos was relieved that the woman he'd been burdened with had worked out much better than he had thought. When he had heard she was joining his Lochos, he'd bewailed his fate, expecting to receive some pampered palace pet who would have to be sheltered and protected. To his eternal relief, Semiramis had turned out to be tough and capable. She'd won grudging acceptance from the other nine members of the Lochos by refusing any special treatment and displaying more-than-average competence with xyston, kipos and javelin. In fact, the Lochos suspected she was more skilled with those than she was letting on but had suppressed her skills to the "a bit better than average" level in order to win acceptance. *That shows she is smart as well as tough.* "And, snake-eater, you are absolutely forbidden to eat any of my men. Right, we're going in again. Same as before. Charge the phalanx, break left just before you hit the Sarissas and throw your javelins into their front ranks."

It was the fifth charge of the kind they had carried out since the fighting had started. Semiramis had worked out what was going on. The Parthian horse-archers were keeping the phalanx under a constant shower of arrows, but every so often they needed to break off to pick up a new supply. While they did so, the prodromoi regiments took their place, hurling their javelins at the serried ranks of sarissaphoros. Neither the javelins nor the arrow flights were having much effect on the phalanx in terms of casualties but she could only guess at the effect on their morale. Standing there, having to take the continued goading would be bad. She could sense they were getting dispirited. There was something about their stance that telegraphed that message. *The executions will continue until morale improves* she thought, remembering an old Assyrian Army practice. Then she pulled her neckcloth up to cover her nose and mouth and kicked her horse into motion.

The constant movement of horses had broken the ground up and dust was becoming a greater problem as the morning wore on. Most of the prodromoi were covering their nose and mouth against the dust cloud. There was a strong belief that breathing battlefield dust caused the lung-sickness that afflicted veteran cavalrymen. Tactically, it was an advantage in that the cavalry wouldn't be seen until they emerged from the cloud and that cut down the time they were vulnerable to arrow fire. Also, not knowing when the next charge would come exaggerated the morale effect. She felt the horse under her surge into a full gallop. She was very fond of her horse Montoi; in her considered and expert opinion, he was the finest piece of horseflesh she had ever ridden. She hunched slightly down in the saddle, feeling Montoi's powerful back legs driving them forward. On either side of them, her nine companions were doing the same. Then, they burst out of the dust and saw the phalanx waiting before them.

They were shaky, she was in no doubt about that. The front line actually bowed back a bit before the ones behind steadied it. Montoi spun left, dug his heels in and charged parallel to the front line of the phalanx. Semiramis took careful aim and threw her javelin. It flew straight and true but the sarissaphoros it was aimed at deflected it with his shield. It went sideways, bounded off the man beside him and fell to the ground. One of the other prodromoi in her lochos had even worse luck. His javelin also flew straight and true but it caught the shaft of a sarissa held by a man three ranks back and was deflected away. Of the ten javelins thrown by her lochos, not one brought down an enemy.

Chastened, the lochos of prodromoi cantered back to their lines. The charge had been an exercise in futility but at least it had given the horses some exercise and stopped the prodromoi from getting bored. As Semiramis wheeled Montoi into place, her Lochagos nodded at her. "Good throw that. Bad luck he caught it. What do you think, snake-eater?"

"I think that phalanx is ready to cave in. It's like salt in water. It looks solid right up to when it falls apart. Then, it suddenly lets go and there's nothing left."

"That's what our Hipparch thinks. So we carry on tossing javelins at them until they dissolve."

Headquarters of Antigonus Monopthalmus, Ipsus, Late Morning

The elephants poured out in an unending stream. Hundreds of them faced his right-hand phalanx in a long, straight line several ranks deep. Although an elderly man, Antigonus still had excellent vision and he could see light infantry running along in front of the Seleucid elephant armada. Every so often, one would stop and take a swing with an axe at the ground. Antigonus knew what he was doing – checking for spiked chains on the ground and, on finding them, cutting them away so they would not injure the elephant's feet. The elephants themselves were advancing slowly and carefully and that added all the more menace to their bulk and numbers.

"Where is Demetrius and his cavalry?" Antigonus shouted out the question, his voice beginning to show a hint of desperation.

"Dead." The one word answer was crushing in its finality.

Antigonus Monopthalmus felt the single word slice into his stomach. "What do you mean dead? He can't be dead. He's my son."

The messenger who had brought the news collapsed on to his knees. "Forgive me your majesty, but his cavalry was surrounded by hundreds of elephants. They showed no mercy and all that is left of our cavalry are piles of bodies, horses and men mixed together."

Antigonus looked at his map, trying to absorb what had happened. *Now, I have nothing. All that is left for me is to seek death on this battlefield.*

Another messenger ran in. "Your majesty, a message from Brykinius, commander of the left wing. He says his phalanx is collapsing under constant attack by horse-archers and cavalry. He demands support immediately if disaster is to be averted."

Antigonus looked up. "He demands? Who is he to demand?"

'Brykinius' was really Bricius, a Celtic mercenary. After the death of Peucestes, Antigonus had put him in command of the left wing simply because he had no other candidate even remotely capable of handling the work. The problem was, despite being given a Hellenified version of his name, he was still a barbarian mercenary and the Macedonians and Greeks under his command had little faith in him. *What wouldn't I give now for one good commander trusted by the men under him.*

"I will see." Antigonus left his tent and climbed on to the back of an elephant that was standing outside. The height of the elephant combined with that of the ridgeline allowed him to see the situation on the left. That one look told him that the message was indeed justified. Where, once before, the phalanx had been a perfect rectangle with sides so straight they could have been made of stone, now it was a distorted mass, still recognizably a phalanx

393

but quickly losing shape and coherence. Once, when he had been a boy, Antigonus had put a square of soft wax in the sun and watched it soften and sag into a shapeless mass. His father, Philip of Elimeia, had seen him and explained that what had just happened to the wax also happened to a poorly-led army when exposed to the heat of battle. The memory shocked Antigonus because of the implied message within it. *Is my father coming back from the afterlife to tell me I have been a poor leader and deserve defeat?*

"Tell Brykinius he must lead his men and shore up his command. That is his duty and why he was appointed to command."

Antigonus used the observation point provided by the elephant to survey the battlefield. That allowed him to see the disasters that were engulfing his right and center as well as his left. He scanned desperately, hoping against hope that he would see Demetrius bringing his cavalry back to save his right but all he saw there were the mass of Seleucid elephants advancing on the phalanx in front of them. The front ranks of that phalanx were already starting to crumble as the crossbows mounted on the elephants poured their bolts into the enemy ranks. *It looks as if somebody has finally found the answer to the Macedonian Phalanx*, Antigonus thought as he watched his defeat beginning to unfold.

Center, Army of Lysimachus, Ipsus, Late Morning

The fifty elephants drawn up before the center phalanx of Antigonus were very unhappy about the situation. It had been great fun pretending to be war elephants for so many years and their pretension had won them excellent treatment and lots of good food. Now, fate had finally turned against them and they faced twice their number of real war elephants. They knew the great, dark-gray beasts opposing them had seen through their pretence and knew them for what they were. Draft animals unfit for the honor of fighting on the battlefields. The Antigonid elephants knew that the war elephants they faced were seriously upset with them and greatly offended by the imposture. The draft elephants knew they had only one course of action that could save them from a ghastly fate and that was to flee immediately. Only the constant hard work of their mahouts prevented them doing so.

As the hundred Seleucid war-elephants closed in on their enemy, the Antigonid elephants heard the sky split by a terrifying scream. All along their line, bolts from the heavy oxybeles catapults were slashing into them. The gunners had targeted the mahouts sitting unprotected on the elephant's necks but the torsion-catapult wasn't that accurate when firing at a point target and the motions of the elephants made it even less so. Some of the bolts hit the mahouts, throwing them, already dead or dying fast, to the ground. Others hit the elephants themselves and that, the stricken beasts found shocking. They'd all been hit by arrows before. Then, their heavy skins had protected them and the arrow wounds had been little more than a mild itch that quickly healed. These bolts were different. They penetrated the elephant skin easily and sunk inches deep into their bodies. The pain they inflicted was indescribable and it drove the Antigonid elephants wild.

Some of the elephants panicked because they had lost their mahouts and there was nobody to stop them fleeing the great war-elephants bearing down upon them. Some panicked because they were gravely wounded by the bolts. The great majority however, panicked because they saw the first two groups had already done so and they had no intention of being left behind to face the war-elephants on their own. The entire line of fifty Antigonid elephants turned and fled to the rear. Unfortunately for both them and the center phalanx of Antigonus, their course took them straight into that phalanx.

One of the virtues of advancing downhill from a ridge crest was that the view from the back ranks of a phalanx was much better than on level ground. Ahead of him, Nikomedes could see the maddened Antigonid elephants plowing into the front ranks of the phalanx they were supposed to be protecting. A virtual battle was breaking out between the sarissaphoros and the elephants as the former tried to avoid being crushed and the latter attempted to escape from the battle. Some of the elephants whose mahouts hadn't been thrown or killed, suddenly collapsed in the middle of the fighting, apparently dead. Nikomedes had heard that the mahouts carried a heavy chisel and mallet so they could kill an elephant that went berserk and he couldn't help but feel sorry for the terrified beasts.

Nevertheless, the sight before him was one to gladden the heart of any sarissaphoros. The enemy phalanx was badly disrupted and the discipline that held its ranks solid was breaking down. The Seleucid elephant crews were making things worse by firing their heavy crossbows at the phalanx, effectively trying to support the rampage of the enemy elephants. There were too few of them to make a real difference but they were adding to the confusion within the enemy ranks. The swishing noise of the sarissas held by the men in front of Nikomedes told him that the ranks were about to collide. Normally, this was where the forward movement of the phalanx stopped and the battle became a grim effort to force the other phalanx back a step or two. The battle could be a murderous slaughtering match or a semi-game where the two sides jousted without shedding much blood but the two phalanxes would be stalemated. This time, though, Nikomedes noted that his phalanx barely slowed down. The ranks split to pass their own elephants, rejoined, then started to force the chaotic front ranks of the Antigonid phalanx back.

Eventually, of course, the Lysimachan phalanx did come to a halt as the rear ranks of their opponents solidified and reformed. The advance achieved before that happened was still the greatest Nikomedes could remember in all the battles he had fought over the years. Ho noticed something else; usually at this point in the battle, the files started to shorten as men in the front ranks fell and those behind them stepped forward to take their place. The line of the rear would become ragged as some files lost more men than others. Yet, today, this was not happening, making it obvious that, while the Antogonid phalanx was defending itself, it was just going through the motion as far as attacking was concerned.

That was when Nikomedes realized that the great Seleucid war elephants were standing behind him. It was a good chance to get some news from somebody who could actually see what was going on. "Hey, elephant humper. What's going on up front?"

One of the archers looked down (in every sense of the phrase) on Nikomedes and his fellow sarissaphoros. "Hey, pointy stick man. Their phalanx is holding but only just. They've got a dozen dead elephants or more in their formation and the rest of their elephants have run away. Your officers have given orders for you to hold their phalanx in place while we shoot them up. So, you can go back to thinking about women and playing with your sarissa."

Nikomedes and the elephant-archer exchanged friendly waves. Then, Nikomedes took a pace forward, occupying the ground once held by the man in front of him. The battle might be stalled but men were still dying.

Left Wing, Army of Seleucus, Ipsus, Noon

The right hand phalanx of the Army of Antigonus was crumpling under the concentrated blow of four hundred elephants. The salvoes of oxybeles bolts had chewed through the front ranks, leaving a gaping hole in the center of the mass of men that offered a path into and through the phalanx. Even more critically, the phalanx itself had been pushed back and to the left so that its left-hand side was pushing into the center phalanx. That phalanx was, itself, being pinned by a frontal attack and raked by bolts from the war-elephants. The result was a steadily-growing area of chaos where the two phalanxes mixed and merged.

Derya Shafrid looked over to his right and saw that the three hundred elephants that had destroyed Demetrius's cavalry were reforming and moving towards the flank and rear of the Antogonid left. It was also painfully obvious that Antigonus had no reserves left to counter any of these movements. The elephants alone were presenting a threat he had no real hope of countering but it was the lack of a reserve that was the undoing of him. He couldn't even fight his way out of the disaster that was engulfing his Army.   He looked ahead as another salvo of oxybeles bolts ripped into the cave that marked where the center of the phalanx had once been.   The range was so close now that every bolt was going through two or more men before finally coming to a halt.   In addition, the archers on the elephants were close enough to be picking men off individually.   Shafrid took a sarissa, screwed the two halves together and started watching the flanks of Jayanta Prabhakar.   The phalanx might be failing and it might bemostly raw recruits and mercenaries but there would still be some hardened veterans inside there.   This was the point where the war-elephants were most vulnerable.   Inside the enemy infantry, a brave man might run up and stab them in the vulnerable belly.   Such a man would almost certainly die, either by sword, spear, arrow or simply a crippled elephant rolling on him, but he stood a good chance of bringing down an elephant.

Sure enough, one man did run from the crumbling phalanx.   He held a short spear in his hands, actually, the front half of a sarissa.   The extra length of both halves screwed together was of no use to him here and simply got in the way.   Shafrid thrust at him with the sarissa he held and watched the man duck around the thrust.   For a moment that seemed much longer than it really was, there was a standoff.   The man on the ground couldn't get past the sarissa to attack the elephant and Shafrid couldn't impale him on the sarissa to get rid of him.   Then, the man grew an arrow out of his chest and he fell to his knees.   He knelt there while the sarissa thrust killed him.

Shafrid saw the archer on an elephant that was bringing up the rear and gave him grateful wave.   There was more to it than that, of course.   That archer would know that his services had been seen and noted.   There would be an extra piece or two of silver for him when the loot was distributed.   It was part of a commander's work to note such things and see that rewards were properly and fairly distributed.   Then Shafrid turned his attention back to his main work.

The elephants were inside the phalanx, past the points of the sarissas and there was little to stop them.   The archers and sarissaphoros on their backs were cutting down the infantry on the ground while the elephants themselves trampled men down.   Occasionally one of them would pick up a man with his trunk and throw the victim through the air.   Shafrid realized he was seeing something he had never seen before.   He'd seen phalanxes forced to retreat, he had seen phalanxes surrender when their position was hopeless and he had seen phalanxes break and run.   He had never, ever seen a phalanx being destroyed like this.

The screams that surrounded him merged with the dust, the triumphant trumpeting of the elephants and the constant whistling of the oxybeles bolts. Beneath it all, he knew that the men packed into the ranks of the phalanx were virtually helpless.   Their sarissas, so lethal when deployed by men in organized formations were now worse than useless. The only threat to the elephants were hypaspists and men who had managed to break away from the organized blocks. *How ironic,* Shafrid thought, *the only hope that Antigonus might have now would be the argyraspides but he killed them all a decade or more ago.*

Daimones Prodromoi, Right Wing, Army of Lysimachus, Ipsus, Noon

"Right, we're going in again. Same as before. Charge the phalanx, break left just before you hit the Sarissas and throw your javelins into their front ranks." The Lochagos repeated the orders wearily. It wasn't just that they had made this charge over and over again but throwing javelins at what was little more than a helpless target seemed demeaning somehow. Semiramis took a firm hold on her javelin and kicked Montoi into motion. She could almost hear him thinking *Really? Again?* He surged into a full gallop and they burst out of the dust to see the phalanx waiting before them. This time, everything was different. They were a rabble, they were out of formation and the points of their sarissas rested firmly on the ground. They were surrendering.

Semiramis managed to stop her javelin throw at the last second. A couple of others in her Lochos didn't, but they managed to change their aim so the javelin went harmlessly into the ground. The Daimones Prodromoi formed up in front of them, xystons at the ready. A faked surrender was very rare but it did happen sometimes. Then Aeschylus rode up and met with a Tetraches who had walked out to meet him. The conversation was quick and simple. The officer commanding the phalanx offered to join the Army of Seleucus in exchange for their baggage, women and a land grant per man in one of the new Katoikoi soldier's settlements Seleucus was founding. Aeschylus nodded his agreement and it was over. The left hand phalanx of the Antigonid Army was out of the battle. Seeing the phalanx fold, a number of small cavalry and light infantry detachments in the vicinity followed suit. Looking up at the ridgeline on her left, Semiramis could see why the phalanx had collapsed. The area occupied by the other two phalanxes was an ever-shrinking island in a sea of elephants.

"What happened to your commander?" One of the Lochogos called the question out to the sarissaphoros as they sorted themselves out.

"He fell off his horse."

The men of the Daimones Prodromoi burst out laughing. 'Fell off his horse' was a well-established euphemism for a commander who was killed by his own men for not surrendering in a hopeless situation. The man who had answered joined in the laughter. "No, he *really* fell off his horse. So drunk he couldn't stay in the saddle. He's sleeping it off back there somewhere."

"Some of you, go and find him. Anything else?" Aeschylus finished the details of the surrender and rejoined the Daimones Prodromoi. "Right, and now we will be in at the finish. I have orders to take you up on to the ridge to help the elephants finish off what's left.

Headquarters of Antigonus Monopthalmus, Ipsus, Early Afternoon

"Your Majesty, we have to surrender. Our left has collapsed completely and most of the survivors are defecting to Seleucus Nikator. Our right is being destroyed by the elephants. The men there are trapped in a great ring and they cannot escape. Already our dead there are beyond counting. Our center is being forced back by the phalanx of Lysimachus supported by the elephants of Seleucus. We are almost surrounded. Light cavalry are moving behind us to cut off our retreat. If we disengage now and use the survivors of our right and center to cut our way out, then there is still a chance. But, our losses will be still greater and our chance of success slight. We owe it to our men to surrender."

Antigonus looked at the Tagmatarchis, the most senior of his surviving officers. "Only if we had won this battle would we have owed anything to our men. We have lost, they have failed us. All we have left to do now is show them how real men fight."

He stormed out of his tent and mounted the horse that was waiting outside. His few surviving senior officers followed him and mounted up also. The small group then moved to where the remains of the center phalanx were trying to hold off the phalanx of Lysimachus supported by a hundred elephants. Looking around him, Antigonus saw a sight he had never seen before, not in the sixty years he had fought in the Army. The ground was carpeted with bodies, mostly those of his men who had died where they stood. Some had sarissa wounds, others arrow or javelin injuries. The most obvious were those who had been brought down by the bolts from the oxybeles crossbows mounted on the elephants that seemed to be everywhere. Many of them had been completely transfixed by the bolts despite their shields and armor.

Looking at them, Antigonus saw that a disproportionate number of them were his Chiliarches and Pentakosiarches, the commanders of a thousand and five hundred respectively. They were the medium-level leadership upon which the efficiency of any army depended. *Seleucus and Lysimachus have deliberately targeted my officer corps for destruction. After today, even if I raise more men, I will have nobody to command them.*

A quick look around showed him that his right flank was gone. It had been crushed by the elephants who had left its ruins in their wake and were now advancing on the remains of his center. The phalanx of Lysimachus was advancing also, picking up speed as the remains of the center phalanx in front of it collapsed. On the left and rear, light cavalry was already closing in to cut off any escape routes.

His assessment of the situation was interrupted by a loud clattering noise. His last phalanx was throwing down its weapons and surrendering. *If I am to escape, it must be now.* He turned his horse and began to gallop towards the light cavalry that were fanning out behind the ruins of his army. That was when he saw the yellow shields with the black daimones head painted on them. *The Daimones Prodromoi. Those bastards have taken the credit for every victory I have ever won. I will not let them defeat me.*

His small group of cavalry charged the regiment that blocked his escape. Some of his companions were brought down by thrown javelins, others by arrows from horse-archers following the prodromoi. Only Antigonus are two others survived to reach sword range. Those two died almost instantly, run through by xystons. Antigonus survived only because, at the last moment, his horse fell from a javelin strike. He was thrown, rolling on the ground before his collapsing horse pinned his leg. By the time he had extracted himself, he was surrounded by the cavalrymen of the Daimones Prodromoi. A shadow fell on him and he turned slightly to see some of the elephants had arrived. Antigonus planted his xyston in the earth and stood looking at the great beast.

"Derya! Derya! Derya!" The cavalrymen had recognized the first commander of their regiment and honored him with their chants and by waving their xystons. Derya Shafrid saw Semiramis in their number and gave her a quick wave of acknowledgment. Then, he slid off Jayanta Prabhakar and approached Antigonus.

"Your Majesty, the Emperor Seleucus has commanded me to find you and bring you to him with all the honors and ceremony befitting a king of your rank and achievements. He promises that you will be given a retirement that will be fitting and appropriate for you. Please, ride on Jayanta Prabhakar with me." Shafrid stepped forward, his arms stretched out in comradely greeting.

Antigonus saw him do so and his mind fogged with rage. *This is the man who had either defeated me or has stolen all the credit for my victories. This man who snatched away my victory with his herd of elephants. And this is the man who killed my son.* In one smooth motion he seized the xyston beside him and plunged its point into Derya Shafrid's chest.

Shafrid saw the gaping wound and the blood spurting out. Without doubt, it was mortal. *Not even Naamah's skills can fix this.* "Igrat, I'm so sorry."

He fell to his knees, still looking at the great wound and said again, "Igrat." Then, as the shadows closed in on him, his last thought was *at least she still has a family to look after her.*

There was a stunned silence at the foul treachery of the murder. Then, Antigonus was struck down by a barrage of oxybeles bolts, arrows and javelins. Nobody could count how many struck home; the number might have been a dozen or more, perhaps many times that. Semiramis jumped off her horse and went over to where his body lay. It took her one quick swing of her kopis and she held the head of Antigonus Monopthalmus, once a soldier and a general, then a king but who had died a foul and despised murderer.

Semiramis mounted Montoi and spoke to Aeschylus. "This needs to go to Parmenio right now. Permission to detach from your regiment?"

"Permission granted. And, Semiramis, thank you for riding with us today. We'll bring Derya's body in. Igrat's going to be heartbroken."

Semiramis nodded and turned Montoi away to ride through the wreckage of the battlefield, bearing both the ultimate battle trophy and the saddest of news.

Parmenio's Headquarters Tent, Center of the Army of Seleucus-Lysimachus, Ipsus, Mid-afternoon

Igrat was waiting when she heard the cries go up. "They're coming in! The Daimones Prodromoi are coming in."

She glanced at Parmenio who was studying his battlefield model. He was stooped over it so she couldn't see his face but he waved her out. So, she left the tent to watch the cavalry regiment ride in. As soon as she stepped outside and saw the faces of those around her, she knew what had happened.

Derya Shafrid's body had been quickly but carefully prepared and laid out on a pier made from three shields lashed to a pair of sarissas. It was being carried by four horseman with two more on either side as an honor guard. The entire regiment held their spears reversed in mourning. Igrat wanted to scream, to cry, to kneel on the ground and tear at her hair but she knew that she had to honor her husband's bravery with her own. Instead, she drew herself erect and her voice echoed around the camp. "Did my husband die bravely?"

"He did, my Lady. He fought bravely and victoriously, showing such skill that no man could stand before him. He could not be killed in fair combat and died from an act of the foulest and most disgusting treachery. He was murdered by a man to whom he had stretched out the hand of friendship. That man's name is not fit to be spoken in the presence of Derya Shafrid." There was a note of warning in the Prodromoi's voice, not aimed at Igrat but to the other spectators. The Daimones Prodromoi would take it ill if the name of Antigonus was spoken in the vicinity of the man he had murdered. "My Lady, his last words were to call out your name."

Igrat felt an arm around her shoulders and knew it was Parmenio. Suddenly, she realized he must have known Derya Shafrid was dead and the same flash of insight told her why he had kept his head bowed over his maps. "Come into the tent, Igrat. You'll have much to do later but his men will prepare his body for cremation in the proper manner for a soldier of such renown."

Before she could comply, there was a stir around the camp. Seleucus Nikator had arrived. He slid off his horse and made straight for Igrat. He embraced her, her head resting on his chest. "Igrat, this is the first time I have ever been sorry to see you. I had hoped never to have to meet with you in these circumstances. Know that I grieve deeply for your loss today and will remember your man in my prayers to our Gods. It has already been reported to me how bravely he fought and how much I owe him. If there is anything I can do for you, you may enter my presence at any time to ask. In the meantime, please take a few pieces of silver to help you through the next few days."

Igrat pulled her head back and looked at him oddly. It wasn't just that he had used the personal pronoun speaking to her rather than the royal 'we' but he knew she was wealthy and a few pieces of silver were of no great consequence to her. Even through her grief, that passing thought shocked her. *There had been a time when I had nothing and would have sold myself – have sold myself, body and soul – for far less than that.* Seleucus Nikator saw her confusion and misunderstood it. He gave her a sad smile and whispered so only she could hear. "Take it, please. Not for your sake, but for the other women who lost their men today. So that they know that, no matter what rank their men held, their loss is seen as equally great in my eyes. Which it is."

Seleucus patted her gently on the back and went over to where some of the newly-widowed women were gathered. He had no bodyguard with him and that was fitting for he had no more determined bodyguards than the women he took the time to comfort and aid. Behind him, Igrat turned to Aeschylus. "Could one of your men show me where Derya died please?"

"We can do better than that." Aeschylus turned and spoke to three of his Lochagos. "Take the Lady Igrat to where Derya died and guard her there. Give her room to grieve but stay close enough to make sure she is not harmed by her own hand or by that of others."

In the background, Parmenio was talking to Semiramis and looking at the head she had brought in. The quest that had driven him for years seemed to be a small and unimportant thing now. It had cost Igrat her husband yet the search for revenge hadn't changed the fact that his son was dead. It had all been for nothing. And so, his words were very simple. "Ten down. It's over."

The Battlefield, Ipsus, Late Dusk

Igrat was sitting on the spot where Derya Shafrid had died, her knees drawn up under her chin. Cavalrymen from the Daimones Prodromoi were watching her discretely. They had been afraid she would try and take her own life and watched her closely but Parmenio seriously doubted if they could have stopped her if that had been the course she had chosen. If she'd wanted to put her knife in her throat, she'd have done so. Now, though, they guarded her against a greater threat. The scavengers were already out, searching the bodies of the slain for anything they had of value. A few of them had seen the woman sitting on the ground and closed in on her, only to be intercepted and beaten. One had tried to come back a second time and now lay amongst the dead.

Parmenio slid off his horse and sat down beside her. She looked at him and smiled very sadly. "It's all right, Father, I'm not going to kill myself. I always knew this would happen one day. You told me that yourself, or was it Lillith? Or Naamah? It's the price we pay. Those we love always die before us. It's just I know now how you felt, when you found out how your son had died. I want to kill the man who did it but our friends got there before me. I suppose, in a way, that makes me lucky. What's left of his body is over there. The elephants trampled it. Father, how many men died here today?"

Parmenio thought about that. "We've lost about three thousand men. Seleucus is still hard at work, aiding and comforting their women. Antigonus lost at least thirty thousand. We're trying to clear the battlefield but nobody has ever dealt with casualties like this before. Demetrius survived by the way, we found him, badly wounded, where his cavalry was destroyed. Seleucus has allowed him to leave with four hundred horse and five hundred foot. He'll be going to Ephesus for his exile. Meleager is dead. He tried to change sides once too often and Lysimachus listened patiently to his demands for high rank and privilege. Then, when Meleager had finished, Lysimachus took a javelin and killed him. Did you find what you were looking for here?"

Igrat shook her head. "I came here because I thought Derya might be waiting for me here, to say goodbye. All the time I was riding here, I was afraid his shade would ask me to join him and I would have to refuse. But he isn't here, Father. I should have known. There's nothing after death. All we have is life. What are we going to do now?"

"Seleucus intends to move his western capital to Antioch. He'll rule from there. Antiochus will rule the eastern half of the empire from Seleucia. We'll stay in Seleucia as well and try to become inconspicuous. But, what will you do now?"

"Whatever you want me to do. Or, whatever the family needs me to do. Go back to being a messenger and delivering packages I suppose. Somebody will have to make sure Antioch and Seleucia stay in touch. Before then, I'll have to sort out all of the things Derya and I collected. Most of his things we'll send back to his family. They never liked me you know. I'll keep the jewelry he gave me. That's all."

"All?" Parmenio got up as he asked the question. He reached down and helped Igrat to her feet. Around them, her cavalry guard closed in to make sure they were safe.

Igrat thought for a moment. "I'll keep his name as well. Until I find a better man."

EPILOGUE

Encampment, Army of Lysimachus, Ipsus, Late Afternoon

Dara had been waiting for Nikomedes to return for her. She knew he had survived unscathed, for word of the dead had quickly spread around the encampment. Seleucus had already made his visits to the women who had lost their men and they now were trying to put their lives back together again. Already, the first suitors had made their appearance and were making their cases to the widows. But, Nikomedes was coming back to her. Then, she saw him and saw that there was somebody with him. A young girl, barely into her teens.

"Who is this?" Dara forced her voice to be warm and welcoming although her suspicions were trying to devour her mind.

Nikomedes looked at his wife and knew exactly what she was thinking. He started to explain what had happened, in far greater detail than was necessary, but it was somehow necessary for his wife to understand what he had seen and he needed to unload his soul by telling it to somebody. "I have just come from the Antigonid camp. You have never seen anything like it over there; the enemy dead are numbered in tens of thousands and the cries of the widows can be heard from afar.

"Normally, the capture of a baggage train is well-ordered and there are only a few chaotic minutes when the cavalry rides in. If there is a guard, there will be fighting while they try to protect the people in the train. By this point, the guards know the battle is over and their side had lost. By putting up resistance, they hope to soften the terms of the surrender and gain a measure of protection for those they defend.

"Usually, the strategy works and the cavalry negotiate a deal rather than take more casualties in a battle that is already over. Only, this time everything is different. The system for a defeat where the dead were measured in dozens or perhaps a few hundred has broken down. The destruction of the enemy army and the death of Antigonus and his entire senior command meant there was nobody left to negotiate a surrender. The guards fled, leaving the baggage train undefended and at the mercy of the sarissaphoros, hypaspists, archers and slingers. They have descended on the Antigonid baggage train and are pillaging it. The women are being dragged out of their tents and wagons and raped right there, in front of everybody. If they resist, the men kill them and look for another. Everything of value is being taken and that of no value is smashed or burned. Only the baggage of the left hand phalanx has been spared and that only because it is guarded by Leonnatus's elephants and cavalry."

Nikomedes paused and drew breath. The sight of the Antigonid baggage train being sacked and pillaged haunted him and the memory made him want to be sick. "We were all over it. My file stuck together, to protect each other and to guard our loot while we collected more. Polybius, you remember Polybius? He found a woman whose man had been killed in the fighting. He was good to her, he offered her an honorable arrangement to become his camp-wife and she accepted. She was one of the few fortunate ones. Dara, the number of women over there who have lost their men today far exceeds the number of our men who will take a camp-wife. Most of them face a dreadful future.

"This girl's father is amongst the dead. Her mother has been taken by into slavery by one of our soldiers. Slavery, not offered the status of a camp-wife. She tried to hide her daughter in a wagon but some of our men found her and dragged her out. She is too young to become a camp-wife but not too young to be raped. I remembered what happened to Eunike. I couldn't let that happen to this girl so I gave those men some of my loot, valued at a silver piece, for her. They were happy, there were more women around they could use so it was no great loss to them. We don't have any children yet, Dara, I thought she could be the start of our family. And then she told me her name."

Dara felt her suspicions subsiding and instead was cosumed with guilt over the things that she had thought. *My husband is a good man, how could I have thought that of him?* "What is your name, child?"

"Eunike, mistress. Really, it is." Eunike was about to cry; she knew camp life well enough to understand the fate she had narrowly escaped and didn't want to see this chance at a decent life turn to ashes.

"Well, Eunike, soon you will have brothers and sisters. Won't she Niko?"

"We must trust in the Gods for that. But we can try very hard. On our new farm." Nikomedes handed his wife a scroll. "His Majesty, King Seleucus gave me this, from his own hand. It's a land grant for a farm on one of his new Katoikoi soldier-settlements in his province of Phrygia. He is forming them all over his empire and is giving land grants to all the veterans. I've been to Phrygia, Dara, the soil is thick and black and just bursts with the desire to produce crops. We'll have a good life there. I also got hold of a cart. It's not a big one but it's large enough for us. And, it came with a donkey to pull it. He'll be useful when we start our farm.

"Where is it?" Dara looked around curiously. She had a shrewd suspicion that her husband had bought a cart, entrusted it to one of his comrades who had promptly vanished with it. She was about to say something to that effect when she was stopped by a 'Halloo' from the outskirts of the camp. To her considerable surprise, a donkey-drawn cart had appeared and was heading for them.

"Ahh, there it is. Timotei brought it back for me while I hurried on ahead." Once again, Nikomedes knew exactly what his wife had been thinking and, being honest with himself, he was relieved that she wasn't right, "Hey, Timotei over here!"

The cart changed course slightly and stopped beside Nikomedes. Timotei jumped down and handed the reins of the donkey to Nikomedes. "Dara, your husband fought bravely today. And I see you have met the girl he rescued. He showed great bravery there too."

Dara frowned slightly at that. Obviously the rescue of Eunike had been harder and more dangerous than Nikomedes had let on. That didn't actually surprise her. She had noted her husband rarely talked about the battles he had fought in. There was another man sitting on the cart with a woman beside him. She recognized him as Polybius and assumed that the woman beside him was the one he had just taken as his camp-wife. Her expression was a strange mixture, grief for the husband she had lost, curiosity about the one she had just acquired and, above all, relief at having survived the sack of the baggage train safely. Dara realized that, even based on the undoubtedly carefully edited version her husband had given her, the quiet, well-ordered Lysimachan encampment must seem like paradise compared with what was happening over at the Antigonid camp.

"What is your name?" Dara asked the woman while she was getting down from the cart.

"I am Myrrine."

"Well, Myrinne, I'm Dara. If you need any help settling in, just ask me. Niko and I will be leaving in a day or two though." Suddenly, at that point, an anvil dropped on Dara. "Niko, *you've met King Seleucus?*"

Nikomedes grinned. He'd been wondering how long it would take for that to sink in. "While we were on our way back. He was with some of the women following the Seleucid Army who had lost their men. Speaking kindly to them and giving them silver. His Strategos, Parmenio the Younger was with him. His Majesty saw me walking back with Eunike here and asked me what was happening. I explained and said that you and I would adopt her as our daughter and bring her up in the Macedonian tradition. He greatly approved of that. Then, he took one of these scrolls from his guard and said we could have a farm on a Katoikoi if we wanted it. Parmenio the Younger said that it was probable that adopting a daughter would be as interesting an experience for me as it had been for him and I might find a farm useful. Not least for somewhere to hide. And so, we have our farm."

Dara looked at him and smiled. "In which case, we'd better start to pack and leave. Come, Eunike, help me pack our things. We had better start getting to know each other."

THE END

Cast List

Aeschylus – Fictional Commander of the Daimones Prodromoi following Derya Shafrid. Later, commander of the six regiments forming Seleucus Nikator's personal guard.

Alcetas – Historical. Originally a senior officer of Eumenes, assigned by him to command in Asia Minor after Eumenes moved south to join with Perdiccas in First Diodochi War. Changed sides and joined with Antigonus. Changed sides again and joined with Seleucus for start of Second Diodochi War. Courted and became lover of Lillith but she refused proposal of marriage. Much embittered, changed sides again and rejoined Antigonus. Eventually went rogue and was executed by Seleucus Nikator.

Alexander – Historical. Son of Polyperchon. A good general and a strong supporter of his father. Killed in battle, 314BC.

Anatolios Metrophanes – Fictional. Cavalry commander serving under Antigonus Monopthalmus. Later served under Demetrius Poliorcetes in Cyprus. Killed at the Battle of Ipsus

Antigenes – Historical. Commander of the Argyraspides, the elite infantry unit fighting for Eumenes. Murdered by Antigonus Monopthalmus after Battle of the Gabiene

Antiochus – Historical Son of Selucus Nikator and ruled Seleucid Empire after his father's death

Antigonus Monopthalmus – Historical. The Big Bad. Member of the Diodochi. Leader of the faction that wishes to break away from the Alexandrine legacy and found their own kingdoms. Initially allied with Antipater and Craterus in First Diodochi War. Allied with Seleucus Nikator and Polyperchon against Eumenes and Cassander in Second Diodochi War. Allied with Polyperchon against Seleucus Nikator and Ptolemy in Third Diodochi War. More or less fought everybody in Fourth Diodochi War. Killed during the Battle of Ipsus.

Epilogue

Antipater – Historical. Leading member of Diodochi after 'death' of Parmenio. Also leader of loyalist faction after death of Alexander the Great. Allied with Antigonus and Cassander in First Diodochi War. Poisoned by son Cassander after Antipater made Polyperchon his heir.

Apollo – Fictional. Young boy found severely burned and injured after forest fire. Healed by Naamah and raised by Lillith. Rash, impulsive and somewhat immature. Gusoyn's lover.

Apollonides – Historical. Cavalry commander of Eumenes in early part of Second Diodochi War. Betrayed Eumenes and changes sides to join Antigonus. Left Antigonus and joined Ptolemy Soter. Murdered by Hippostratus at Cyrenê.

Arrhidaeus – AKA Phillip Arrhidaeus. Brother of Alexander, poisoned by Olympias; left crippled and brain damaged thus disqualified from throne. Married and allied to Eurydice and murdered by Olympias.

Attalus – Fictional. Sutler and friend of Callicrates. Patronized and insulted Igrat but still got rich with her help. Devoted supporter of Seleucus Nikator.

Barsine -- Historical. Allegedly mistress of Alexander the Great and mother of his illegitimate son Heracles. In fact, relationship highly questionable and the two were more likely imposters. Murdered by Cassander and probably deserved it.

Barsine Stateira Second wife of Alexander the Great. Murdered by Perdiccas and definitely didn't deserve it.

Callicrates – Fictional. A sutler and an early 'friend with benefits' of Igrat. Helped her make her first significant sums of money and understand the rear end of a battlefield. With her help, became very rich. Devoted supporter of Seleucus Nikator.

Cassander – Historical. Son of Antipater but passed over by him in favor of Polyperchon. In revenge he poisoned his father and fought against the alliance favored by Antipater. Hated the Alexandrine legacy. Fought his own war against the Alexandrine Regents for his own motives and reasons. Not formally allied with anybody during first, second and third Diodochi Wars although got support from others when their interests coincided with his. Allied with Seleucus, Lysimachus and Ptolemy in Fourth Diodochi War.

Chandragupta Maurya – Historical. Emperor of India and founder of the Mauryan Dynasty. Married Helen, daughter of Seleucus Nikator

Cleitus – Historical. Satrap of Lydia in Second Diodochi War, declared for Eumenes. Became commander of elephant troops of Eumenes. Killed after Battle of Paraitacene.

Craterus – Historical. Member of the Diodochi and prime instigator behind the death of Philotas. Killed after the battle of the Hyllus River.

Demetrius Poliorcetes – Historical Son of Antigonus Monopthalmus. Highly competent commander in his own right and expert at siege warfare, Eventually replaced Lysimachus as ruler of Macedonia and re-established the Antigonid dynasty there.

Derya Shafrid – Fictional. Skilled prodromoi cavalry commander and husband of Igrat. After severe battle injuries, became the commander of the elephant regiments of Seleucus Nikator. Killed at the Battle of Ipsus.

Dromichaetes – Fictional. Sarissaphoros veteran killed at the Fortress of Camels.

Eumenes – Historical. Court scholar and historian to Alexander the Great and loyal to the Alexandrine tradition. Turned out to be a much better general than anybody expected. Opposed Antigonus in First Diodochi War and defeated (and killed) Craterus at the Hyllus River. Antigonus Monopthalmus planned his gruesome death as a warning to those who opposed him; Naamah got in first with a mercy-killing.

Eurydice – Historical. Wife of Phillip Arrhidaeus and fanatically loyal to him. Chose to die a horrible and humiliating death at hands of Olympias rather than betray him. After death, only person on any of the sides fighting the wars to be regarded and venerated as a true hero.

Gusoyn –Fictional. Former charioteer and now member of Parmenio's household. A mature and dignified man who takes responsibility seriously. Although usually assumes a subordinate position as a servant, in fact he is Parmenio's trusted right-hand man. If Parmenio wants something done carefully and well, Gusoyn is the man he turns to.

Helen – Historical. Daughter of Seleucus Nikator; married Chandragupta Maurya. Took the Indian name Durdhara on her marriage and gave birth to one son, Bindusara who succeeded his father on the Indian throne. She saved her husband's life by drinking poisoned wine intended for him.

Hesperos – Historical Eldest son of Callicrates. Eventually became treasurer of the Seleucid Empire for Antiochus I

Hieronymus of Cardia – Historical. Court historian. Originally Eumenes was his patron but changed sides and was supported by Antigonus. Disillusioned with Antigonus after the murder of the Argyraspides and settled in the Seleucid Empire.

Epilogue

Hippostratus – Historical.   General serving under Antigonus Monopthalmus.   Scheming and treacherous but not bad as a field commander. Began move to center stage after death of Antigenes. Became disillusioned with Antigonus and left his service to join Ptolemy. Killed at Cyrenê

Igrat – Fictional.   Petty thief, beggar and street whore saved by Parmenio from grisly execution. Superbly gifted as a courier and adopted by Parmenio as his daughter. Married Derya Shafrid.

Kavita – Historical. Originally wife of Cleitus then joined court of Seleucus Nikator. Became lady-in-waiting to Helen, teaching her to speak the Indian language and instructing her on Indian culture. Instrumental in solidifying the Seleucid-Mauryan alliance.

Leonnatus – Historical.   Commander of a Sarissaphoros regiment, initially in the employ of Eumenes during the First Diodochi War. Changed sides after the battle of Cilicia and joined Army of Antigonus. Changed sides again after defeat of Antigonus in Third Diodochi War and joined Lysimachus to fight Antigonid troops commander by Meleager.

Lillith – Fictional.   Former Canaanite queen. Treasurer of Parmenio's household. Finds walking painful and difficult since her feet were badly burned in her youth.

Lysimachus – Historical Ruler of Thrace, Asia Minor and Macedonia

Meleager – Historical.   Junior commander under Perdiccas, betrayed him and switched sides to Ptolemy Soter, the changed sides to join Eumenes, then switched sides again to Antigonus Monopthalmus.   Rebelled against Antigonus Monopthalmus and gave allegiance to Peithon in his rebellion against Antigonus. Betrayed Peithon and rejoined Antigonus. Switched sides and served Seleucus Nikator. Then attempted to usurp power for himself. After that failed, switched sides and rejoined Antigonus. Then, betrayed Antigonus and joined Lysimachus. For some reason nobody trusted him. Killed by Lysimachus to prevent further betrayals.

Menander – Historical.   General and supporter of Antigonus Monopthalmus. Left by him to control Asia Minor while Antigonus dealt with problems elsewhere. Defeated and killed by Eumenes at the Battle of Cilicia.

Naamah – Historical.   Midian/Canaanite.   Distant cousin of Lillith. Formerly queen of Canaanite city-state, herbalist, healer and poisoner. Killed Alexander the Great by poisoning him with hellbore. (Note there is just enough historical evidence to suggest that a city-state queen of this description and name actually existed).

Neoptolemus – Historical. Minor king of Armenia. Originally allied with Perdiccas and Eumenes but changed sides and joined Craterus. Killed at the Hyllus River.

Nikomedes – Fictional. Sarissaphoros, first appears as a callow recruit and becomes a hardened veteran over the course of the story.

Olympias – Historical. Mother of Alexander the Great, best described as 'mother from hell'. Absolutely determined to see Alexander's son by Roxane become ruler of whole Alexandrine Empire (with Olympias calling all the shots). Defeated by Cassander and killed by raving mob who tore her apart (according to legend, there was nothing recognizable left of her body – which raises an interesting question, was she actually killed?).

Parmenio – Historical. Strategic genius and architect of Alexander the Great's victories Former leading member of the Diodochi, the generals of Alexander, and believed murdered by Alexander in 330BC following Alexander's murder of his son Philotas. In this story, he survived and wants all the other Diodochi dead for their participation in the death of his son. Picked Seleucus Nikator as his tool for the job being the Diodochi he held least responsible for his son's death. Grew to like and admire Seleucus and forgave him for his part in the death of Philotas.

Perdiccas – Historical. Member of Diodochi. Initial leader of faction who wished to break up the Empire into individual independent kingships. In First Diodochi War, allied with Eumenes and Seleucus against Antipater, Antigonus and Craterus. Deposed and killed by Seleucus Nikator.

Perdicatus – Historical. Actually, this man was named Perdiccas but name changed slightly to avoid confusion. Killed by Phoenix after leading mutiny of Eumenes's troops.

Peucestes – Historical. Cavalry commander under Eumenes. Inept and of little importance, vanished into oblivion after the Battle of the Gabiene. Reappeared almost ten years later serving Demetrius. Killed at the Battle of Ipsus

Phoenix – Historical. Junior officer under Eumenes. Performed very well in putting down mutiny of Eumenes's troops. Rose steadily on merit and became one of the Generals of Lysimachus. Specialist in siege warfare.

Pharnabazus – Fictional. Friend of Phoenix. Killed in Babylon during Third Diodochi War.

Philotarsas – Historical. Argyraspides officer who deserted and joined Antigonus. Killed at the Fortress of Camels after he tried to desert to Ptolemy.

Epilogue

Polyperchon – Historical. Member of Diodochi. One of Alexander's most trusted generals and long-time friend of Antipater. Appointed heir to Antipater in place of Cassander resulting in blood feud between the two. Polyperchon supported Olympias because she wanted Roxane's son by Alexander to be Emperor. In doing so, Polyperchon made Olympias also an enemy of Cassander. Retired from Diodochi Wars, yielding place to Cassander. Eventually died of natural causes.

Ptolemy Soter – Historical. Member of Diodochi. First Diodochi to set himself up as King. Allied to Antigonus, Antipater and Craterus in First Diodochi War. Admitted guilt in death of Philotas to Parmenio and was forgiven by him. Formed shadow alliance with Seleucus Nikator. Strategy is to stay out of things as much as possible while building up his strength. Had particularly strong Navy that was destroyed in Battle of Salamis in 305BC.

Roxane – Historical. Wife of Alexander the Great. Mother of heir to throne. A helpless pawn if ever there was one, yet conducted herself with dignity and nobility that impressed everybody who met her. Murdered by Cassander in 305 BC.

Seleucus Nikator – Historical. Member of the Diodochi, became satrap of Babylon and then founder of Seleucid Empire. Initially allied with Perdiccas and Eumenes in First Diodochi War but changed sides and joined Antipater, Antigonus and Craterus. Formed secure shadow alliance with Ptolemy Soter.

Semiramis –Historical. Also known as Shammuramat. Once Empress of the Assyrian Empire. Met up with Parmenio's household when she was running an inn in Babylon. At the time of this story, was Parmenio's partner.

Teutamus – Historical. Second-in-Command of the Argyraspides, the elite infantry unit fighting for Eumenes. Murdered by Antigonus Monopthalmus after Battle of the Gabiene.

Telesphorus of Peloponnesus. -- Historical Skilled naval commander under Cassander and later overall naval commander for the allied Kings in the Fourth Diodochi War. Ended up forming his own maritime empire of small islands in the Aegean.

Xenophilus – Historical. Treasurer of Seleucus Nikator and keeper of the Alexandrine Treasury at Susa. Probably the richest man in the world; in modern terms at least a trillionaire.

www.ingramcontent.com/pod-product-compliance
Lightning Source LLC
Chambersburg PA
CBHW020928020726
47495CB00002B/390